WASTELANDS 2
MORE STORIES OF THE APOCALYPSE

Also available from John Joseph Adams
and Titan Books

Dead Man's Hand: An Anthology of the Weird West
Wastelands: Stories of the Apocalypse

WASTELANDS 2

MORE STORIES OF THE APOCALYPSE

EDITED BY
JOHN JOSEPH ADAMS

TITAN BOOKS

WASTELANDS 2: MORE STORIES OF THE APOCALYPSE

Print edition ISBN: 9781783291519
E-book edition ISBN: 9781783291526

Published by Titan Books
A division of Titan Publishing Group Ltd
144 Southwark St, London SE1 0UP

First Titan Books edition: June 2016
2 4 6 8 10 9 7 5 3 1

Visit our website: www.titanbooks.com

A CIP catalogue record for this title is available from the British Library.

Printed and bound in the USA.

CONTENTS

INTRODUCTION
JOHN JOSEPH ADAMS

It's hard to imagine following up something like the end of the world.

But fans of post-apocalyptic fiction know that end-of-the-world stories aren't really about *the end*—they're about new beginnings and the end of the world *as we know it*. Our stories, our lives, our world continues on, even if the trappings change and the facade of civilization falls by the wayside. As the title of George R. Stewart's masterpiece reminds us: the Earth abides.

And as the Earth abides, so does our interest in post-apocalyptic fiction. The genre has continued to flourish in the years since the original *Wastelands* (hereinafter referred to as "Volume One") was published, and when I began reading for the new anthology I discovered a wealth of material to choose from. Yet it was very difficult to even contemplate following up a book like Volume One, which, to my astonishment, was widely hailed as not only the definitive post-apocalyptic anthology but as one of the finest anthologies *of any kind*. And, although it was my first anthology, it contained works by the likes of Stephen King, George R. R. Martin, Orson Scott Card, Octavia E. Butler, and other legendary figures of the SF/fantasy field. When you come out of the gates with that kind of success, it's daunting to say the least to contemplate a follow-up.

But my love for post-apocalyptic fiction has not waned since editing Volume One, and it's clear the genre is still at the forefront of many authors' minds as well. Five of the stories included here are from the 20th Century, but the remaining twenty-five were all published from the year 2000 onward, and eighteen of those were originally published in the years since Volume One came out. That seems to indicate that the boom in post-apocalyptic fiction that I detected back when I decided to put Volume One together is still ongoing, and writers and readers now are seemingly as fascinated with the apocalypse as we were back in the genre's heyday in the 1950s. Or, in other words, it's certainly not the end of the world for the end-of-the-world genre.

In Volume One's introduction (which you can find online at johnjosephadams.com/wastelands), I traced the rise and resurgence of post-apocalyptic fiction, citing the dawn of the Atomic Age as the former, and 9/11 as the latter. I also speculated at length about why we're so fascinated by the end of the world. There, I said, "To me, the appeal is obvious: it fulfills our taste for adventure, the thrill of discovery, the desire for a new frontier. It also allows us to start over from scratch, to wipe the slate clean and see what the world may have been like if we had known then what we know now." But it's since occurred to me that many of us have a strong attraction to things that scare us; there wouldn't be a horror genre otherwise. And in many ways, post-apocalyptic fiction is the scariest kind of fiction there is, because the more plausible a horrific story is, the scarier it is. Stories about demons and supernatural monsters can be entertaining, but deep down I don't find them particularly scary, because I'm *pretty* certain those things don't—and never will—exist.

The end of the world, however? That could happen.

Will we ever sate our appetite for stories about the end? It's hard to imagine that we will. At least not until the end actually comes…

THE TAMARISK HUNTER
PAOLO BACIGALUPI

A big tamarisk can suck 73,000 gallons of river water a year. For $2.88 a day, plus water bounty, Lolo rips tamarisk all winter long.

Ten years ago, it was a good living. Back then, tamarisk shouldered up against every riverbank in the Colorado River Basin, along with cottonwoods, Russian olives, and elms. Ten years ago, towns like Grand Junction and Moab thought they could still squeeze life from a river.

Lolo stands on the edge of a canyon, Maggie the camel his only companion. He stares down into the deeps. It's an hour's scramble to the bottom. He ties Maggie to a juniper and starts down, boot-skiing a gully. A few blades of green grass sprout neon around him, piercing juniper-tagged snow clods. In the late winter, there is just a beginning surge of water down in the deeps; the ice is off the river edges. Up high, the mountains still wear their ragged snow mantles. Lolo smears through mud and hits a channel of scree, sliding and scattering rocks. His jugs of tamarisk poison gurgle and slosh on his back. His shovel and rockbar snag on occasional junipers as he skids by. It will be a long hike out. But then, that's what makes this patch so perfect. It's a long way down, and the riverbanks are largely hidden.

It's a living; where other people have dried out and blown away, he has remained: a tamarisk hunter, a water tick, a stubborn bit of weed. Everyone else has been blown off the land as surely as dandelion seeds, set free to fly south or east, or most of all north where watersheds sometimes still run deep and where even if there are no more lush ferns or deep cold fish runs, at least there is still water for people.

Eventually, Lolo reaches the canyon bottom. Down in the cold shadows, his breath steams.

He pulls out a digital camera and starts shooting his proof. The Bureau of Reclamation has gotten uptight about proof. They want different angles on the offending tamarisk, they want each one photographed before and after, the whole process documented, GPS'd, and uploaded directly by the camera. They want it done on-site. And then they still sometimes come out to spot check before they calibrate his headgate for water bounty.

But all their due diligence can't protect them from the likes of Lolo. Lolo has found the secret to eternal life as a tamarisk hunter. Unknown to the Interior Department and its BuRec subsidiary, he has been seeding new patches of tamarisk, encouraging vigorous brushy groves in previously cleared areas. He has hauled and planted healthy root balls up and down the river system in strategically hidden and inaccessible corridors, all in a bid for security against the swarms of other tamarisk hunters that scour these same tributaries. Lolo is crafty. Stands like this one, a quarter-mile long and thick with salt-laden tamarisk, are his insurance policy.

Documentation finished, he unstraps a folding saw, along with his rockbar and shovel, and sets his poison jugs on the dead salt bank. He starts cutting, slicing into the roots of the tamarisk, pausing every thirty seconds to spread Garlon 4 on the cuts, poisoning the tamarisk wounds faster than they can heal. But some of the best tamarisk, the most vigorous, he uproots and sets aside, for later use.

$2.88 a day, plus water bounty.

It takes Maggie's rolling bleating camel stride a week to make it back to Lolo's homestead. They follow the river, occasionally climbing above it onto cold mesas or wandering off into the open desert in a bid to avoid the skeleton sprawl of emptied towns. Guardie choppers buzz up and down the river like swarms of angry yellowjackets, hunting for porto-pumpers and wildcat diversions. They rush overhead in a wash of beaten air and gleaming National Guard logos. Lolo remembers a time when the guardies traded potshots with people down on the riverbanks, tracer-fire and machine-gun chatter echoing in the canyons. He remembers the glorious hiss and arc of a Stinger missile as it flashed across red-rock desert and blue sky and burned a chopper where it hovered.

But that's long in the past. Now, guardie patrols skim up the river unmolested.

Lolo tops another mesa and stares down at the familiar landscape of an eviscerated town, its curving streets and subdivision cul-de-sacs all sitting silent in the sun. At the very edge of the empty town, one-acre ranchettes and snazzy five-thousand-square-foot houses with dead-stick trees and dust-hill landscaping fringe a brown tumbleweed golf course. The sandtraps don't even show anymore.

When California put its first calls on the river, no one really worried. A couple towns went begging for water. Some idiot newcomers with bad water rights stopped grazing their horses, and that was it. A few years later, people started showering real fast. And a few after that, they showered once a week. And then people started using the buckets. By then, everyone had stopped joking about how "hot" it was. It didn't really matter how "hot" it was. The problem wasn't lack of water or an excess of heat, not really. The problem was that 4.4 million acre-feet of water were supposed to go down the river to California. There was water; they just couldn't touch it.

They were supposed to stand there like dumb monkeys and watch it flow on by.

"Lolo?"

The voice catches him by surprise. Maggie startles and groans and lunges for the mesa edge before Lolo can rein her around. The camel's great padded feet scuffle dust and Lolo flails for his shotgun where it nestles in a scabbard at the camel's side. He forces Maggie to turn, shotgun half-drawn, holding barely to his seat and swearing.

A familiar face, tucked amongst juniper tangle.

"Goddamnit!" Lolo lets the shotgun drop back into its scabbard. "Jesus Christ, Travis. You scared the hell out of me."

Travis grins. He emerges from amongst the junipers' silver bark rags, one hand on his gray fedora, the other on the reins as he guides his mule out of the trees. "Surprised?"

"I could've shot you!"

"Don't be so jittery. There's no one out here 'cept us water ticks."

"That's what I thought the last time I went shopping down there. I had a whole set of new dishes for Annie and I broke them all when I ran into an ultralight parked right in the middle of the main drag."

"Meth flyers?"

"Beats the hell out of me. I didn't stick around to ask."

"Shit. I'll bet they were as surprised as you were."

"They almost killed me."

"I guess they didn't."

Lolo shakes his head and swears again, this time without anger. Despite the ambush, he's happy to run into Travis. It's lonely country, and Lolo's been out long enough to notice the silence of talking to Maggie. They trade ritual sips of water from their canteens and make camp together. They swap stories about BuRec and avoid discussing where they've been ripping tamarisk and enjoy the view of the empty town far below, with its serpentine streets and quiet houses and shining untouched river.

It isn't until the sun is setting and they've finished roasting a magpie that Lolo finally asks the question that's been on his mind ever since Travis's sun-baked face came out of the tangle. It goes against etiquette, but he can't help himself. He picks magpie out of his teeth and says, "I thought you were working downriver."

Travis glances sidelong at Lolo and in that one suspicious, uncertain look, Lolo sees that Travis has hit a lean patch. He's not smart like Lolo. He hasn't been reseeding. He's got no insurance. He hasn't been thinking ahead about all the competition, and what the tamarisk endgame looks like, and now he's feeling the pinch. Lolo feels a twinge of pity. He likes Travis. A part of him wants to tell Travis the secret, but he stifles the urge. The stakes are too high. Water crimes are serious now, so serious Lolo hasn't even told his wife, Annie, for fear of what she'll say. Like all of the most shameful crimes, water theft is a private business, and at the scale Lolo works, forced labor on the Straw is the best punishment he can hope for.

Travis gets his hackles down over Lolo's invasion of his privacy and says, "I had a couple cows I was running up here, but I lost 'em. I think something got 'em."

"Long way to graze cows."

"Yeah, well, down my way even the sagebrush is dead. Big Daddy Drought's doing a real number on my patch." He pinches his lip, thoughtful. "Wish I could find those cows."

"They probably went down to the river."

Travis sighs. "Then the guardies probably got 'em."

"Probably shot 'em from a chopper and roasted 'em."

"Californians."

They both spit at the word. The sun continues to sink. Shadows fall across the town's silent structures. The rooftops gleam red, a ruby cluster decorating the blue river necklace.

"You think there's any stands worth pulling down there?" Travis asks.

"You can go down and look. But I think I got it all last year. And someone had already been through before me, so I doubt much is coming up."

"Shit. Well, maybe I'll go shopping. Might as well get something out of this trip."

"There sure isn't anyone to stop you."

As if to emphasize the fact, the thud-thwap of a guardie chopper breaks the evening silence. The black-fly dot of its movement barely shows against the darkening sky. Soon it's out of sight and cricket chirps swallow the last evidence of its passing.

Travis laughs. "Remember when the guardies said they'd keep out looters? I saw them on TV with all their choppers and Humvees and them all saying they were going to protect everything until the situation improved." He laughs again. "You remember that? All of them driving up and down the streets?"

"I remember."

"Sometimes I wonder if we shouldn't have fought them more."

"Annie was in Lake Havasu City when they fought there. You saw what happened." Lolo shivers. "Anyway, there's not much to fight for once they blow up your water treatment plant. If nothing's coming out of your faucet, you might as well move on."

"Yeah, well, sometimes I think you still got to fight. Even if it's just for pride." Travis gestures at the town below, a shadow movement. "I remember when all that land down there was selling like hotcakes and they were building shit as fast as they could ship in the lumber. Shopping malls and parking lots and subdivisions, anywhere they could scrape a flat spot."

"We weren't calling it Big Daddy Drought, back then."

"Forty-five thousand people. And none of us had a clue. And I was a real estate agent." Travis laughs, a self-mocking sound that ends quickly. It sounds too much like self-pity for Lolo's taste. They're quiet again, looking down at the town wreckage.

"I think I might be heading north," Travis says finally.

Lolo glances over, surprised. Again he has the urge to let

Travis in on his secret, but he stifles it. "And do what?"

"Pick fruit, maybe. Maybe something else. Anyway, there's water up there."

Lolo points down at the river. "There's water."

"Not for us." Travis pauses. "I got to level with you, Lolo. I went down to the Straw."

For a second, Lolo is confused by the non sequitur. The statement is too outrageous. And yet Travis's face is serious. "The Straw? No kidding? All the way there?"

"All the way there." He shrugs defensively. "I wasn't finding any tamarisk, anyway. And it didn't actually take that long. It's a lot closer than it used to be. A week out to the train tracks, and then I hopped a coal train, and rode it right to the interstate, and then I hitched."

"What's it like out there?"

"Empty. A trucker told me that California and the Interior Department drew up all these plans to decide which cities they'd turn off when." He looks at Lolo significantly. "That was after Lake Havasu. They figured out they had to do it slow. They worked out some kind of formula: how many cities, how many people they could evaporate at a time without making too much unrest. Got advice from the Chinese, from when they were shutting down their old communist industries. Anyway, it looks like they're pretty much done with it. There's nothing moving out there except highway trucks and coal trains and a couple truck stops."

"And you saw the Straw?"

"Oh sure, I saw it. Out toward the border. Big old mother. So big you couldn't climb on top of it, flopped out on the desert like a damn silver snake. All the way to California." He spits reflexively. "They're spraying with concrete to keep water from seeping into the ground and they've got some kind of carbon-fiber stuff over the top to stop the evaporation. And the river just disappears inside. Nothing but an empty canyon below it. Bone-dry. And choppers and Humvees everywhere, like a damn hornets' nest. They wouldn't let me get any closer than a half mile on account of the eco-crazies trying to blow it up. They weren't nice about it, either."

"What did you expect?"

"I dunno. It sure depressed me, though: They work us out here and toss us a little water bounty and then all that water next year goes right down into that big old pipe. Some Californian's probably filling his swimming pool with last year's water bounty right now."

Cricket-song pulses in the darkness. Off in the distance, a pack of coyotes starts yipping. The two of them are quiet for a while. Finally, Lolo chucks his friend on the shoulder. "Hell, Travis, it's probably for the best. A desert's a stupid place to put a river, anyway."

Lolo's homestead runs across a couple acres of semi-alkaline soil, conveniently close to the river's edge. Annie is out in the field when he crests the low hills that overlook his patch. She waves, but keeps digging, planting for whatever water he can collect in bounty.

Lolo pauses, watching Annie work. Hot wind kicks up, carrying with it the scents of sage and clay. A dust devil swirls around Annie, whipping her bandana off her head. Lolo smiles as she snags it; she sees him still watching her and waves at him to quit loafing.

He grins to himself and starts Maggie down the hill,

but he doesn't stop watching Annie work. He's grateful for her. Grateful that every time he comes back from tamarisk hunting she is still here. She's steady. Steadier than the people like Travis who give up when times get dry. Steadier than anyone Lolo knows, really. And if she has nightmares sometimes, and can't stand being in towns or crowds and wakes up in the middle of the night calling out for family she'll never see again, well, then it's all the more reason to seed more tamarisk and make sure they never get pushed off their patch like she was pushed.

Lolo gets Maggie to kneel down so he can dismount, then leads her over to a water trough, half-full of slime and water skippers. He gets a bucket and heads for the river while Maggie groans and complains behind him. The patch used to have a well and running water, but like everyone else, they lost their pumping rights and BuRec stuffed the well with Quickcrete when the water table dropped below the Minimum Allowable Reserve. Now he and Annie steal buckets from the river, or, when the Interior Department isn't watching, they jump up and down on a footpump and dump water into a hidden underground cistern he built when the Resource Conservation and Allowable Use Guidelines went into effect.

Annie calls the guidelines "RaCAUG" and it sounds like she's hawking spit when she says it, but even with their filled-in well, they're lucky. They aren't like Spanish Oaks or Antelope Valley or River Reaches: expensive places that had rotten water rights and turned to dust, money or no, when Vegas and L.A. put in their calls. And they didn't have to bail out of Phoenix Metro when the Central Arizona Project got turned off and then had its aqueducts blown to smithereens when Arizona wouldn't stop pumping out of Lake Havasu.

Pouring water into Maggie's water trough, and looking around at his dusty patch with Annie out in the fields, Lolo reminds himself how lucky he is. He hasn't blown away. He and Annie are dug in. Calies may call them water ticks, but fuck them. If it weren't for people like him and Annie, they'd dry up and blow away the same as everyone else. And if Lolo moves a little bit of tamarisk around, well, the Calies deserve it, considering what they've done to everyone else.

Finished with Maggie, Lolo goes into the house and gets a drink of his own out of the filter urn. The water is cool in the shadows of the adobe house. Juniper beams hang low overhead. He sits down and connects his BuRec camera to the solar panel they've got scabbed onto the roof. Its charge light blinks amber. Lolo goes and gets some more water. He's used to being thirsty, but for some reason he can't get enough today. Big Daddy Drought's got his hands around Lolo's neck today.

Annie comes in, wiping her forehead with a tanned arm. "Don't drink too much water," she says. "I haven't been able to pump. Bunch of guardies around."

"What the hell are they doing around? We haven't even opened our headgates yet."

"They said they were looking for you."

Lolo almost drops his cup.

They know.

They know about his tamarisk reseeding. They know he's been splitting and planting root-clusters. That he's been dragging big healthy chunks of tamarisk up and down the river. A week ago he uploaded his claim on the canyon tamarisk—his biggest stand yet—almost worth an acre-foot in itself in water bounty. And now the guardies are knocking on his door.

Lolo forces his hand not to shake as he puts his cup down. "They say what they want?" He's surprised his voice doesn't crack.

"Just that they wanted to talk to you." She pauses. "They had one of those Humvees. With the guns."

Lolo closes his eyes. Forces himself to take a deep breath. "They've always got guns. It's probably nothing."

"It reminded me of Lake Havasu. When they cleared us out. When they shut down the water treatment plant and everyone tried to burn down the BLM office."

"It's probably nothing." Suddenly he's glad he never told her about his tamarisk hijinks. They can't punish her the same. How many acre-feet is he liable for? It must be hundreds. They'll want him, all right. Put him on a Straw work crew and make him work for life, repay his water debt forever. He's replanted hundreds, maybe thousands of tamarisk, shuffling them around like a cardsharp on a poker table, moving them from one bank to another, killing them again and again and again, and always happily sending in his "evidence."

"It's probably nothing," he says again.

"That's what people said in Havasu."

Lolo waves out at their newly tilled patch. The sun shines down hot and hard on the small plot. "We're not worth that kind of effort." He forces a grin. "It probably has to do with those enviro crazies who tried to blow up the Straw. Some of them supposedly ran this way. It's probably that."

Annie shakes her head, unconvinced. "I don't know. They could have asked me the same as you."

"Yeah, but I cover a lot of ground. See a lot of things. I'll bet that's why they want to talk to me. They're just looking for eco-freaks."

"Yeah, maybe you're right. It's probably that." She nods slowly, trying to make herself believe. "Those enviros, they don't make any sense at all. Not enough water for people, and they want to give the river to a bunch of fish and birds."

Lolo nods emphatically and grins wider. "Yeah. Stupid." But suddenly he views the eco-crazies with something approaching brotherly affection. The Californians are after him, too.

Lolo doesn't sleep all night. His instincts tell him to run, but he doesn't have the heart to tell Annie, or to leave her. He goes out in the morning hunting tamarisk and fails at that as well. He doesn't cut a single stand all day. He considers shooting himself with his shotgun, but chickens out when he gets the barrels in his mouth. Better alive and on the run than dead. Finally, as he stares into the twin barrels, he knows that he has to tell Annie, tell her he's been a water thief for years and that he's got to run north. Maybe she'll come with him. Maybe she'll see reason. They'll run together. At least they have that. For sure, he's not going to let those bastards take him off to a labor camp for the rest of his life.

But the guardies are already waiting when Lolo gets back. They're squatting in the shade of their Humvee, talking. When Lolo comes over the crest of the hill, one of them taps the other and points. They both stand. Annie is out in the field again, turning over dirt, unaware of what's about to happen. Lolo reins in and studies the guardies. They lean against their Humvee and watch him back.

Suddenly Lolo sees his future. It plays out in his mind the way it does in a movie, as clear as the blue sky above. He puts his hand on his shotgun. Where it sits on Maggie's far side, the guardies can't see it. He keeps Maggie angled away from them and lets the camel start down the hill.

The guardies saunter toward him. They've got their Humvee with a .50 caliber on the back and they've both got M-16s slung over their shoulders. They're in full bulletproof gear and they look flushed and hot. Lolo rides down slowly. He'll have to hit them both in the face. Sweat trickles between his shoulder blades. His hand is slick on the shotgun's stock.

The guardies are playing it cool. They've still got their rifles slung, and they let Lolo keep approaching. One of them has a wide smile. He's maybe forty years old, and tanned. He's been out for a while, picking up a tan like that. The other raises a hand and says, "Hey there, Lolo."

Lolo's so surprised he takes his hand off his shotgun. "Hale?" He recognizes the guardie. He grew up with him. They played football together a million years ago, when football fields still had green grass and sprinklers sprayed their water straight into the air. Hale. Hale Perkins. Lolo scowls. He can't shoot Hale.

Hale says, "You're still out here, huh?"

"What the hell are you doing in that uniform? You with the Calies now?"

Hale grimaces and points to his uniform patches: Utah National Guard.

Lolo scowls. Utah National Guard. Colorado National Guard. Arizona National Guard. They're all the same. There's hardly a single member of the "National Guard" that isn't an out-of-state mercenary. Most of the local guardies quit a long time ago, sick to death of goose-stepping family and friends off their properties and sick to death of trading potshots with people who just wanted to stay in their homes. So even if there's still a Colorado National Guard, or an Arizona or a Utah, inside those uniforms with all their expensive nightsight gear and their brand-new choppers flying the river bends, it's pure California.

And then there are a few like Hale.

Lolo remembers Hale as being an OK guy. Remembers stealing a keg of beer from behind the Elks Club one night with him. Lolo eyes him. "How you liking that Supplementary Assistance Program?" He glances at the other guardie. "That working real well for you? The Calies a big help?"

Hale's eyes plead for understanding. "Come on, Lolo. I'm not like you. I got a family to look after. If I do another year of duty, they let Shannon and the kids base out of California."

"They give you a swimming pool in your back yard, too?"

"You know it's not like that. Water's scarce there, too."

Lolo wants to taunt him, but his heart isn't in it. A part of him wonders if Hale is just smart. At first, when California started winning its water lawsuits and shutting off cities, the displaced people just followed the water—right to California. It took a little while before the bureaucrats realized what was going on, but finally someone with a sharp pencil did the math and realized that taking in people along with their water didn't solve a water shortage. So the immigration fences went up.

But people like Hale can still get in.

"So what do you two want?" Inside, Lolo's wondering why they haven't already pulled him off Maggie and hauled him away, but he's willing to play this out.

The other guardie grins. "Maybe we're just out here seeing how the water ticks live."

Lolo eyes him. This one, he could shoot. He lets his hand fall to his shotgun again. "BuRec sets my headgate. No reason for you to be out here."

The Calie says, "There were some marks on it. Big ones."

Lolo smiles tightly. He knows which marks the Calie is talking about. He made them with five different wrenches when he tried to dismember the entire headgate apparatus in a fit of obsession. Finally he gave up trying to open the bolts and just beat on the thing, banging the steel of the gate, smashing at it, while on the other side he had plants withering. After that, he gave up and just carried buckets of water to his plants and left it at that. But the dents and nicks are still there, reminding him of a period of madness. "It still works, don't it?"

Hale holds up a hand to his partner, quieting him. "Yeah, it still works. That's not why we're here."

"So what do you two want? You didn't drive all the way out here with your machine gun just to talk about dents in my headgate."

Hale sighs, put upon, trying to be reasonable. "You mind getting down off that damn camel so we can talk?"

Lolo studies the two guardies, figuring his chances on the ground. "Shit." He spits. "Yeah, OK. You got me." He urges Maggie to kneel and climbs off her hump. "Annie didn't know anything about this. Don't get her involved. It was all me."

Hale's brow wrinkles, puzzled. "What are you talking about?"

"You're not arresting me?"

The Calie with Hale laughs. "Why? Cause you take a couple buckets of water from the river? Cause you probably got an illegal cistern around here somewhere?" He laughs again. "You ticks are all the same. You think we don't know about all that crap?"

Hale scowls at the Calie, then turns back to Lolo. "No, we're not here to arrest you. You know about the Straw?"

"Yeah." Lolo says it slowly, but inside, he's grinning. A great weight is suddenly off him. They don't know. They don't know shit. It was a good plan when he started it, and it's a good plan still. Lolo schools his face to keep the glee off, and tries to listen to what Hale's saying, but he can't, he's jumping up and down and gibbering like a monkey. They don't know—

"Wait." Lolo holds up his hand. "What did you just say?"

Hale repeats himself. "California's ending the water bounty. They've got enough Straw sections built up now that they don't need the program. They've got half the river enclosed. They got an agreement from the Department of Interior to focus their budget on seep and evaporation control. That's where all the big benefits are. They're shutting down the water bounty payout program." He pauses. "I'm sorry, Lolo."

Lolo frowns. "But a tamarisk is still a tamarisk. Why should one of those damn plants get the water? If I knock out a tamarisk, even if Cali doesn't want the water, I could still take it. Lots of people could use the water."

Hale looks pityingly at Lolo. "We don't make the regulations, we just enforce them. I'm supposed to tell you that your headgate won't get opened next year. If you keep hunting tamarisk, it won't do any good." He looks around the patch, then shrugs. "Anyway, in another couple years they were going to pipe this whole stretch. There won't be any tamarisk at all after that."

"What am I supposed to do, then?"

"California and BuRec is offering early buyout money."
Hale pulls a booklet out of his bulletproof vest and flips it
open. "Sort of to soften the blow." The pages of the booklet
flap in the hot breeze. Hale pins the pages with a thumb
and pulls a pen out of another vest pocket. He marks
something on the booklet, then tears off a perforated
check. "It's not a bad deal."

Lolo takes the check. Stares at it. "Five hundred dollars?"

Hale shrugs sadly. "It's what they're offering. That's just
the paper codes. You confirm it online. Use your BuRec
camera phone, and they'll deposit it in whatever bank you
want. Or they can hold it in trust until you get into a town
and want to withdraw it. Any place with a BLM office, you
can do that. But you need to confirm before April 15. Then
BuRec'll send out a guy to shut down your headgate before
this season gets going."

"Five hundred dollars?"

"It's enough to get you north. That's more than they're
offering next year."

"But this is my patch."

"Not as long as we've got Big Daddy Drought. I'm sorry,
Lolo."

"The drought could break any time. Why can't they give
us a couple more years? It could break any time." But even
as he says it, Lolo doesn't believe. Ten years ago, he might
have. But not now. Big Daddy Drought's here to stay. He
clutches the check and its keycodes to his chest.

A hundred yards away, the river flows on to California.

DEEP BLOOD KETTLE
HUGH HOWEY

They say the sky will fill with dust in a bad way if we don't do something soon. My teacher Mrs. Sandy says that if the meteor hits, it'll put up enough dirt to block the sun, and everything will turn cold for a long, long while. When I came home and told Pa about this, he got angry. He called Mrs. Sandy a bad word, said she was teaching us nonsense. I told him the dinosaurs died because of dust in the sky. Pa said there weren't no such thing as dinosaurs.

"You boys watch," he told me and my brother. "That rock'll burn up. It'll be no more than a flash of light. I've seen a million shooting stars if I've seen a dozen." Pa stopped rubbing his rifle and traced a big arc in the air with his oil-stained rag. "She'll hit the sky and light up like fireworks, and the worst she'll do is leave a crater like that one down in Arizona. Then we'll show them suckers how we watch over our land."

Only Pa don't use the word "suckers." Pa uses worse words for the invaders than he ever did for Mrs. Sandy. He never calls them aliens. Sometimes he says it's the Russians or the Chinese or the Koreans. He believes in aliens about as much as dinosaurs.

Pa spat in the dirt and asked if I was taking a break or something. I told him "nossir" and went back to oiling my gun. He and my brother did the same.

Pa says our land is fertile because of the killin' we soak it in. That's why things grow as tall as they do. The little critters are killed dead and give their life to the soil.

I seen it every year when we plow it under for the new crops. When I was a boy, before father let me drive the John Deere, I'd play in the loose soil his plowing left behind. Acres and acres for a sandbox. The dust he kicked up would blot the sky and dry my mouth, but I'd kick through the furrows and dig for arrowheads until my fingernails were chipped or packed full of dirt.

Where he hadn't yet plowed, you could see the dead stalks from the last harvest. The soil there was packed tight from the rains and the dry spells. Pa used to laugh at the newfangled ways of planting that kept the ground like that by driving the seeds straight through. It weren't the way the Samuels tended their land, he told us. We Samuels dragged great steel plows across the hard pack and the old stalks and we killed everything in the ground. That was what made the land ready again.

When I was younger, I found half a worm floppin' on top of the ground after a plow. It moved like the tail on a happy dog, but it was already dead. Took a while for it to realize, was all. I pinched it between my fingers and watched it wind down like the grandfather clock in the great room.

When it was still, the worm went into a furrow, and I kicked some dirt over it. That was the whole point. The little things would feed the corn, and the corn would feed us, and we would all get taller because of it. Pa, meanwhile, drove that tractor in great circles that took him nearly out of sight; the dust he kicked up could blot out the whole Montana sky, and my boots would fill up with gravel as I kicked through the loose furrows he left behind.

Pa only believes in things he can see. He didn't believe in the meteor until it became brighter than any star in the sky. Before long, you could see it in the daytime if you knew where to look and squinted just right. The people on the TV talked to scientists who said it was coming straight for us. They had a date and time and everything. One of them said you could know where it would land, but that nobody wanted a panic. It just meant people panicked everywhere. And then it leaked that the rock would hit somewhere between Russia and China, and Pa reckoned those people were panicking a little worse.

He called it a rock, not a meteor. Like a bunch of people, Pa don't think it'll amount to much. Folks been predicting doom since his grandpa was a boy, and the world outside still looked pretty much the same.

This was before we got "First Contact." That's what they called it even though the rock hadn't set down yet. It was nothing but a phone call from what I could tell. On the TV they said it was coming from the other side of the rock. That's when even the scientists and all the smart people started acting a little crazy.

First Contact happened back when Mrs. Sandy was still

our teacher. We listened to the news at school, I talked to her, and I didn't tell Pa any of what I learned. It made him angry hearing about the demands, but Mrs. Sandy said it was the best thing that ever happened to our planet, them deciding to come here. She told me a lot before she left and the substitute took her place. She was going to be one of them that welcomed the invaders, even sold her house and bought a pickup with a camper back. I eventually reckoned Pa was right to call her some of those bad things.

But I did sort out a bunch between the TV and what Mrs. Sandy said. The rock weren't no accident like the scientists used to suppose. It was aimed. Like the stones I chucked after a plowing, trying to hit one rock with another. The invaders, they was right behind the big rock.

Mrs. Sandy liked to say that our governments would make the right choice. And all of a sudden, the same channels on TV that I watched for news showed new people. They wore headphones and spoke funny and argued over what to do. My brother wouldn't stop asking about the little flags in front of each of them, and I had to tell him to shut up so I could hear.

The invaders were giving us a choice, it sounded like. All they wanted was half our land and for us to get rid of all of our weapons, and they would leave most of us alone. They gave a date. It was the same one the scientists had already figured. The rock could be moved, they said. It didn't have to hit. It could go into orbit, and then we could have it for our own.

On a different channel, men with suits and ties argued real loud over how much the rock was worth. They used words I'd never heard of before, something more than "trillion." I knew what gold and some of the other valuable things were, but some were called rare and sounded like they were from Earth. I couldn't sort out how something that could kill us one day could be worth so much the next, but the invaders said the rock only needed a nudge.

When I turned thirteen, Pa said I was finally old enough to drive. He taught me in the old pickup with the missing tailgate and the tires that were always starving for air. It was a shifter, which seemed a hard way to start driving, but Pa believed in learning the worst to begin with. I had to yank up on the steering wheel to push the old clutch all the way in. Damn thing made it so my arms would be as sore at night as my legs. Pa cursed every time the gears growled, and it was hot in the truck even with the windows down. But I got to where he would send me to fetch the mail. And once I'd mastered the old pickup, he taught me on the John Deere, and I learned to plow. Pa was right that it made driving the tractor easier. But it was still scary as hell.

The first time you drive something so big, you wonder if one man ought to be able. There was a red lever that went from rabbit to turtle, and Pa would stand in the cabin with me and yell for me to nudge it up. But we were already bouncing around something fierce. The noise was terrible. And looking back, I couldn't see the house through the haze I was stirring. It weren't even like we were moving so much as the great big tires of the tractor were spinning the earth beneath their knobby treads. Pa would bend over the seat and knock the red lever up, and the bucking would grow worse. The steering wheel jittered side to side, and I had to clutch it just to stay in my seat.

But like the truck, my fear of the tractor didn't keep.

Before long, Pa hitched the great plow to the back, twenty-four feet wide, and I learned how to kill the soil to make it ready for planting. The seat would bounce me along like I was in a saddle, and the radio would blare in the little cabin that smelled like my dad when he was sweaty. I did circles like I was mowing grass, but twenty-four feet at a time. The mesa behind our house would disappear behind the dust, and it got so I couldn't see the cliffs along the back of the homestead. But I could see the soil in front packed hard and tight, and I could see out the side where I'd already been. Plowing was a lot like mowing—I just had to overlap where I'd been before.

"Not too much overlap," Pa would tell me. The price of gas had gone way up since First Contact, and too much overlap meant an extra run for no good reason. And so I bounced along and put death in the soil. I cut the worms in half and made things ready for planting. Now and then, a deer would startle across the loose furrows, legs having a hard time of it, and white rabbits would dash from the thrush. The rabbits were the dumbest little things. They would dart back and forth in front of the tractor—they could see me coming, but they couldn't make up their minds. I would yell and yell at them, but they would just jitter back and forth until the tractor went over them and then the plow. Turning in my seat, I always expected a tuft of white to spit out somewhere, but the soil that kicked up would just turn a little red.

"That's where the corn will grow the tallest," Pa would say when I told him how dumb the rabbits were. The blood in the soil was a good thing. That's when you knew it was ready.

* * *

The cliffs behind our house were a source of constant play, and they had a funny name. *Too Close for Comfort*, they were called. I reckoned kids made up that name, but it was a real thing. Scientists called it that. Men who were supposedly smart had come up with it.

When I was a boy too young to drive—before I turned thirteen—they came from the university and dug in the dirt at the base of the cliffs that rise up behind our land. They found so many bones beneath the dirt that they couldn't take them all. Steve Harkin and I plotted to sneak in one night and nab a skull or two, but the men in the shiny city trucks with no 4X4 put a stop to that by giving us a skull each. It weren't as fun without the danger and flashlights, but we got our skulls.

I remember cradling that great hunk of bone as heavy as stone and asking one of the university men there why they were digging there.

"This here was a buffalo jump," the man told me. He reminded me of Mrs. Sandy, and he had this clipboard with all kinds of little squares full of numbers and was the smartest man I ever spoke to 'ccpt for my Pa.

"The buffalo used to come over this cliff and smash into the rocks down here," he told me and Steve Harkin. "That's where these bones came from."

Steve thought that was pretty cool. We gazed up at the cliffs that I had known all my life, the ones that delayed the sunrise in the morning, and I saw them different for the first time. I asked this man from the university why buffalo were so dumb.

"Oh, buffalo aren't dumb," he claimed. I was about to argue with him, but then he explained. "Indians used to chase the buffalo to the edge of the cliff in great herds," he said. They tumbled off hundreds at a time and smashed their legs so they couldn't walk. While they squealed and snorted and tried to pick themselves up on busted bones, the Indians would run in with spears and jab 'em in the neck.

Steve whistled. I asked the man if that was real.

"Very real," he said. "The people who used to live here long before us called it pishkun."

"Pushkin," Steve Harkin said. "What does that mean?"

"It means 'deep blood kettle,'" the man told us. He pointed to where the men and women were digging in these funny squares with ropes and stakes marking everything off. "You can still see the blood in the soil," he said.

I didn't know if that man from the university was playing with us or not, but I told him we needed to go. That skull he'd given me was getting heavier and heavier the longer he talked.

The people on TV with the little flags and the headphones reminded me of white rabbits in the plow season. You could watch 'em go back and forth on the screen. Everyone wanted the gold and the trillions and trillions and trillions and all the rare Earth stuff. But nobody wanted to give up their land. And the invaders insisted on half. They wanted half or they would take it all.

People on the TV argued about why the aliens would do something like this, why they would let the rock hit us and kick up the dirt and make things cold, but I knew. I reckon I knew better than most. Just the year before, I'd watched a movie about invaders coming down. They'd made a different kind of contact. There were fights with lasers and explosions and our side found a way at the end to lick them for good.

It was a good movie, but those invaders were dumb. I tried to picture us Samuels taming our plot of land something like that. Pa and Riley and me would take to the soil with guns and shoot the worms one by one. And the worms would fight back with the rabbits, the deer, the turtles, and the foxes. And I could imagine them swarming us and licking us good. They were dumb, but there was an awful lot of them.

Which was why we used the plow. It was why we throw the dirt up into the air. We make all things die in the soil so when we put in our own seed, that's all the life there is. And where the ground is reddest, that deep blood kettle, the corn reaches up so high you think it might leave us behind. And that's what the rock will do, plow us under. It weren't going to be like that movie at all.

Mrs. Sandy used to say before she left town that the dust would kick up and blot out the sky if the rock fell, but she didn't think we would let that happen. Mrs. Sandy always thought the best of people. She even liked my Pa, no matter what he called her. Me, I wished she would come back from wherever she went. I'd like to have her sit in the John Deere with me and feel it buck and buck and chase down those rabbits too dumb to move. I'd take Mrs. Sandy by the hand and lead her to the cliffs on the edge of our land and show her the piles of bones and see what the Indians had done.

But Mrs. Sandy was gone, and nobody went to school no more. And outside, the spot of light in the sky had grown so bright that it was like a star in the daytime. The people on the TV moved like rabbits. They were chased like buffalo. And you didn't need to know where to look no more to see that something bad was coming.

ANIMAL HUSBANDRY

SEANAN McGUIRE

The city of Clayton was burning. I saw the smoke from over fifteen miles away, but I kept riding towards it, less from hope that the fire was a sign of civilization than from sheer, cussed stubbornness. My instructions said I needed to go this way. Since all the GPS systems failed around the time the networks and satellite uplinks died, I really didn't think that deviating was a good idea. Not if I was actively interested in living, anyway.

Fortunately for me, the wind was blowing out to sea, carrying the bulk of the doubtless carcinogenic smoke with it. I left the trailer about a mile down the road from the lookout point, choosing the minor risk that one of the other poor souls left in this godforsaken world would stumble over it—you can't exactly LoJack a draft horse—over the greater risks of smoke inhalation and panicked animals rocketing out of my control. My mare, the unimaginatively named Midnight, would put up with just about anything I asked from her. She'd be able to stand the heat as long as I could.

Even with the wind in our favor, the air was so thick with ash that I could practically chew it by the time we got to the top of the lookout point. I shielded my eyes to block the flames, squinting through the smoke as I strained to see the city beyond. There wasn't much left to see. The fire had almost burned itself out, but it was still vigorous enough to make that particular route impassable.

There were two choices. We could try to find another route. Or we could backtrack twenty miles to the superstore I'd seen in San Ramon, resupply, and let the fire finish burning itself to death.

"We need a break, don't we, Midnight?" I asked, running a hand down the anxious mare's throat. She snorted, front legs dancing a half-panicked tattoo against the gravel. She was ready to bolt, holding herself in place solely because she assumed I wanted her to stay.

There was no need for that. We'd seen everything we'd come to see, and it was just more devastation. Tugging gently on the reins, I turned Midnight towards the caravan, and the road.

Before we rode out of the region completely, I stopped at the sign marking the city limits, pulled out my staple gun and another of my precious flyers, and set to work. Even if we didn't come back this way, even if the store managed to yield a better route, I would have done my self-imposed duty by the people who might still be living here. Wherever they were. When we finally turned towards San Ramon, white copy-paper ghosts glared from the city sign behind us, eye-poppingly clean in a landscape gone to ash.

It would never be enough, but it would have to do.

IMPORTANT—IMPORTANT—IMPORTANT—PLEASE READ YOUR SURVIVAL COULD DEPEND ON IT

"If you're alive and reading this, there are a few things you should be aware of. Firstly, those diseases everyone died of? The ones that barely had time to make the papers before it was over? They weren't natural, and that means there's no way to estimate their out-of-body survival rates. <u>Be careful.</u> Keep contact with the dead to an absolute minimum. If you must handle human remains, wear gloves and be prepared to dispose of your outer garments immediately afterwards. Avoid closed-up spaces where people died, especially those which have remained moist. Diseases survive better in dark, warm, moist places.

"Stick with bottled water whenever possible. Boil everything when you can't. All that plastic they said we needed to keep out of the landfills? Forget it. Bottled water could save you. (Not just from the manmade toxins. Cholera, dysentery, lots of other nasty things could be lurking in the water by now. Drink Crystal Springs or shit out your intestines. The choice is yours.) When selecting canned foods, check to be sure that the cans are whole and have not been dented. Exterior rust is fine. Interior rust is not.

"On the bottom of this flyer you will find a list of basic nutritional supplements which are likely to be missing in your current diet. All items on the list can be found at any large grocery store or moderately-sized health food store. I recommend you begin taking them.

"Watch out for dogs and other previously domesticated animals, as they may have turned feral in the absence of human custodianship. I have also included a list of standard poison baits and their doses. I do not recommend their use. They may still provide a measure of security while traveling.

"I am on my way to Grants Pass, Oregon. I recommend you do the same as soon as you can. Time was short before the pandemics, and there's no telling how much we have left.

"Hurry."

My name was at the bottom: Mercy Neely, Doctor of Veterinary Medicine. Possibly the last vet in the world. Possibly the last medical practitioner of any kind in California.

I really wish I'd paid more attention in class.

The San Ramon superstore showed signs of moderate looting, which was reassuring. I've come to see looting as a sort of hopeful omen, a little piece of proof that the human race will manage to recover from what it's done to itself. I was less pleased to see that my would-be looters had focused their attentions on the junk food aisles and cosmetics, almost completely ignoring the canned goods and well-stocked pharmacy. Maybe that was better for me, but it didn't bode well for the survival of the species.

After my brief solo reconnaissance was done, I cranked up the loading bay door enough to drive the wagon inside and parked it in what used to be the stock room. Midnight wandered off to investigate while I was unhitching the other horses and pouring their oats out on the concrete. I don't know what their names were originally; I call them Tweedledee and Tweedledum, and that seems to work well enough for everyone involved. The goats were hard at work trying to chew through their ropes again. I set them loose to wreak what havoc they could inside the closed superstore ecosystem. Goats can do a lot of damage, but even they can't chew through walls.

Finally, with everyone else roaming free, I opened the wagon's back door and released the hounds. Even indoors, it's difficult to overstate the value of a good guard dog in this brave new world we're all marooned in. They came bounding out with tails wagging madly, even Brewster, whose close-cropped stub of a tail could barely do more than vibrate rapidly back and forth.

The dogs inquired whether I might be interested in company while I explored the store, largely through the mechanism of trying to jump up and lick my face. I allowed that this might be acceptable. An agreement was reached. Who says animals don't communicate?

"All you be good, now," I cautioned the rest of the traveling zoo, and stepped through the swinging doors that separated the loading dock from the rest of the store, all three dogs at my heels. Time to go shopping. New-world style.

The world ended about fourteen months ago. Sadly, I missed this momentous occasion. I was home sick with the plague, and was thus not allowed to participate in the grand pandemic which wiped out the majority of the human race. Yeah. I get the irony. Still, I like to think I'm doing pretty well, all things considered. I've made it more than halfway to my eventual destination, despite some pretty major complications, and I've managed to do it without having a psychotic break. Talking to the animals doesn't count. That's what I went to school for.

As for how I missed the pandemic… bubonic plague has been endemic in California's small mammal population since the 1800s, when it was imported along with other luxury items such as silk, spices, and cheap immigrant labor. The state managed to hold on to all four imports until just recently. I doubt there's going to be much of a market for any of them these days, but hey, I also didn't think mankind was going to wipe itself out in a blaze of dick-waving glory, so what do I know?

California's ongoing plague problems are how I know for certain that the pandemic was manmade. Supposedly, Texas was hit by a form of bubonic plague that mowed down the population like a wheat thresher. It spread too fast for anything but a droplet-based transmission—person-to-person by way of sneezing or coughing—and it was resistant to all known antibiotics. Welcome to fourteenth-century Europe, where the Black Death was everybody's least-favorite neighbor. Only that's not possible, because that's not how bubonic plague works. Bubonic plague is carried by rat fleas, transmitted by rat fleas, and spreads slowly, since rat fleas are notoriously unreliable about when they bite you. Pneumonic plague is droplet-based, but that's not what killed Texas. Bubonic plague that wasn't bubonic plague killed Texas, and that means it wasn't bubonic plague at all. It was something somebody built in a lab, and I'm sure its creator won the Terrorist Science Fair before letting it out of the vial.

The Texas plague killed horses, cattle, goats, and most dogs, by the way. Texas may be the last place in this country where it's safe to sleep outside without fear of your neighbor's abandoned Rottweiler. Thanks, Texas plague. Thanks a lot.

As the only veterinarian in Pumpkin Junction, California,

my practice covered basically anything that people wanted to bring me. Mercy Neely, Swiss Army veterinarian. If someone had a sick cat, dog, or other standard pet, I was their girl. If they had a horse that needed gelding, a cow that needed a checkup, or a flock of sheep that needed their shots, that was also me. I did parrots, reptiles, and anything else animal-like that happened to need medical attention. I examined an African praying mantis once; I extracted a mousetrap from the stomach of an escaped boa constrictor; I euthanized an emu with a broken leg. My practice was boring more often than it was interesting, but it was always vital. I was the only game in town.

I guess I technically still would be, if I'd stayed.

I'd been out at the O'Shea place the Sunday before the pandemic started, giving the goats their yearly exam. With thirty of the things in the flock, it was easier for me to go to them. The barn was hopping with fleas, and I must've been bitten a good thirty times before I finished for the day. Three days later, I got sick. You can't be a California vet and not know what's endemic to the population; I know bubonic plague when I see it. I diagnosed myself, gave myself an illegal prescription for tetracycline, doped myself to the gills, and went to bed. Not, sadly, before hanging a sign with a cute little hand-drawn rat on my door. "Doc's got the PLAGUE!"

I even slept through the quake that leveled half the damn state. Remember, kids, vets get the good tranquilizers.

I like to think that there were other survivors in my home town. The pathogens that hit California seem to have caught and killed almost instantly, and I went to bed for six days starting two days before the pandemic came out to play. I like to think that some people made it through the sickness, saw the sign on my door, and decided that there was no point in checking. I wouldn't blame them if they did, but I would see them again when I got to Grants Pass.

Most of all, I like to think that I was exposed along with everybody else. I didn't miss infection because I was locked in my little room over the office; I missed infection because I had a natural immunity. In a healthy population, naturally immune parents tend to have naturally immune children. Maybe Dan didn't make it through, but if I was naturally immune, there's a chance that Linda was, too. There's a chance that she'll be waiting for me at the end of this road.

Wishful thinking, but hell. Everybody's allowed a little wishful thinking after they've survived the end of the world.

The dogs roved ahead of me as we walked through the dimly lit store, never ranging more than about ten feet away. It wasn't just because they felt the need to protect me, although that was a part of it; the last six people we'd seen had been armed, and had taken shots at my little pack before I had time to tell them not to. When I left Pumpkin Junction, I had six dogs in my personal escort. They'd been picked off one by one, and the three I had left were the ones who'd figured out that hiding behind the human was the best way to survive.

Brewster was the most timid of the three, despite also being the largest. He looked back at me, buffing uncertainly. "It's okay, Brewster," I said, in a soothing tone. I was only half-paying attention to his unease. My eyes were too busy crawling over the shelves, noting the things we needed, the things we could use, and comparing them to the wagon's carrying capacity. If I hitched Midnight alongside the Tweedles and walked for a while, we could manage another few hundred pounds of kibble; that would probably get us all the way to Sacramento, where we could—

A gun hammer was cocked behind me. A very small sound, but one that had come to hold a great deal of importance in my life over the past year. It was the sound of someone who might decide that my surviving the pandemic was just a fluke that needed to be corrected.

I stopped in my tracks, raising my hands to shoulder-height. Brewster hunched his massive head down, a growl rumbling from the bottom of his throat. I could hear the other two dogs moving up ahead, still uncertain and unwilling to approach the stranger. "I'm sorry," I said, voice calm and level. Never be the first to show panic. Never let them think that you might be an easy target. "I didn't know this store was yours. If you'll just let me gather up my animals, I'll be on my way." *Please*, I prayed silently, *please let me gather up my animals.* I lost two goats to a man who saw them as fresh meat on the hoof; I lost my second riding horse to a man who fancied himself the Lone Ranger and decided that an old gray mare would do just fine as Silver. I'm sure one of her legs was broken before I'd even made it out of the valley that he took her from me in. The old gray mare, she ain't what she used to be.

"Turn around, miss. Real slow, no sudden movements."

Male; middle-aged, probably one of the white-collar workers who'd packed this sort of business park before the pandemic; artificially polite, which was a natural development under the circumstances. Even when you were the one holding the gun, it paid to be polite. Next time, the gun might belong to someone else. I turned as I'd been instructed, not dropping my hands or making any effort to avoid meeting his eyes. Confident without being challenging, that was the goal. Once you've stared down a bull that smells cows in estrus, you can handle anything humanity has left to throw at you.

The man behind me looked almost exactly like I would have expected, even down to the stained, slightly tattered white dress shirt. Even a year after the disaster, people still dressed like they expected the old world to be called back to order any second. The poor bastards. They'd been domesticated, and they didn't even know it.

"Those your dogs?" he demanded. The skin of his left cheek jumped and fluttered in a nervous tic, making it look like he might jitter apart at any moment.

"Yes," I said, not lowering my hands. "They're also my horses, my goats, and, if you've been inside the wagon already, my birds. They're well-fed and not a threat to you."

The pistol he had angled towards my chest wavered, almost perfectly in time with the tic on his cheek. "Are you some sort of farmer?"

"No. I'm a veterinarian."

Shock and relief chased each other across his face for a moment before he lowered his gun, saying, "Miss, I'm going to need you to come with me." He hesitated, finally adding, more quietly, "Please."

"Sir, I don't want to get your hopes up here. I'm not a people doctor. I'm—"

"It's my daughter. She's nine."

Linda will be nine this year. If the world can make it that long. I sighed.

"Come back to my wagon with me. I'll need some things from my bag."

* * *

His name was Nathan Anderson; he'd been a tech writer, churning out endless pages of instructions for machines he'd never use. Like almost every other survivor I've encountered, he never got sick at all. No pandemic for Nathan. No wife, friends, or job, either. Nothing but scrounging from the stores of San Ramon and taking care of Miranda. Until Miranda started getting sick; until he was lucky enough to catch a traveling veterinarian who'd been to some form of medical school, even if it wasn't the human kind.

He was quiet as we walked the three blocks back to the office building they called home, only the gun in his hand serving as a reminder of his status as my captor. Brewster, Mike, and Little Bobby trailed along behind me, an anxious canine escort. I wasn't willing to leave them behind. Too much of a chance that Nathan had friends who'd learned the hard way that dogs needed to be shot on sight.

Nathan paused at the office door. "She was awake when I went out scouting for supplies. She gets a little disoriented sometimes, but she's a good girl. She'll probably even like your dogs."

I could smell the sickness from here, that horrible combination of sweat and vomit and a dozen other bodily fluids that says "something's dying nearby." I kept my face as neutral as I could. "Let's see if she's up now."

Nathan looked relieved—like he'd been afraid right up until that moment that I was going to disarm him and run—and opened the door.

Miranda's room had been a corner office before the pandemic, probably much-prized for the floor-to-ceiling windows that comprised two of the four walls. Now it was a little girl's paradise. The once-white walls had been inexpertly painted pink, and flower-shaped plastic decals studded the window glass. Toys and books were heaped haphazardly around the floor. At the center of it all was a glorious fairy tale of a four-poster bed—God knows where they found that—and in the center of the bed was Miranda.

Any hopes this little jaunt would prove my theory about immunity being hereditary died when I saw her. Adopted daughter, maybe. Adopted after the pandemic, almost certainly. But biological daughter? No. Not unless he'd had a Korean wife whose genes had been able to beat his nine falls out of ten.

Miranda raised her head at the sound of the door, summoning a smile from somewhere deep inside herself. "Daddy." She paused, brow knotting. "We have company?" The question was uncertain, like she thought I might be a hallucination.

I swallowed the lump in my throat before it could turn to full-fledged tears. "I'm Mercy Neely, honey. I'm a veterinarian."

Sudden interest brightened her eyes. "Is that why you have dogs? I like dogs. I used to have a dog. Before—" She stopped, the brightness fading. "Before."

"A lot of people did." Nathan was standing frozen next to me. He'd ceased to be a factor as soon as I saw the little girl. Ignoring the possibility that he'd decide to shoot me, I started for the bed, setting my traveling medicine kit down on the mattress. "Now, your dad says you don't feel so good."

"Uh-huh."

"You want to tell me about it?"

"My head hurts. I can't breathe sometimes. I keep choking when I try to sleep." She sounded ashamed of her own symptoms. Poor kid. "I—" A cough cut off her words, and she sat up to catch it in her hands, bending almost double in the process. It had a rich, wet sound, like it was being dredged up through quicksand.

"Just breathe," I said, and turned back towards Nathan. "It could be a lot of things. Without a lab, I can't really tell you which one. It's probably pneumonia, complicated by general malnutrition. I'm going to give you a list of medicines that I need you to go back to the store and find for me."

His eyes widened, then narrowed. "I'm not leaving you alone with her."

"My way out of here is back at that store. I'm unarmed. I'm not exactly going to take a sick little girl hostage, now, am I?" I shook my head, expression disgusted. "She shouldn't be left alone. Either you trust me here, or you trust that I'll come back."

"I'll lock the office door behind me."

"You do that."

Still he hesitated, eyes flicking from me to Miranda and back again.

I sighed, and played the ultimate trump card: "I don't know how long she has."

His expression hardened.

"I'll be right back."

Things I don't need to explain: what it was like to step outside for the first time after I got better and the rest of the world didn't. I'm pretty sure everyone that's still alive has their own version of *that* story, and they don't need to be repeated. I woke up, I felt better, I went outside, I threw up six times, I went a little crazy, and I got over it. There wasn't time to have a nervous breakdown. Maybe if I'd been a doctor, but I wasn't a doctor; I never wanted to be a doctor. I'm a veterinarian, and my patients still needed me.

Four days isn't long enough for most animals to turn vicious; that made my job a lot easier. It took eighteen hours to canvas the town, letting cats out of houses, assessing dogs and livestock and making my decisions as impartially as I could. Domestic cattle aren't made to live without somebody to take care of them. They need milking, or their udders will split open and they'll die of infection. Sheep are worse. Goats are fine on their own; so are horses, most poultry, and pigs. Cats will go feral. Dogs will go mean. If it could be released, I either released it or fed it and promised to be back in a little while. If it couldn't be released...

Ending future suffering is one luxury veterinarians have that human doctors don't. I spent a lot of that first day crying, but I guarantee you that while the people of Pumpkin Junction died just as badly as the rest of the world, our animals died better than they did anywhere else.

I held back some of the stock. A few milking goats, some horses I knew were gentle and well-mannered, several of the larger, healthier, friendlier dogs. I was already planning, you see. Figuring out what I'd need, and what *we'd* need when I finished the trip. Can't build a society without animals, and there's no point in re-domesticating when we have the potential to save the work we've already done. Some of it, anyway.

God, I hope she's there.

* * *

Miranda turned wide, dark eyes on me after her adoptive father was gone, and asked, "Am I going to get better?"

"That's what medicine is for, isn't it?" I opened my bag, pulling out a needle and a small, unlabeled bottle. I never labeled that particular bottle. They taught us that in veterinary school. Even when they were the ones who'd decided that dear old Kitty was ready for that great scratching post in the sky, people didn't want to see the label.

They also taught us to be natural about it. To fill the syringe like it was any other vaccination. "Miranda's a pretty name," I said. "I like it."

"So do I," she said, watching me with gravity beyond her years. "Are you going to give me a shot?"

"Mm-hmm. Just a little one, to help you sleep." I glanced up, offering her a warm smile. "I have a daughter just about your age. Her name is Linda."

"You do?" Her expression turned carefully neutral, like she was about to walk into a minefield. "Is she... did she..."

"She's just fine. She's waiting for me in a place called Grants Pass. It's up in Oregon. I'm on my way there now." Linda would be there. Linda had to be there. She was the one who had told me to go there in the first place. Eight years old, smart as a whip, and gullible enough to believe everything she ever read. Gullible enough to believe the pandemic was coming, for one thing, and that it would probably come in our lifetime. "When they go crazy, Mom, you have to promise to come to Oregon," she said, with those big blue eyes just as wide and serious as they could go. Like my agreeing to come to Grants Pass was a matter of life or death. So I agreed. What else can you do? I only got her every other weekend, and if she wanted me to promise to take a post-apocalyptic road trip, I'd promise.

Linda had to be there. What I'd seen in Pumpkin Junction on the day I went a little crazy was just the shock talking. I didn't see it again. And if part of me insisted that I only didn't see it because I didn't go back there, who cares? There were no animals in that shitty little apartment. There was nothing there to save.

Miranda looked unsure. "How come she isn't traveling with you?"

"Well, see, Linda's daddy and I didn't think it was a good idea for us to live together anymore. So Linda was with her daddy when everybody got sick, and she had to start without me. I'll catch up to her sooner or later." I tapped the syringe, easing out the bubbles. "She promised to meet me there, and she takes her promises seriously."

Linda takes everything seriously, and has since she was born. So we sat down with the maps of the state, and we worked out four routes that we could take to get to Oregon. The Route Where They Closed the Roads. The Route Where Quarantine Kept the Roads Open. The Route Where There's Been An Earthquake and We Have To Go Around. The Route Where Too Many People Survived and We Need to Avoid Them. Even after the earthquake that took out most of the Los Angeles metro area, the bulk of California was mostly somewhere between routes one and two. Linda wouldn't have had any problems if she'd avoided the coast roads and skirted the area around Red Bluff.

"Can we come with you? Me and my daddy?"

"We'll talk about it when you wake up," I said soothingly.

She didn't even cry when the needle went in; she bore the brief pain like a trooper. Domesticated animals always do.

* * *

58

There are a lot of ways for people to die in the post-pandemic world; I've seen most of them. The human race was domesticated a long time ago, and like the cows that need someone to milk them, or the sheep too dumb to run away from a predator, the humans forgot how to stay alive without the trappings of their civilization. So they stagger along pretending they still have some quality of life while their teeth get loose from scurvy and their bowels get scarred by parasitic infections. Most of the people who lived through the sicknesses shouldn't have. They're just suffering now, without all the little luxuries they were so accustomed to.

Euthanasia is kinder. It's quicker. It takes the pain away. If we don't let our pets suffer, why should we let people do it? Part of being a vet is knowing that the thing to do with suffering is end it, not prolong it just for the sake of being able to say that all your patients survive. I'm not a moralist. I see suffering, and I end it. It's that simple. Human doctors aren't allowed to have that luxury, but there's a reason I never wanted to work with people.

Miranda's eyes fluttered shut in a matter of seconds as the drugs took effect, her body effectively sliding into a comatose state that was deeper than any sleep. I put the syringe away and took her hand, my index finger pressed against the pulse point of her wrist. Her heart sped up, fighting against the lidocaine. Her fingers tightened on mine with no more force than a kitten's jaws.

She gasped once, sighed, and was still.

"See?" I said, slipping my hand out of hers. "Nothing to be afraid of."

* * *

Nathan returned about ten minutes later, clutching a bag that bulged with medical supplies. I met him at the office door, motioning for him to be quiet. "She's sleeping," I whispered. He looked past me to where she was stretched out on her bed, expression peaceful, and believed me.

Outside, in the hall, I offered him a sympathetic smile, and said, "It's bad, but she should pull through. I've given her something to help her sleep, and I can show you which medicines to give her. But there's a fee for my help."

The hope in his eyes died like a switch had been flipped. "What's that?" he asked, warily.

I held up my bag. "After spending a year scrounging in all this rust? You need a tetanus shot. Let me give it to you, and I'll stay as long as it takes to get her better."

Nathan laughed, sounding utterly relieved. "I think I can stand a shot if it gets my baby girl better."

"Good." I smiled. "This won't hurt a bit."

"...FOR A SINGLE YESTERDAY"

GEORGE R. R. MARTIN

Keith was our culture, what little we had left. He was our poet and our troubadour, and his voice and his guitar were our bridges to the past. He was a time-tripper too, but no one minded that much until Winters came along.

Keith was our memory. But he was also my friend.

He played for us every evening after supper. Just beyond sight of the common house, there was a small clearing and a rock he liked to sit on. He'd wander there at dusk, with his guitar, and sit down facing west. Always west; the cities had been east of us. Far east, true, but Keith didn't like to look that way. Neither did the rest of us, to tell the truth.

Not everybody came to the evening concerts, but there was always a good crowd, say three-fourths of the people in the commune. We'd gather around in a rough circle, sitting on the ground or lying in the grass by ones and twos. And Keith, our living hi-fi in denim and leather, would stroke his beard in vague amusement and begin to play.

He was good, too. Back in the old days, before the Blast,

he'd been well on his way to making a name for himself. He'd come to the commune four years ago for a rest, to check up on old friends and get away from the musical rat race for a summer. But he'd figured on returning.

Then came the Blast. And Keith had stayed. There was nothing left to go back to. His cities were graveyards full of dead and dying, their towers melted tombstones that glowed at night. And the rats—human and animal—were everywhere else.

In Keith, those cities still lived. His songs were all of the old days, bittersweet things full of lost dreams and loneliness. And he sang them with love and longing. Keith would play requests, but mostly he stuck to his kind of music. A lot of folk, a lot of folk-rock, and a few straight rock things and show tunes. Lightfoot and Kristofferson and Woody Guthrie were particular favorites. And once in a while he'd play his own compositions, written in the days before the Blast. But not often.

Two songs, though, he played every night. He always started with "They Call the Wind Maria" and ended with "Me and Bobby McGee." A few of us got tired of the ritual, but no one ever objected. Keith seemed to think the songs fit us, somehow, and nobody wanted to argue with him.

Until Winters came along, that is. Which was in a late-fall evening in the fourth year after the Blast.

His first name was Robert, but no one ever used it, although the rest of us were all on a first name basis. He'd introduced himself as Lieutenant Robert Winters the evening he arrived, driving up in a jeep with two other men. But his Army didn't exist anymore, and he was looking for refuge and help.

That first meeting was tense. I remember feeling very

scared when I heard the jeep coming, and wiping my palms on my jeans as I waited. We'd had visitors before. None of them very nice.

I waited for them alone. I was as much a leader as we had in those days. And that wasn't much. We voted on everything important, and nobody gave orders. So I wasn't really a boss, but I was a greeting committee. The rest scattered, which was good sense. Our last visitors had gone in big for slugging people and raping the girls. They'd worn black-and-gold uniforms and called themselves the Sons of the Blast. A fancy name for a rat pack. We called them SOB's too, but for other reasons.

Winters was different, though. His uniform was the good ol' U.S. of A. Which didn't prove a thing, since some Army detachments are as bad as the rat packs. It was our own friendly Army that went through the area in the first year after the Blast, scorching the towns and killing everyone they could lay their hands on.

I don't think Winters was part of that, although I never had the courage to flat-out ask him. He was too decent. He was big and blond and straight, and about the same age as the rest of us. And his two "men" were scared kids, younger than most of us in the commune. They'd been through a lot, and they wanted to join us. Winters kept saying that he wanted to help us rebuild.

We voted them in, of course. We haven't turned anyone away yet, except for a few rats. In the first year, we even took in a half-dozen citymen and nursed them while they died of radiation burns.

Winters changed us, though, in ways we never antic-ipated. Maybe for the better. Who knows? He brought books and supplies. And guns, too, and two men who knew how to use them. A lot of the guys on the commune had come there to get away from guns and uniforms, in the days before the Blast. So Pete and Crazy Harry took over the hunting, and defended us against the rats that drifted by from time to time. They became our police force and our Army.

And Winters became our leader.

I'm still not sure how that happened. But it did. He started out making suggestions, moved on to leading discussions, and wound up giving orders. Nobody objected much. We'd been drifting ever since the Blast, and Winters gave us a direction. He had big ideas, too. When I was spokesman, all I worried about was getting us through until tomorrow. But Winters wanted to rebuild. He wanted to build a generator, and hunt for more survivors, and gather them together into a sort of village. Planning was his bag. He had big dreams for the day after tomorrow, and his hope was catching.

I shouldn't give the wrong impression, though. He wasn't any sort of a tin tyrant. He led us, yeah, but he was one of us, too. He was a little different from us, but not *that* different, and he became a friend in time. And he did his part to fit in. He even let his hair get long and grew a beard.

Only Keith never liked him much.

Winters didn't come out to concert rock until he'd been with us over a week. And when he did come, he stood outside the circle at first, his hands shoved into his pockets. The rest of us were lying around as usual, some singing, some just listening. It was a bit chilly that night, and we had a small fire going.

Winters stood in the shadows for about three songs. Then, during a pause, he walked closer to the fire. "Do you take requests?" he asked, smiling uncertainly.

I didn't know Winters very well back then. But I knew Keith. And I tensed a little as I waited for his answer.

But he just strummed the guitar idly and stared at Winters' uniform and his short hair. "That depends," he said at last. "I'm not going to play 'Ballad of the Green Berets,' if that's what you want."

An unreadable expression flickered over Winters' face. "I've killed people, yes," he said. "But that doesn't mean I'm proud of it. I wasn't going to ask for that."

Keith considered that, and looked down at his guitar. Then, seemingly satisfied, he nodded and raised his head and smiled. "Okay," he said. "What do you want to hear?"

"You know 'Leavin' on a Jet Plane'?" Winters asked.

The smile grew. "Yeah. John Denver. I'll play it for you. Sad song, though. There aren't any jet planes anymore, Lieutenant. Know that? 's true. You should stop and think why."

He smiled again, and began to play. Keith always had the last word when he wanted it. Nobody could argue with his guitar.

A little over a mile from the common house, beyond the fields to the west, a little creek ran through the hills and the trees. It was usually dry in the summer and the fall, but it was still a nice spot. Dark and quiet at night, away from the noise and the people. When the weather was right, Keith would drag his sleeping bag out there and bunk down under a tree. Alone.

That's also where he did his timetripping.

I found him there that night, after the singing was over and everyone else had gone to bed. He was leaning against his favorite tree, swatting mosquitoes and studying the creekbed.

I sat down next to him. "Hi, Gary," he said, without looking at me.

"Bad times, Keith?" I asked.

"Bad times, Gary," he said, staring at the ground and idly twirling a fallen leaf. I watched his face. His mouth was taut and expressionless, his eyes hooded.

I'd known Keith for a long time. I knew enough not to say anything. I just sat next to him in silence, making myself comfortable in a pile of fresh-fallen leaves. And after a while he began to talk, as he always did.

"There ought to be water," he said suddenly, nodding at the creek. "When I was a kid, I lived by a river. Right across the street. Oh, it was a dirty little river in a dirty little town, and the water was as polluted as all hell. But it was still water. Sometimes, at night, I'd go over to the park across the street, and sit on a bench, and watch it. For hours, sometimes. My mother used to get mad at me."

He laughed softly. "It was pretty, you know. Even the oil slicks were pretty. And it helped me think. I miss that, you know. The water. I always think better when I'm watching water. Strange, right?"

"Not so strange," I said.

He still hadn't looked at me. He was still staring at the dry creek, where only darkness flowed now. And his hands were tearing the leaf into pieces. Slow and methodical, they were.

"Gone now," he said after a silence. "The place was too close to New York. The water probably glows now, if there is any water. Prettier than ever, but I can't go back. So much is like that. Every time I remember something, I have to remember that it's gone now. And

I can't go back, ever. To anything. Except... except with that..." He nodded toward the ground between us. Then he finished with the leaf, and started another.

I reached down by his leg. The cigar box was where I expected it. I held it in both hands, and flipped the lid with my thumbs. Inside, there was the needle, and maybe a dozen small bags of powder. The powder looked white in the starlight. But seen by day, it was pale, sparkling blue.

I looked at it and sighed. "Not much left," I said.

Keith nodded, never looking. "I'll be out in a month, I figure." His voice sounded very tired. "Then I'll just have my songs, and my memories."

"That's all you've got now," I said. I closed the box with a snap and handed it to him. "Chronine isn't a time machine, Keith. Just a hallucinogen that happens to work on memory."

He laughed. "They used to debate that, way back when. The experts all said chronine was a memory drug. But they never *took* chronine. Neither have you, Gary. But I know. I've timetripped. It's not memory. It's more. You go back, Gary, you really do. You live it again, whatever it was. You can't change anything, but you know it's real, all the same."

He threw away what was left of his leaf, and gathered his knees together with his arms. Then he put his head atop them and looked at me. "You ought to timetrip someday, Gary. You really ought to. Get the dosage right, and you can pick your yesterday. It's not a bad deal at all."

I shook my head. "If I wanted to timetrip, would you let me?"

"No," he said, smiling but not moving his head. "I found the chronine. It's mine. And there's too little left to share. Sorry, Gary. Nothing personal, though. You know how it is."

"Yeah," I said. "I know how it is. I didn't want it anyway."

"I knew that," he said.

Ten minutes of thick silence. I broke it with a question. "Winters bother you?"

"Not really," he said. "He seems okay. It was just the uniforms, Gary. If it wasn't for those damn bastards in uniform and what they did, I *could* go back. To my river, and my singing."

"And Sandi," I said.

His mouth twisted into a reluctant smile. "And Sandi," he admitted. "And I wouldn't even need chronine to keep my dates."

I didn't know what to say to that. So I didn't say anything. Finally, wearying, Keith slid forward a little, and lay back under the tree. It was a clear night. You could see the stars through the branches.

"Sometimes, out here at night, I forget," he said softly, more to himself than to me. "The sky still looks the same as it did before the Blast. And the stars don't know the difference. If I don't look east, I can almost pretend it never happened."

I shook my head. "Keith, that's a game. It *did* happen. You can't forget that. You know you can't. And you can't go back. You know that, too."

"You don't listen, do you, Gary? I *do* go back. I really do."

"You go back to a dream world, Keith. And it's dead, that world. You can't keep it up. Sooner or later you're going to have to start living in reality."

Keith was still looking up at the sky, but he smiled gently as I argued. "No, Gary. You don't see. The past is as real as the present, you know. And when the present is bleak and empty, and the future more so, then the only sanity is living in the past."

I started to say something, but he pretended not to hear. "Back in the city, when I was a kid, I never saw this many stars," he said, his voice distant. "The first time I got into the country, I remember how shocked I was at all the extra stars they'd gone and stuck in my sky." He laughed softly. "Know when that was? Six years ago, when I was just out of school. Also last night. Take your pick. Sandi was with me, both times."

He fell silent. I watched him for a few moments, then stood up and brushed myself off. It was never any use. I couldn't convince him. And the saddest part of it was, I couldn't even convince myself. Maybe he was right. Maybe, for him, that was the answer.

"You ever been in the mountains?" he asked suddenly. He looked up at me quickly, but didn't wait for an answer. "There was this night, Gary—in Pennsylvania, in the mountains. I had this old beat-up camper, and we were driving through, bumming it around the country.

"Then, all of a sudden, this fog hit us. Thick stuff, gray and rolling, all kind of mysterious and spooky. Sandi loved stuff like that, and I did too, kind of. But it was hell to drive through. So I pulled off the road, and we took out a couple of blankets and went off a few feet.

"It was still early, though. So we just lay on the blankets together, and held each other, and talked. About us, and my songs, and that great fog, and our trip, and her acting, and all sorts of things. We kept laughing and kissing, too, although I don't remember what we said that was so funny. Finally, after an hour or so, we undressed each other and made love on the blankets, slow and easy, in the middle of that dumb fog."

Keith propped himself up on an elbow and looked at

me. His voice was bruised, lost, hurt, eager. And lonely. "She was beautiful, Gary. She really was. She never liked me to say that, though. I don't think she believed it. She liked me to tell her she was pretty. But she was more than pretty. She *was* beautiful. All warm and soft and golden, with red-blond hair and these dumb eyes that were either green or gray, depending on her mood. That night they were gray, I think. To match the fog." He smiled, and sank back, and looked up at the stars again.

"The funniest thing was the fog," he said. Very slowly. "When we'd finished making love, and we lay back together, the fog was gone. And the stars were out, as bright as tonight. The stars came out for us. The silly goddamn voyeuristic stars came out to watch us make it. And I told her that, and we laughed, and I held her warm against me. And she went to sleep in my arms, while I lay there and looked at stars and tried to write a song for her."

"Keith…" I started.

"Gary," he said. "I'm going back there tonight. To the fog and the stars and my Sandi."

"Damnit, Keith," I said. "Stop it. You're getting yourself hooked."

Keith sat up again and began unbuttoning his sleeve. "Did you ever think," he said, "that maybe it's not the drug that I'm addicted to?" And he smiled very broadly, like a cocky, eager kid.

Then he reached for his box, and his timetrip. "Leave me alone," he said.

That must have been a good trip. Keith was all smiles and affability the next day, and his glow infected the rest of us. The mood lasted all week. Work seemed to go faster and easier than usual, and the nightly song sessions were as boisterous as I can remember them. There was a lot of laughter, and maybe more honest hope than we'd had for quite a while.

I shouldn't give Keith all the credit, though. Winters was already well into his suggestion-making period, and things were happening around the commune. To begin with, he and Pete were already hard at work building another house—a cabin off to the side of the common house. Pete had hooked up with one of the girls, and I guess he wanted a little more privacy. But Winters saw it as the first step toward the village he envisioned.

That wasn't his only project, either. He had a whole sheaf of maps in his jeep, and every night he'd drag someone off to the side and pore over them by candlelight, asking all sorts of questions. He wanted to know which areas we'd searched for survivors, and which towns might be worth looting for supplies, and where the rat packs liked to run, and that sort of thing. Why? Well, he had some "search expeditions" in mind, he said.

There was a handful of kids on the commune, and Winters thought we ought to organize a school for them, to replace the informal tutoring they'd been getting. Then he thought we ought to build a generator and get the electricity going again. Our medical resources were limited to a good supply of drugs and medicines; Winters thought that one of us should quit the fields permanently and train himself as a village doctor. Yeah, Winters had a lot of ideas, all right. And a good portion of 'em were pretty good, although it was clear that the details were going to require some working out.

Meanwhile, Winters had also become a regular at the

evening singing. With Keith in a good mood, that didn't pose any real problems. In fact, it livened things up a little.

The second night that Winters came, Keith looked at him very pointedly and swung into "Vietnam Rag," with the rest of us joining in. Then he followed it up with "Universal Soldier." In between lyrics, he kept flashing Winters this taunting grin.

Winters took it pretty well, however. He squirmed and looked uncomfortable at first, but finally entered into the spirit of the thing and began to smile. Then, when Keith finished, he stood up. "If you're so determined to cast me as the commune's very own friendly reactionary, well I guess I'll have to oblige," he said. He reached out a hand. "Give me that guitar."

Keith looked curious but willing. He obliged. Winters grabbed the instrument, strummed it a few times uncertainly, and launched into a robust version of "Okie from Muskogee." He played like his fingers were made of stone, and sang worse. But that wasn't the point.

Keith began laughing before Winters was three bars into the song. The rest of us followed suit. Winters, looking very grim and determined, plowed on through to the bitter end, even though he didn't know all the words and had to fake it in spots. Then he did the Marine hymn for an encore, ignoring all the hissing and moaning.

When he was finished, Pete clapped loudly. Winters bowed, smiled, and handed the guitar back to Keith with an exaggerated flourish.

Keith, of course, was not one to be topped easily.

He nodded at Winters, took the guitar, and promptly did "Eve of Destruction."

Winters retaliated with "Welfare Cadillac." Or tried to.

Turned out he knew hardly any of the words, so he finally gave that up and settled for "Anchors Aweigh."

That sort of thing went on all night, as they jousted back and forth, and everybody else sat around laughing. Well, actually we did more than laugh. Generally we had to help Winters with his songs, since he didn't really know any of them all the way through. Keith held his own without us, of course.

It was one of the more memorable sessions. The only thing it really had in common with Keith's usual concerts was that it began with "They Call the Wind Maria," and ended with "Me and Bobby McGee."

But the next day, Keith was more subdued. Still some kidding around between him and Winters, but mostly the singing slipped back into the older pattern. And the day after, the songs were nearly all Keith's kind of stuff, except for a few requests from Winters, which Keith did weakly and halfheartedly.

I doubt that Winters realized what was happening. But I did, and so did most of the others. We'd seen it before. Keith was getting down again. The afterglow from his latest timetrip was fading. He was getting lonely and hungry and restless. He was itching, yet again, for his Sandi.

Sometimes, when he got that way, you could almost see the hurt. And if you couldn't see it, you could hear it when he sang. Loud and throbbing in every note.

Winters heard it too. He'd have had to be deaf to miss it. Only I don't think he understood what he heard, and I know he didn't understand Keith. All he knew was the anguish he heard. And it troubled him.

So, being Winters, he decided to do something about it. He came to Keith.

I was there at the time. It was midmorning, and Keith and I had come in from the field for a break. I was sitting on the well with a cup of water in my hand, and Keith was standing next to me talking. You could tell that he was getting ready to timetrip again, soon.

He was very down, very distant, and I was having trouble reaching him.

In the middle of all this, Winters comes striding up, smiling, in his Army jacket. His house was rising quickly, and he was cheerful about it, and he and Crazy Harry had already mapped out the first of their "search expeditions."

"Hello, men," he said when he joined us at the well. He reached for the water, and I passed my cup.

He took a deep drink and passed it back. Then he looked at Keith. "I enjoy your singing," he said. "I think everybody else does, too. You're very good, really." He grinned. "Even if you are an anarchistic bastard."

Keith nodded. "Yeah, thanks," he said. He was in no mood for fooling around.

"One thing, though, has been bothering me," Winters said. "I figured maybe I could discuss it with you, maybe make a few suggestions. Okay?"

Keith stroked his beard and paid a little more attention. "Okay. Shoot, Colonel."

"It's your songs. I've noticed that most of them are pretty… down, let's say. Good songs, sure. But sort of depressing, if you know what I mean. Especially in view of the Blast. You sing too much about the old days, and things we've lost. I don't think that's good for morale. We've got to stop dwelling so much on the past if we're ever going to rebuild."

Keith stared at him, and slumped against the well. "You gotta be kidding," he said.

"No," said Winters. "No, I mean it. A few cheerful songs would do a lot for us. Life can still be good and worthwhile if we work at it. You should tell us that in your music. Concentrate on the things we still have. We need hope and courage. Give them to us."

But Keith wasn't buying it. He stroked his beard, and smiled, and finally shook his head. "No, Lieutenant, no way. It doesn't work like that. I don't sing propaganda, even if it's well-meant. I sing what I feel."

His voice was baffled. "Cheerful songs, well… no. I can't. They don't work, not for me. I'd like to believe it, but I can't, you see. And I can't make other people believe if I don't. Life is pretty empty around here, the way I see it. And not too likely to improve. And… well, as long as I see it that way, I've got to sing it that way. You see?"

Winters frowned. "Things aren't *that* hopeless," he said. "And even if they were, we can't admit it, or we're finished."

Keith looked at Winters, at me, then down into the well. He shook his head again, and straightened. "No," he said simply, gently, sadly. And he left us at the well to stalk silently in the fields.

Winters watched him go, then turned to me. I offered him more water, but he shook his head. "What do you think, Gary?" he said. "Did I have a point? Or didn't I?"

I considered the question, and the asker. Winters sounded very troubled and very sincere. And the blond stubble on his chin made it clear that he was trying his best to fit in. I decided to trust him, a little.

"Yes," I said. "I know what you were driving at. But it's not that easy. Keith's songs aren't just songs. They mean things to him."

I hesitated, then continued. "Look, the Blast was hell

for everybody, I don't have to tell you that. But most of us out here, we chose this kind of life, 'cause we wanted to get away from the cities and what they stood for. We miss the old days, sure. We've lost people, and things we valued, and a lot that made life joyful. And we don't much care for the constant struggle, or for having to live in fear of the rat packs. Still, a lot of what we valued is right here on the commune, and it hasn't changed that much. We've got the land, and the trees, and each other. And freedom of a sort. No pollution, no competition, no hatred. We like to remember the old days, and the *good* things in the cities—that's why we like Keith's singing—but now has its satisfactions tōo.

"Only, Keith is different. He didn't choose this way, he was only visiting. His dreams were all tied up with the cities, with poetry and music and people and noise. And he's lost his world; everything he did and wanted to do is gone. And… and well, there was this girl. Sandra, but he called her Sandi. She and Keith lived together for two years, traveled together, did everything together. They only split for a summer, so she could go back to college. Then they were going to join up again. You understand?"

Winters understood. "And then the Blast?"

"And then the Blast. Keith was here, in the middle of nowhere. Sandi was in New York City. So he lost her, too. I think sometimes that if Sandi had been with him, he'd have gotten over the rest. She was the most important part of the world he lost, the world they shared together. With her here, they could have shared a new world and found new beauties and new songs to sing. But she wasn't here, and…"

I shrugged.

"Yeah," said Winters solemnly. "But it's been four years,

Gary. I lost a lot too, including my wife. But I got over it. Sooner or later, mourning has to stop."

"Yes," I said. "For you, and for me. I haven't lost that much, and you… you think that things will be good again. Keith doesn't. Maybe things were *too* good for him in the old days. Or maybe he's just too romantic for his own good. Or maybe he loved harder than we did. All I know is that *his* dream tomorrow is like his yesterday, and mine isn't. I've never found anything I could be that happy with. Keith did, or thinks he did. Same difference. He wants it back."

I drank some more water, and rose. "I've got to get back to work," I said quickly, before Winters could continue the conversation. But I was thoughtful as I walked back to the fields.

There was, of course, one thing I hadn't told Winters, one important thing. The timetripping. Maybe if Keith was forced to settle for the life he had, he'd come out of it. Like the rest of us had done.

But Keith had an option; Keith could go back. Keith still had his Sandi, so he didn't *have* to start over again.

That, I thought, explained a lot. Maybe I should have mentioned it to Winters. Maybe.

Winters skipped the singing that night. He and Crazy Harry were set to leave the next morning, to go searching to the west. They were off somewhere stocking their jeep and making plans.

Keith didn't miss them any. He sat on his rock, warmed by a pile of burning autumn leaves, and out-sung the bitter wind that had started to blow. He played hard and loud, and sang sad. And after the fire went out, and the audience drifted off, he took his guitar and his cigar box and went off toward the creek.

I followed him. This time the night was black and cloudy, with the smell of rain in the air. And the wind was strong and cold. No, it didn't sound like people dying. But it moved through the trees and shook the branches and whipped away the leaves. And it sounded... restless.

When I reached the creek, Keith was already rolling up his sleeve.

I stopped him before he took his needle out. "Hey, Keith," I said, laying a hand on his arm. "Easy. Talk first, okay?"

He looked at my hand and his needle, and returned a reluctant nod. "Okay, Gary," he said. "But short. I'm in a rush. I haven't seen Sandi for a week."

I let go his arm and sat down. "I know."

"I was trying to make it last, Gary. I only had a month's worth, but I figured I could make it last longer if I only timetripped once a week." He smiled. "But that's hard."

"I know," I repeated. "But it would be easier if you didn't think about her so much."

He nodded, put down the box, and pulled his denim jacket a little tighter to shut out the wind. "I think too much," he agreed. Then, smiling, he added, "Such men are dangerous."

"Ummm, yeah. To themselves, mostly." I looked at him, cold and huddled in the darkness. "Keith, what will you do when you run out?"

"I wish I knew."

"I know," I said. "Then you'll forget. Your time machine will be broken, and you'll have to live today. Find somebody else and start again. Only it might be easier if you'd start now. Put away the chronine for a while. Fight it."

"Sing cheerful songs?" he asked sarcastically.

"Maybe not. I don't ask you to wipe out the past, or pretend it didn't happen. But try to find something in the present. You know it can't be as empty as you pretend. Things aren't black and white like that. Winters was part right, you know—there *are* still good things. You forget that."

"Do I? What do I forget?"

I hesitated. He was making it hard for me. "Well… you still enjoy your singing. You know that. And there could be other things. You used to enjoy writing your own stuff. Why don't you work on some new songs? You haven't written anything to speak of since the Blast."

Keith had picked up a handful of leaves and was offering them to the wind, one by one. "I've thought of that. You don't know how much I've thought of that, Gary. And I've *tried*. But nothing comes." His voice went soft right then. "In the old days, it was different. And you know why. Sandi would sit out in the audience every time I sang. And when I did something new, something of mine, I could see her brighten. If it was good, I'd know it, just from the way she smiled. She was proud of me, and my songs."

He shook his head. "Doesn't work now, Gary. I write a song now, and sing it, and… so what? Who cares? You? Yeah, maybe you and a few of the others come up after and say, 'Hey, Keith, I liked that.' But that's not the same. My songs were *important* to Sandi, the same way her acting was important to me. And now my songs aren't important to anyone. I tell myself that shouldn't matter. I should get my own satisfaction from composing, even if no one else does. I tell myself that a lot. But saying it doesn't make it so."

Sometimes I think, right then, I should have told Keith that his songs were the most important thing in the world to me. But hell, they weren't. And Keith was a friend, and I couldn't feed him lies, even if he needed them.

Besides, he wouldn't have believed me. Keith had a way of recognizing truth.

Instead, I floundered. "Keith, you could find someone like that again, if you tried. There are girls in the commune, girls as good as Sandi, if you'd open yourself up to them. You could find someone else."

Keith gave me a calm stare, more chilling than the wind. "I don't need someone else, Gary," he said. He picked up the cigar box, opened it, and showed me the needle. "I've got Sandi."

Twice more that week Keith timetripped. And both times he rushed off with a feverish urgency. Usually he'd wait an hour or so after the singing, and discreetly drift off to his creek. But now he brought the cigar box with him, and left even before the last notes of "Me and Bobby McGee" had faded from the air.

Nobody mentioned anything, of course. We all knew Keith was timetripping, and we all knew he was running out. So we forgave him, and understood. Everybody understood, that is, except Pete, Winters' former corporal. He, like Winters and Crazy Harry, hadn't been filled in yet. But one evening at the singing, I noticed him looking curiously at the cigar box that lay by Keith's feet. He said something to Jan, the girl he'd been sleeping with. And she said something back. So I figured he'd been briefed.

I was too right.

Winters and Crazy Harry returned a week, to the day, after their departure. They were not alone. They brought three young teen-agers, a guy and two girls, whom they'd found down west, in company with a group of rats. "In company," is a euphemism, of course. The kids had been slaves. Winters and Crazy had freed them.

I didn't ask what had happened to the rats. I could guess.

There was a lot of excitement that night and the night after. The kids were a little frightened of us, and it took a lot of attention to convince them that things would be different here. Winters decided that they should have their own place, and he and Pete began planning a second new cabin. The first one was nearing its crude completion.

As it turned out, Winters and Pete were talking about more than a cabin. I should have realized that, since I caught Winters looking at Keith very curiously and thoughtfully on at least two occasions.

But I didn't realize it. Like everyone else, I was busy getting to know the newcomers and trying to make them feel at ease. It wasn't simple, that.

So I didn't know what was going on until the fourth evening after Winters' return. I was outside, listening to Keith sing. He'd just barely finished "They Call the Wind Maria," and was about to swing into a second song, when a group of people suddenly walked into the circle. Winters led them, and Crazy Harry was just behind him with the three kids. And Pete was there, with his arm around Jan. Plus a few others who hadn't been at the concert when it started but had followed Winters from the common house.

Keith figured they wanted to listen, I guess. He began to play. But Winters stopped him.

"No, Keith," he said. "Not right now. We've got business to take care of now, while everybody's together. We're going to talk tonight."

Keith's fingers stopped, and the music faded. The only sounds were the wind and the crackle of the nearby burning leaves. Everyone was looking at Winters.

"I want to talk about timetripping," Winters said.

Keith put down his guitar and glanced at the cigar box at the base of concert rock. "Talk," he said.

Winters looked around the circle, studying the impassive faces, as if he was weighing them before speaking. I looked too.

"I've been told that the commune has a supply of chronine," Winters began. "And that you use it for timetripping. Is that true, Keith?"

Keith stroked his beard, as he did when he was nervous or thoughtful. "Yeah," he said.

"And that's the *only* use that's ever been made of this chronine?" Winters said. His supporters had gathered behind him in what seemed like a phalanx.

I stood up. I didn't feel comfortable arguing from the ground. "Keith was the first one to find the chronine," I said. "We were going through the town hospital after the Army had gotten through with it. A few drugs were all that were left. Most of them are in the commune stores, in case we need them. But Keith wanted the chronine. So we gave it to him, all of us. Nobody else cared much."

Winters nodded. "I understand that," he said very reasonably. "I'm not criticizing that decision. Perhaps you didn't realize, however, that there are other uses for chronine besides timetripping."

He paused. "Listen, and try to judge me fairly, that's all I ask," he said, looking at each of us in turn. "Chronine is a powerful drug; it's an important resource, and we need all our resources right now. And timetripping—anyone's timetripping—is an *abuse* of the drug. Not what it was intended for."

That was a mistake on Winters' part. Lectures on drug abuse weren't likely to go over big in the commune. I could feel the people around me getting uptight.

Rick, a tall, thin guy with a goatee who came to the concerts every night, took a poke at Winters from the ground. "Bullshit," he said. "Chronine's time travel, Colonel. Meant to be used for tripping."

"Right," someone else said. "And we gave it to Keith. I don't want to timetrip, but he does. So what's wrong with it?"

Winters defused the hostility quickly. "Nothing," he said. "*If* we had an unlimited supply of chronine. But we don't. Do we, Keith?"

"No," Keith said quietly. "Just a little left."

The fire was reflected in Winters' eyes when he looked at Keith. It made it difficult to read his expression. But his voice sounded heavy. "Keith, I know what those time trips mean to you. And I don't want to hurt you, really I don't. But we need that chronine, all of us."

"How?" That was me. I wanted Keith to give up chronine, but I'd be damned before I'd let it be taken from him. "How do we *need* the chronine?"

"Chronine is not a time machine," Winters said. "It is a memory drug. And there are things we *must* remember." He glanced around the circle. "Is there anyone here who ever worked in a hospital? An orderly? A candy-striper? Never mind. There might be, in a group this size. And they'd have seen things. Somewhere in the back of their skulls they'd *know* things we need to know. I'll bet some of you took shop in high school. I'll bet you learned all sorts of useful things. But how much do you remember?

With chronine, you could remember it all. We might have someone here who once learned to make arrows. We might have a tanner. We might have someone who knows how to build a generator. We might have a *doctor!*"

Winters paused and let that sink in. Around the circle, people shifted uneasily and began to mutter.

Finally Winters continued. "If we found a library, we wouldn't burn the books for heat, no matter how cold it got. But we're doing the same thing when we let Keith timetrip. *We're* a library—all of us here, we have books in our heads. And the only way to read those books is with chronine. We should use it to help us remember the things we must know. We should hoard it like a treasure, calculate every recall session carefully, and make sure—make *absolutely* sure—that we don't waste a grain of it."

Then he stopped. A long, long silence followed; for Keith, an endless one. Finally Rick spoke again. "I never thought of that," he said reluctantly. "Maybe you have something. My father was a doctor, if that means anything."

Then another voice, and another; then a chorus of people speaking at once, throwing up half-remembered experiences that might be valuable, might be useful. Winters had struck paydirt.

He wasn't smiling, though. He was looking at me.

I wouldn't meet his eyes. I couldn't. He had a point— an awful, awful point. But I couldn't admit that, I couldn't look at him and nod my surrender. Keith was my friend, and I had to stand by him.

And of all of us in the circle, I was the only one standing. But I couldn't think of anything to say.

Finally Winters' eyes moved. He looked at concert rock. Keith sat there, looking at the cigar box.

The hubbub went on for at least five minutes, but at last it died of its own weight. One by one the speakers glanced at Keith, and remembered, and dropped off into awkward silence. When the hush was complete, Keith rose and looked around, like a man coming out of a bad dream.

"No," he said. His voice was hurt and disbelieving; his eyes moved from person to person. "You can't. I don't... don't *waste* chronine. You know that, all of you. I visit Sandi, and that's not wasting. I need Sandi, and she's gone. I have to go back. It's my only way, my time machine." He shook his head.

My turn. "Yes," I said, as forcefully as I could manage. "Keith's right. Waste is a matter of definition. If you ask me, the biggest waste would be sending people back to sleep through college lectures a second time."

Laughter. Then other voices backed me. "I'm with Gary," somebody said. "Keith needs Sandi, and we need Keith. It's simple. I say he keeps the chronine."

"No way," someone else objected. "I'm as compassionate as anyone, but *hell*—how many of our people have died over the last few years 'cause we've bungled it when they needed doctoring? You remember Doug, two years ago? You shouldn't need chronine for that. A bad appendix, and he dies. We butchered him when we tried to cut it out. If there's a chance to prevent that from happening again—even a long shot—I say we gotta take it."

"No guarantee it won't happen anyway," the earlier voice came back. "You have to hit the right memories to accomplish anything, and even *they* may not be as useful as you'd like."

"Shit. We have to *try*..."

"I think we have an obligation to Keith..."

"I think Keith's got an obligation to *us*..."

And suddenly everybody was arguing again, hassling back and forth, while Winters and Keith and I stood and listened. It went on and on, back and forth over the same points. Until Pete spoke.

He stepped around Winters, holding Jan. "I've heard enough of this," he said. "I don't even think we got no argument. Jan here is gonna have my kid, she tells me. Well, damnit, I'm not going to take any chances on her or the kid dying. If there's a way we can learn something that'll make it safer, we take it. Especially I'm not gonna take no chances for a goddamn weakling who can't face up to life. Hell, Keithie here wasn't the only one hurt, so how does *he* rate? I lost a chick in the Blast too, but I'm not begging for chronine to dream her up again. I got a new chick instead. And that's what you better do, Keith."

Keith stood very still, but his fists were balled at his sides. "There are differences, Pete," he said slowly. "Big ones. My Sandi was no chick, for one thing. And I loved her, maybe more than you can ever understand. I know you don't understand pain, Pete. You've hardened yourself to it, like a lot of people, by pretending that it doesn't exist. So you convinced everybody you're a tough guy, a strong man, real independent. And you gave up some of your humanity, too." He smiled, very much in control of himself now, his voice sure and steady. "Well, I won't play that game. I'll cling to my humanity, and fight for it if I must. I loved once, really loved. And now I hurt. And I won't deny either of those things, or pretend that they mean any less to me than they do."

He looked to Winters. "Lieutenant, I want my Sandi, and I won't let you take her away from me. Let's have a vote."

Winters nodded.

It was close, very close. The margin was only three votes. Keith had a lot of friends.

But Winters won.

Keith took it calmly. He picked up the cigar box, walked over, and handed it to Winters. Pete was grinning happily, but Winters didn't even crack a smile.

"I'm sorry, Keith," he said.

"Yeah," said Keith. "So am I." There were tears on his face. Keith was never ashamed to cry.

There was no singing that night.

Winters didn't timetrip. He sent men on "search expeditions" into the past, all very carefully planned for minimum risk and maximum reward.

We didn't get any doctor out of it. Rick made three trips back without coming up with any useful memories. But one of the guys remembered some valuable stuff about medicinal herbs after a trip back to a bio lab, and another jaunt recalled some marginally good memories about electricity.

Winters was still optimistic, though. He'd turned to interviewing by then, to decide who should get to use the chronine next. He was very careful, very thorough, and he always asked the right questions. No one went back without his okay. Pending that approval, the chronine was stored in the new cabin, where Pete kept an eye on it.

And Keith? Keith sang. I was afraid, the night of the argument, that he might give up singing, but I was wrong. He couldn't give up song, any more than he could give up Sandi. He returned to concert rock the very next evening, and sang longer and harder than ever before. The night after that he was even better.

During the day, meanwhile, he went about his work with a strained cheerfulness. He smiled a lot, and talked a lot, but he never *said* anything much. And he never mentioned chronine, or timetripping, or the argument.

Or Sandi.

He still spent his nights out by the creek, though. The weather was getting progressively colder, but Keith didn't seem to mind. He just brought out a few blankets and his sleeping bag, and ignored the wind, and the chill, and the increasingly frequent rains.

I went out with him once or twice to sit and talk. Keith was cordial enough. But he never brought up the subjects that really mattered, and I couldn't bring myself to force the conversations to places he obviously didn't want to go. We wound up discussing the weather and like subjects.

These days, instead of his cigar box, Keith brought his guitar out to the creek. He never played it when I was there, but I heard him once or twice from a distance, when I was halfway back to the common house after one of our fruitless talks. No singing, just music. Two songs, over and over again. You know which two.

And after a while, just one. "Me and Bobby McGee." Night after night, alone and obsessed, Keith played that song, sitting by a dry creek in a barren forest. I'd always liked the song, but now I began to fear it, and a shiver would go through me whenever I heard those notes on the frosty autumn wind.

Finally, one night, I spoke to him about it. It was a short conversation, but I think it was the only time, after the argument, that Keith and I ever really reached each other.

I'd come with him to the creek, and wrapped myself in a heavy woolen blanket to ward off the cold, wet drizzle that was dripping from the skies. Keith lay against his tree, half into his sleeping bag, with his guitar on his lap. He didn't even bother to shield it against the damp, which bothered me.

We talked about nothing, until at last I mentioned his lonely creek concerts. He smiled. "You know why I play that song," he said.

"Yeah," I said. "But I wish you'd stop."

He looked away. "I will. After tonight. But tonight I play it, Gary. Don't argue, please. Just listen. The song is all I have left now, to help me think. And I've needed it, 'cause I been thinking a lot."

"I warned you about thinking," I said jokingly.

But he didn't laugh. "Yeah. You were right, too. Or I was, or Shakespeare... whoever you want to credit the warning to. Still, sometimes you can't help thinking. It's part of being human. Right?"

"I guess."

"I know. So I think with my music. No water left to think by, and the stars are all covered. And Sandi's gone. Really gone now. You know, Gary... if I kept on, day to day, and didn't think so much, I might forget her. I might even forget what she looked like. Do you think Pete remembers his chick?"

"Yes," I said. "And you'll remember Sandi. I'm sure of that. But maybe not quite so much... and maybe that's for the best. Sometimes it's good to forget."

Then he looked at me. Into my eyes. "But I don't *want* to forget, Gary. And I won't. I won't."

And then he began to play. The same song. Once. Twice. Three times. I tried to talk, but he wasn't listening. His fingers moved on, fiercely, relentlessly. And the music and the wind washed away my words.

Finally I gave up and left. It was a long walk back to the common house, and Keith's guitar stalked me through the drizzle.

Winters woke me in the common house, shaking me from my bunk to face a grim, gray dawn. His face was even grayer. He said nothing; he didn't want to wake the others, I guess. He just beckoned me outside.

I yawned and stretched and followed him. Just outside the door, Winters bent and handed me a broken guitar.

I looked at it blankly, then up at him. My face must have asked the question.

"He used it on Pete's head," Winters said. "And took the chronine. I think Pete has a mild concussion, but he'll probably be all right. Lucky. He could be dead, real easy."

I held the guitar in my hands. It was shattered, the wood cracked and splintered, several strings snapped. It must have been a hell of a blow. I couldn't believe it. "No," I said. "Keith... no, he couldn't..."

"It's his guitar," Winters pointed out. "And who else would take the chronine?" Then his face softened. "I'm sorry, Gary. I really am. I think I understand why he did it. Still, I want him. Any idea where he could be?"

I knew, of course. But I was scared. "What... what will you do?"

"No punishment," he said. "Don't worry. I just want the chronine back. We'll be more careful next time."

I nodded. "Okay," I said. "But nothing happens to Keith. I'll fight you if you go back on your word, and the others will too."

He just looked at me, very sadly, like he was disappointed

FOR A SINGLE YESTERDAY"

that I'd mistrust him. He didn't say a thing. We walked the mile to the creek in silence, me still holding the guitar.

Keith was there, of course. Wrapped in his sleeping bag, the cigar box next to him. There were a few bags left. He'd used only one.

I bent to wake him. But when I touched him and rolled him over, two things hit me. He'd shaved off his beard. And he was very, very cold.

Then I noticed the empty bottle.

We'd found other drugs with the chronine, way back when. They weren't even guarded. Keith had used sleeping pills.

I stood up, not saying a word. I didn't need to explain. Winters had taken it all in very quickly. He studied the body and shook his head.

"I wonder why he shaved?" he said finally.

"I know," I said. "He never wore a beard in the old days, when he was with Sandi."

"Yes," said Winters. "Well, it figures."

"What?"

"The suicide. He always seemed unstable."

"No, Lieutenant," I said. "You've got it all wrong, Keith didn't commit suicide."

Winters frowned. I smiled.

"Look," I said. "If you did it, it would be suicide. You think chronine is only a drug for dreaming. But Keith figured it for a time machine. He didn't kill himself. That wasn't his style. He just went back to his Sandi. And this time, he made sure he stayed there."

Winters looked back at the body. "Yes," he said. "Maybe so." He paused. "For his sake, I hope that he was right."

* * *

The years since then have been good ones, I guess. Winters is a better leader than I was. The timetrips never turned up any knowledge worth a damn, but the search expeditions proved fruitful. There are more than two hundred people in town now, most of them people that Winters brought in.

It's a real town, too. We have electricity and a library, and plenty of food. And a doctor—a real doctor that Winters found a hundred miles from here. We got so prosperous that the Sons of the Blast heard about us and came back for a little fun. Winters had his militia beat them off and hunt down the ones who tried to escape.

Nobody but the old commune people remember Keith. But we still have singing and music. Winters found a kid named Ronnie on one of his trips, and Ronnie has a guitar of his own. He's not in Keith's league, of course, but he tries hard, and everybody has fun. And he's taught some of the youngsters how to play.

Only thing is, Ronnie likes to write his own stuff, so we don't hear many of the old songs. Instead we get postwar music. The most popular tune, right now, is a long ballad about how our Army wiped out the Sons of the Blast.

Winters says that's a healthy thing; he talks about new music for a new civilization. And maybe he has something. In time, I'm sure, there will be a new culture to replace the one that died. Ronnie, like Winters, is giving us tomorrow.

But there's a price.

The other night, when Ronnie sang, I asked him to do "Me and Bobby McGee." But nobody knew the words.

CHISLEHURST MESSIAH
LAUREN BEUKES

It wasn't the blood seas that got to him. Or the dead birds that fell out of the sky and rotted on the lawn in crumpled bundles of feathers. Or the plague of flying ants crusting themselves up against the window panes. Or even Marlowe dying in agony as her organs liquidised inside her and gushed out all over the carpet so Simon had to rip the damn thing out. You'd be surprised how much the smell of spleen will permeate a room. Especially when you can't open the windows because of the ants.

That was all Very Upsetting, make no mistake. Even though he had been about to divorce the silly bitch and nail her for half her estate and the account in Jersey that she thought he didn't know about. And even though her death was messy and ugly and awkward—embarrassed, he'd left her to it, going into the den to play that jewel-swapping game on Facebook while she screamed and writhed and spat up black strings of blood—frankly, her dying saved him a lot of time and effort because the dumb cunt hadn't changed her will yet. Easier to inherit than squeeze a decent alimony out of a shit-hot investment banker with a shit-hot investment banker's lawyer.

Not that all that cash was any use to him at the moment. That was the supreme fucker of it. The banks were locked up. The bankers were either dead or hiding out in holiday houses in Spain and France, fortified in a hurry, private security guards patrolling the perimeters with automatic weapons. At least, that's what he'd seen on the news before the news cut out.

He missed television. He missed the stock ticker running along the bottom of the business report. Missed the explosions in dusty Third World deserts and the *Women Who Kill* and plastic surgery reality shows and especially the scruffy animals being rescued from nasty abusive owners by trained task teams of dedicated volunteers. He felt a bit like one of those pathetically mangy pets himself, trapped in Marlowe's Chislehurst block of flats all alone, with nothing to eat except cans of foie gras and baked beans. (Marlowe had thrown out anything with "organic" on the label back in the early days when rumours about terrorists targeting the food markets was still the prevailing theory.)

And surely it'd be Only A Matter of Time before the government restored order and his satellite TV and sent an elite unit, CO19 maybe, to the rescue? He just needed to outlast the hoodie scum running rampant in the streets.

At least the building still had electricity. After last year's riots, the body corporate had passed a motion to install generators in the building. (Couldn't have warm Stoli!) Simon reckoned there was at least a few weeks' worth of diesel stashed in the basement.

So far he hadn't had to leave home for supplies. He

went shopping in the neighbouring apartments, with a handkerchief doused in Issey Miyake pressed over his mouth and nose to try to obscure the smell. The bodies left him strangely unmoved. It was all very abstract, like some grotesque modern art exhibition, all black puddled insides and swarms of flies that lifted off the bloated grey corpses in a halo when he stepped into the room.

He was much more interested in snooping around, reaffirming the suspicions he'd long fostered about their friends and neighbours. The Pepoys, for example, had a lifetime supply of prescription uppers in their medicine cabinet, which would explain the delirious cheer Alice had brought to dinner parties. He'd never liked her or her over-eager speculative conversation starters: "If you could go to anywhere on holiday where would it be?" Right where I've just been, you stupid bint. That's the whole point of marrying into money. The only pick-me-up Alice Pepoys needed now was a spatula, he thought, grinning spitefully.

He cleaned out her stash of pharmaceuticals just in case. He didn't mind feeling a bit sorry for himself with Everything He'd Been Through, but he didn't want to get stuck in wallowing self pity. Especially if CO19 got delayed.

The Bennetts were even more pathetic. Four of the five bedrooms were lavishly appointed straight from a bespoke decorator's catalogue; pinstripe walls and inoffensive abstract prints. The fifth was kitted out with a king size bed with a black rubber sheet and a closet containing a parking attendant's outfit and a camera rigged in the mirrored door.

He took the tapes home with him, along with four tins of sardines, sun-dried cherry tomatoes imported from Italy, water biscuits, a loaf of rye bread, frozen, and, an even dirtier secret than the half-hearted sex dungeon:

three months' worth of Sainsbury's microwave meals.

On the way back, he thought he heard a baby screaming from the house a block over. But cats fighting make almost exactly the same noise. And he wasn't going to risk his life for a bloody cat. It wasn't that he was a man of no conscience. He'd seen that heart-breaking documentary on the pets left behind after 9/11. It had reduced even that cold bitch Marlowe to a sobbing, snotty bundle tucked under his arm on the couch. Even worse than that dolphin movie. He'd be sure to tell CO19 about poor little kitty when they got here, and they could sort it out.

The Bennetts' sex videos were tedious. He'd seen way worse on the Internet. Which was the only thing still running. All the major networks were down. No TV. No radio. No mobile phone reception. He'd picked up some radio chatter in the beginning; government broadcasts advising people to stay in their homes: pip, pip, keep calm and carry on, which segued into increasingly panicky emergency services reports asking people to report to local medical centres as soon as possible. Then it petered off into static. Occasionally, bizarrely, he'd pick up heavy metal music, as if some radio engineer had walked out and left *Shouty Goth Freaks Greatest Hits Volume 13* playing at full blast.

And yet, somehow, by some mechanism he didn't understand, probably learned from dodgy Arab protestors, the Internet was still working. And the bloody chavs were in control of it.

He'd been glued to Marlowe's Powerbook, trawling YouTube, his only link to the outside world. He spent hours bouncing from clip to clip, compulsively shoving cashew nuts into his mouth, washing them down with her

Ardbeg. If the footage was anything to go by, the looting was still in full swing.

Occasionally he heard the roar of engine noise in the distance, which inspired him to keep the curtains closed at night. But Marlowe's neighbours weren't the type who coveted designer trainers and iPods and the other shit the kids on the clips were still going after. And anyway, why would they bother with the suburbs when the little scum had the whole city as their playground?

He spent the next couple of days mainlining Colombian coffee and Ardbeg and popping Alice Pepoy's uppers and a course of expired antibiotics, because he'd seen enough zombie movies to know that the only thing worse than rampaging hordes of dead-eyed creatures is dying of something embarrassing like an infected toenail. (And he *had* stubbed his toe on the doorframe, when he dragged Marlowe's corpse, wrapped in twelve layers of garbage bags, out onto the front lawn where it wouldn't be so very much in the way, no doubt exposing himself to all kinds of horrible bacteria in the process.)

Mostly he stayed in bed, the laptop balanced on his stomach, which was admittedly a little more padded than normal. He needed to get to the gym; his abs were turning into jelly. Too much stale bruschetta and salty snack foods. But the one in the building's basement stank like an abbatoir and the Stairmaster was practically alive with maggots.

He scrolled through the comments sections of the videos. "The yoof shall inherit the earth" was the most common slogan, outnumbering the diehard spam streams ten to one. He clicked on a link titled "Chelsea Deth Rap", spooning duck pâté into his mouth with his fingers while he waited for it load.

A grainy image of a teenaged moron cruising along in a black BMW SUV, arm lolling out the window, miming along to out-of-sync lyrics, mediocre bass tinny in the backgroud. The yoof shall inherit the earth, all right. Pity they can't fucking rhyme. Or spell, Simon thought, checking out the mangled language superimposed on the screen: "When the birds is dieng/the peoples is crying/when the rich are fuked/they ain't got no luck/our time is here/yeah, our time is here/is right fukin now.

Christ.

He clicked the link to another one ("apacolypse now innit"), the Gherkin burning in the background, a kid wearing a balaclava dancing in front of it, a Sprite bottle filled with what had to be petrol in one raised hand. Simon couldn't hear what the kid was shouting at the camera or iPhone or whatever; the sound of exploding glass and screaming smothered his voice.

Another clip showed a group of kids roaring through Harvey Nichols on dirt bikes, casually swiping perfume and make-up displays off the shelves with golf clubs. Marlowe had practically lived at Harvey Nicks. Her closets heaved with Vivienne Westwood corsets that were decades too young for her.

The only survivors seemed to be the kind of kids you saw shambling around the sink estates. Hollow-eyed yobs with acne-faced girlfriends cluttering up the pavements with pushchairs and streaming-nosed toddlers. "Underprivileged", my arse, Simon thought, bitterly. Not exactly starving African children. Living off benefits, leeches on society. Breeding like cockroaches and sucking the life out of the country. Human scum, the lot of them. Taking the piss.

Parasites like them were the reason he voted Conservative. That and tax cuts.

He did find some diversity, hidden deep in the results pages: a young Nigerian or Somali girl or something (who can tell, honestly?) with a shaved head and metal shit in her face, demonstrating first aid techniques and basic water filtration in a series of clips. In another video, a gloating young Eastern European lunatic with a husky voice and a ponytail and a grease-stained t-shirt, sitting in his basement, ranting into his webcam in a *hilarious* accent about "viral Ragnarok" and "zis is vot happens ven you don't vaccinate your children."

Simon realised that he hadn't seen a single person over thirty on any of the recent clips. He hoped this was because people his age couldn't be arsed. But he was beginning to doubt it.

Feverishly, he clicked on clip after clip, desperate to find someone—anyone—who looked like his sort of person. His age. His type. Nothing. And that's when he had The Epiphany.

CO19 were never coming.

He, Simon Thomas St. Martinborough, was the last of his kind.

He half-skidded, half-ran to the full-length mirror in the walk-in-closet, taking a moment to admire himself before searching out the truth in his reflection. You'd never say he was 38. (A wannabe silver fox, Marlowe had called him. At 23 years his senior, she could fucking talk.) His scruffy beard was peppered with silver. His hair was dirty and sticking up in places. But his skin glowed with oily pink health and his eyes were wild, full of intensity and fire. He looked like a man who had survived a Terrible Thing. He looked Enlightened. He looked, in short, like The Chosen One.

His reverie was interrupted by roaring engines. Aston Martins, if he was any judge of fine luxury motor vehicles (and he was). He quickly reached for the light to turn it off. No point letting them know he was here. He poured the last slug of whisky into his glass and sat waiting in the dark for the damn *yoof* to fuck right off. Which is when they lobbed the Molotov through the downstairs window into the study, where it just so happened he'd been storing all the liquor he'd rescued from the neighbouring apartments. It went down, or rather up, like a bomb.

The house filled with churning clouds of hot black smoke faster than he could have imagined was possible. He grabbed the closest thing to hand—one of Marlowe's trendy terrorist-chic scarves that had been all the rage several years back—and wrapped it round his face and scrambled for the exit.

He launched himself down the stairs, hearing the crack and pop as the glass buckled in the study, feeling the white heat against his skin. He almost got lost in the hallway, disoriented by the smoke and, yes, all right, the whisky too. But all the way through the dreadful choking gauntlet he felt himself buoyed by a sense of invincibility. And yes, even a kind of inner peace.

He fell out the front door, gasping great big lungfuls of the cool night air (mixed in with the sweet stench of Marlowe on the grass half a foot away) and turned to see her 750,000 quid love nest alive with flames. He felt a surge of exhilaration. He was alive. He was It. The Guy. Untouchable! And watching the flat spewing great gobs of greasy smoke out of its faux-Tudor windows, Simon had his second epiphany of the day. There was a Master Plan at work. A Grand Design. Simon had a destiny to fulfill.

Just as soon as the sun came up.

Eyes gritty from smoke and lack of sleep, he wandered out into the morning, making for the high street, passing a dead horse from the nearby riding stables lying in the centre of the road, its skin undulating with maggots.

Obviously, it was intended for him to walk. He'd smashed the window of every luxury car for three blocks (the Messiah—yes, Messiah—couldn't be expected to show up driving a Toyota) but not a single one had the keys in it. He wondered if Miss Nigeria's instructional YouTube videos included how-to-hot-wire-a-car. Too late now. The Powerbook was long gone, together with his previous life. Besides, the roads were clogged with burned-out buses and overturned cars.

He couldn't believe Chislehurst High Street was the same place. The storefront windows were jagged dark holes; the delicatessen's doorway was blocked by fallen debris; the Waitrose a burnt out, stinking shell. An Audi R8 had rammed through the estate agent's window; he could make out the shadowy figure of the driver crumpled over the wheel. And everywhere, bloated bodies.

He crunched over the still-rotting corpses of a flock of swallows smeared across the road. A designer dog—some kind of chihuahua—covered in sores and burrs, trotted after him for a while, but he shooed it away. He felt for it, of course, but he had More Important Things to do right now. The future of England depended on him.

The people needed him. He could show them how to put society back together again. He would explain why looting was wrong, why a good university education mattered and why having too many children too young was short-sighted and wholly untenable. (Although he realised that they would probably need to start in on repopulating the planet fairly soon and his seed would be an absolute requirement. He'd already resigned himself to having sex with only the most beautiful and promising young chav girls, with their big hair and over-abundance of make-up and their Juicy velour-tracksuited bottoms.)

He headed towards Orpington, then Mottingham—he remembered seeing the high street on one of the clips, and it looked fairly intact. The kids would be tired of looting and rampaging by now. They'd want someone to tell them what to do. Too many years living in a nanny state would mean that eventually they'd welcome a forward-thinking leader to Show Them The Way.

It took him most of the day to make it into Mottingham. He'd had to wrap his shirt around his mouth to block out the stink of burning plastic and putrefying bodies that filled the air in the Bromley town centre. He'd almost made it past the smouldering wreck of Marks & Spencer when he heard the grumble of an engine and the squeal of tyres. He whirled around in time to see a motorbike—a Ducati for fuck's sake—roaring towards him. He ran into the centre of the street, almost tripping over the seeping body of a policeman in riot gear, and waved his arms over his head. The bike screamed straight past him, its riders turning back briefly. Then he heard the crash of splintering glass. He ducked instinctively, nostrils filled with the reek of petrol, heat crisping the hairs on his arms. Bastard had chucked a petrol bomb at him. But at least he knew he was getting closer. This was it. He gobbled another fistful of Alice Pepoy's pills, just to take the edge off.

He followed the sound of drum 'n' bass through a labyrinth of council houses and narrow alleyways, weirdly free of rubbish. Then he saw the first one: a black kid wearing an ill-fitting Armani suit and smoking a cigar, leaning up against the bonnet of a black BMW parked at an angle and blocking the street. Simon heard the sound of children's laughter. Smelled the delicious odour of some kind of roasting meat. He could hear music pumping out of the nearby houses. It looked like business as usual. He felt his heart soar. Soon he would take his Rightful Place.

"What do you want, man?" the kid said. Behind him, a group of kids emerged from the houses. Some had children slung casually on their hips. Simon felt heat spread through his stomach like a good single malt. His people. His heart went out to them. He thought about how they would look back on this moment, tell the story over and over again. All part of his legend. The Coming of Simon.

A plump girl wearing a white mini-skirt in defiance of the cold stepped up next to the black kid. Her arms dripped with gold jewellery, her blue-white legs were mottled with cellulite. She had a really big gun, drooping casually from her fingers with their luminous orange nail polish. Simon kept up his beatific smile. He should have expected a little resistance. Change is hard.

The girl with the firearm spoke first. "What's 'e want, then?"

"Dunno. Ask him," the black kid said.

"I'm here to save you," Simon said. No one was returning his smile.

"Yeah?" The girl looked unimpressed. A spike of panic pierced Simon's happy glow. He wasn't used to feeling out of his depth. He remembered how he'd hooked up with Marlowe. How he'd read the situation the second he saw her. Knew what she needed. It was almost a sixth sense.

A skill. And he knew what these kids needed. Someone to Bring Them Out of Darkness. They just didn't know it yet. He should probably keep it simple.

"I know this is going to be hard for you to understand. But I need you to trust me. I'm the Messiah."

The black kid rolled his eyes.

"Right," the girl said. Then she raised the gun at his heart.

"No, really," Simon stammered. "I can help. I'm—"

He didn't get to finish the sentence. A bright ball of light exploded in his head. He couldn't breathe. It felt like a bloody great rhinoceros had ploughed into his chest. He suddenly felt very heavy and woozy, perversely all at the same time. His knees folded up under him like one of those balloon men outside cheap car dealerships.

The girl looked down at him blankly. "Had quite enough of you lot," she said and turned on her heel, dismissing him. The black kid shook his head. He looked a bit sad. Then he dropped the cigar and walked away after her. The kids in the houses followed suit, vanishing back through the doorways like ghosts. Nothing to see here.

These were the last things Simon St. Martinborough, Messiah, thought before he died. First: *This isn't right*. And, then, as the smoke from the still smouldering Hamlet cigar got up his nose: *Stupid fucking chavs. Couldn't even loot a decent brand.*

COLLIDING BRANES

RUDY RUCKER & BRUCE STERLING

"But why call this the end of the universe?" said Rabbiteen Chandra, feeling the dry night air beat against her face. The rollicking hearse stank of cheap fried food, a dense urban reek in the starry emptiness of the Nevada desert. "At dawn our universe's two branes collide in an annihilating sea of light. That's not death, technically speaking—that's a kalpa rebirth."

Angelo Rasmussen tightened his pale, keyboard-punching hands on the hearse's cracked plastic wheel. His hearse was a retrofitted 1978 Volvo, which ran on recycled biodiesel cooking oil. "You're switching to your Hindu mystic thing now? After getting me to break that story?"

"I double-checked my physics references," Rabbiteen offered, with an incongruous giggle. "Remember, I have a master's degree from San Jose State."

Rabbiteen knew that this was her final road trip. She'd been a good girl too long. She tapped chewing tobacco into a packet of ground betel nut. Her tongue and her gums were stained the color of fresh blood.

"The colliding branes will crush the stars and planets to a soup of hard radiation," she assured Angelo. "Then they rebound instantly, forming brand-new particles of matter, and seeding the next cycle of the twelve-dimensional cosmos." She spread her two hands violently, to illustrate. "Our former bodies will expand to the size of galactic superclusters."

Angelo was eyeing her. "I hope our bodies overlap." He wore a shy, eager smile. "Given what you and I know, Rabbiteen, we might as well be the last man and woman on Earth." He laid his hand on her thigh, but not too far up.

"I've thought that issue through," said Rabbiteen, inexpertly jetting betel spit out the window. Blowback stained her hand-stitched paisley blouse. "We'll definitely make love—but not inside this hearse, okay? Let's find some quaint tourist cabins."

As professional bloggers, Rabbiteen and Angelo knew each other well. For three years, they'd zealously followed each other's daily doings via email, text messages, video posts, social networking and comment threads.

Yet they'd never met in the flesh. Until today, their last day on Earth—the last day for the Earth, and, in stark fact, also for Earth's solar system, Earth's galaxy, Earth's Local Group galactic cluster, and Earth's whole twelve-dimensional universe shebang.

The end was near, and Rabbiteen didn't care to watch the cosmos collapse from inside her cramped room in her parents' house in Fremont. Nor did Angelo want to meet the end in his survivalist bunker in the foothills of the Sierras near Fresno—a bunker which, to untrained eyes, resembled an abandoned barn in the middle of a sun-killed almond farm.

So, after a dense flurry of instant-messages, the two bloggers had joined forces and hit the great American road together, blasting one last trump from the hearse's dirge-like horn, a mournful yet powerful blast which echoed from Rabbiteen's parents' pink stucco house and all through the table-flat development of a thousand similar homes.

Chastely sipping biodiesel through the apocalyptic traffic, they'd made it over Tioga Pass onto Nevada's Route 6 by midnight. They were out well ahead of mankind's last lemming-like rush to universal destruction.

"I've been obsessing over Peak Oil for years," Angelo confessed. He was feeling warm and expansive, now that Rabbiteen had promised him some pre-apocalypse sex. "As a search term, my name is practically synonymous with it. But now I can't believe I was such a sap, such a piss-ant, when it came to comprehending the onrushing scope of this planet's disaster! I was off by... what is it? By a million orders of magnitude?"

Rabbiteen patted his flannelled arm supportively. Angelo was just a political scientist, so he was really cute when he carried on about "orders of magnitude."

He was rueful. "I was so worried about climate change, financial singularities and terror attacks in the Strait of Hormuz. And all the time the parallel branes were converging!" He smacked the Volvo's cracked dashboard with the flat of his pale hand. "I'm glad we escaped from the dense urban cores before the apocalypse. Once people fully realize that cosmic string theory is unraveling, they'll butcher each other like vicious animals."

"Don't insult our friends the animals," said Rabbiteen, flirtatiously bending her wrists to hold her hands like little paws.

Rabbiteen's "What Is Karmic Reality?" blog cleverly leveraged her interest in scientific interpretations of the Upanishads into a thriving medium for selling imported Indian clothes, handicrafts and mosaics.

Angelo, unable to complete his political science doctorate due to skyrocketing tuition costs, had left Stanford to run his own busy "Ain't It Awful?" website. His site tracked major indicators for the imminent collapse of American society. The site served to market his print-on-demand tracts about the forthcoming apocalypse, which earned him a meager living.

The end of the universe had begun with a comment from trusted user "Cody" on Rabbiteen's blog. Cody had linked to a preliminary lab report out of Bangalore's Bahrat University. The arXiv.pdf report documented ongoing real-time changes in the fine-structure constant. Subtle dark and light spectral lines hidden in ordinary light were sashaying right up the spectrum.

Rabbiteen had pounced on this surprising news as soon as it hit her monitor, deftly transforming the dry physics paper into an interactive web page with user-friendly graphic design. To spice up her post for user eyeballs, she'd cross-linked it to the well-known Cyclic Universe scenario. This cosmological theory predicted that the fundamental constants of physics would change rapidly whenever two parallel membranes of the cosmic twelve dimensions were about to—as laymen put it—"collide."

Although Rabbiteen didn't feel supremely confident about the cataclysmic Cyclic Universe scenario, that theory was rock-solid compared to the ramshackle Inflationary notion that had grown up to support the corny, old-school Big Bang.

Cosmologists had been tinkering with the tired Big

Bang theory for over fifty years. Their rickety overwrought notions had so many patches, upgrades, and downright mythologies that even the scheme of a cosmos churned from a sea of galactic cow milk by a giant Hindu cobra seemed logical by comparison.

After Rabbiteen's post, Angelo had horned into the act, following a link to Rabbiteen posted by that same user Cody on Angelo's "Ain't It Awful" blog. With the help of vocal contributors from a right-wing activist site, Angelo quickly unearthed a pirated draft of speechwriters' notes for an impending presidential oration.

Tonight the U.S. President was planning to blandly deny that the cosmos was ending.

The leaked speech made commentary boil like a geyser on Angelo's catastrophe blog—especially since, unable to keep his loyal users in the dark, he'd been forced to announce to them that their entire universe was kaput. The likelihood of this event was immediately obvious to loyal fans of "Ain't It Awful," and the ripples were spreading fast.

"Listen, Rabbiteen," said Angelo, tentatively slowing the hearse. "Why bother to find a motel? It's not like we want to sleep during our last night on Earth. It'd be crazy to waste those precious few remaining hours."

"Don't you want to dream one more great dream?"

He turned his thin, abstracted face from the bug-splattered windshield, his expression gentler than she'd expected. "I'd rather post one last great blog-post. Exactly how many minutes do we have left in our earthly existence?"

Their Linux laptops nestled together on the gray-carpeted floor of the hearse, the screens glowing hotly, the power cords jacked into a luxurious double-socketed cigarette-lighter extension. USB jacks sucked Internet access from a Fresnel antenna that Angelo had made from metal tape, then jammed on the hearse's roof.

Rabbiteen plopped her warm laptop onto her skirted thighs. She scrolled through a host of frantic posts from her over-excited readers.

"Still almost five hundred minutes," she said thoughtfully. "It's two a.m. here, and the latest doom estimate is for ten-twenty a.m. local time. Hmm. This scientist woman net-friend of mine—Hintika Kuusk from Estonia—she says that, near the end, the force of gravity will become a quantized step function. Six minutes after that, the strong force drops to the point where our quarks and gluons fly apart."

"And then the Big Splat hits us?"

"Full interbrane contact comes seven yoctoseconds after our protons and neutrons decay."

"Seven yoctoseconds?" Angelo's gauzy, policy-oriented knowledge of hard science was such that he couldn't be entirely sure when Rabbiteen was serious.

"That's seven septillionths of a second," clarified Rabbiteen. "A short time, but a definite gap. It's a shame, really. Thanks to our crude nucleon-based human bodies, we'll miss the hottest cosmic action since the start of our universe, fourteen billion years ago. But, Angelo, if we hug each other ever so tightly, our quarks will become as one." And with this, she laughed.

"You think that's funny?"

"I don't know. Isn't it funny? How could it not be funny? If I let myself cry, that'll be worse."

"There's no time left to weep and mourn, not even for ourselves," mused Angelo. "I realize that you approach the problem of death in your own way. That motto you posted—'the dewdrop slides into the shining sea.'"

Rabbiteen was moved by the proof that he'd been reading her blog. She clapped her glowing laptop shut and gazed out at the stricken moon above a purple ridge of low mountains. "The moon looks so different now, doesn't it? It's redder! The changes in the fundamental constants will affect all electromagnetic phenomena. No more need for fancy big-science instruments, Angelo. We can see the changes in the fundamental constants of physics with our own wet, tender eyeballs."

She wiped her eyes, smudging her lashes. "In a way, it's wonderful that everything will dissolve together. The mountains and the moon, the rich and the poor, all the races and colors."

The road's fevered white line pulsed against Angelo's pale blue eyes. When he spoke again his voice had turned grating and paranoid. "I keep trying for the high road, Rabbiteen, but I can't fully buy that this is the End. I've got a feeling that certain shadowy figures have been preparing for this. There are so many hints on the Internet... You want to know the real truth about where we're going?"

"Tell me, Angelo." Rabbiteen valued his insights into human society, which was a system she herself had trouble confronting.

"Cody calls it the Black Egg. It's hidden in the Tonopah Test Range, a secret base in Nevada, right near Area 51. He says the fascist slavemasters have built a back-door escape route off our condemned cosmos."

"*That's* where we're headed?" said Rabbiteen, sounding dubious. "On Cody's say-so?"

"Those in the know have an inside track to the Black Egg survival pod against the collapse of the universe. As major intellectual figures on the blogosphere, we should definitely be going there, right? Why should we be left outside the Dr. Strangelove mine-shaft bunker when the lords of creation have their own transhuman immortality?"

Rabbiteen was unconvinced. "Oh, Angelo, why do you always blog so much about rulers and power? Everything's emergent. The old white men on top are helpless idiots. They're like foam on a tsunami. Can bacteria stop a bucket of bleach?"

"You're naive," said Angelo loftily. "Do you think it's mere coincidence that we were contacted and guided by a heavy operator like Cody? You're a key blogger on weird physics, and I—I rank with the world's foremost citizen-journalists."

"But Cody is just some blog commenter," said Rabbiteen slowly. The frank lunacy of the Black Egg story made her uneasy. "Cody never seemed like a particularly helpful guy to me. He's more like a snoop, a troll, and a snitch."

"He's just geeky, Rabbiteen. Cody doesn't have a whole lot of human social skills."

"On my blog he comes across like a stalker."

"He told me he's a veteran working physicist employed on black-ops projects by the federal government. A lonely old man whose whole life has been top-secret. I had to work hard at it, but I've won Cody over. He never had any trace of freedom in his life, except for the Internet. He thinks of you and me as his most intimate friends."

"Okay, fine," said Rabbiteen. "Why not the Tonopah Test Range? If that makes you happy."

But rather than smiling at her agreeability, Angelo was antsy. "I wish you hadn't said that. Now you've got me all worried. What if Cody is lying to me? All that amazing physics data could be clever disinformation. Maybe he's just some kind of crazy online pervert who, for whatever twisted reason—"

Rabbiteen aimed a brave smile at her friend's tormented face. "Look, that sign says Tonopah! And there's a nice little motel."

Angelo instantly slewed the heavy hearse into the dark, empty parking lot. Despite the late hour, the motel office door yawned open, with a trapezoid of light on the gravel.

Springy on his sneakered feet, Angelo hopped out of the hearse and into the motel office. Stretching the travel kinks from her back, Rabbiteen noticed a dull glow in the valley beyond this ridge. That must be the whipped old mining town of Tonopah. An all-but-defunct burg like that shouldn't be emitting so much flickering light and hot glare—oh. Tonopah was on fire.

Squinting into the distance, Rabbiteen could make out motorcycles, buzzing Tonopah's back streets like hornets. Some of the night-riders carried torches, leaving spark-spewing trails in the gloom.

"We don't want to stay around here," said Angelo, returning to her. Carefully, disturbingly, he wiped his feet on the gravel, leaving dark stains. Blood.

A vagrant breeze wafted whoops and screams across the dark hills.

"The owner's been killed?" said Rabbiteen. Hollowness filled her chest. "Oh god, oh god, I don't want to be slaughtered by psychos! I want to flash out with the Big Splat!"

"Don't panic," said Angelo, hugging her. "Don't panic yet." He stepped back and showed her a trophy tucked in the back of his belt. A forty-five automatic pistol. "You see, the owner was web-surfing. He had this handgun right next to his mouse—somebody lopped his head clean off while he was staring into his screen." Angelo handed her the pistol, butt-first. "The clip's full; that survival newbie never fired one shot in his own defense!"

Rabbiteen shuddered as she handled the weapon. Beyond the motel's sordid lot, a pair of monster trucks bounced side by side down the two-lane highway, their multiple headlights beaming crazed jittering cones. "Maybe we shouldn't go through Tonopah."

"I'll drive like a maniac, and you'll fire wildly," Angelo advised. "So it'll be fine. Let me give you the précis on this Colt military automatic. As a survivalist, I've logged a lot of hours on this model. It's easy except for the recoil. You hold it in both hands and gently squeeze the trigger. Try that."

Off at the edge of the motel lot, Rabbiteen saw a suspicious shadow. Something looping, boiling, rippling like heat haze. The head lopper? She hastily squeezed off a shot. The pistol kicked upwards with a flash and a deafening bang. The window of a motel unit blew out with a musical crash of glass.

Then, ominous, total silence.

If there had been any guests in this lonely motel, they were all gone. Or murdered. Yet there was still a roiling, phantom shape in the farthest corner of the parking lot. A midnight dust devil, or a smear of tears across her vision.

It was definitely time to go.

"Let's access some mash-up Internet maps," said Angelo, powering up the hearse with a biodiesel splutter. "I know the Test Range is on the far side of Tonopah, but of course the site's fully concealed from the sheep-like American public."

Rabbiteen piled into the paint-blistered hearse with him, suddenly cheered by the utter recklessness of their plan. The last night of mankind's existence—how could it be any other way than this? Car doors locked, and windows up, smelly gun near to hand, she crouched elbow to elbow with her friend, connecting to the global mind, comforted by her talismanic laptop.

"Why do you suppose that Google Maps doesn't even list any super-secret labs?" she complained.

Angelo toyed with the wheel, inching the car across the gravel, waiting patiently as a midnight slew of cars blasted from the darkness down Highway 6. "That's easy. I mean, I'm a dropout from Stanford... and Sergey and Larry are both dropouts from Stanford, too. But unlike me, they're covering for the Man! Because they sold out!"

"Oh, wait," said Rabbiteen, "Google just linked me to a nutcase map site with tons of great info. Hmm. The Tonopah Test Range is just past the Tonopah airport. It butts into Groom Lake where people see, like, aliens from other dimensions. And, get this, the Test Range has their own secret part, and that's *Area 52.*"

"Wow," said Angelo. A raging eighteen-wheeler pattered gravel across their windshield. "That's one digit higher than 51."

Rabbiteen's iPhone emitted the stunning *clank clank* of a steam-hammer. She'd once missed a vitally important instant-message, so her alert preferences were set to maximum stun.

She bumped her head on the grimy dashboard as she lunged for her sleek device. "It's Cody! Cody is trying to hit me!"

"Hunh," said Angelo. "Don't read it."

"I hot 2 c u 2 n4k3d," read Rabbiteen. She glared at Angelo. "Hot to see you two naked? What does that mean? What on earth did you tell that guy?"

"I had to social-engineer him so he'd help us break into the Black Egg. Like I said, Cody is a very lonely old man."

"You told him that you'd post photos of us naked?"

"No I didn't say that exactly," said Angelo, his voice almost wistful. "It's worse. I told him I'd stream us having sex on live webcam video." He straightened his shoulders. "I had to tell him something like that, Rabbiteen. I lied to him. And, really, at this point, so what? What possible difference does it make? The whole universe is about to melt."

Rabbiteen frowned down at her pistol, turning it over in her hands. She was momentarily tempted to shoot Angelo, but stifled the impulse. It was amazing how many user-friendly little clicks and snicks the pistol had.

"Anyway, my gambit worked on him," said Angelo. He patted the iPhone, which lay on the seat, its message still showing. "See the digits on the bottom of the screen? Cody also sent you the GPS coordinates to the site."

He punched tiny buttons on a squat plastic gizmo suction-cupped to the dash of his hearse.

"Continue Highway 6 through Tonopah," said the genteel female voice of Angelo's GPS navigation unit. "Turn right at unmarked dirt road number 37A."

Jaw set, Angelo peeled out of the lot and barreled through the crumbling heart of the stricken desert settlement. Knots of drunken, flare-wielding marauders were barricading the streets with smoldering debris. Angelo accelerated through a flaming police sawhorse, and Rabbiteen braced her heavy pistol in both hands, firing wildly and shrieking flamewar abuse through the open window.

Overawed by the style of the loons in the hearse, the rioters let them pass.

Then they motored sedately through the eastern outskirts of blacked-out Tonopah, past burning tract homes and empty desert shacks, past the silent airport and the abandoned mines.

As they turned off onto the dirt side road, Rabbiteen mimicked the feminine voice of the GPS navigator. "Suggestion. What if I posted naked pictures of myself with this gun?" She shoveled in a fresh chew of betel. "What kind of user response would I get?"

"You mean if your users weren't torn apart into their constituent quarks?" Angelo smiled and took her hand.

. He was feeling buoyant. The world was definitely ending, in fire and blood just as he'd always guessed, yet he'd finally found a woman meant for him. With that sweet, frank way she had of cutting to the core of an issue without ever delivering anything useful, Rabbiteen Chandra was the very soul of bloggerdom.

His last night on Earth felt as vast and endless as a crumpled galaxy, while the full moon had gone the shape and color of a dry-squeezed blood orange. The clumps of sage were pale purple. The world Angelo inhabited had finally come to look and feel just like the inside of his own head. Incredible to think that he and Rabbiteen might be the last human beings ever to witness this landscape. It was as if they owned it.

"Isn't that a guard house ahead?" said Rabbiteen. "If you want to crash through that, I can lay down some covering fire. At least till I run out of bullets."

The GPS crooned sedately from the dash. "Proceed though Security Gate 233-X, traveling twenty-two miles further into the Tonopah Test Range to destination Area 52."

"I'd hoped Cody would be waiting for us at this security

gate," said Angelo, slowing the hearse. "But I guess he never leaves his supercomputer console." His nerves were fraying again. "The guards around here are brainwashed killing machines. Mindlessly devoted to the fugitive neoconservatives of the Area 52 escape pod. If I stop, they'll extradite us to Guantanamo. If I pull a U-turn, they'll chase us down with Predator aircraft. If I barrel through the gate, we'll smash head-on into their truck-bomb tank traps."

"Oh, stop talking like that," said Rabbiteen. "It's three a.m. on their last night on Earth! How devoted to duty can those guys be? Don't they have any girlfriends? Or kids?"

The glum little concrete guardhouse that defended the Test Range was in fact deserted. The razor-wire chain-link moaned in the wind and the striped traffic arm pointed uselessly at the starry sky.

The hearse rolled into the empty desert compound, the narrow military road gently curving around peaks that sat on the sand like giant Zen boulders. Here and there old war-gamed jeeps had been shot to pieces from helicopters. Except for this ritualized military debris, there was only the moon and the mountains, the silence broken by periodic updates from the GPS unit.

To cover his growing embarrassment, Angelo propped his laptop on the dash. Automatically he clicked for his blog. "Oh my God!"

Terror gripped Rabbiteen's heart. "What? What now?"

"Look at my traffic spike! My Webalizer stats are right off the charts! Drudge Report, Boing Boing, Huffington Post, they're all sucking my dust! I rule the net tonight! Everybody's linking to me!"

"How about *my* blog?" she asked. "I blogged the Big Splat before you did—"

"This is fantastic!" continued Angelo. "I'm finally fully validated as an independent citizen-journalist!"

Rabbiteen jealously moused around his screen. "Dammit, my own site has totally crashed! Why doesn't your traffic max out when you get Slashdotted so hard?"

"My 'Ain't It Awful' site is scalable, babe. I pay full service on the Amazon web-cloud and they just keep adding servers. This is the last night on Earth. No one will ever beat my post for traffic. I'm the greatest blogger in the history of the planet."

Rabbiteen considered this boast. Though galling, it had to be true. Her boyfriend was the greatest blogger in the world. Except nobody would really call Angelo her boyfriend, because they'd never even kissed.

Feeling letdown, she stroked the glossy screen of her iPhone, scroll-flicking her way through a rolling list of friends and landing on, why not, Prof. Dr. Hintika Kuusk, the Estonian string theorist. Dr. Kuusk was a kindly, grandmotherly scholar; a woman of the world who'd always been very kind to the gawky physics enthusiast named "Rabbiteen Chandra."

Rabbiteen pecked out a text message on the phone's eerie virtual keyboard. "About to have sex with Angelo Rasmussen inside Area 52."

She thumb-smeared SEND and launched her confession into cellphonespace. She was glad she'd told a confidante. Blogger that she was, it always felt better to tell somebody than to do something.

Moments passed, and then the phone emitted its signature clank. A sober incoming reply from Hintika Kuusk: "Fare thee well, Rabbiteen."

"Farewell 4ever Dr. Kuusk," typed Rabbiteen, her heart

filling. She slid a glance over at Angelo, who was steering with one hand while trying to type with the other. She considered cozying up to him and working her wiles, but just then, with another clank, here came a mass-mailing to Hintika Kuusk's extensive buddy list: "OMG OMG OMG! Rabbiteen-Karmic-Reality is hooking up with Angelo-Ain't-It-Awful!"

Within seconds, a follow-up fusillade tumbled onto Rabbiteen's phone display and laptop screen—from handhelds, from Twitterstreams, from MySpace pages—gossipy whoops and snarks, cheerful shout-outs and me-toos, messages from half the women Rabbiteen knew.

Angelo glanced over, his eyebrows kinked. "What's the excitement?"

"Oh, it's just my silly, romantic women friends. Don't let me distract you from fondling your famous blog."

Angelo was gentlemanly enough to close his laptop. "We're being fools. What do you say we pull over now?"

He tapped a button on the GPS unit for a distance update. "Area 52 is now twelve miiiii—" The robotic voice twisted into a sudden anguished squawk. The device sputtered, chirped, and went dark.

Reflexively concerned about any loss in connectivity, Rabbiteen lifted her cell phone. Its display had gone black. "Those wonky Apple batteries..."

"Try your laptop?" said Angelo.

Rabbiteen read from its screen. "You are not connected to the Internet." And then, like a cranky, spoiled child finally falling asleep, her laptop, too, went dark.

And then—oh dear—the car died.

Wrestling the stiff power steering, Angelo guided them to rest in a curved billow of roadside sand.

It was quiet here, so very quiet. The wind whispered, the red moon glowed.

Rabbiteen spoke aloud, just to hear her own voice. "I was sort of expecting this. Electrical circuits can't work any more. Too much drift in the fundamental constants of electromagnetism."

"Like a power failure affecting the whole Earth?" said Angelo.

"It's much more than a power failure. And it's not just our sweet little Earth. It's the entire universe."

Angelo sighed. "For years people called me paranoid. Now I finally know I was a realist. I was truly perceptive and insightful. I was never a fringe crank intellectual, I was a major public thinker! I should have had a wife, kids… I should have had tenure and a MacArthur Grant."

Should Rabbiteen declare her love for him? It was on the tip of her tongue. He was oh so close in the rosily moon-dappled car. She reached out and touched his face.

"There's one important part I still don't get," said Angelo doggedly. "Aren't our nerves electrical? We should be fainting or passing out. But I'm still thinking—and my heart's still beating… It's beating for you."

"Human nerves are mostly chemical," said Rabbiteen, her voice rising to a squeak. She made a lunge for him. At last they kissed.

"We could lose our ability to think and feel at any moment," Angelo said presently. "So it's the back of my hearse, or it's the sand. Unless you want to get out and hunt for Cody's Black Easter Egg."

Rabbiteen turned and gazed behind herself. The hearse did have white silk ruffles. In the weirdly altered moonlight, those were kind of—romantic.

As they bucked against each other, bellies slapping, vivid and relentless, it occurred to Rabbiteen that she and Angelo were just like the two cosmic branes.

It could be claimed that the once-distant branes were violently colliding, but that was a very male way to frame what was happening. If you laid out your twelve-dimensional coordinate system differently, the branes passed through one another and emerged reenergized and fecund on the other side of that event.

It was like the urge to have sex, which was loud and pestering and got all the press, as opposed to the urge to have children, which was even more powerful, obliteratingly powerful, only nobody could sell that to men.

Afterward came the urge to abandon all awareness and slide into deep black sleep, which no one could resist. Cuddled in the sweaty crook of Angelo's arm, Rabbiteen tumbled straight over the edge of nightmare.

She saw a lipless, billowing, yellow-eyed face peering into the side window of the hearse. Its enormous mouth gaped in woozy appetite, yawning and slamming like some drug-drenched door of perception. The otherworldly visitation of a Hindu demon. Had she dreamed that?

"Angelo!" She poked his ribs.

But he was offline, a blissful, snoring mass. She retrieved the gun from the front seat, and stared with grainy-eyed, murderous intent into the moonlit desert. Despite her fear and wariness, she couldn't keep her lids open.

Red distorted sunlight woke them through the windows of the hearse.

"Oh no, here it comes!" yipped Angelo, sitting up with a start. He'd mistaken the rising sun for the final cosmic conflagration, and not without reason, for the solar disk was ten times its usual diameter, and the light it shed was as dim as the clouded gaze of a stroke victim.

The world outside their hearse was rendered in faded Technicolor. The skewed interaction between light, matter, and their human retinas was tinting the sage red, the sand a pale green, the sky canary yellow.

With icy, tingling fingers, Rabbiteen grabbed Angelo's wrist, trying to read his watch. "It can't already be time for the end, can it?"

"My watch has a wrecked battery now," said Angelo. "But if the sun's coming up, then it must be about six a.m., right? We've still got, what, four hours to hunt for the Black Egg."

Rabbiteen's bare belly rumbled. "Do you have any breakfast?"

"Of course! Angelo Rasmussen is the Compleat Survivalist. I don't always have great sex with gorgeous Californian tech chicks, but I always have food and water."

As she preened a little, he dug into the wheel-well. "Here we go. Fruit-leather and freeze-dried granola."

They munched companionably, sitting with their legs dangling out the hearse's open back door. Rabbiteen felt happier than ever before in her life, out of her mind with head-over-heels, neck-yourself-silly romantic bonding. It was beyond ironic that this would happen to her just now.

"Do you really think a lame stalker like Cody could dodge the Big Splat?" she essayed. "I'd love to hope that's the truth. I mean, now that we're together, it would be such a great ending if somehow—"

"Not looking good," said Angelo, staring into the particolored desert gloom. "If Cody's story was for real, we should see scads of black helicopters flying in here, with all kinds of fat cats saving themselves from destruction."

"Even your *black* helicopters can't work today," said Rabbiteen a little impatiently. "It's not just the batteries, Angelo. It's spark-plugs, ignition, control chips—everything. No electrical machine will ever function again." Seeing his stricken look, she tried to soothe him. "Maybe all the refugees are here already. Maybe they're all crowded into the brane collision survival pod. Imagine the fun when they see us."

"The Black Egg of Area 52," said Angelo, drawing fresh strength from the idea. "Let's walk there."

"I'm ready. We'll walk to the end of the earth."

Angelo loaded a stained khaki knapsack with food and water, daintily lotioned his skin, and even produced a couple of wide-brimmed hats, blister packs and a telescoping metal walking-stick.

"Rabbiteen Rasmussen," he murmured as they gamely trudged the sandy road. "What a fantastic name. That would be a king-hell blogger handle."

Rabbiteen's heart glowed with joy.

They came to a fork in the troubled road—with both alternatives equally bleak. "My compass is useless now," Angelo griped. "Also, I think the sun is exploding."

Indeed the swollen, ruddy sun was spiky with fractalized flares. Its face was mottled with dark writhing sunspots, vast cavities into the star's inner layers. Old Man Sol was visibly breathing his last. It was like seeing a beloved parent succumb to a disfiguring disease.

They picked the road to the left and slogged forward.

Rabbiteen's love-smitten psyche was bubbling over with happy thoughts, yet the fear goblins ran fast behind, eating them. Compulsively, her mind returned to that demonic toad face she'd glimpsed in the midnight of her soul—but she didn't share this inner terror with Angelo. He'd only make fun of her, or worse, drive himself frantic with speculation.

Their few remaining moments of togetherness were passing all too fast. There was no sign of any secret base, or of any human beings at all. They were trudging endless, badly colored terrain in utter forlornness, like the last two holdout players in some outdated Internet game.

Angelo was stumbling, leaning heavily on his fancy high-tech walking-stick.

"My feet are asleep," he complained.

"Me too." Rabbiteen rubbed one tingling hand against another. "I guess—I guess the changes in the electrical constants are finally getting to our nerves and our bodies." Against her will, a sudden wail forced itself from her. "Oh, Angelo, do you love me?"

"Did I forget to say that? I get so distracted sometimes. Yes, I love you. I do love you. I'd post it in letters of fire bigger than the sun."

This declaration revived her a little; they wobbled on, teetering on their rubbery ankles.

Angelo was thinking hard. How strange it was that a woman's welcoming body could nail a man to the fabric of space and time. This was a mystical proof to him that sexual intercourse was an inherent part of the fabric of the universe. His brain was working very fast—as if some kind of electrochemical friction had vanished inside his skull— but the fringes of his nervous system were fading. It was terrible to know he would soon die, and worse to know that Rabbiteen's kindly, ardent body would smear across the cosmos like a spin-painting.

"Look!" she cried. Another unguarded, open gate. They tottered through, their knees wobbling. In the fractured, crystalline distance they could see sun-blasted buildings and a sandy airstrip. "It's too far," added Rabbiteen, bursting into tears. "And we're too slow! We won't make it."

They sat in the shadow of a boulder, arms around each other, awaiting the end—or the strength to rise and slog on. But now a deep rumble filled their ears. Sand rose into the air as if blown by an impalpable gale; rocks flew off the mountains with the ease of tumbling dice.

The two lovers fell upwards.

There was frantic, incomprehensible activity all around them, as if they were mice in the grinding engine of a merry-go-round. Like the maculated sun overhead, the planet's surface had come unmoored. Geological strata had gently unpacked like the baked layers of a baklava, sending the surface debris crashing about in search of new equilibria.

Eerie pink sunlight glittered from the hearse's window as, plucked from beyond the horizon, it tumbled past them, its hood and doors slamming rhythmically, bouncing up the slopes of the nearest peak.

In ordinary times, the earthquake noise alone might have crushed their clinging bodies, but the booming of this planetary destruction was oddly muted and gentle. The fundamental constants had plateaued for a moment. A new order of gravity settled in, with everything that could come loose from the Earth being messily sorted according to its mass.

Belatedly, a reluctant mountain tore itself loose and rose ponderously into the lemon sky.

Rabbiteen and Angelo were floating a few score yards above the remains of the ancient desert—a patch of fine dust beneath a layer of sand with pebbles admixed, topped by bones, sticks, stones and target-range military rubble.

A venomous little Gila monster tumbled past them, dislodged from some flying mountain redoubt, its stubby tail twisting, its skin glittering like a beaded armband.

Angelo's blown mind irritably snatched for facts. "Are those nerve-gas canisters up there? They're like weather balloons." He beat his helpless legs against the empty air and began to twist in place. "Can you explain this to me, Ms. Karmic Science?"

Rabbiteen's mind had frozen with awe. The mountains of the firmament were floating across the spotted face of the bloated sun. She had no way to think clearly—with thunderhead shelves of granite and feldspar poised to crush her.

"Hold me, Angelo! You're drifting away! I want to be with you till the very end!"

"We're doomed," said Angelo. He squinted into the hazy, polymorphous distances. The stark concrete hangars and wooden shacks of Area 52 were piled in midair like badly assembled Ikea shelving.

The humbled remnants of the secret federal base showed no signs of life. No super scientists, no fat cats there, no Black Egg. All those cogent hints about close encounters in the American Southwest with psychic saucer-craft, and nobody was even here. People were so cynical about the miraculous that they couldn't even bother to show up.

"I can almost feel that other brane arriving now," said Rabbiteen. "Once the force of gravity has changed, we only have six minutes."

"Cody!" hollered Angelo, his voice echoing off the floating islands of stone. He cupped his hands around his mouth. "Help us, Cody!"

"Come on, Cody!" shrieked Rabbiteen. Giggling shrilly,

she grappled at Angelo. Her fingers were numb, and the flesh of his neck and shoulders felt spongy and strange. "The desert's so beautiful, Cody! Especially upside down! We had great sex, and next time you can watch us, I promise!"

"Cody, Cody, Cody!!!"

A lens-like shape formed in mid-air, magnifying the tumbleweeds and boulders. Slowly, it opened a dark throat.

"Hello?" said Angelo.

The blackness folded in on itself and took form. The hole became crooked, then everted, like a giant origami tentacle. It swayed around in mid-air like a hungry feeler.

It took note of the two of them.

The warped tentacle wriggled and dimpled; the tip flexed to assume the shape of a staring, glistening face. Complex forces within the bulging shape were manipulating it like a sock puppet. The eyes bulged like a rubber mask, the mouth stretched and gaped like a toad's.

"Cody?" said Angelo, yet again, one arm wrapped around Rabbiteen. "Are you here to save us?"

The demonic toad twisted his head this way and that. He had large, golden eyes. "Do I look properly embodied within your planet's three spatial dimensions?"

"No!" Rabbiteen squeaked, stiff with unearthly terror. "You look like hell!"

"Interaction was so much easier on the Internet," said the toad, smacking his thin lips. "It's a lot of trouble to manifest this low-dimensional form to you." The creature's voice was modulated white noise, like sand sculpted into letters.

"I saw him last night, Angelo," cried Rabbiteen. "I saw him peeking into the hearse! And he was in the motel parking lot. Cody was stalking us."

"I was monitoring you," said Cody, his head billowing

like a black pillowcase. "You two alone have reached Area 52, naturally selected from the many billions on your planet. You are like sperm cells beating their way up a long canal—"

"—to reach the Black Egg," completed Angelo hurriedly. His molecules felt overstretched. "Okay, yes! Here we are! Let us inside!"

Cody leered at them provokingly. "The Cosmic Mother," he said, "is the immortal entity that fills the band of hyperspace between the twin branes of the cosmos. I am the tip of one of Mother's many tentacles. If you can imagine that."

"Of course we can imagine that!" jabbered Rabbiteen. "Don't let us die!"

"Let us in," repeated Angelo. His fingers felt and looked like orange circus peanuts.

"This Black Egg is prepared for you, my blogger friends," said Cody simply. "The universe is collapsing, so the Cosmic Mother has placed a Black Egg on every space and place that supports intelligence. Billions of eggs, spewed in the cosmos like dewdrops in the shining sea."

"Oh, Cody," said Rabbiteen. "You read my blog too."

"Of course I do. Physics is collapsing, but the network will persist. All the Black Eggs are linked via quantum entanglement. Telepathy, if you will."

Momentarily, Angelo forgot his fears. "Wow, I always wanted some telepathy."

"There's also infinite connectivity and infinite storage in the network of eggs," Cody evangelized. "The network has an infinite number of users. They're all upset and angry, just like you, because they're all indignant to see their universe collapse. They all believed they were the most important aspect of the universe. Imagine the confusion. We have an infinite number of anthropic principles—one for each race!"

"Then you'll need moderators," said Rabbiteen practically. "You need some users that know how to link and comment."

"Absolutely we do," said Cody. "This cosmic cycle was planned out and architected rather poorly. It's closing down much earlier than the Cosmic Mother expected. Instead of crashing like this, the universes are supposed to get more stable with each new release."

"We're just the kickass bloggers you need!" crowed Angelo. "We can keep up our moaning and complaining for millions of years! Assuming that we're rewarded for our efforts. I mean—is there any kind of revenue stream inside there?"

"You'll lack nothing inside your race's Black Egg," leered Cody. "Except your human need to eat or breathe. There will be sex, of course. There's always sex on the Net. The Cosmic Mother adores sex."

"Wow," said Rabbiteen.

"Now come closer to me," said the toad-headed tentacle. "Technical detail: your Black Egg is a hyperdisk where the branes are riveted together via a wormhole link in the twelfth dimension. In this one special region—it's down my gullet—the branes can't collide. I know your primitive minds can't understand that. Think of me as a pine cone that protects a tree's seeds from the heat of a fierce wildfire."

Angelo shook his bloating hands. "Never mind the license agreements, just sign us up and log us in!"

Rabbiteen had to annotate. "Really, Cody, I think it's

more accurate to say the cosmic branes pass through each other serenely."

"Ah, you refer to the Twisterman coordinatization," said Cody, his bloated demon head expanding with a ragged jolt. "Yes, under that viewpoint, we'll all be transformed into our mirror-images. If you calculate in terms of the diffeomorphic quiver bundles, then it's—"

"Hurry up!" screamed Angelo—losing his composure as his left thumb snapped off.

"Fine," said Cody. "Over the next ten million years we can discuss these issues fully." His wide mouth gaped open. The inside looked dank and slimy.

Rabbiteen felt another flicker of unease. Could it be that Cody was an underworld demon after all? Under his promise of cosmic transformation, was he luring them to a fate infinitely worse than mere death? How would the toad behave any differently, if he were doing that?

Cody waited with his silent mouth agape.

Up in the sky, the sun went out. The stars and moon were gone as well. Utter darkness reigned. A shrill buzz filled the nonexistent air and slid menacingly down the scale.

Pressing together, Angelo and Rabbiteen crawled into the toad's mouth. Pushing and pulling, moving as one, the lovers wriggled their way down to the womb of the Black Egg. And of our world they saw no more.

Within the Egg's twelve-dimensional kalpas, time and space regressed. There was neither room nor duration in which to hunger, to tire, or draw a human breath. Yet in another sense, this was a weightless and limitless utopian paradise in which happy Neetibbar and wry Olegna could gambol and embrace.

The mortal races of the next universe would occasionally

comment on two glorious superclusters, titanic arcs of creative energy stenciling the void like a net—sharp and sleek, stable and sweet, weaving the warp and weft of the reborn cosmos.

ELLIE

JACK McDEVITT

If the lights at Bolton's Tower go out, the devil gets loose. At least, that was the story. The idea spooked me when I was a kid, and even years later on those rare occasions when I traveled into its general neighborhood, which was well north on the Great Plains, far off the trading routes.

The Tower put out a lot of light, so much that it could be seen from the Pegborn-Forks road. In a world illuminated mostly by kerosene and candles, it was unique, and it was easy to believe there might be a supernatural force at work.

I'd been away from the Dakotas for *years*, and had long since forgotten about the thing, when the press of business and a series of unseasonal storms drove me north into my old home grounds. The weather had been overcast for a week, had cleared off during the course of a long cold afternoon, and when the sun went down, Bolton's star rose in the east. I knew it immediately for what it was, and I knew I was close.

There's something else odd about Bolton's Tower.

It's just inside the southern rim of a long, curving ridge. The ridge isn't high. It seldom exceeds thirty feet, and sometimes it's no more than a ripple in the grass. But it's a strange ridge: if you follow it far enough, you discover it forms a *perfect circle*. You can't see that from any single place; the ring is too big. More than sixty miles around. I've heard tent preachers explain that the circle symbolizes God, because it's endless, and cannot be improved on. Just the thing to imprison Satan, they add darkly.

I crossed the ridge on foot, leading my mount. Snow was beginning to fall again, and the wind was picking up. The Tower rose out of a cluster of dark, weather-beaten buildings and a screen of trees. These structures were low and flat, dreary boxes, some made of clapboard and others of brick. Their windows were gone; their doors hung on broken hinges or were missing altogether. A roof had blown off one, another lay partly demolished by a fallen tree. A small barn, set to one side, had been kept in reasonable repair, and I heard horses moving within as I drew near.

The Tower soared above the ruin, seven stories of bone-white granite and thick glass. Porches and bays and arches disconnected it from the prairie, as if it belonged to a less mundane reality. The roof melted into banks of curved glass panels capped by a crystal spire. Its lines whispered of lost power and abandoned dreams, passion frozen in stone.

I released the straps on my crossbow, and loosened it in its sheath.

Several windows on the second and third floors were illuminated. The Tower lights themselves, red and white signature beams, blazed into the murky night.

In the windows, no one moved.

The base of the Tower culminated in a broad terrace surrounded by a low wall, elevated from the road by about twenty wide stone steps. The steps were flanked by dead hedge.

I rode past, down a grass-covered street, and dismounted in front of the barn. Max made some noises to indicate he was glad the day was over. I hoped he was right.

The barn had sliding doors. I opened one and we went inside. Three horses moved restlessly in their stalls. The place smelled of them, warm and pungent. I tied Max up, but did not remove his saddle. Just in case. I debated whether to take the crossbow, but in the end left it, on the ground that guests arriving with weapons were a lot more likely to be turned away.

Wind shook the building, and snow rattled against it like sleet. On the plains, the stuff has the consistency of rock salt. And when the wind is up the way it was that night, it can beat you down pretty good. I burrowed into my coat, pulled my hat low to protect my eyes, and strode back out into the storm.

I climbed the steps and crossed the terrace. There was a statue of someone out there, in an old dried-up fountain, a rumpled woman in Old World clothes, with the name *Margaret Hanbury*, and the inscription: FROM THIS NARROW SPACE, WE TOUCH THE INFINITE.

Six heavy glass doors guarded the entrance. I looked up at the Tower, cold and remote, its aspect growing and shifting in the changing texture of its spectral lights.

The doors had no give. Beyond them lay a dark lobby. I could see furniture, wall-hangings, a stairway illuminated from above. I banged on the glass.

For several minutes nothing happened. I tried again,

and was thinking about moving in with the horses when the terrace lit up. A man descended the staircase, came to a stop midway across the lobby, and stood for a time studying me. Finally, he came forward, threw a bolt, and pulled the door open.

"Good evening," he said, in a rich baritone. "Sorry to leave you standing out here, but I'm inclined to be careful these days."

He was a half-foot taller than I, with lean, almost cruel features, and dark intelligent eyes. His buckskin jacket covered a white denim shirt. His black trousers were creased. He was a dark and somber man, and his manner suggested he was accustomed to command. He wore a neatly trimmed beard, and his hair was black and quite thick.

"Thank you," I said, moving past him. It was good to be in out of the wind.

More lights went on. The interior was quite long, perhaps two hundred feet, although it was only as wide as an ordinary room. It was decorated with Indian art, totems, weavings, pottery, and a few oils depicting teepees by sunset and young braves in canoes. Chairs were scattered about in no particular order, and with no effort to match their styles. There were rattans, fabric of a half-dozen different colors, a wooden bench, and several small tables.

He extended a hand. "This is not a good day to be on the road."

"No," I said. "It's downright brisk out there." I shook the snow off my shoulders. "I'm Jeff Quincey."

"Edward Marsh. Where are you headed, Quincey?" His voice changed texture, not precisely softening, but rather growing consciously more amiable.

"I'm bound for the Forks. I'd expected to spend the night

in Sandywater, but I got off to a late start this morning. And the weather—"

He nodded. Snow whipped across the glass. "You'll want to stay the night with us, of course."

"If it's no trouble, I'd be grateful."

"None at all. We don't get many visitors here." He turned on his heel and led the way to the staircase.

On the second floor, carpeted corridors ran off in three directions. The carpet was frayed and, in some places, threadbare. Closed doors marched uniformly along the walls. "This way," Marsh said, striding off into the right-hand passageway. "What business are you in, Quincey?"

"I'm a trader. And an occasional agent for Overland."

He nodded. "It's the traders that'll open up this country." Halfway down the hall, the place began to look lived-in. The gray walls gave way to dark-stained paneling, rugs were thrown over the weary carpet, and someone had hung a series of prints. The prints alternated between abstracts and sketches of Old World city scenes. One depicted Chicago, crowded with traffic; another, New York at night; and a third, a Parisian sidewalk café. "I've been there," I told him.

"Where?"

"Chicago."

"Really?" He glanced at the image. "Odd, all the times I've walked by this, and I don't think I ever really looked at it." He pushed his hands deep into his jacket pockets. "Why?"

Why indeed? It had been one of the more oppressive experiences of my life, wandering through those gray, cold canyons. Climbing past the rusting metal that filled its ravine streets, looking up at thousands of empty windows, and knowing what lay mouldering behind them. "I was hired to help with a survey. An historical project."

He nodded. "I do believe you're a man after my own heart, Quincey." We entered a sitting room half-lit by a low fire. Several pieces of oversized upholstered furniture filled most of the available space. Crossbows and bison trophies were mounted in strategic locations, and a battered garrison hat hung on a peg. Yellowing books were stacked on wall-shelves, more than I'd seen in one place this side of Port Remote. Some appeared to be military histories. But there were also travel journals, and technical titles whose meaning escaped me, like *An Orderly Approach to Chaos*, and *The n-Particle*. That was old stuff, pre-Crash, and I wondered whether anyone now living really understood them.

He switched on an electric lamp, and motioned me to a chair. "I stay out of the cities," he said. "I don't like places where you can't see what's coming at you. Anyway," he winked, "you never know when some of the concrete is going to let go." He took glasses and a decanter from a cabinet. "Port?"

"Yes. Fine."

"Good. We don't have much of a selection." He filled them and held one out for me. "To the outside world," he said.

That was a strange toast. I glanced through the window at the endless plain. "Cheers," I said.

We talked for a few moments of inconsequentials. How short the summer had been this year; the apparent withdrawal of the raiders who had harassed stages and attacked settlements in the area ("too cold for them here in winter," offered Marsh); the rumor that a firearms manufacturing plant had been set up in Nevada, and was now turning out weapons and ammunition in quantity. We refilled the glasses. My host was friendly enough,

God knew, and solicitous for my welfare. But I sensed a barrier, and a lack of warmth in his smile. "You're in time for dinner," he said at last. "We'll eat shortly." He studied me thoughtfully. "If you like, I believe we can replenish your wardrobe."

Marsh enjoyed his role as host, but I sensed he would have been uncomfortable in my position, as suppliant. "Thank you," I said. "You're very kind." And I thought of Max. "I'd like to take some water out to my horse."

"Is he in the barn?"

"Yes."

"I'll take care of it. Meantime, if you're ready, let's look at your quarters."

He provided me with a spacious and, by prairie standards, luxurious room on the third floor. A big double bed stood in its center, with pillows piled high and a quilt thrown over. I lacked a fireplace, but there was a steady flow of warm air from a vent. The atmosphere was masculine: varnished walls, a mounted deer's head, an antique pistol over the bed, and a military ensign bearing rifles and bugles and the numeral *IV* by the door. A small desk had been placed near the window. An ancient dictionary lay on the desk, and a battered copy of Pierce's *Travels Through the Dakotas* on a side table.

I threw off my clothes, leaving them in a pile on the floor, and retreated into a tan-tiled bathroom. I showered in glorious hot water, toweled off, and tried the garments my host had provided. They were a size large, but they were clean and smelled faintly of pine. I washed my own clothes and hung them to dry.

The smell of steak and potatoes drifted up from the kitchen. I wandered downstairs, pausing to look through a window at the rooftop lights. They blazed through the rushing snow. What a prodigious waste of power it all was. I wondered how they were able to manage it?

Marsh must have heard me coming: he was waiting when I arrived on the second floor. "I hope you feel better, Quincey," he said.

I did. Very much so.

We returned to the room in which we had talked earlier. A pot of coffee was waiting. He poured, and we sat down by the fire. We were barely settled when he looked up, past my shoulder. "Eleanor," he said, "this is Mr. Quincey."

I rose and turned, and was astonished. So, I might add, was Eleanor.

"*Jeff*," she said, and I watched dismay, relief, fear, affection, and everything between, ripple across her face.

And *I*: my God, it was *Ellie Randall*.

For those few seconds, I could only stare.

Probably, no one ever quite recovers from the first big passion. Ellie had been mine. We'd had three months together when we were both growing up in the Forks. And that was all there was. She lost interest and walked out of my life. I didn't even have the consolation of losing her to someone else. Shortly after that I left the area, and when I went back ten years later she was gone and nobody knew where.

So I stood gaping back, shackled by the old resentment, breathless again. She was as gorgeous as I remembered. And that too shook me: I think in some dark corner of the mind, I'd hoped eventually to come across her and discover that the near-supernatural creature of my twentieth year had been a figment of youthful daydreaming. That, to a mature adult, she would really be quite ordinary. Perhaps even a trifle dull. That I'd conclude I'd been lucky to have got away.

But in that darkened room she seemed composed of firelight and shifting shadows, more spirit than flesh. (Although the flesh was not to be overlooked.) Her familiar features were classic, dark, and, now that she'd recovered from her initial shock, amused. She shook her head in sheer pleasure and her black hair swirled across her shoulders. Delight filled her eyes, and I felt the entire room, the chairs, the lamps, the fire, and certainly me, come erect.

I knew already I would lie alone on the plains during years to come and replay this meeting. From that moment, I developed a loathing for Edward Marsh that nothing could ever efface.

We embraced, a fleeting, phantasmagoric thing, her lips brushing my cheek, her shoulders vibrant and alive in my hands. Her eyes touched mine. "Jeff, it really *is* you, isn't it? What have you been doing all these years?"

Her smile melted me into my socks, and I was twenty years old again. I didn't trust my voice, so I grinned, foolishly no doubt, retreated to my coffee, and mumbled something about traveling extensively.

Marsh moved into the gap. "Well, *that's* interesting," he said, eyes brightening. "How odd that you two would know each other."

"We grew up together. Jeff and I were good friends for a long time." Her eyes settled on me. "It *is* good to see you again, Jeff." The smile never faded. "Listen, I have to finish dinner. But we have a lot to talk about." She swung round and trooped out. And the room sank back into the normal flow of time.

"She hasn't changed," I told Marsh. He was watching me with interest, and I knew what he was wondering. The rational tack, of course, was to change the subject. "What kind of installation was this originally?" I asked, heading in the first direction that suggested itself.

He took a long breath and examined his coffee. "A research facility of some sort," he said. "Ellie can tell you more about it than I can."

"Oh?"

He shrugged. "Yes, she's closer to the history of the place than I am." There was something dismissive in his tone, as if there were more important matters to consider. His eyes glided over me.

"Will there be others at dinner?" I asked.

"No," he said distractedly. "There is no one else here."

I looked down at my shirt.

"It belonged to *Ellie's* brother-in-law, actually," he said. "He left a few years ago."

Ellie's *brother-in-law*? Why not "my brother"? "Where is he now?" I asked conversationally.

"We don't know. Occasionally, someone comes by with a letter from him. Last we heard, he was in Zona."

I gradually received the impression, one that was reinforced through the evening, that he was measuring me, that he was involved in a calculation and that I was somehow a variable.

Marsh had traveled widely. He explained that he had been born in Canada, in a town not far from Ottawa. "We all grew up in the shadows of that enormous wreck. And I've stayed away from the ruins since. Don't like them." He shook his head. "No sir. Don't like them one bit."

"I know what you mean," I said, not sure at all that I did.

"We're headed backward, Quincey. All of us. Still losing ground even while you and I sit here. And I don't like being reminded of it." He raised his arms in a sweeping gesture that took in the walls, or maybe the world. "They're all yellow now," he said. "Fading. And when they're gone, I suspect none of us will even remember who we were."

I realized finally he was referring to his books, marshaled around the room like a military guard. I repressed a shrug. I've never read a book, and am barely able to manage trade documents, if the truth be known. "I'm not so sure," I said. "Life is hard, but it could be worse. I mean, there's always food and drink, if a man's willing to work. And women enough, God knows." I wished Ellie had been there to hear that. I hoped he would repeat it to her, and she would understand that I had been having a very fine time on my own, thank you.

A few minutes later, Ellie announced that dinner was ready. We retired to the dining room, and she flashed me another big smile. I thought I saw in it a glint of regret. I applied the construction most favorable to myself, and attacked dinner with a sense of good cheer.

The table would have supported dinner for ten. We ate by candlelight, warmed by two fireplaces.

The meal consisted of steak and potatoes and green beans and buttered corn and hot rolls. Marsh broke out a decanter and filled the glasses, and we toasted "old friends." *His* proposal. I was still wondering about the nature of the facility. "What," I asked, "is the ring? The ring-shaped ridge?"

Ellie tried her drink, and obviously approved. "They used this place to break into atoms," she said. "They were trying to discover what matter really is."

"Why?" I asked.

"I'm not entirely sure."

"Did they leave records?"

"In a way. They wrote their results into computer banks."

"Oh." The computers don't work anymore.

She sliced off a piece of steak, turned it on her fork, and slid it between her lips. "Not bad," she said, eyes gleaming. "Given time, maybe we'll figure out how to fix them."

We ate quietly for a few minutes. "How do you come to own a place like the Tower?" I asked Marsh.

"I don't own it," he said. "It's Ellie's, actually."

She tried her wine and let me see she approved. "I married into it. Two or three years after you left, I married Corey Bolton. His family had been here for generations." She propped her chin on her fist and looked right through me. "Corey died in a raid several years later. After that his brothers cleared out, and I more or less inherited the place."

"It's *big*," I said.

She smiled. "You don't know the half of it. Most of the complex is underground."

Marsh smiled reflexively. He looked uneasy.

I expected him to say something. But he only patted his mouth with his napkin. The silence stretched out.

"I wonder what *does* lie inside atoms?" I said.

"Energy," said Marsh.

"Yes." Ellie nodded agreement. She *had* changed, of course. The buoyancy of the adolescent had given way to cool dignity. Her eyes, which had been unabashedly playful, glowed now with mystery and intelligence. The sense of what I had lost began to overwhelm me, and I was sorry I had stumbled into the place. Better a cold night on the plain than this. "But there's obviously more to it than that."

"And the ridge?" I asked again.

"Oh. It's a tunnel. We can reach it from here, actually. They fired atoms, or parts of atoms, I'm not sure which, through it. When they collided, they broke apart, and it was possible to see what was inside."

"It's hard to believe," I said, "that anyone could ever do that."

"So." She announced the subject change with her tone. "What have *you* been doing since you left the Forks, Jeff?" She touched a wall panel and Mozart filled the room. We talked about greenhouses (the Tower had *two*), and the source of their power (solar), and Marsh's trip to the Pacific, and how Chicago looks from offshore.

I learned that Marsh had been a colonel with irregulars formed to defend a group of Minnesota settlements. That Ellie was trying to pull together a comprehensive account of pre-Crash activities at the Tower, that the trail seemed to lead to Minneapolis, and that eventually she would make the trip. Ellie's comment to that effect ignited the colonel's disapproval, and I understood that I had blundered into an old argument. "Too dangerous," he said, dismissing the matter.

When we'd finished, he insisted on clearing the table, and carrying the dishes into the kitchen. I was impressed by the manner in which he stayed with her and made himself useful. But I noticed also, on several occasions, silent exchanges taking place between them. Was she reassuring him about our relationship? I suspected so, and was pleased that he might, even momentarily, consider me a potential rival.

In all, it was a delicious and entertaining evening. I was sorry to see it end.

* * *

The storm had eased off, and the sky had cleared. But the wind had lost none of its force, and it drove the loose snow across the landscape.

The clothes I'd washed were still damp. I waited, listening for the last footsteps to come upstairs, and then I went down and arranged my garments in front of the fire. I threw an extra log on, and sank into a chair in front of the blaze. It was warm and pleasant. And it was not long before sleep overtook me.

I dreamt of her that night, as I had on other nights. And, as was the usual climax to these nocturnal reunions, I awoke depressed with the weight of her loss. I sat staring at the fire, which was now little more than embers, aware of the wind and sounds deep in the belly of the building and the flow of moonlight through the windows.

And I realized I was not alone.

A patch of darkness disconnected itself and came forward.

Ellie.

"Hello," I said.

She wore a heavy woolen robe, drawn up around the neck, her black hair thrown over the collar. I could not see her expression, but the glow from the window touched her eyes. "Hi, Jeff," she said. "Is there anything wrong with your room?"

For a wild moment, I wondered whether she had just come from there. "No," I said. I pointed at the clothes strung by the fire. "I just got too comfortable here. There's no problem."

After a brief silence, she said, "I didn't expect to see you again."

I had got up, but she gestured me back into my seat,

and stirred the fire. "You've a lovely home," I said. "You've done well."

She nodded. The robe was frayed, oversized. But it didn't matter: she was breathtakingly beautiful. "Corey was *good*. I couldn't have asked for more."

"I'm sorry you lost him," I said.

"Thanks. It's a long time ago now." She slipped into an adjoining chair. "Jeff, I'm glad to find you here. I was afraid I wouldn't really get a chance to talk to you."

I was prodding myself to be generous, to avoid letting any of the old anger show. But it was hard. "We don't really have much to talk about," I said.

"Yes, we do." She gazed at me steadily, and I imagined I could see sparks reflected in her eyes. "I can't change what happened between us. I can't even say that I *would*, if I could. I loved Corey, and I wouldn't have missed my years with him for anything." She touched my forearm, just her fingertips, but the effect was electric. "You understand what I'm telling you?"

"Yes," I said. But I had no idea.

She stared past my shoulder. "You know that Ed is not my husband."

"I'd guessed."

"When we were attacked, when Corey was killed, Ed was the one who came to the rescue. He rode in with a detachment from Sandybrook and personally killed two of the sons of bitches."

"And afterward," I said, "he stayed."

"Not immediately. Corey's brothers couldn't take it anymore out here and they left. When that happened, he tried to persuade me to leave, too."

"Why didn't you?"

She took a deep breath. "This is my *home*." But her eyes looked away. "When I wouldn't leave, he came out. Used to sleep in here. Like you. Eventually…" She shrugged.

"This place is dangerous. For two people."

"We have defenses. Corey wouldn't have been killed if we hadn't been surprised." She shook her head, maybe reassuring herself. "No. I'll never leave here, Jeff. I *love* this place."

We sat quiet.

"But I did want you to know," she said, "that I've never been able to forget you."

That and fifty bucks, I thought. But I didn't say it.

The room got very quiet. It occurred to me that Marsh might be standing within earshot. Marsh, who had killed two raiders. "I'm happy to hear it," I said.

"I know what you're thinking," she said, mischievously.

"What am I thinking?"

"He won't care," she said. "Ed doesn't care about *me*."

That made no sense. He doesn't own the property. If he had no feelings for her, why on earth would he stay in this godforsaken place? I replayed the evening. The way Marsh had introduced her. The way he'd responded when he had discovered we'd known each other. The way he talked to her. "I don't believe it," I said.

"Nevertheless it's true. He feels trapped here, and he blames me." She pushed up out of her chair. "He stays out of a sense of duty."

Her grip tightened on my hand, and a tear ran down her cheek. It was a moment I'd contemplated many times when I was younger. Ellie perhaps realizing at last what she had lost. Asking me to forgive. In my imagination, the moment had always seemed delicious. But when it came, I took no pleasure in it.

"You never married," she said.

"I never stayed in one place long enough. Anyway, no one ever seemed much interested."

"Well, we both know that's not true," she said. She stared at me for a long moment, and, without another word, got out of her chair, pressed her lips against my cheek, and left the room.

I went to bed. I didn't sleep well, though, and I was tempted to clear out during the night. But that might have raised questions and embarrassed Ellie. So I determined to get through breakfast, and leave as quickly as I reasonably could.

Bacon and coffee were already on when I started down. I poked my head into the dining room first, saw no one, and made for the kitchen. Ellie was there, manning an electric stove. But I saw immediately that something was wrong. She looked tired, and the *joie de vivre* of the previous day had been replaced with knife-edged intensity. "Good morning, Jeff," she said. Her tone was cordial, but not warm.

She wore a white jumper open at the throat, and a knee-length knit skirt. Her hair was brushed back, revealing pale, drawn features. "You okay?" I asked.

"I'm fine." She delivered a dispirited smile. "How do you like your eggs?"

"Medium well." I looked at her. "What's wrong?"

She poked at the bacon. "He's gone, Jeff."

"Gone? Ed?"

"Yes."

"Where?"

"Out. Skedaddled. Left for parts unknown."

"My God. What happened?"

She turned her attention to the eggs, scooping at them and wiping her eyes with the backs of her hands. I pulled the pan from the burner and set it down where things wouldn't burn, and then I caught her up. "Talk to me," I said.

"He left before dawn."

"Did he think something happened between us?"

"No," she said. "No. Nothing like that."

"What makes you think he's not coming back?"

"I *know* he's not coming back." She shook her head. "Listen, I'll be okay. Best thing is for you to eat and head out."

"Tell me why," I said.

"I've already told you. He felt trapped here. I warned him what it would be like, but he wouldn't listen, or didn't really understand. When you came, last night, when he saw that we had been friends, maybe *more* than friends, he saw his chance."

"To *bolt*?"

She nodded.

"Knowing that I wouldn't leave you here alone?"

"I'm sure that's what he thought."

"A creep with a conscience." I sank into a chair.

"That's not true," she said. "He waited. He stayed for *years*. Most men would have just walked out. Jeff, he never committed to this."

"Sure he did," I said. "When he moved in, he made a commitment." But I could see it hurt her. She wanted to think well of the son of a bitch, so I let it go.

We abandoned the kitchen, left breakfast in ruins, and wandered into the room with the fireplaces.

"Okay," I said. "What happens now?"

She shrugged. "I'll manage."

"You can't stay here alone."

"Why not?"

"*Alone?* Rattling around in this place?"

"It's my home."

"It will be a prison. Close it up and come back with me. To the Forks. It'll be safe for a while. Give yourself a chance to get away from it."

"No." Her voice caught. "I can't leave here."

"Sure you can. Just make up your mind and do it."

She nodded and took a long breath. "Maybe you're right," she said. "Maybe it *is* time to let go."

"Good." I saw possibilities for myself. "Listen, we'll—"

"Take my chances." She was beginning to look wild. "There's no reason *I* should have to be buried here—"

"None at all," I said.

"If it gets loose, it gets loose. I mean, nobody else cares, do they?"

"Right," I said. "If *what* gets loose?"

She looked at me a long time. "Maybe you should know what's in the basement."

I didn't like the sound of that.

I tried to get her to explain, but she only shook her head. "I'll show it to you," she said.

So I followed her down to the lobby. Outside, the snow cover ran unbroken to the horizon. I looked at the Native American display. "Corey's idea," she said. "He thought it provided a counterpoint to the technology."

We went downstairs, down four more levels in fact, into the bowels of the building. At each floor I paused and looked along the corridors, which were dark, illuminated only by the lights in the stairway area. The passageways might have gone on forever. "How big is this place?" I asked.

"*Big*," she said. "Most of it's underground. Not counting the tunnel." As we got lower, I watched her spirits revive. "I think you're right, Jeff. It *is* time to get out. The hell with it."

"I agree." I put an arm around her and squeezed, and her body was loose and pliable, the way a woman is when she's ready.

"Jeff," she said, "I meant what I said last night."

During the time we had known one another, I had never told her how I felt. Now, deep below the Tower, I embraced her, and held her face in my hands, and kissed her. Tears rolled again, and when we separated, my cheeks were wet. "Ellie," I said, "for better or worse, I love you. Always have. There has never been a moment when I would not have traded everything I had for you."

She shook her head. No. "You'd better see what you're getting into first before you say any more."

We turned on lights and proceeded down a long corridor, past more closed rooms. "These were laboratories," she said, "and storage rooms, and libraries."

The floor was dusty. Walls were bare and dirty. The doors were marked with the letter designator "D", and numbered in sequence, odd on the left, even on the right. There had been carpeting, I believe, at one time. But there was only rotted wood underfoot now.

"Doesn't look as if you come down here very much," I said.

She pointed at the floor, and I saw footprints in the dust. "Every day."

She threw open a door and stepped back. I walked past her into the dark.

I could not immediately make out the dimensions of the room, or its general configuration. But ahead, a blue glow flickered and wavered and crackled. Lights came on. The room was quite large, maybe a hundred feet long. Tables and chairs were scattered everywhere, and the kind of antique equipment that turns up sometimes in ruins was piled high against both side walls.

The blue glow was on the other side of a thick smoked window. The window was at eye level, about thirty feet long, and a foot high. She watched me. I crossed to the glass and looked in.

A luminous, glowing cylinder floated in the air. It was a foot off the floor, and it extended almost to the ceiling. Thousands of tiny lights danced and swirled within its folds. It reminded me of a Christmas tree the Sioux had raised outside Sunset City a couple of years ago. "What is it?" I asked.

"The devil," she said softly.

A chill worked its way up my back. "What do you mean?"

"It's a result of the research they did here. A by-product. Something that wasn't supposed to happen. Jeff, they *knew* there was a possibility things might go wrong. But the bastards went ahead anyway."

"Wait," I said. "Slow down. Went ahead with what?"

"With what we were talking about last night. Smashing atoms. Jeff, this was state-of-the-art stuff." She moved close to me, and I touched her hair. "Do you know what protons are?"

"Yeah. Sort of. They're made of atoms."

"Other way around," she said. "The thing about protons is that they are extremely stable. Protons are the basic building blocks of matter. There is *nothing* more stable than a proton. Or at least, there used to be nothing."

"I'm not following this."

"The people who worked here knew there was a possibility they might produce an element that would *be* more stable." Her voice was rising, becoming breathless. "And they also knew that if it actually happened, if they actually produced such an element, it would *de*stabilize any proton it came into contact with."

"Which means what?"

"They'd lose the lab." I was still watching the thing, fascinated. It seemed to be rotating slowly, although the lights moved independently at different speeds, and some even rotated against the direction of turn. The effect was soothing. "In fact," she continued, "they were afraid of losing the Dakotas."

"You mean that it might *destroy* the Dakotas?"

"Yes."

"Ridiculous."

"I would have thought so too. But apparently not. Not if the records are correct."

I couldn't figure it out. "Why would they make something like that?" I asked.

"They didn't set out to *make* it. They thought it was *possible*. A by-product. But the chances seemed remote, and I guess the research was important, so they went ahead."

I still couldn't see the problem. After all, it was obvious that nothing untoward had occurred.

"They took steps to protect themselves in case there was an incident. They developed a defense. Something to contain it."

"How?"

"You're looking at it. It's a magnetic field that plays off the new element. They called it Heisium."

"After its discoverer?"

"Yes."

"So it's contained. What's the problem?"

She stood with her back to it, looking away. "What do you suppose would happen if the power failed here?"

"The lights would go out." And I understood. *The lights would go out.* "Isn't there a backup?"

"It's *on* the backup. Has been for almost two hundred years. The Crash took out their electrical source, and it's been running on the Tower's solar array ever since."

"Why do you come down here every day?"

"Check the gauges. Look around. Make sure everything's okay."

That shook me. "What do you do if it isn't?"

"Flip a circuit breaker. Tighten a connection. Rewire whatever." She inhaled. *"Somebody has to do this."*

"Jesus."

"They kept this place manned for forty years. Then, after the Crash, the son of one of the people responsible for the original decision, Avery Bolton, the guy the Tower's named for, stayed on. And kept the place going. When he died, his daughter succeeded him. And brought her family. In one way or another, that family has been here ever since. Until Corey. And his brothers. His brothers weren't worth much, and now I'm all that's left." She shook her head. "Seen enough?"

"Ellie, do you *really* believe all this?"

"I believe there's a good chance the threat is real." We were sitting in the lobby. "Why else would I *be* here?"

"Things get twisted over a long time. Maybe they were wrong." Outside, the day was bright and cold. "I just can't believe it."

"That's good," she said. "You should continue to think that. But I'm going to have to continue to assume that Corey knew what he was talking about."

"My God, Ellie, it's a *trap*."

She looked at me, and her eyes were wet. "Don't you think I *know* that?"

I looked up at an oil of a Sioux warrior on horseback, about to plunge a lance into a bison. "There's a way to settle it," I said.

She shook her head. "No."

"Ellie. We can shut it down. Nothing will happen."

"*No*. I won't consider it. And I want you to promise you won't do anything like that."

I hesitated.

"I want your word, Jeff. *Please*."

"Okay," I said.

"Not ever. No matter what."

"Not ever." She looked fragile. Frightened. "No matter what."

She looked out across the snowfields. "It must be time to go."

"I won't leave you," I said.

That evening was a night to kill for. The consummation of love, denied over a lifetime, may be as close as you can come to the point of existence. I took her, and took her again, and went limp in her arms, and woke to more passion. Eventually the curtains got gray, and I made promises that she said she didn't want to hear, but I made them anyway. We had a magnificent breakfast, and made love again in the room with the fireplaces. Eventually, sometime around lunch, we went down and looked again at Bolton's devil. She took along a checklist, and explained the gauges and circuit breakers and pointed out where the critical wiring was, and where things might go wrong. Where they'd gone wrong in the past. "Just in case," she said. "Not that I expect you to get involved in this, but it's best if someone else knows. Edward hated to do this. He rarely came here."

She showed me where the alarms were throughout our living quarters, and how, if the power supply got low, the system automatically shunted everything into the storage batteries in the lab. "It's happened a couple of times when we've had consecutive weeks without sunlight."

"It must get cold," I said. The temperatures here dropped sometimes to forty below for a month at a time.

"We've got fireplaces," she said. "And we'll have each other."

It was all I needed to hear.

I stayed on, of course. And I did it with no regrets. I too came to feel the power of the thing in the lab. I accepted the burden voluntarily. And not without a sense of purpose, which, I knew, would ultimately bind us together more firmly than any mere vow could have.

We worried because the systems that maintained the magnetic bottle were ageing. Eventually, we knew, it would fail. But not, we hoped, in our lifetimes.

We took turns riding the buckboard over to Sandywater for supplies. Our rule was that someone was always available at the Tower. In case.

And one day, about three months after my arrival, she did not come back. When a second day had passed without word, I went after her. I tracked her as far as the town, where I found the buckboard. There was no sign of her.

Jess Harper, who works for Overland, thought he'd seen her get into a buckboard with a tall bearded man. "They rode west," he said. "I thought it was odd."

That was almost a year ago. I still make the rounds in the Tower, and I still believe she'll come back. In the meantime, I check the gauges and occasionally throw a circuit breaker. The power in the living quarters shut down once, but I got through it okay. *We* got through it okay.

What I can't understand is how I could have been so wrong. I know who the bearded man was, and I try to tell myself that they must have been very desperate to get away. And I try to forgive them. Forgive *her*.

But it's not easy. Some nights when the moon is up, and the wind howls around the Tower, I wonder what they are doing, and whether she ever thinks about me. And occasionally, I am tempted to break my promise, and turn things off. Find out once and for all.

FOUNDATION

ANN AGUIRRE

I don't remember how the sun feels.

It's an abstract concept for me, something I know exists, but doesn't have the meaning it once did. When we first came down, my mom and dad said it was just for a few weeks, just a precaution. The outbreaks in the city came from some biological agent released in Times Square, I guess, and the news was full of conflicting reports on whether it came from North Korea or Iran. Other sites had other theories, but it was a coordinated strike, targeting cities all over the world.

At the time, I didn't know why—or even what—was happening. I was thirteen when my parents quietly bought a unit in the bunkers. By that point, the city was bad enough that my mother no longer went out to do the marketing. Instead, she called a service that brought our food, and she didn't let the courier come into the apartment, either. He left our groceries in the foyer with the doorman, who then scanned to make sure there were no foreign objects in the boxes or suspicious contaminants present.

By this point, I had stopped attending school. I was nine when they declared a state of national emergency and the country went to martial law, trying to contain the damage. Whole sectors of the city were designated hazardous and quarantined accordingly. My dad said the heavily armed soldiers in the streets patrolled to protect me, so I wasn't to worry about them. They would soon restore order and things would get back to normal. Though I didn't know it at the time, he was totally wrong.

For us, normal ended on May 5 when the chemicals exploded in Times Square.

The world never recovered.

It's funny, but when I look back over my childhood, I see a progression of my world getting smaller. At five, I went on a plane with my parents and the whole universe lay open before me. There was a white beach with sand soft as powder and an endless blue ocean; the air was balmy, and it was an island, covered in mountains. I remember asking if this was heaven, and my mother laughed. She said, "It's not heaven, Robin, but it *is* paradise."

There were other wonders on that trip, but I was so young that they've begun to fade, colors running together like a painting left out in the rain. I mind this fiercely because it feels like time is stealing what little I have left. After we came home, I went to school, and my world was my teacher and twenty-four other students. Then it narrowed further to my parents and the walls of the apartment with the occasional supervised trip outdoors.

And when I was thirteen, they took away the sun. I argued. I sulked. I tried to convince my parents they were overreacting—we didn't need to go live underground like rabbits, but they were afraid. The streets teemed with people who had been infected with the Metanoia Virus, and public services couldn't cope with them all. My parents told me these unfortunates were unable to hold a job; their health and mental abilities had been permanently compromised. In time, they promised, the government would help the sick. I wasn't sure shooting them or rounding them up in trucks counted as help, but I got used to hearing automatic-weapons fire and the rumble of large engines as I fell asleep.

That morning, the bunker company sent an armed escort to take us from our apartment. We put on special clothing and masks that would allegedly protect us. I rode in an armored vehicle for the first time—and the last— that day. We went into a tall building, down some stairs, and through a heavy, heavy door. My parents signed some documents, and then we took possession of our new home.

"It's so small," my mother said.

My father put an arm around her. "We'll get used to it. We'll make do. This is just a precaution, just for a little while, until they get things back in order."

Now, I wonder if he knew, if he suspected.

For the first year, we maintained contact with the outside world. The air we breathed was regulated and filtered, our food was expensive and packaged "like the astronauts eat," according to my mother. That was supposed to make it more exciting, but I had to force mine down. Sometimes I wondered what the point of survival was, if this was what we had to do; it seemed there was nothing in the world worth saving.

Then silence fell. Reports stopped coming. I was fourteen years old. My mother spent all day weeping when the news sites went quiet. Another day, she pressed random keys on the terminal, trying to get anyone to respond. And that was when we found the local intercom.

Oh, we had known there were others in units nearby. We had seen the doors when we took possession of our unit, but the manager said it was best we didn't mingle because opening the hermetic seal on our doors increased the risk of contagion. The company did its best to guarantee a 100 percent contaminant-free atmosphere, but that warranty existed only in our bunker, not in the public areas like the hallway. Which should be safe, but there was no guarantee.

The terminal beeped, and then a voice said, "Hello?"

He sounded young.

My mother lost interest when she realized she hadn't contacted the authorities for a status update. Someone who sounded like that couldn't know any more than we did. So she stepped away and I took her place. A few more keystrokes and I had an image on-screen. I had spent most of my time sleeping, drawing, or reading, as I hadn't been a tech person even before we came down here. In the bunker, I sketched furiously, as if I could keep the world alive by capturing my memories of it.

"Are you inside too?" the boy asked.

I nodded and told him our unit number. "You?"

"I'm in three F. Austin Shelley," he added, as if I had asked.

"Robin Schiller." I couldn't think of a good way to ask this, so I just came out with it. "Have you talked to anyone or heard anything—"

"No. This is the first contact I've had with anyone outside our flat in almost a year."

He had dark brown hair, green eyes, and a thin face with the concentrated pallor of one who hasn't been outdoors in a while. I'd probably be showing the same lack, if I didn't have my father's dark skin. From my mother, I'd gotten hazel eyes and my interest in drawing. I'd never been outdoorsy or sporty, and I was lucky my dad didn't care about such things too much. Before, he had some idea I might be a doctor like him, but with the way things had changed, I didn't think much about the future.

Even then, I suspected I might not have one.

"How long have you been here?" I asked.

"Almost a year, since I was fourteen."

That made him a year older than me. Surprising, how much I liked knowing I wasn't the only one my age down here. He might understand how alone I felt and how impossible everything seemed. I wanted to chat more, but there was no chance that day.

"Robin," my mother said. "Come away. Your father wants to talk to you."

"Will you call me again?" Austin asked.

"Yes," I said quickly. I memorized the colors currently lit on the terminal. "Soon, I promise."

My parents sat me down and explained that it was likely we wouldn't be going back up. If the world was in such bad shape that the infrastructure had collapsed, they didn't see us returning. Which meant I had to adjust to the small life we currently knew. Two years ago, I would've protested. But I had grown up a bit since then. I understood the limitations, and I only nodded.

Early the next morning while my mom and dad were still asleep, I used the terminal to call Austin. It wasn't so much that I thought they would mind as the fact that I wanted something of my own. Since we lived in one room, it had gotten harder to remember when I had hours to myself, no one looking at my drawings over my shoulder.

He answered on the first ring, his voice a sleepy whisper. "Robin?"

"You asked me to—"

"I know. Not about anything specific. I'm just tired of talking to my parents. My mother's trying to pretend this will be over shortly."

"It might be," I said. "But probably not in the way she hopes."

The video aspect of the call stayed dark, as lights and moving images would wake our parents in a way that whispers might not. So his sigh came across with poignant clarity. I imagined his fear echoed my own, but I didn't mention it. We didn't know each other well enough to share such things.

"What did you do, before?" It was an open question.

"I was at a charter school, studying art. I'm fourteen," I added, because he might not have been able to tell from the quick glimpse yesterday.

"My parents called me home from military academy just before they dropped the bomb about the bunker."

"I don't know anything about boarding school. Did you like it?"

His hesitation told me the answer was no. "I got used to it."

At that point, my parents stirred, so I whispered, "Tomorrow?"

"Yes. Please." It was the tacked-on "please" that made me determined not to miss a day.

I suspected Austin Shelley was lonely like me.

After that, the days fell into a routine. Austin would have been a year ahead of me in school, for what little such things mattered these days. He had wanted to become an architect—though that seemed unlikely now—and he was fascinated by how things worked. I ticked off the days in my journal, each one bringing a fresh conversation with my new friend.

Thirty-four days after I first called Austin Shelley, my father sat me down. At first, I thought it meant they'd learned my secret and I was about to get a lecture, but instead, my parents wanted to discuss our current living conditions. Apparently, they thought it wasn't healthy for us to be cooped up like animals in an exhibit.

"We've discussed the risks at length," my father said, "and your mother and I agree that we should get to know the other families down here."

"Yes. If we're stuck, we might as well make the best of it," my mother added with a determinedly cheerful expression.

I'd seen that look many times, just before she offered me the lesser of two evils, but I was tired of our four walls, however expensive they had been. Safety at the cost of new experiences tasted like stale, unleavened bread. So later that day, my father unsealed the door and we stepped into the hallway beyond. Inside our bunker it was easier to pretend, but here, it was definitely grim and institutional, constructed quickly in answer to the growing unease. Other doors opened around us, and in their *shhh* sounds I heard a tacit acceptance that this was our new reality.

Six families. Six bunkers.

Four of them had children, but most were younger. I might end up watching them to give their parents a break, but they'd never be my friends. Not like Austin. He came toward me with a shy half-smile, like he felt odd about meeting someone with whom he'd been talking in whispers for over a month. I knew exactly how he felt. This was possibly the worst party ever; since we all had the same rations, there was nothing to offer but our company.

I offered my hand, and he shook it, solemn-faced. As far as our parents were concerned, we were strangers, but he had been a lifeline across days that seemed so alike as to have no end. And sometimes I had dark thoughts, like, *is survival at this cost even* worth *it*? Most days, the answer was yes, but occasionally it was just because I knew he was waiting to hear from me.

Austin was taller than me by at least four inches. At military school, they probably made him participate in team sports too. I beckoned for him to come into our unit, away from the kids chasing one another up and down the hall. There were five of them, not including us, which meant some families had more than one. I couldn't imagine how they were coping with the reduced space. Probably, their mothers put them on the exercise machine and made them use it until they exhausted all their energy.

"So this is you," he said, and then his pale cheeks colored.

I pretended I thought he meant our apartment instead of acknowledging it as a lame version of *so we meet at last*. "Is it like your place?"

"Pretty much."

"This is the sketch book I was telling you about. I'm almost out of pages. But I like this one—" I broke off, conscious that he was studying me, not the book. "Do I look… different than you expected?"

It was an issue for some people that my father was a different color than my mother. Fervently I hoped that wouldn't be the case for Austin; he shook his head quickly, eyes dropping to the floor and then back to mine again.

"It's just… odd," he managed finally.

He's shy, I guessed.

Ordinarily, I could be too, but we'd talked enough in the mornings that he felt like an old friend. So maybe if I treated him that way, he would relax. I hoped so. For me, he offered the bright spot at the start of each day.

"Everything is."

"I don't draw people," he said then. "But I have some designs. Buildings. Would you like to see?" Again, the touch of color.

I couldn't figure out why he was so awkward with me, unless it was the weight of knowing the private things we'd whispered to each other without ever expecting the doors would open. Maybe I had played a priestly role in his mind, that of confessor, but now that I was standing here, it felt different. I followed Austin next door to find that his unit was a precise mirror of ours, every amenity, each feature.

Carefully, I paged through his sketches, then tapped one. "This is amazing. I've never seen anything like it. Where did you see it?"

"That's one I wanted to build. After I became an architect."

His green eyes swam with desperation and sorrow because now, that was an impossible dream. And there was nothing I could say to turn the world right side up again. My goals had always been smaller—to draw or paint. Maybe I could still do that on a reduced scale, but Austin couldn't. Everything he wanted had been stolen from him.

"I'm sorry," I said, but it wasn't enough.

For a few seconds, I covered his hand with mine. I'd seen my dad do it countless times with patients, but this felt…

different. A little spark went through me. I'd always known I was odd—not in the sense that I preferred boys over girls, but in the sense that it didn't matter. Most times, I'd rather keep company with a beautiful painting, lost in my own head. But on the two occasions when my interest had been roused, it was by what went on in their hearts and minds, not the physical trappings. In my admittedly light romantic past, there had been a couple of crushes and one kiss.

His chin dipped so he wasn't looking at me anymore. "It's probably for the best. I'd only have fought with my dad about it."

But he didn't pull his hand away. In fact, he shifted until it lay palm up beneath mine. I had never been so conscious of the heat of my skin against someone else's. The touch gave me a fluttery feeling in my stomach, and I didn't know if I should lace our fingers together, but I think he was waiting for some kind of cue he didn't receive because a few seconds later, he drew back.

"You don't get along?"

That opened the door to a flood of confidences he imparted in his morning voice, soft enough that it created a familiar bond. We had been talking for an hour when our families decided we should return to isolation with promises to repeat the meeting soon. I wished I could stay with Austin, but things would change soon enough—and in ways I couldn't have predicted then. If I've learned anything since those days, it's not to wish too hard for a shift in circumstances since it never happens as you imagine.

A month later, the Markowitz parents fell ill. The oldest child called our unit, sobbing, as she begged my father to come and save them. He was the only doctor in the bunkers; my mother implored him not to go. I understood her caution, but I also knew why he would ultimately refuse her.

"I have to try, Mel. You know that."

"Don't go," she pleaded, as if she *knew*. "Call the administrator."

Ostensibly, there was a corporate representative here to make sure nothing went wrong. He did periodic checks, but he didn't socialize with us, didn't communicate more than necessary. Likely he had orders to that effect as it would be impossible to hand down unpopular edicts if he got too close.

Before my father could reply, the comm sounded, an official tone. "I regret to inform you that there was a fault in the ventilation systems. All units may have been exposed to outside toxins. Naturally, a full refund will be issued."

"A refund," my mother repeated, looking numb. "What good will that do us? Jeremy, I can't watch you and Robby die."

I ached because she hadn't called me that in so long, not since I was a little kid. My dad wore a tight, brave expression, but I saw terror in his dark eyes. His hands curled into fists, as my calm, unflappable father fought the urge to take out his rage on the furnishings. I had never been so frightened in my life.

"I have to check on the Markowitz family," he said softly.

"Jeremy—"

"Stop it. If we've already been exposed, then it doesn't matter. You know that."

Exposed. Such a small word to contain so much horror and vulnerability. My mother took to her bed after my father left; first she cried until she had no voice, then she took a pair of pills that let her sleep. Looking back, I can say she was a sweet woman, but she wasn't strong. That day, Austin called me for the first time while our parents were awake. Time seemed too precious for secrets now.

"I guess you heard," he said.

"Yeah. My dad is making rounds, trying to help."

"Mine is—" The audio cut in and out, revealing the fury his dad didn't bother to contain.

"Come over. You shouldn't be around him when he's so mad." I could hear bits of the rant about how Mr. Shelley would sue the company, but it was all sound and fury. Even the colonel knew there would be no legal recourse in the new world rising from the ashes of the old. That was part of why he was so angry.

Austin didn't ask permission from his parents; if we were all dying anyway, what did obedience matter? He slipped into our unit with minimum fuss. Here, it was quiet at least.

"I don't want to die," he whispered in our morning voice.

A lump comprised of equal parts fear and sympathy rose in my throat. "Me either."

"I'm not ready. I mean, I always knew it might come to this, but part of me believed my old man. He could buy his way out of anything. Even this." His voice broke. "Turns out, not so much."

"I tried to pretend it wasn't happening. Live in my own head."

Somehow he went into my arms or I went into his and we tangled, hard. He was shaking, or I was. So hard, knowing the air you breathed might be what killed you. Austin smelled exactly like me; he used the same company-provided soap and toiletries, but it was a little better on him, deeper and richer, or it might've been the alchemy of his skin. If it hadn't been for my mother asleep behind us—or the fact that my father could come back at any moment—I might've done more than hold him, if I'd been that brave, then. In truth, I wasn't; and it might've felt like taking advantage anyway when he was so obviously upset.

He didn't go back to his unit that night. Austin slept in my bed, curled against my back. My mother didn't wake. In the morning, I roused to a comforting arm over my waist; it was the first time I'd slept the night through with another person. I wondered if he would regret the need and vulnerability, but he didn't seem to. Nor did he appear in any hurry to go back next door.

By the time my father returned, he looked exhausted, dark rings about his eyes. The slump of his shoulders told me it hadn't gone well at the Markowitz place.

"Bad?" I guessed.

"The parents died in the night."

I bit out a word I wasn't supposed to use, and my father didn't even chide me. "That was fast."

"The oldest girl has it, and there's nothing I can do for her, but the younger two seem to be all right. The administrator collected the bodies."

"So we just wait to die?" Austin demanded.

My father shook his head. "I don't know, son. The girls will be over here shortly, once they finish packing. I hope you don't mind looking after them. I need to get some sleep. Is your mother—"

"She's not handling it well."

But she was suffering from more than self-medication. Illness followed, so she grew weaker and weaker. My mother never said my name again. Never called me Robby. As she lingered near death, I held in the tears through sheer force of will. Even Austin's hand on my shoulder didn't help, though it felt nice. She died just before midnight.

The oldest Markowitz girl also died that night—or maybe the administrator hurried her along. He was a cold-faced man and quick with a needle; I resolved never to be alone with him. Soon, we had two little orphaned girls underfoot, and Austin stayed with us until his mother came for him, wearing a look unlike any I've ever seen.

"I know you and the colonel have had your differences, but you need to say good-bye."

He shot me a panicked glance and I stood reflexively. "Do you mind if I come?"

Mrs. Shelley shook her head. "He's sick, you know."

I shrugged. "My father's been tending people. Both these girls lost their family to the plague. If I haven't gotten it by now, maybe I'm immune."

I shouldn't have said that.

Austin's father passed that night, and by morning, I was burning with fever. I gloss over this part of the story because I can't remember much about it. Some things are crystal clear, even at a remove of years, but not this. There were broken mirrors in my head, sweat and pain, a glimpse of my father's heartbroken face and green eyes luminous with tears.

I'm told I lay near death for seven days, and on the seventh, I came out of it. I recovered. In our small cross section of the populace, I'm the only one who did. A few simply never got sick. By the time the dying stopped, our small community had been decimated.

Of the original twenty-five, six of us lived. Me, Austin, my father, his mother, and the two Markowitz girls. After overhearing some cryptic comments from the administrator, we talked it over and decided to abandon the bunkers. There was apparently a vaccine, but it hadn't been thoroughly tested, and in some cases, it was making things worse. Instead of merely dying, some people were… changing. It sounded alarming—and I didn't want the company using us as test subjects for their faulty medicine or cleaning us up as a failed experiment.

We had to get away. To hide. So the next morning, we packed up everything we could carry—and it wasn't much. The walk was… harrowing. I'd never realized there was a whole world beneath the city, but there clearly was. People lived down here in warrens and tunnels—pale folk with shining eyes and suspicious stares. Most didn't look kindly on strangers and moved us along.

But after endless turns, endless twists through a dark world, we found a place that welcomed us. They were a fairly new settlement, calling themselves the College enclave, because of a nearby subway stop, I guess. And when they found out we had a doctor among us, they drew back the barricades and welcomed us. On the surface, most had been homeless, drug addicts or alcoholics, those that society threw away. Down here, they had the power.

In a heartbeat, everything changes.

"They're evacuating the city," one of the settlers told us. "Apparently it's uninhabitable up there right now."

Another shrugged. "We wouldn't have qualified for evac anyway. They're shortlisting those who can contribute to society."

A dusky-skinned man with dreadlocks said, "Down here, we all can. We do. Doctor, do you mind checking out my little girl?"

Because he always did, my father said yes—and the rest

of us found a little piece of ground to call our own. It was dark, cramped, and smelled a bit, of smoke and other, less pleasant things. I felt sure I'd get used to it. Life had already shifted so much.

Austin laced his fingers through mine and drew me away from the others. "It's better than the bunkers," he said softly, his tone more hopeful than certain.

"I hope so. At least we're not at the company's mercy. Let them try to find us here."

His expression became exultant, defiant, even. He put a hand on my shoulder and pushed me against the wall, then kissed me with such surety and promise. No more waiting for cues, apparently. Since he had been for me, almost from the moment I heard his voice in the dark, I curled my hand into his hair. There had been one touch of lips to mine before this, but *this* was the kiss I would cherish and remember, a kiss to obliterate all others. I was breathless when he stopped.

"I wasn't sure if you…" he started, then he shifted to, "I was afraid."

"Don't ever be. Not with me."

That night, the original settlers decided we needed some rules to follow; each of us should serve a purpose. Austin was confident that night, possibly because of us. And so he said, "You should divide up jobs like an old-school tribe. Some people hunt, others build."

Most people laughed, but the chief said, "What about the rest?"

"They breed to keep numbers up, naturally. But not too much. We want to survive, not overpopulate."

To my surprise, they ratified his idea. And it worked well for a long time. My father lasted ten years down there;

Mrs. Shelley passed on shortly thereafter. The Markowitz girls had sons and daughters. And Austin? He was a builder, even down here; oh, he crafted the most marvelous things. I helped him in that. Austin Shelley was also the love of my life.

I lost him two years ago.

And I am so very tired now. My name is Robin Schiller, and I have come to the end of my life. In this final recounting, I entrust my tale to you, my pupil; you are the first Wordkeeper. In this world, words matter. Sometimes they're all we have. So I entrust mine to you. Let them be remembered.

Let it be so.

BEAT ME DADDY
(EIGHT TO THE BAR)
CORY DOCTOROW

We were the Eight-Bar Band: there was me and my bugle; and Timson, whose piano had no top and got rained on from time to time; and Steve, the front-man and singer. And then there was blissed-out, autistic Hambone, our "percussionist" who whacked things together, more or less on the beat. Sometimes, it seemed like he was playing another song, but then he'd come back to the rhythm and *bam*, you'd realise that he'd been subtly keeping time all along, in the mess of clangs and crashes he'd been generating.

I think he may be a genius.

Why the Eight-Bar Band? Thank the military. Against all odds, they managed to build automated bombers that *still fly*, roaring overhead every minute or so, bomb-bay doors open, dry firing on our little band of survivors. The War had been over for ten years, but still, they flew.

So. The Eight-Bar Band. Everything had a rest every eight bars, punctuated by the white-noise roar of the most expensive rhythm section ever imagined by the military-industrial complex.

We were playing through "Basin Street Blues," arranged for bugle, half-piano, tin cans, vocals, and bombers. Steve, the front-man, was always after me to sing backup on this, crooning a call-and-response. I blew a bugle because I didn't *like* singing. Bugle's almost like singing, anyway, and I did the backup vocals *through* it, so when Steve sang, "Come along wi-ith me," I blew, "Wah wah wah wah-wah wah," which sounded dynamite. Steve hated it. Like most front-men, he had an ego that could swallow the battered planet, and didn't want any lip from the troops. That was us. The troops. Wah-wah.

The audience swayed in time with the music, high atop the pile of rubble we played on in the welcome cool of sunset, when the work day was through. They leaned against long poles, which made me think of gondoliers, except that our audience used their poles to pry apart the rubble that the bombers had created, looking for canned goods.

Steve handed Hambone a solo cue just as a bomber flew by overhead, which was his idea of a joke. He didn't like Hambone much. "Take it, Hambone!" he shouted, an instant before the roar began. It got a laugh. Hambone just grinned his blissed-out smile and went gonzo on the cans. The roar of the bomber faded, and he played on, and then settled into a kicky lick that set me on an expedition on the bugle that left me blue in the face. Steve gave us dirty looks.

Then a stranger started dancing.

It was pretty shocking: not the dancing; people do that whenever they find some booze or solvents or whatever; it was the stranger. We didn't get a lot of strangers around there. Lyman and his self-styled "militia" took it upon themselves to keep wanderers out of our cluster of rubble. She was dirty, like all of us, but she had good teeth, and she wasn't so skinny you could count her ribs. Funny how that used to be sexy when food was plentiful.

And she could dance! Steve skipped a verse, and Timson looked up from the book he keeps on his music stand and gawped. I jammed in, and Hambone picked up on it, and Steve didn't throw a tantrum, just scatted along. She danced harder, and we didn't break for the next bomber, kept playing, even though we couldn't hear ourselves, and when we could, we were still in rhythm.

We crashed to an ending, and before the applause could start, we took off on "Diggin' My Potatoes," which Steve sang as dirty and lecherous as he could. We *hopped* and the stranger danced and the audience joined in and the set went twice as long as it normally would have, long after the sun set. Man!

Steve made a beeline for her after the set, while I put away the bugle and Timson tied a tarp down over his piano. Hambone kept banging on his cans, making an arrhythmic racket. He only did that when he was upset, so I helped him to his feet.

"C'mon, Ham," I said. "Let's get you home."

Hambone smiled, but to a trained Hambone-ologist like me, it was a worried grin. The stranger was staring at Hambone. Hambone was looking away. I led him to his cave, guiding him with one hand at the base of his skull, where he had a big knot of scar tissue—presumably, whatever had given him that lump had also made him into what he was. I made sure he went in, then went back, nervous. Hambone was a barometer for trouble, and when he got worried, I got worried, too.

The stranger had peeled Steve off of her, and was having an animated conversation with Timson. Uh-oh. That meant that she was a reader. It's all Timson ever talked about. He was a world-class bookworm. He'd moved into the basement of what was left of a bookstore-café, and was working his way through their stock. You never saw Timson without a book.

"Anemic Victorian girly book—that's all that was," he was saying when I caught up with him.

The stranger shoved his shoulder, playfully. Timson is a big one, and not many people are foolhardy enough to shove him, playfully or otherwise. "You've got to be kidding me! Are you some kind of *barbarian*? *Emma* is a classic, you bunghole!" My sainted mother would have said that she had a mouth on her like a truck-driver. It turned me on.

"Hi!" I said.

Timson's retort was derailed as he turned to look at me. He said, "Brad, meet Jenna. Jenna, meet Brad."

I shook her hand. Under the dirt, she was one big freckle, and the torchlight threw up red highlights from her hair. Mmmm. Redheads. I had it bad.

"You blow good," the stranger—Jenna—said.

"Hell," Timson said, slapping me on the back hard enough to knock a whoosh of air out of my lungs. "Brad is the best trumpet player for a hundred klicks!" Jenna raised a dubious eyebrow.

"I'm the *only* trumpet player for a hundred klicks," I explained. Talking to a stranger was a novel experience: we got to recycle all the band jokes. She smiled.

I don't know where she slept that night. She was pretty good at taking care of herself—there weren't hardly any wanderers around anymore, and I'd never seen a solo woman. When I retired to my shack, I was pretty sure that she'd found herself shelter.

"This is how *all of you* survive?" she asked me the next day. I'd taken her out prospecting with me, going after a mountain of concrete rubble that had recently shifted after a baby quake. I had a good feeling about it.

"Yeah," I said, wedging my pole in and prying down hard. If you do it just right, you start a landslide that takes off a layer of the pile, revealing whatever's underneath. Do it wrong, you break your pole, give yourself a hernia, or bury yourself under a couple tons of rebar and cement. I'd seen a movie where people used the technique after some apocalypse or another. A plane went by overhead and stopped the conversation.

"But it's not bloody *sustainable*," she said. Her face was red with exertion, as she pried down hard.

I stopped prying and looked around pointedly. Mountains of rubble shimmered in the damp heat, dotting the landscape as far as the eye could see.

She followed my gaze around. "OK, fine. You've got a good supply. But not everyone else does. Sooner or later, someone, somewhere, is going to run out. And then what? Turf wars? The last thing we need around here is another fucking war."

It wasn't the first time I'd heard that theory. Lyman and his buddies were particular proponents of it. They drilled half-ass military maneuvers in their spare time, waiting for the day when they'd get to heroically repel an invasion. I told her what I told them. "There's plenty of rubble to go around."

Another plane went by. She went back to her rock with renewed vigor and I went back to mine. After several moments of grunting and sweating, she said, "For this generation, maybe. What'll your kids eat?"

I leaned against my pole. "Who said anything about kids? I don't plan on having any."

She leaned against hers. Actually, it was my spare—two-and-a-half metres of 1" steel gas-pipe—but I'd let her use it for the day. "So that's it for the human race, as far as you're concerned? The buck stops here?"

I got the feeling that she had this argument a lot. "Other people can do whatever they want. I'm not gonna be anyone's daddy."

Another plane passed. "That's pretty damned selfish," she said.

I rose to the bait. "It's selfish not to have kids I can't look after in a world that's gone to hell?"

"If you took an interest in the world, you could make it a livable place for your kids."

"Yeah, and if I wanted to have kids, I'd probably do that. But since I don't, I won't. QED."

"And if my grandma had wheels, she'd be a friggin' roller skate. Come on, Brad. Live like a savage if you must, but let's at least keep the rhetoric civilised."

She sounded like Timson, then. I hate arguing with Timson. He always wins. I pushed against my pole and the chunk I'd been working on all morning finally shifted and an ominous rumbling began from up the hill. "Move!" I shouted.

We both ran downslope like nuts. That was my favorite part of any day, the rush of pounding down an uneven mountain face with tons of concrete chasing after me. I scrambled down and down, leaping over bigger obstacles, using all four limbs and my pole for balance. Jenna was right behind me, and then she was overtaking me, grinning hugely. We both whooped and dove into the lee of another mountain. The thunder of the landslide was temporarily drowned out by the roar of another plane.

I turned around quick, my chest heaving, and watched my work. The entire face of the mountain was coming down in stately march. Lots of telltale glints sparkled in the off-pour. Canned goods. Fossil junk food from more complex times.

"Tell me that that's not *way* funner than gardening," I panted at Jenna.

She planted her hands on her thighs and panted.

I loved going out prospecting with other people. Some folks liked to play it safe, nicking away little chunks of a mountain. I liked to make a *big* mess. It's more dangerous, more cool, and more rewarding. I'm a big show-off.

I went back and started poking at the newly exposed stratum, popping cans into my sack. The people who'd lived in this city before it got plagued and Dresdenned had been ready for a long siege, every apartment stuffed with supplies. I kept my eyes open for a six-pack of beer or a flask of booze, and I found both. The beer would be a little skunky after a decade of mummification, but not too bad. The tequila would be smooth as silk. I found it hard not to take a long swallow, but it was worth too much in trade for me to waste it on my liver.

Jenna joined me, scooping up the cans and stashing them in her pack. I didn't begrudge her the chow: there was more than I could carry home before the day was through in this load, and whatever I didn't take would get snapped up by some entrepreneur before morning. I wandered off, selecting the best of the stuff for my larder. I heard Jenna throwing up on the other side of the mountain. I scampered over to her.

It was what I'd expected: she'd turned up some corpses. Ten years of decomposition had cleaned them up somewhat, but they weren't pretty by any stretch. The plague bombs they dropped on this town had been full of nasty stuff. It killed fast, and left its victims twisted into agonised hieroglyphs. I turned, and pulled Jenna's hair out of the way of her puke.

"Thanks," she said, when she was done, five planes later. "Sorry, I can't get used to dead bodies, even after all this."

"Don't apologise," I said. "Plague victims are worse than your garden variety corpse."

"Plague victims! Damn!" she said, taking several involuntary steps backward. I caught her before she fell.

"Whoa! They're not contagious anymore. That plague stuff was short-lived. The idea was to kill everyone in the city, wait a couple months, then clean out the bodies and take up residence. No sense in destroying prime real estate."

"Then how did all this—" she waved at the rubble "— happen?"

"Oh, that was our side. After the city got plagued, they Dresdenned the hell out of it so that the enemy wouldn't be able to use it." After the War, I'd hooked up for a while with a crazy guy who wouldn't tell me his name, who'd been in on all the dirty secrets of one army or another. From all he knew, he must've been in *deep*, but even after two years of wandering with him, I never found out much about him. He died a month before I found my current home. Lockjaw. Shitty way to go.

"They bombed their own fucking city?" she asked,

incredulous. I was a little surprised that she managed to be shocked by the excesses of the War. Everyone else I knew had long grown used to the idea that the world had been trashed by some very reckless, immoral people. As if to make the point, another plane buzzed over us.

"Well, everyone was already dead. It was their final solution: if they couldn't have it, no one else could. What's the harm in that?" I said. Whenever my nameless companion had spilled some dirty little secret, he'd finish it with *What's the harm in that?* and give a cynical chuckle. He was a scary guy.

She didn't get the joke.

"Come on," I said. "We gotta get this stuff back home."

That evening, the band played again. Our audience was bigger, maybe a hundred people. Steve liked a big crowd. He jumped around like bacon in a pan, and took us through all our uptempo numbers: "South America, Take It Away," "All the Cats Join In," "Cold Beverages," "Atomic Dog," and more. The crowd loved it; they danced and stomped and clapped, keeping the rhythm for us during the long rests when the planes went by.

We played longer than usual. When we were done, I was soaked with sweat, my lips and cheeks were burning, and the sun had completely set. Some enterprising soul had built a bonfire. We used to do that all the time, back when booze was less scarce: build a big fire and party all night. Somewhere along the line, we'd stopped, falling into a sunup-to-sundown rhythm.

That night, though, I lay on my back beside the fire and watched the constellations whirl overhead. The planes counterpointed the soft crackling noises the fire made, and I felt better than I had in a long time.

The crowd had mostly gone home, but the band was still out, as were Lyman and his boys, and a few other diehards. And Jenna. She'd led the dancing all night.

"That was *fun*," she said, hunkering down with me and Timson and Hambone. Steve was fondling one of his groupies, a skinny girl with bad teeth named Lucy. In my nastier moods, I called her "Loose." She was dumb enough not to get the joke.

Jenna passed Timson the canteen and he swigged deeply. "It sure was," he said. "We haven't been that tight in a while."

"You know, I've been all through the southland, but you guys are the only band I've seen. Everyone else is just scratching out a living. How'd you guys get together?"

"Hambone," I said. He was rappity-tappiting some firewood.

"*Hambone*?" she said. "I gotta hear this."

"I got here about seven years ago," I said, taking a pull from the canteen. "I'd been wandering around for a while, but for some reason, I thought I'd stay here for a while. Hambone was already here—near as anyone can tell, he's been here since the War. He managed to keep himself alive, just barely.

"I'd been here for a couple of weeks, and I'd spent most of that time building my house. I spent a lot of time hanging around out front of my place, blowing my horn, thinking. I didn't have any friends around here: I didn't want any. I just wanted to blow and watch the flies." I paused while a plane howled by.

"Then, one morning, I was blowing 'Reveille' and watching the sun come up, and I heard this crazy beat behind me. I looked around, and it was Hambone, sitting on top of the hill out back of my place, keeping time. I didn't know about him, then, so I figured he was just one of the locals. I waved at him, but he just kept on pounding, so I picked up my horn and we jammed and jammed.

"It became a regular morning gig. Once I ran out of steam, he'd get up and wander away. After a while, he was playing right on my doorstep, and I noticed how skinny he was. I tried to talk to him, and that's when I figured out he was *special*. So after we finished, I gave him a couple cans of Spam." A plane flew past.

"After a month of this, I decided I'd follow him when he left. He didn't seem to mind. We came to a ladder that led down into a big, bombed out basement, all full of books. And this big asshole was playing a piano, just pounding on it."

I nodded at Timson, who picked up the tale. "It'd been tough to get the piano down there, but when I found it, I knew I needed to have it. I'd been going nuts, looking for a chance to play. Hambone had been coming by regular to jam around, and I tried to make sure he got fed. I figured he was shell-shocked and needed a hand. Then, one day, he shows up with this guy and his horn. Next thing you know, we're all playing our asses off. It was the most fun I'd ever had." He waited for a plane to pass, and built up the fire.

"The rest, as they say, is history," he continued. "Steve heard us jamming and invited himself along. He kept after us to play publicly."

Jenna looked over at Steve, who was lying on his back with Lucy twined around him. "Well, he can sing, anyway," she said, and grinned wickedly.

We all nodded.

"So," she said, stretching casually. "What are you guys

gonna do when you run out of cans?"

I groaned. She'd been picking at the subject all day.

Timson poked at the fire, and Lyman sauntered over. "Our supply will hold out a while yet," he said, "if we keep interlopers out." He loomed threateningly over her. Timson stood up and loomed back. Lyman retreated a little.

"How about gardens?" she said. "A decent garden could really stretch out your food supply."

"Who," I said, lazily, "is going to work on a garden when there's all this food just lying around?"

"I will, for one. Think about it: fresh vegetables! Fruit! When was the last time you had a tomato, a big fat red one?"

My mouth watered. Lyman said, "When we run out of cans, we'll just move along. Gardens'll only tie us down here." His boys all nodded, the way they did when he made a pronouncement.

Jenna glared at him. "That's pretty goddamn short-sighted. How long can you live off the past? When are you going to start living for the future?"

Lyman's rebuttal was cut off by another plane.

Timson slapped her on the back. "'When are you going to start living for the future?' You've practiced that, right?"

She pretended she didn't hear him. "How come the planes don't run out of fuel?" she said.

I said, "They've got an automated maintenance station somewhere around here. They land there for scheduled repairs and refueling. It's supposed to restock their ammo, too, but it looks like they've run out. Lucky for us."

Jenna's ears pricked up. "You know where this station is? They'd have power? Radios? Maybe we could call for help."

Everyone looked at her like she was nuts. "Where, exactly, are you going to call?" Timson asked.

"New Zealand. They didn't get into the War at all. They're probably sitting pretty. Maybe they could help us out."

"*On the Beach*, Nevil Shute," Timson said. "You've been reading too much science fiction, girl."

She slapped his shoulder. "It was *The Chrysalids* actually. John Wyndham. Kiwis and Aussies *always* come out okay."

"Seriously," she continued, "what else are you doing around here? Aren't you getting bored of slipping back into savagery?"

"We've got plenty to do," Lyman called from across the fire. "We've got to drill the militia!"

"Band's gotta practice," Steve called, from under Lucy.

"Sure you do!" Jenna retorted. "If you're gonna play the Sydney Opera House, you're gonna need a whole *shitload* of practice!"

Steve glared at her, and Timson pounded her on the back. I produced my Mickey of tequila and magnanimously shared it all around, even letting Lyman and his thugs have a swig.

She dropped in the next morning while I was blowing 'Reveille.' I hadn't had the energy the night before to take Hambone back to his cave, so he'd crashed on the floor of my shack. It's a pretty good shack: three of the walls are concrete, there from before the War. I'd put together a roof of tin and cardboard and whatever else I could find, and added another wall the same way. Be it ever so humble.

"You gonna help me dig a garden?" she asked.

I squinted at her. She'd gotten some water somewhere to clean up. Timson had a big reservoir in his basement, a flooded sub-basement. I had thought I'd seen them go off together.

Pink and scrubbed, with her hair tied back tight, she

was, well, pneumatic. Sweat beaded on her forehead, and on her pink eyebrows. She was wearing a tee-shirt and cutoffs, and the prospect of passing a day beside her while she bent over a garden was very tempting. But if she and Timson had something going on, I'd best put myself out of temptation's way. Besides, I was sure that the hill I'd been working on still had some good stuff in it.

"Got a full dance card today, sorry," I said.

"Well, don't get caught under any rockslides," she said, giving me a slightly pissed-off look.

I spent the day undermining the mountain, but I couldn't get it to come down. Finally, exhausted, I staggered to the hill where we played and warmed up on the horn.

Jenna and Timson arrived together, eating olives and stewed tomatoes with their fingers. Timson set up an architecture book on his stand and tapped at the piano. Hambone ambled up. Steve showed up with Lucy clinging to him like a limpet, and then we played our asses off.

Jenna danced and so did lots of other people, and then Steve waded out into the crowd and danced with them, and I joined him, and then the crowd and the band were all mixed up, and it was *fine*.

It turned out I was wrong about Jenna and Timson. She used his water but that was it. He *was* feeding her, though. Now, he can do whatever he wants with his food, it's his, but the two of us had always fed Hambone, and Timson couldn't afford to feed both of them, so I ended up running my larder down to dangerous levels over the next couple months.

I started to get a little grumpy about it, but that all ended when Jenna and Timson showed up at Hambone's cave one night while I was feeding him. They had three big sacks, filled right to the top with fresh vegetables: tomatoes, string beans, squash, rutabaga, cabbage and onions. There was even lemon grass, parsley and basil. And strawberries! My eyes nearly fell out of my head.

"Holy crap!" I said.

Timson pounded me on the back, then popped a cherry tomato into my gaping mouth. I bit down involuntarily and gasped. "That is the best thing I've ever tasted," I said.

"Tell me something I don't know," Jenna said. "We've noticed you sulking around the last couple months. I figured that I could bribe you and you'd quit pissing around."

"Did you *grow these*?" I said.

"No, I pulled them out of my ass," Jenna said, and ate a big, fat strawberry.

Timson fed Hambone a few strawberries, and that signaled the beginning of a chowdown that went on and on until we could hardly move. My hands stank of a wondrous cocktail of strawberries and herbs and onions. It had been a long time since I'd put fresh vegetables inside my body. I felt like I was sweating *green*.

"Sun's going down," Timson said. "Showtime. I'll catch up."

Jenna and Hambone and I climbed slowly up the hill, luxuriating in satiety. Hambone's smile was a new one, pure joy.

Timson met up, lugging more sacks. He shelled them out before we started playing, and I never saw more snaggletoothed grins. Even Steve had some. He made a crack about the wisdom of handing out fruit to an audience before a show, but no one was going to waste any of that beautiful food by throwing it.

Between sets, Timson stood up. "Jenna's been growing this food for the last couple months. I think you'll agree that it's pretty goddamn good." There were hoots of agreement. "So here's the deal. We've got some plots over on the south, ready to be hoed and planted. We've got seeds. But we need people to work the plots and gather water. Anyone who's interested can meet us tomorrow morning."

Well, that kind of put a damper on the celebration. I felt a little down, realising that this wonderful chow meant stooping in fields, hoeing and planting like some kind of Dark Ages peasant. In the back of my mind, I still thought that I could just keep on prospecting for cans until someone rebuilt civilisation and started making more cans. Rebuilding civilisation was going to take a long, long time. Then I burped up an onion-basil-tomato-tasting burp, and knew that I'd be out the next morning, anyway.

We kept on playing, and people kept dancing, and I may have been the only one who noticed Lyman and his boys shaking their heads and stalking off into the night.

Nearly everyone showed up the next morning and collected a precious handful of Jenna's seeds. She explained that she'd been hoarding them for years, looking for a place to plant them. The way she said it, you got the feeling that she was trusting you with her children.

We attacked the plots. They were rocky and rubble-strewn, and the poles were poorly suited to hoeing. People improvised: empty bottles became scoops; flattened cans, blades.

We worked, and Jenna came by and kibitzed, pointing out rocks that we'd missed, and generally being a pain in the ass. Eventually, enough grumbling got grumbled, and she went and tended her own garden, so to speak.

The work got hypnotic after that. The roar of the planes, the sounds of digging, it all blended into a deep rhythm. Hambone meandered by and idly tapped out a beat, and I found myself singing "Minnie the Moocher," and everyone joined in on the call-and-response. It was great, until I realised that I was singing for a crowd and shut my mouth. I didn't like singing for other people.

Not everyone was cut out to be a farmer. Good thing, too, or we would've starved to death waiting for the harvest. Still, there were people down at the gardens from sunup to sundown, clucking over their veggies.

The shit hit the fan one night as we were setting up to play. Lyman was sitting on Timson's piano, grinning wide enough to show us all his rotten chiclets. Three of his boys hung around close, and another four or five stood at a distance, sniggering.

Timson gave him a long, considering look. It was the kind of look I'd seen him give a humongous hunk of concrete in his plot one day, before he squatted down and hauled it out of the earth, like a 100 kilo spud.

Lyman grinned bigger. "I wanna talk to you," he said.

Timson nodded slowly. Hambone rapped out a nervous tatter with his fingernails on a beer bottle he'd been carrying around, but I didn't need his help to know that things were getting bad.

"This gardening thing is getting out of hand," Lyman said. "People are neglecting their duties."

"What duties?" Timson asked, in a low tone.

"Drilling with us. We got to be ready to defend our land."

Timson gave a little shake of his head.

Lyman jumped in with more: "People're getting too attached to this place. We'll have to move when the food runs out, and we can't take no garden with us."

Timson's look got more considering. He cocked his head. "Why do they have to defend it and get ready to leave? That seems like a bit of a contradiction to me."

Lyman's brow furrowed. If I'm making him sound a little dim, that's only because he was. "We'll defend it until the food runs out, then we'll move on."

Jenna snickered. One of Lyman's boys reached out to smack her. Hambone drummed louder; Jenna batted his hand away.

I found myself saying, "What if the food doesn't run out? What if we grow enough of our own to stay alive?"

Lyman glared at me. "Is that how you want to live?"

I said, "Sooner or later, all the cans will be gone."

Lyman waved a dismissive hand. "Someone will take care of that. I'm worried about *this* group. *This* city."

"So why not let us make sure we've got enough to eat?"

Lyman started forward and I jumped. "I told you! We need to defend the place! And we need to be ready to go if we can't!"

Timson interceded. "What does this have to do with me?"

Lyman spread his hands out. "I want you to shut down the garden. We were doing just fine without it. I don't like to see people wasting their time."

Timson said, "It's not mine to shut down." He nodded at Jenna, who was glaring daggers at the goon who'd tried to smack her.

"Not mine, either," she said, with barely controlled fury. "It's everyone's."

Lyman said, "Well, you just tell everyone that the garden's got to be shut down."

He slid off the piano and took off, goons in tow. One of them contrived to bump into me hard enough to make me drop my horn, and I had to snag it up quick before he stomped it.

Steve showed up, looking pissed, which meant that he was worried. "What was that all about?" he said.

"What was what all about?" Timson said, and propped a book up on his music stand.

They trashed the gardens two nights later, while we played. I wouldn't have thought that pack of lazy bastards had it in them to haul enough gravel to cover all the beds, especially not at night, but that's what they did. They kicked up the plants, and smashed the makeshift tools that the gardeners had left.

They didn't even have the smarts to steer clear of us the next day. Instead, they waited until a shocked crowd had gathered, and then showed up with big grins. Lyman had a pistol shoved in his waistbelt. I'd seen it before, and I didn't think it worked, but you never knew.

"Good morning!" Lyman said, stomping across the murdered beds. "How's everybody doing today?"

Timson hefted his pole and looked significantly at the militia. A number of people in the crowd got the idea. Lyman's boys looked uneasy.

Lyman said, "We've been chasing off rovers to the north every day and more are coming. Things are getting rough. We'll need volunteers for the militia. You've all got spare time now."

I'd never even harvested a single tomato from my plot. I could see the smashed green buds that I'd been nurturing.

Jenna said, "Who's got any spare time? It's going to take us *days* to clean up this mess." She stooped and picked up a stone and tossed it away from the beds. "Lucky I got more seeds."

I bent and picked up a rock of my own and tossed it. I wanted to toss it at Lyman, but Jenna had set an example.

Not everyone followed it. A lot wandered off, to prospect or to go with Lyman. I couldn't blame them—I felt like giving up.

Over the next week or two, the plots started to get back into shape. Occasionally, Lyman would cruise by and glare, and we'd try to ignore him. He and his boys would walk across the plots, talking loudly about running off wanderers. Some of his boys had been planting gardens not long before. It made me boil.

I got it out at nights, when we played. The crowd had diminished. Anyone who had anything to do with Lyman stayed away. Those left behind were more into it than ever. A lot of them sang along, to Steve's chagrin. Some of them were pretty good.

Lyman hadn't trashed the beds again. I knew he hadn't given up. I waited, nervously, for the other shoe to drop.

It didn't take long. One night, our set ended early because of rain, which always made Hambone nervous. I led him back to his cave and was met on the trail by Lyman, dripping and grinning.

There was no small talk. He put a hand on my chest. "When you going to stop pussying around and help us defend ourselves?"

"I'm a little busy right now. Why don't you ask me again in a couple of centuries?" Hambone started doing a little shuffle.

Lyman gave him a fist in the ear. His head spun around, and I saw the knot of scar at the base of his skull strain. He turned back around and started shuffling. Lyman drew his arm back.

"Jesus, Lyman, what the hell is your problem?" I said.

He turned and popped me right in the mouth, splitting my lip and loosening one of my teeth. I was so proud of my teeth: I brushed 'em every morning and every night, and they were in better shape than most. I clutched my mouth. Lyman kicked me down, then walked away, stepping hard on my chest as he walked past me.

I led Hambone back up to his cave, and slept there.

I felt so bad the next morning, I almost didn't go back to the gardens. My face ached, and I couldn't blow a single note.

But I dragged myself down anyway. I was feeling stubborn.

Timson had a black eye and a limp, but he grinned like a pirate when he saw me. "How many?" he said.

"Just Lyman," I said.

He snorted. "They sent six for me. None of 'em are feeling too good this morning, I bet. Couple of them won't be walking for a while." He showed me his hands. His knuckles were raw.

"Can you play?" I asked, wincing in sympathy.

"Probably." He yanked a weed out of a plot. "I can garden."

Jenna got away unscathed. No one, not even Timson, was sure where she slept. I'd thought it was a weird quirk, but I realised that she knew what she was doing.

We worked together in the garden that day, the three of us and Hambone. No one else showed up. Some of the early berries were ripe, so we ate them. "Hey," I said, pointing at a plane. "You still plan on making that long-distance call? New Zealand?"

Jenna wiped the sweat off her forehead. "Once we've got this crop in. I don't know that we'd be let back in if we left."

I conceded the point.

That night, Timson played as best as he could, and I confined myself to the occasional sour blat on the horn. The crowd was subdued, and grew more so when Lyman and his boys showed up.

Steve called the set over early, then went and chatted with Lyman. Pretty soon they were whooping it up. Timson and I shared disgusted looks. "Fuck this," he said, and stalked away.

Jenna and me and Hambone went and sat in the gardens, where Hambone played a soft racket with my pole.

"I don't think we'll play again," I said.

"Come on," she said, dismissively. "This'll blow over. You guys are good, you should play."

"Who gives a damn if we're good or not? It's just a band."

She stared at Hambone for a while. "You ever wonder why I stayed here?" she said, finally.

"Tired, I guess. Same as me."

"I'd been looking for a place to grow a garden for a long time. A place where they were starting over, not just doing the same old stuff. And one day, I'm wandering along, and I heard you guys. I thought I'd found civilization. Before I could figure out exactly where the sound was coming from, I spotted some of Lyman's boys and hid. I hid out until I heard the music the next day, and then I snuck in. And I said, 'Girl, here's a place where they still have something besides eating and killing and screwing.' So I settled. I let you use my precious seeds. I think if you guys give up playing, this place will dry up and fly away in a couple of years."

"Unless we get rescued by Kiwis first," I said, playfully. I grinned, and my lip started bleeding again. "Ow," I said.

She laughed, and I laughed.

Steve avoided the band for a week. We didn't play, even after my lip had healed. Everyone was tense, ready to blow.

Then the gardens got trashed again. This time, they did it in broad daylight, while Timson and Jenna and I glared at them. It wasn't just Lyman and his pals, either: almost everyone came out, including a number of former gardeners. And Steve.

Timson walked away. Even Lyman's boys had the sense not to taunt him. Jenna and I stared as our beds were murdered again. They did a thorough job, sowing the soil with gravel and crap like nails and glass. Some of the former gardeners avoided our gaze, but other than that, there was no remorse. I shook.

Jenna led me away, with Hambone in tow. They weren't too scared to taunt *us*, and someone hit me with a dirt clod.

Jenna took me to a little cave whose entrance was hidden by an overhang from an I-beam. Jenna cleared some debris from the doorway, then led me inside.

It was claustrophobic and dark inside, and a bedroll was spread out on the floor beside a giant internal-frame pack.

The three of us sat in silence. Jenna's shoulders shook. Tentatively, I reached out for her and she hugged tight to me. Hambone clapped the buckles of her pack's straps together.

I held her there for a long time. Eventually, she tried to pull away, but I held on, and she relaxed into me. It had been a long time since I'd held a woman like that, and I found myself clutching her tighter. A warm, fluttery feeling filled my belly. I tried to kiss her.

She shoved me away abruptly. "Fuck off!" she said.

"What?" I said.

"Jesus, put it back in your pants!"

"What's your problem?" I said.

"My problem is I thought you were my *friend*. All of a sudden, you start grabassing. Get out, you goddamned letch!" She shoved at me. I scrambled out and slogged home.

I stayed in bed until noon, wallowing in self-pity. Then I cracked a bottle of vodka out of my larder and killed it. It had been a while since my last bender, but it all came back just fine. Before I knew it, I was huffing from a rag soaked in solvent, reeling and dazed. I stayed stoned until I fell asleep, then got up and felt so rotten that I started over again.

I knew I was sulking, but I didn't see any reason to stop. The band was gone, the gardens were gone, Jenna was gone.

I realized that I'd spent the decade since the War waiting for someone to rebuild civilization, and that it wasn't going to happen. It was just going to get worse, every single year. Even if we planted a million gardens, the best I could hope for was to die of old age in a cave, surrounded by my illiterate offspring.

It was enough to make me want to join the militia.

Eventually, I staggered out into the blinding light. I went to work on a hill, and that's where Timson found me.

He was flustered and angry, showing more emotion than he usually did. "Have you seen her?" he said.

"Who?" I said, blearily.

"Jenna. You haven't seen her?"

"No," I said, guiltily, "not since Lyman—"

"Shit!" he said, and spun on his heel, taking off.

His urgency penetrated my fog and I chased after him. "You think something's up?" I said.

He nodded grimly. "Lyman's been too smug lately, like the cat that ate the cream. I think he's got her."

"Where would he keep her?" I said. There wasn't much standing that you could keep a person locked up inside of.

"Those assholes have an 'armory' where they keep all their goddamn weapons. He's said as much to me, when he was bragging. I want to find it."

"Hang on a sec," I said. "Have you checked her place?"

"You know where it is?" he asked, surprised.

"Come on," I said, feeling perversely proud that he didn't.

She wasn't at her place, but there were signs of a struggle. Her pack was shredded, her seeds ground into the concrete floor.

Timson took one look and tore off. I followed his long strides as best as I could. I knew where he was headed: Steve's.

Steve lived in part of a half-buried underground shopping mall. Timson pummeled down the stairs with me close behind.

Steve and Lucy were twined on a pile of foam rubber. Timson hauled him up by the arm and slammed his head against a wall.

"Where's the armory?" he roared.

Steve held his head. "Fuck you," he sneered.

Timson slammed his head again. Lucy rushed him from behind and I tripped her.

"Where is it?" Timson said. "Don't make me any angrier."

Steve dangled, nude, from Timson's meaty paws. Terror and anger warred on his features. Terror won. He spilled his guts. "They'll kill you," he said. "They've been fighting off wanderers all week. They're in a bad mood."

Timson snorted and dropped him.

Lyman was expecting us. He blocked the entrance to the armory, a bomb shelter with a heavy, counterweighted steel door. I'd seen a few doors like it in my travels, but I'd never managed to get one open.

Timson got ready to rush him, then checked himself. Lyman had his gun hanging lazily off one hand.

"Afternoon, boys," he said, grinning.

"Are you going to shoot me?" Timson said.

Lyman held up his gun with an expression of mock surprise. "Probably not," he said. "Not unless you give me a reason to. I'm here to protect."

"Well, I'm about to give you a reason to. I'm going in there to get Jenna. I'll kill you if you try to stop me."

Lyman stuck his gun back into his waistband. "You're too late," he said.

I saw red and started forward, but he held a hand up.

"She got away. We only wanted to scare her off and get rid of her seeds, but she went nuts. It's a good thing she got away, or I would've forgotten my manners."

Timson *growled*.

Lyman took a step backwards. "Look, if you don't believe me, go on in and take a look around, be my guest."

Jenna wasn't inside, but they weren't kidding when they called it an arsenal. I hadn't seen that many weapons since the War. It made me faintly sick.

Then I spotted something that froze me in my tracks. Beneath one of the long tables, a dented silver canister with ugly biohazard decals. You saw fragments of them sometimes, exploded in the midst of plague-wracked corpses. A plague bomb.

Lyman strutted around like a proud papa. "Lots of these were here when I found the place, but we've picked up a few here and there along the way. Nobody's chasing us out of here." He followed my horrified gaze.

"You like it?" he said. "That's just in case someone *does* manage to run us off—it won't do them any good! Our Final Solution." He patted the bomb with a proprietary air.

All of a sudden, it got to me. I started laughing. "Nobody's chasing you out!" I gasped. "This is your rubble, and nobody's chasing you out!" Timson started laughing, too. Lyman and his boys reddened. We left.

We found Jenna with Hambone, in his cave. She had the remains of her pack with her, and was shoveling Hambone's things into it.

She startled when we came in, but once she'd seen us, she went back to packing. "Getting outta Dodge," she said, in answer to our unspoken question.

"Are you all right?" I asked, feeling guilty and awful.

"They killed my seeds," she said, in a hopeless voice. I started to reach for her, then stopped and stared at the floor.

She finished packing and grabbed Hambone. "You coming?"

Timson shouldered her pack, answering for both of us.

I'd settled seven years before. I thought I'd stayed in good shape, but I'd forgotten how punishing life on the road could be.

Jenna set a brutal pace. She wouldn't talk to me any more than necessary. We ate sparingly, from what she scrounged on the way. She knew a lot about what was edible and what wasn't, skills I'd never picked up, but my belly still growled.

"Where are we going?" I said, after a week. My feet had toughened, but my legs felt like they'd been beaten by truncheons.

Instead of answering, she pointed up at a plane overhead. Of course, I thought, time to make a long-distance call.

A week later, I said, "Have you thought this thing through?

I mean, the station may be automated, but it'll have defenses. Locks, at least. How do you plan on getting in?"

Timson, who'd been silent the whole morning, said, "I'm curious, too. I've been thinking: this Australia thing is kind of far-fetched, isn't it? If they wanted to rescue us, they would've done it a long time ago, don't you think?"

"Screw Australia," she said impatiently. "Any station capable of maintaining those jets is bound to have lots of things we can use. I want a fence for my garden."

"But how are we going to get in?" I said.

"Hambone," she said, with a smug smile.

Hambone grinned affably. "Guh?" I said.

"He's a *pilot*. High ranking one, too."

"Not to repeat myself," I said, "but, guh?"

She spun Hambone around and pulled his shaggy hair away from the collar of his grimy tee-shirt. "Look." I did. She dug at the knot of scar tissue at the base of his skull. Horrified, I watched as the scar flapped back, revealing a row of plugs, ringed with cracked and blackened skin.

"Brainstem interface. I noticed it the first time I saw you guys. You never noticed?"

"I noticed the scar, sure—"

"Scar?" she said. She flapped it around. "It's a dustcover! Hambone's wired! We'll just point his retinas at the scanner and *voilà*, instant entry. Damn, you didn't think I was going to try and hop the fence, did you?"

Timson grinned sheepishly. "Well, *actually*..."

We reached the station the next day. The familiar roar of the jets was joined by the ear-shattering sound of them landing and taking off, like clockwork.

The airfield was fenced in by a lethal wall, ten meters tall and ringed with aged corpses. A lot of slow learners had found out the hard way about the station's defenses.

We wandered the perimeter for several kilometers before we came to a gate. It had a retinal scanner, like I sometimes found when I unearthed the remains of a bank machine. Hambone grew more and more agitated as we neared it.

"Go on," Jenna whispered. "Come on, you can do it."

His nervous drumming became more and more pronounced, until he was waving his arms, flailing wildly.

Jenna caught his hands and held them tightly. "That's all right," she cooed. "It's all right, come on."

Centimeter by slow centimeter, Jenna coaxed Hambone to the scanner. Finally, he put his eyes against the battered holes. Red light played over his features, and the gates sighed open.

We were all still standing around and grinning like idiots before we noticed that Hambone was running across the airfield.

He was already halfway to a jet. We caught up with him as he was vaulting the extruded ladder. An armored cart that had been attached to the fuselage reeled in its umbilicus and rolled away.

Hambone was already seated in the pilot's chair, punching at the buttons. A cable snaked from the back of his seat into the plugs on his neck. I had time to think, *That's_weird*, and then the plane lurched forward. The cockpit had seats for a copilot and a bombardier, and we all crammed in like sardines, Jenna on my lap, and we crushed together when the plane jolted.

"Holy shit!" Jenna shouted.

Hambone drummed his fingers against an instrument panel while he pulled back on a joystick. "Strap in!" Timson shouted.

I did, pulling crash webbing across us.

"Hambone, what the hell are you doing?" Jenna shouted.

He grinned affably, and the plane lifted off.

Hambone flew the plane confidently, with small, precise movements. Jenna, Timson and I stared at each other helplessly. The jet had taken off at a screaming climb that flattened us back against our seats—I noted with curious detachment that Hambone's seat had a recessed niche so that the cables depending from his skull weren't compressed.

In an instant, we were above the clouds, with only tiny patches of scorched earth visible.

The silence inside the cockpit rang inside my ears. For the first time in seven years, I couldn't hear jets crashing overhead.

"Hey, Hambone?" I said, cautiously.

Jenna shushed me. "Don't distract him," she whispered.

It was good advice. Timson stared at the instrument panels.

"I think," he whispered, "that we're headed out to sea."

Jenna and I groaned. Hambone reached out with one hand and unlatched a compartment that spilled out freeze-dried rations.

"At least we won't starve to death," Timson whispered.

"Why are we whispering?" I said.

"So Hambone doesn't get panicked," Jenna said.

"He never gets panicked," I said in a normal tone. Hambone unwrapped a bar of fruit leather and munched thoughtfully at it, while his fingers danced over the controls.

"He never flies planes, either," she hissed.

"We're over the ocean now. Pacific, I think," Timson said. He'd done something with the seat that caused it to slide back into a crawlspace, and we were still cramped, but at least we weren't in each other's laps. I looked out the window. Yup, ocean.

I started shivering.

"We're going to die," I said.

"Probably," Jenna said. She giggled.

I punched her playfully and my panic receded.

Timson started playing with one of the panels.

"What are you doing?" I said, alarmed.

"Trying to figure out where we're going. Don't worry, this is the copilot's seat. I don't think I can screw up the navigation from here unless he turns it over to me." Ragged and filthy, he looked like a caveman next to the sleek controls.

"You don't think?" I said.

He waved impatiently at me, poked some more. "OK," he said. "Hambone's taking us to Australia."

I always knew that Hambone had heard the things we'd said. Still, it was easy to forget. We took turns trying to convince him to head back. After a few hours, we gave up. Timson said that we'd crossed the halfway mark, anyway. We were closer to Australia than home.

Then there was nothing to do but eat and wait.

Eventually, some of the instruments lit and I thought, *This is it, we're dead.* Curiously, I wasn't scared. I'd been scared so long, and now I was bored, almost glad that it was ending.

"Bogeys," Timson said, staring out the window.

I looked up. Two sleek new fighters were paralleling us. Inside their cockpits, I could see pilots in what looked like space suits. I waved to one. He tapped his headset.

Jenna said, "They're trying to radio us."

Timson picked up a lightweight headset from a niche above his seat. He screwed it into his ear and held up a finger.

"Hello?" he said. We held our breath.

"Yes, that's us," he said.

"What?" I said. He shushed me.

"All right," he said.

"*What*?" I shouted, startling Hambone. Jenna clapped a hand over my mouth.

"I'm sorry, I don't know how. Do you know which button I push? I see. All right, I think this is it. I'm going to push it. Is that all right? OK, thanks. Bye."

I peeled Jenna's hand off my mouth. "What?" I demanded.

"That's the Panoceanic Air Force. They're landing us at Sydney. We'll be quarantined when we get there, but I think it's just a formality."

The lights in the cockpit dimmed and the cable zipped out of Hambone's neck. Absently, he reached back and smoothed the dustcover over the plugs. "They're landing us," Timson said.

I leaned back and sighed. I like Hambone a lot, but I'd rather not have an autistic flying my plane, thank you very much.

I was reaching for another bar of fruit leather when the plane took a tremendous lurch that pressed Jenna and me against the crash webbing hard enough to draw blood on our exposed skin. I heard a sickening crack and looked around wildly, terrified that it was someone's skull. In the juddering chaos, I saw Timson, face white, arm hanging at a nauseating, twisted angle.

We jolted again, and I realized that I was screaming. I closed my mouth, but the screaming continued. Out of the bombardier's porthole, I saw the air convecting across the shuddering wings, and realized that the screaming was the air whistling over the fuselage. The ground rushed towards us.

Jenna's head snapped back into my nose, blinding me with pain, and then we were tumbling through the cockpit. Jenna had released the crash webbing altogether and was ping-ponging around Hambone. I saw her claw at the dustcover on his neck before she was tossed to the floor.

I pried my fingers loose from the armrests on my chair and came forward to Hambone. I straddled him, legs around his waist, and suppressed my gorge as I scrabbled at what I still thought of as his "scar" until it peeled back. My fingertips skated over the plugs and the knots of skin around them, and then I did toss up, spraying vomit and losing my grip on Hambone.

I ended up atop Jenna. The plane screamed down and down and I locked eyes with Hambone, silently begging him to do something. His gaze wandered, and my eyes stopped watering long enough to see Hambone do something to his armrest which caused the cabling on his seat to snake out and mate with his brainstem. The plane leveled off and he smiled at us.

It couldn't have taken more than thirty seconds, but it seemed like a lifetime. Timson cursed blue at his arm, which was swollen and purple, and Jenna cradled her bumped head in arms that streamed blood from dozens of crisscrossed webbing cuts. I got us strapped in as we touched down.

We got escorted off the ship by a bunch of spacemen with funny accents. They didn't take us to the hospital until they'd scrubbed us and taken blood. They wanted to take Hambone away, but we were very insistent. The spacemen told us that he was very "high functioning," and that the plugs in the back of his neck were only rated for about five years.

"They'll have to come out," one of them explained to us.

"Otherwise, he'll only get worse."

Jenna said, "If you take them out, will he get better?"

The spaceman shrugged. "Maybe. It's a miracle that he's still bloody alive, frankly. Bad technology."

They de-quarantined us a month later. I'd never been cleaner. Those Aussies are pretty worried about disease.

The four of us took a flat near Bondi Beach. Timson found a job in a bookstore, and Jenna spends most of her time working with Hambone. Some days, I think she's getting through to him.

I'm on the dole and feeling weird about it. I can't get used to the idea of just showing up at someone else's place and taking handouts. But the Aussies don't seem to mind. Very progressive people. They ran our story on the news and a music store in Canberra donated a bugle and an electric piano.

I'm teaching Jenna to blow. It's not that I don't like playing anymore, but it's hard to sing and play at the same time. All four of us practice every night, out in our garden. We still flinch every eight bars, waiting for the roar of a jet to interrupt us, then smile sheepishly when it doesn't come. The important thing is, we're playing.

Even an interloper like me knows how you get to Sydney Opera House: practice.

A BEGINNER'S GUIDE TO SURVIVAL BEFORE, DURING, AND AFTER THE APOCALYPSE

CHRISTOPHER BARZAK

First, remember what it means to be human. Even when your country has turned against you, even when some other part of the world has been decimated (by bomb, by terrorist cells, by forcible entry and removal of dissidents to dark and forgotten chambers, by hurricane or tornado or tsunami), even then remember that you can retain your humanity if you continue to be humane.

Despite that, you will have certain struggles, like finding work when you're not the right sort (too young, too old, too female, too ethnic, too queer), or like that time you went to the grocery store and the cashier refused to touch your money because you were one of them: one of those Other People. Stay calm. If you are not a part of a normalized group, your chances of being strung up for giving the wrong look or replying with the wrong tone might be more than enough reason for a society gone wrong to cast you out even further, or perhaps kill you. Instead, say, "Thank you." Say, "I'm sorry, that's not what I meant." Say, "You're absolutely right, I'm sorry. I wasn't thinking. I'm sorry." Say it again: "I'm sorry. I'm sorry. I'm sorry."

Wear the requisite uniform. Brush the dust off your shoulders and polish your shoes. Look like you mean this pose you're taking. You love this country more than you love life itself. Practice these phrases: "I am a patriot of the first order," and, "God has shown me the light," and, maybe the most important one, "If you don't like it here, go somewhere else." This last one is most effective in proving your loyalty. Do not hesitate to degrade your fellow man if it means your life or his is at stake.

Go to underground meetings in the back rooms of bars and coffee shops. It will not be like the 1960s. There is no free love, just fear, fear, fear. Despair reigns over these conversations, and occasionally you find yourself trying to annihilate your desperation by taking other meeting-goers to bed after too many drinks. Say, "Do you think this is it?" And when they ask, "This is what?" say, "The end of the world. Do you think this is it?"

They'll say, "If it isn't the end of the world, I don't want to know what is."

They will cry after you make love to them. They will tell you secrets. Secrets about the child they aborted ten years ago, when that was still legal, before they began to arrest women post-facto. That was what they called it in the Reformation Papers: post-facto. After the fact. Retrospective retribution. They will tell you secrets about the last lover they had, before their lover was outed during the Reclamation Period, when all of the homos and queers were given the choice: normalize or die. It was fairly simple. Most chose life. It is one of the most unfortunate aspects of being human, this drive to survive no matter what the cost. Their last lover will have been called Jason, and you'll wonder what sort of person Jason was, what kind of lover. Do you remind this person with whom you've chosen to abandon reality of Jason? Do you have the same eyes? The same smile? The same voice? The same scent? Are you Jason-esque?

Take drugs. They will keep you not-feeling. Numbness is important when the world is coming apart. Refuse the hallucinogens. Accept the dampeners. You need to see the world as it is. You cannot afford to see it as it isn't.

Remember. This is one of the verbs they will try to remove from your brain. Remember. If you cannot remember, they can tell you anything about the past—your own or the world's—and you will not be able to know if they are telling the truth. Sit in the library, that most taboo of places, and read as many books as they still allow to be kept on the shelves. Download illegal information. Use false service provider addresses. Move around. If you stay still, you're certain to be caught.

When the first of the bombs go off, go into hiding. When you are safe, grieve. Sit in your cave, the one in the hills that used to belong to your family, and grieve the loss of so many lives. Lives you never knew personally. Imagine their faces. Imagine the faces of those you knew and loved. Imagine the mushroom clouds and the clouds of viruses. Imagine the way skin crackles and crisps, the way the body can turn against itself in mere minutes or hours when exposed to the right amount of radiation or illness.

Stay where you are. Keep silent. When you hear others pass by your carefully obscured cave entrance, bite your bottom lip and pray. Pray, even if you don't believe in a god. It may help you to keep silent if you are speaking the language of angels, which can never be heard by human ears. It is the language of thought, plucked like rays of light from the sky and carried off to some other place, where you hope some higher power may hear you.

At night, build a small fire out of moss and straw and twigs. Do not risk the luxury of true warmth and light. It will reach the eyes and ears and noses of those who would take what little luxury you have planned for: a six-month supply of canned meats and vegetables, a mattress and a pile of blankets, a lantern and gobs of oil to burn. Soap. A creek you can wash yourself in at night, even though it chills you to the bone.

Be vigilant during the daytime. Erase the tracks you make between your regular routes from the cave to the nearby river where you sometimes try to fish but rarely catch anything worth starting a fire over. Gather berries and nuts from different bushes and trees, so that no one can see them disappearing so obviously from one place. Notice the curl of blue smoke coming over the hillside. Walk toward it until you see the farm from which it comes. It is a four-mile walk to this place. Not far. Remember that they can see anything you might smoke just as you saw theirs.

Ignore the human howls of pain and starvation that pierce the early morning air. Ignore the disappearance of the animals that had occasionally blundered into your cave in those first few months after the bombs went off. Surely this is bad news. But what can you expect? This is the end of the world you're trying to live through. Animals may disappear. It is your job not to let yourself disappear with them.

Learn how to swim, strong and hard. Don't trust old women who live in shacks in the woods. If someone pulls out a dagger, even in an innocuous manner, run. Hide in disgusting places, because no one will want to look there, even if they know they should.

When the world grows quiet, remember what it used to be like before the apocalypse, remember what it felt like to live in a town with streets on a grid, a tree growing strong and proud in front of each house. Remember the scent of your mother's rosebushes, and how she called them her babies. Remember how your father picked you up when you fell off your bicycle and the asphalt of the street ate a chunk of the palm of your hand. Remember how he said, "Shh, shh, it's okay, baby," and try not to make any noise when you feel the tears falling down your cheeks. There are bandits moving around outside. If they hear, everything you've managed to accomplish—constructing this semblance of existence after the world has ended—is finished.

Start talking to your shadow. It sits on the wall of your cave each night like an angry imp. Arms folded. Chin tucked into its chest like a sulking child. Tell it to cheer up. Tell it to stop whining. Tell your shadow it needs to buck the hell up or get lost. You don't have time for stragglers in this screwed-up world. You can't wait around while it sorts out its feelings. Ask it, "Are you a man or are you a shadow?" When it remains silent, say, "I thought so."

Stare at the sky over the hillside for a number of days and notice how the ribbon of smoke that occasionally found its way over the farm behind that hill has stopped appearing. Don't do anything right away. Just count the days. One. Two. Three. Four. Like that, until you get to ten full days with no smoke dawning on the horizon. Walk over the hill to the farm. Creep around its perimeter. Wait for an hour or two, just watching, to make sure there are no signs of life. Peer into the kitchen window. Dirty dishes are stacked and scattered everywhere. The body of an old woman lies at an odd angle beside a table overflowing with old newspapers, plastic grocery bags and rubber bands. Enter the house quietly, and make your rounds until you're sure no one living remains. Then raid the kitchen, take the food stored in the basement, the guns in the living room, the newspapers and boxes of matches for starting fires more easily, then—

Stop. Why are you taking everything when you can move what you have to the house instead?

Bury the old woman. Lie in her bed each night staring up at a foreign ceiling, but remember how familiar it is to do this, unable to sleep, a ceiling above you. Not the cold walls of a cave. You are still a bit human, then. You can remember creature comforts, luxuries. You didn't completely devolve.

And here you have a house! And a river nearby, and a garden, and a barn where six chickens and a rooster all sit on their nests like the little members of royal families, clucking their way through the dead days of the apocalypse. They lay eggs, and you fry them in a pan on an antique stove. The old woman was a collector. Everything in this house is old, old, old.

Sit down in the old woman's old rocking chair. Push yourself back and forth on the balls of your feet like you are her. Grip your fingertips over the arms of the chair. Smile as you turn your face to look out the nearest window, where the sun falls through in a long golden shaft, and dust motes spin like stars inside it. Beyond it, though, take notice of the smoke curling up and into the sky above the hillside. Someone has taken your old cave.

Be cautious, but not illogical. Whoever it is up there, they're just another person trying to eke out an existence under ridiculous circumstances, just like you. Watch the perimeter of your property, though. Pay attention to all of the places you yourself used to hide when you were spying on the old woman. Take notice that you think of the old woman's land as your property now. No one owns the world any longer. It is all yours.

On a cool evening, drift through the purple gloaming that hovers beneath the trees around your property and climb the hillside from a secret angle. When you see the person living in your cave, wince in confusion. They are so familiar. Those eyes, that hair, the curl of the lips, the set of the shoulders. It's you, actually, after all. To be precise, it's your shadow. It never left the cave when you moved into the old woman's house. It stayed behind in the surroundings to which it had grown accustomed. It can never forget what it went through. It can never move with you into the old woman's house. If it did, it would forget everything that happened to it, and in the moment of its total forgetting, it would cease to exist.

Leave your shadow be. Let it continue on as it wishes. Go back to the old woman's house and make yourself dinner. A nice salad. Some eggs, hard-boiled. Sigh when you're all finished. It's hard to get the image of your shadow out of your memory. The food doesn't distract you. The warm water of the bath you boil up with plenty of kettles an hour later can't either. So you sit in the dented copper basin in the pantry like some kind of pioneer days person, knobbly knees sticking out of the sudsy water, and weep. Weep for everyone you used to know. Many names can be included on this list that you conjure, including your own.

There is such a thing as survivor's guilt, even at the end of the world, even after the end of the world is over. But don't worry. Like everything else, this too shall pass.

WONDROUS DAYS
GENEVIEVE VALENTINE

"We should make a map," she says. "Just to keep track of things."

I keep my mouth shut, try not to look at her.

We live in a sooty half-dawn that never wakes. Nights are so dark it's better not to think about it. (The nights had only just begun to get dark at all; for a while it was just as bright as the day, from all the fires eating through the dry forest, and we walked until we dropped just to keep ahead of the smoke.)

Sleeping is the worst. You don't know if you've been asleep for ten hours or ten minutes. I'm never rested—the darkness and the smoke have swallowed everything—and there's nothing to go on, and whenever I open my eyes everything's still pointless, and she's already awake.

"It's morning," she says, or, "It's afternoon," like she knows any better than I do what time it is, and she's looking away from me and out at the wreckage.

Maybe that's why she wanted to make a map; just to pretend that there was something better coming, that we'd meet someone who would need it.

The real map of the new world is tacked to a wall in the Darkroad Project wing of the Ames Research Center. It's already yellowing; NASA's acid-free paper can't hold up against the atmosphere.

The map is stuck with little green pins where explosions are most likely to affect the tectonic plates. There are circles drawn in black and red, in orange and purple and green. The map key names them: twenty years, ten years, five years, one. The black circles are widest, and marked Xibalba.

The papers posted around it are from algorithms that have been run on the Pleiades supercomputer. They're printed thickly with core temperatures, trade winds, a Refractive Index to gauge the best chances to preserve the ice caps. There's a list of temperate vegetation six pages long, Latin names and English names side by side.

There are smaller maps, anonymous close-ups of deserts and forests and plains and islands. Beneath each map there are pages of notes on maximum water levels, likely periods of drought, natural shelters; each one has a tacked-up list of flora and fauna marked with Xs, or E for Edible.

It's a drastic future, carefully planned, waiting patiently for its day.

She looked like she had been ready for something. She had hiking boots that laced up her calves, and a backpack big enough to live from. My canvas sneakers lasted less than a week; I had to wrap them with drawstrings from my jacket until we found a corpse with my shoe size.

She never said what she had been doing in the forest. She hardly ever talked. I talked; when we met I talked about what had happened, about where my girlfriend was. ("Dead," she said.) I talked about where we should go to look for others.

There were none. Just corpses with my shoe size.

After we'd walked where I wanted for ten days, she said, "I think we should try another way." It was the longest speech she'd made, and the way she said it sounded like the whole thing was my fault.

"Like you know where to go," I said, but we headed another way.

That was when she started the map; like wherever I'd been going, didn't matter.

She kept a book in her cargo pocket where she made hatchmarks for the dead. She had a page for women, a page for men. Sometimes there was no telling from the parts who it had been to start with; those hatchmarks had a page of their own.

"You should give up," I said.

She knelt, turned the body over.

(Eventually you stop throwing up when you see corpses; your body holds onto whatever nutrients you can get.)

We found a deer. Most of the meat had turned, but maggots had kept part of the loin clean enough to eat.

She cut off what she could with the knife in her pocket, and she found a cave deep enough to block the wind, and after she had twisted grass so it would burn, I used my lighter to start the fire.

Weird what you're good for, when circumstances change.

In the morning she's sitting at the mouth of the cave, looking out at the boggy forest. She doesn't like to be near me; when we've got tree cover she sleeps out of reach; when we're in caves she sleeps as far away as the walls allow.

(Cave living. Shit. Sometimes you wish you had died.)

After a second I realize she's looking at the sky; maybe she could navigate just by the stars, back when there had been stars.

Something turns over in my stomach. Hunger, maybe.

Point Zero, an activist group of historians and academics, had held a rally in New York to protest the Darkroad Project's access to Pleiades. They carried signs that read 13 TO ZERO; SCIENCE NOT SUPERSTITION; THE MAYANS WOULD BE ASHAMED.

"The Mayan Solstice is just resetting a clock!" one guy shouted into the cameras. "We're wasting taxpayer money on an astronomy lab that only generates scare tactics! Mindless superstition like this is catching!"

Point Zero vaulted to Public Enemy Number One. The Pope declared the intervening year a gift, and bid his congregation, "Use these wondrous days to make peace before the End Times, when Jesus calls His faithful children to Heaven." Superstition about 2012 spread faster than the media could track it, and Point Zero's rationalism looked like a losing fighter until twelve of them took over the NSA's Sequoia computer.

(They'd had an insider on the development team, which the NSA never admitted.)

They hacked C-SPAN, announced the takeover, activated the nuclear grid, and held the Svalbard Seed Vault hostage.

"We have no wish to harm Norway or any other country," they broadcasted, "but we are willing to take drastic measures to force humanity to confront its own future and to work for the planet's survival."

Norway provided boats for evacuees. (The Wildlife Federation sent in their own boat teams to rescue the reindeer, bears, and foxes that had been forgotten in the crisis.)

The Point Zero faction also demanded the dismantling of the Darkroad Project at the Ames Research Center, and the public acknowledgement of any quakeproof cities being constructed.

The manifesto they disseminated talked about "the fetishization of disaster as religious experience" and "the inevitable emergence of suspicion as commodity."

It named the Darkroad Project "an underreporting think tank whose members should be using their intelligence to educate the world about astronomic research, rather than burying their disaster-scenario findings under government hush money."

"Unless this 2012 Doomsday theory is debunked publicly," the manifesto concluded, "we will protest the waste of international resources in any way necessary to make it clear that we are serious about our goal, and ensure that we eliminate the rising and dangerous power of mass delusion in the hands of the under-informed."

The manifesto was roundly decried as sensationalist.

Construction on several subterranean cities came quietly to a halt.

(No one could tell what Point Zero might already know; no one knew what Sequoia could do in the hands of the right people.)

I was driving across the mountain when it hit.

The earth snapped once from side to side, like a wet dog shaking off the rain, and my car flew into the rock face sideways because the road had spat it out.

(I was lucky. The others must have been spat out the other side, down the rock face.)

When I finally came around, I broke out of the car and limped back onto the road, and I couldn't even recognize where I was; the mountain had crumbled to dust around me, and I was standing in the center of a world I didn't know. It was like a pile of puzzle pieces snapped together by a careless kid; everything looked unfinished, forced together with gaps between them, so two halves of a tree were suddenly standing a mile apart.

Everything was colorless and dim, so I thought it must have been almost night, and I dragged my way back to the car to sleep until it was morning. (I didn't know yet that there were no more mornings.)

I go ahead of her with a walking stick, in case of animals or sinkholes. Whenever I look back, she's frowning off to one side, making notes on her cheap road map (my cheap road map, the most useful thing I'd offered).

Finally she says, "We should go back to the cave tonight. The ground is too soft here to sleep on."

Her profile is sharp and bright against the grimy day, and I feel like I've faded to nothing, like she's the only living thing left.

I watched her fall asleep near the cave mouth (where there was still enough light to see). She had her book tented on her chest, her head turned away.

I slid the book out of her fingers (her fingers were cold, she was too close to the cave mouth), and tucked it into the inner pocket of my jacket.

(She trusted me only because she had to, because otherwise there was nothing left. Let her ask for it back; find out what it's worth.)

After the manifesto came out, the Ames was publicly cleared out; the governor insisted it was for the safety of employees, not as a concession to Point Zero.

The Nobel Mathematics Committee issued a statement disowning the "Point Zero extremists, who turn a legitimate standpoint into a terrorist platform."

The board members of the mainstream Point Zero held a vote and had a very long discussion. Zeropointzero.org went offline.

Reset13.org popped up the next day, its homepage dotted with strings of 13s and 0s and a palatable explanation of b'ak'tuns and k'atuns. It had a comic strip featuring a pair of sarcastic Mayans who cracked jokes about resetting a long-form clock.

Their members list grew.

A week after the taking of Sequoia, there were only those twelve members of Point Zero left, and they were surrounded by police, locked into a little operating room with a world at their fingertips.

She doesn't mention the book. All day I walk in front of her, tense and waiting, ready for a fight that never comes.

I had figured she'd be better than this, somehow. (Better than what? My mind is muddy; I breathe through the coat of grime on my lungs, put one foot in front of the other, grind my walking stick into the ground so I don't fall through.)

Behind me she breathes a steady in-and-out, like she's drilling slowly through my skull.

We don't start fires at night. You find cover and you huddle in and you hope not to freeze. At first it was awful, but now I don't really even shiver any more; my body's bracing itself for a very long winter.

She hunkers down into her coat, and I try to make out the line of her profile against the crawling night, until it gets too dark and I give up. I can't see a thing at night since the fires stopped.

(Strange, the things you miss.)

"Why were you skywatching, before? What were you looking for?"

After too long she says, "What makes you think I was looking for something?"

Bullshit. She'd been looking for something since the day I staggered through the woods delirious from hunger and half-sick from my own smell, and she appeared out of nowhere to take me back to the hollow trunk where she had made shelter from the grimy light.

"Don't lie to me," I say. I hardly recognize my own voice, like the dark distorted it.

But I had listened to the news back when Point Zero was protesting. I knew that if you looked up at the night sky you saw Xibalba Be, the Dark Road that the Mayans had seen, the biggest clock humanity could set by. Someone from the think tank had gone on the news and explained the galactic alignment with a computer graphic. The planets had already lined up like a string of beads; nobody knew if anything would happen before they split, but you had to think that something could.

I wait for her to call me a liar; to ask about her book. I count to ten. To ten. To ten. She's so quiet I can hardly hear her breathing.

I keep my eyes squeezed shut (you get vertigo at night trying to look around with no light anywhere), but there are little white flecks in my vision, a tiny constellation of angry stars.

It's the dark that does you in. It's the dark that slides over you worse than the ash or the wind, because you know that all the ways to keep back the dark are gone, that when your lighter is gone there will be no more fire without flint and sticks and admitting that there's no hope for anything better.

The dark swallows up the new geography that's been shaken out over the old one, swallows up everything but you (she's sleeping next to you, propped up against the cave wall, but the cave is so small you could reach out and slide your hand into her pocket), and you wake from nothing and know that the dark has pooled like oil in your ears and your nostrils, and even with your eyes squeezed shut you know it's stained your vision until you can't see, that you're walking in circles as the ground under you is crumbling, that with the next step you're going to fall, and then you wake and open your eyes, gasping, your hands scraping at the roof of your mouth to claw the darkness out, and she's leaning over you, marking on your body with pencil where she'll carve away the good meat, and when you scream at her the darkness slides into your stomach, and you wake to the sooty sky and her silhouette already standing outside the cave, untouched and impenetrable, and as you sit up something coils around your lungs and squeezes tight.

Point Zero knew they had been abandoned; they knew that whatever happened, their lives were over, and it was only left to decide how they would go out.

They didn't want to damage the seed vault, no matter what. They never had. Of all the doomsday propositions Point Zero dismissed, the swift extinction of nature was not one. (They cheered when they heard that the animals were being evacuated from Svalbard.)

Resolute, they wrote a new broadcast, where they would announce additional targets; they'd force oil fields to stop production, they'd frighten the world into a worldwide ceasefire. They would sit in the Ops Room with Sequoia and slowly starve out, to buy enough time for the world to come to its senses.

"These wondrous days you're waiting for don't come from prayer, but from deed," they wrote. "They are the provenance of those who care enough to make sacrifices for a better world. We are your caretakers; we will craft these days for all of you."

(Hunger was setting in; they were getting evangelical.)

They didn't know about the room in the basement of the Ames with maps tacked to it, with pinpoints and predictions from the Darkroad Project about how a new world could be carved from the old one.

Point Zero didn't know there were plans that had already been made.

The next day is dark and heavy, heavier than yesterday; I can't breathe (she had stuffed soot down my lungs overnight) and with every step I can feel her staring at my back like she knows something I don't—

I turn on her.

"Is this about your fucking book?"

She doesn't say anything, just gives me that hard, closed-off look I'm getting pretty sick of.

"If you want it back," I snap, "you can ask for it."

"Why did you take it?" she asks, like there's an answer, and all I can think of is, "It's a stupid thing to carry," which is the truth but it isn't an answer.

But she doesn't question me, just says, "You can't do that," so calm it stings, and I sink an inch into the mud and I hate her for pushing me like this. I hate her and my hand flies at her and as she ducks I scream, "I'll do what the fuck I want to you!"

She staggers a few paces back. Then she looks at me for

a long time, and I feel like I've sunk into the ground up to my knees. I make fists at my sides.

Finally she says, "I'd like it back."

The last fucking thing I need from her is that tone, that tone like she's disappointed in me, like I'm the one who's not making sense.

I yank the book out of my jacket and throw it on the ground at my feet. It hits the mud with a wet thwack, hovers for a second before it starts to sink.

She never looks at the book; never looks away from me.

I step on it as I turn around, just for the satisfaction of forcing it down, and then I keep walking.

Eventually, I hear her footsteps behind me. When I look back at her later, there's no mud on her; she's finally wised up about that worthless thing.

There's no need for it. Not like the past is going to change.

After the second broadcast from Point Zero that stated their intentions and put a dozen cities under the gun, there were stampedes from the cities into the countryside. There were ceasefires in war zones as countries pulled their troops back to handle the home fronts. Churches were overrun with congregations hoping to make amends before Point Zero pushed the button.

No one was thinking any more about an empty Research Center; it was nominally under guard, but since Point Zero had ignored it, so had the police. All five members of the Darkroad Project slipped in through a side door without even being seen.

As world governments argued about how to protect against the threat posed by Sequoia's nuclear grid, as Point

Zero's broadcast was picked up by news stations with panicking anchors, as people rioted over canned food in grocery stores, the Darkroad Project stood at the control console of Pleiades and executed the program they had been working on for two years.

Xibalba.exe ran flawlessly; they knew as soon as the earthquake hit and the room buckled.

(They were too close to a fault line to expect to survive; but a true scientist must accept the risks of the experiment.)

We walk for hours. We walk until the dark is almost on us; I want to see how long she'll keep up. (Every step, I have to stop myself from looking over my shoulder.)

The dark rolls in from all around us (the dust hides everything), but she doesn't stop, and I can't—I can't show any weakness, not after all this. I keep walking. Soot has coated my nostrils, and the whole world smells like char, and the darkness is sliding over me.

"It's getting dark," I say, "we should stop," and my voice is small in the dark.

She says, "If you're tired."

Fuck her. I keep walking.

My legs are numb; I feel like I can hardly walk, like I'm falling asleep from the bottom up, and my walking stick isn't helping. I let it fall; I need my hands for balance, and I swing them out a little away from my sides, my hands fisted. I won't stop until she stops.

Behind me, she says, "I voted yes, you know."

Her voice is far away, and it pushes me deeper into the ground. I turn—I try to turn, but I'm thigh-deep in mud, and I realize her voice is far away because she hasn't followed me. She's been paying attention to the lay of the land.

"Get me out of here," I say.

She says, "I voted yes. It was a two-two split until I voted. I thought it would be worth it to suffer for a while, until everything could be set right. We thought it would be worth it, to start over."

The mud is slimy against my stomach.

"I was willing to die," she said. "Then I made it out, and I was willing to help anyone I found. I helped you."

I realize she's speaking in past tense; that she's done helping me.

I try to step back out of the sinkhole, but the mud is slick and heavy, and it pulls me off-balance, and I sink deeper. I take a breath, trying to calm down. You can't fight sinkholes, you have to spread your arms or something to slow yourself down; I remember this from a movie, I can get out of here.

"Point Zero was right," she says, and her voice is angled toward the sky. "The threat would have been better. We gave too much credit to people."

I choke out, "Fuck, I'm sorry," in a tone that cuts the roof of my mouth.

It falls quiet. The inky dark has made my other senses sharper; I can hear the mud sucking at my clothes, my pulse pounding in my ears. Far off, I hear an owl.

"I'm sorry, too," she says, and I hear leaves crunching under her feet as she steps back.

I scream, I kick wildly, I dig into the mud to try to swim out, but it's too slick and I'm in too deep and the oily blackness swallows me; when I scream, I choke on it.

"The new world has to be better than the old one," she says. "That's my project now."

I can hardly hear her. The darkness has slid into my nose and my ears, leaking past my squeezed-shut eyes, and I know the next time I open my mouth I'll swallow clay and it will be over.

"Next time," she says, not unkindly, "I'll know better what kind of person to look for," and there are two footsteps before the mud closes over me.

(Strange what you're good for, when circumstances change.)

DREAMS IN DUST

D. THOMAS MINTON

The arrival of the dust-covered girl caught Keraf by surprise. The girl's slender face, sun-beaten to a deep brown, blended seamlessly into the cloth wrapped around her head. She couldn't have been more than seventeen, but she wielded her rifle with ease.

Keraf didn't even try for his own rifle, slung over his shoulder. Shooting her would be a waste of his last bullet because she didn't appear to have a canteen.

"My sand sled got demasted four days ago," he said in response to her unspoken question. His tongue, dry and dusty, made it difficult to speak. "I have things I can trade for water."

Her eyes roved over Keraf's gauzy robes, his keffiyeh wrapped around the lower half of his face, his rifle, the narrow metal cylinder at his waist, and the empty water bag slung over his back.

"I could just shoot you," she said.

With roles reversed, Keraf might have said the same.

In the wastes of the Atlantic Basin, bandits outnumbered honest men. He didn't think she would believe him, but told her what he thought was the truth. "I'm carrying something that could save the Earth."

"Nothing can save the Earth," the girl said.

"Water can."

Keraf thought he saw the tip of her rifle dip, but the sun was strong and the shadows stark.

The girl's eyes narrowed. "Start walking, and don't try anything. I've deaded better liars than you."

The girl led him across the dunes to an earthen embankment. Keraf hadn't realized it was there until he was upon it; the mound of earth blended with the beige and umber monotony of the rippled dunescape. They were met by a boy covered more in sand than clothing. After a whispered exchange with the girl, the boy set off running up and over the hill.

Keraf waited with the girl, collecting a thicker skin of dust.

After a few minutes, the boy returned with a bundle of cloth-wrapped poles slung over his shoulder. A stoneware bottle bounced from a cord against his left thigh. He gave the girl the bottle, then set about erecting a canopy from the poles.

The girl's lips glistened when she lowered the bottle.

Keraf watched the water evaporate. He licked cracked lips with a sandpaper tongue. Six swallows, he had counted, more than a day's ration in the lamasery.

He unslung his water bag and dropped it in the sand at the edge of the canopy. It wasn't any cooler in the shade, but at least he was out of the sun.

The girl eyed him, but said nothing. She shared the same fine bones and gold-flecked eyes as the boy. A family compound, then, Keraf thought, hidden somewhere over the embankment. They couldn't have had more than a condenser or two, but maybe a trade was still possible.

After a few minutes, an older man and woman came over the embankment and down the sand face. The woman carried a naked toddler on her hip. When the girl saw them, she ran to meet them and exchanged her rifle for the little boy.

As they came into the shade, Keraf pushed his shoulders back and rose up to his full height. The man peeled his checkered keffiyeh aside to reveal cheeks covered with coarse gray stubble and skin pitted from where the cancers had been cut away.

In his hands he carried another stoneware bottle capped with a small metal cup. He wiped the dust from the inside of the cup with the sleeve of his robe and poured a finger of water. He extended it to Keraf.

Keraf pressed his palms together and touched his fingertips to his forehead. "Your water is life," he murmured. When he reached for the cup, the old man pulled it back.

"Your face," he said. "I want to see who drinks our water."

Keraf unclipped his keffiyeh, exposing his face. Even though the air was hot, it felt cool on his black skin.

"The mark of the Mechanists," the man said, nodding at the metal ankh hanging at Keraf's throat. "We don't see many of your kind here." He extended the cup a second time. "I am called Faruk," he said. "You have met Imani, my grandniece." He motioned to the girl with the toddler in her arms.

The child's top lip was split from his mouth to his nose, a defect of birth. Keraf had seen such deformities in small enclaves before. It gave him hope that the one thing he could trade had value.

Keraf stared down into the water, and forced himself to sip. It cooled his burning tongue. He licked every drop of moisture from his lips before tipping the last of the water into his mouth. He handed the cup back to Faruk.

"I am Keraf," he said, now that his throat was lubricated. "Your water is life; I owe you my life."

Faruk handed the cup to the little boy in Imani's arms. The boy's slender red tongue snapped in and out through the cleft in his lip, licking dry the beads of water that clung to the metal.

Keraf found it difficult not to stare. "I am on a mission to Costa de Santo," he said, pulling his eyes from the toddler. "Four days ago, my sled capsized crossing the mid-Atlantic mountains. What water I had was lost. I seek water so I can complete my mission."

Faruk's eyes narrowed. "We have no water to spare."

Keraf did not expect anyone to *give* him water. A single condenser could produce a gallon a day from the basin's arid atmosphere, enough for only a handful of people and a few plants.

"I can trade," he said. "I carry a fully-functional uric acid modification, enhanced melanin, and high efficiency sweat glands." The genetic modifications had become fixed in the Earth's human population prior to the final dewatering by the Orbitals, but small enclaves could regress through inbreeding. "My semen is worth a few days of water."

"It's worth nothing if we dry out."

From Faruk's expression, Keraf could not tell if the man

was simply negotiating. The Atlantic Basin was isolated, and opportunities to maintain his clan's genetic viability could not have presented themselves often. Pressing the issue this early in a negotiation could offend.

"You have the advantage," Keraf said. "My rifle is worth something, as is my water bag. I'm willing to work for a ration."

Faruk looked unimpressed.

"I beg your compassion. My mission is important."

"He says he carries something that could save us," Imani said. The toddler squirmed in her arms, and she set him down. The boy hid behind her robes and poked his tongue out at Keraf through his cleft.

"The Earth is dead," Faruk said. "Those who believe otherwise are chasing fantasies in the dust."

"What if he speaks the truth? We can spare—"

Faruk hissed and the girl fell silent. The toddler started to cry. The tears on his cheek made Keraf's mouth water.

Imani knelt and pulled the boy into her arms, quieting him. She collected his tears on her fingertips and put them in her mouth.

Keraf pretended to ignore the exchange, even as his mind tried to construct what Imani had intended to say. Could they spare water? No one could spare water, for there was none to spare.

"Let me show you." Keraf slowly unclipped the metal cylinder from his belt and unscrewed the cap on one end. "These are copies of a document discovered by my Order." Keraf removed a tube of handmade paper and carefully unrolled it. It was covered with intricate lines and neat blocks of hand-printed text. "It is a plan for a deep drilling machine, but my lamasery lacks the resources to construct it. The Mechanist Court at Costa de Santo can build it, and if they do, they can bring water to the surface."

Faruk studied the document for a moment, but Keraf suspected the man could not decipher it. Without water, industrialization and the skills associated with it had collapsed. Other than condensers, little remained from the wet-Earth.

Faruk's lips pulled downward into a frown. He waved the paper aside. "The deep ocean? A myth. I won't spend time looking at what I don't have, only to lose sight of what I do. My grandniece should do the same, for her son. We cannot help you. We have no water to spare."

"Please, I am at your mercy." Keraf reached for Faruk, but the man stepped back.

Faruk pushed aside a fold of his robe to reveal a revolver in his belt. "It's best you be on your way."

Imani grabbed her great uncle's arm. "You talk of the future, but my son has no—"

Faruk pulled his arm free. "Enough!"

Imani lowered her face.

"How long will your condensers last?" Keraf tried to keep the desperation out of his voice. "Ours run on sweat and prayer. Out here, it must be—" An odd sound drew Keraf's eyes to the toddler. The boy was peeing on the sand.

Keraf dropped the paper. His eyes grew wide. "You have found water," he whispered, as he fell to his knees.

Faruk drew the pistol from his belt. In a single fluid motion, he leveled it at Keraf's chest.

Keraf could not take his eyes off the arc of lemon-yellow water. The toddler did not have the genetic modification to produce uric acid instead of urine. He would need over a gallon of water a day to survive; yet he lived.

The toddler finished peeing, and Imani scooped him into her arms. Keraf watched the puddle sink into the dust. He ached to hold the wet sand in his hands.

Faruk pulled back the hammer on his revolver.

"Don't, Uncle," Imani said.

"He will bring others. They will take what we have."

"But the drilling machine…"

"Those drawings are probably not even real," Faruk said. "A ruse to steal water from our mouths."

"Already the seep gives less than it once did. If the paper he carries can bring back the water…" Imani squeezed the toddler in her arms. The boy squirmed but could not slip free.

Keraf stared, no longer seeing the toddler's cleft lip. "Your child is the future," he said, "one where we have enough water to wet the ground with our urine." He looked up the revolver's barrel, past the three bullets arrayed in the chambers. "I have dedicated my life to bringing water back to the world," he said. "I have heard it used to fall from the sky. I have never seen such a thing, but I dream that our children will. If you shoot me, at least deliver these plans to Costa de Santo. I believe they can save us."

Faruk's eyebrows pinched together. "Why do you believe?"

"If I do not, then everything is just dust." Keraf waited for the bullet. He imagined a heaven with cool rain.

The pistol wavered. "The last time I saw the rain, I was a small boy," Faruk said. "We ran outside with pots and plates and cloths—anything that could hold water. It rained for less than a minute—only a fine mist really—but enough to dampen my face." He touched his cheeks, as if wiping moisture from them. "I will never forget that."

Keraf licked his lips, trying to imagine what rain would

taste like. "Sometimes it is hard not to lose hope," he said.

Faruk lowered the revolver. "Hope is a powerful thing." He picked up the paper at his feet, carefully rolled it, and handed it back to Keraf. "Come."

Keraf followed Faruk up the embankment, leaving the others to dismantle the canopy. As he crested the top, Keraf stopped.

Below, in the dusty trough, a dozen dome-shaped dwellings ringed a small greenhouse. Through beads of water sparkling on the greenhouse glass, Keraf saw a pool of water nestled among green leaves. He drew an audible breath.

"Without hope, we are dust," Faruk said. "Before you leave, we will share water."

BY FOOLS LIKE ME

NANCY KRESS

Hope creeps quietly into my bedroom without knocking, peering around the corner of the rough doorjamb. I'm awake; sleep eludes me so easily now. I know from the awful smell that she has been to the beach.

"Come in, child, I'm not asleep."

"Grandma, where's Mama and Papa?"

"Aren't they in the field?" The rains are late this year and water for the crops must be carried in ancient buckets from the spring in the dell.

"Maybe. I didn't see them. Grandma, I found something."

"What, child?"

She gazes at me and bites her lip. I see that this mysterious find bothers her. Such a sensitive child, though sturdy and healthy enough, God knows how.

"I went to the beach," she confesses in a rush. "Don't tell Mama! I wanted to dig you some trunter roots because you like them so much, but my shovel went clunk on something hard and I... I dug it up."

"Hope," I reprimand, because the beach is full of dangerous bits of metal and plastic, washed up through the miles of dead algae on the dead water. And if a soot cloud blows in from the west, it will hit the beach first.

"I'm sorry," she says, clearly lying, "but, Grandma, it was a metal box and the lock was all rusted and there was something inside and I brought it here."

"The box?"

"No, that was too heavy. The... just wait!"

No one can recognize most of the bits of rusted metal and twisted plastic from before the Crash. Anything found in a broken metal box should be decayed beyond recognition. I call, "Hope! Don't touch anything slimy—" but she is already out of earshot, running from my tiny bedroom with its narrow cot, which is just blankets and pallet on a rope frame to keep me off the hard floor. It doesn't; the old ropes sag too much, just as the thick clay walls don't keep out the heat. But that's my fault. I close the window shutters only when I absolutely have to. Insects and heat are preferable to dark. But I have a door, made of precious and rotting wood, which is more than Hope or her parents have on their sleeping alcoves off the house's only other room. I expect to die in this room.

Hope returns, carrying a bubble of sleek white plastic that fills her bare arms. The bubble has no seams. No mold sticks to it, no sand. Carefully she lays the thing on my cot.

Despite myself, I say, "Bring me the big knife and be very careful, it's sharp."

She gets the knife, carrying it as gingerly as an offering for the altar. The plastic slits more readily than I expected. I peel it back, and we both gasp.

I am the oldest person on Island by two decades, and I have seen much. Not of the world my father told me about, from before the Crash, but in our world now. I have buried two husbands and five children, survived three great sandstorms and two years where the rains didn't come at all, planted and first-nursed a sacred tree, served six times at the altar. I have seen much, but I have never seen so much preserved sin in one place.

"What… Grandma… what is that?"

"A book, child. They're all books."

"Books?" Her voice holds titillated horror. "You mean… like they made before the Crash? Like they cut down *trees* to make?"

"Yes."

"Trees? Real *trees*?"

"Yes." I lift the top one from the white plastic bubble. Firm, thick red cover, like… dear God, it's made from the skin of some animal. My gorge rises. Hope mustn't know that. The edges of the sin are gold. My father told me about books, but not that they could look like this. I open it.

"Oh!" Hope cries. "Oh, Grandma!"

The first slate—no, first *page*, the word floating up from some childhood conversation—is a picture of trees, but nothing like the pictures children draw on their slates. This picture shows dozens of richly colored trees, crowded together, each with *hundreds* of healthy, beautifully detailed green leaves. The trees shade a path bordered with glorious flowers. Along the path runs a child wearing far too many wraps, following a large white animal dressed in a wrap and hat and carrying a small metal machine. At the top of the picture, words float on golden clouds: *Alice in Wonderland*.

"Grandma! Look at the—Mama's coming!"

Before I can say anything, Hope grabs the book, shoves it into the white bubble, and thrusts the whole thing under my cot. I feel it slide under my bony ass, past the sag that is my body, and hit the wall. Hope is standing up by the time Gloria crowds into my tiny room.

"Hope, have you fed the chickens yet?"

"No, Mama, I—"

Gloria reaches out and slaps her daughter. "Can't I trust you to do anything?"

"Please, Gloria, it's my fault. I sent her to see if there's any more mint growing in the dell."

Gloria scowls. My daughter-in-law is perpetually angry, perpetually exhausted. Before my legs gave out and I could still do a full day's work, I used to fight back. The Island is no more arid, the see-oh-too no higher, for Gloria than for anyone else. She has borne no more stillborn children than have other women, has endured no more soot clouds. But now that she and my son must feed my nearly useless body, I try to not anger her too much, to not be a burden. I weave all day. I twist rope, when there are enough vines to spare for rope. I pretend to be healthier than I am.

Gloria says, "We don't need mint, we need fed chickens. Go, Hope." She turns.

"Gloria—"

"What?" Her tone is unbearable. I wonder, for the thousandth time, why Bill married her, and for the thousandth time I answer my own question.

"Nothing," I say. I don't tell her about the sin under the bed. I could have, and ended it right there. But I do not.

God forgive me.

* * *

Gloria stands behind the altar, dressed in the tattered green robe we all wear during our year of service. I sit on a chair in front of the standing villagers; no one may miss services, no matter how old or sick or in need of help to hobble to the Grove. Bill half carried me here, afraid no doubt of being late and further angering his wife. It's hard to have so little respect for my son.

It is the brief time between the dying of the unholy wind that blows all day and the fall of night. Today the clouds are light gray, not too sooty, but not bearing rain, either.

The altar stands at the bottom of the dell, beside the spring that makes our village possible. A large flat slab of slate, it is supported by boulders painstakingly chiseled with the words of God. It took four generations to carve that tiny writing, and three generations of children have learned to read by copying the sacred texts onto their slates. I was among the first. The altar is shaded by the six trees of the Grove and from my uncomfortable seat, I can gaze up at their branches against the pale sky.

How beautiful they are! Ours are the tallest, straightest, healthiest trees of any village on Island. I planted and first-nursed one of them myself, the honor of my life. Even now I feel a thickness in my shriveled chest as I gaze up at the green leaves, each one wiped free of dust every day by those in service. Next year, Hope will be one of them. There is nothing on Earth lovelier than the shifting pattern of trees against the sky. Nothing.

Gloria raises her arms and intones, "'Then God said, "I give you every plant and every tree on the whole Earth. They will be food for you."'"

"Amen," call out two or three people.

"'Wail, oh pine tree,'" Gloria cries, "'for the cedar has

247

fallen, the stately trees are ruined! Wail, oaks—'"

"Wail! Wail!"

I have never understood why people can't just worship in silence. This lot is sometimes as bad as a flock of starlings.

"—oaks of Bashan, the—"

Hope whispers, "Who's Bashan?"

Bill whispers back, "A person at the Crash."

"'—dense forest has been cut down! And they were told—told!—not to harm the grass of Earth or any plant or tree.'"

Revelation 9:4, I think automatically, although I never did find out what the words or numbers mean.

"'The vine is dried up!'" Gloria cries, "'the fig tree is withered! The pomegranate and the palm and the apple tree, all the trees of the field, are dried up! Surely the joy of mankind is withered away!'"

"Withered! Oh, amen, withered!"

Joel 1:12.

"'Offer sacrifices and burn incense on the high places, under any spreading tree!'"

Amy Martin, one of the wailers, comes forward with the first sacrifice, an unrecognizable piece of rusted metal dug up from the soil or washed up on the beach. She lays it on the altar. Beside me Hope leans forward, her mouth open and her eyes wide. I can read her young thoughts as easily as if they, too, are chiseled in stone: *That metal might have been part of a "car" that threw see-oh-two and soot into the air, might have been part of a "factory" that poisoned the air, might have even been part of a "saw" that cut down the forests!* Hope shudders, but I glance away from the intensity on her face. Sometimes she looks too much like Gloria.

Two more sacrifices are offered. Gloria takes an ember from the banked fire under the altar—the only fire allowed in the village—and touches it briefly to the sacrifices. "'Instead of the thornbush will grow the pine tree, and instead of briars the myrtle will grow. This will be for the Lord's glory, for an everlasting sign which—'"

I stop listening. Instead I watch the leaves move against the sky. What is "myrtle"—what did it look like, why was it such a desirable plant? The leaves blur. I have dozed off, but I realize this only when the whole village shouts together, "We will never forget!" and services are over.

Bill carries me back through the quickening darkness without stars or moon. Without the longed-for rain. Without the candles I remember from my childhood on Island, or the dimly remembered (dreamed?) fireless lights from before that. There are no lights after dark on Island, nothing that might release soot into the air.

We will never forget.

It's just too bad that services are so boring.

Alice in Wonderland
    Pride and Prejudice
    Birds of India and Asia
    Moby Dick
    Morning Light
    Jane Eyre
    The Sun Also Rises

I sit on my cot, slowly sounding out the strange words. Of course the sun rises—what else could it do? It's rising now outside my window, which lets in pale light, insects, and the everlasting hot wind.

"Can I see, Grandma?" Hope, naked in the doorway. I didn't hear the door open. She could have been Gloria. And is it right for a child to see this much sin?

But already she's snuggled beside me, smelling of sweat and grime and young life. Even her slight body makes the room hotter. All at once a memory comes to me, a voice from early childhood: *Here, Anna, put ice on that bruise. Listen, that's a—*

What bruise? What was I to listen to? The memory is gone.

"M—m—m—oh—bee—Grandma, what's a 'moby'?"

"I don't know, child."

She picks up a different one. "J—j—aye—n... Jane! That's Miss Anderson's name! Is this book about her?"

"No. Another Jane, I think." I open *Moby Dick*. Tiny, dense writing, pages and pages of it, whole burned forests of it.

"Read the sin with the picture of trees!" She roots among the books until she finds *Alice in Wonderland* and opens it to that impossible vision of tens, maybe hundreds, of glorious trees. Hope studies the child blessed enough to walk that flower-bordered path.

"What's her name, Grandma?"

"Alice." I don't really know.

"Why is she wearing so many wraps? Isn't she *hot*? And how many days did her poor mother have to work to weave so many?"

I recognize Gloria's scolding tone. The pages of the book are crisp, bright and clear, as if the white plastic bubble had some magic to keep sin fresh. Turning the page, I begin to read aloud. "'Alice was beginning to get very tired of sitting by her sister on the bank—'"

"She has a *sister*," Hope breathes. Nearly no one does now; so few children are carried to term and born whole.

"'—and tired of having nothing to do: once—'"

"How could she have nothing to do? Why doesn't she carry water or weed crops or hunt trunter roots or—"

"Hope, are you going to let me read this to you or not?"

"Yes, Grandma. I'm sorry."

I shouldn't be reading to her at all. *Trees* were cut down to make this book; my father told me so. As a young man, not long after the Crash, he himself was in service as a book sacrificer, proudly. Unlike many of his generation, my father was a moral man.

"'—or twice she had peeped into the book her sister was reading, but it had no pictures or conversation in it.' *And what is the use of a book*, thought Alice, *without pictures or conversation?* 'So she was considering—'"

We read while the sun clears the horizon, a burning merciless ball, and our sweat drips onto the gold-edged page. Then Gloria and Bill stir in the next room and Hope is on the floor in a flash, shoving the books under my sagging cot, running out the door to feed the chickens and hunt for their rare, precious eggs.

The rains are very late this year. Every day Gloria, scowling, scans the sky. Every day at sunset she and Bill drag themselves home, bone-weary and smeared with dust, after carrying water from the spring to the crops. The spring is in the dell, and water will not flow uphill. Gloria is also in service this year and must nurse one of the trees, wiping the poisonous dust from her share of the leaves, checking for dangerous insects. More work, more time. Some places on Earth, I was told once, have too much water, too many plants from the see-oh-too. I can't imagine it. Island has heard from no other place since I was a young woman and the last radio failed. Now a radio would be sin.

I sit at the loom, weaving. I'm even clumsier than usual, my fingers stiff and eyes stinging. From too much secret reading, or from a high see-oh-too day? Oh, let it be from the reading!

"Grandma," Hope says, coming in from tending the chickens. "My throat hurts." Her voice is small; she knows.

Dear God, not *now*, not when the rains are already so late… But I look out the window and yes, I can see it on the western horizon, thick and brown.

"Bring in the chickens, Hope. Quick!"

She runs back outside while I hobble to the heavy shutters and wrestle them closed. Hope brings in the first protesting chicken, dumps it in her sleeping alcove, and fastens the rope fence. She races back for the next chicken as Bill and Gloria run over the fields toward the house.

Not *now*, when everything is so dry…

They get the chickens in, the food covered, as much water inside as can be carried. At the last moment Bill swings closed the final shutter, and we're plunged into darkness and even greater heat. We huddle against the west wall. The dust storm hits.

Despite the shutters, the holy protection of wood, dust drifts through cracks, under the door, maybe even through chinks in the walls. The dust clogs our throats, noses, eyes. The wind rages: *oooeeeeeeeeoooooeeeee*. Shrinking beside me, Hope gasps, "It's trying to get in!"

Gloria snaps, "Don't talk!" and slaps Hope. Gloria is

right, of course; the soot carries poisons that Island can't name and doesn't remember. Only I remember my father saying, "Methane and bio-weapons…"

Here, Anna, put ice on that bruise. Listen, that's a—

A what? What was that memory?

Then Gloria, despite her slap, begins to talk. She has no choice; it's her service year and she must pray aloud. "'Wail, oh pine tree, for the cedar has fallen, the stately trees are ruined! Wail, oaks of Bashan, the dense forest has been cut down!'"

I want Gloria to recite a different scripture. I want, God forgive me, Gloria to shut up. Her anger burns worse than the dust, worse than the heat.

"'The vine is dried up and the fig is withered; the pomegranate—'"

I stop listening.

Listen, that's a—

Hope trembles beside me, a sweaty mass of fear.

The dust storm proves mercifully brief, but the see-oh-too cloud pulled behind it lasts for days. Everyone's breathing grows harsh. Gloria and Bill, carrying water, get fierce headaches. Gloria makes Hope stay inside, telling her to sit still. I see in Gloria's eyes the concern for her only living child, a concern that Hope is too young to see. Hope sees only her mother's anger.

Left alone, Hope and I sin.

All the long day, while her parents work frantically to keep us alive, we sit by the light of a cracked shutter and follow Alice down the rabbit hole, through the pool of tears, inside the White Rabbit's house, to the Duchess's peppery kitchen. Hope stops asking questions, since I know none of the answers. What is pepper, a crocodile, a caucus race, marmalade? We just read steadily on, wishing there were more pictures, until the book is done and Alice has woken. We begin *Jane Eyre*: "'There was no possibility of taking a walk that day…'"

Birds of India and Asia has gorgeous pictures, but the writing is so small and difficult that I can't read most of it. Nonetheless, this is the book I turn to when Hope is asleep. So many birds! And so many colors on wings and backs and breasts and rising from the tops of heads like fantastic feathered trees. I wish I knew if these birds were ever real, or if they are as imaginary as Alice, as the White Rabbit, as marmalade. I wish—

"Grandma!" Hope cries, suddenly awake. "It's raining outside!"

Joy, laughter, dancing. The whole village gathers at the altar under the trees. Bill carries me there, half running, and I smell his strong male sweat mingled with the sweet rain. Hope dances in her drenched wrap like some wild thing and chases after the other children.

Then Gloria strides into the Grove, grabs Hope, and throws her onto the altar. "You've sinned! My own daughter!"

Immediately everyone falls silent. The village, shocked, looks from Gloria to Hope, back to Gloria. Gloria's face is twisted with fury. From a fold of her wrap she pulls out *Alice in Wonderland*.

"This was in the chicken coop! This! A sin, trees *destroyed*… you had this in our very house!" Gloria's voice rises to a shriek.

Hope shrinks against the wide flat stone and she puts her hands over her face. Rain streams down on her, flattening her hair against her small skull. The book in Gloria's hand sheds droplets off its skin cover. Gloria tears out pages and throws them to the ground, where they go sodden and pulpy as maggots.

"Because of you, God might not have sent any rains at all this year! We're just lucky that in His infinite mercy—you risked—you—"

Gloria drops the mutilated book, pulls back her arm, and with all her force strikes Hope on the shoulder. Hope screams and draws into a ball, covering her head and neck. Gloria lashes out again, a sickening thud of hand on tender flesh. I cry, "Stop! No, Gloria, stop—Bill—let me go!"

He doesn't. No one else moves to help Hope, either. I can feel Bill's anguish, but he chokes out, "It's right, Mama." And then, invoking the most sacred scripture of all, he whispers, "We will never forget."

I cry out again, but nothing can keep Hope from justice, not even when I scream that it is my fault, my book, my sin. They know I couldn't have found this pre-Crash sin alone. They know that, but no one except me knows when Gloria passes beyond beating Hope for justice, for Godly retribution, into beating her from Gloria's own fury, her withered fig tree, her sin. No one sees but me. And I, an old woman, can do nothing.

Hope lies on her cot, moaning. I crouch beside her in her alcove, its small window unshuttered to the rain. Bill bound her broken arm with the unfinished cloth off my loom, then went into the storm in search of his wife.

"Hope… dear heart…"

She moans again.

If I could, I would kill Gloria with my own hands.

A sudden lone crack of lightning brightens the alcove. Already the skin on Hope's wet arms and swollen face has started to darken. One eye swells.

Here, Anna, put ice on that bruise. Listen, that's a—

"Grandma…"

"Don't talk, Hope."

"Water," Hope gasps and I hold the glass for her. Another flash of lightning and for a moment Gloria stands framed in the window. We stare at each other. With a kind of horror I feel my lips slide back, baring my teeth. Gloria sees, and cold slides down my spine.

Then the lightning is gone, and I lay my hand on Hope's battered body.

The rain lasts no more than a few hours. It's replaced by day after day of black clouds that thunder and roil but shed no water. Day after day. Gloria and Bill let half the field die in their attempt to save the other half. The rest of the village does much the same.

Hope heals quickly; the young are resilient. I sit beside her, weaving, until she can work again. Her bruises turn all the colors of the angry earth: black and dun and dead-algae green. Gloria never looks at or speaks to her daughter. My son smiles weakly at us all, and brings Hope her meal, and follows Gloria out the door to the fields.

"Grandma, we sinned."

Did we? I don't know any more. To cut down *trees* in order to make a book… my gorge rises at just the thought.

Yes, that's wrong, as wrong as anything could ever be. Trees are the life of the Earth, are God's gift to us. Even my father's generation, still so selfish and sinful, said so. Trees absorb the see-oh-too, clean the air, hold the soil, cool the world. Yes.

But, against that, the look of rapture on Hope's face as Alice chased the White Rabbit, the pictures of *Birds of India and Asia*, Jane Eyre battling Mrs. Reed… Hope and I destroyed nothing ourselves. Is it so wrong, then, to enjoy another's sin?

"We sinned," Hope repeats, mourning, and it is her tone that hardens my heart. "No, child. We didn't."

"We didn't?" Her eyes, one still swollen, grow wide.

"We didn't make the books. They already *were*. We just read them. Reading isn't sinful."

"Nooooo," she says reluctantly. "Not reading the altar scriptures. But Alice is—"

Gloria enters the house. She says to me, "Services tonight."

I say, "I'm not going."

Gloria stops dead halfway to the wash bucket, her field hat suspended in her hand. For the briefest moment I see something like panic on her face, before it vanishes into her usual anger. "Not going? To services?"

"No."

Hope, frightened, looks from her mother to me. Bill comes in.

Gloria snaps, with distinct emphasis, "*Your* mother says she's not going to services tonight."

Bill says, "Mama?"

"No," I say, and watch his face go from puzzlement to the dread of a weak man who will do anything to avoid argument. I hobble to my alcove and close the door. Later, from my window, I watch them leave for the Grove, Hope holding her father's hand.

Gloria must have given him silent permission to do that.

My son.

Painfully I lower myself to the floor, reach under my cot, and pull out the white plastic bubble. For a while I gaze at the pictures of the gorgeous birds of India and Asia. Then I read *Jane Eyre*. When my family returns at dusk, I keep reading as long as the light holds, not bothering to hide any of the books, knowing that no one will come in.

One heavy afternoon, when the clouds steadily darken and I can no longer see enough to make out words, a huge bolt of lightning shrieks through the sky—*crack!* For a long moment my head vibrates. Then silence, followed by a shout: "Fire!"

I haul myself to my knees and grasp the bottom of the window. The lightning hit one of the trees in the Grove. As I watch, numb, the fire leaps on the ceaseless wind to a second tree.

People scream and run, throwing buckets of muddy water from the spring. I can see that it will do no good— too much dry timber, too much wind. A third tree catches, a fourth, and then the grass too is on fire. Smoke and ash rise into the sky.

I sink back onto my cot. I planted one of those trees, nursed it as I'd once nursed Bill. But there is nothing I can do. Nothing.

By the light of the terrible flames I pick up *Jane Eyre* and, desperately, I read.

And then Hope bursts in, smeared with ash, sweat and tears on her face.

"Hope—no! Don't!"

"Give it to me!"

"No!"

We struggle, but she is stronger. Hope yanks *Jane Eyre* out of my hands and hurls it to the floor. She drops on top of it and crawls under my cot. Frantically I try to press down the sagging ropes so that she can't get past them, but I don't weigh enough. Hope backs out with the other books in their plastic bubble. She scrambles to her feet.

"We did this! You and me! Our sin made God burn the trees!"

"No! Hope—"

"Yes! We did this, just like the people before the Crash!" *We will never forget.*

I reach for her, for the books, for everything I've lost or am about to lose. But Hope is already gone. From my window I see her silhouetted against the flames, running toward the grass. The village beats the grass with water-soaked cloths. I let go of the sill and fall back onto the cot before I can see Hope throw the books onto the fire.

Gloria beats Hope again, harder and longer this time. She and Bill might have put me out of the house, except that I have no place to go. So they settle for keeping me away from Hope, so that I cannot lead her further into sin.

Bill speaks to me only once about what happened. Bringing me my meal—meager, so meager—he averts his eyes from my face and says haltingly, "Mama... I..."

"Don't," I say.

"I have to… you… Gloria…" All at once he finds words. "A little bit of sin is just as bad as a big sin. That's what *you* taught me. What all those people thought before the Crash—that their cars and machines and books each only destroyed a little air so it didn't matter. And look what happened! The Crash was—"

"Do you really think you're telling me something I don't know? Telling *me*?"

Bill turns away. But as he closes the door behind him, he mumbles over his shoulder, "A little bit of sin is as bad as a big sin."

I sit in my room, alone.

Bill is not right. Nor is Gloria, who told him what to say. Nor is Hope, who is after all a child, with a child's uncompromising, black-and-white faith. They are all wrong, but I can't find the arguments to tell them so. I'm too ignorant. The arguments must exist, they *must*—but I can't find them. And my family wouldn't listen anyway.

Listen, Anna, that's a—

A nightingale.

The whole memory flashes like lightning in my head: my father, bending over me in a walled garden, laughing, trying to distract me from some childish fall. *Here, Anna, put ice on that bruise. Listen, that's a nightingale!* A cube of frozen water pulled with strong fingers from his amber drink. Flowers everywhere, flowers of scarcely believable colors, crimson and gold and blue and emerald. And a burst of glorious unseen music, high and sweet. A bird, maybe one from *Birds of India and Asia.*

But I don't know, can't remember, what a nightingale looks like. And now I never will.

JIMMY'S ROADSIDE CAFÉ

RAMSEY SHEHADEH

After the world ended, Jimmy set up a roadside café in the median of I-95, just north of the Fallston exit, in the grassy depression between the guardrails. His first café, nothing more than a plywood shanty, fell to the first thunderstorm that blew through. The second was better: he dug a sort of foundation and built the walls out of heavy plywood he'd harvested from an overturned Home Depot truck, reinforced the corners with steel joints, laid down a sheet of tin for the roof. He used a Hummer's windshield for the front window, a thick yellow shower curtain for the door. And then he nailed an Open/Closed sign beside the doorway, flipped it to *Open*, settled down in his lawn chair, and waited.

Two days later he got his first customer.

She was half gone already, her face a mass of pinkish sores, one of her eyes pure red and swollen nearly out of its socket. She came out of the north, staggering drunkenly between the ranks of stopped cars, moving with the hitched, staccato gait of creeping atrophy.

"Hello!" he cried, and jumped up, waving frantically, then rushed onto the road and wended his way through the dead cars, toward the woman. He stopped in front of her, panting, smiling broadly, and held out a hand. "Welcome to Jimmy's Roadside Café. I'm Jimmy."

The woman stopped, swayed, put a hand on the side of a Corolla to steady herself. She was wearing a man's trench coat over sweats, sneakers at least two sizes too big for her, a pink floral top. She studied him for a moment, then said: "I need help."

"Of course," said Jimmy, smiling broadly. "Come inside."

It was a grey day, threatening rain. He took her by the arm and led her down into the median and through the café's canted doorway to its only booth, the backseats of a Buick and a Lincoln flanking a small table. He bustled away and came back with a Scooby-Doo glass half-filled with brandy, and a donut that clattered like cutlery when he dropped it on the table.

"House special," said Jimmy.

She looked at the donut, but made no move toward it.

"Don't worry, you'll be able to keep it down," said Jimmy. "You just need to have the brandy in you first." He raised the glass to her lips. "Trust me."

She made a face, but drank. Tentatively at first, then in long drafts.

Jimmy sat down across from her and snapped the donut in two, handed one half to her, and started on the other. It tasted like sweetened cement, hard on the outside and chalky on the inside. But he chewed and swallowed, downing it like medicine, and eventually she followed suit.

"What's your name?" said Jimmy.

"Margaret."

"I'm very pleased to meet you, Margaret."

"I'm looking for my husband," she said.

Jimmy frowned, didn't answer. Her words dropped into the silence, like coins falling down a well.

"His name is Nabil. He's Lebanese. He's a lawyer."

Jimmy held up a finger, and went behind the bar—a long board laid atop two towers of stacked cinder blocks—and pulled his drawing pad and pencils out of a cardboard box with the word *Basement* scrawled on its side in red marker.

"All right," said Jimmy. "What was his head shaped like? Thin and tapered?"—he drew a wedge—"Or plump?"—an oval—"Or square-jawed?"—a trapezoid.

"Plump. But not that plump."

"Okay." He drew a narrower oval. "Nose?"

"Biggish. Wide nostrils."

He drew it. "Like this?"

She shrugged. "I guess."

"Good. Eyes?"

And they worked their way through it, building the dead man's face, feature by feature, until they had a portrait. He sketched in a thicket of short black hair, curly and tousled, and a thick neck with a prominent Adam's apple, then spun it around. "Like that?"

She nodded. "That's him."

Jimmy spun the portrait back and wrote *Have you seen this man?* along the bottom, then went outside and nailed it to the wall beside the curtain. He looked up and down I-95, so thick with dead cars that it seemed paved with them. He went back inside.

Margaret was studying herself in the full-length mirror mounted horizontally behind the bar. The face that stared back at her was ravaged, bewildered, numb. Jimmy said: "So hopefully we get some news. Do you want more brandy?"

She nodded, then coughed, a long wracking heave that spattered blood and mucus on the table between them. Jimmy leapt up and came around and put an arm around her shoulder and held her until the spasm passed.

She was crying. "It hurts," she said.

"I know." He produced a lozenge. "Try this. It helps a little." He rose and unfolded his bed, a portable cot with a thin foam mattress, then helped her onto it and drew a woolen blanket up to her neck. "Try to sleep," he said.

He knew she wouldn't, though. The disease ate sleep, and left dementia and demon visions in its wake. He thought about giving her morphine, but there wasn't much to spare, and she'd need it later.

He waited until her breathing slowed, then went outside, drawing the curtain shut behind him, and eased himself into his lawn chair. He looked out at the empty world.

His second customer appeared out of the north as well, pulling a large red wagon with two children inside, a boy and a girl, both laid neatly out and dressed formally, as if for a wedding, the boy in a black suit and a little red bow tie, the girl in a frilly blue dress with lacework at the sleeves.

"Hello there!" said Jimmy, scurrying up the bank to the road. This new visitor was large, bald and broad-shouldered, and wore a charcoal Giants jersey and a pair of blue sweats, torn at the knees. He slowed, but did not stop, and fixed Jimmy with a hard glare.

"I'm Jimmy," said Jimmy. "Welcome to my roadside café."

The man glanced over at the shack. "Is this a joke?"

"No," said Jimmy, and he frowned. "Is what a joke?"

The man took in Jimmy's uniform: the carefully pressed chinos, the long white apron, the little tie. The nametag. He said: "Why aren't you dead?"

"Can I interest you in a donut?" said Jimmy. "On the house, of course."

"What are you, crazy? Are you out of your fucking mind?"

"No," said Jimmy. A shadow of uncertainty flickered across his face. "We have brandy, too."

The man snorted, and picked up his pace. He was leaving. Jimmy felt a thrill of panic. He said: "You have lovely children."

The man stopped, dropped the wagon's handle, and, in one fluid motion, spun around and slammed his fist into the center of Jimmy's face. Jimmy heard his nose crack, and the world went dark. When he came back to it, he was on the street, and the man was straddling his chest, hitting him and hitting him. Every blow was seismic, the pain monstrous, and then incomprehensible. A gentle thrill of peace passed through Jimmy's body. He felt sure that he would die soon.

And then there was a voice, low and rasped, barely audible. The man paused, and looked over at the café. Margaret stood framed by the slanting doorway, stooped and leaning against the wall, wrapped tightly in Jimmy's blanket.

He looked back. "Is that your wife?"

Jimmy swallowed the blood in his mouth, licked the blood off his lips. "No," he said. "That's Margaret."

"Margaret," said the man, and, after a moment, planted a hand on either side of Jimmy's body and pushed himself to his feet. He wiped the sweat out of his eyes, bent and offered his hand.

Jimmy took it. His left eye was already swollen shut, and he thought that one of his cheekbones might be broken. He swayed for a moment, waiting for the dizziness to pass. "Can I offer you some brandy?" he said, spitting out a tooth. "On the house, of course."

The man's name was Patrick Cramer. He'd moved to New York with his wife a year before the plague, and was on his way back to Florida now.

"New York was my wife's idea," he said. "She wanted the kids to grow up in a city. Museums and plays and culture and shit. But we never got around to any of that, so it was just a really expensive place to live in a really small apartment."

They were sitting outside the café, all of them. Margaret had begun screaming during the night, so Jimmy gave her a couple of doses of morphine, which had done wonders. Even though it was only temporary, he was glad to see her better, smiling, her face a lovely echo of what it had been before the plague.

Jimmy had gone scavenging the day before, and came back with two more lawn chairs and a bag of beef jerky, teriyaki-flavored. They were eating the jerky now, Jimmy tearing it into thin strips for Margaret to swallow. She couldn't chew very well anymore; her teeth were coming loose, swimming uncertainly in the pink soup of her gums.

"I went to New York City once," said Jimmy. "I was seventeen. We were going to look for prostitutes, me and my friends."

"Did you find any?" said Margaret, smiling.

Jimmy nodded. "Lots of them. Big ones and small ones, fat ones and thin ones."

Margaret laughed. "They sound like they're from Dr. Seuss."

"Horton Humps a Whore," said Patrick.

"I chickened out, though. I went to a diner and waited for my friends to get done. That's where I met my wife."

"I have to tell you, Jimmy," said Margaret, still smiling, "that isn't the most romantic story I've ever heard."

"'I met my wife that night I couldn't find any hookers,'" said Patrick, and chuckled quietly to himself. The wagon with his children in it was parked close by, under a cloud of flies.

Jimmy said: "For me, the best thing about New York was the crowds. Lots of people don't like that, the crush, but I loved it. It's hard to be alone in New York."

Patrick snorted. "Easy to be lonely, though."

"Oh, you can be lonely anywhere. I'd rather be lonely in a crowd." He squinted off into the distance. "I liked the hot dogs, too. Is that a hawk?"

Margaret shaded her eyes and looked westward, into the diffuse light of evening. "An osprey, maybe?"

"I don't think there are any ospreys in this part of Maryland. Mostly they live around the bay."

"It's a fucking *bird*," said Patrick, without malice.

"My husband was really crazy about birds," said Margaret, still squinting at the wheeling speck in the distance. "We were going on a birding vacation next month. To California."

"Hunting?"

"No. Just looking."

Patrick stared at her. "Seriously? You drive around *looking* at birds?"

"No. My *husband* drives around looking at birds. I stay at the hotel and get massages." She glanced at Patrick, caught him rolling his eyes. "So what do you do for fun?"

"Make money."

"That's all?"

He considered. "Spending money is okay too, I guess. But it's just the cigarette afterwards, you know?"

"No," said Margaret. "I don't. I *like* that cigarette."

"They'll kill you," said Patrick, too quickly to stop himself.

Jimmy frowned. He'd been enjoying the conversation, but he didn't much like the uncomfortable silence it had become. He said: "My favorite thing about California is the sunsets."

Margaret closed her eyes, and Jimmy saw her eyelids flutter with a spasm of pain. "That's what I wanted to do most of all," she said. "Watch the sun setting over the Pacific." She paused. "My husband was on a business trip, down in Texas. Do you think the plague got down there too?"

Jimmy got up, and said: "Let me get you some more brandy." He disappeared into the café. The sounds of bottles clinking together came faintly from the open doorway.

"Man doesn't talk about what he doesn't want to talk about," said Patrick, after a moment.

Margaret managed a grin, and bundled herself tighter into her blankets, and stared off into the west.

The next morning dawned bright and crisp, alive with bird chatter. Leaves rustled gently against each other in a clean autumn breeze. Jimmy bent over Patrick and shook him gently, whispered: "Time to get up."

Patrick opened his eyes, blinked. The air inside the café

was close and warm, faintly redolent of decay. He craned his head back and glared. "Who says?"

Jimmy held up a shovel, and smiled. "Come on," he said, and went outside.

Patrick groaned, then struggled cursing out of his sleeping bag and went to the window and looked out at his children, still in their wagon, drawn up against the side of the café and covered now with a burlap tarp. When he turned back, Margaret was staring at him with wide and bleary eyes, her head turned sideways against the cot. It seemed detached, somehow, a separate thing laid down beside her body.

"Hundreds of them," she whispered. "Thousands."

Patrick blinked. "What?"

"They're made of eyes. Just mouths and eyes, floating around like newspaper. Everywhere. There's nothing they won't eat." She paused and drew a long ragged breath. "They're so hungry."

"Jesus fuck," said Patrick, a shiver crawling up his spine. He inched sidelong to the doorway and out into the open air. Jimmy was waiting for him. "I think Margaret's lost it," he said.

"Not yet," said Jimmy. He held out a shovel. "We'd better get started, while it's still cool out here."

"Started with what?"

Jimmy pointed across the northbound lanes, to a small stand of trees. "In there, I think. That's a good place."

"A good place for *what*?"

Jimmy cocked his head. "To bury them."

Patrick stiffened, and his gaze turned to stone. "They go in the ground when we get to Florida."

"You won't get to Florida. Florida's a long way away."

"Let me worry about that."

"But they want to finish dying."

Patrick didn't answer. A muscle worked restlessly in his jaw.

"If you were a dead person, would you want to be in a wagon right now, rotting your way down to Florida?" Jimmy shook his head. "I sure wouldn't. I'd want to be in the ground, where I'm supposed to be."

Patrick grabbed a handful of Jimmy's apron. "Shut up. Shut up or I swear to God I'll kill you."

"You're being irrational. And you're scaring away my customers."

"You don't have any customers, you fucking lunatic."

"Well *of course* I don't. There's a wagon full of dead children at my front door."

Patrick let go and stepped back, his eyes wide, and started laughing: hard, mirthless barks that erupted out of him like thick gouts of earth. He crossed his arms over his chest and held his sides and laughed. Tears spilled out the corners of his eyes. He bent over at the waist, went down on one knee, planted an arm on the ground for support. Laughing.

And then he lurched to his feet and grabbed a shovel and stepped onto the highway and swung at the windshield of the nearest car, again and again. When the windshield shattered, he pounded the hood into a warren of dented canyons, and struck off a rearview mirror with the thin of the shovel blade, then swung the flat against the driver's side window. The car's alarm sounded, a bleating horn that rose from a mild whoop to a stuttering scream. He tore open the hood and started on the engine. The alarm cut off.

Jimmy watched the birds while the car died beside him. Many of them were drab and uninteresting, but there were a few blue jays and robins, snatches of color fluttering between the vehicles, picking at what remained of the desiccated bodies inside. Before the plague, he'd never thought much about birds, except when they crapped on his car, and those had been uncharitable thoughts.

Finally, Patrick threw down his shovel and staggered back. The car was a crumpled, shattered nightmare image of itself, sitting dead and canted in the center of a halo of broken glass. He collapsed heavily on the tarmac, slumped forward, breathing hard, head sunk into the hollow of his shoulders.

Jimmy picked up the shovel and held it out to him. "It's getting late."

"It's the boy's birthday today," said Patrick, quietly.

"Dead people don't have birthdays. Only alive people."

Patrick looked up. "You're a fucking monster, you know that?" But he said it without conviction, or heat, and a moment later took the shovel.

They steered the wagon between the rows of frozen traffic, to the opposite verge. The trees in the cluster Jimmy had chosen were denuded and emaciated, and managed to throw only a patchwork skein of shade on the earth beneath them. Three plywood headstones poked out of the ground, like numbered chits from an ancient cash register. They said: *Audrey, Frances, Kevin.*

"Someone's already here," said Patrick.

"There's room," said Jimmy, and plunged his shovel into the earth, stepped on the blade to drive it down.

"Aren't you curious? About who these people are?"

"No." He levered out a clod of dirt. "I know who they are."

Patrick waited, but Jimmy had nothing more to say on the subject, so he bent to the work.

* * *

Two hours later, they had a broad, short, deep grave. Patrick threw down his shovel and wiped the sweat out of his eyes and went to the wagon and drew off the tarp. The little girl stared blindly up at him with red, swollen eyes. He lifted her, then dropped to his knees and lowered her gently into the hole. Laid her legs straight, crossed her arms over her chest, smoothed the hair away from her face. Then he did the same for the boy. As if he were putting them to bed.

"Do you want to say something?" said Jimmy, after a short silence.

"Like what?"

"Like a prayer, maybe."

"I don't pray anymore," said Patrick, and he began to cry, quietly.

"I prayed," said Jimmy. "When I buried Frances, I said, 'Please God give her the pony she always wanted.' And when I buried Kevin, I said, 'Please God let him play with boys his own age,' because he didn't get to do that much when he was alive. And when I buried my wife, I said, 'I'll miss you forever.' Which wasn't a prayer, I guess." He paused, considering. "Well, maybe it was a prayer to her."

They stood for a while. Patrick said: "Go away, Jimmy."

"Okay. Just call me when you're ready." Jimmy put down the shovel and stepped out of the circle of trees and wandered for a while between the cars until he found a cache of magazines in the back of an old Nissan. He climbed onto the roof of a nearby van and lay down on his back and opened a *Reader's Digest*.

He was just finishing an article about the many benefits of fiber when he heard the sounds of labor from the copse: the hiss of a shovel, the dry skitter of falling dirt. He put down the *Reader's Digest* and looked up at the sun, just cresting the apex of its arc, then down at the river of cars that stretched southbound down 95, into the day's bright and empty horizon.

Margaret batted at the air. Her left eye had darkened into an angry shade of purple, nearly black. Her skin was white and marbled with capillaries that stood out against the pallor like a skeletal roadmap. Her hair was falling out in clumps, exposing patches of white scalp.

Jimmy caught up her hands and held them. He said: "Nothing you're seeing is real."

"They're eating me." She spoke in a cracked, guttural whisper. "They won't stop eating me."

"No they're not. Come on, I have something to show you." He knelt and put one arm under her back, the other in the joint of her knees, and lifted her. She was fragile as a bird, and weighed nothing at all. A papier-mâché doll of a woman.

The air outside had turned chilly. The sun hung just over the tops of the trees, red and purplish, tinting the sky in fading orange strata. Jimmy climbed onto the highway and made for the van he'd sunned himself on earlier, moving quickly. Patrick was waiting on the roof. He handed her up, then scrambled after.

"You should leave her alone," said Patrick, his lips pursed in a prim expression of disapproval that seemed wildly out of place on his broad, rough-hewn features. But he helped ease her into the low beach chair they'd brought up earlier.

Jimmy knelt down and shook her, gently. "Time to wake up, Margaret."

Margaret let her head loll to the side. Her good eye,

pink now, rolled toward him. "You're on fire," she said.

"I'm not on fire. Wake up now. There isn't much time."

But she shook her head, and kept shaking it, a gesture that shaded from refusal to anger to despair. Jimmy put his hands on either side of her head, steadying it, and brought his face close to hers and waited until her darting eyes slowed and found his.

"Good," said Jimmy. He swung around to sit beside her, draped an arm over her shoulder, and pointed at the cars below, a frozen river of metal and glass flowing endlessly southward. "Now watch."

Patrick frowned and shook his head, said something, but Jimmy wasn't listening. He was staring westward, at the setting sun. As he watched, its lip touched the top of the treeline and spread instantly across, limning the rich dusky greens in red and gold. He turned back to the road, and said: "Okay, here it comes."

A wash of brilliance exploded up out of the highway, the slant of the sunlight reflecting up from thousands of sloped windshields, and suddenly the road below them was a sparkling, blinding sheen of narrow white light, hemmed in by the trees on either side. A brilliant path laid suddenly down on the surface of the world, plunging southward into the heart of the far horizon.

Margaret caught her breath, and whispered: "Where are we?"

"We're in California," said Jimmy.

Her hand found his, grasped it tightly. Her breathing eased, and her tensed, knotted body began to relax.

"Oh, Nabil," she said at last. "It's beautiful."

"Of course it is," said Jimmy.

They sat watching until the sun dropped below the

trees, and when Margaret closed her eyes Jimmy tucked the blanket about her shoulders and kissed her gently on her forehead. "Goodbye, Margaret," he said.

They buried her the next day, in the graveyard copse, beside the drawing of her husband. Jimmy said a few words when they were done, and then, after a moment's silence, they crossed the highway and settled into their lawn chairs.

"I'm thinking tomorrow we should go into town and pick up some Cheerios," said Jimmy. "Cheerios don't go bad, ever. You can't kill Cheerios. They're the cockroach of breakfast cereals."

"I'm leaving tomorrow," said Patrick.

Jimmy looked over. "Really? Where are you going?"

"Down to Florida. I've got family down there." He shrugged. "I'm immune to this fucking thing, and I'm not the only one with my genes."

Jimmy nodded. "It would be nice if you stayed, though."

"You should come with me, man. There's nothing here for you."

"There's my café. And there was Margaret, and there was you."

"That's over now."

"*That* is, sure."

They lapsed into silence, and watched the birds wheel and dance over the dead rows of cars.

The next day, Jimmy found a big hiker's backpack and stuffed it with donuts and beef jerky and a two-liter Coke bottle filled with fresh creek water. "Be careful," he said, handing the pack over. "Stay near the highway. Sleep inside cars at night. Wild things are starting to come out, now that we're gone."

Patrick nodded. "Thanks."

"Come back and visit if you can. We're always open."

Patrick grinned. "It's been a pleasure, Jimmy," he said. They shook hands and he turned away, moving down the shoulder, southward.

Jimmy watched him disappear into the early morning haze, then went back into the café and tidied up a bit. He took Margaret's sheets off the cot and burned them in a little pyre. He rubbed the window clean, swept the floor, polished the table. Then went outside and settled into his lawn chair, and waited.

Four days later, a stuttering, puttering sound came down off the highway. He jumped to his feet and ran up, peering north. A scooter was winding its way through the cars, dragging a small makeshift wagon behind it. An Indian woman sat hunched over the handlebars, navigating carefully. The man in the seat behind her lolled against her back. His skin was pocked and white, his eyes vermillion.

They were very close before the woman saw him. She started and braked hard, and the sharp squeal of her tires pierced the morning's stillness like a needle. A small boy with tousled hair and large round eyes popped his head up from the wagon, and said: "Are we there yet, Mommy?"

The woman clambered carefully out of her seat, then turned to catch the man behind her, who was listing hard to the side. Jimmy rushed over and took his other arm, and together they eased him onto the street.

"Thank you," said the woman, warily. The boy clambered out of his wagon and hid behind her, peeking shyly up past her skirts.

The sky was a soft shade of blue, the sunlight bright and crisp. A breeze blew through the cars, carrying with it the stench of decay, the bouquet of morning. Jimmy smiled. "Welcome to Jimmy's Roadside Café," he said. "I'm Jimmy."

THE ELEPHANTS OF POZNAN

ORSON SCOTT CARD

In the heart of old Poznan, the capital of Great Poland since ancient times, there is a public square called Rynek Glowny. The houses around it aren't as lovely as those of Krakow, but they have been charmingly painted and there is a faded graciousness that wins the heart. The plaza came through World War II more or less intact, but the Communist government apparently could not bear the thought of so much wasted space. What use did it have? Public squares were for public demonstrations, and once the Communists had seized control on behalf of the people, public demonstrations would never be needed again. So out in the middle of the square they built a squat, ugly building in a brutally modern style. It sucked the life out of the place. You had to stand with your back to it in order to truly enjoy the square.

But we'd all seen the ugly building for so many years that we hardly noticed it anymore, except to apologize to visitors, ruefully remember the bad old days of

Communism, and appreciate the irony that the occupants of such a tasteless building should include a restaurant, a bookshop, and an art gallery. And when the plague came and the city was so cruelly and suddenly emptied, those of us who could not let go of Poznan, who could not bear to eke out the last of our lives in the countryside, drifted to the old heart of the city and took up residence in the houses surrounding the square. As time passed, even the ugly building became part of the beauty of the place, for it had been part of the old crowded city now lost forever. Just as the toilets with little altars for the perusal of one's excrement reminded us of the many decades of German overlordship, so this building was also a part of our past, and now, by its sheer persistence among us, a part of ourselves. If we could venerate the bones and other bodily parts of dead saints, couldn't we also find holiness of a kind even in this vile thing? It was a relic of a time when we thought we were suffering, but to which we now would gladly return, just to hear schoolchildren again in the streets, just to see the flower shop once more selling the bright excesses of overcopious nature, spots of vivid color to show us that Poland was not, by nature, grey.

Into this square came the elephants, a group of males, making their way in what seemed a relentless silence, except that a trembling of the windows told us that they were speaking to each other in infrasound, low notes that the human ear could not hear, but the human hand could feel on glass. Of course we had all seen elephants for years on our forays out into the gardens of suburban Poznan— clans of females and their children following a matriarch, gangs of mature males hanging out to kill time until one of them went into musth and set off in search of the nearest estrous female. We speculated at first about where they came from, whether their forebears had escaped from a zoo or a circus during the plague. But soon we realized that their numbers were far too great to be accounted for that way. Too many different clans had been seen. On Radio Day we learned, from those few stations that still bothered, that the elephants had come down the Nile, swum the Suez, swarmed through Palestine and Syria and Armenia, crossed the Caucasus, and now fed in the lush wheat pastures of Ukraine, bathed in the streams of Belarus, and stood trumpeting on the shores of Estonia and Pomerania, calling out to some god of the sea, demanding passage to lands as yet unpossessed by the great stumpy feet, the probing noses, the piercing ivory, and the deep thrumming music of the new rulers of the world.

Why should they not rule it? We were only relics ourselves, we who had had the misfortune of surviving the plague. Out of every hundred thousand, only fifty or a hundred had survived. And as we scavenged in the ruins, as we bulldozed earth over the corpses we dragged from the areas where we meant to live, as we struggled to learn how to keep a generator or two running, a truck here and there, the radios we used only once a week, then once a month, then once a year, we gradually came to realize that there would be no more children. No one conceived. No one bore. The disease had sterilized us, almost all. There would be no recovery from this plague. Our extinction had not required a celestial missile to shatter the earth and darken the sky for a year; no other species shared our doom with us. We had been taken out surgically, precisely, thoroughly, a tumor removed with a delicate viral hand.

So we did not begrudge the elephants their possession

of the fields and the forests. The males could knock down trees to show their strength; there was no owner to demand that animal control officers come and dispose of the rampaging beasts. The females could gather their children into barns and stables against the winter blast, and no owner would evict them; only the crumbling bones and strands of hairy flesh showed where horses and cattle had starved to death when their masters died too quickly to think of setting them free from their stalls and pens.

Why, though, had these males come into the city? There was nothing for them to eat. There was nothing for us to eat; when our bicycles gave out and we could cobble together no more makeshift carts, we would have to leave the city ourselves and live closer to the food that we gathered from untended fields. Why would the elephants bother with such a ruin? Curiosity, perhaps. Soon they would see that there was nothing here for them, and move on.

We found ourselves growing impatient as the hours passed, and the days, and still we kept encountering them on the city streets. Didn't they understand that we lived in the heart of Poznan specifically because we wanted a human place? Didn't they feel our resentment of their trespass? All the rest of Earth is yours; can you not leave undesecrated these crypts we built for ourselves in the days of our glory?

Gradually it dawned on us—dawned on me, actually, but the others realized I was right—that the elephants had come, not to explore Poznan, but to observe us. I would pedal my bicycle and glance down a cross street to see an elephant lumbering along on a parallel path; I would turn, and see him behind me, and feel that shuddering in my breastbone, in my forehead, that told me they were speaking to each other, and soon another elephant would be shadowing me, seeing where I went, watching what I did, following me home.

Why were they interested in us? Humans were no longer killing them for their ivory. The world was theirs. We were going to die—I, who was only seven years old when the plague came, am now past thirty, and many of the older survivors are already, if not at death's door, then studying the travel brochures and making reservations, their Bibles open and their rosaries in hand. Were these males here as scientists, to watch the last of the humans, to study our death ways, to record the moment of our extinction so that the elephants would remember how we died with only a whimper, or less than that, a whisper, a sigh, a sidelong glance at God?

I had to know. For myself, for my own satisfaction. If I found the truth, whom else would I tell it to, and for what purpose? They would only die as I would die, taking memory with them into the fire, into the ash, into the dust. I couldn't get any of the others to care about the questions that preyed upon me. What do the elephants want from us? Why do they follow us?

Leave it alone, Lukasz, they said to me. Isn't it enough that they don't bother us?

And I answered with the most perplexing question of all, to me at least. Why elephants? The other wild animals that roamed the open country were the ones one might expect to see: The packs of dogs gone wild, interbreeding back to mongrel wolfhood; the herds of cattle, breeding back to hardiness, and of horses, quick and free and uninterested in being tamed. The companions of man, the servants and slaves of man, now masterless, now free. Unshorn sheep.

Unmilked goats. Sudden-leaping housecats. Scrawny wild chickens hiding from ever-vigilant hawks. Ill-tempered pigs rooting in the woods, the boars making short work of dogs that grew too bold. That was the wildlife of Europe. No other animals from Africa had made the journey north. Only the elephants, and not just from Africa—the elephants of India were roaming the Orient, and on the most recent Radio Day we learned, through messages relayed many times, that they had somehow crossed the Bering Strait and were now, in ever greater numbers, grazing the prairies of America, small-eared cousins to the great-canopied beasts that now shadowed us on the streets of Poznan. I pictured them swimming, or piling onto boats that some last human pilot guided for them onto the Stygian shore.

They had inherited the Earth, and were bent on surveying their new domain.

So I took to spending my days in the library, reading all I could about elephants, and then about all the processes of life, all the passages of history, trying to understand not only them but ourselves, and what had happened to us, and what our cities might mean to them, our houses, our streets, our rusting cars, our collapsing bridges, our sorry cemetery mounds where winter brought fresh crops of human bone to the surface, white stubble on a fallow field. I write this now because I think I know the answers, or at least have found guesses that ring true to me, though I also know they might be nothing more than a man hungry for meanings inventing them where they don't exist. Arguably, all meanings are invented anyway; and since I have no one to please but myself, and no one to read this who will care, except perhaps one, then I may write as I please, and think as I please, and reread this whenever I can bear it.

They made no effort to follow me inside the library. What good would it do them? Clever as they were with their inquisitive trunks, I could imagine them being deft enough to turn pages without tearing them. But what would the markings on the pages mean to them? Elephants sang their literature to each other in octaves we humans could not hear. Their science was the science of the temporal gland, the probing nose. They observed, but—or so I thought—did not experiment.

I did learn enough to warn the others before the first of the males went into musth. When you see one of them acting agitated, when his temporal glands pour out a steady black streak down his cheeks, when the other males are shy of him and give him room, then we must do the same, staying out of his way, not meeting his gaze. Let him pass. The city is his, wherever he wants to go. He won't stay here long, in musth. He must go and find a female then, and they were all outside in the open fields. He would give his deep rumbling call and pour out his lusty scent into the air and dribble musky fluid onto the ground where every other elephant could smell it and know: This way passed a male bent on making babies. This way passed God, looking for the Holy Virgin.

So we studied each other, and avoided offending each other, and grew used to each other's ways, the elephants and the fifty remaining residents of Poznan.

And then one day they began to push.

The males all gathered in the public square. We, too, gossiping to each other that something important was going to happen, gathered in our houses and leaned at our windows to watch.

They wandered aimlessly through the square, eleven of

them—the twelve apostles, I thought, sans Iscariot—until noon made the smallest shadows. Then, as if of one mind, they surrounded the ugly old Communist building, facing it. When all were in place, they moved forward, slowly, each bull resting his massive brow against the miserable façade. Then, slowly, each began to tense his muscles, to shift his weight, to make little adjustments, to plant his feet, and then to push with greater and greater strength against the wall.

They're trying to push it down, I realized. And so did the others, all of us calling out to each other in our high-pitched human voices.

They're critics of architecture!

They've come to beautify Poznan!

We began to address the elephants with our calls, as if they were our football team, as if the plaza were a playing field. We cheered them, laughed in approval, shouted encouragement, placed meaningless bets about whether they could actually break through the walls.

Then, abruptly, I was no longer part of the playfulness. For without meaning to, I changed perspective suddenly, and saw us as the elephants must have seen us. This was Africa after all, and we were the primates perched in the trees, hooting and screeching at the giants, unaware of our own insignificance, or at least unbothered by it.

When I pulled my head back inside my window, I was filled with grief, though at that moment I could not have told you why. I thought at first it was because we humans were so diminished, reduced to chattering from safe perches. But then I realized that the human race had always been the same, had never risen, really, from our primate ways. No, what I was grieving for was that ugly old building, that relic of noble dreams gone sour. I had never lived under Communism, had only heard the stories of the Russian overlords and the Polish Communists who claimed to be fulfilling the will of the masses and perhaps, sometimes, believed their own propaganda—so my father told me, and I had no reason to doubt him. When the Communists decided what was good and what was bad, they acted as rigidly as any Puritan. Aesthetic concerns in architecture led to wasteful overspending of the labor of the working class; therefore, the ugliness of all new buildings was a badge of virtue. We human beings had reinvented ourselves, Homo sovieticus, Homo coprofabricus, or whatever the scientific name would be. A new species that never guessed how quickly it would be extinct.

The elephants would keep pushing until the walls came down—I knew that. Intransigence was built into the elephants' shoulders the way screeching and chattering were built into the primate mouth. And even though the other humans were cheering them, egging them on, I was sad. No, wistful. If we had really wanted that ugly building taken down, we knew where the dynamite was kept, we could have blown it out of existence. Elephants are mighty and strong, as beasts go, but when it comes to destruction, their foreheads are no match for the explosives in the locked sheds at the construction sites of buildings that will never be finished.

We don't need you to take it down, you meddlers, I wanted to say. We built it, we humans. It's ours. What right have you to decide which artifacts should stand, and which should fall?

The fascination of it was irresistible, though. I couldn't stay away from the window for long. I had to check, again, again, to see if they were making any progress, to see if some crack had appeared. The beasts had enormous patience, pushing and pushing until their shadows were swallowed up in the shade of the buildings as the sun headed out past Germany, past France, out to the Atlantic to be plunged steaming into the sea of night. That was the clock they lived by, these elephants; they had put in their day's work, and now they wandered off, heading out of the city as they did most nights, to eat and drink and sleep in some more hospitable place.

The next morning they were back, earlier this time, and formed their circle much more quickly, and pushed again. The betting among us began in earnest, then. Would they succeed? Would they give up? How long till the first crack? How long till a wall fell? We had nothing of value to bet; or rather, we had everything: we had inherited the city from the dead, so that we could bet enormous sums of money and pay in cash or diamonds if we wanted to, but when we wagered we never bothered to carry such useless objects from one house to another. Enough to say who won and who lost. The only reason we had such wealth was because the dead had left it all behind. If they didn't value it any more than that, what was it worth to us, except as counters in games of chance?

There was unguessed-at meaning in their pushing after all. For on the third day of the elephants' pushing—still to no visible effect—Arek came home to Poznan. Arek, whom I had named for my father. Arek, who dashed my last hope. Arek, who killed my wife.

For years after the plague, no children were conceived. From Berlin, where one of the survivors was a doctor, we learned that when the plague was new and they were still trying to study it, the medical researchers determined that the virus rooted in the reproductive systems of men and women, specifically attacking their bodies where the human seed was made. This was not how the plague did its slaughtering, but it guaranteed that the few survivors would be sterile. The message left us in despair.

But I was young, and though I had seen more death before I turned ten than I would ordinarily have seen even if I devoted my whole life to watching American movies, my hope was still undashable. Or rather, my body's hope, which in my teens was much stronger than my reason. As the people from the hinterlands and smaller towns came seeking human company, Poznan became a gathering place. In those days we lived on the outskirts of the city, in a place where we could actively farm, before we realized that farming was redundant with miles and miles of fields and gardens reseeding themselves faster than we could harvest them. So I was hoeing the turnips—the kind of task the adults gratefully left to my strong and flexible young arms and legs—when Hilde and her family came to town in a horse-drawn wagon.

It wasn't Hilde herself that I saw at first, it was the miracle of seeing a family. At first, of course, we assumed they were a nonce family, clinging to each other because no one else in their area survived. But no, no, they looked like each other, that miracle of resemblance that told us all that they were genetically connected. And soon we learned that yes, they were a mother, a father, a daughter, all of whom had survived the plague. They knew it was wrong of them to grieve for the two sons and three daughters who died, for they had not lost everyone they loved, as all the rest of us had done. There was something in them that was stronger than the disease. And Hilde, a plump nordic blonde, soon became beautiful to all of us, because we knew that if any woman had a viable ovum left, it would be her.

She and her parents understood that her womb, if it was not barren, could not belong to her alone, and that her only hope of continuing our poor, weak species was to find a mate whose body still could spew forth living sperm. She had been sexually immature when the plague came, but now was womanly, ready to bear if bear she could. One man at a time would husband her, for three months; then a month of solitude, and then the next man's turn to try. That way there would be no doubt of fatherhood if she conceived; he would be her husband, to father more children on her. She agreed to this because there was no other hope.

I was third to try, at fifteen a frightened child myself, approaching her like the temple priestess that she was, begging the god to choose me, to let life come into her from me. She was sweet and patient, and told no one how clumsy I was. I liked her, but did not yet love her, for she was still a stranger to me. I could mate with her, but not speak to her—or at least not be understood, for she came from a German-speaking area in the westernmost mountains, and had but little Polish—though more of Polish than I had of German.

The second month she had no period, and the third, and the fourth. She was kept away from me, from all men, until in the fifth month she asked for me. "You are half of this miracle," she said in halting Polish, and from then on I was her companion. No more fieldwork for me—what if I was injured? What if I caught cold? Instead I stayed with her, taught her to speak Polish and learned to read German, more or less.

In the eighth month the doctor finally came from Berlin. He had never worked in obstetrics, but he was the best hope we had, and since no one in Berlin was pregnant, they understood what was at stake; even a half-Polish baby in Poznan was better than no more babies anywhere at all. We made him welcome; he taught us how to make beer.

The ninth month. Nothing happened. He spoke of inducing labor. We worked to get a room in the hospital powered up, the old equipment working, and he gave Hilde an ultrasound examination. He could not face us after that. "You counted wrong?" he offered, as a possibility.

No, we did not count wrong. We knew the last time she had sex with anyone—with me—and it was nine months and two weeks ago.

"The baby is not ready yet," he said. "Weeks to go. Maybe many weeks. The limb-length tells me this. The development of the face and hands."

And then the worst news. "But the head—it is very large. And strangely shaped. Not a known condition, though. I looked in the books. Not seen before, not exactly this. If it is still growing—and how can I tell, since it is already as big as an adult human head—this does not look happy for her. She cannot bear this child normally. I will have to cut the baby out."

Cut it out now, her parents said. It has been nine months.

"No," the doctor said. "If I cut now, I think that it will die. I think it has the lungs of a fetus of five months. I did not come here to abort a fetus. I came to deliver a baby."

But our daughter…

Hilde agreed with the doctor. "If he has to cut me open

anyway, there is no hurry. Wait until the baby himself thinks that he is ready."

We knew now it would be a boy, and were not glad of it. A daughter would have been better, everyone knew that. Everyone but me—I was not ready to play Lot with a daughter of mine, and I was the only man proven to have viable sperm, so I thought it was better that I would have a son and then could wander with Hilde and the boy, through all the world if need be, searching for a place where another mating had happened, where there might be a girl for him. I could imagine that future happily.

Ten months. Eleven. No woman had carried a child for so long. She could not sit up in bed now, for still it grew, and the ultrasound looked stranger and stranger. Wide hips, and eyes far apart on a face appallingly broad. The ultrasound, with its grainy, black-and-white image, made it look like a monster. This was no baby. It would never live.

Worse, it was draining the life out of Hilde. Most of what she ate went across the placenta to feed this cancerous growth inside her. She grew wan of face, weak of muscle even as her belly grew more and more mountainous. I would sit beside her and when she was tired of the book I read, I would hold her hand and talk to her of walks along the streets of the city, of my visit to Krakow when I was six, before the plague; how my father took me along as he escorted a foreign author through the city; how we ate at a country restaurant and the foreigner could not eat the floury bread and the chewy noodles and the thick lard spread. She laughed. Or, as she grew weaker, smiled. And finally, near the end, just clung to my hand and let me babble. I wanted nothing more than to have Hilde. Forget the baby. It's already dead to me, this monster. Just let me have Hilde, the time with her that a man should have with his wife, the life together in a little house, the coming home at night to her embrace, the going forth in the morning with her kiss on my lips and her blessing in my ears.

"I will take it now," said the doctor. "Perhaps the next child will be normal. But she grows too weak to delay any longer."

Her parents agreed. Hilde, also, gave consent at last. The doctor had taught me to be his nurse, and trained me by making me watch the bloody surgeries he did on hares and once on a sheep, so I would not faint at the blood when the time came to cut into my wife. For wife she was, at her insistence, married to me in a little ceremony just before she went under the anaesthetic. She knew, as did I, that the marriage was not permanent. Perhaps the community would give me one more try to make a normal child with her, but if that one, too, should fail, the rotation would begin again: three months of mating, a month fallow, until a father with truer seed was found.

What we did not understand was how very weak she had become. The human body was not designed to give itself so completely to the care of such a baby as this one. Somehow the baby was sending hormonal messages to her, the doctor said, telling her body not to bear, not to present; the cervix not to efface and open. Somehow it caused her body to drain itself, to make the muscles atrophy, the fat to disappear.

The doctor's incision was not large enough at first. Nor with the second cut. Finally, with the third, her womb lay open like the belly of a dissected frog, and at last he lifted the little monster out. He handed it to me. Almost I tossed it aside. But it opened its eyes. Babies aren't supposed to be able to do that, I know now. But it opened its eyes and looked at me. And I felt a powerful trembling, a vibration in my chest and arms. It was alive, whatever it was, and it was not in me, its father, to kill it. So I set it aside, where a couple of women washed it, and did the rituals that the doctor had prescribed—the drops into the eyes, the blood samples. I did not watch. I returned to Hilde.

I thought she was unconscious. But then the baby made a sound, and even though it was lower than a baby's mewling ought to be, she knew it was his voice, and her eyes fluttered open. "Let me see," she whispered. So I ran and took the baby from the women and brought it to her.

It was as large as a toddler, and I was loath to lay such a heavy burden on her chest. But Hilde insisted, reaching with her fingers because she could not raise her arms. I leaned over her, bearing as much of the baby's weight as I could. He sought her breast and, when she found the strength to raise a hand and guide a nipple into his mouth, he sucked mightily. It hurt her, but her face spoke of ecstasy as well as pain. "Mama loves the baby," her lips said silently.

She died as the doctor was still stitching her. He left the wound and tried to revive her, shoving the baby and me out of the way and pumping at her heart. Later, after the autopsy, he told me that her heart had been used up like all her other muscles. The child had ruled the mother, had demanded her life from her, and she had given it.

My Hilde. Till death parted us.

There was some debate on whether to feed the child, and then on whether to baptize it. In both cases, mercy and hope triumphed over fear and loathing. I wanted to oppose them, but Hilde had tried to feed the baby, and even after she was dead I did not wish to contradict her. They made me choose a name. I gave it my father's name because I could not bear to give it mine. Arkadiusz. Arek.

He weighed nearly ten kilograms at birth.

At two months he walked.

At five months his babbling noises became speech. They taught him to call me papa. And I came to him because he was, after all, my own.

Hilde's parents were gone by then. They blamed me—my bad seed—for their daughter's death. In vain did the doctor tell them that what the plague had done to me it no doubt also did to her; they knew, in their hearts, that Hilde was normal, and I was the one with the seed of monstrosity. They could not bear to look at me or at Arek, either, the killers of their last child, their beautiful little girl.

Arek walked early because his wideset legs gave him such a sturdy platform, while crawling was near impossible for him. His massive neck was strong enough to hold his wide-faced, deep-skulled head. His hands were clever, his arms long and probing. He was a font of questions. He made me teach him how to read when he was not yet two.

The two strange apertures in his head, behind the eyes, before the ears, seeped with fluid now and then. He stank sometimes, and the stench came from there. At the time we did not know what to call these things, or what they meant, for the elephants had not yet come. The whole community liked Arek, as they must always like children; they played with him, answered his questions, watched over him. But beneath the love there was a constant gnawing pain. He was our hope, but he was no hope at all. Whatever his strange condition was, it might have made him quicker than a normal child, but we knew that it could not be healthy, that like most strange children he would no doubt die before his time. And definitely, mutant that he was, he must surely be as sterile as a mule.

And then the elephants came, great shadowy shapes out in the distant fields. We marveled. We wondered. They came nearer, day by day. And Arek became quite agitated. "I hear them," he said.

Hear what? We heard nothing. They were too far off for us to hear.

"I hear them," he said again. He touched his forehead. "I hear them here." He touched his chest. "And here."

The flow from the apertures in his head increased.

He took to wandering off. We had to watch him closely. In the middle of a reading lesson, he would stand up and face the distant elephants—or face the empty horizon where they might be—and listen, rapt. "I think I understand them," Arek said. "Here's a place with good water."

All of Poland has good water now, I pointed out.

"No," he said impatiently. "It's what they said. And now they talk of one who died. They have the scent of him. The one who died." He listened more; I still heard nothing. "And me," he said. "They have the scent of me."

Elephants care nothing for you, I said.

He turned to me, his eyes awash with tears. "Take that back," he said.

Sit and do your lessons, Arek.

"What do I care what dead people say? I have no need of what they said!"

You're five years old, Arek. I know better than you what you need to know.

"Your father had to know all this," he said. "But what is it to me? What good has reading done for you?"

I tried to hold him, but at five years old he was too

strong. He ran from the room. He ran out into the field. He ran toward the elephants.

I followed him as best I could. Others joined me, calling out Arek's name. He was not swift, and we could have caught him if we were willing to tackle him like rugby players. But our goal was only to keep him safe, and so we jogged alongside him, his short and heavy legs lumbering forward, ever closer to the elephants. A matriarch and her clan, with several babies of varying sizes. We tried to stop him then, to hold him back, but by then the matriarch had noticed us, and as she approached, Arek screamed and tried more violently to get away, to run to her. She trumpeted at us, and finally, tentatively, in fear of her we set him down.

She let him embrace her trunk; he clambered upward, over her great impassive brow, and sprawled his body across the top of her head. Her trunk reached up to him; I feared that she would sweep him from her head like lint. Instead she touched the leaking aperture on his right cheek, then brought the tip of her trunk down to her mouth. To smell and taste it.

That was when I realized: The matriarch, too, had an aperture between eye and ear, a leaking stinkhole. When I did my reading, I learned that it was the temporal gland. The elephants had it, and so did my son.

Neither Hilde nor I was elephantine. Nor was there any logical way, given the little science that I knew, for me to explain how a gland that only elephants had should suddenly show up on a human child. It wasn't just the temporal glands, either. As he sat perched atop the matriarch, I could see how closely his brow resembled hers. No great flapping ears, no abnormality of nose, and his eyes were still binocular, not side-aimed like the elephant's. Yet there was no mistaking how his forehead was a smaller echo of her own.

He has been waiting for them, I murmured.

And then I thought, but did not say: They came in search of him.

He would not go home with me. One by one the others drifted back to our village, some returning to bring me food and offer food to Arek. But he was busy riding on the matriarch, and playing with the babies, always under the watchful gaze of the mothers, so that no harm would come to him. He made a game of running up the trunks and turning somersaults onto an elephant's back. He swung on tusks. He rode them like horses, he climbed them like trees, and he listened to them like gods.

After two days they moved on. I tried to follow. The matriarch picked me up and put me back. Three times she did it before I finally acquiesced. Arek was their child now. They had adopted him, he had adopted them. Whatever music they were making, he heard it and loved it. The pied piper had come to lead away our only son, our strange inhuman child, the only hope we had.

From that day I did not see him, until the twelfth bull elephant arrived with Arek astride his neck.

Full-grown Arek—just a little taller, I estimated, than his father, but built like a tractor, with massive legs and arms, and a neck that made his enormous head look almost natural. "Father!" he cried. "Father!" He had not seen me at the window. I wanted to hide from him. He must be fifteen now. The age I was when I met Hilde. I had put him from my mind and heart, as I had already done with my parents, and my baby sister, whom I had left behind unburied when I was too hungry to wait any longer for them to wake again, for God to raise them up from their sickbeds. Of all those I had lost, why was he the one that could return? For a moment I hated him, though I knew that it was not his fault.

He was their child anyway, not mine. I could see that now. Anyone could see it. His skin was even filthy grey like theirs.

He didn't see me. He slid down the brow and trunk of the bull he was riding and watched as his steed—his companion? His master?—took its place in the circle that pushed against the walls of the ugly building. He walked around them, a wide circle, looking up at the windows on the opposite side of the square. But it was not by sight that he found me. It was when he was directly under my window, looking the other way, that he stopped, and turned, and looked up at me, and smiled. "Father," he said. "I have seen the world!"

I did not want him to call me father. Those were his fathers, those bull elephants. Not me. I was the bearer of the seed, its depositor, but the seed itself had been planted in both Hilde and me by the plague. Born in Africa and carried to the world on airplanes, virulent and devastating, the plague was no accident of nature. Paranoid as it sounded even to myself, I had the evidence of Arek's elephantinism to bolster what I knew but could not prove. Somehow in the kettle of the temporal gland, the elephants created this new version of man, and sent the seed out into the world, carried by a virus. They had judged us, these beasts, and found us wanting. Perhaps the decision was born as grieving elephants gathered around the corpses of their kinfolk, slain and shorn of their tusks. Perhaps the decision came from the shrinking land and the drying earth. Perhaps it was their plan all along, from the time they made us until they finally were done with us.

For in the darkness of the library, as I moved along the table, keeping my yellowing books always in the slant of light from the window, I had conjured up a picture of the world. The elephants, the true gods of antiquity. They had reached the limit of what they could do with their prehensile noses. What was needed now was hands, so virus by virus, seed by seed, they swept away one species and replaced it with another, building and improving and correcting their mistakes. There was plenty of the primate left in us: the baboon, the chimpanzee. But more and more of the elephant as well: the kindness, the utter lack of warfare, the benevolent society of women, the lonely wandering harmless helpful men, and the absolute sanctity of the children of the tribe. Primate and elephant, always at war within us. We could see the kinship between us and the apes, but failed to see how the high-breasted elephant could possibly also be our kind.

Only now, with Arek, could the convergence at last be seen. They had made at last an elephant with hands, a clever toolmaker who could hear the voices of the gods.

I thought of the bulldancers of Crete, and then of Arek running up the trunks of elephants and somersaulting on their heads. The mastodons and mammoths were all gone, and the elephants were south of the Mediterranean; but they were not forgotten. In human memory, we were supposed to dance with joy upon the horns and head of a great loving beast, our father, our maker. Our prophets were the ones who heard the voice of God, not in the tempest, but in the silent thrumming, the still small voice of infrasound, carried through stone and earth as easily as through the air. On the mountain they heard the voice of God, teaching us how to subdue the primate and become the sons of God, the giants on the earth. For the sons of God did marry the daughters of men. We remembered that God was above us, but thought that meant he was above the sky. And so my speculation and imagining led me to this mad twisting of the scripture of my childhood—and no less of the science and history in the library. What were the Neanderthals? Why did they disappear? Was there a plague one day, carried wherever the new-made Cro-Magnon wandered? And did the Neanderthals understand what their woolly mammoth deities had done to them? Here was their ironic vengeance: It was the new, godmade men, the chosen people, who hunted the mammoths and the mastodons to extinction, who bowed the elephants of India to slavery and turned the elephants of Africa into a vast wandering ivory orchard. We men of Cro-Magnon descent, we thought we were the pinnacle. But when God told us to be perfect, as he was perfect, we failed him, and he had to try again. This time it was no flood that swept our souls away. And any rainbow we might see would be a lie.

I spoke of this to no one—I needed human company too much to give them reason to think me mad. Elephants as gods? As God himself? Sacrilege. Heresy. Madness. Evil. Nor was I sure of it myself; indeed, most days, most hours of the day, I mocked my own ideas. But I write them here, because they might be true, and if someday these words are read, and I was right, then you'll hear my warning: You who read this, you are not the last and best, any more than we were. There is always another step higher up the ladder, and a helpful trunk to lift you upward on your way, or dash you to the ground if you should fail.

Arek called me father, and I was not his father. But he came from Hilde's body; she gave her life to give him breath, and loved him, ugly and misshapen as he was, as she held him to her empty breasts while her heart pushed the last few liters of blood through her worn-out body. Not a drop of pap came from her into his mouth. He had already sucked her dry. But for that moment she loved him. And for her sake—and for his, at first, I will be honest here—I tried to treat him well, to teach him and provide for him and protect him as best I could. But at five years of age they took him and he was raised by elephants. In what sense now was he my son?

"Father," he said to me again. "Don't be afraid. It's only me, your boy, Arek."

I'm not afraid, I almost said.

But he would know it was a lie. He could smell a lie on me. Silence was my refuge.

I left my room and went down the stairs to the level of the street. I came blinking into the sunlight. He held out a hand to me. His legs were even stockier now; whenever he stood still, he looked as planted as a pair of old trees. He was taller than I am, and I am tall. "Father," he said. "I want them to meet you. I told them all the things you taught me."

They already know me, I wanted to say. They've been following me for years. They know when and where I eat and sleep and pee. They know all they want to know of me, and I want nothing at all from them, so...

So I followed him anyway, feeling my hand in his, the

firm kind grasp, the springy rolling rhythm of his walk. I knew that he could keep walking forever on those legs. He led me to the new elephant, the one he had arrived with. He bade me stand there as the trunk took samples of my scent for tasting, as one great eye looked down on me, the all-seeing eye. Not a word did I say. Not a question did I ask.

Until I felt the thrumming, strong now, so powerful that it took my breath away, it shook my chest so strongly.

"Did you hear him, Father?" asked my son.

I nodded.

"But did you understand?"

I shook my head.

"He says you understand," said Arek, puzzled. "But you say that you don't."

At last I spoke: I understand nothing.

The elephant thrummed out again.

"You understand but do not know you understand," said Arek. "You're not a prophet."

The elephant had made me tremble, but it was Arek's word that made me stumble. Not a prophet. And you are, my son?

"I am," said Arek, "because I hear what he says and can turn it into language for the rest of you. I thought you could understand him, too, because he said you could."

The elephant was right. I did understand. My mad guesses were right, or somewhat right, or at least not utterly wrong. But I said nothing of this to Arek.

"But now I see you do understand," said Arek, nodding, content.

His temporal glands were dripping, the fluid falling onto his naked chest. He wore trousers, though. Old polyester ones, the kind that cannot rot or fade, the kind that will outlast the end of the universe. He saw me looking, and again supposed that I had understood something.

"You're right," he said. "I've had it before. Only lightly, though. And it did me no good." He smiled ruefully. "I've seen the world, but none like me."

Had what before?

"The dripping time. The madness."

Musth, I said.

"Yes," he answered. He touched the stream of fluid on his cheek, then streaked it on my cheek. "It takes a special woman to bear my child."

What if there isn't one?

"There is," he said. "That's why I came here."

There's no one here like you.

"Not yet," he said. "And besides, I had this gift to give you."

What gift?

He gestured, as if I should have understood all along. The building that the elephants were pushing at. "You always told me how much you hated this building. How ugly it was. I wanted to give you something when I came again, but I couldn't think of anything I could do for you. Except for this."

At his words, the elephants grunted and bellowed, and now it was clear that all their pushing before had been preliminary to this, as they braced themselves and rammed, all at once, again and again. Now the building shuddered. Now the façade cracked. Now the walls buckled.

Quickly Arek drew me back, out of danger. The elephants, too, retreated, as the walls caved in, the roof collapsed. Dust blew out of the place like smoke, blinding me for a moment, till tears could clear my vision.

No silence now, no infrasound. The bulls gave voice, a great triumphant fanfare.

And now the families came: the matriarch, the other females, their babies, their children. Into the square, now unobstructed except for the rubble pile, they came by the dozens. There must be three clans here, I thought. Four. Five. Trumpeting. Triumphant.

All this, because they knocked down a building?

No. The fall of the building was the gift to the father. It was the signal for the real festivities to begin.

"I made them bring her here," said Arek. "You're my family, and these are my friends." He indicated the people leaning out of the windows over the square. "Isn't that what weddings are for?"

The elephants made way for one last arrival. An Indian elephant lumbered into the square, trunk upraised, trumpeting. It progressed in stately fashion to the place where Arek and I were standing. On its back sat Arek's bride-to-be. At first glance she was human, boldly and charmingly nude. But under the shock of thick, straight hair her head was, if anything, larger than Arek's, and her legs were set so wide that she seemed to straddle the elephant's neck the way a woman of my species might bestride a horse. Down the forehead and the trunk of the beast she slid, pausing only to stand playfully upon the tusks, then jump lightly to the ground. Those legs, those hips—she clearly had the strength to carry a baby as large as Arek had been for the entire year. But wide as her body was, could such a head pass through the birth canal?

Because she was naked, the answer was before my eyes. The entrance to her birth canal was not between her thighs, but in a pouch of skin that drooped from the base of her abdomen; the opening was in front of the pubis. No longer would the pelvic circle limit the size of a baby's head. She would not have to be cut open to give birth.

Arek held out his hand. She smiled at him. And in that smile, she became almost human to me. It was the shy smile of the bride, the smile that Hilde had given me when she was pregnant, before we knew it was no human child she carried.

"She's in heat," said Arek. "And I'm… in musth. You have no idea how crazy it makes me."

He didn't sound crazy, or act it, either. Instead he had the poise of a king, the easy confidence of an elephant. At the touch of her hand, his temporal glands gave forth such a flow that I could hear the fluid dripping onto the stones of the plaza. But otherwise he betrayed no eagerness.

"I don't know how it's done," said Arek. "Marriage, I mean. They said I should marry as humans do. With words."

I remembered the words that had been said for me and Hilde. As best I could, I said them now. The girl did not understand. Her eyes, I saw now, had the epicanthic fold—how far had they brought her? Was she the only one? Were there only these two in all the world? Is that how close they came to the edge of killing us all, of ending the whole experiment?

I said the words, and she shaped the answers. But I could tell that it didn't matter to her, or to him either, that she understood not a bit of the Polish words she had to say. Below the level of audible speech, they had another kind of language. For I could see how her forehead thrummed with a tone too low for my ears to hear. But he could hear. Not words, I assumed. But communication nonetheless. The thing with speech, they'd work that out. It would still be useful to them, when communication needed to be precise. But for matters of the heart, they had the language of the elephants. The language of the gods. The Adamic tongue. The idiom God had used one time to say, Multiply and replenish the earth, and subdue it. We did the first; we did the last. Now, perhaps, this new couple in their new garden, would learn the replenishing part as well. Only a few of us lingering beasts, of us the dust of the earth, would remain, and not for long. Then the whole world would be their garden.

Today they're gone. Out of Poznan, the elephants and their new creatures, the son and daughter of the gods. My Arek and his wife, whose name he never spoke aloud to us. No doubt he has some deep and rumbling name for her that I could never hear. They will have many children. They must watch them carefully. Or perhaps this time it will be different. No stone crashed against a brother's head this time. No murder in the world. Only the peace of the elephants.

They're gone, and the rejoicing is over—for we did rejoice, because even though we know, we all know, that Arek and his bride are not of our kind, they still carry the only portion of our seed that will remain alive in the earth; better to live on in them than to die utterly, without casting seed at all.

They're gone, and now each day I go out into the square and work amid the wreckage of the building. Propping up the old façade, leaning it against a makeshift wall. Before I die, I'll have it standing again, or at least enough of it so that the square looks right. Already I have much of one wall restored, and sometimes the others come and help me, when they see I'm struggling with a section of wall too heavy or awkward for a man to raise alone.

It may have been an ugly thing, that Communist monstrosity, but it was built by humans, in a human place, and they had no right to knock it down.

THE POSTMAN
DAVID BRIN

PRELUDE: THE THIRTEEN-YEAR THAW

Chill winds still blew. Dusty snow fell. But the ancient sea was in no hurry.

The Earth had spun six thousand times since flames blossomed and cities died. Now, after sixteen circuits of the Sun, plumes of soot no longer roiled from burning forests, turning day into night.

Six thousand sunsets had come and gone—gaudy, orange, glorious with suspended dust—ever since towering, superheated funnels had punched through to the stratosphere, filling it with tiny bits of suspended rock and soil. The darkened atmosphere passed less sunlight—and it cooled.

It hardly mattered anymore what had done it—a giant meteorite, a huge volcano, or a nuclear war. Temperatures and pressures swung out of balance, and great winds blew. All over the north, a dingy snow fell, and in places even summer did not erase it.

Only the Ocean, timeless and obstinate, resistant to change, really mattered. Dark skies had come and gone. The winds pushed ocher, growling sunsets. In places, the ice grew, and the shallower seas began to sink.

But the Ocean's vote was all important, and it was not in yet.

The Earth turned. Men still struggled, here and there.

And the Ocean breathed a sigh of winter.

THE CASCADES
1

In dust and blood—with the sharp tang of terror stark in his nostrils—a man's mind will sometimes pull forth odd relevancies. After half a lifetime in the wilderness, most of it spent struggling to survive, it still struck Gordon as odd how obscure memories would pop into his mind right in the middle of a life-or-death fight.

Panting under a bone-dry thicket—crawling desperately to find a refuge—he suddenly experienced a recollection as clear as the dusty stones under his nose. It was a memory of contrast—of a rainy afternoon in a warm, safe university library, long ago—of a lost world filled with books and music and carefree philosophical ramblings.

Words on a page.

Dragging his body through the tough, unyielding bracken, he could almost *see* the letters, black against white. And although he couldn't recall the obscure author's name, the *words* came back with utter clarity.

"Short of Death itself, there is no such thing as a 'total' defeat… There is never a disaster so devastating that

a determined person cannot pull something out of the ashes—by risking all that he or she has left...

"Nothing in the world is more dangerous than a desperate man."

Gordon wished the long-dead writer were here right now, sharing his predicament. He wondered what pollyannaish glow the fellow might find around *this* catastrophe.

Scratched and torn from his desperate escape into this dense thicket, he crawled as quietly as he could, stopping to lay still and squeeze his eyes shut whenever the floating dust seemed about to make him sneeze. It was slow, painful progress, and he wasn't even sure where he was headed.

Minutes ago he had been as comfortable and well-stocked as any solitary traveler could hope to be, these days. Now, Gordon was reduced to not much more than a ripped shirt, faded jeans, and camp moccasins—and the thorns were cutting them all to bits.

A tapestry of fiery pain followed each new scratch down his arms and back. But in this awful, bone-dry jungle, there was nothing to do but crawl onward and pray his twisting path did not deliver him back to his enemies—to those who had effectively killed him already.

Finally, when he had come to think the hellish growth would never end, an opening appeared ahead. A narrow cleft split the brush and overlooked a slope of tumbled rock. Gordon pulled free of the thorns at last, rolled over onto his back, and stared up at the hazy sky, grateful simply for air that wasn't foul with the heat of dry decay.

Welcome to Oregon, he thought bitterly. *And I thought* Idaho *was bad.*

He lifted one arm and tried to wipe the dust out of his eyes.

Or is it that I'm simply getting too old for this sort of thing? After all, he was over thirty now, beyond the typical life expectancy of a postholocaust traveler.

Oh Lord, I wish I was home again.

He wasn't thinking of Minneapolis. The prairie today was a hell he had struggled for more than a decade to escape. No, *home* meant more to Gordon than any particular place.

A hamburger, a hot bath, music, Merthiolate…

…a cool beer…

As his labored breathing settled, other sounds came to the fore—the all too clear noise of happy looting. It rose from a hundred feet or so down the mountainside. *Laughter* as the delighted robbers tore through Gordon's gear.

…a few friendly neighborhood cops… Gordon added, still cataloging the amenities of a world long gone.

The bandits had caught him off guard as he sipped elderberry tea by a late afternoon campfire. From that first instant, as they charged up the trail straight at him, it had been clear that the hot-faced men would as soon kill Gordon as look at him.

He hadn't waited for them to decide which to do. Throwing scalding tea into the face of the first bearded robber, he dove right into the nearby brambles. Two gunshots had followed him, and that was all. Probably, his carcass wasn't worth as much to the thieves as an irreplaceable bullet. They already had all his goods, anyway.

Or so they probably think.

Gordon's smile was bitterly thin as he sat up carefully, backing along his rocky perch until he felt sure he was out of view of the slope below. He plucked his travel belt free of twigs and drew the half-full canteen for a long, desperately needed drink.

Bless you, paranoia, he thought. Not once since the Doomwar had he ever allowed the belt more than three feet from his side. It was the only thing he had been able to grab before diving into the brambles.

The dark gray metal of his .38 revolver shone even under a fine layer of dust as he drew it from its holster. Gordon blew on the snub-nosed weapon and carefully checked its action. Soft clicking testified in understated eloquence to the craftsmanship and deadly precision of another age. Even in killing, the old world had made well.

Especially in the art of killing, Gordon reminded himself. Raucous laughter carried up from the slope below.

Normally he traveled with only four rounds loaded. Now he pulled two more precious cartridges from a belt pouch and filled the empty chambers under and behind the hammer. "Firearm safety" was no longer a major consideration, especially since he expected to die this evening anyway.

Sixteen years chasing a dream, Gordon thought. *First that long, futile struggle against the collapse... then scratching to survive through the Three-Year Winter... and finally, more than a decade of moving from place to place, dodging pestilence and hunger, fighting goddamned Holnists and packs of wild dogs... half a lifetime spent as a wandering, dark-age minstrel, play-acting for meals in order to make it one day more while I searched for...*

...for someplace...

Gordon shook his head. He knew his own dreams quite well. They were a fool's fantasies, and had no place in the present world.

...for someplace where someone was taking responsibility...

He pushed the thought aside. Whatever he had been looking for, his long seeking seemed to have ended here, in the dry, cold mountains of what had once been eastern Oregon.

From the sounds below he could tell that the bandits were packing up, getting ready to move off with their plunder. Thick patches of desiccated creeper blocked Gordon's view downslope through the ponderosa pines, but soon a burly man in a faded plaid hunting coat appeared from the direction of his campsite, moving northeast on a trail leading down the mountainside.

The man's clothing confirmed what Gordon remembered from those blurred seconds of the attack. At least his assailants weren't wearing army surplus camouflage… the trademark of Holn survivalists.

They must be just regular, run of the mill, may-they-please-roast-in-Hell bandits.

If so, then there was a sliver of a chance the plan glimmering in his mind just might accomplish something.

Perhaps.

The first bandit had Gordon's all-weather jacket tied around his waist. In his right arm he cradled the pump shotgun Gordon had carried all the way from Montana. "Come on!" the bearded robber yelled back up the trail. "That's enough gloating. Get that stuff together and move it!"

The leader, Gordon decided.

Another man, smaller and more shabby, hurried into view canning a cloth sack and a battered rifle. "Boy, what a haul! We oughta celebrate. When we bring this stuff back, can we have all the 'shine we want, Jas?" The small robber hopped like an excited bird. "Boy, Sheba an' the girls'll *bust* when they hear about that lil' rabbit we drove off into the briar patch. I never seen anything run so fast!" He giggled.

Gordon frowned at the insult added to injury. It was the same nearly everywhere he had been—a postholocaust callousness to which he'd never grown accustomed, even after all this time. With only one eye peering through the scrub grass rimming his cleft, he took a deep breath and shouted.

"I wouldn't count on getting drunk yet, Brer Bear!" Adrenaline turned his voice more shrill than he wanted, but that couldn't be helped.

The big man dropped awkwardly to the ground, scrambling for cover behind a nearby tree. The skinny robber, though, gawked up at the hillside.

"What…? Who's up there?"

Gordon felt a small wash of relief. Their behavior confirmed that the sons of bitches weren't true survivalists. Certainly not *Holnists*. If they had been, he'd probably be dead by now.

The other bandits—Gordon counted a total of five—hurried down the trail carrying their booty. "Get down!" their leader commanded from his hiding place. Scrawny seemed to wake up to his exposed position and hurried to join his comrades behind the undergrowth.

All except one robber—a sallow-faced man with salt-and-pepper sideburns, wearing an alpine hat. Instead of hiding he moved forward a little, chewing a pine needle and casually eyeing the thicket.

"Why bother?" he asked calmly. "That poor fellow had on barely more than his skivvies, when we pounced him. We've got his shotgun. Let's find out what he wants."

Gordon kept his head down. But he couldn't help noticing the man's lazy, affected drawl. He was the only one who was clean shaven, and even from here Gordon could tell that his clothes were cleaner, more meticulously tended.

At a muttered growl from his leader, the casual bandit shrugged and sauntered over behind a forked pine. Barely hidden, he called up the hillside. "Are you there, Mister Rabbit? If so, I am so sorry you didn't stay to invite us to tea. Still, aware how Jas and Little Wally tend to treat visitors, I suppose I cannot blame you for cutting out."

Gordon couldn't believe he was trading banter with this twit. "That's what I figured at the time," he called. "Thanks for understanding my lack of hospitality. By the way, with whom am I speaking?"

The tall fellow smiled broadly. "With whom…? Ah, a grammarian! What joy. It's been so long since I've heard an educated voice." He doffed the alpine hat and bowed. "I am Roger Everett Septien, at one time a member of the Pacific Stock Exchange, and presently your robber. As for my colleagues…"

The bushes rustled. Septien listened, and finally shrugged. "Alas," he called to Gordon. "Normally I'd be tempted by a chance for some real conversation; I'm sure you're as starved for it as I. Unfortunately, the leader of our small brotherhood of cutthroats insists that I find out what you want and get this over with.

"So speak your piece, Mister Rabbit. We are all ears."

Gordon shook his head. The fellow obviously classed himself a wit, but his humor was fourth-rate, even by postwar standards. "I notice you fellows aren't carrying *all* of my gear. You wouldn't by some chance have decided to take only what you needed, and left enough for me to survive, would you?"

From the scrub below came a high giggle, then more hoarse chuckles as others joined in. Roger Septien looked left and right and lifted his hands. His exaggerated sigh seemed to say that *he*, at least, appreciated the irony in Gordon's question.

"Alas," he repeated. "I recall mentioning that possibility to my compatriots. For instance, our women might find some use for your aluminum tent poles and pack frame, but I suggested we leave the nylon bag and tent, which are useless to us.

"Um, in a sense we have done this. However, I don't think that Wally's... er, *alterations* will meet your approval."

Again, that shrieking giggle rose from the bushes. Gordon sagged a little.

"What about my boots? You all seem well enough shod. Do they fit any of you, anyway? Could you leave them? And my jacket and gloves?"

Septien coughed. "Ah, yes. They're the main items, aren't they? Other than the shotgun, of course, which is nonnegotiable."

Gordon spat. *Of course, idiot. Only a blowhard states the obvious.*

Again, the voice of the bandit leader could be heard, muffled by the foliage. Again there were giggles. With a pained expression, the ex-stockbroker sighed. "My leader asks what you offer in *trade*. Of course I know you have nothing. Still, I must inquire."

As a matter of fact, Gordon had a few things they might want—his belt compass for instance, and a Swiss army knife.

But what were his chances of arranging an exchange and getting out alive? It didn't take telepathy to tell that these bastards were only toying with their victim.

A fuming anger filled him, especially over Septien's false show of compassion. He had witnessed this combination of cruel contempt and civilized manners in other once-educated people, over the years since the Collapse. By his lights, people like this were far more contemptible than those who had simply succumbed to the barbaric times.

"Look," he shouted. "You don't need those damn boots! You've no real need for my jacket or my toothbrush or my notebook, either. This area's clean, so what do you need my Geiger counter for?

"I'm not stupid enough to think I can have my shotgun back, but without some of those other things I'll die, damn you!"

The echo of his curse seemed to pour down the long slope of the mountainside, leaving a hanging silence in its wake. Then the bushes rustled and the big bandit leader stood up. Spitting contemptuously upslope, he snapped his fingers at the others. "Now I know he's got no gun," he told them. His thick eyebrows narrowed and he gestured in Gordon's general direction.

"Run away, little rabbit. Run, or we'll skin you and have you for supper!" He hefted Gordon's shotgun, turned his back, and sauntered casually down the trail. The others fell in behind, laughing.

Roger Septien gave the mountainside an ironic shrug and a smile, then gathered up his share of the loot and followed his compatriots. They disappeared around a bend in the narrow forest path, but for minutes afterward Gordon heard the softly diminishing sound of someone happily whistling.

You imbecile! Weak as his chances had been, he had spoiled them completely by appealing to reason and charity. In an era of tooth and claw, nobody ever did that except out of impotence. The bandits' uncertainty had evaporated just as soon as he foolishly asked for fair play.

Of course he could have fired his .38, wasting a precious bullet to *prove* he wasn't completely harmless. That would have forced them to take him seriously again…

Then why didn't I do that? Was I too afraid?

Probably, he admitted. *I'll very likely die of exposure tonight, but that's still hours away, far enough to remain only an abstract threat, less frightening and immediate than five ruthless men with guns.*

He punched his left palm with his fist.

Oh stuff it, Gordon. You can psychoanalyze yourself this evening, while you're freezing to death. What it all comes down to, though, is that you are one prize fool, and this is probably the end.

He got up stiffly and began edging cautiously down the slope. Although he wasn't quite ready to admit it yet, Gordon felt a growing certainty that there could only be one solution, only one even faintly possible way out of this disaster.

As soon as he was free of the thicket, Gordon limped to the trickling stream to wash his face and the worst of his cuts. He wiped sweat-soaked strands of brown hair out of his eyes. His scrapes hurt like hell, but none of them looked bad enough to persuade him to use the thin tube of the precious iodine in his belt pouch.

He refilled his canteen and thought.

Besides his pistol and half-shredded clothes, a pocket knife, and compass, his pouch held a miniature fishing kit that might prove useful, if he ever made it over the mountains to a decent watershed.

And of course ten spare rounds for his .38, small, blessed relics of industrial civilization.

Back at the beginning, during the riots and the great starvation, it had seemed that the one thing in inexhaustible supply was ammunition. If only turn-of-the-century America had stockpiled and distributed food half so well as its citizens had cached mountains of bullets…

Rough stones jabbed his throbbing left foot as Gordon gingerly hurried toward his former campsite. Clearly these half-shredded moccasins would get him nowhere. His torn clothes would be about as effective against freezing mountain autumn nights as his pleas had been against the bandits' hard hearts.

The small clearing where he had made camp only an hour or so ago was deserted now, but his worst fears were surpassed by the havoc he found there.

His tent had been converted into a pile of nylon shreds, his sleeping bag a small blizzard of scattered goose down. All Gordon found intact was the slim longbow he had been carving from a cut sapling, and a line of experimental venison-gut strings.

Probably thought it was a walking stick. Sixteen years after the last factory had burned, Gordon's robbers had completely overlooked the potential value of the bow and strings, when the ammo finally ran out.

He used the bow to poke through the wreckage, looking for anything else to salvage.

I can't believe it. They took my journal! That prig Septien probably looks forward to poring over it during the snowtime, chuckling over my adventures and my naiveté while my bones are being picked clean by cougars and buzzards.

Of course the food was all gone: the jerky; the bag of split grains that a small Idaho village had let him have in exchange for a few songs and stories; the tiny hoard of rock candy he had found in the mechanical bowels of a looted vending machine.

It's just as well about the candy, Gordon thought as he plucked his trampled, ruined toothbrush out of the dust.

Now why the hell did they have to do that?

Late in the Three-Year Winter—while the remnants of his militia platoon still struggled to guard the soy silos of Wayne, Minnesota, for a government nobody had heard from in months—*five* of his comrades had died of raging oral infections. They were awful, inglorious deaths, and no one had even been sure if one of the war bugs was responsible, or the cold and hunger and near total lack of modern hygiene. All Gordon knew was that the specter of his teeth rotting in his head was his own personal phobia.

Bastards, he thought as he flung the little brush aside.

He kicked the rubbish one last time. There was nothing here to change his mind.

You're procrastinating. Go. Do it.

Gordon started off a little stiffly. But soon he was moving downtrail as quickly and silently as he could, making time through the bone-dry forest.

The burly outlaw leader had promised to eat him if they met again. Cannibalism had been common in the early days, and these mountain men might have acquired a taste for the "long pork." Still, he had to persuade them that a man with nothing to lose must be reckoned with.

Within half a mile or so, their tracks were familiar to him: two traces with the soft outlines of deer hide and three with prewar Vibram soles. They were moving at a leisurely pace, and it would be no trouble simply to catch up with his enemies.

That was not his plan, however. Gordon tried to

remember this morning's climb up this same trail.

The path drops in altitude as it winds north, along the east face of the mountain, before switching back south and east into the desert valley below.

But what if I were to cut above the main trail, and traverse the slope higher up? I might be able to come down on them while it's still light… while they're still gloating and expecting nothing.

If the shortcut is there…

The trail wove gradually downhill toward the northeast, in the direction of the lengthening shadows, toward the deserts of eastern Oregon and Idaho. Gordon must have passed below the robbers' sentinels yesterday or this morning, and they had taken their time following him until he was settled into camp. Their lair had to be somewhere off this same trail.

Even limping, Gordon was able to move silently and quickly, the only advantage of camp moccasins over boots. Soon he heard faint sounds below and ahead.

The raiding party. The men were laughing, joking together. It was painful to hear.

It wasn't so much that they were laughing over *him*. Callous cruelty was a part of life today, and if Gordon couldn't reconcile himself to it, he at least recognized *he* was the Twentieth-Century oddball in today's savage world.

But the sounds reminded him of other laughter, the rough jokes of men who shared danger together.

Drew Simms—freckle-faced pre-med with a floppy grin and deadly skill at chess or poker—the Holnists got him when they overran Wayne and burned the silos…

Tiny Kielre—saved my life twice, and all he wanted when he was on his deathbed, the War Mumps tearing him apart, was for me to read him stories...

Then there had been Lieutenant Van—their half-Vietnamese platoon leader. Gordon had never known until it was too late that the Lieutenant was cutting his own rations and giving them to his men. He asked, at the end, to be buried in an American flag.

Gordon had been alone for so long. He missed the company of such men almost as much as the friendship of women.

Watching the brush on his left, he came to an opening that seemed to promise a sloping track—a shortcut perhaps—to the north across the mountain face. The rust-dry scrub crackled as he left the path and broke his own trail. Gordon thought he remembered the perfect site for a bushwhack, a switchback that passed under a high, stony horseshoe. A sniper might find a place a little way above that rocky outcrop, within point-blank range of anyone hiking along the hairpin.

If I can just get there first...

He might pin them down by surprise and force them to negotiate. That was the advantage in being the one with nothing to lose. Any sane bandit would prefer to live and rob another day. He had to believe they would part with boots, a jacket, and some food, against the risk of losing one or two of their band.

Gordon hoped he would not have to kill anybody.

Oh grow up, please! His worst enemy, over the next few hours, could be his archaic scruples. *Just this once, be ruthless.*

The voices on the trail faded as he cut across the slope of the mountain. Several times he had to detour around jagged gullies or scabrous patches of ugly bramble. Gordon concentrated on finding the quickest way toward his rocky ambuscade.

Have I gone far enough?

Grimly, he kept on. According to imperfect memory, the switchback he had in mind came only after a long sweep northward along the east face of the mountain.

A narrow animal track let him hurry through the pine thickets, pausing frequently to check his compass. He faced a quandary. To stand a chance of catching his adversaries, he had to stay above them. Yet if he kept too high, he might go right past his target without knowing it.

And twilight was not long away.

A flock of wild turkeys scattered as he jogged into a small clearing. Of course the thinned human population probably had something to do with the return of wildlife, but it was also one more sign that he had come into better-watered country than the arid lands of Idaho. His bow might someday prove useful, should he live long enough to learn to use it.

He angled downslope, beginning to get worried. Surely by now the main trail was quite a bit below him, if it hadn't already switched back a few times. It was possible he had already gone too far north.

At last Gordon realized the game path was turning inexorably *westward*. It appeared to be rising again as well, toward what looked like another gap in the mountains, shrouded in late afternoon mist.

He stopped a moment to catch his breath and his bearings. Perhaps this was yet another pass through the cold, semi-arid Cascade Range, leading eventually into the Willamette River Valley and thence the Pacific Ocean. His map was gone but he knew that at most a couple weeks' walk in that direction ought to bring him to water, shelter, fishing streams, game to hunt, and maybe...

And maybe some people trying to put something right in the world again. The sunlight through that high fringe of clouds was like a luminous halo, akin to the dimly remembered skyglow of city lights, a promise that had led him ever inward from the Midwest, searching. The dream—hopeless as he knew it was—simply would not go away.

Gordon shook his head. For certain there would be snow in that range, and cougars, and starvation. There could be no turning away from his plan. Not if he wanted to live.

He tried hard to cut downslope, but the narrow game paths kept forcing him north and westward. The switchback *had* to be behind him, by now. But the thick, dry undergrowth diverted him farther into the new pass.

In his frustration Gordon almost missed the sound. But then he stopped suddenly, listening.

Were those voices?

A steep ravine opened up the forest just ahead. He hurried toward it until he could see the outlines of this mountain and others in the chain, wrapped in a thick haze, amber high on their westward flanks and darkening purple where the sun no longer shone.

The sounds seemed to be coming from below, to the east. And yes, they *were* voices. Gordon searched and made out the snakelike line of a trail on the mountain's flank. Far off, he caught a brief flash of color moving slowly upward through the woods.

The bandits! But why were they moving uphill again? They couldn't be, unless...

Unless Gordon was already far north of the trail he had taken the day before. He must have missed the ambush site altogether and come out above a side path. The bandits were climbing a fork he had failed to notice yesterday, one leading up into *this* pass rather than the one he had been caught in.

This must be the way to their base!

Gordon looked up the mountain. Yes, he could see how a small hollow could fit over to the west, on a shoulder near the lesser-used pass. It would be defensible and very hard to discover by chance.

Gordon smiled grimly and turned west as well. The ambush was a lost opportunity, but if he hurried he could beat the bandits home, perhaps get a few minutes to steal what he needed—food, clothes, something to carry them in.

And if the hideout wasn't deserted?

Well, maybe he could take their women hostage and try to cut a deal.

Yeah, that's lots better. Like holding a ticking bomb beats jogging with nitroglycerin.

Frankly, he hated all of his alternatives.

He started to run, ducking under branches and dodging withered stumps as he charged along the narrow game path. Soon Gordon felt a strange exuberance. He was committed, and none of his typical self-doubt would get in the way now. Battle adrenaline nearly made him high as his stride opened and small shrubs swept by in a blur. He stretched to leap over a toppled, decayed tree trunk, cleared it easily...

Landing sent sharp pain lancing up his left leg as something stabbed him through the flimsy moccasins. He sprawled, face first, into the gravel of a dry stream bed.

Gordon rolled over clutching his injury. Through wet, pain-diffracted eyes, he saw that he had tripped over a thick strand of looped, rusted steel cable, no doubt left over from some ancient prewar logging operation. Again, while his leg throbbed agonizingly, his surface thoughts were absurdly rational.

Eighteen years since my last tetanus shot. Lovely.

But no, it hadn't cut him, only tripped him. That was bad enough, though. He held onto his thigh and clamped his mouth shut, trying to ride out a savage cramp.

At last the tremors subsided and he dragged himself over to the toppled tree, gingerly hoisting himself into sitting position. He hissed through clenched teeth as the waves of agony slowly faded.

Meanwhile he could hear the bandit party passing not far below, taking away the head start that had been his only advantage.

So much for all those great plans to beat them to their hideout. He listened until their voices faded up the trail.

At last Gordon used his bow as a staff and tried standing up. Letting weight settle slowly on his left leg, he found it would support him, though it still quivered tenderly.

Ten years ago I could've taken a fall like that and been up and running without another thought. Face it. You're obsolete, Gordon. Worn out. These days, thirty-four and alone is the same as being ready to die.

There would be no ambush now. He couldn't even chase the bandits, not all the way up to that notch in the mountain. It would be useless to try to track them on a moonless night.

He took a few steps as the throbbing slowly subsided. Soon he was able to walk without leaning too hard on his makeshift staff.

Fine, but where to? Perhaps he should spend the remaining daylight looking for a cave, a pile of pine needles, anything to give him a chance to live through the night.

In the growing chill Gordon watched shadows climb higher above the desert valley floor, merging and darkening the flanks of the nearby mountains. The reddening sun probed through chinks in the range of snowy peaks to his left.

He was facing north, unable quite yet to summon the energy to move, when his eye was caught by a sudden flash of light, a sharp glinting against the rolling forest green on the opposite flank of this narrow pass. Still favoring his tender foot, Gordon took a few steps forward. His brow furrowed.

The forest fires that had seared so much of the dry Cascades had spared the thick forests on that part of the mountainside. And yes, something across the way was catching the sunlight like a mirror. From the folds in the hillsides, he guessed that the reflection could only be seen from this very spot, and only in the late afternoon.

So he had guessed wrong. The bandits' roost wasn't in that hollow higher up in the pass to the west after all, but much closer. Only a stroke of luck had given it away.

So you're giving me clues, now? Now? he accused the world. *I don't have enough troubles as it is, without being offered straws to grasp at?*

Hope was an addiction. It had driven him westward for half his life. Moments after all but giving up, Gordon found himself piecing together the outlines of a new plan.

Could he try to rob a cabin filled with armed men? He pictured himself, kicking in the door to their wide-eyed astonishment, holding them all at bay with the pistol in one hand, while he tied them all up with the other!

Why not? They might be drunk, and he was desperate enough to try. Could he take hostages? Hell, even a milk goat would be more valuable to them than his boots! A captured woman should bring more in trade than that.

The idea was a sour taste in his mouth. It depended on the bandit leader behaving rationally for one thing. Would the bastard recognize the secret power of a desperate man, and let him go with what he needed?

Gordon had seen pride make men do stupid things. More often than not. *If it comes down to a chase, I'm cooked. I couldn't outrun a badger, right now.*

He eyed the reflection across the pass, and decided he had very little choice, after all.

It was slow going from the first. His leg still ached and he had to stop every hundred feet or so to scan merging and crisscrossing trails for his enemy's spoor. He also found he was checking shadows as potential ambushes, and made himself quit. These men weren't Holnists. Indeed, they seemed lazy. Gordon guessed that their pickets would be close to home, if they maintained any at all.

As the light faded, the footprints were lost in the gravelly soil. But Gordon knew where he was going. The glinting reflection could no longer be seen, but the ravine on the opposite shoulder of the mountain saddle was a dark, tree-lined V silhouette. He chose a likely path and hurried ahead.

It was growing dark quickly. A stiff, cold breeze blew damply off the misty heights. Gordon limped up a dry stream bed and leaned on his staff as he climbed a set of switchbacks. Then, when he guessed he was within a quarter mile of his goal, the path suddenly failed.

He kept his forearms up to protect his face while he tried to move quietly through the dry undergrowth. He fought down a lingering, threatening urge to sneeze in the floating dust.

Chilly night fog was flowing down the mountainsides. Soon the ground would shimmer with faintly luminous ground frost. Still, Gordon shivered less from the cold than from nerves. He knew he was getting close. One way or another, he was about to have an encounter with death.

In his youth he had read about heroes, historical and fictional. Nearly all of them, when the time came for action, seemed able to push aside their personal burdens of worry, confusion, angst, for at least the time when action impended. But Gordon's mind didn't seem to work that way. Instead it just filled with more and more complexities, a turmoil of regrets.

It wasn't that he had doubts about what had to be done. By every standard he lived by, this was the right thing to do. Survival demanded it. And anyway, if he was to be a dead man, at least he could make the mountains a little safer for the next wayfarer by taking a few of the bastards with him.

Still, the nearer he drew to the confrontation, the more he realized that he hadn't wanted his dharma to come to this. He did not really wish to kill any of these men.

It had been this way even as, with Lieutenant Van's little platoon, he had struggled to help maintain a peace—and a fragment of a nation—that had already died.

And afterward, he had chosen the life of a minstrel, a traveling actor and laborer—partly in order to keep moving, searching for a light, somewhere.

A few of the surviving postwar communities were known to accept outsiders as new members. Women were always welcome, of course, but some accepted new men.

And yet there was so often a catch. A new male frequently had to duel—kill for the right to sit at a communal table, or bring back a scalp from a feuding clan to prove his prowess. There were few real Holnists anymore in the plains and Rockies. But many survivor outposts he had encountered nevertheless demanded rituals of which Gordon wanted no part.

And now here he was, counting bullets, a part of him coldly noting that, if he made them count, there were probably enough for all the bandits.

Another sparse berry thicket blocked his path. What the patch lacked in fruit it made up for in thorns. This time Gordon moved along its edge, carefully picking his way in the gathering gloom. His sense of direction—honed after thirteen years of wandering—was automatic. He moved silently, cautious without rising above the maelstrom of his own thoughts.

All considered, it was amazing a man like him had lived this long. Everyone he had known or admired as a boy had died, along with all the hopes any of them had had. The soft world made for dreamers like himself broke apart when he was only eighteen. Long since then he'd come to realize that his persistent optimism had to be a form of hysterical insanity.

Hell, everybody's crazy, these days.

Yes, he answered himself. *But paranoia and depression are adaptive, now. Idealism is only stupid.*

Gordon paused at a small blob of color. He peered into the bramble and saw, about a yard inside, a solitary clump of blueberries, apparently overlooked by the local black bear. The mist heightened Gordon's sense of smell and he could pick their faint autumn mustiness out of the air.

Ignoring the stabbing thorns, he reached in and drew back a sticky handful. The tart sweetness was a wild thing in his mouth, like Life.

Twilight was almost gone, and a few wan stars winked through a darkling overcast. The cold breeze riffled his torn shirt and reminded Gordon that it was time to get this business over with, before his hands were too chilled to pull a trigger.

He wiped the stickiness on his pants as he rounded the end of the thicket. And there, suddenly, a hundred feet or so away it seemed, a broad pane of glass glinted at him in the dim skyglow.

Gordon ducked back behind the thorns. He drew his revolver and held his right wrist with his left hand until his breathing settled. Then he checked the pistol's action. It clicked quietly, in an almost gentle, mechanical complacency. The spare ammo was heavy in his breast pocket.

A hazard to quick or forceful motion, the thicket yielded as he settled back against it, heedless of a few more little scratches. Gordon closed his eyes and meditated for calm and, yes, for forgiveness. In the chilly darkness, the only accompaniment to his breathing was the rhythmic ratchet of the crickets.

A swirl of cold fog blew around him. *No,* he sighed. *There's no other way.* He raised his weapon and swung around.

The structure looked distinctly odd. For one thing, the distant patch of glass was dark.

That was queer, but stranger still was the silence. He'd

have thought the bandits would have a fire going, and that they would be loudly celebrating.

It was nearly too dark to see his own hand. The trees loomed like hulking trolls on every side. Dimly, the glass pane seemed to stand out against some black structure, reflecting silvery highlights of a rolling cloud cover. Thin wisps of haze drifted between Gordon and his objective, confusing the image, making it shimmer.

He walked forward slowly, giving most of his attention to the ground. Now was not the time to step on a dry twig, or to be stabbed by a sharp stone as he shuffled in the dimness.

He glanced up, and once more the eerie feeling struck him. There was something *wrong* about the edifice ahead, made out mostly in silhouette behind the faintly glimmering glass. It didn't look right, somehow. Boxlike, its upper section seemed to be mostly window. Below, it struck him as more like painted metal than wood. At the corners…

The fog grew thicker. Gordon could tell his perspective was wrong. He had been looking for a house, or large cottage. As he neared, he realized the thing was actually much closer than he'd thought. The shape was familiar, as if—

His foot came down on a twig. The "snap!" filled his ears and he crouched, peering into the gloom with a desperate need that transcended sight. It felt as if a frantic power drove out of his eyes, propelled by his terror, demanding the mist be cloven so he could see.

Obediently, it seemed, the dry fog suddenly fell open before him. Pupils dilated, Gordon saw that he was less than two *meters* from the window… his own face reflected, wide-eyed and wild haired… and saw, superimposed on his own image, a vacant, skeletal, death mask—a hooded skull grinning in welcome.

Gordon crouched, hypnotized, as a superstitious thrill coursed up his spine. He was unable to bring his weapon to bear, unable to cause his larynx to make sound. The haze swirled as he listened for proof that he had really gone mad—wishing with all his might that the death's head was an illusion.

"Alas, poor Gordon!" The sepulchral image overlaid his reflection and seemed to shimmer a greeting. Never, in all these awful years, had Death—owner of the world—manifested to him as a specter. Gordon's numbed mind could think of nothing but to attend the Elsinorian figure's bidding. He waited, unable to take his gaze away, or even to move. The skull and his face... his face and the skull... The thing had captured him without a fight, and now seemed content to grin about it.

At last it was something as mundane as a monkey reflex that came to Gordon's aid.

No matter how mesmerizing, how terrifying, no unchanging sight can keep a man riveted forever. Not when it seemed that nothing at all was happening, nothing changing. Where courage and education failed him, where his nervous system had let him down, *boredom* finally took command.

His breath exhaled. He heard it whistle between his teeth. Without willing them to, Gordon felt his eyes turn slightly from the visage of Death.

A part of him noted that the window was set in a door. The handle lay before him. To the left, another window. To the right... to the right was the hood.

The... *hood*...

The hood of a jeep.

The hood of an abandoned, rusted jeep that lay in a faint rut in the forest gully...

He blinked at the hood of the abandoned, rusted jeep with ancient U.S. government markings, and the skeleton of a poor, dead civil servant within, skull pressed against the passenger-side window, facing Gordon.

The strangled sigh he let out felt almost ectoplasmic, the relief and embarrassment were so palpable. Gordon straightened up and it felt like unwinding from a fetal position—like being born.

"Oh. Oh Lordie," he said, just to hear his own voice. Moving his arms and legs, he paced a long circle around the vehicle, obsessively glancing at its dead occupant, coming to terms with its reality. He breathed deeply as his pulse settled and the roar in his ears gradually ebbed.

Finally, he sat down on the forest floor with his back against the cool door on the jeep's left side. Trembling, he used both hands as he put the revolver back on safety and slid it into its holster. Then he pulled out his canteen and drank in slow, full swallows. Gordon wished he had something stronger, but water right now tasted as sweet as life.

Night was full, the cold, bone-chilling. Still, Gordon spent a few moments putting off the obvious. He would never find the bandits' roost now, having followed a false clue so far into a pitch-dark wilderness. The jeep, at least, offered some form of shelter, better than anything else around.

He hauled himself up and placed his hand on the door lever, calling up motions that had once been second nature to two hundred million of his countrymen and which, after a stubborn moment, forced the latch to give. The door let out a loud screech as he pulled hard and forced it open. He slid onto the cracked vinyl of the seat and inspected the interior.

The jeep was one of those reversed, driver-on-the-right types the post office had used back in the once-upon-a-time of before the Doomwar. The dead mailman—what was left of him—was slumped over on the far side. Gordon avoided looking at the skeleton for the moment.

The storage area of the truck was nearly full with canvas sacks. The smell of old paper filled the small cabin at least as much as the faded odor of the mummified remains.

With a hopeful oath, Gordon snatched up a metal flask from the shift well. It sloshed! To have held liquid for sixteen years or more it had to be well sealed. Gordon swore as he twisted and pried at the cap. He pounded it against the door frame, then attacked it again.

Frustration made his eyes tear, but at last he felt the cap give. Soon he was rewarded with a slow, rough turning, and then the heady, distantly familiar aroma of whiskey.

Maybe I've been a good boy after all.

Maybe there is indeed a God.

He took a mouthful and coughed as the warming fire streamed down. Two more small swallows and he fell back against the seat, breathing almost a sigh.

He wasn't ready yet to face removing the jacket draped over the skeleton's narrow shoulders. Gordon grabbed sacks—bearing the imprint U.S. POSTAL SERVICE—and piled them about himself. Leaving a narrow opening in the door to let in fresh mountain air, he burrowed under the makeshift blankets with his bottle.

At last he looked over at his host, contemplating the dead civil servant's American flag shoulder patch. He unscrewed the flask and this time raised the container toward the hooded garment.

"Believe it or not, Mr. Postman, I always thought you folks gave good and honest service. Oh, people used you as whipping boys a lot, but I know what a tough job you all had. I was proud of you, even before the war.

"But this, Mr. Mailman"—he lifted the flask—"this goes beyond anything I'd come to expect! I consider my taxes very well spent." He drank to the postman, coughing a little but relishing the warm glow.

He settled deeper into the mail sacks and looked at the leather jacket, ribs serrating its sides, arms hanging loosely at odd angles. Lying still, Gordon felt a sad poignancy—something like homesickness. The jeep, the symbolic, faithful letter carrier, the flag patch... they recalled comfort, innocence, cooperation, an easy life that allowed millions of men and women to relax, to smile or argue as they chose, to be tolerant with one another—and to hope to be better people with the passage of time.

Gordon had been ready, today, to kill and to be killed. Now he was glad that had been averted. They had called him "Mr. Rabbit" and left him to die. But it was his privilege, without their ever knowing it, to call the bandits "countrymen," and let them have their lives.

Gordon allowed sleep to come and welcomed back optimism—foolish anachronism that it might be. He lay in a blanket of his own honor, and spent the rest of the night dreaming of parallel worlds.

2

Snow and soot covered the ancient tree's broken branches and seared bark. It wasn't dead, not quite yet. Here and there tiny shoots of green struggled to emerge, but they weren't doing well. The end was near.

A shadow loomed, and a creature settled onto the drifts, an old, wounded thing of the skies, as near death as the tree.

Pinions drooping, it laboriously began building a nest—a place of dying. Stick by stick, it pecked among the ruined wood on the ground, piling the bits higher until it was clear that it was not a nest at all.

It was a pyre.

The bloody, dying thing settled in atop the kindling, and crooned soft music unlike anything ever heard before. A glow began to build, surrounding the beast soon in a rich purple lambience. Blue flames burst forth.

And the tree seemed to respond. Aged, ruined branches curled forward toward the heat, like an old man warming his hands. Snow shivered and fell, the green patches grew and began to fill the air with a fragrance of renewal.

It was not the creature in the pyre that was reborn, and even in sleep, that surprised Gordon. The great bird was consumed, leaving only bones.

But the tree blossomed, and from its flowering branches things uncurled and drifted off into the air.

He stared in wonderment when he saw that they were balloons, airplanes, and rocket ships. Dreams.

They floated away in all directions, and the air was filled with hope.

3

A camp robber bird, looking for blue jays to chase, landed on the jeep's hood with a hollow thump. It squawked—once for territoriality and once for pleasure—then began poking through the thick detritus with its beak.

Gordon awakened to the tap-tapping sound. He looked up, bleary-eyed, and saw the gray-flanked bird through the dust-smeared window. It took him moments to remember where he was. The glass windshield, the steering wheel, the smell of metal and paper, all felt like a continuation of one of the night's most vivid dreams, a vision of the old days before the war. He sat dazedly for a few moments, sifting through feelings while the sleep images unraveled and drifted away, out of grasp.

Gordon rubbed his eyes, and presently began to consider his situation.

If he hadn't left an elephant's trail on his way into this hollow last night, he should be perfectly safe right now. The fact that the whiskey had lain here untouched for sixteen years obviously meant the bandits were lazy hunters. They had their traditional stalks and blinds, and had never bothered fully to explore their own mountain.

Gordon felt a bit thick-headed. The war had begun when he was eighteen, a college sophomore, and since then there had been little chance to build a tolerance to eighty-proof liquor. Added to yesterday's series of traumas and adrenaline rushes, the whiskey had left him cottonmouthed and scratchy behind the eyelids.

He regretted his lost comforts as much as ever. There would be no tea this morning. Nor a damp washcloth, or venison jerky for breakfast. No toothbrush.

Still, Gordon tried to be philosophical. After all, he was alive. He had a feeling there would be times when each of the items stolen from him would be "missed most of all."

With any luck, the Geiger counter wouldn't fall into that category. Radiation had been one of his main reasons for going ever westward, since leaving the Dakotas. He had grown tired of walking everywhere a slave to his precious counter, always afraid it would be stolen or would break down. Rumor had it that the West Coast had been spared the worst of the fallout, suffering more, instead, from plagues wind-borne from Asia.

That had been the way with that strange war. Inconsistent, chaotic, it had stopped far short of the spasm everyone had predicted. Instead it was more like a shotgun blast of one midscale catastrophe after another. By itself, any one of the disasters might have been survivable.

The initial "techno-war" at sea and in space might not have been so terrible had it remained contained, and not spilled over onto the continents.

The diseases weren't as bad as in the Eastern Hemisphere, where the Enemy's weapons went out of control in his own populace. They probably wouldn't have killed so many in America, had the fallout zones not pushed crowds of refugees together, and ruined the delicate network of medical services.

And the starvation might not have been so awful had terrified communities not blocked rails and roads to keep out the germs.

As for the long-dreaded atom, only a tiny fraction of the world's nuclear arsenals were used before the Slavic Resurgence collapsed from within and unexpected victory was declared. Those few score bombs were enough to trigger the Three-Year Winter, but not a Century-Long Night that might have sent Man the way of the dinosaurs. For weeks it appeared that a great miracle of restraint had saved the planet.

So it seemed. And indeed, even the combination—a few bombs, some bugs, and three poor harvests—would not have been enough to ruin a great nation, and with it a world.

But there was another illness, a cancer from within.

Damn you forever, Nathan Holn, Gordon thought. Across a dark continent it was a common litany.

He pushed aside the mail sacks. Ignoring the morning chill, he opened his left belt pouch and pulled out a small package wrapped in aluminum foil, coated with melted wax.

If there ever had been an emergency, this was one. Gordon would need energy to get through the day. A dozen cubes of beef bouillon were all he had, but they would have to do.

Washing down a bitter, salty chunk with a swig from his canteen, Gordon kicked open the left door of the jeep, letting several sacks tumble out onto the frosted ground. He turned to his right and looked at the muffled skeleton that had quietly shared the night with him.

"Mr. Postman, I'm going to give you as close to a decent burial as I can manage with my bare hands. I know that's not much payment for what you've given me. But it's all I can offer." He reached over the narrow, bony shoulder and unlocked the driver's door.

His moccasins slipped on the icy ground as he got out and stepped carefully around to the other side of the jeep.

At least it didn't snow last night. It's so dry up here that the ground ought to thaw enough for digging in a little while.

The rusty right-hand door groaned as he pulled. It was

tricky, catching the skeleton in an emptied mail sack as it pitched forward. Gordon somehow managed to get the bundle of clothes and bones laid out on the forest floor.

He was amazed at the state of preservation. The dry climate had almost mummified the postman's remains, giving insects time to clean up without much mess. The rest of the jeep appeared to have been free from mold for all these years.

First he checked the mailman's apparel.

Funny—why was he wearing a paisley shirt under his jacket?

The garment, once colorful but now faded and stained, was a total loss, but the leather jacket was a wonderful find. If big enough, it would improve his chances immeasurably.

The footgear looked old and cracked, but perhaps serviceable. Carefully, Gordon shook out the gruesome, dry remnants and laid the shoes against his feet.

Maybe a bit large. But then, anything would be better than ripped camp moccasins.

Gordon slid the bones out onto the mail sack with as little violence as he could manage, surprised at how easy it was. Any superstition had been burned out the night before. All that remained was a mild reverence and an ironic gratitude to the former owner of these things. He shook the clothes, holding his breath against the dust, and hung them on a ponderosa branch to air out. He returned to the jeep.

Aha, he thought then. *The mystery of the shirt is solved.* Right next to where he had slept was a long-sleeved blue uniform blouse with Postal Service patches on the shoulders. It looked almost new, in spite of the years. *One for comfort, and another for the boss.*

Gordon had known postmen to do that, when he was a

boy. One fellow, during the muggy afternoons of summer, had worn bright Hawaiian shirts as he delivered the mail. The postman had always been grateful for a cool glass of lemonade. Gordon wished he could remember his name.

Shivering in the morning chill, he slipped into the uniform shirt. It was only a little bit large.

"Maybe I'll grow to fill it out," he mumbled, joking weakly with himself. At thirty-four he probably weighed less than he had at seventeen.

The glove compartment contained a brittle map of Oregon to replace the one he had lost. Then, with a shout Gordon grabbed a small square of clear plastic. A scintillator! Far better than his Geiger counter, the little crystal would give off tiny flashes whenever its crystalline interior was struck by gamma radiation. It didn't even need power! Gordon cupped it in front of his eye and watched a few sparse flickerings, caused by cosmic rays. Otherwise, the cube was quiescent.

Now what was a prewar mailman doing with a gadget like that? Gordon wondered idly, as the device went into his pants pocket.

The glove compartment flashlight was a loss, of course; the emergency flares were crumbled paste.

The bag, of course. On the floor below the driver's seat was a large, leather, letter-carrier's sack. It was dry and cracked, but the straps held when he tugged, and the flaps would keep out water.

It wouldn't come close to replacing his lost Kelty, but the bag would be a vast improvement over nothing at all. He opened the main compartment and bundles of aged correspondence spilled out, breaking into scattered piles as brittle rubber bands snapped apart. Gordon picked up a few of the nearest pieces.

"From the Mayor of Bend, Oregon, to the Chairman of the School of Medicine, University of Oregon, Eugene." Gordon intoned the address as though he were playing Polonius. He flipped through more letters. The addresses sounded pompous and archaic.

"Dr. Franklin Davis, of the small town of Gilchrist sends—with the word URGENT printed clearly on the envelope—a rather bulky letter to the Director of Regional Disbursement of Medical Supplies… no doubt pleading priority for his requisitions."

Gordon's sardonic smile faded into a frown as he turned over one letter after another. Something was wrong here.

He had expected to be amused by junk mail and personal correspondence. But there didn't seem to be a single advertisement in the bag. And while there were many private letters, most of the envelopes appeared to be on one or another type of official stationery.

Well, there wasn't time for voyeurism anyway. He'd take a dozen or so letters for entertainment, and use the backsides for his new journal.

He avoided thinking about the loss of the old volume—sixteen years' tiny scratchings, now doubtless being perused by that onetime stockbroker robber. It would be read and preserved, he was sure, along with the tiny volumes of verse he had carried in his pack, or he had misread Roger Septien's personality.

Someday, he would come and get them back.

What was a U.S. Postal Service jeep doing out here, anyway? And what had killed the postman? He found part of his answer around at the back of the vehicle—bullet holes in the tailgate window, well grouped midway up the right side.

Gordon looked over to the ponderosa. Yes, the shirt and the jacket each had two holes in the back of the upper chest area.

The attempted hijacking or robbery could not have been prewar. Mail carriers were almost never attacked, even in the late eighties' depression riots, before the "golden age" of the nineties.

Besides, a missing carrier would have been searched for until found.

So, the attack took place *after* the One-Week War. But what was a mailman doing driving alone through the countryside after the United States had effectively ceased to exist? How long afterward had this happened?

The fellow must have driven off from his ambush, seeking obscure roads and trails to get away from his assailants. Maybe he didn't know the severity of his wounds, or simply panicked.

But Gordon suspected that there was another reason the letter carrier had chosen to weave in and out of blackberry thickets to hide deep in forest depths.

"He was protecting his cargo," Gordon whispered. "He measured the chance he'd black out on the road against the possibility of getting to help… and decided to cache the mail, rather than try to live."

So, this was a bona fide *postwar* postman. A hero of the flickering twilight of civilization. Gordon thought of the old-time ode of the mails… "Neither sleet, nor hail…" and wondered at the fact that some had tried this hard to keep the light alive.

That explained the official letters and the lack of

junk mail. He hadn't realized that even a semblance of normality had remained for so long. Of course, a seventeen-year-old militia recruit was unlikely to have seen anything normal. Mob rule and general looting in the main disbursement centers had kept armed authority busy and attrited until the militia finally vanished into the disturbances it had been sent to quell. If men and women elsewhere were behaving more like human beings during those months of horror, Gordon never witnessed it.

The brave story of the postman only served to depress Gordon. This tale of struggle against chaos, by mayors and university professors and postmen, had a "what if" flavor that was too poignant for him to consider for long.

The tailgate opened reluctantly, after some prying. Moving mail sacks aside, he found the letter carrier's hat, with its tarnished badge, an empty lunchbox, and a valuable pair of sunglasses lying in thick dust atop a wheel well.

A small shovel, intended to help free the jeep from road ruts, would now help to bury the driver.

Finally, just behind the driver's seat, broken under several heavy sacks, Gordon found a smashed guitar. A large-caliber bullet had snapped its neck. Near it, a large, yellowed plastic bag held a pound of desiccated herbs that gave off a strong, musky odor. Gordon's recollection hadn't faded enough to forget the aroma of marijuana.

He had envisioned the postman as a middle-aged, balding, conservative type. Gordon now recreated the image, and made the fellow look more like himself: wiry, bearded, with a perpetual, stunned expression that seemed about to say, "Oh, wow."

A neohippy perhaps—a member of a subgeneration that had hardly begun to flower before the war snuffed it out and everything else optimistic—a neohippy dying to protect the establishment's mail. It didn't surprise Gordon in the slightest. He had had friends in the movement, sincere people, if maybe a little strange.

Gordon retrieved the guitar strings and for the first time that morning felt a little guilty.

The letter carrier hadn't even been armed! Gordon remembered reading once that the U.S. Mail operated across the lines for three years into the 1860s Civil War. Perhaps this fellow had trusted his countrymen to respect that tradition.

Post-Chaos America had no tradition but survival. In his travels, Gordon had found that some isolated communities welcomed him in the same way minstrels had been kindly received far and wide in medieval days. In others, wild varieties of paranoia reigned. Even in those rare cases where he had found friendliness, where decent people seemed willing to welcome a stranger, Gordon had always, before long, moved on. Always, he found himself beginning to dream again of wheels turning and things flying in the sky.

It was already midmorning. His gleanings here were enough to make the chances of survival better without a confrontation with the bandits. The sooner he was over the pass then, and into a decent watershed, the better off he would be.

Right now, nothing would serve him half so well as a stream, somewhere out of the range of the bandit gang, where he could fish for trout to fill his belly.

One more task, here. He hefted the shovel.

Hungry or not, you owe the guy this much.

He looked around for a shady spot with soft earth to dig in, and a view.

4

"...They said, 'Fear not, Macbeth, till Birnam Wood comes to Dunsinane'; and now a wood comes to Dunsinane!

"Arm, arm, arm yourselves! If this is what the witch spoke of—that thing out there—there'll be no running, or hiding here!"

Gordon clutched his wooden sword, contrived from planking and a bit of tin. He motioned to an invisible aide-de-camp.

"I'm gettin' weary of the sun, and wish the world were undone.

"Ring the alarum bell! Blow, wind! Come wrack! At least we'll die with harness on our back!"

Gordon squared his shoulders, flourished his sword, and marched Macbeth offstage to his doom.

Out of the light of the tallow lamps, he swiveled to catch a glimpse of his audience. They had loved his earlier acts. But this bastardized, one-man version of Macbeth might have gone over their heads.

An instant after he exited, though, enthusiastic applause began, led by Mrs. Adele Thompson, the leader of this small community. Adults whistled and stamped their feet. Younger citizens clapped awkwardly, those below twenty years of age watching their elders and slapping their hands awkwardly, as if they were taking part in this strange rite for the first time.

Obviously, they had liked his abbreviated version of the ancient tragedy. Gordon was relieved. To be honest, some parts had been simplified less for brevity than because of his imperfect memory of the original. He had last seen a copy of the play almost a decade ago, and that a half-burned fragment.

Still, the final lines of his soliloquy had been canon. That part about "wind and wrack" he would never forget.

Grinning, Gordon returned to take his bows onstage—a plank-covered garage lift in what had once been the only gas station in the tiny hamlet of Pine View.

Hunger and isolation had driven him to try the hospitality of this mountain village of fenced fields and stout log walls, and the gamble had paid off better than he'd hoped. An exchange of a series of shows for his meals and supplies had tentatively passed by a fair majority of the voting adults, and now the deal seemed settled.

"Bravo! Excellent!" Mrs. Thompson stood in the front row, clapping eagerly. White-haired and bony, but still robust, she turned to encourage the forty-odd others, including small children, to show their appreciation. Gordon did a flourish with one hand, and bowed deeper than before.

Of course his performance had been pure crap. But he was probably the only person within a hundred miles who had once minored in drama. There were "peasants" once again in America, and like his predecessors in the minstrel trade, Gordon had learned to go for the unsubtle in his shows.

Timing his final bow for the moment before the applause began to fade, Gordon hopped off the stage and began removing his slap-dash costume. He had set firm limits; there would be no encore. His stock was theater, and he meant to keep them hungry for it until it was time to leave.

"Marvelous. Just wonderful!" Mrs. Thompson told him as he joined the villagers, now gathering at a buffet table along the back wall. The older children formed a circle around him, staring in wonderment.

Pine View was quite prosperous, compared with so many of the starving villages of the plains and mountains. In some places a good part of a generation was nearly missing due to the devastating effects the Three-Year Winter had had on children. But here he saw several teenagers and young adults, and even a few oldsters who must have been past middle age when the Doom fell.

They must have fought to save everybody. That pattern had been rarer, but he had seen it, too, here and there.

Everywhere there were traces of those years. Faces pocked from diseases or etched from weariness and war. Two women and a man were amputees and another looked out of one good eye, the other a cloudy mass of cataracts.

He was used to such things—at least on a superficial level. He nodded gratefully to his host.

"Thank you, Mrs. Thompson. I appreciate kind words from a perceptive critic. I'm glad you liked the show."

"No, no seriously," the clan leader insisted, as if Gordon had been trying to be modest. "I haven't been so delighted in years. The Macbeth part at the end there sent shivers up my spine! I only wish I'd watched it on TV back when I had a chance. I didn't know it was so good!

"And that inspiring speech you gave us earlier, that one of Abraham Lincoln's... well, you know, we tried to start a school here, in the beginning. But it just didn't work out. We needed every hand, even the kids'. Now though, well, that speech got me to thinking. We've got some old books put away. Maybe now's the time to give it a try again."

Gordon nodded politely. He had seen this syndrome before—the best of the dozen or so types of reception he had experienced over the years, but also among the saddest. It always made him feel like a charlatan when his shows brought out grand, submerged hopes in a few of the decent, older people who remembered better days... hopes that, to his knowledge, had always fallen through before a few weeks or months had passed.

It was as if the seeds of civilization needed more than goodwill and the dreams of aging high school graduates to water them. Gordon often wondered if the right symbol might do the trick—the right *idea*. But he knew his little dramas, however well received, weren't the key. They might trigger a beginning, once in a great while, but local enthusiasm always failed soon after. He was no traveling messiah. The legends he offered weren't the kind of sustenance needed in order to overcome the inertia of a dark age.

The world turns, and soon the last of the old generation will be gone. Scattered tribes will rule the continent. Perhaps in a thousand years the adventure will begin again. Meanwhile...

Gordon was spared hearing more of Mrs. Thompson's sadly unlikely plans. The crowd squeezed out a small, silver-haired, black woman, wiry and leather skinned, who seized Gordon's arm in a friendly, viselike grip.

"Now, Adele," she said to the clan matriarch, "Mister Krantz hasn't had a bite since noontime. I think, if we want him able to perform tomorrow night, we'd better feed him. Right?" She squeezed his right arm and obviously thought him undernourished—an impression he was loathe to alter, with the aroma of food wafting his way.

Mrs. Thompson gave the other woman a look of patient

indulgence. "Of course, Patricia," she said. "I'll speak with you more about this later, Mr. Krantz, after Mrs. Howlett has fattened you up a bit." Her smile and her glittering eyes held a touch of intelligent irony, and Gordon found himself re-evaluating Adele Thompson. She certainly was nobody's fool.

Mrs. Howlett propelled him through the crowd. Gordon smiled and nodded as hands came out to touch his sleeve. Wide eyes followed his every movement.

Hunger must make me a better actor. I've never had an audience react quite like this before. I wish I knew exactly what it was I did that made them feel this way.

One of those watching him from behind the long buffet table was a young woman barely taller than Mrs. Howlett, with deep, almond eyes and hair blacker than Gordon remembered ever seeing before. Twice, she turned to gently slap the hand of a child who tried to help himself before the honored guest. Each time the girl quickly looked back at Gordon and smiled.

Beside her, a tall, burly young man stroked his reddish beard and gave Gordon a strange look—as if his eyes were filled with some desperate resignation. Gordon had only a moment to assimilate the two as Mrs. Howlett pulled him over in front of the pretty brunette.

"Abby," she said, "let's have a little bit of everything on a plate for Mr. Krantz. Then he can make up his mind what he wants seconds of. I baked the blueberry pie, Mr. Krantz."

Dizzily, Gordon made a note to have two helpings of the blueberry. It was hard to concentrate on diplomacy, though. He hadn't seen or smelled anything like this in years. The odors distracted him from the disconcerting looks and touching hands.

There was a large, spit-turned, stuffed turkey. A huge, steaming bowl of boiled potatoes, dollied up with beer-soaked jerky, carrots, and onions, was the second course. Down the table Gordon saw apple cobbler and an opened barrel of dried apple flakes. *I must cozen a supply of those, before I leave.*

Skipping further inventory, he eagerly held out his plate. Abby kept watching him as she took it.

The big, frowning redhead suddenly muttered something indecipherable and reached out to grab Gordon's right hand in both of his own. Gordon flinched, but the taciturn fellow would not let go until he answered the grip and shook hands firmly.

The man muttered something too low to follow, nodded, and let go. He bent to kiss the brunette quickly and then stalked off, eyes downcast.

Gordon blinked. *Did I just miss something?* It felt as if some sort of event had just occurred, and had gone completely over his head.

"That was Michael, Abby's husband," Mrs. Howlett said. "He's got to go and relieve Edward at the trap string. But he wanted to stay to see your show, first. When he was little he so used to love to watch TV shows…"

Steam from the plate rose to his face, making Gordon quite dizzy with hunger. Abby blushed and smiled when he thanked her. Mrs. Howlett pulled him over to take a seat on a pile of old tires. "You'll get to talk to Abby, later," the black woman went on. "Now, you eat. Enjoy yourself."

Gordon did not need to be encouraged. He dug in while people looked on curiously and Mrs. Howlett rattled on.

"Good, isn't it? You just sit and eat and pay us no mind.

"And when you're all full and you're ready to talk again,

I think we'd all like to hear, one more time, how you got to be a mailman."

Gordon looked up at the eager faces above him. He hurriedly took a swig of beer to chase down the too-hot potatoes.

"I'm just a traveler," he said around a half-full mouth while lifting a turkey drumstick. "It's not much of a story how I got the bag and clothes."

He didn't care whether they stared, or touched, or talked at him, so long as they let him eat!

Mrs. Howlett watched him for a few moments. Then, unable to hold back, she started in again. "You know, when I was a little girl we used to give milk and cookies to the mailman. And my father always left a little glass of whiskey on the fence for him the day before New Year's. Dad used to tell us that poem, you know, 'Through sleet, through mud, through war, through blight, through bandits and through darkest night…'"

Gordon choked on a sudden, wayward swallow. He coughed and looked up to see if she was in earnest. A glimmer in his forebrain wanted to dance over the old woman's accidentally magnificent remembrance. It was rich.

The glimmer faded quickly, though, as he bit into the delicious roast fowl. He hadn't the will to try to figure out what the old woman was driving at.

"*Our* mailman used to sing to us!"

The speaker, incongruously, was a dark-haired giant with a silver-streaked beard. His eyes seemed to mist as he remembered. "We could hear him coming, on Saturdays when we were home from school, sometimes when he was over a block away.

"He was black, a lot blacker than Mrs. Howlett, or Jim

Horton over there. Man, did he have a nice voice! Guess that's how he got the job. He brought me all those mail order coins I used to collect. Ringed the doorbell so he could hand 'em to me, personal, with his own hand."

His voice was hushed with telescoped awe.

"Our mailman just whistled when I was little," said a middle-aged woman with a deeply lined face. She sounded a little disappointed.

"But he *was* real nice. Later, when I was grown up, I came home from work one day and found out the mailman had saved the life of one of my neighbors. Heard him choking and gave him mouth-to-mouth until th' ambulance came."

A collective sigh rose from the circle of listeners, as if they were hearing the heroic adventures of a single ancient hero. The children listened in wide-eyed silence as the tales grew more and more embroidered. At least the small part of him still paying attention figured they had to be. Some were simply too far-fetched to be believed.

Mrs. Howlett touched Gordon's knee. "Tell us again how you got to be a mailman."

Gordon shrugged a little desperately. "I just found the mailman's fings!" he emphasized around the food in his mouth. The flavors had overcome him, and he felt almost panicky over the way they all *hovered* over him. If the adult villagers wanted to romanticize their memories of men they had once considered lower-class civil servants at best, that was all right. Apparently they associated his performance tonight with the little touches of extroversion they had witnessed in their neighborhood letter carriers, when they had been children. That, too, was okay. They could think anything they damn well pleased, so long as they didn't interrupt his eating!

"Ah!" Several of the villagers looked at each other knowingly and nodded, as if Gordon's answer had had some profound significance. Gordon heard his own words repeated to those on the edges of the circle.

"He found the mailman's things… so naturally he became…"

His answer must have appeased them, somehow, for the crowd thinned as the villagers moved off to take polite turns at the buffet. It wasn't until much later, on reflection, that he perceived the significance of what had taken place there, under boarded windows and tallow lamps, while he crammed himself near to bursting with good food.

5

"…we have found that our clinic has an abundant supply of disinfectants and painkillers of several varieties. We hear these are in short supply in Bend and in the relocation centers up north. We're willing to trade some of these—along with a truckload of de-ionizing resin columns that happened to be abandoned here—for one thousand doses of tetracycline, to guard against the bubonic plague outbreak to the east. Perhaps we'd be willing to settle for an active culture of balomycine-producing yeast, instead, if someone could come up and show us how to maintain it.

"Also, we are in desperate need of…"

The Mayor of Gilchrist must have been a strong-willed man to have persuaded his local emergency committee to offer such a trade. Hoarding, however illogical and uncooperative, was a major contributor to the collapse. It astonished Gordon that there still had been people with this much good sense during the first two years of the Chaos.

He rubbed his eyes. Reading wasn't easy by the light of a pair of homemade candles. But he found it difficult getting to sleep on the soft mattress, and damn if he'd sleep on the floor after so long dreaming of such a bed, in just such a room!

He had been a little sick, earlier. All that food and home-brewed ale had almost taken him over the line from delirious happiness to utter misery. Somehow, he had teetered along the boundary for several hours of blurrily remembered celebration before at last stumbling into the room they had prepared for him.

There had been a *toothbrush* waiting on his nightstand, and an iron tub filled with hot water.

And soap! In the bath his stomach had settled, and a warm, clean glow spread over his skin.

Gordon smiled when he saw that his postman's uniform had been cleaned and pressed. It lay on a nearby chair; the rips and tears he had crudely patched were now neatly sewn.

He could not fault the people of this tiny hamlet for neglecting his one remaining longing… something he had gone without too long to even think about. Enough. This was almost Paradise.

As he lay in a sated haze between a pair of elderly but clean sheets, waiting leisurely for sleep to come, he read a piece of correspondence between two long-dead men.

The Mayor of Gilchrist went on:

"We are having extreme difficulty with local gangs of 'Survivalists.' Fortunately, these infestations of egotists are mostly too paranoid to band together. They're as much trouble to each other as to us, I suppose. Still, they are becoming a real problem.

"Our deputy is regularly fired on by well-armed men in army surplus camouflage clothing. No doubt the idiots think he's a Russian lackey or some such nonsense. They have taken to hunting game on a massive scale, killing everything in the forest and doing a typically rotten job of butchering and preserving the meat. Our own hunters come back disgusted over the waste, often having been shot at without provocation.

"I know it's a lot to ask, but when you can spare a platoon from relocation riot duty, could you send them up here to help us root out these self-centered, hoarding, romantic scoundrels from their little filtered armories? Maybe a unit or two of the US Army will convince them that we won the war, and have to cooperate with each other from now on..."

He put the letter down.

So it had been that way here, too. The clichéd "last straw" had been this plague of "survivalists"—particularly those following the high priest of violent anarchy, Nathan Holn.

One of Gordon's duties in the militia had been to help weed out some of those small gangs of city-bred cutthroats and gun nuts. The number of fortified caves and cabins his unit had found—in the prairie and on little lake islands—had been staggering... all set up in a rash of paranoia in the difficult decades before the war.

The irony of it was that we had things turned around! The depression was over. People were at work again and cooperating. Except for a few crazies, it looked like a renaissance was coming, for America and for the world.

But we forgot just how much harm a few crazies could do, in America and in the world.

Of course when the collapse did come, the solitary survivalists' precious little fortresses did not stay theirs for long. Most of the tiny bastions changed hands a dozen or more times in the first months—they were such tempting targets. The battles had raged all over the plains until every solar collector was shattered, every windmill wrecked, and every cache of valuable medicines scattered in the never-ending search for heavy dope.

Only the ranches and villages, those possessing the right mixture of ruthlessness, internal cohesion, and common sense, survived in the end. By the time the Guard units had all died at their posts, or themselves dissolved into roving gangs of battling survivalists, very few of the original population of armed and armored hermits remained alive.

Gordon looked at the letter's postmark again. *Nearly two years after the war.* He shook his head. *I never knew anyone held on so long.*

The thought hurt, like a dull wound inside him. Anything that made the last sixteen years seem avoidable was just too hard to imagine.

There was a faint sound. Gordon looked up, wondering if he had imagined it. Then, only slightly louder, another faint knock rapped at the door to his room.

"Come in," he called. The door opened about halfway. Abby, the petite girl with the vaguely oriental cast to her eyes, smiled timidly from the opening. Gordon refolded the letter and slipped it into its envelope. He smiled.

"Hello, Abby. What's up?"

"I… I've come to ask if there was anything else you needed," she said a little quickly. "Did you enjoy your bath?"

"Did I now?" Gordon sighed. He found himself slipping back into Macduff's burr. "Aye, lass. And in particular I appreciated the gift of that toothbrush. Heaven sent, it was."

"You mentioned you'd lost yours." She looked at the floor. "I pointed out that we had at least five or six unused ones in the storage room. I'm glad you were pleased."

"It was your idea?" He bowed. "Then I am indeed in your debt."

Abby looked up and smiled. "Was that a letter you were just reading? Could I look at it? I've never seen a letter before."

Gordon laughed. "Oh surely you're not that young! What about before the war?"

Abby blushed at his laughter. "I was only four when it happened. It was so frightening and confusing that I... I really don't remember much from before."

Gordon blinked. Had it really been that long? Yes. Sixteen years was indeed enough time to have beautiful women in the world who knew nothing but the dark age.

Amazing, he thought.

"All right, then." He pushed the chair by his bed. Grinning, she came over and sat beside him. Gordon reached into the sack and pulled out another of the frail, yellowed envelopes. Carefully, he spread out the letter and handed it to her.

Abby looked at it so intently that he thought she was reading the whole thing. She concentrated, her thin eyebrows almost coming together in a crease on her forehead. But finally she handed the letter back. "I guess I can't really read that well. I mean, I can read labels on cans, and stuff. But I never had much practice with handwriting and... sentences."

Her voice dropped at the end. She sounded embarrassed, but in a totally unafraid, trusting fashion, as if he were her confessor.

He smiled. "No matter. I'll tell you what it's about." He held the letter up to the candlelight. Abby moved over to sit by his knees on the edge of the bed, her eyes rapt on the pages.

"It's from one John Briggs, of Fort Rock, Oregon, to his former employer in Klamath Falls... I'd guess from the lathe and hobby horse letterhead that Briggs was a retired machinist or carpenter or something. Hmmm."

Gordon concentrated on the barely legible handwriting. "It seems Mr. Briggs was a pretty nice man. Here he's offering to take in his ex-boss's children, until the emergency is over. Also he says he has a good garage machine shop, his own power, and plenty of metal stock. He wants to know if the man wants to order any parts made up, especially things in short supply..."

Gordon's voice faltered. He was still so thick-headed from his excesses that it had just struck him that a beautiful female was sitting on his bed. The depression she made in the mattress tilted his body toward her. He cleared his throat quickly and went back to scanning the letter.

"Briggs mentions something about power levels from the Fort Rock reservoir... Telephones were out, but he was still, oddly enough, getting Eugene on his computer data net..."

Abby looked at him. Apparently much of what he had said about the letter writer might as well have been in a foreign language to her. "Machine shop" and "data net" could have been ancient, magical words of power.

"Why didn't you bring us any letters, here in Pine View?" she asked quite suddenly.

Gordon blinked at the non sequitur. The girl wasn't stupid. One could tell such things. Then why had everything he said, when he arrived here, and later at the party, been completely misunderstood? She still thought he was a *mailman*, as, apparently, did all but a few of the others in this small settlement.

From whom did she imagine they'd get mail?

She probably didn't realize that the letters he carried had been sent long ago, from dead men and women to other dead men and women, or that he carried them for... for his own reasons.

The myth that had spontaneously developed here in Pine View depressed Gordon. It was one more sign of the deterioration of civilized minds, many of whom had once been high school and even college graduates. He considered telling her the truth, as brutally and frankly as he could, to stop this fantasy once and for all. He started to.

"There aren't any letters because..."

He paused. Again Gordon was aware of her nearness, the scent of her and the gentle curves of her body. Of her trust, as well.

He sighed and looked away. "There aren't any letters for you folks because... because I'm coming west out of Idaho, and nobody back there knows you, here in Pine View. From here I'm going to the coast. There might even be some large towns left. Maybe..."

"Maybe someone down there will write to us, if we send them a letter first!" Abby's eyes were bright. "Then, when you pass this way again, on your way back to Idaho, you could give us the letters they send, and maybe do another play-act for us like tonight, and we'll have so much beer and pie for you you'll bust!" She hopped a little on the edge of the bed. "By then I'll be able to read better, I promise!"

Gordon shook his head and smiled. It was beyond his right to dash such dreams. "Maybe so, Abby. Maybe so. But you know, you may get to learn to read easier than that. Mrs. Thompson's offered to put it up for a vote to let me stay on here for a while. I guess officially I'd be a school teacher, though I'd have to prove myself as good a hunter and farmer as anybody. I could give archery lessons…"

He stopped. Abby's expression was open-mouthed in surprise. She shook her head vigorously. "But you haven't heard! They voted on it after you went to take your bath. Mrs. Thompson should be ashamed of trying to bribe a man like you that way, with your important work having to be done!"

He sat forward, not believing his ears. "What did you say?" He had formed hopes of staying in Pine View for at least the cold season, maybe a year or more. Who could tell? Perhaps the wanderlust would leave him, and he could finally find a home.

His sated stupor dissipated. Gordon fought to hold back his anger. To have the chance revoked on the basis of the crowd's childish fantasies!

Abby noticed his agitation and hurried on. "That wasn't the only reason, of course. There was the problem of there being no woman for you. And then…" Her voice lowered perceptibly. "And then Mrs. Howlett thought you'd be perfect for helping me and Michael finally have a baby…"

Gordon blinked. "Um," he said, expressing the sudden and complete contents of his mind.

"We've been trying for five years," she explained. "We really want children. But Mr. Horton thinks Michael can't 'cause he had the mumps *really* bad when he was twelve. You remember the real bad mumps, don't you?"

Gordon nodded, recalling friends who had died. The resultant sterility had made for unusual social arrangements everywhere he had traveled.

Still…

Abby went on quickly. "Well, it would cause problems

if I asked any of the other men here to… to be the body father. I mean, when you live close to people, like this, you have to look on the men who aren't your husband as not being really 'men'… at least not that way. I… I don't think I'd like it, and it might cause trouble."

She blushed. "Besides, I'll tell you something if you promise to keep a secret. I don't think any of the other men would be able to give Michael the kind of son he deserves. He's really very smart, you know. He's the only one of us youngers who can *really* read…"

The flow of strange logic was coming on too fast for Gordon to follow completely. Part of him dispassionately noted that this was all really an intricate and subtle tribal adaptation to a difficult social problem. That part of him though—the last Twentieth-Century intellectual—was still a bit drunk, and meanwhile the rest was starting to realize what Abby was driving at.

"You're different." She smiled at him. "I mean, even Michael saw that right from the start. He's not too happy, but he figures you'll only be through once a year or so, and he could stand that. He'd rather that than never have any kids."

Gordon cleared his throat. "You're sure he feels this way?"

"Oh, yes. Why do you think Mrs. Howlett introduced us in that funny way? It was to make it clear without really saying it out loud. Mrs. Thompson doesn't like it much, but I think that's because she wanted you to stay."

Gordon's mouth felt dry. "How do *you* feel about all this?"

Her expression was enough of an answer. She looked at him as if he were some sort of visiting prophet, or at least a hero out of a story book. "I'd be honored if you'd say yes," she said, quietly, and lowered her eyes.

"And you'd be able to think of me as a man, 'that way'?"

Abby grinned. She answered by crawling up on top of him and planting her mouth intensely upon his.

There was a momentary pause as she shimmied out of her clothes and Gordon turned to snuff out the candles on the bed stand. Beside them lay the letter man's gray uniform cap, its brass badge casting multiple reflections of the dancing flames. The figure of a rider, hunched forward on horseback before bulging saddlebags, seemed to move at a flickering gallop.

This is another one I owe you, Mr. Postman.

Abby's smooth skin slid along his side. Her hand slipped into his as he took a deep breath and blew the candles out.

6

For ten days, Gordon's life followed a new pattern. As if to catch up on six months' road weariness, he slept late each morning and awoke to find Abby gone, like the night's dreams.

Yet her warmth and scent lingered on the sheets when he stretched and opened his eyes. The sunshine streaming through his eastward-facing window was like something new, a springtime in his heart, and not really early autumn at all.

He rarely saw her during the day as he washed and helped with chores until noon—chopping and stacking wood for the community supply and digging a deep pit for a new outhouse. When most of the village gathered for the main meal of the day, Abby returned from tending the flocks. But she spent lunchtime with the younger children, relieving old one-legged Mr. Lothes, their work supervisor. The little ones laughed as she kidded them, plucking the wool that coated their clothes from a morning spent carding skeins for the winter spinning, helping them keep the gray strands out of their food.

She barely glanced at Gordon, but that brief smile was enough. He knew he had no rights beyond these few days, and yet a shared look in the daylight made him feel that it was all real, and not just a dream.

Afternoons he conferred with Mrs. Thompson and the other village leaders, helping them inventory books and other long-neglected salvage. At intervals, he gave reading and archery lessons.

One day he and Mrs. Thompson traded methods in the art of field medicine while treating a man clawed by a "tiger," what the locals called that new strain of mountain lion which had bred with leopards escaped from zoos in the postwar chaos. The trapper had surprised the beast with its kill, but fortunately, it had only batted him into the brush and let him run away. Gordon and the village matriarch felt sure the wound would heal.

In the evenings all of Pine View gathered in the big garage and Gordon recited stories by Twain and Sayles and Keillor. He led them in singing old folk songs and lovingly remembered commercial jingles, and in playing "Remember When." Then it was time for drama.

Dressed in scrap and foil, he was John Paul Jones, shouting defiance from the deck of the *Bonne Homme Richard*. He was Anton Perceveral, exploring the dangers of a faraway world and the depths of his own potential with a mad robot companion. And he was Doctor Hudson, wading through the horror of the Kenyan

Conflict to treat the victims of biological war.

At first Gordon always felt uneasy, putting on a flimsy costume and stomping across the makeshift stage waving his arms, shouting lines only vaguely recalled or made up on the spot. He had never really admired play-acting as a profession, even before the great war.

But it had got him halfway across a continent, and he was good at it. He felt the rapt gaze of the audience, their hunger for wonder and something of the world beyond their narrow valley, and their eagerness warmed him to the task. Pox-scarred and wounded—bent from year after year of back-breaking labor merely to survive—they looked up, the need greatest in eyes clouded with age, a yearning for help doing what they could no longer accomplish alone—remembering.

Wrapped in his roles, he gave them bits and pieces of lost romance. And by the time the last lines of his soliloquy faded, he too was able to forget the present, at least for a while.

Each night, after he retired, she came to him. For a while she would sit on the edge of his bed and talk of her life; about the flocks, and the village children, and Michael. She brought him books to ask their meanings and questioned him about his youth—about the life of a student in the wonderful days before the Doomwar.

Then, after a time, Abby would smile, put away the dusty volumes, and slide under the covers next to him while he leaned over and took care of the candle.

On the tenth morning, she did not slip away with the predawn light, but instead wakened Gordon with a kiss.

"Hmmmn, good morning," he commented, and reached for her, but Abby pulled away. She picked up her clothes, brushing her breasts across the soft hairs of his flat stomach.

"I should let you sleep," she told him. "But I wanted to ask you something." She held her dress in a ball.

"Mmm? What is it?" Gordon stuffed the pillow behind his head for support.

"You're going to be leaving today, aren't you?" she asked.

"Yes." He nodded seriously. "It's probably best. I'd like to stay longer, but since I can't, I'd better be heading west again."

"I know." She nodded seriously. "We'll all hate to see you go. But… well, I'm going to meet Michael out at the trapline, this evening. I miss him terribly." She touched the side of his face. "That doesn't bother you, does it? I mean, it's been wonderful here with you, but he's my husband and…"

He smiled and covered her hand. To his amazement, he had little difficulty with his feelings. He was more envious than jealous of Michael. The desperate logic of their desire for children, and their obvious love for one another, made the situation, in retrospect, as obvious as the need for a clean break at the end. He only hoped he had done them the favor they sought. For despite their fantasies, it was unlikely he would ever come this way again.

"I have something for you," Abby said. She reached under the bed and pulled out a small silvery object on a chain, and a paper package.

"It's a whistle. Mrs. Howlett says you should have one." She slipped it over his neck and adjusted it until satisfied with the effect.

"Also, she helped me write this *letter*." Abby picked up the little package. "I found some stamps in a drawer in the gas station, but they wouldn't stick on. So I got some money, instead. This is fourteen dollars. Will it be enough?"

She held out a cluster of faded bills.

Gordon couldn't help smiling. Yesterday five or six of the others had privately approached him. He had accepted their little envelopes and similar payments for postage with as straight a face as possible. He might have used the opportunity to charge them something he needed, but the community had already given him a month's stock of jerky, dried apples, and twenty straight arrows for his bow. There was no need, nor had he the desire to extort anything else.

Some of the older citizens had had relatives in Eugene, or Portland, or towns in the Willamette Valley. It was the direction he was heading, so he took the letters. A few were addressed to people who had lived in Oakridge and Blue River. Those he filed deep in the safest part of his sack. The rest, he might as well throw into Crater Lake, for all the good they would ever do, but he pretended anyway.

He soberly counted out a few paper bills, then handed back the rest of the worthless currency. "And who are you writing to?" Gordon asked Abby as he took the letter. He felt as if he were playing Santa Claus, and found himself enjoying it.

"I'm writing to the university. You know, at Eugene? I asked a bunch of questions like, are they taking new students again yet? And do they take married students?" Abby blushed. "I know I'd have to work real hard on my reading to get good enough. And maybe they aren't recovered enough to take many new students. But Michael's already so smart... and by the time we hear from them maybe things will be better."

"By the time you hear..." Gordon shook his head.

Abby nodded. "I'll for sure be reading a lot better by then. Mrs. Thompson promises she'll help me. And her husband has agreed to start a school, this winter. I'm

369

going to help with the little kids.

"I hope maybe I can learn to be a teacher. Do you think that's silly?"

Gordon shook his head. He had thought himself beyond surprise, but this touched him. In spite of Abby's totally disproportioned view of the state of the world, her hope warmed him, and he found himself dreaming along with her. There was no harm in wishing, was there?

"Actually," Abby went on, confidentially, twisting her dress in her hands. "One of the big reasons I'm writing is to get a… a pen pal. That's the word, isn't it? I'm hoping maybe someone in Eugene will write to me. That way we'll get letters, here. I'd love to get a letter.

"Also"—her gaze fell—"that will give you another reason to come back, in a year or so… besides maybe wanting to see the baby."

She looked up and dimpled. "I got the idea from your Sherlock Holmes play. That's an 'ulterior motive,' isn't it?"

She was so delighted with her own cleverness, and so eager for his approval, Gordon felt a great, almost painful rush of tenderness. Tears welled as he reached out and pulled her into an embrace. He held her tightly and rocked slowly, his eyes shut against reality, and he breathed in with her sweet smell a light and optimism he had thought gone from the world.

7

"Well, this is where I turn back." Mrs. Thompson shook hands with Gordon. "Down this road things should be pretty tame until you get to Davis Lake. The last of the old loner survivalists that way wiped each other out some years back, though I'd still be careful if I were you."

There was a chill in the air, for autumn had arrived in full. Gordon zipped up the old letter carrier's jacket and adjusted the leather bag as the straight-backed old woman handed him an old roadmap.

"I had Jimmie Horton mark the places we know of, where homesteaders have set up. I wouldn't bother any of them unless you have to. Mostly they're a suspicious type, likely to shoot first. We've only been trading with the nearest for a short time."

Gordon nodded. He folded the map carefully and slipped it into a pouch. He felt rested and ready. He would regret leaving Pine View as much as any haven in recent memory. But now that he was resigned to going, he actually felt a growing eagerness to be traveling, to see what had happened in the rest of Oregon.

In the years since he had left the wreckage of Minnesota, he had found ever wilder signs of the dark age. But now he was in a new watershed. This had once been a pleasant state with dispersed light industry, productive farms, and an elevated level of culture. Perhaps it was merely Abby's innocence infecting him. But logically, the Willamette Valley would be the place to look for civilization, if it existed anywhere anymore.

He took the old woman's hand once again. "Mrs. Thompson, I'm not sure I could ever repay what you people have done for me."

She shook her head. Her face was deeply tanned and so lined Gordon was certain she had to be more than the fifty years she claimed.

"No, Gordon, you paid your keep. I would've liked it if

you could've stayed and helped me get the school going. But now I see maybe it won't be so hard to do it by ourselves."

She gazed out over her little valley. "You know, we've been living in a kind of a daze, these last years since the crops have started coming in and the hunting's returned. You can tell how bad things have gotten when a bunch of grown men and women, who once had jobs, who read magazines—and filled out their own taxes, for Heaven's sake—start treating a poor, battered, wandering play-actor as if he was something like the Easter Bunny." She looked back at him. "Even Jim Horton gave you a couple of letters to deliver, didn't he?"

Gordon's face felt hot. For a moment he was too embarrassed to face her. Then, all at once, he burst out laughing. He wiped his eyes in relief at having the group fantasy lifted from his shoulders.

Mrs. Thompson chuckled as well. "Oh, it was harmless I think. And more than that. You've served as a… you know, that old automobile thing… a *catalyst* I think. You know, the children are already exploring ruins for miles around—between chores and supper—bringing me all the books they find. I won't have any trouble making school into a privilege.

"Imagine, *punishing* them by suspending 'em from class! I hope Bobbie and I handle it right."

"I wish you the best of luck, Mrs. Thompson," Gordon said sincerely. "God, it would be nice to see a light, somewhere in all this desolation."

"Right, son. That'd be bliss."

Mrs. Thompson sighed. "I'd recommend you wait a year, but come on back. You're kind… you treated my people well. And you're discreet about some things, like that business with Abby and Michael."

She frowned momentarily. "I *think* I understand what went on there, and I guess it's for the best. Got to adjust, I suppose. Anyway, like I said, you're always welcome back."

Mrs. Thompson turned to go, walked two paces, then paused. She half turned to look back at Gordon. For a moment her face betrayed a hint of confusion and wonder. "You aren't *really* a postman, are you?" she asked suddenly.

Gordon smiled. He set the cap, with its bright brass emblem, on his head. "If I bring back some letters, you'll know for sure."

She nodded, gruffly, then set off up the ruined asphalt road. Gordon watched her until she passed the first bend, then he turned about to the west, and the long downgrade toward the Pacific.

8

The barricades had been long abandoned. The baffle wall on Highway 58, at the east end of Oakridge, had weathered into a tumbled tell of concrete debris and curled, rusting steel. The town itself was silent. This end, at least, was clearly long abandoned.

Gordon looked down the main street, reading its story. Two, possibly three, pitched battles had been fought here. A storefront with a canted sign—EMERGENCY SERVICES CLINIC—sat at the center of a major circle of devastation.

Three intact panes reflected morning sunlight from the top floor of a hotel. Elsewhere though, even where store windows had been boarded, the prismatic sparkle of shattered glass glistened on the buckled pavement.

Not that he had really expected anything better, but some of the feelings he had carried with him out of Pine View had led to hopes for more islands of peace, especially now that he was in the fertile watershed of the Willamette Valley. If no living town, at least Oakridge might have shown other signs conducive to optimism. There might have been traces of methodical reclamation, for instance. If an industrial civilization existed here in Oregon, towns such as this one should have been harvested of anything usable.

But just twenty yards from his vantage point Gordon saw the wreckage of a gas station—a big mechanic's tool cabinet lay on its side, its store of wrenches, pliers, and replacement wiring scattered on the oil-stained floor. A row of never-used tires still hung on a rack high above the service lifts.

From this, Gordon knew Oakridge to be the worst of all possible Oakridges, at least from his point of view. The things needed by a machine culture were available at every hand, untouched and rotting... implying there was no such technological society anywhere near. At the same time, he would have to pick through the wreckage of fifty waves of previous looters in his search for anything useful to a single traveler like himself.

Well, he sighed. *I've done it before.*

Even sifting through the downtown ruins of Boise, the gleaners before him had missed a small treasure trove of canned food in a loft behind a shoe store... some hoarder's stash, long untouched. There was a pattern to such things, worked out over the years. He had his own methods for conducting a search.

Gordon slipped down on the forest side of the barricade baffle and entered the overgrowth. He zigzagged, on the off chance he had been watched. At a place where he could verify landmarks in three different directions, Gordon dropped his leather shoulder bag and cap under an autumn-bright red cedar. He took off the dark brown letter-carrier's jacket and laid it on top, then cut brush to cover the cache.

He would go to any lengths to avoid conflict with suspicious locals, but only a fool would leave his weapons behind. There were two types of fighting that could come out of a situation like this. For one, the silence of the bow might be better. For the other, it could be worth expending precious, irreplaceable .38 cartridges. Gordon checked the pistol's action and reholstered it. His bow he carried, along with arrows and a cloth sack for salvage.

In the first few houses, on the outskirts, the early looters had been more exuberant than thorough. Often the wreckage in such places discouraged those who came after, leaving useful items within. He had found it true often before.

Still, by the fourth house Gordon had a poor collection to show for this theory. His sack contained a pair of boots almost useless from mildew, a magnifying glass, and two spools of thread. He had poked into all the usual and some unconventional hoarder's crannies, and found no food of any sort.

His Pine View jerky wasn't gone, but he had dipped down farther than he liked. His archery was better, and he had bagged a small turkey two days ago. Still, if he didn't have better luck gleaning, he might have to give up on the Willamette Valley for now and get to work on a winter hunting camp.

What he *really* wanted was another haven such as Pine

View. But fate had been kind enough, lately. Too much good luck made Gordon suspicious.

He moved on to a fifth house.

The four-poster bed stood in what had once been a prosperous physician's two-story home. Like the rest of the house, the bedroom had been stripped of nearly everything but the furniture. Nevertheless, as he crouched down over the heavy area rug, Gordon thought he might have found something the earlier looters had missed.

The rug seemed out of place. The bed rested upon it, but only with the right pair of legs. The left pair lay directly on the hardwood floor. Either the owner had been sloppy in placing the big oval carpet, or...

Gordon put down his burdens and grabbed the edge of the rug.

Whew. It's heavy.

He started rolling it toward the bed.

Yes! There was a thin, square crack in the floor, under the carpet. A bed leg pinned the rug over one of two brass door hinges. A *trapdoor*.

He pushed hard on the bedpost. The leg hopped and fell again with a boom. Twice more he shoved and loud echoes reverberated.

On his fourth heave the bedpost snapped in two. Gordon barely escaped impalement on the jagged stub as he toppled onto the mattress. The canopy followed and the aged bed collapsed in a crash. Gordon cursed, fighting with the smothering shroud. He sneezed violently in a cloud of floating dust.

Finally, regaining a bit of sense, he managed to slither

out from under the ancient, moldy fabric. He stumbled out of the room, still sputtering and sneezing. The attack subsided slowly. He gripped the upstairs bannister, squinting in that torturous, semi-orgasmic state that comes before a whopping sternutation. His ears rang with an extra murmur that seemed almost like voices.

Next thing you'll be hearing church bells, he told himself.

The final sneeze came at last, in a loud "Ah—chblthooh!" Wiping his eyes, he reentered the bedroom. The trapdoor lay fully exposed, layered under a new coating of dust. Gordon had to pry the edge of the secret panel. Finally, it lifted with a high, rusty skreigh.

Again, it seemed as though some of the sound came from *outside* the house. But when he stopped and listened carefully, Gordon heard nothing. Impatiently, he bent down and brushed aside cobwebs to peer into the cache.

There was a large metal box inside. He poked around hoping for more. After all, the things a prewar doctor might have kept in a locked chest—money and documents— would be of less use to him than canned goods stashed here in a spree of wartime hoarding. But there was nothing other than the box. Gordon hauled it out, puffing.

Good. It's heavy. Now let's hope it's not gold or any similar crap. The hinges and lock were rusted. He lifted the haft of his knife to smash the small lock. Then he stopped abruptly.

Now they were unmistakable. The voices were close, too close.

"I think it came from this house!" someone called from the overgrown garden outside. Feet shuffled through the dry leaves. There were steps on the wooden porch.

Gordon sheathed the knife and snatched up his gear.

Leaving the box by the bed, he hurried out of the room to the stairwell.

This was not the best of circumstances to meet other men. In Boise and other mountain ruins there had been almost a code—gleaners from ranches all around could try their luck in the open city, and although the groups and individuals were wary, they seldom preyed on one another. Only one thing could bring them all together—a rumor that someone had sighted a Holnist, somewhere. Otherwise they pretty much left each other alone.

In other places, though, territoriality was the rule—and fiercely enforced. Gordon might be searching in some such clan's turf. A quick departure would, in any case, be discreet.

Still... he looked back at the strongbox anxiously. *It's mine, damnit!*

Boots clomped noisily downstairs. It was too late to close the trapdoor or hide the heavy treasure chest. Gordon cursed silently and hurried as quietly as he could across the upstairs landing to the narrow attic ladder.

The top floor was little more than a simple, A-frame garret. He had searched among the useless mementos here earlier. Now all he wanted was a hiding place. Gordon kept near the sloping walls to avoid creaks in the floorboards. He chose a trunk near a small, gabled window, and there laid his sack and quiver. Quickly, he strung his bow.

Would they search? In that case, the strongbox would certainly attract attention.

If so, would they take it as an offering and leave him a share of whatever it contained? He had known such things to happen, in places where a primitive sort of honor system worked.

He had the drop on anyone entering the attic, although

it was dubious how much good that would do—cornered in a wooden building. The locals doubtless retained, even in the middle of a dark age, the craft of fire making.

At least three pairs of booted feet could be heard now. In rapid, hollow steps, they took the stairs, skirmishing up one landing at a time. When everyone was on the second floor, Gordon heard a shout.

"Hey, Karl, looka this!"

"What? You catch a couple of the kids playing doctor in an old bed ag… sheeit!"

There was a loud thump, followed by the hammering of metal on metal.

"Sheeit!" Gordon shook his head. Karl had a limited but expressive vocabulary.

There were shuffling and tearing sounds, accompanied by more scatalogical exclamations. At last, though, a third voice spoke up loudly.

"Sure was nice of that fellow, findin' this for us. Wish we could thank him. Ought to get to know him so we don't shoot first if we ever see him again."

If that was bait, Gordon wasn't taking. He waited.

"Well, at least he deserves a warning," the first voice said even louder. "We got a shoot first rule, in Oakridge. He better scat before someone puts a hole in him bigger than the gap between a survivalist's ears."

Gordon nodded, taking the warning at face value. The footsteps receded. They echoed down the stairwell, then out onto the wooden porch.

From the gable overlooking the front entrance, Gordon saw three men leave the house and walk toward the surrounding hemlock grove. They carried rifles and bulging canvas day packs. He hurried to the other windows as they disappeared into the woods, but saw no other motion. No signs of anyone doubling back from another side.

There had been three pairs of feet. He was sure of it. Three voices. And it wasn't likely only one man would stay in ambush, anyway. Still, Gordon was careful as he moved out. He lay down beside the open attic trapdoor, his bow, bag, and quiver next to him, and crawled until his head and shoulders extended out over the opening, slightly above the level of the floor. He drew his revolver, held it out in front of him, and then let gravity swing his head and torso suddenly downward in a fashion an ambusher would hardly expect.

As the blood rushed to his head Gordon was primed to snap off six quick shots at anything that moved.

Nothing did. There was nobody in the second-floor hallway.

He reached for his canvas bag, never taking his gaze from the hallway, and dropped it to clatter on the landing. The sound triggered no ambush.

Gordon took up his gear and dropped to the next level in a crouch. He quickly moved down the hall, skirmish-style.

The strongbox lay open and empty next to the bed, beside it a scattering of paper trash. As he had expected, there were such curiosities as stock certificates, a stamp collection, and the deed to this house.

But some of the other debris was different.

A torn cardboard container, the cellophane wrapper newly removed, colorfully depicted a pair of happy canoeists with their new collapsible rifle. Gordon looked at the weapon pictured on the box and stifled a strangled cry. Doubtless there had also been boxes of ammunition.

Goddamn thieves, he thought bitterly.

But the other trash almost drove him wild. EMPIRIN WITH CODEINE, ERYTHROMYCIN, MEGAVITAMIN COMPLEX, MORPHINE... the labels and boxes were strewn about, but the bottles had been taken.

Carefully handled... cached and traded in dribbles... these could have bought Gordon admission into almost any hamlet. Why he might even have won a probationary membership in one of the wealthy Wyoming ranch communities!

He remembered a good doctor, whose clinic in the ruins of Butte was a sanctuary protected by all the surrounding villages and clans. Gordon thought of what that sainted gentleman could have done with these.

But his eyesight nearly went dim with dark tunnels of rage when he saw an empty cardboard box whose label read... TOOTH POWDER...

My tooth powder!

Gordon counted to ten. It wasn't enough. He tried controlled breathing. It only helped him focus on his anger. He stood there, slope-shouldered, feeling impotent to answer this one more unkindness by the world.

It's all right, he told himself. *I'm alive. And if I can get back to my backpack, I'll probably stay alive. Next year, if it comes, I can worry about my teeth rotting out of my head.*

Gordon picked up his gear and resumed his stalking exit out of that house of false expectations.

A man who spends a long time alone in the wilderness can have one great advantage over even a very good hunter—if that hunter nevertheless goes home to friends and companions most nights. The difference is a trait in kinship with the animals, with the wilds themselves. It was something as undefinable as that which made him nervous. Gordon sensed that something was odd long before he could attribute it. The feeling would not go away.

He had been retracing his steps toward the eastern edge of town, where his gear was cached. Now, though, he stopped and considered. Was he overreacting? He was no Jeremiah Johnson, to read the sounds and smells of the woods like street signs in a city. Still, he looked around for something to back up his unease.

The forest was mostly western hemlock and bigleaf maple with alder saplings growing like weeds in nearly every former open area. It was a far cry from the dry woodlands he had passed through on the east side of the Cascades, where he had been robbed under the sparse ponderosa pines. Here there was a scent of life richer than anything he remembered since before the Three-Year Winter.

Animal sounds had been scant until he stopped moving. But as he kept still, a flow of avian chatter and movement soon began to flow back into this patch of forest. Gray-feathered camp robbers flitted in small groups from spot to spot, playing guerrilla war with lesser jays for the best of the tiny, bug-rich glades. Smaller birds hopped from branch to branch, chirping and foraging.

Birds in this size range had no great love for man, but neither did they go to great lengths to avoid him, if he was quiet.

Then why am I nervous as a cat?

There was a brief snapping sound to his left, near one of the ubiquitous blackberry thickets, about twenty yards away. Gordon whirled, but there, too, there were birds.

Correction. A bird. A mockingbird.

The creature swooped up through the branches and landed in a bundle of twigs Gordon guessed to be its nest. It stood there, like a small lordling, haughty and proud, then it squawked and dove toward the thicket again. As it passed out of sight, there was another tiny rustle, then the mockingbird swooped into view again.

Gordon idly picked at the loam with his bow while loosening the loop on his revolver, trying hard to maintain a frozen expression of nonchalance. He whistled through fear-dry lips as he walked slowly, moving neither toward the thicket nor away from it, but in the direction of a large grand fir.

Something behind that thicket had set off the mockingbird's nest defense response, and that something was trying hard to ignore the nuisance attacks—to stay silently hidden.

Alerted, Gordon recognized a hunting blind. He sauntered with exaggerated carelessness. But as soon as he passed behind the fir, he drew his revolver and ran into the forest at a sharp angle, crouching, trying to keep the bulk of the tree between himself and the blackberry bramble.

He remained in the tree's umbra only a moment. Surprise protected him a moment longer. Then the cracking of three loud shots, all of different caliber, diffracted down the lattice of trees. Gordon sprinted to a fallen log at the top of a small rise. Three more bangs pealed out as he dove over the decaying trunk, and hit the ground on the other side to a sharp snapping sound and stabbing pain in his right arm.

He felt a moment's blind panic as the hand holding his revolver cramped. If he had broken his *arm*...

Blood soaked the cuff of his U.S. Government Issue

tunic. Dread exaggerated the pain until he pulled back his sleeve and saw a long, shallow gash, with slivers of wood hanging from the laceration. It was the bow that had broken, stabbing him as he fell on it.

Gordon threw the fragments aside and scrambled on hands and knees up a narrow gully to the right, keeping low to take advantage of the creekbed and underbrush. Behind him whoops of gleeful chase carried over the tiny hillock.

The following minutes were a blur of whipping branches and sudden zigzags. When he splashed into a narrow rivulet, Gordon whirled, then hurried against the flow.

Hunted men often will run downstream, he remembered, racing upslope, hoping his enemies knew that bit of trivia. He hopped from stone to stone, trying not to dislodge mud into the water. Then he jumped off into the forest again.

There were shouts behind him. Gordon's own footfalls seemed loud enough to wake sleeping bears. Twice, he caught his breath behind boulders or clumps of foliage, thinking as well as practicing silence.

Finally, the shouts diminished with distance. Gordon sighed as he settled back against a large oak and pulled out his belt-pouch aid kit. The wound would be all right. There was no reason to expect infection from the polished wood of the bow. It hurt like hell but the tear was far from vessels or tendons. He bound it in boiled cloth and simply ignored the pain as he got up and looked around.

To his surprise, he recognized two landmarks at once... the towering, shattered sign of the Oakridge Motel, seen over the treetops, and a cattle grate across a worn asphalt path just to the east.

Gordon moved quickly to the place where he had

cached his goods. They were exactly as he had left them. Apparently, the Fates were not so unsubtle as to deal him another blow just yet. He knew they didn't operate that way. They always let you hope for a while longer, then strung it out before they *really* let you have it.

Now the stalked turned stalker. Cautiously, Gordon sought out the blackberry blind, with its irate resident mockingbird. As expected, it was empty now. He crept around behind to get the ambushers' point of view, and sat there for a few minutes as the afternoon waned, looking and thinking.

They had had the drop on him, that was for certain. From this point of view it was hard to see how they had missed when the three men fired on him.

Were they *so* surprised by his sudden break for it? They must have had semi-automatic weapons, yet he only remembered six shots. Either they were being *very* stingy with ammo or...

He approached the grand fir across the clearing. Two fresh scars blemished the bark, ten feet up.

Ten feet. They couldn't be such bad marksmen.

So. It all fit. They had never meant to kill him at all. They had aimed high on purpose, to give him a scare and drive him off. No wonder his pursuers never really came close to catching him during his escape into the forest.

Gordon's lip curled. Ironically, this made his assailants easier to hate. Unthinking malice he had come to accept, as one must accept foul weather and savage beasts. So many former Americans had become little better than barbarians.

But calculated *contempt* like this was something he had

to take personally. These men had the concept of mercy; still they had robbed, injured, and terrorized him.

He remembered Roger Septien, taunting him from that bone-dry hillside. These bastards were no better at all.

Gordon picked up their trail a hundred yards to the west of the blind. The bootprints were clear and uncovered… almost arrogant in their openness.

He took his time, but he never even considered turning back.

It was approaching dusk before the palisade that surrounded New Oakridge was in sight. An open area that had once been a city park was enclosed by a high wooden fence. From within could be heard the lowing of cattle. A horse whinnied. Gordon smelled hay and the rich odors of livestock.

Nearby a still higher palisade surrounded three blocks of what had once been the southwest corner of Oakridge town. A row of two-story buildings half a block long took up the center of the village. Gordon could see the tops of these over the wall, and a water tower with a crow's nest atop it. A silhouetted figure stood watch, looking out over the dimming forest.

It looked like a prosperous community, perhaps the best-off he had encountered since leaving Idaho.

Trees had been cut to make a free-fire zone around the village wall, but that was some time ago. Undergrowth half as high as a man had encroached on the cleared field.

Well there can't be many survivalists in the area, anymore, Gordon thought, *or they'd be a whole lot less careless.*

Let's see what the main entrance is like.

He skirted around the open area toward the south side of the village. On hearing voices he drew up cautiously behind a curtain of undergrowth.

A large wooden gate swung open. Two armed men sauntered out, looked around, then waved to someone within. With a shout and a snap of reins, a wagon pulled by two draft horses sallied through then stopped. The driver turned to speak to the two guards.

"Tell the Mayor I appreciate the loan, Jeff. I know my stead is in the hole pretty deep. But we'll pay him back out of next year's harvest, for sure. He already owns a piece of the farm, so it ought to be a good investment for him."

One of the guards nodded. "Sure thing, Sonny. Now you be careful on your way out, okay? Some of the boys spotted a loner down at the east end of old town, today. There was some shootin'."

The farmer's breath caught audibly. "Was anyone hurt? Are you sure it was just a loner?"

"Yeah, pretty sure. He ran like a rabbit according to Bob."

Gordon's pulse pounded faster. The insults had reached a point almost beyond bearing. He put his left hand inside his shirt and felt the whistle Abby had given him, hanging from its chain around his neck. He took some comfort from it, remembering decency.

"The feller did the Mayor a real favor, though," the first guard went on. "Found a hidey hole full of drugs before Bob's guys drove him off. Mayor's going to pass some of them around to some of the owners at a party tonight, to find out what they'll do. I sure wish I moved in those circles."

"Me too," the younger watchman agreed. "Hey, Sonny, you think the Mayor might pay you some of your bonus in drugs, if you make quota this year? You could have a real party!"

"Sonny" smiled sheepishly and shrugged. Then, for some reason, his head drooped. The older guard looked at him quizzically.

"What's the matter?" he asked.

Sonny shook his head. Gordon could barely hear him when he spoke. "We don't wish for very much anymore, do we, Gary?"

Gary frowned. "What do you mean?"

"I mean as long as we're wishing to be like the Mayor's cronies, why don't we wish we had a Mayor without cronies at all!"

"I…"

"Sally and I had three girls and two boys before th' Doom, Gary."

"I remember, Sonny, but—"

"Hal an' Peter died in th' war, but I counted me an' Sally blessed that all three girls grew up. Blessed!"

"Sonny, it's not your fault. It was just bad luck."

"*Bad luck*?" The farmer snorted. "One raped to death when those reavers came through, Peggy dead in childbirth, and my little Susan… she's got *gray hair,* Gary. She looks like Sally's sister!"

There was a long stretch of silence. The older guard put his hand on the farmer's arm. "I'll bring a jug around tomorrow, Sonny. I promise. We'll talk about the old days, like we used to."

The farmer nodded without looking up. He shouted "Yaah!" and snapped the reins.

For a long moment the guard looked after the creaking wagon, chewing on a grass stem. Finally, he turned to his younger companion. "Jimmy, did I ever tell you about Portland? Sonny and I used to go there, before the war. They had this mayor, back when I was a kid, who used to pose for…"

They passed through the gate, out of Gordon's hearing.

Under other circumstances Gordon might have pondered hours over what that one small conversation had revealed about the social structure of Oakridge and its environs. The farmer's crop indebtedness, for instance—it was a classic early stage of share-kind serfdom. He had read about things like this in sophomore history tutorial, long ago and in another world. They were features of feudalism.

But right now Gordon had no time for philosophy or sociology. His emotions churned. Outrage over what had happened today was nothing next to his anger over the proposed use of the drugs he had found. When he thought of what that doctor in Wyoming could do with such medicines… why most of the substances wouldn't even make these ignorant savages high!

Gordon was fed up. His bandaged right arm throbbed.

I'll bet I could scale those walls without much trouble, find the storage hut, and reclaim what I found… along with some extra to make up for the insults, the pain, my broken bow.

The image wasn't satisfying enough. Gordon embellished. He envisioned dropping in on the Mayor's "party," and *wasting* all the power-hungry bastards who were making a midget empire out of this corner of the dark age. He imagined acquiring power, power to do good… power to *force* these yokels to use the education of their younger days before the learned generation disappeared forever from the world.

Why, why *is nobody anywhere taking responsibility for putting things right again? I'd help. I'd dedicate my life to such a leader.*

But the big dreams all seem to be gone. All the good men— like Lieutenant Van and Drew Simms—died defending them. I must be the only one left who still believes in them.

Leaving was out of the question, of course. A combination of pride, obstinacy, and simple gonadal fury rooted him in his tracks. Here he would do battle, and that was that.

Maybe there's an idealists' militia, in Heaven or in Hell. I guess I'll find out soon.

Fortunately, the war hormones left a little space for his forebrain to choose *tactics.* As the afternoon faded, he thought about what he was going to do.

Gordon stepped back into the shadows and a branch brushed by, dislodging his cap. He caught it before it fell to the ground, was about to put it back on, but then stopped abruptly and looked at it.

The burnished image of a horseman glinted back at him, a brass figure backed by a ribbon motto in Latin. Gordon watched shifting highlights in the shiny emblem, and slowly, he smiled.

It would be audacious—perhaps much more so than attempting the fence in the darkness. But the idea had a pleasing symmetry that appealed to Gordon. He was probably the last man alive who would choose a path of greater danger purely for aesthetic reasons, and he was glad. If the scheme failed, it would still be spectacular.

It required a brief foray into the ruins of old Oakridge— beyond the postwar village—to a structure certain to be among the least looted in town. He set the cap back on his head as he moved to take advantage of the remaining light.

An hour later, Gordon left the gutted buildings of the old town and stepped briskly along the pitted asphalt road, retracing his steps in the gathering dusk. Taking a long detour through the forest, he came at last to the road Sonny had used, south of the village wall. Now he approached boldly, guided by a solitary lantern hanging over the broad gate.

The guard was criminally lax. Gordon came within thirty feet unchallenged. He saw a shadowy sentry, standing on a parapet over near the far end of the palisade, but the idiot was looking the other way.

Gordon took a deep breath, put Abby's whistle to his lips, and blew three hard blasts. The shrill screams pealed through the buildings and forest like the shriek of a stooping raptor. Hurried footsteps pounded along the parapet. Three men carrying shotguns and oil lanterns appeared above the gate and stared down at him in the gathering twilight.

"Who are you? What do you want?"

"I must speak with someone in authority," Gordon hailed. "This is official business, and I demand entry to the town of Oakridge!"

That certainly put them off their routine. There was a long, stunned silence as the guards blinked, first at him and then at each other. Finally, one man hurried off while the first speaker cleared his throat. "Uh, come again? Are you feverish? Have you got the Sickness?"

Gordon shook his head. "I am not ill. I am tired and hungry. And angry over being shot at. But settling all that can wait until I have discharged my duty here."

This time the chief guard's voice cracked in blank

perplexity. "Dis-discharged your… What the *hell* are you talking about, man?"

Hurried footsteps echoed on the parapet. Several more men arrived, followed by a number of children and women who began to string out to the left and right. Discipline, apparently, wasn't well practiced in Oakridge. The local tyrant and his cronies had had things their way for a long time.

Gordon repeated himself. Slowly and firmly, giving it his best Polonius voice.

"I demand to speak with your superiors. You are trying my patience keeping me out here, and it will definitely go into my report. Now get somebody here with authority to open this gate!"

The crowd thickened until an unbroken forest of silhouettes topped the palisade. They stared down at Gordon as a group of figures appeared on the parapet to the right, carrying lanterns. The onlookers on that side made way for the newcomers.

"Look, loner," the chief guard said, "you're just asking for a bullet. We got no 'official business' with *anyone* outside this valley, haven't since we broke relations with that Commie place down at Blakeville, years ago. You can bet your ass I'm not bothering the Mayor for some crazy…"

The man turned in surprise as the party of dignitaries reached the gate. "Mr. Mayor… I'm sorry about the ruckus, but…"

"I was nearby anyway. Heard the commotion. What's going on here?"

The guard gestured. "We got a fellow out there babbling like nothing I've heard since the crazy times. He must be sick, or one of those loonies that always used to come through."

"I'll take care of this."

In the growing darkness the new figure leaned over the parapet. "I'm the Mayor of Oakridge," he announced. "We don't believe in charity, here. But if you're that fellow who found the goodies this afternoon, and graciously donated them to my boys, I'll admit we owe you. I'll have a nice hot meal lowered over the gate. And a blanket. You can sleep there by the road. Tomorrow, though, you gotta be gone. We don't want no diseases here. And from what my guards tell me, you must be delirious."

Gordon smiled. "Your generosity impresses me, Mr. Mayor. But I have come too far on official business to turn away now. First off, can you tell me if Oakridge has a working wireless or fiber optic facility?"

The silence brought on by his non sequitur was long and heavy. Gordon could imagine the Mayor's puzzlement. At last, the bossman answered.

"We haven't had a radio in ten years. Nothing's worked since then. Why? What has that to do with anythi—"

"That's a shame. The airwaves have been a shambles since the war, of course..." he improvised, "...all the radioactivity, you know. But I'd hoped I could try to use your transmitter to report back to my superiors."

He delivered the lines with aplomb. This time they brought not silence but a surge of amazed whispers up and down the parapet. Gordon guessed that most of the population of Oakridge must be up there by now. He hoped the wall was well built. It was not in his plan to enter the town like Joshua.

He had quite another legend in mind.

"Get a lantern over here!" the Mayor commanded. "Not that one, you idiot! The one with the reflector! Yes. Now shine it on that man. I want a look at him!"

A bulky lamp was brought forth and there was a rattle as light speared out at Gordon. He was expecting it though and neither covered his eyes nor squinted. He shifted the leather bag and turned to bring his costume to the best angle. The letter carrier's cap, with its polished crest, sat at a rakish angle on his head.

The muttering of the crowd grew louder.

"Mr. Mayor," he called. "My patience is limited. I already will have to have words with you about the behavior of your boys this afternoon. Don't force me to exercise my authority in ways both of us would find unpleasant. You're on the verge of losing your privilege of communication with the rest of the nation."

The Mayor shifted his weight back and forth rapidly. "Communication? Nation? What is this blither? There's just the Blakeville commune, those self-righteous twits down at Culp Creek, and Satan knows what savages beyond them. Who the hell *are* you anyway?"

Gordon touched his cap. "Gordon Krantz, of the United States Postal Service. I'm the courier assigned to reestablish a mail route in Idaho and lower Oregon, and general federal inspector for the region."

And to imagine he had been embarrassed playing Santa Claus back in Pine View! Gordon hadn't thought of the last part about being a "federal inspector" until it was out of his mouth. Was it inspiration, or a dare?

Well, might as well be hanged for a sheep as a goat, he thought.

The crowd was in tumult. Several times, Gordon heard the words "outside" and "inspector"—and especially "mailman." When the Mayor shouted for silence, it came slowly, trailing off into a rapt hush.

"So you're a mailman." The sneer was sarcastic. "What kind of idiots do you take us for, Krantz? A shiny suit makes you a government official? What government? What proof can you give us? Show us you're not a wild lunatic, raving with radiation fever!"

Gordon pulled out the papers he had prepared only an hour before, using the seal stamp he had found in the ruins of the Oakridge Post Office.

"I have credentials, here…" But he was interrupted at once.

"Keep your papers to yourself, loonie. We're not letting you come close enough to infect us with your fever!"

The Mayor straightened and waved an arm in the air, addressing his subjects. "You all remember how crazies and imposters used to come around, during the Chaos years, claiming to be everything from the Antichrist to Porky Pig? Well, there's one fact we can all depend on. Crazies come and crazies go, but there's only one "government"… that's what we got right here!"

He turned back to Gordon. "You're lucky this isn't like the plague years, loonie. Back then a case like yours would've called for immediate cure… by cremation!"

Gordon cursed silently. The local tyrant was slick and certainly no easy bluff. If they wouldn't even look at the "credentials" he had forged, the trip into old town this afternoon had been wasted. Gordon was down to his last ace. He smiled for the crowd, but he really wanted to cross his fingers.

From a side pocket of the leather bag he pulled out a small bundle. Gordon made a pretense of shuffling through the packet, squinting at labels he knew by heart.

"Is there a… a Donald Smith, here?" he called up at the townspeople.

Heads turned left and right in sudden, hushed conversation. Their confusion was obvious even in the gathering darkness. Finally someone called out.

"He died a year after the war! In the last battle of the warehouses."

There was a tremor in the speaker's voice. Good. Surprise was not the only emotion at work here. Still, he needed something a lot better than that. The Mayor was still staring at him, as perplexed as the others, but when he figured out what Gordon was trying to do, there would be trouble.

"Oh well," Gordon called. "I'll have to confirm that, of course." Before anyone could speak, he hurried on, shuffling the packet in his hand.

"Is there a Mr. or Mrs. Franklin Thompson in town? Or their son or daughter?"

Now the tide of hushed whispering carried almost a superstitious tone. A woman replied. "Dead! The boy lived until last year. Worked on the Jascowisc stead. His folks were in Portland when it blew."

Damn! Gordon had only one name left. It was all very well to strike their hearts with his knowledge, but what he needed was somebody alive!

"Right!" he called. "We'll confirm that. Finally, is there a Grace Horton here? A Miss *Grace Horton…*"

"No there ain't no Grace Horton!" the Mayor shouted, confidence and sarcasm back in his voice. "I know everyone in my territory. Never been no Grace Horton in the ten years since I arrived, you imposter!

"Can't you all see what he did? He found an old telephone book in town, and copied down some names to stir us up with." He shook a fist at Gordon. "Buddy, I rule that you are disturbing the peace and endangering the public health! You've got five seconds to be gone before I order my men to fire!"

Gordon exhaled heavily. Now he had no choice. At least he could beat a retreat and lose nothing more than a little pride.

It was a good try, but you knew the chances of it working were slim. At least you had the bastard going there, for a little while.

It was time to go, but to his surprise Gordon found his body would not turn. His feet refused to move. All will to run away had evaporated. The sensible part of him was horrified as he squared his shoulders and called the Mayor's bluff.

"Assault on a postal courier is one of the few federal crimes that the pro tem Congress hasn't suspended for the recovery period, Mr. Mayor. The United States has always protected its mailmen."

He looked coldly into the glare of the lamp. "*Always,*" he emphasized. And for a moment he felt a thrill. He *was* a courier, at least in spirit. He was an anachronism that the dark age had somehow missed when it systematically went about rubbing idealism from the world. Gordon looked straight toward the dark silhouette of the Mayor, and silently dared him to kill what was left of their shared sovereignty.

For several seconds the silence gathered. Then the Mayor held up his hand. "One!"

He counted slowly, perhaps to give Gordon time to run, and maybe for sadistic effect.

"Two!"

The game was lost. Gordon knew he should leave now, at once. Still, his body would not turn.

"Three!"

This is the way the last idealist dies, he thought. These sixteen years of survival had been an accident, an oversight of Nature, about to be corrected. In the end, all of his hard-won pragmatism had finally given way… to a gesture.

There was movement on the parapet. Someone at the far left was struggling forward.

The guards raised their shotguns. Gordon thought he saw a few of them move hesitantly—reluctantly. Not that that would do him any good.

The Mayor stretched out the last count, perhaps a bit unnerved by Gordon's stubbornness. The raised fist began to chop down.

"Mr. Mayor!" a woman's tremulous voice cut in, her words high-pitched with fear as she reached up to grab the bossman's hand. "P-please… I…"

The Mayor shrugged her hands away. "Get away, woman. Get her out of here."

The frail shape backed away from the guards, but she cried out clearly. "I… I'm Grace Horton!"

"What?" The Mayor was not alone in turning to stare at her.

"It's my m-maiden name. I was married the year after the second famine. That was before you and your men arrived…"

The crowd reacted noisily. The Mayor cried out, "Fools! He copied her name from a telephone book, I tell you!"

Gordon smiled. He held up the bundle in his hand and touched his cap with the other.

"Good evening, Mizz Horton. It's a lovely night, yes? By the way, I happen to have a letter here for you, from a Mr. Jim Horton, of Pine View, Oregon… He gave it to me twelve days ago…"

The people on the parapet all seemed to be talking at once. There were sudden motions and excited shouts. Gordon cupped his ear to listen to the woman's amazed exclamation, and had to raise his voice to be heard.

"Yes, ma'am. He seemed to be quite well. I'm afraid that's all I have on this trip. But I'll be glad to carry your reply to your brother on my way back, after I finish my circuit down in the valley."

He stepped forward, closer to the light. "One thing though, ma'am. Mr. Horton didn't have enough postage, back in Pine View, so I'm going to have to ask you for ten dollars... C.O.D."

The crowd roared.

Next to the glaring lantern the figure of the Mayor turned left and right, waving his arms and shouting. But nothing he said was heard as the gate swung open and people poured out into the night. They surrounded Gordon, a tight press of hot-faced, excited men, women, children. Some limped. Others bore livid scars or rasped in tuberculin heaviness. And yet at that moment the pain of living seemed as nothing next to a glow of sudden faith.

In the middle of it all Gordon maintained his composure and walked slowly toward the portal. He smiled and nodded, especially to those who reached out and touched his elbow, or the wide curve of his bulging leather bag. The youngsters looked at him in superstitious awe. On many older faces, tears streamed.

Gordon was in the middle of a trembling adrenaline reaction, but he squelched hard on the little glimmering of conscience... a touch of shame at this lie.

The hell with it. It's not my fault they want to believe

in the Tooth Fairy. I've finally grown up. I only want what belongs to me!

Simpletons.

Nevertheless, he smiled all around as the hands reached out, and the love surged forth. It flowed about him like a rushing stream and carried him in a wave of desperate, unwonted hope, into the town of Oakridge.

WHEN WE WENT TO SEE THE END OF THE WORLD

ROBERT SILVERBERG

Nick and Jane were glad that they had gone to see the end of the world, because it gave them something special to talk about at Mike and Ruby's party. One always likes to come to a party armed with a little conversation. Mike and Ruby give marvelous parties.

Their home is superb, one of the finest in the neighborhood. It is truly a home for all seasons, all moods. Their very special corner of the world. With more space indoors and out... more wide-open freedom. The living room with its exposed ceiling beams is a natural focal point for entertaining. Custom-finished, with a conversation pit and fireplace. There's also a family room with beamed ceiling and wood paneling... plus a study. And a magnificent master suite with twelve-foot dressing room and private bath. Solidly impressive exterior design. Sheltered courtyard. Beautifully wooded ⅓-acre grounds. Their parties are highlights of any month. Nick and Jane waited until they thought enough people had arrived. Then

Jane nudged Nick and Nick said gaily, "You know what we did last week? Hey, we went to see the end of the world!"

"The end of the world?" Henry asked.

"You went to see it?" said Henry's wife Cynthia.

"How did you manage that?" Paula wanted to know.

"It's been available since March," Stan told her. "I think a division of American Express runs it."

Nick was put out to discover that Stan already knew. Quickly, before Stan could say anything more, Nick said, "Yes, it's just started. Our travel agent found out for us. What they do is they put you in this machine, it looks like a tiny teeny submarine, you know, with dials and levers up front behind a plastic wall to keep you from touching anything, and they send you into the future. You can charge it with any of the regular credit cards."

"It must be very expensive," Marcia said.

"They're bringing the costs down rapidly," Jane said. "Last year only millionaires could afford it. Really, haven't you heard about it before?"

"What did you see?" Henry asked.

"For a while, just greyness outside the porthole," said Nick. "And a kind of flickering effect." Everybody was looking at him. He enjoyed the attention. Jane wore a rapt, loving expression. "Then the haze cleared and a voice said over a loudspeaker that we had now reached the very end of time, when life had become impossible on Earth. Of course, we were sealed into the submarine thing. Only looking out. On this beach, this empty beach. The water a funny grey color with a pink sheen. And then the sun came up. It was red like it sometimes is at sunrise, only it stayed red as it got to the middle of the sky, and it looked lumpy and saggy at the edges. Like a few of us, hah hah.

Lumpy and sagging at the edges. A cold wind blowing across the beach."

"If you were sealed in the submarine, how did you know there was a cold wind?" Cynthia asked.

Jane glared at her. Nick said, "We could see the sand blowing around. And it looked cold. The grey ocean. Like winter."

"Tell them about the crab," said Jane.

"Yes, the crab. The last life-form on Earth. It wasn't really a crab, of course, it was something about two feet wide and a foot high, with thick shiny green armor and maybe a dozen legs and some curving horns coming up, and it moved slowly from right to left in front of us. It took all day to cross the beach. And toward nightfall it died. Its horns went limp and it stopped moving. The tide came in and carried it away. The sun went down. There wasn't any moon. The stars didn't seem to be in the right places. The loudspeaker told us we had just seen the death of Earth's last living thing."

"How eerie!" cried Paula.

"Were you gone very long?" Ruby asked.

"Three hours," Jane said. "You can spend weeks or days at the end of the world, if you want to pay extra, but they always bring you back to a point three hours after you went. To hold down the babysitter expenses."

Mike offered Nick some pot. "That's really something," he said. "To have gone to the end of the world. Hey, Ruby, maybe we'll talk to the travel agent about it."

Nick took a deep drag and passed the joint to Jane. He felt pleased with himself about the way he had told the story. They had all been very impressed. That swollen red sun, that scuttling crab. The trip had cost more than a month in Japan, but it had been a good investment. He and Jane were the first in the neighborhood who had gone. That was important. Paula was staring at him in awe. Nick knew that she regarded him in a completely different light now. Possibly she would meet him at a motel on Tuesday at lunchtime. Last month she had turned him down but now he had an extra attractiveness for her. Nick winked at her. Cynthia was holding hands with Stan. Henry and Mike both were crouched at Jane's feet. Mike and Ruby's twelve-year-old son came into the room and stood at the edge of the conversation pit. He 'said, "There just was a bulletin on the news. Mutated amoebas escaped from a government research station and got into Lake Michigan. They're carrying a tissue-dissolving virus and everybody in seven states is supposed to boil their water until further notice." Mike scowled at the boy and said, "It's after your bedtime, Timmy." The boy went out. The doorbell rang. Ruby answered it and returned with Eddie and Fran.

Paula said, "Nick and Jane went to see the end of the world. They've just been telling us about it."

"Gee," said Eddie, "we did that too, on Wednesday night."

Nick was crestfallen. Jane bit her lip and asked Cynthia quietly why Fran always wore such flashy dresses. Ruby said, "You saw the whole works, eh? The crab and everything?"

"The crab?" Eddie said. "What crab? We didn't see the crab."

"It must have died the time before," Paula said. "When Nick and Jane were there."

Mike said, "A fresh shipment of Cuernavaca Lightning is in. Here, have a toke."

"How long ago did you do it?" Eddie said to Nick.

"Sunday afternoon. I guess we were about the first."

"Great trip, isn't it?" Eddie said. "A little somber, though. When the last hill crumbles into the sea."

"That's not what we saw," said Jane. "And you didn't see the crab? Maybe we were on different trips."

Mike said, "What was it like for you, Eddie?"

Eddie put his arms around Cynthia from behind. He said, "They put us into this little capsule, with a porthole, you know, and a lot of instruments and—"

"We heard that part," said Paula. "What did you see?"

"The end of the world," Eddie said. "When water covers everything. The sun and the moon were in the sky at the same time—"

"We didn't see the moon at all," Jane remarked. "It just wasn't there."

"It was on one side and the sun was on the other," Eddie went on. "The moon was closer than it should have been. And a funny color, almost like bronze. And the ocean creeping up. We went halfway around the world and all we saw was ocean. Except in one place, there was this chunk of land sticking up, this hill, and the guide told us it was the top of Mount Everest." He waved to Fran. "That was groovy, huh, floating in our tin boat next to the top of Mount Everest. Maybe ten feet of it sticking up. And the water rising all the time. Up, up, up. Up and over the top. Glub. No land left. I have to admit it was a little disappointing, except of course the idea of the thing. That human ingenuity can design a machine that can send people billions of years forward in time and bring them back, wow! But there was just this ocean."

"How strange," said Jane. "We saw the ocean too, but there was a beach, a kind of nasty beach, and the crab-thing walking along it, and the sun—it was all red, was the sun red when you saw it?"

"A kind of pale green," Fran said.

"Are you people talking about the end of the world?" Tom asked. He and Harriet were standing by the door taking off their coats. Mike's son must have let them in. Tom gave his coat to Ruby and said, "Man, what a spectacle!"

"So you did it, too?" Jane asked, a little hollowly.

"Two weeks ago," said Tom. "The travel agent called and said, 'Guess what we're offering now, the end of the goddamned world!' With all the extras it didn't really cost so much. So we went right down there to the office, Saturday, I think—was it a Friday?—the day of the big riot, anyway, when they burned St Louis—"

"That was a Saturday," Cynthia said. "I remember I was coming back from the shopping center when the radio said they were using nuclears—"

"Saturday, yes," Tom said. "And we told them we were ready to go, and off they sent us."

"Did you see a beach with crabs," Stan demanded, "or was it a world full of water?"

"Neither one. It was like a big ice age. Glaciers covered everything. No oceans showing, no mountains. We flew clear around the world and it was all a huge snowball. They had floodlights on the vehicle because the sun had gone out."

"I was sure I could see the sun still hanging up there," Harriet put in. "Like a ball of cinders in the sky. But the guide said no, nobody could see it."

"How come everybody gets to visit a different kind of end of the world?" Henry asked. "You'd think there'd be only one kind of end of the world. I mean, it ends, and this is how it ends, and there can't be more than one way."

"Could it be fake?" Stan asked. Everybody turned around and looked at him. Nick's face got very red. Fran looked so mean that Eddie let go of Cynthia and started to rub Fran's shoulders. Stan shrugged. "I'm not suggesting it is," he said defensively. "I was just wondering."

"Seemed pretty real to me," said Tom. "The sun burned out. A big ball of ice. The atmosphere, you know, frozen. The end of the goddamned world."

The telephone rang. Ruby went to answer it. Nick asked Paula about lunch on Tuesday. She said yes. "Let's meet at the motel," he said, and she grinned. Eddie was making out with Cynthia again. Henry looked very stoned and was having trouble staying awake.

Phil and Isabel arrived. They heard Tom and Fran talking about their trips to the end of the world and Isabel said she and Phil had gone only the day before yesterday. "Goddamn," Tom said, "everybody's doing it! What was your trip like?"

Ruby came back into the room. "That was my sister calling from Fresno to say she's safe. Fresno wasn't hit by the earthquake at all."

"Earthquake?" Paula asked.

"In California," Mike told her. "This afternoon. You didn't know? Wiped out most of Los Angeles and ran right up the coast practically to Monterey. They think it was on account of the underground bomb test in the Mojave Desert."

"California's always having such awful disasters," Marcia said.

"Good thing those amoebas got loose back east," said Nick. "Imagine how complicated it would be if they had them in LA now too."

"They will," Tom said. "Two to one they reproduce by airborne spores."

"Like the typhoid germs last November," Jane said.

"That was typhus," Nick corrected.

"Anyway," Phil said, "I was telling Tom and Fran about what we saw at the end of the world. It was the sun going nova. They showed it very cleverly, too. I mean, you can't actually sit around and experience it, on account of the heat and the hard radiation and all. But they give it to you in a peripheral way, very elegant in the McLuhanesque sense of the word. First they take you to a point about two hours before the blowup, right? It's I don't know how many jillion years from now, but a long way, anyhow, because the trees are all different, they've got blue scales and ropy branches, and the animals are like things with one leg that jump on pogo sticks—"

"Oh, I don't *believe* that," Cynthia drawled.

Phil ignored her gracefully. "And we didn't see any sign of human beings, not a house, not a telephone pole, nothing, so I suppose we must have been extinct a long time before. Anyway, they let us look at that for a while. Not getting out of our time machine, naturally, because they said the atmosphere was wrong. Gradually the sun started to puff up. We were nervous—weren't we, Iz?—I mean, suppose they miscalculated things? This whole trip is a very new concept and things might go wrong. The sun was getting bigger and bigger, and then this thing like an arm seemed to pop out of its left side, a big fiery arm reaching out across space, getting closer and closer. We saw it through smoked glass, like you do an eclipse. They gave us about two minutes of the explosion, and we could feel it getting hot already. Then we jumped a couple of years forward in time. The sun was back to its regular shape, only it was smaller, sort of like a little white sun instead of a big yellow one. And on Earth everything was ashes."

"Ashes," Isabel said, with emphasis.

"It looked like Detroit after the union nuked Ford," Phil said. "Only much, much worse. Whole mountains were melted. The oceans were dried up. Everything was ashes." He shuddered and took a joint from Mike. "Isabel was crying."

"The things with one leg," Isabel said. "I mean, they must have all been wiped out." She began to sob. Stan comforted her.

"I wonder why it's a different way for everyone who goes," he said. "Freezing. Or the oceans. Or the sun blowing up. Or the thing Nick and Jane saw."

"I'm convinced that each of us had a genuine experience in the far future," said Nick. He felt he had to regain control of the group somehow. It had been so good when he was telling his story, before those others had come. "That is to say, the world suffers a variety of natural calamities, it doesn't just have one end of the world, and they keep mixing things up and sending people to different catastrophes. But never for a moment did I doubt that I was seeing an authentic event."

"We have to do it," Ruby said to Mike. "It's only three hours. What about calling them first thing Monday and making an appointment for Thursday night?"

"Monday's the President's funeral," Tom pointed out. "The travel agency will be closed."

"Have they caught the assassin yet?" Fran asked.

"They didn't mention it on the four o'clock news," said Stan. "I guess he'll get away like the last one."

"Beats me why anybody wants to be President," Phil said.

Mike put on some music. Nick danced with Paula.

Eddie danced with Cynthia. Henry was asleep. Dave, Paula's husband, was on crutches because of his mugging, and he asked Isabel to sit and talk with him. Tom danced with Harriet even though he was married to her. She hadn't been out of the hospital more than a few months since the transplant and he treated her extremely tenderly. Mike danced with Fran. Phil danced with Jane. Stan danced with Marcia. Ruby cut in on Eddie and Cynthia. Afterward Tom danced with Jane and Phil danced with Paula. Mike and Ruby's little girl woke up and came out to say hello. Mike sent her back to bed. Far away there was the sound of an explosion. Nick danced with Paula again, but he didn't want her to get bored with him before Tuesday, so he excused himself and went to talk with Dave. Dave handled most of Nick's investments. Ruby said to Mike, "The day after the funeral, will you call the travel agent?" Mike said he would, but Tom said somebody would probably shoot the new President too and there'd be another funeral. These funerals were demolishing the gross national product, Stan observed, on account of how everything had to close all the time.

Nick saw Cynthia wake Henry up and ask him sharply if he would take her on the end-of-the-world trip. Henry looked embarrassed. His factory had been blown up at Christmas in a peace demonstration and everybody knew he was in bad shape financially. "You can *charge* it," Cynthia said, her fierce voice carrying above the chitchat. "And it's so *beautiful*, Henry. The ice. Or the sun exploding. I want to go."

"Lou and Janet were going to be here tonight, too," Ruby said to Paula. "But their younger boy came back from Texas with that new kind of cholera and they had to cancel."

Phil said, "I understand that one couple saw the moon come apart. It got too close to the Earth and split into chunks and the chunks fell like meteors. Smashing everything up, you know. One big piece nearly hit their time machine."

"I wouldn't have liked that at all," Marcia said.

"Our trip was very lovely," said Jane. "No violent things at all. Just the big red sun and the tide and that crab creeping along the beach. We were both deeply moved."

"It's amazing what science can accomplish nowadays," Fran said.

Mike and Ruby agreed they would try to arrange a trip to the end of the world as soon as the funeral was over. Cynthia drank too much and got sick. Phil, Tom, and Dave discussed the stock market. Harriet told Nick about her operation. Isabel flirted with Mike, tugging her neckline lower. At midnight someone turned on the news. They had some shots of the earthquake and a warning about boiling your water if you lived in the affected states. The President's widow was shown visiting the last President's widow to get some pointers for the funeral. Then there was an interview with an executive of the time-trip company. "Business is phenomenal," he said. "Time-tripping will be the nation's number one growth industry next year." The reporter asked him if his company would soon be offering something besides the end-of-the-world trip. "Later on, we hope to," the executive said. "We plan to apply for Congressional approval soon. But meanwhile the demand for our present offering is running very high. You can't imagine. Of course, you have to expect apocalyptic stuff to attain immense popularity in times like these."

The reporter said, "What do you mean, times like these?"

but as the time-trip man started to reply, he was interrupted by the commercial. Mike shut off the set. Nick discovered that he was extremely depressed. He decided that it was because so many of his friends had made the journey, and he had thought he and Jane were the only ones who had. He found himself standing next to Marcia and tried to describe the way the crab had moved, but Marcia only shrugged. No one was talking about time-trips now. The party had moved beyond that point. Nick and Jane left quite early and went right to sleep, without making love. The next morning the Sunday paper wasn't delivered because of the Bridge Authority strike, and the radio said that the mutant amoebas were proving harder to eradicate than originally anticipated. They were spreading into Lake Superior and everyone in the region would have to boil all their drinking water. Nick and Jane discussed where they would go for their next vacation. "What about going to see the end of the world all over again?" Jane suggested, and Nick laughed quite a good deal.

THE REVELATION OF MORGAN STERN

CHRISTIE YANT

It is July 31, your birthday, and I can't reach you. I've been trying all day, but the cell networks are down, the Internet is down. I even tried a pay phone—there are two left in town that I know of. I collected all of my change and walked to the 76 in the village.

It was on fire. I watched it for a while from a distance as it painted a brown, toxic streak across the sky. It was a long walk back to the house, or what's left of it. My feet hurt, and it was too quiet.

The back of the house fell in, but I managed to climb into the kitchen and recover a few things. I have no way to tell you that I salvaged a donut and lit a candle and sang to you. Tonight we would have celebrated your birthday over video chat, the best we could do so far apart. I don't know if you're alive or dead.

I thought it was just an earthquake. We've been waiting for "the Big One" my entire life, so what else would I think it was? Just the inevitable result of tectonic pressure—

slippage, two goliaths moving past each other, barely a shrug in geological terms but enough to rattle the life out of us. I thought that an earthquake like that, one that could bring down a town that had known it was coming forever, surely that must be the worst of it.

I was wrong. We didn't see the worst of it until after the sun went down, when furious angels filled the sky—from where, I don't know—and with them, the screams that broke the silence.

I wonder if you're safe. I wonder how far they can fly.

AUGUST 2

I didn't know what to take from the house. The first thing I thought of was your birthday present. It was a stupid, sentimental thought, but when I opened it I had to laugh. If there's anything I need to take with me, it's your birthday present.

This isn't at all how we imagined it, is it? We talked about this sort of thing a lot, sometimes joking, sometimes serious: the trouble the world was in, and how it would eventually end. A biological accident, some virus cooked up in a lab; nuclear war, maybe a meteor strike. We'd look at the stars during those rare and precious times together and talk about how it might happen, and what we would do if it did. So for your birthday I started to put a survival kit together, as a romantic, silly joke. A cheap enameled cash box with everything you'd need: a compass, nylon rope, waterproof matches, a space blanket. Things like that, plus this notebook, and a pen. On the top I wrote in Sharpie: In Case of Apocalypse.

We joked about the nonsensical ways: zombies, aliens, the Rapture.

I don't think that's what this is. They don't seem to discriminate the way I would expect the God of the Old Testament to do.

So far I've been safe. Luck seems to be on my side, and I am on my way to you. My fourth grade California history lessons will finally pay off: I am going to spend tonight at the old adobe Mission, and then walk south down El Camino Real from Mission to Mission during the day until I reach Los Angeles.

It's quiet again, except for a sort of background noise, like a radio, or a conversation I'm not near enough to hear. There's something familiar and almost comforting about it.

AUGUST 4

I only got as far as Summerland. Is it weird to say that I'm enjoying this part? Everything around me is in ruins; the survivors are grouped together in terrified clusters, some of them already talking about rebuilding. I try to avoid them as much as I can. But walking this stretch of the freeway is peaceful; the dolphins seem unaware of what's happened, they swim just offshore as they always have on placid days. The air is cool, the sun is bright, the water the teal of early summer, and I know that this is the last time it's going to be easy.

Once I get past Ventura the way will be treacherous. The city scares me; crossing through the Mojave scares me more. But all that's important is that I get to you.

I'm going to Wichita, like we said we would. It was a

joke, I know, but it's all I can think of to do. I'm going, and I hope you are too. I hope you remember where we said we'd meet, what the place was called.

I've only seen a couple of angels today, black against the clear blue sky. I think they mostly come out at night.

AUGUST 7

I'm so tired. I've only just started and I'm already so tired. And scared, for reasons that I'm not sure I'm even ready to commit to paper. Reasons that have nothing to do with the end of the world. Suddenly I'm a child again, talking to imaginary friends, and believing for all the world that they're talking back.

It's nothing. Just the exhaustion. Tomorrow will be better.

AUGUST 16, BARSTOW, CALIFORNIA

There it is. The desert.

It scares me in ways I can't even articulate. I know what it is to burn for a day, to have our nearest star turn from friend to enemy, to be blistered and nauseated. For a day. What about a week? Two weeks? I don't know how long it will take. Water, shade, sunblock, and getting across that expanse as fast as I possibly can are what's on my mind right now. If anything's going to finish me, it'll be the angels or the desert. I haven't survived one just to let the other kill me. You're on the other side of the desert, or at least I hope you are. I have to assume you're there, safe, waiting for me, or there won't be a point.

I stole a bike in the valley. Is it stealing? I don't know. It has a patch kit and an odometer. I haven't ridden much since I was a teenager, and I've never ridden more than forty miles in a day. Today I'm going to try for 100. I need to get across this wasteland as fast as I can. I'm pretty sure my life depends on it.

AUGUST 17

They came out at sunset, just as I was getting ready to ride. There must have been survivors there after all, though I didn't run into any. The lack of bodies has been a puzzle until now. They take them, I think—I could see some of them carrying people, silhouetted against the dusk-lit sky, like a hawk carrying a mouse in its talons. Where? Why? I don't know. Barstow is in flames; I can still see the glow from here. All I could do was ride as hard as I could, and not look back, not look up.

AUGUST 18

I think I may have figured out where they came from. They look like biblical angels, so I had assumed they came from above us somewhere, even if it doesn't make sense. The air teeming with impossible creatures that set things on fire with their touch and carry people off into the sky doesn't make sense either. But tonight at sunset I waited and watched.

They don't come from above; they come from below.

Maybe you knew that already. Maybe it was obvious, the way the ground has split open, here in Arizona just as in California. Maybe it's out where you are, too, the Earth cracked and broken, and soot-black angels emerging from the heart of the planet every night.

AUGUST 20

The tire on the bike just couldn't take another patch, so I'm back on foot.

I should have told you back then when we were forming our "plan" that twenty-five miles a day on foot is about the maximum. I learned this in fourth grade, as did every kid educated in California: it's how they decided where to put the Missions, always a day's walk from each other. From the Santa Barbara Mission to the Mission Santa Inez is twenty-five miles; from Santa Inez to La Purisima is twenty-five miles. I knew that. We each have 1500 miles to cross. I think I'm still in Arizona. It's going to take a long time.

I should have told you.

SEPTEMBER 1

It's too hot to travel by day, and by night there are the angels. I've been trying to split the difference by starting out late in the afternoon, before sunset, and going as long as I can, until I spot one of them and have to find shelter. Shelter is usually a rock, and it is usually already claimed by the non-human residents of the desert. It is a good thing I'm not afraid of snakes.

I'm down to my last few looted Power Bars, and I don't really know how far I have left to go.

I have a lash of blood blisters across three fingers of my right hand, and I cut the hell out of my left. It hurts to hold the pen, but I've got nothing else to do. I used to think being alone would be great, with time to do nothing but think, and it was at first; now the sound of my own voice grates on me, and I'm tired of my own thoughts. I wish I could talk to you— you always had new thoughts, fresh thoughts I'd never had before, but they still seemed to settle in my mind as if they belonged to me all along. I've seen nothing but the brown of sand and stone by day and the world in grayscale at night. I can't wait to see something green again that isn't a cactus.

Did I ever tell you that I used to hear voices when I was a kid? I think it started after my parents died; trauma does strange things to a person's mind. They were sort of comforting, those voices, even if they never made sense. In my memory they sound a little like my mom and dad. They made me feel like I wasn't really alone in the world after all, just like you always made me feel. I decided at some point that they were the voices of the animals that lived in the ground, and I would lay on my belly in the yellow grass and whisper my life into their burrows, my hopes and dreams, my anger and pain. And I would listen to them answer with meaningless sounds—the language, I thought, of rabbits and ground squirrels.

I must not be holding it together as well as I thought I was. I have to face it: I'm hearing them again.

There are fewer angels now. I only saw three last night, though they were close and I thought for certain I was moments away from being carried off by those burning hands.

But only three. That's good. Maybe it's almost over.

* * *

SEPTEMBER 15

I'm in Texas.

I met a guy on the road, maybe your age. He has a horse. He offered to let me ride it—I declined. My feet feel like they're on fire all the time, but at the end of the world it seems unwise to accept favors from strangers. He says his name is Brian; I'm not sure why I don't believe him. There is no reason to lie about our names out here. Maybe it's that superstitious part of me that grew up on fairy tales that says I shouldn't give him my own real name. Maybe it's in our blood, the rules of magic. I think it's a good instinct, in these strange times. I told him my name was Morgan. We've been traveling together for about three days. Some things are easier, like finding food. He's good at that. I had time to study the survival book (why didn't I put fishing line in the Apocalypse box? Why?!) so between the two of us I think we're not going to starve. I don't like him, though—he's an arrogant prick. I was starved for company but now I just wish he'd shut up.

We used to joke about how someday the world would be ours. It seemed so possible, didn't it? Everything we attempted together just worked. We were going to be together permanently soon.

Instead the world is empty, and we're farther apart than we've ever been.

SEPTEMBER 17

How many miles to Wichita? Three score and ten. Can I get there by candlelight? Yes, there and back again.

How many really? Too many. I'd give anything for a magic ring or a pair of Seven-league Boots right now.

SEPTEMBER 19

They took Brian. We had left the road, to stay safer at night, and I was off tying the horse. Two of them came from above, with a rush of wings and a sound like—a sound like voices, a thousand voices, voices that resonated in my bones.

I ran like hell into the trees. By the time I stopped I was totally disoriented. I waited for daylight. When I found the camp again, the tree-tops around our camp were burnt black as an angel's wing. The horse was where I left her, but Brian was gone.

Apart from the ring of charred trees there was no other sign of them. Again I'm reminded of the fairy tales we grew up on, and I wonder if it wasn't the angels that inspired the tales of fire-breathing dragons.

How long have they been here, and where have they been hiding?

SEPTEMBER 23

According to the map I'm now seventeen towns away from you.

I shouldn't think that way. You may not be there. You may have died that first week, or on the road on your way to Wichita. I should probably assume you did; if you didn't then you're an anomaly like I am.

So many things that I didn't tell you. How far we can walk

in a day, how long it will take to reach each other. That I hoped you would marry me, eventually—no, that's a lie, I hoped that you would marry me soon. That I used to hear voices.

That I had seen the angels before.

Would it increase your chances of surviving them if you knew? Or would you have thought I was crazy, and left me? Or thought I was crazy and try to get me help? Or would you believe me, and live life a little more afraid, the way that I did?

There was a quake in 1978. I was at my friend's house, in her bedroom on the second floor. The windows rattled; the whole house swayed. We could see the water sloshed out of the pool through her window. It wasn't much of a quake, not compared to what we just went through, but the experience terrified me.

I guess I thought I was having a nightmare that night when it appeared at my window, black except where the golden glow from its core leaked out, through its eyes, the webs between its fingers, its mouth. It just stared at me through the window and I could do nothing but stare back, afraid to move, afraid to scream, paralyzed in my seven-year-old fear.

That was one of the many things you gave to me, that you didn't even know—I felt safe from them when I was with you. For the first time in my life I finally felt safe. The nightmares didn't come when you were beside me.

You know that feeling you get when you suspect that you've done something really, profoundly wrong? That ice-water sick feeling that drains the blood from your head and knocks you to your knees, and you just hope it's a mistake, and believe on some level that it must be, because you couldn't possibly have done something so wrong?

I have that feeling tonight.

I have to get to you.

Please, please be alive.

SEPTEMBER 24

Hundreds, I think. None at all for several nights, and now there are so many that they block out the stars. I can see their red-gold glow. I smell smoke.

I think they're looking for me.

SEPTEMBER 27

They're watching me as I write this. I think the one closest to me used to be Brian. I see other faces that look familiar. Thank whatever gods there may be that none of them look like yours.

I can hear the voices again, feel them. Their mouths don't move, but I'm certain it's them I'm hearing. Sometimes I think I can almost isolate one from the rest, but then it all becomes noise again, murmured nonsense.

They aren't moving. They don't seem inclined to hurt me. They look like they're waiting. For what? For me to do something? For me to speak? To ask them what they are, what they want?

SEPTEMBER 28

They're gone, the voices are gone, and I can think again, move again, breathe again. Nothing changed all night—they stood there looking at me, waiting for what, I'm not sure.

The one I saw when I was a child did the same thing. Just looked at me, waiting. When I think back it seems almost as if there was a look of expectation, like it thought I had been waiting for it; memory is tricky, though, and the more you revisit a memory the less accurate it becomes. We add details that weren't there, things that might have made sense but didn't really happen. So perhaps that's what I'm doing. Just trying to make it make sense.

In my childish reasoning, I did the only thing I could do—the only thing you can do with the monster under the bed, or the bogeyman in the closet, or the angel at your window with eyes like burning coals and a face like cooling embers. I told it to go away.

It opened its mouth, and it seemed confused and almost disappointed. But it did what I said. It went away.

They took Brian. They took everyone. Why didn't they take me? Why did the angel turn away, confused, all those years ago?

The worst part of this for me is not the hunger, the exhaustion, or the loneliness. It's not the hardship or the fear. It's not even the fact that the world as we knew it has come to an end, and all my nightmares have become real. It's the fact that I'm pretty sure it's my fault.

Every time I think of it I'm dizzy and sick. I'm responsible. I summoned them all those years ago. I didn't know it then, but that hardly matters now. Everyone in the world is dead, or else transformed—which is as good as dead or maybe even worse—and it's my fault.

I play with the knife from your birthday box and think about how much easier it would be to just kill myself and get it over with, but I can't risk it. You may still be alive.

For now, I'd better make the best time I can. The road here is tree-lined and shady. I suppose I'll know more when the sun goes down.

LATER.

They brought me rabbits. A lot of them. The air is filled with the acrid smell of burnt hair from where they gripped them in their hands. They knew I was hungry. So I looked up how to skin an animal and did the best I could. I made a mess of it, and I can't say it tasted very good, but my head has stopped hurting and my stomach doesn't feel like it's trying to eat my back bone anymore.

They've spread out a little this time, but they still have me surrounded. I'm considering just trying to walk through them and continue down the road. I think they would let me.

The sound of voices comes and goes; it's almost like trying to tune an old radio with knobs and dials. If I move a certain way I'm overwhelmed by them, but if I tilt my head just a little sometimes one will come clear for a moment. But then I shake my head because what I hear them saying is too unbelievable, and I lose it again.

They never take their eyes off me. I think they're waiting for me to tell them what to do.

SEPTEMBER 29

I couldn't stand it, the way they were looking at me. I just—I don't know, I broke. I screamed at them; I threw rocks. They just stood there, stoic, waiting.

So I left. They stepped aside to let me pass, and then they followed me. So I screamed again, and told them to stop—and they did. Stopped in their tracks, the grass burning beneath their feet. I kept walking, looking back every few yards to make sure they were still there. They never moved from where I told them to stay.

Eventually I turned back.

I think I understand. Now I'm the one watching them.

SEPTEMBER 30

They tell me that you're alive. I'm sending one of them ahead, with this notebook, and the box.

They heard me, all those years ago. They listened to my fears and my dreams. They heard the anger of a child who had lost everything, telling them how the world would be if she were in charge; no one would leave her because there would be no one else in the world, just her and the people she loves. They were trapped, with no one but me to tell them about the world above, and now that they're free they have given me what I said I wanted.

Do not be afraid, love. Do not run. Their touch burns, and if you run, they will bring you back to me.

We made so many plans, you and I. We always felt invincible together, like we could do anything at all. I always said I would give you the world if I could.

I couldn't have known that it would one day be mine to give.

FINAL EXAM
MEGAN ARKENBERG

PART I - MULTIPLE CHOICE

1. The first time you visited the ocean, that Fourth-of-July weekend when purple storm clouds swallowed the horizon and the great cerulean expanse below them was freckled with parti-colored sails, you looked out over the water and felt...

   (a) The smallness of humanity in the face of a universe that is older and vaster and more full of life than any of us can imagine, much less understand
   (b) A sudden urge to jump
   (c) The awful terror of living
   (d) Nothing; there was only the sea-spray on your face, salty, cold and needle-fine
   (e) All of the above

2. At what point did you know—and I mean really *know*, in your gut, in the tautness of your heartstrings—that things had gone horribly wrong?

(a) When you ran the faucet in the motel bathroom to wash the salty tear-tracks from your face, and the water came out cold and red, staining the sink

(b) When the equipment at work started breaking down; first the conveyor belts on the registers, then the adding machine in the office, then the registers themselves. IT had the same advice over and over again: unplug it, turn it off, and plug it in again. Of course it never worked.

(c) When Donald looked up from the papers he was correcting at the kitchen counter and said, "Baby girl, what do you think about couples' therapy?" and you were so startled that you dropped the whole carton of orange juice

(d) When the pink-suited reporter interrupted the inspirational drama on the television in the marriage counselor's waiting room, her hair frizzled with electricity and her left eyebrow bloodied from a shallow cut to the forehead. "Tell us what you're seeing," somebody said, and she said, "God…"

(e) When you asked him to pass you a butter knife from the drawer, and he must have heard you, but he was marking something in the margin of his book and you had to ask a second time. He slammed the book shut and pulled the drawer so hard that it came off the slides. Here, he said, flinging the knife across the counter. It landed with its tongue-like blade pointed at your breast.

3. When the pink-suited reporter's station showed the first footage of the things shambling out of the water, you compared them to...

    (a) Your neighbor's dog, a blond-gray whippet with a scratched bald patch high on his left shoulder. You thought of Sultan when you saw the first shambling thing bend, drawing back its black and rubbery lips, and sinking its long yellow teeth into its own thigh, biting down to the bone.
    (b) Fish, especially the fat, foul-smelling, tasteless white fish Donald used to bring home by the bucket-load and smoke over a charcoal fire on the patio
    (c) Skinny girls, like the neighbor three blocks over who took her early morning jogs in a white tank top that, by the time she reached your house, had turned transparent with sweat, displaying her prominent ribs
    (d) Godzilla, whose movie you had never seen, but whose general shape you vaguely remembered from a commercial for a Japanese automobile
    (e) The sea-witch from a picture book your favorite teacher read to the class one day, when it was raining too hard to go outside for recess. The artist had drawn the sea-witch with a water snake

wound around her shoulders like a mink; the sea-witch was offering it a taste of a tiny red crab, which she held between her own sharp teeth.

4. After several months watching them, first through the reporter's camera and then, later, through the slats in the boards you had pounded over your windows, you came to the conclusion that the shambling things had originated…

(a) On Mars
(b) In an alternate dimension, where the laws of physics and geometry and merging into freeway traffic are subtly different, and it is possible to have four-sided triangles
(c) In the nightmares of mankind, where we let our guard down and unleash the latent psychic powers of creation which, when we are awake, limit themselves to such pieces of good fortune as the perfect seat in the movie theatre, or a bra that fits
(d) On this planet, in the natural course of evolution, which has already produced such monsters as the platypus, the hyena, and your skinny neighbor
(e) After Chernobyl, or Three-Mile Island, or a worse disaster that a national government, or the Illuminati, had been more successful at covering up

5. Now that it has been months since the last sighting, many people have chosen to believe that

the shambling monsters are gone for good. You, however, know that they are…

(a) Still in the ocean, huddled at the bottom of chasms too deep for sonar, waiting to rise again and feel the cold moonlight on their bulbous faces

(b) Taking on the appearance of everyday people: the cashier at the newly re-opened liquor store, the gang of skinny gun-dragging teenagers who moved into the old marriage counselor's office, the woman who walks up and down the sidewalk in the late afternoon, calling out names you can never quite understand

(c) In our nightmares, slowly shaping us to our true forms

(d) Hiding under your bed

(e) Both c and d

6. What could you have done to prevent all this from happening?

(a) Become a better cook, as Donald's mother always hinted with her gifts of Julia Child and Betty Crocker collections, the elaborate kitchen gadgets whose names, much less their functions, remain shrouded in mystery. Though you never really learned to love food, you did learn to cook, to boil and bubble the bacteria out of a can of condensed soup. Incidentally, your mother-in-law would be proud.

(b) Become a better liar. It is true that the pink-

and-emerald tie he wanted to buy at the church flea-market was the ugliest thing you had ever seen, uglier even than the monsters from the sea, uglier even than Sultan. But it would not have hurt you to bite your lip and nod your head and say Yes, for seventy-five cents it certainly is a steal.

(c) Prayed more, and harder, and to the right people. Saint Helena is the patron of dysfunctional marriage. Saint Neot is the patron of fish.

(d) All of the above

(e) None of the above

7. The worst part was…

(a) When the first shambling thing ate the pink-suited reporter, and the cameraman didn't turn away, and you sat there petrified in the marriage counselor's office, watching the flesh blossom and drip over the creature's scaly lips. "Jesus Christ," you said, reaching for Donald's hand. He was gripping a magazine cover too tightly to notice.

(b) When he flung the little velvet box at you over the dinner table, and you looked at him and you asked, "What is this for?" and he said, "I knew you'd forget."

(c) When you checked into the motel, and you couldn't stop licking your bottom lip even though you knew your saliva was keeping the split open, and the man at the front desk was clearly worried for you but he just as clearly didn't know what to say, so he handed you a pair of key-cards and told you, earnestly, to have a good night

(d) Later that night, when you opened the bottle of pinot grigio that the liquor clerk had recommended and drank it all in one long throat-tearing gulp. Your cell phone started to sing from its compartment in your purse, the sweet black-and-white movie love song Donald had tried to serenade you with, once, in the back seat of your car. Even drunk, your thumb found the phone's power button and turned it off.

(e) This moment, now, as you look back on all of it, and can't think of anything that you would do the same

8. When you came home from the motel the next morning, a hangover ringing in your ears, you found his packed suitcase sitting on the coffee table in the living room. You stumbled into the bathroom to vomit, and when you came out again, the suitcase was gone. That was, in a way, the last you ever saw of Donald. What happened to him?

(a) Shortly after he left, he was eaten by one of the shambling creatures.

(b) He met another woman on a bus to Chicago. She was taller than you are, and skinnier, and she smelled like cinnamon and vanilla.

(c) He joined that cult down in Louisiana, the one

with the blood sacrifices and the idol built of concrete blocks, and he was one of the men who walked into the ocean on June 21, and became a pillar of salt.

(d) He committed suicide with a shaving razor in the bathtub of the same motel room where you hid from him, that last night. He never forgave himself for hitting you, not even when he remembered that you'd hit him first.

(e) He slipped, somehow, into an alternate dimension, where the laws of physics and geometry are subtly different, and there is a house just like yours, but the woman inside is a better liar.

9. His last thoughts were…

(a) Incomprehensible with fear, the nauseating smell of his own blood

(b) Of you

(c) Revelations about the falseness of Euclidean geometry, the sheer *wrongness* of all human conceptions of time and history and causal relationships, that could never have been comprehended by another human being, even if Donald had lived, and admitted to himself what he had understood

(d) Of Christine Kaminski, the slender brunette who took him to junior prom, and who forged a deeper connection with him on that one night in the rented Marriott ballroom than you did in seven years of marriage. She wore pale blue, his favorite color, and only kissed him once, during the last dance of the night. If he had married her, he would have been happy.

(e) Of his little brother, who died at birth, whom he never told you about. He intended to, but there was never a moment in that first year of marriage when you weren't too busy with something else—arranging furniture, organizing closets and cupboards, filing for loans, writing thank-you cards. Afterward, it seemed too late to bring it up. The closest he ever came was during that Christmas dinner at your sister's, when you teased him about being an only child.

10. Looking back on all of it, you still don't understand...

(a) Why all the equipment at work broke down that day. You even stayed an extra fifteen minutes to play with the reset buttons and a bent paperclip; it made you late to the marriage counselor's office, which in some ways didn't matter, because her previous appointment was running over and you had to wait anyway, but in some ways it did matter, because Donald was expecting you to arrive on time. It didn't help in any case. Everything was still broken the next day.

(b) Why the water in the motel bathroom turned to blood. Afterward, you asked around town, and learned that no one else had discovered blood or any other bodily fluids running through their pipes. But there was a lot going on at the time;

maybe they simply hadn't noticed.

(c) Why you told Donald about the Little Mermaid picture book as you collapsed drunken and giggling into your own back seat. Your throat was hoarse from swearing at your baseball team as they permitted run after humiliating run, and you had spilled beer on the sleeve of your sweatshirt. You tried to wiggle out of it and it got stuck around your hips, and you said, This reminds me of a story...

(d) What attracted you to Donald in the first place. Was it his eyes, his soft lips, the way he ran his fingers through his hair when he was nervous, the way all his undershirts smelled like chalkboards, the way he tightened his tie with both hands before saying something important?

(e) All of the above

11. After that incident in Portland, when the shambling thing almost caught up to you by clinging to the bottom of your bus, your favorite shirt became stained with...

(a) Seawater
(b) Blood (yours)
(c) Ichor (its)
(d) Semen
(e) Merlot

12. Your sister, who knows these things, told you that the best technique for fighting the shambling monsters is...

(a) Frying them with a blowtorch
(b) Dowsing them with holy water
(c) Dragging them behind a truck
(d) Flinging them into a nuclear reactor
(e) Running until they tire of chasing you

13. You most regret...

(a) Missing that shot at the fast-food joint in Vancouver, when the little boy died. It was not your fault; no one had ever taught you to fire a revolver, much less where to aim on a bulbous heavy-lidded nightmare as it slithered over a drive-thru window. But it *was* your fault, because the creature had followed you, and if you hadn't stopped to eat at that particular restaurant at that particular time, it would never have killed that child.
(b) Not letting him buy that hideous watermelon tie at the church flea-market, when you knew it reminded him of his grandfather, and made him smile
(c) Wearing your favorite shirt on the bus in Portland
(d) Shaking Donald as you got into the car in the marriage counselor's parking lot, then slapping him across the face. No matter how terrified you were, no matter how much you thought he'd earned it, you should have known better than to hit him. You did know better. You knew it reminded him of his father.
(e) Turning into your pillow that last time he tried

to kiss you goodnight, so that his lips caught you on the cheek

14. In your dreams, the shambling monsters appear at your bedside, and their voices sound like...

    (a) Radio static, interspersed with love songs from old black-and-white movies
    (b) The screaming of the pink-suited reporter as those yellow teeth crunched through her clavicle
    (c) The marriage counselor, with her gentle eastern accent, the sharp tick of her pen against her clipboard punctuating each clause
    (d) Footsteps over broken glass
    (e) The whisper of a fish's breath

15. Now, when you look out at the sea, you feel...

    (a) The smallness of humanity in the face of a universe that is older and vaster and more full of life than any of us can imagine, much less understand
    (b) A sudden urge to jump
    (c) The awful terror of living
    (d) His absence; there is only the sea-spray on your face, salty, cold and needle-fine
    (e) All of the above

PART II - SHORT ANSWER

16. Is this really the end of the world? Defend your answer with evidence from the following texts:

the *Apocalypse of John*, the *Collected Works of H. P. Lovecraft*, *The Shepherd of Hermas*, Ibn Al-Nafis' *Theologus Autodidactus*, Mary Shelley's *The Last Man*, the fortieth through fifty-eighth stanzas of *Völuspá*, and last week's edition of the *New York Times*.

17. Just what is it about filling in bubbles on a multiple choice test that makes you believe that every terrible decision you've made might, with luck, with sheer cussedness, have turned out right in the end?

PART III - EXTRA CREDIT

18. What color were Donald's eyes?

PART IV - ANSWER KEY

1. The correct answer is (e) All of the above. You were nine years old, and had wanted to see the ocean ever since the day your third-grade teacher read you a picture book with the *real* story of the Little Mermaid—Andersen, not Disney. You wore a pink-and-yellow bathing suit that you had outgrown the previous summer and carried a purple plastic pail, not because you had any intention of building sandcastles but because the children in the picture book (who appeared in the seashore-margins on every page, though they had nothing to do with the mermaid or her prince or her beautiful raven-haired rival) had carried pails and shovels, made of tin, in which they collected seashells. At that moment,

standing at the edge of the pier while your parents argued through a transaction at the overpriced snack-shack behind you, you registered nothing but the caress of the waves on your face. Only later, with reflection, did you feel the smallness, the terror, the urge to jump.

On your honeymoon, Donald tried to recreate this experience (which you had shared with him in the backseat of your car, after a drunken night at the worst baseball game your team had ever played). He took you to the same pier, bought you a paper cone of roasted peanuts at the same overpriced snack-shack, but the weather was different, clean and peaceful, and your red two-piece fit your body like a second skin.

2. The correct answer is (e) When you asked him to pass you a butter knife, and he must have heard you, but he was marking something in the margin of his book and you had to ask a second time. It cost sixty-seven dollars to fix the drawer slides, sixty-seven dollars you didn't have but managed to find somewhere, probably in the old plastic KFC cup you kept by the telephone to collect money for date nights, back when you went on dates. In days to come, that cup would hold many things: pinot grigio, as you drank yourself into a stupor; vomit; distilled water for an impromptu eye wash; strips of bloody gauze.

3. The correct answer, I'm sorry to say, is (d) Godzilla. You had never done your best or most original

thinking under stress. Donald would not have hesitated to point this out, but then again, when Donald saw the shambling things on the television his first thought was of the illustration of the sea-witch, which he had seen only days before as he wandered through the mall, looking for your anniversary present. He found the old picture book in a store that specialized in plush animals and greeting cards, and he thought of buying it for you, but he remembered that day on the pier by the ocean, and bought you a pearl bracelet instead.

There's an old superstition that a bride shouldn't wear pearls on her wedding day, because for each pearl she wears, her husband will give her a reason to cry.

4. The correct answer is (b) In an alternate dimension. At least, that was your theory; the true answer is somewhat closer to (d) On this planet, in the natural course of evolution. You, however, are not expected to know this, or to retain your sanity if you had glimpsed some hint of it by mistake.

What happened between you and Donald was also by and large the result of a natural chain of events, an estrangement, a distancing of the sort that shambles into so many relationships. The truth—which you are also not expected to know—is that you never had very much in common to begin with. Your date nights stopped because you could no longer agree on a restaurant, or a movie, or a group of friends to visit.

Breaking the cutlery drawer was the natural result of too many nights listening to you root for a baseball team he had never cared for in the first place.

5.   The correct answer is (b) Taking on the appearance of every-day people. The marriage counselor, who spoke to you briefly on the office phone when you called her during your lunch break, said that Donald thought you had trust issues. It's not paranoia if they're really out to get you, you said. "Who is out to get you?" asked the marriage counselor.

If your memory had a better sense of irony, it would have recalled that conversation two months later as you darted from shadow to shadow down your near-deserted block, clutching a gun you didn't know how to use, listening for the gelatinous thump of the creature's footsteps behind you. You'd learned by then that they could distinguish humans through scent, and that they gave off distinctive odors of their own; this particular creature, a female who smelled as chalky as a jar of antacid, had been trailing you for weeks. In the end, you only lost her when you packed the truck and moved up to Oregon for a few months, to stay with your sister, who'd compulsively saved canned goods and ammunition in her basement. Even later, after you worked up the courage to return home, when you cracked open the front door and slipped into the foyer, your nostrils were assaulted by the stench of mold and chalk.

6. The correct answer is (e) None of the above. Of course, you could have tried cooking, or lying, or praying; it would not have hurt to try. But you never did.

7. The correct answer is (a) When the first shambling thing ate the pink-suited reporter, and the cameraman didn't turn away. You will see that scene in your nightmares for the rest of your life. You will never again look at that particular shade of pink without your stomach churning, your tongue fumbling compulsively past your lips, your ribs curling inward, your vision spotting like blood on bathroom tissue. In all of this, the reporter's death is the only thing about which you have never spoken to anyone. Sometimes, you think it is the real reason you drink.

8. The correct answer is (b) He met another woman on a bus to Chicago. Her name was Nora and she used to work in a bakery; she was not a very good baker, but her hand was perfectly steady as she drew looping cursive letters in pink gel across the smooth buttercream canvases. The last cake she decorated was for a little girl named Rebecca, who ate the frosting in huge gobs with her fingers, but had wanted the lettering to be blue. Nora didn't care that Donald was married, and he didn't care that her last relationship had been with a woman who died of suspiciously severe food poisoning. They settled for a while in an apartment over an abandoned antique store. Then, after a year and a half, Nora joined the Louisiana blood-cult, and Donald never heard from her again.

Though he did eventually commit suicide with a shaving razor, it is too much of a coincidence to think that he did it in that same motel room where you'd sobbed over the sink all those months before.

9. The correct answer is (b) Of you. For better or for worse, you were the love of his life. In the early whirlwind years, he imagined that some corner of his heart had always known and loved you, even at junior prom, when he was kissing Christine Kaminski and smelling the soapy-bubblegum scent of her shampoo. Later, when Nora disappeared, he began to write letters to you. He never sent them, which is just as well. You would never have opened them, and they would not have told you anything you didn't already know.

Here is what the last one said: Baby girl, I've forgotten the color of your eyes. Sorry for everything. Don.

10. The correct answer is (e) All of the above. It's ironic, when you consider that an Apocalypse is meant to be a revelation, an unveiling, that at the end of everything so much remains veiled. No one knows why, in offices and stores around the country, computers and cash registers went down in droves that Tuesday afternoon. You were the only one to see the blood come out of the faucet, and you wouldn't even swear that it was blood. It might have been zinfandel. You will never learn why you always need to be drunk before you can share really important information with the people

you love. Even this answer key won't give you all the answers.

(What first attracted you to Donald was the way he mispronounced your last name.)

11. The correct answer is (b) Blood (yours). You were sitting at the window above the left rear wheel, your head jolting with each pothole against the padded headrest, when you caught the stench of chalk coming through the air conditioning. You panicked and fought your way to the front door, and the driver misinterpreted your flailing and laid you low with a punch between the eyes. Everyone was jumpy, those first few months. You woke a half-hour later to learn that the bus had crossed six bridges while you were out, and the smell of chalk was gone, replaced by the sour-metallic taste in the back of your nostrils and gummed in your lace neckline.

12. The correct answer is, of course, (d) Flinging them into a nuclear reactor, but you had to make do with (e) Running until they tired of chasing you.

13. The correct answer is (e) turning into your pillow that last time he tried to kiss you goodnight. In the days and months and years to come, you would miss the taste of his mouth, miss the cool scratch of his unshaved chin across your cheek. Of course the little boy's death bothers you, and the pink-and-green tie, and the hideous satisfaction of the hard granite sound your hand made when it collided with his jaw. But

none of these produced in you the same yearning, the
same hunger, the deep chilling pain of a hollowness
you yourself created.

14. The correct answer is (a) Radio static, interspersed
with love songs from old black-and-white movies.
If Donald ever calls you, the ring tone will be the
same: a sweet plucking of violin strings, a woman's
too-mellow voice. The worst thing about these
nightmares is that you often think he *is* calling you,
and it pulls you out of your dream of running into
the cold and poorly lit reality of the place you ran
to. And once there, in the silence, in your narrow
bed, you are all alone.

15. The correct answer is (d).

16. Answers will vary.

17. Answers will vary.

A FLOCK OF BIRDS

JAMES VAN PELT

The starlings wheeled like a giant blanket flung into the sky, like sentient smoke, banking and turning in unison. They passed overhead so close that Carson heard their wings ripping the air, and when the flock flew in front of the sun, the world grew gray. Carson shivered even though it was only early September and warm enough for a short-sleeved shirt. This close he could smell them, all dark-feathered and frantic and dry and biting.

He estimated maybe 50,000 birds. Not the largest flock he'd seen this year, but one of the bigger ones, and certainly bigger than anything he'd seen last year. Of course, the summer before that he didn't watch the birds. No one did. No chance to add to his life list that year. No winter count either. The Colorado Field Ornithology office closed.

He leaned back in his lawn chair. The bird vortex moved east, over the wheatgrass plain until the sun brightened again, pressing pleasant heat against the back of his hands and arms. He was glad for the hat that protected his head and its middle-aged bald spot. This wasn't the time to mess with skin cancer, he thought, not a good time at all. He was glad his teeth were generally healthy and his eyesight was keen.

The binoculars were excellent, Bausch & Lomb Elite. Wide field of vision. Top notch optics. Treated lenses. He'd picked them up from a sporting goods store in Littleton's South Glenn Mall. Through them the birds became singular. He followed discrete groups. They swirled, coming straight toward him for a moment, then sliding away. Slowly he scanned the flight until he reached the leading edge. Birds on one half and sky on the other. They switched direction and the leaders became the followers. He took the binoculars away and blinked at their loss of individuality. In the middle, where the birds were thickest, the shape was black, a sinuous, twisting dark chord. One dot separated itself from the others, flying against the current. Carson only saw it for a second, but it was distinctly larger than the starlings, and its wing beat was different. He focused the binoculars again, his breath coming fast, and scanned the flock. It would be unusual for a single bird of a different species to fly with the starlings.

Nothing for several minutes other than the hordes streaming by, then the strange bird emerged. Long, slender wings, a reddish breast, and it was *fast*. Much faster than the starlings and twice their size. The cloud shifted, swallowing it, as the entire flock drifted slowly east, farther into the plains.

The bird looked familiar. Not one from his journals, but one he'd seen a picture of before. Something tropical perhaps that had drifted north? Every once in a while a single representative of a species would be spotted, hundreds, sometimes thousands of miles from where it was normally found. The birder who saw it could only hope that someone else confirmed the sighting or that he got a picture, otherwise it would be discounted and couldn't be legitimately added to a life list. If he could add a new bird to his list, maybe that would make things better. A new bird! He could concentrate on that. Something good to cling to.

The flock grew small in the distance.

Carson sighed, put the binoculars back in their case, then packed the rest of his gear into the truck. He checked the straps that held his motorcycle in place. They were tight. The tie-down holding the extra batteries for the truck and motorcycle were secure too. From his spot on the hill he could see the dirt road he'd taken from the highway and the long stretch of I-25 that reached north toward Denver and south to Colorado Springs. No traffic. The air above the Denver skyline was crystalline. He strained his ears, tilting his head from one side then the other. He hadn't heard a car on the highway behind him all afternoon. Grass rustle. Moldy-leaf smells, nothing else, and when he finally opened the truck's door, the metallic click was foreign and loud.

Back at his house in Littleton, he checked the photoelectric panels' gauges inside the front door. It had been sunny for the last week, so the system was full. The water tower showed only four hundred gallons though. He'd have to go water scavenging again in the next few days.

"I'm home," he called. His voice echoed off the tiled foyer. "Tillie?"

The living room was empty, and so were the kitchen and bedrooms. Carson stepped into the bathroom, his hand on his chest where his heart beat fast, but the sleeping pills in the cabinet looked undisturbed. "Tillie?"

He found her sitting in the back yard beneath the globe willow, still in her robe. The nightgown beneath it was yellowed and tattered. In her dresser he'd put a dozen new ones, but she'd only wear the one she had in her suitcase when he'd picked her up, wandering through the Denver Botanical Gardens two years ago.

He sat on the grass next to her. She was fifty or so. Lots of gray in her blond hair. Slender wrists. Narrow face. Strikingly blue eyes that hardly ever focused on anything.

"How's that cough?" he asked.

"We never play bridge anymore, Bob Robert."

Carson stretched out. A day with binoculars pressed to his face and his elbows braced on his knees hurt his back. "Tough to get partners," he said. Then he added out of habit, "And I'm not Bob Robert."

She picked at a loose thread in the robe, pulling at it until it broke free. "Have you seen the garden? Not a flower in it. A single geranium or a daisy would give me hope. If just one dead thing would come back."

"I've brought you seeds," he said. "You just need to plant them."

She wrapped the thread around her fingertip tightly. "I waited for the pool man, but he never came. I hate skimming." She raised her fist to her mouth and coughed primly behind it twice, grimacing each time.

Carson raised his head. Other than the grass under the tree, most of the yard was dirt. The lot was longer than it was wide. At the end farthest from the house a chicken wire enclosure surrounded the poultry. A couple hens sat in the shade by the coop. No pool. When he'd gone house hunting, he'd toyed with the idea of a pool, but the thought of trying to keep it filled and the inevitable problems with water chemistry made him decide against it. The house on the other side of the privacy fence had a pool, as did most of the houses in the neighborhood, now empty except for the scummy pond in the deep end. In the spring he'd found a deer, its neck bent unnaturally back, at the bottom of one a block over. Evidently it had jumped the fence and gone straight in.

"Are you hungry?" Carson asked.

Tillie tilted her head to the side. "When will the garden grow again?"

He pushed himself off the ground. "I'll fix eggs."

Later that evening, he tucked Tillie into bed. The room smelled of peppermint. From the bulge in her cheek, he guessed she was sucking on one. In a little-girl voice, she said, "Can you put in my video?" Her expression was alert, but her eyes were red-rimmed and watery. He smiled. This was as good as she got. Sometimes he could play gin rummy with her and she'd stay focused for an hour or so before she drifted away. If he asked her about her past, she'd be unresponsive for days. All he knew about her came from the suitcase she carried when he'd found her. There was a sheet of letterhead with a name at the top: "Tillie Waterhouse, Marketing Executive," and an athletic club identification card with her picture and name. But there was no Tillie Waterhouse in the Denver phone book. Could she have wandered away from the airport when air travel was canceled? The first words she had said to him, when she finally spoke, were, "How do you bear it?"

"Did you have a good day?" He turned on the television and pressed rewind on the VCR.

Her hands peeked out from under the covers and pulled

them tight under her chin. "Something magical is going to happen. The leaves whispered to me."

The video clicked to a stop. "I'm glad to hear that," he said. The television flickered as the tape started, a documentary on the 2001 New York City Marathon a decade earlier. It opened with a helicopter flyover of the racers crossing the Verrazano-Narrows Bridge into Brooklyn. The human crowd surged forward, packed elbow-to-elbow, long as the eye could see. Then the camera cut to ankle level. Feet ran past for five minutes. Then it went to face level at a turn in the course. The starting crush had spread out, but the runners still jogged within an arm's length of each other, thousands of them. Carson had watched the video with her the first few times. The video was a celebration of numbers. Thirty-thousand athletes straining over the twenty-six-mile course through New York City's five boroughs.

"Here's the remote if you want to watch it again."

"So many American flags," she said.

"It was only a month after that first terrorist thing." Carson sat on the end of her bed. Some runners wore stars and stripes singlets or racing shorts. Others carried small flags and waved them at the camera as they passed.

"I won't be able to sleep," she said.

He nodded. "Me either."

Before he left, he pressed his hand to her forehead. She looked up briefly, the blanket still snug against her chin. A little fever and her breath sounded wheezy.

Later that night he made careful entries in his day book. A breeze through the open window freshened the room. He'd spotted a mountain plover, a long-billed curlew, a burrowing owl and a horned lark, plus the usual assortment of lark sparrows, yellow warblers, western meadowlarks, red-winged blackbirds, crows, black terns and mourning doves. Nothing unusual beside the strange bird in the starling flock. Idly he thumbed through his bird identification handbook. No help there. Could it actually be a new bird? Something to add to his life list?

Tomorrow he'd take the camera. Several major flocks roosted in the elms along the Platte River. He hadn't done a riparian count in a couple months anyway. After visiting the distribution center, he'd go to the river. With an early enough start, he would still have ten hours of sun to work with.

He shut the book and turned off his desk light. Gradually his eyes adjusted as he looked out the window. A full moon illuminated the scene. From his chair he could see three houses bathed in the leaden glow, their windows black as basalt. His neighbor's minivan rested on its rims, all four tires long gone flat. Carson tried to come up with the guy's name, but it remained elusive. Generally he tried not to think about his neighbors or their empty houses.

He couldn't hear anything other than the wind moving over the silent city. Not sleepy at all, he watched the shadows slide slowly across the lawn. Just after 2:00 A.M., a pair of coyotes trotted up the middle of the street. Their toenails clicked loudly against the asphalt. Carson finally rose, took two sleeping pills and went to bed.

"The woman who stays with me is sick," said Carson. He rested his arm against his truck, supplies requisition list in hand.

The distribution center manager nodded dourly. "Oh, the sweet sorrow of parting." He hooked his grimy thumbs in his overalls. Through the warehouse doors behind him

Carson saw white plastic-wrapped bales, four feet to a side, stacked five bales high and reaching to the warehouse's far end. They contained bags of flour, corn, cloth, paper, a little bit of everything. Emergency stores.

Carson blanched. "It's not that. She just has a cough and a bit of fever. If it's bacterial, an antibiotic might knock it right out."

"T.B. or not T.B. That is congestion, Carson," he said, laughing through yellow teeth. Carson guessed he might be fifty-five or sixty.

Carson smiled. "You're pretty sharp today."

"Finest collection of video theater this side of hell. Watched Laurence Olivier last night until 3:00 or 4:00." The manager consulted his clipboard. "No new pharmaceuticals in a couple months, and I haven't seen antibiotics in over a year. I could have my assistant keep an eye open for you, but he hasn't come in for a week. Lookin' sickly his last day, you know?" The manager rubbed his fingers on his chest. "Could be that I've lost him. Have you tried a tablespoon of honey in a shot glass of bourbon? Works for me every time."

A car pulled into the huge, empty parking lot behind Carson's truck, but whoever was inside didn't get out. Carson nodded in the car's direction. Evidently they wanted to wait for Carson to finish his business.

He handed the manager the list. "Can you also give me cornmeal and sugar? A mix of canned vegetables would be nice too."

"That I've got." The manager hopped on a forklift. "Tomorrow may creep in a pretty pace, but I shouldn't be a minute."

When he returned with the goods he said, "The quality of mercy is not strained here. I'm not doing anything this afternoon. I'll dig some for you. Few months back I heard a pharmacy in an Albertson's burned down. Looters overlooked it. Might be something there. I've got your address." He waved the requisition list. "I could bring it by your house."

Carson loaded boxes of canned soup and vegetables into the truck. "What about the warehouse?"

The manager shrugged. "Guess we're on an honor system now. Only a dozen or so customers a day. Maybe a couple hundred total. I'll bet there aren't 50,000 people alive in the whole country. I'll leave the doors open." For a moment the manager stared into the distance, as if he'd lost his thought. Behind them, the waiting car rumbled. "You know how they say that if you put a jellybean in a jar every time you make love the first year that you're married, and you take one out every time you make love after that, that the jar will never be empty? This warehouse is a little like that."

When Carson started the truck, the manager leaned into the window, resting his arms on the car door. This close, Carson could see how greasy the man's hair was, and it smelled like old lard.

The manager's smile was gone. "How long have you known me?" he said, looking Carson straight in the eye. His voice was suddenly so serious.

Carson tried not to shrink away. He thought back. "I don't know. Sixteen months?"

The manager grimaced. "That makes you my oldest friend. There isn't anyone alive that I've known longer."

For a second, Carson was afraid the man would begin crying. Instead, he straightened, his hands still on the door.

Tentatively, Carson said, "I'm sorry. I don't think I've ever asked what your name was."

"Nope, nope, no need," the manager barked, smiling again. "A rose by any other moniker, as they say. I'll see what I can find you in the coughing line. Don't know about antibiotics. Come back tomorrow."

It wasn't until Carson had driven blocks away toward the river, as he watched the boarded-up stores slide by, as he moved down the empty streets, past the mute houses that he realized, other than Tillie, the manager was his oldest friend too.

Sitting on his camp chair, Carson had a panoramic river view. On the horizon to the west, the mountains rose steeply, only a remnant of last winter's snow clinging to the tops of the tallest peaks. Fifty yards away at the bottom of a short bluff, the river itself, at its lowest level of the season, rolled sluggishly. Long gravel tongues protruded into the water where little long-legged birds searched for insects between the rocks. A bald eagle swept low over the water going south. Carson marked it in his notebook.

Across the river stood clumps of elm and willows. He didn't need his binoculars to see the branches were heavy with roosting starlings. Counting individuals was impossible. He'd have to estimate. He wondered what the distribution manager would make of the birds. After all, they had something in common. If it weren't for Shakespeare, the starlings wouldn't be here at all. In the early 1890s, a club of New York Anglophiles thought it would be comforting if all the birds mentioned in Shakespeare's plays lived in America. They tried nightingales and chaffinches and various thrushes, but none succeeded like the 100 European starlings they released in Central Park. By the last count there were over two hundred million of them. He'd read an article in one of his bird books that called them "avian cockroaches."

He set up his camera on a tripod and scanned the trees with the telephoto. Not only were there starlings, but also red-winged blackbirds, an aggressive, native species. They could hold their own against invaders.

Carson clicked a few shots. He could edit the photos out of the camera's memory later if he needed the space. A group of starlings lifted from some of the trees. Maybe something disturbed them? He looked for a deer or raccoon on the ground below, but couldn't see anything. The birds swirled upwards before sweeping down river. He thought about invaders, like infection, spreading across the country. Carp were invaders. So were zebra mussels that hitchhiked in ships' ballast water and became a scourge, attaching themselves to the inside of pipes used to draw water into power plants.

It wasn't just animals either. Crabgrass, dandelions, kudzu, knotweed, tamarisk, leafy spurge, and Norway maple, pushing native species to extinction.

Infection. Extinction. And extinct meant you'd never come back. No hope.

Empty houses. Empty shopping malls. Empty theaters. Contrail-free skies. Static on the radio. Traffic-free highways. The creak of wind-pushed swing sets in dusty playgrounds. He pictured Tillie's video, the endless runners pouring across the bridge.

Carson shook his head. He'd never get the count done if he daydreamed. Last year he spotted 131 species in the fall count. Maybe this year he'd find more. Maybe he'd see something rare, like a yellow-billed loon or a fulvous whistling duck.

Methodically, he moved his focus from tree to tree. Mostly starlings, their beaks resting on their breasts. Five hundred in one tree. A thousand in the next. He held the binoculars in his left hand while writing the numbers with his right. Later he'd fill out a complete report for the Colorado Field Ornithologists. A stack of reports sat on his desk at home, undeliverable.

He couldn't hear the birds from here, but their chirping calls would be overwhelming if he could walk beneath them.

A feathered blur whipped through his field of vision. Carson looked over the top of his binoculars. Two birds skimmed the treetops, heading upriver. He stood, breath coming quick. Narrow wings. Right size. He found them in the binoculars. Were they the same kind of bird he'd seen yesterday? What luck! But they flew too fast and they were going away. He'd never be able to identify them from this distance. If only they'd circle back. Then, unbelievably, they turned, crossing the river, coming toward him. The binoculars thumped against his chest when he dropped them, as he picked up the camera, tripod and all. He found the birds, focused, and snapped a picture. They kept coming. He snapped again, both birds in view. Closer even still until just one bird filled the frame. Snap. Then they whipped past, only twenty feet overhead. And fast! Faster than any bird he'd seen except a peregrine falcon on a dive.

His hands trembled. Definitely a bird new to him. A new species to add to his life list. And the bird he'd seen yesterday couldn't be a single, misplaced wanderer, not if there were two of them here. Maybe a flock had been blown into the area. He knew Colorado birds, and these weren't native.

He stayed another hour, counting starlings and recording

the other river birds that crossed his path, but his heart wasn't in it. In his camera waited the image of the new bird, but he'd have to transfer it to the computer where he could study it.

Tillie was in bed. Beside her, on the night stand, were packets of seeds. She hadn't moved them since he'd brought them to her in the spring. The television was on. There were, of course, no broadcasts, so gray snow filled the screen, and the set softly hissed. Carson turned it off, darkening the room. Sunlight leaked around the closed curtains, but after the brightness outside, he could barely see. In the silence, Tillie's breathing rasped. He tiptoed around her bed to put his hand to her forehead. Distinctly warm. She didn't move when he touched her.

"Tillie?" he said.

She mumbled but didn't open her eyes.

Carson turned on her reading light, painting her face in highlights and sharp shadows. He knelt beside her. Her lips were parted slightly, and she licked them before taking her next rattling breath. He wanted to jostle her awake. She slept so poorly most nights that he resisted. The fever startled him. As long as it was just a cough, he hadn't worried much. A cough, that could be a cold or an allergy. But a fever, that was a red flag. He remembered all the home defense brochures with their sobering titles: *Family Triage* and *Know Your Symptoms*. "Tillie, I need to check your chest."

His fingers shook as he pulled the blanket away from her chin. Her neck was clammy, and underneath the covers she was sweating. She *smelled* warm and damp. Clumsily he unbuttoned her nightgown's top buttons, then he moved the light so he could see better. No rash. She wasn't wearing a bra, so he could see that the tops of her breasts looked smooth. "Tillie?" he whispered, really not wanting to wake her. Her eyes moved under her eyelids. Maybe she dreamed of other places, the places she would never talk to him about. Gently he rubbed his fingertips over the skin below her collarbones. No boils. No "bumpy swellings" the brochures described.

Tillie mumbled again. "Bob Robert," she said.

"I'll get some aspirin and water." He pulled the blanket back up. She didn't move.

"You're nice," she said, but her head was turned away, and he wasn't sure if she was talking to him or continuing a conversation in her dream.

As he poured water from a bottle in the refrigerator, he realized that it would be difficult to tell if Tillie became delirious. If she started talking sense, *then* he'd have to worry about her.

The distribution manager had said to come back the next day, so there was nothing to do other than to give her aspirin and keep her comfortable. She woke up enough to take the medicine, but closed her eyes immediately. Carson patted her on the top of her hands, made sure the water pitcher was full, then went to his office where he printed the pictures from his camera. The last one was quite good. Full view of the bird's beak, head, neck, breast, wing shape and tail feathers. Identification should have been easy, but nothing matched in his books. He needed better resources.

Driving to Littleton library meant passing the landfill. Most days Carson tried to ignore it—it reminded him of

Arlington Cemetery without the tombstones—but today he stopped at the side of the road. He needed a place to think, and the broad, featureless land lent itself to meditations. Last year swarms of gulls circled, waiting for places to set down. The ones on the ground picked at the remnants of flags that covered the low hills. The year before, wreaths and flags and sticks festooned with ribbons dotted the mounds while earth movers ripped long ditches and chugged diesel exhaust. Today, though, no birds. He supposed there was nothing left for them to eat. No smells to attract them. The earth movers were parked off to the side in a neat row. Dust swirled across the dirt in tiny eddies that danced for a moment, then dissipated into nothing. The ground looked as plain as his back yard. Not a tree anywhere or grass. He thought about Tillie searching for a geranium.

He looked up. The sky was completely empty. No hawks. Could it be that not even a mouse lived in the landfill?

What would he do if she left? He leaned against the car, his hands deep in his pockets, chin on his chest. What if she were gone? So many had departed: the girl at the magazine stand, the counter people at the bagel shop, his coworkers. What was it he used to do? He could barely remember, just like he couldn't picture his wife's face clearly anymore. All of them, slipping away.

He slid his fingers inside his shirt. No bumps there either. Why not, and were they inevitable?

A wind kicked across the plain, scurrying scraps of paper and more dust toward him in a wave. He could taste rain in the air. Weather's changing, he thought, and climbed back into the car before the wind reached him.

* * *

Skylights illuminated the library's main room. Except for the stale smell and the thin coating of neglect on the countertops and the leather chairs arranged in cozy reading circles, it could be open for business. Carson saw no evidence that anyone had been here since his last visit a month ago. He checked his flashlight. Sunlight didn't penetrate to the back stacks where the bird books were, and he wanted to make sure he didn't miss any.

On the bulletin board inside the front doors hung civil defense and the Center for Disease Control posters filled with the familiar advice: avoid crowds, get good sleep, report symptoms immediately. The civil defense poster reminded him that *Patriots Protect Their Immune Systems* and the depressing, *Remember, It Got Them First*.

The cart he found had a wheel that shook and didn't track with the others. It pulled to the left and squeaked loudly as he pushed it between the rows. In the big building, the noise felt out of place. Absurdly, Carson almost said, "Shhh!" A library was *supposed* to be quiet, even if he was the only one in it.

Back at the bird books, he ran his flashlight across the titles, all his favorite tomes: the Audubon books and the National Geographic ones. The two huge volumes of Bailey and Niedrich's *Birds of Colorado* with their beautiful photographs and drawings. He placed them in the cart lovingly. By the time he finished, he'd arranged thirty-five books on the cart, every bird reference they had. He shivered as he straightened the collection. The back of the library had never felt cold before.

At the checkout desk, he agonized over what to do. When he was a child, the librarian filled out a card that was tucked in the book's front cover. Everything was computerized now. How was he going to check the books out? Not that it was likely anyone would want them, but it didn't feel right, just taking them. Finally he wrote a note with all the titles listed. He stuck it to the librarian's computer, thought about it for a second, then wrote a second one to put into the gap he'd left in the shelves. He added his address and a "P.S. If you really need these books, please contact me."

Before going, he wandered into the medical section. Infectious diseases were in the 600 area. There wasn't a title left. He took a deep breath that tickled his throat. It felt odd, so he did it again, provoking a string of deep coughs. It's just the dust in here, he thought, but his lungs felt heavy, and he realized he'd been holding off the cough all day.

Carson stopped at the distribution center on the way home. The parking lot was empty. He wandered through the warehouse, between the high stacks, down the long rows. No manager. No assistant. Last year Carson had hauled a diesel generator into a theater near his house. He'd rigged it to power a projector so he could watch a movie on the big screen, but the empty room with all the empty seats gave him the creeps. He'd fled the theater without even turning off the generator. The warehouse felt like that. As he walked toward the exit, his strides became faster and faster until he was running.

As the sun set into the heavy clouds on the horizon, he accepted the obvious. Whatever Tillie had, he had too. She breathed shallowly between coughing fits, and, although the fever responded to aspirin, it rebounded quickly. The aspirin helped with his own fever, but he felt headachy and tired.

Sitting beside her bed, he put his hand on her arm. "I'm going to go back to the distribution center tomorrow, Tillie. He said he might find some medicine."

Tillie turned toward him, her eyes gummy and bloodshot. "Don't go," she said. Her voice quivered, but she looked directly at him. No drifting. Speaking deliberately, she said, "Everybody I know has gone away."

Carson looked out the window. It would be dark soon.

Tillie's arm burned beneath his fingertips. He could almost feel the heated blood rushing through her. "I've got to do something. You might have pneumonia."

She inhaled several times. Carson imagined the pain; an echo of it pulsed in his own chest.

"Could you stay in the neighborhood?" she asked.

He nodded.

Tillie closed her eyes. "When it started, I watched TV all the time. That's all I did, was watch TV. My friends watched TV. They played it at work. 'A Nation Under Quarantine' the newscasters called it. And then I couldn't watch any more."

Carson blinked his eyes shut against the burning. That's where he didn't want to go, into *those* memories. It's what he didn't think about when he sat in his camp chair counting birds. It's what he didn't picture when he bolted solar cells onto the roof, when he gathered wood for the new wood stove he'd installed in the living room, when he pumped gasoline out of underground tanks at silent gas stations. Sometimes he had a hard time imagining anything was wrong at all. When he drove, the car still responded to his touch. The wind whistled tunelessly past his window. How could the world still be so familiar and normal and yet so badly skewed?

"Well, we keep doing what has to be done, despite it all," he said.

"I was innocent." Her gaze slid away from his, and she smiled. Carson saw her connection to him sever. The shift was nearly audible. "I don't want to see the news tonight. Maybe there will be a nice rerun later. *Friends* or *Cheers* would be good. I'll go to the mall in the morning. The fall fashions should be in." She settled into her pillow as if to go to sleep.

Carson set up a vaporizer, hoping that would make her breathing easier, then quietly shut her door before leaving.

Crowbar in hand, he crossed the dirt expanse that was his front yard, stepped over the dry-leafed hedge between his yard and the neighbors. The deadbolt splintered out of the frame when he leaned on the crowbar, and one kick opened the door. The curtains were closed, darkening the living room. Carson wrinkled his nose at the house's mustiness. Under that smell lingered something rotten, like mildew and bad vegetables gone slimy and black.

He flicked on his flashlight. The living room was neat, magazines fanned across a coffee table for easy selection, glass coasters piled on a small stand by a lounge chair and family photos arranged on the wall. Three bedroom doors opened into the main hallway. In one, a crib stood empty beneath a Mickey Mouse mobile. In the second, his light played across an office desk, a fax machine and a laptop computer, its top popped open and keyboard waiting.

The third door led to the master bedroom. In the bathroom medicine cabinet he found antacids, vitamins and birth control pills, but no antibiotics. When he left the house, he closed the front door as best he could.

An hour later he'd circled the block, breaking into

every house along the way. Two of the houses had already been looted. The door on the first hung from only one hinge. In the second, the furniture was overturned, and a complicated series of cracks emanated from a single bullet hole in the living-room window. In some of the houses the bed sheets covered long lumps. He stayed out of the bedrooms. No antibiotics.

His chest heavy, barely able to lift his feet, he trudged across the last lawn to his house where one window was lit. Whatever the illness was, it felt serious. Not a cold or flu, but down deep malignant, sincere, like nothing he'd ever had before. This was how he felt, and he'd started in good shape, but Tillie hardly ever ate well. She never exercised. Her system would be especially vulnerable. He pictured his house empty. No Tillie gazing over her cards before drawing. No Tillie wandering in the yard, looking for a single geranium to give her hope. "How do you bear it?" she'd asked.

Tillie was sleeping, her fever down again, but her breathing was just as hoarse. In his own lungs, each inhalation fluttered and buzzed. He imagined a thousand tiny pinwheels whirling away inside him.

Carson started the New York City Marathon video, then returned to the chair next to Tillie's bed. He wet a washcloth then pressed it against her forehead. She didn't move. "What a celebration of life," said the announcer. "In the shadow of disaster, athletes have gathered to say we can't be beat in the long run." A map of the course winding through the five boroughs appeared on the screen. Then a camera angle from a helicopter skimming over the streets showing the human river. At one point a dozen birds flew between the camera and the ground. "Doves," thought

Carson, feeling flush. Even his eyes felt warm, and when he finally rested his head on Tillie's arm, he couldn't feel a difference in their temperatures.

He dreamed about bird books spread across a desk in front of him, but he wasn't in his office. Other desks filled the room, and at each one a person sat, studying books. In the desk beside his, a man with tremendous sideburns that drooped to the sides of his neck picked up a dead bird, spread its wing feathers apart, scrutinizing each connection. He placed the bird back on his desk, then added a few lines to a drawing of it on an easel.

"Purple finch," said the man, and Carson knew with dreamlike certainty that it was John Audubon. "A painting is forever, even if the bird is not." Audubon poked at the feathered pile. "It's a pity I have to kill them to preserve them."

"I'm searching for a bird's name," said Carson. Some of the people at the other desks looked up in interest. He described the bird. "I've only seen three of them flying with European starlings."

"Only three?" Audubon looked puzzled. "They flew in flocks that filled the sky for days. Outside of Louisville, the people were all in arms. The banks of the Ohio were crowded with men and boys, incessantly shooting at the birds. Multitudes were destroyed, and for a week or more the population fed on no other flesh, and you saw only three?"

Carson nodded.

"With European starlings?"

Carson was at a loss. How could he explain to Audubon about birds introduced to America after his death? He said instead, "But what is the bird's name?"

"Purple finch, I told you."

"No, I mean the bird I described."

Audubon picked up his pencil and added another line to the drawing. He mumbled an answer.

"Excuse me?" said Carson.

More mumbling. Audubon continued drawing. The bird didn't look like a finch, purple or otherwise. His lines grew wilder as the bird became more and more fantastic. He sketched flames below it with quick, sure strokes, all the while mumbling, louder and louder.

Carson strained to understand him. What was the bird? What was it? And he became aware that the mumbling was hot and moist in his ear. With a jerk, he sat up. Tillie's lips were moving, but her eyes were shut. What time was it? Where was he? For a moment he felt completely dissociated from the world.

Two aspirins in hand, he tried waking her up, but she refused to open her eyes. Her cheeks were red, and in between incoherent bursts of speech, her breathing was labored, as if she were a deep-sea diver, bubbling from the depths. Her forehead felt hot again. A sudden shivering attack took him, and for a minute it was all he could do to grit his teeth against the shaking. When it passed, he swallowed the aspirins he'd brought for her. Maybe there might be antibiotics in one of the houses a block over.

He put on a coat against his chills, grabbed the crowbar and flashlight, then crossed the street. In the night air, his head seemed light and large, but walking was a strain. The crowbar weighed a thousand pounds.

In the second house he found a plastic bottle marked Penicillin in a medicine cabinet. He laughed in relief, then coughed until he sat on the bathroom floor, the flashlight beside him casting long, weird shadows. Only two tablets, 250 mg each. They hardly weighed anything in his hand. What was an adult dosage? Was penicillin the right treatment for pneumonia? What if she didn't have pneumonia, or she did but it was viral instead of bacterial?

Carson staggered back home. After fifteen minutes, he was able to rouse Tillie enough to take the pills and the aspirin. Exhausted, he collapsed on the chair by her bed. He put his head back and stared at the ceiling. Swirls and broad lines marked the plaster. For a moment he thought they were clouds, and in the clouds he saw a bird, the narrow-winged one that he'd seen by the river, the one Audubon said he knew, and suddenly, Carson knew too. He'd always known, and he laughed. No wonder it looked familiar. Of course he couldn't find it in his bird books.

Smiling, holding Tillie's hand, he fell asleep.

A pounding roused him.

Thump, thump, thump. Like a heartbeat. His eyelids came apart reluctantly and gradually he focused on the length of bedspread that started at his cheek and reached to the bed's end. Without moving, without even really knowing where he was, he knew he was sick. Sickness can't be forgotten. Even in his sleep, he must have been aware of the micro war within. It surged through him, alienating his organs, his skin. The machine is breaking down, he thought.

"Someone's at the door," said Tillie. She stirred beside him. "It might be the pool man."

Carson pushed himself from the bed, his back cracking in protest. His legs felt wooden. How long had he been next to her?

She was sitting up, blankets over her legs, an open book face down under her hands. "You've been sleeping, Bob Robert," she said brightly.

He put a hand against her forehead, then against his own. "I'm not Bob Robert." She was cooler, and the wheezing in her chest didn't sound quite as bad. The empty penicillin bottle sat on the night stand beneath her reading light. Could antibiotics work that fast? Even if they did, one dose wouldn't cure whatever they had. She'd relapse. He'd get sicker. He needed to find more.

A pounding from the front of the house again.

He stood shakily, his chest aching on each breath.

"I'll be back," he said.

"Oh, I'm all right. A bit of reading will do me good." She opened the book. It was one from his office. Sometime during the night she must have gotten out of bed.

Carson braced himself against the hallway wall as he walked to the front door, hunched over the illness. His head throbbed and the sunlight through the front window was too bright.

"Carson, are you in there?" a voice yelled. "Birnam Wood has come to Elsinore," it shouted.

Through the pain and fever, Carson squinted. He opened the door. "Isn't it Dunsinane that Birnam comes to?"

The warehouse manager balanced a box on his hip. "I saw the damnedest thing on the way here." He started. "Jeeze, man! You look terrible."

Carson nodded, trying to put the scene together. The manager's truck was parked next to his own in the driveway. The sun lingered high in the sky.

How long had he been sleeping? Carson forced the words out in little gasps. "What are you doing?"

Grabbing Carson's arm, the manager helped him into the living room onto the couch. "I found the antibiotics I told you about," he said. "It wasn't in the pharmacy. The place burned to the ground." The manager ripped open the box lid. Inside were rows of small white boxes. Inside the first box were hundreds of pills. He plucked two out. "But in the delivery area behind the store, there was a UPS truck chock-full of medicine."

Carson blinked, and the manager offered him a glass of water for the pills. When did he get up to fetch the water?

"Your chest is heavy, right, and you're feverish and tired?"

"Yes," croaked Carson.

"I can hear your lungs from here. Pneumonia, for sure, I'll bet. If we're lucky, this'll knock it right out."

Carson swallowed the pills. Sitting, he felt better. It took the pressure off his breathing. Tillie had looked healthier. Maybe the penicillin helped her, and if it helped her, it could help him.

The manager walked around the room, stopping at the photoelectric panels' gauges. "You have a sweet set up here. Did you do the wiring yourself?"

Carson nodded. He croaked, "Why aren't you at the warehouse?" The light in the room flickered. Ponderously, Carson turned his head. Through the picture window, it seemed for a moment as if shadows raced over the houses, but when he checked again, the sun shone steadily.

Without looking at him, the manager said, "Time to move on. That warehouse paralyzed me. I've been waiting, I think. Olivier's Hamlet said last night, 'If it be now, 'tis not to come; if it be not to come it will be now.' "

"What was he talking about?" asked Carson.

"Fear of death. Grief," said the manager. "The readiness is all, he said. Ah, who is this?"

Tillie stood at the entrance to the hallway. She'd changed into jeans and a work shirt. Her face was still feverish and she swayed a little. "Oh, good, the pool man," she said. Without pausing for a reply, she waved a handful of packets at them. "I'm tired of waiting for flowers, Carson. I'm going to plant something."

Confused, he said, "It's nearly winter," but she'd already disappeared. He rubbed his brow, and his hand came away wet with sweat. "Did she call me Carson?"

Shadows hurried across the street again, and this time the manager looked too.

"What is that?" asked Carson.

"I was going to ask you." The manager stepped out the door and glanced up. "I saw them on the way over. They're funny birds."

Carson heaved himself out of the couch. His head swam so violently that he nearly fell, but he caught himself and made it to the door. He held the manager's arm to stay steady.

Overhead, the flock streamed across the sky, barely above the rooftops. Making no sound. Hundreds of them. Narrow wings. Red breasts.

"What are they?" asked the manager.

Carson straightened. Even sickness couldn't knock him down for this. The birds zoomed like feathered jets. Where had they been all these years? Had there just been a few hidden in the remotest forests, avoiding human eyes? Had they teetered on the edge of extinction for a century without actually disappearing despite all evidence to the contrary? Was it conceivable to return to their glory?

Carson said, "They're passenger pigeons."

The manager said, "What's a passenger pigeon?"

It's an addition to my life list, thought Carson. Audubon said they'd darkened the skies for days. Carson remembered the New York City Marathon. The people kept running and running and running. They filled the Verrazano-Narrows Bridge.

"I guess sometimes things can come back," said Carson.

The impossible birds wheeled to the east.

PATIENT ZERO
TANANARIVE DUE

September 19

The picture came! Veronica tapped on my glass and woke me up, and she held it up for me to see. It's autographed and everything! For you, Veronica mouthed at me, and she smiled a really big smile. The autograph says, TO JAY—I'LL THROW A TOUCHDOWN FOR YOU. I couldn't believe it. Everybody is laughing at me because of the way I yelled and ran in circles around my room until I fell on the floor and scraped my elbow. The janitor, Lou, turned on the intercom box outside my door and said, "Kid, you gone crazier than usual? What you care about that picture for?"

Don't they know Dan Marino is the greatest quarterback of all time? I taped the picture to the wall over my bed. On the rest of my wall I have maps of the United States, and the world, and the solar system. I can find Corsica on the map, and the Palau Islands, which most people have never heard of, and I know what order all the planets are in. But there's nothing else on my wall like Dan Marino. That's the best. The other best thing I have is the cassette tape from that time the President called me on the telephone when I was six. He said, "Hi, is Jay there? This is the President of the United States." He sounded just like on TV. My heart flipped, because it's so weird to hear the President say your name. I couldn't think of anything to say back. He asked me how I was feeling, and I said I was fine. That made him laugh, like he thought I was making a joke. Then his voice got real serious, and he said everyone was praying and thinking about me, and he hung up. When I listen to that tape now, I wish I had thought of something else to say. I used to think he might call me another time, but it only happened once, in the beginning. So I guess I'll never have a chance to talk to the President again.

After Veronica gave me my picture of Marino, I asked her if she could get somebody to fix my TV so I can see the football games. All my TV can play is videos. Veronica said there aren't any football games, and I started to get mad because I hate it when they lie. It's September, I said, and there's always football games in September. But Veronica told me the NFL people had a meeting and decided not to have football anymore, and maybe it would start again, but she wasn't sure, because nobody except me was thinking about football. At first, after she said that, it kind of ruined the autograph, because it seemed like Dan Marino must be lying, too. But Veronica said he was most likely talking about throwing a touchdown for me in the future, and I felt better then.

This notebook is from Ms. Manigat, my tutor, who is Haitian. She said I should start writing down my thoughts and everything that happens to me. I said I don't have any thoughts, but she said that was ridiculous. That is her favorite word, ridiculous.

Oh, I should say I'm ten today. If I were in a regular school, I would be in fifth grade like my brother was. I asked Ms. Manigat what grade I'm in, and she said I don't have a grade. I read like I'm in seventh grade and I do math like I'm in fourth grade, she says. She says I don't exactly fit anywhere, but I'm very smart. Ms. Manigat comes every day, except on weekends. She is my best friend, but I have to call her Ms. Manigat instead of using her first name, which is Emmeline, because she is so proper. She is very neat and wears skirts and dresses, and everything about her is very clean except her shoes, which are dirty. Her shoes are supposed to be white, but whenever I see her standing outside of the glass, when she hasn't put on her plastic suit yet, her shoes look brown and muddy.

Those are my thoughts.

September 20

I had a question today. Veronica never comes on Fridays, and the other nurse, Rene, isn't as nice as she is, so I waited for Ms. Manigat. She comes at one. I said, "You know how they give sick children their last wish when they're dying? Well, when Dr. Ben told me to think of the one thing I wanted for my birthday, I said I wanted an autograph from Dan Marino, so does that mean I'm dying and they're giving me my wish?" I said this really fast.

I thought Ms. Manigat would say I was being ridiculous. But she smiled. She put her hand on top of my head, and her hand felt stiff and heavy inside her big glove. "Listen, little old man," she said, which is what she calls me because she says I do so much worrying, "you're a lot of things, but you aren't dying. When everyone can be as healthy as you, it'll be a happy day."

The people here always seem to be waiting, and I don't know what for. I thought maybe they were waiting for me to die. But I believe Ms. Manigat. If she doesn't want to tell me something, she just says, "Leave it alone, Jay," which is her way of letting me know she would rather not say anything at all than ever tell a lie.

October 5

The lights in my room started going on and off again today, and it got so hot I had to leave my shirt off until I went to bed. Ms. Manigat couldn't do her lessons the way she wanted because of the lights not working right. She said it was the emergency generator. I asked her what the emergency was, and she said something that sounded funny: "Same old same old." That was all she said. I asked her if the emergency generator was the reason Dr. Ben took the television out of my room, and she said yes. She said everyone is conserving energy, and I have to do my part, too. But I miss my videos. There is nothing at all to do when I can't watch my videos. I hate it when I'm bored. Sometimes I'll even watch videos I've seen a hundred times, *really* a hundred times. I've seen *Big* with Tom Hanks more times than any other video. I love the part in the toy store with the really big piano keys on the floor. My mom taught me how to play "Three Blind Mice" on our piano at home, and it reminds me of that. I've never seen a toy store like the one in *Big*. I thought it was just a made-up place, but Ms. Manigat said it was a real toy store in New York.

I miss my videos. When I'm watching them, it's like I'm inside the movie, too. I hope Dr. Ben will bring my TV back soon.

October 22

I made Veronica cry yesterday. I didn't mean to. Dr. Ben said he knows it was an accident, but I feel very sorry, so I've been crying too. What happened is, I was talking to her, and she was taking some blood out of my arm with a needle like always. I was telling her about how me and my dad used to watch Marino play on television, and then all of a sudden she was crying really hard.

She dropped the needle on the floor and she was holding her wrist like she broke it. She started swearing. She said Goddammit, goddammit, goddammit, over and over, like that. I asked her what happened, and she pushed me away like she wanted to knock me over. Then she went to the door and punched the number code really fast and she pulled on the doorknob, but the door wouldn't open, and I heard something in her arm snap from yanking so hard. She had to do the code again. She was still crying. I've never seen her cry.

I didn't know what happened. I mashed my finger on the buzzer hard, but everybody ignored me. It reminded me of when I first came here, when I was always pushing the buzzer and crying, and nobody would ever come for a long time, and they were always in a bad mood when they came.

Anyway, I waited for Ms. Manigat, and when I told her

about Veronica, she said she didn't know anything because she comes from the outside, but she promised to find out. Then she made me recite the Preamble to the Constitution, which I know by heart. Pretty soon, for a little while, I forgot about Veronica.

After my lessons, Ms. Manigat left and called me on my phone an hour later, like she promised. She always keeps her promises. My telephone is hooked up so people on the inside can call me, but I can't call anybody, inside or outside. It hardly ever rings now. But I almost didn't want to pick it up. I was afraid of what Ms. Manigat would say.

"Veronica poked herself," Ms. Manigat told me. "The needle stuck through her hot suit. She told Dr. Ben there was sudden movement."

I wondered who made the sudden movement, Veronica or me?

"Is she okay?" I asked. I thought maybe Ms. Manigat was mad at me, because she has told me many times that I should be careful. Maybe I wasn't being careful when Veronica was here.

"We'll see, Jay," Ms. Manigat said. From her voice, it sounded like the answer was no.

"Will she get sick?" I asked.

"Probably, yes, they think so," Ms. Manigat said.

I didn't want her to answer any more questions. I like it when people tell me the truth, but it always makes me feel bad, too. I tried to say I was sorry, but I couldn't even open my mouth.

"It's not your fault, Jay," Ms. Manigat said.

I couldn't help it. I sobbed like I used to when I was still a little kid. "Veronica knew something like this could happen," she said.

But that didn't make anything better, because I remembered how Veronica's face looked so scared inside her mask, and how she pushed me away. Veronica has been here since almost the beginning, before Ms. Manigat came, and she used to smile at me even when nobody else did. When she showed me my picture from Dan Marino, she looked almost as happy as me. I had never seen her whole face smiling like that. She looked so pretty and glad.

I was crying so much I couldn't even write down my thoughts like Ms. Manigat said to. Not until today.

November 4

A long time ago, when I first came here and the TV in my room played programs from outside, I saw the first grade picture I had taken at school on TV. I always hated that picture because Mom put some greasy stuff in my hair that made me look like a total geek. And then I turned on the TV and saw that picture on the news! The man on TV said the names of everyone in our family, and even spelled them out on the screen. Then, he called me Patient Zero. He said I was the first person who got sick.

But that wasn't really what happened. My dad was sick before me. I've told them that already. He got it away on his job in Alaska. My dad traveled a lot because he drilled for oil, but he came home early that time. We weren't expecting him until Christmas, but he came when it was only September, close to my birthday. He said he'd been sent home because some people on his oil crew got sick. One of them had even died. But the doctor in Alaska had looked at my dad and said he was fine, and then his boss sent him home. Dad was really mad about that. He hated to lose money. Time away from a job was always losing money, he said. He was in a bad mood when he wasn't working.

And the worse thing was, my dad wasn't fine. After two days, his eyes got red and he started sniffling. Then I did, too. And then my mom and brother.

When the man on TV showed my picture and called me Patient Zero and said I was the first one to get sick, that was when I first learned how people tell lies, because that wasn't true. Somebody on my dad's oil rig caught it first, and then he gave it to my dad. And my dad gave it to me, my mom and my brother. But one thing he said was right. I was the only one who got well.

My Aunt Lori came here to live at the lab with me at first, but she wasn't here long, because her eyes had already turned red by then. She came to help take care of me and my brother before my mom died, but probably she shouldn't have done that. She lived all the way in California, and I bet she wouldn't have gotten sick if she hadn't come to Miami to be with us. But even my mom's doctor didn't know what was wrong then, so nobody could warn her about what would happen if she got close to us. Sometimes I dream I'm calling Aunt Lori on my phone, telling her please, please not to come. Aunt Lori and my mom were twins. They looked exactly alike.

After Aunt Lori died, I was the only one left in my whole family.

I got very upset when I saw that news report. I didn't like hearing someone talk about my family like that, people who didn't even know us. And I felt like maybe the man on TV was right, and maybe it was all my fault. I screamed and cried the whole day. After that, Dr. Ben made them fix my TV so I couldn't see the news anymore or any programs from outside, just cartoons and kid movies on video. The only good thing was, that was when the President called me. I think he was sorry when he heard what happened to my family.

When I ask Dr. Ben if they're still talking about me on the news, he just shrugs his shoulders. Sometimes Dr. Ben won't say yes or no if you ask him a question. It doesn't matter, though. I think the TV people probably stopped showing my picture a long time ago. I was just a little kid when my family got sick. I've been here four whole years!

Oh, I almost forgot. Veronica isn't back yet.

November 7

I have been staring at my Dan Marino picture all day, and I think the handwriting on the autograph looks like Dr. Ben's. But I'm afraid to ask anyone about that. Oh, yeah— and yesterday the power was off in my room for a whole day! Same old same old. That's what Ms. M. would say.

November 12

Ms. Manigat is teaching me a little bit about medicine. I told her I want to be a doctor when I grow up, and she said she thinks that's a wonderful idea because she believes people will always need doctors. She says I will be in a good position to help people, and I asked her if that's because I have been here so long, and she said yes.

The first thing she taught me is about diseases. She says

in the old days, a long time ago, diseases like typhoid used to kill a lot of people because of unsanitary conditions and dirty drinking water, but people got smarter and doctors found drugs to cure it, so diseases didn't kill people as much anymore. Doctors are always trying to stay a step ahead of disease, Ms. Manigat says.

But sometimes they can't. Sometimes a new disease comes. Or, maybe it's not a new disease, but an old disease that has been hidden for a long time until something brings it out in the open. She said that's how nature balances the planet, because as soon as doctors find cures for one thing, there is always something new. Dr. Ben says my disease is new. There is a long name for it I can't remember how to spell, but most of the time people here call it Virus-J.

In a way, see, it's named after me. That's what Dr. Ben said. But I don't like that.

Ms. Manigat said after my dad came home, the virus got in my body and attacked me just like everyone else, so I got really, really sick for a lot of days. Then, I thought I was completely better. I stopped feeling bad at all. But the virus was already in my brother and my mom and dad, and even our doctor from before, Dr. Wolfe, and Ms. Manigat says it was very *aggressive,* which means doctors didn't know how to kill it.

Everybody wears yellow plastic suits and airtight masks when they're in my room because the virus is still in the air, and it's in my blood, and it's on my plates and cups whenever I finish eating. They call the suits hot suits because the virus is *hot* in my room. Not hot like fire, but dangerous.

Ms. Manigat says Virus-J is extra special in my body because even though I'm not sick anymore, except for when I feel like I have a temperature and I have to lie down sometimes, the virus won't go away. I can make other people sick even when I feel fine, so she said that makes me a carrier. Ms. Manigat said Dr. Ben doesn't know anybody else who's gotten well except for me.

Oh, except maybe there are some little girls in China. Veronica told me once there were some little girls in China the same age as me who didn't get sick either. But when I asked Dr. Ben, he said he didn't know if it was true. And Ms. Manigat told me it might have been true once, but those girls might not be alive anymore. I asked her if they died of Virus-J, and she said no, no, no. Three times. She told me to forget all about any little girls in China. Almost like she was mad.

I'm the only one like me she knows about for sure, she says. The only one left.

That's why I'm here, she says. But I already knew that part. When I was little, Dr. Ben told me about antibodies and stuff in my blood, and he said the reason him and Rene and Veronica and all the other doctors take so much blood from me all the time, until they make purple bruises on my arms and I feel dizzy, is so they can try to help other people get well, too. I have had almost ten surgeries since I have been here. I think they have even taken out parts of me, but I'm not really sure. I look the same on the outside, but I feel different on the inside. I had surgery on my belly a year ago, and sometimes when I'm climbing the play-rope hanging from the ceiling in my room, I feel like it hasn't healed right, like I'm still cut open. Ms. Manigat says that's only in my mind. But it really hurts! I don't hate anything like I hate operations. I wonder if that's what happened to the other little girls, if they kept getting cut up and cut up until they died. Anyway, it's been a year since I had any operations. I keep telling Dr. Ben they can have as much blood as they want, but I don't want any more operations, please.

Dr. Ben said there's nobody in the world better than me to make people well, if only they can figure out how. Ms. Manigat says the same thing. That makes me feel a little better about Virus-J.

I was happy Ms. Manigat told me all about disease, because I don't want her to treat me like a baby the way everybody else does. That's what I always tell her. I like to know things.

I didn't even cry when she told me Veronica died. Maybe I got all my crying over with in the beginning, because I figured out a long time ago nobody gets better once they get sick. Nobody except for me.

November 14

Today, I asked Ms. Manigat how many people have Virus-J.

"Oh, Jay, I don't know," she said. I don't think she was in the mood to talk about disease.

"Just guess," I said.

Ms. Manigat thought for a long time. Then she opened her notebook and began drawing lines and boxes for me to see. Her picture looked like the tiny brown lines all over an oak-tree leaf. We had a tree called a live oak in our backyard, and my dad said it was more than a hundred years old. He said trees sometimes live longer than people do. And he was right, because I'm sure that tree is still standing in our yard even though my whole family is gone.

"This is how it goes, Jay," Ms. Manigat said, showing me with her pencil-tip how one line branched down to the next.

"People are giving it to each other. They don't usually know they're sick for two weeks, and by then they've passed it to a lot of other people. By now, it's already been here four years, so the same thing that happened to your family is happening to a lot of families."

"How many families?" I asked again. I tried to think of the biggest number I could. "A million?"

Ms. Manigat shrugged just like Dr. Ben would. Maybe that meant yes.

I couldn't imagine a million families, so I asked Ms. Manigat if it happened to her family, too, if maybe she had a husband and kids and they got sick. But she said no, she was never married. I guess that's true, because Ms. Manigat doesn't look that old. She won't tell me her age, but she's in her twenties, I think. Ms. Manigat smiled at me, even though her eyes weren't happy.

"My parents were in Miami, and they got it right away," Ms. Manigat said. "Then my sister and nieces came to visit them from Haiti, and they got it, too. I was away working when it happened, and that's why I'm still here."

Ms. Manigat never told me that before.

My family lived in Miami Beach. My dad said our house was too small—I had to share a room with my brother—but my mother liked where we lived because our building was six blocks from the ocean. My mother said the ocean can heal anything. But that can't be true, can it?

My mother wouldn't like it where I am, because there is no ocean and no windows neither. I wondered if Ms. Manigat's parents knew someone who worked on an oil rig, too, but probably not. Probably they got it from my dad and me.

"Ms. Manigat," I said, "maybe you should move inside

like Dr. Ben and everybody else."

"Oh, Jay," Ms. Manigat said, like she was trying to sound cheerful. "Little old man, if I were that scared of anything, why would I be in here teaching you?"

She said she *asked* to be my teacher, which I didn't know. I said I thought her boss was making her do it, and she said she didn't have a boss. No one sent her. She wanted to come.

"Just to meet me?" I asked her.

"Yes, because I saw your face on television, and you looked to me like a one-of-a-kind," she said. She said she was a nurse before, and she used to work with Dr. Ben in his office in Atlanta. She said they worked at the CDC, which is a place that studies diseases. And he knew her, so that was why he let her come teach me.

"A boy like you needs his education. He needs to know how to face life outside," she said.

Ms. Manigat is funny like that. Sometimes she'll quit the regular lesson about presidents and the Ten Commandments and teach me something like how to sew and how to tell plants you eat from plants you don't, and stuff. Like, I remember when she brought a basket with real fruits and vegetables in it, fresh. She said she has a garden where she lives on the outside, close to here. She said one of the reasons she won't move inside is because she loves her garden so much, and she doesn't want to leave it.

The stuff she brought was not very interesting to look at. She showed me some cassava, which looked like a long, twisty tree branch to me, and she said it's good to eat, except it has poison in it that has to be boiled out of the root first and the leaves are poisonous too. She also brought something called akee, which she said she used to eat from trees in Haiti. It has another name in Haiti that's too hard for me to spell. It tasted fine to me, but she said akee can never be eaten before it's opened, or before it's ripe, because it makes your brain swell up and you can die. She also brought different kinds of mushrooms to show me which ones are good or bad, but they all looked alike to me. She promised to bring me other fruits and vegetables to see so I will know what's good for me and what isn't. There's a lot to learn about life outside, she said.

Well, I don't want Ms. Manigat to feel like I am a waste of her time, but I know for a fact I don't have to face life outside. Dr. Ben told me I might be a teenager before I can leave, or even older. He said I might even be a grown man.

But that's okay, I guess. I try not to think about what it would be like to leave. My room, which they moved me to when I had been here six months, is really, really big. They built it especially for me. It's four times as big as the hotel room my mom and dad got for us when we went to Universal Studios in Orlando when I was five. I remember that room because my brother, Kevin, kept asking my dad, "Doesn't this cost too much?" Every time my dad bought us a T-shirt or anything, Kevin brought up how much it cost. I told Kevin to stop it because I was afraid Dad would get mad and stop buying us stuff. Then, when we were in line for the King Kong ride, all by ourselves, Kevin told me, "Dad got fired from his job, stupid. Do you want to go on welfare?" I waited for Dad and Mom to tell me he got fired, but they didn't. After Kevin said that, I didn't ask them to buy me anything else, and I was scared to stay in that huge, pretty hotel room because I thought we wouldn't have enough money to pay. But we did. And then Dad got a job on the oil rig, and we thought everything would be better.

My room here is as big as half the whole floor I bet. When I run from one side of my room to the other, from the glass in front to the wall in back, I'm out of breath. I like to do that. Sometimes I run until my ribs start squeezing and my stomach hurts like it's cut open and I have to sit down and rest. There's a basketball net in here, too, and the ball doesn't ever touch the ceiling except if I throw it too high on purpose. I also have comic books, and I draw pictures of me and my family and Ms. Manigat and Dr. Ben. Because I can't watch my videos, now I spend a lot of time writing in this notebook. A whole hour went by already. When I am writing down my thoughts, I forget about everything else.

I have decided for sure to be a doctor someday. I'm going to help make people better.

November 29

Thanksgiving was great! Ms. Manigat cooked real bread and brought me food she'd heated up. I could tell everything except the bread and cassava was from a can, like always, but it tasted much better than my regular food. I haven't had bread in a long time. Because of her mask, Ms. Manigat ate her dinner before she came, but she sat and watched me eat. Rene came in, too, and she surprised me when she gave me a hug. She never does that. Dr. Ben came in for a little while at the end, and he hugged me too, but he said he couldn't stay because he was busy. Dr. Ben doesn't come visit me much anymore. I could see he was growing a beard, and it was almost all white! I've seen Dr. Ben's hair when he's outside of the glass, when he isn't wearing his hot suit, and his hair is brown, not white. I asked him how come his beard was white, and he said that's what happens when your mind is overly tired.

I liked having everybody come to my room. Before, in the beginning, almost nobody came in, not even Ms. Manigat. She used to sit in a chair outside the glass and use the intercom for my lessons. It's better when they come in.

I remember how Thanksgiving used to be, with my family around the table in the dining room, and I told Ms. Manigat about that. Yes, she said, even though she didn't celebrate Thanksgiving in Haiti like Americans do, she remembers sitting at the table with her parents and her sister for Christmas dinner. She said she came to see me today, and Rene and Dr. Ben came too, because we are each other's family now, so we are not alone. I hadn't thought of it like that before.

December 1

No one will tell me, not even Ms. M., but I think maybe Dr. Ben is sick. I have not seen him in five whole days. It is quiet here. I wish it was Thanksgiving again.

January 23

I didn't know this before, but you have to be in the right mood to write your thoughts down. A lot happened in the days I missed.

The doctor with the French name is gone now, and I'm glad. He wasn't like Dr. Ben at all. I could hardly believe he was a real doctor, because he always had on the dirtiest clothes when I saw him take off his hot suit outside of the glass. And he was never nice to me—he wouldn't answer at all when I asked him questions, and he wouldn't look in my eyes except for a second. One time he slapped me on my ear, almost for nothing, and his glove hurt so much my ear turned red and was sore for a whole day. He didn't say he was sorry, but I didn't cry. I think he wanted me to.

Oh yeah, and he hooked me up to IV bags and took so much blood from me I couldn't even stand up. I was scared he would operate on me. Ms. Manigat didn't come in for almost a week, and when she finally came, I told her about the doctor taking too much blood. She got really mad. Then I found out the reason she didn't come all those days—he wouldn't let her! She said he tried to bar her from coming. *Bar* is the word she used, which sounds like a prison.

The new doctor and Ms. Manigat do not get along, even though they both speak French. I saw them outside of the glass, yelling back and forth and moving their hands, but I couldn't hear what they were saying. I was afraid he would send Ms. Manigat away for good. But yesterday she told me he's leaving! I told her I was happy, because I was afraid he would take Dr. Ben's place.

No, she told me, there isn't anyone taking Dr. Ben's place. She said the French doctor came here to study me in person because he was one of the doctors Dr. Ben had been sending my blood to ever since I first came. But he was already very sick when he got here, and he started feeling worse, so he had to go. Seeing me was his last wish, Ms. Manigat said, which didn't seem like it could be true because he didn't act like he wanted to be with me.

I asked her if he went back to France to his family, and

Ms. Manigat said no, he probably didn't have a family, and even if he did, it's too hard to go to France. The ocean is in the way, she said.

Ms. Manigat seemed tired from all that talking. She said she'd decided to move inside, like Rene, to make sure they were taking care of me properly. She said she misses her garden. The whole place has been falling apart, she said. She said I do a good job of keeping my room clean—and I do, because I have my own mop and bucket and Lysol in my closet—but she told me the hallways are filthy. Which is true, because sometimes I can see water dripping down the wall outside of my glass, a lot of it, and it makes puddles all over the floor. You can tell the water is dirty because you can see different colors floating on top, the way my family's driveway used to look after my dad sprayed it with a hose. He said the oil from the car made the water look that way, but I don't know why it looks that way here. Ms. Manigat said the water smells bad, too.

"It's ridiculous. If they're going to keep you here, they'd damn well better take care of you," Ms. Manigat said. She must have been really mad, because she never swears.

I told her about the time when Lou came and pressed on my intercom really late at night, when I was asleep and nobody else was around. He was talking really loud like people do in videos when they're drunk. Lou was glaring at me through the glass, banging on it. I had never seen him look so mean. I thought he would try to come into my room but then I remembered he couldn't because he didn't have a hot suit. But I'll never forget how he said, *They should put you to sleep like a dog at the pound.*

I try not to think about that night, because it gave me nightmares. It happened when I was pretty little, like eight.

Sometimes I thought maybe I just dreamed it, because the next time Lou came he acted just like normal. He even smiled at me a little bit. Before he stopped coming here, Lou was nice to me every day after that.

Ms. Manigat did not sound surprised when I told her what Lou said about putting me to sleep. "Yes, Jay," she told me, "for a long time, there have been people outside who didn't think we should be taking care of you."

I never knew that before!

I remember a long time ago, when I was really little and I had pneumonia, my mom was scared to leave me alone at the hospital. "They won't know how to take care of Jay there," she said to my dad, even though she didn't know I heard her. I had to stay by myself all night, and because of what my mom said, I couldn't go to sleep. I was afraid everyone at the hospital would forget I was there. Or maybe something bad would happen to me.

It seems like the lights go off every other day now. And I know people must really miss Lou, because the dirty gray water is all over the floor outside my glass and there's no one to clean it up.

February 14

6-4-6-7-2-9-4-3 6-4-6-7-2-9-4-3 6-4-6-7-2-9-4-3

I remember the numbers already! I have been saying them over and over in my head so I won't forget, but I wanted to write them down in the exact right order to be extra sure. I want to know them without even looking.

Oh, I should start at the beginning. Yesterday, no one brought me any dinner, not even Ms. Manigat. She came with a huge bowl of oatmeal this morning, saying she was very sorry. She said she had to look a long time to find that food, and it wore her out. The oatmeal wasn't even hot, but I didn't say anything. I just ate. She watched me eating.

She didn't stay with me long, because she doesn't teach me lessons anymore. After the French doctor left, we talked about the Emancipation Proclamation and Martin Luther King, but she didn't bring that up today. She just kept sighing, and she said she had been in bed all day yesterday because she was so tired, and she was sorry she forgot to feed me. She said I couldn't count on Rene to bring me food because she didn't know where Rene was. It was hard for me to hear her talk through her hot suit today. Her mask was crooked, so the microphone wasn't in front of her mouth where it should be.

She saw my notebook and asked if she could look at it. I said sure. She looked at the pages from the beginning. She said she liked the part where I said she was my best friend. Her face-mask was fogging up, so I couldn't see her eyes and I couldn't tell if she was smiling. I am very sure she did not put her suit on right today.

When she put my notebook down, she told me to pay close attention to her and repeat the numbers she told me, which were 6-4-6-7-2-9-4-3.

I asked her what they were. She said it was the security code for my door. She said she wanted to give the code to me because my buzzer wasn't working, and I might need to leave my room if she overslept and nobody came to bring me food. She told me I could use the same code on the elevator, and the kitchen was on the third floor. There wouldn't be anybody there, she said, but I could look on the shelves, the top ones up high, to see if there was any food. If not, she said I should take the stairs down to the first floor and find the red EXIT sign to go outside. She said the elevator doesn't go to the first floor anymore.

I felt scared then, but she put her hand on top of my head again just like usual. She said she was sure there was plenty of food outside.

"But am I allowed?" I asked her. "What if people get sick?"

"You worry so much, little man," she said. "Only you matter now, my little one-of-a-kind."

But see I'm sure Ms. Manigat doesn't really want me to go outside. I've been thinking about that over and over. Ms. Manigat must be very tired to tell me to do something like that. Maybe she has a fever and that's why she told me how to get out of my room. My brother said silly things when he had a fever, and my father too. My father kept calling me *Oscar*, and I didn't know who Oscar was. My dad told us he had a brother who died when he was little, and maybe his name was Oscar. My mother didn't say anything at all when she got sick. She just died very fast. I wish I could find Ms. Manigat and give her something to drink. You get very thirsty when you have a fever, which I know for a fact. But I can't go to her because I don't know where she is. And besides, I don't know where Dr. Ben keeps the hot suits. What if I went to her and she wasn't wearing hers?

Maybe the oatmeal was the only thing left in the kitchen, and now I ate it all. I hope not! But I'm thinking maybe it is because I know Ms. Manigat would have brought me more food if she could have found it. She's always asking me if I have enough to eat. I'm already hungry again.

6-4-6-7-2-9-4-3
6-4-6-7-2-9-4-3

* * *

February 15

I am writing in the dark. The lights are off. I tried to open
my lock but the numbers don't work because of the lights
being off. I don't know where Ms. Manigat is. I'm trying
not to cry.

What if the lights never come back on?

February 16

There's so much I want to say but I have a headache from
being hungry. When the lights came back on I went out
into the hall like Ms. M told me and I used the numbers
to get the elevator to work and then I went to the kitchen
like she said. I wanted to go real fast and find some peanut
butter or some Oreos or even a can of beans I could open
with the can opener Ms. M left me at Thanksgiving.

There's no food in the kitchen! There's empty cans and
wrappers on the floor and even roaches but I looked on
every single shelf and in every cabinet and I couldn't find
anything to eat.

The sun was shining really REALLY bright from the
window. I almost forgot how the sun looks. When I went
to the window I saw a big, empty parking lot outside. At
first I thought there were diamonds all over the ground
because of the sparkles but it was just a lot of broken glass.
I could only see one car and I thought it was Ms. M's. But
Ms. M would never leave her car looking like that. For one
thing it had two flat tires!

Anyway I don't think there's anybody here today. So I thought of a plan. I have to go now.

Ms. M, this is for you—or whoever comes looking for me. I know somebody will find this notebook if I leave it on my bed. I'm very sorry I had to leave in such a hurry.

I didn't want to go outside but isn't it okay if it's an emergency? I am really really hungry. I'll just find some food and bring it with me and I'll come right back. I'm leaving my door open so I won't get locked out. Ms. M, maybe I'll find your garden with cassavas and akee like you showed me and I'll know the good parts from the bad parts. If someone sees me and I get in trouble I'll just say I didn't have anything to eat.

Whoever is reading this don't worry. I'll tell everybody I see please please not to get too close to me. I know Dr. Ben was very worried I might make somebody sick.

SOULLESS IN HIS SIGHT

MILO JAMES FOWLER

Fatha he always knows best, he knowed it when I was born and he knows it now as he takes his hatchet to this man's skull to break it open like an egg and let the brains run out all gooey and grey like porridge and smelly like the insides of a cat. This man he came tearing down our street on a motorbike making all manner of ruckus in the early morning light, juking his way round all them broken-down cars in the road and the rotting dead folks inside them, but we keep all the windows up so's we don't have to smell them. This man he sure took the wrong turn if he thought he'd be passing by our way alive. First it was the arrow Fatha planted in his back from fifty yards; Fatha with his crossbow is a sure-dead shot. The gas-chugging bike it flipped off one way and smashed into a rusty car and this man he dropped the other way clawing at his back like he had a chance to rip out the thing.

"You got him good!" I whooped and I danced, kicking up dust and ash that makes this whole world smell like an old fireplace.

"Ain't dead yet." Fatha he whipped out the hatchet he keeps clean and sharp, dangling round his neck on a thick leather strap. "Come, Boy."

That's what he calls me—Boy—because that's what I am, his child, his only begotten son in all the world. So he loves me the most and does what he must to get me into Heaven.

This dying man he cursed a blue streak and kicked, pawing at the ground. Fatha's hatchet came down once and broke through the helmet, shattering black glass that hid this man's face, and the struggling stopped and this man he lay still and quiet then.

"Let's get it off." Fatha tugs his hatchet free and reaches under this man's chin—and I help because that is what I do—and we pry the helmet off his sunsore head.

The blade of Fatha's hatchet messed up his face good, cutting clear into his skull with that one stroke. Fatha he's a big man with big muscles that kill like nobody's business. This man wasn't near so big while alive and not half so big now he's dead. Funny how death does that to a body. He has long greasy hair kind of like we've got and a dirty beard kind of like Fatha's got only Fatha keeps his clean. When I can grow one—and Fatha he says I'm awful close—I'm gonna keep it clean too, and there ain't no way I'll be letting my skin get all nasty like this man. I do right and keep my skin covered like Fatha tells me to all the time, and it keeps them sores away.

With the helmet off, Fatha's hatchet comes down again, once, twice, the hot blood spraying up like rain from the wrong direction. He's got this man's skull wide open now, and he wipes his blade off on this man's thick flannel shirt and takes a looksee inside, reaching in, prying the gap with his fingers through all that goo.

Fatha hums and mutters to himself like he does when he's thinking and when he's looking for something important to find.

"Does he got one?" I'm on my haunches copping a squat and petting the flannel, wishing it wasn't so bloody or it might have been nice and warm for the nighttimes.

"Don't you rush me, Boy." Fatha's voice is always so quiet when it comes to this part, and he's got to work fast but he's also got to work slow—that's how he described it once when I asked him about it.

He told me there's very little time in the space between, once a body's heart stops beating, so it's got to be done quick—but not so quick you scare off the thing, because then you'll never get it back. But then again, it's only if there's one in the first place, because like me, Fatha says there be plenty of folks in this world today with no souls.

This man he don't look like he'd have much of one, to tell the truth, but as Fatha says, no beggars can ever be choosers. And so I'll take what I can get and be glad of it. If I ever want to see Mama again, then it's got to be so.

Fatha curses loud and foul and shoves the man's floppy head off to the side to spill its mess onto the cracked asphalt.

"No good?" I rise with Fatha and I look up at him while he looks off into the faraway with his eyes there and not here, with his thick knuckles knotted on the hatchet.

I asked him one time why it was I needed a soul anyways. I seem to be getting along fine without one.

Fatha he said, "No soul, and you don't get into Heaven, Boy."

And I asked him, "How come I was born with no soul?"

And he told me, "The Good Gawd seen fit to leave the planting of it to me, child, and soon as I find you one, I'm gonna plant it right in there." He tapped me on the forehead just so, like his sausage finger could do it too, put an honest-to-gawd soul right into my brain where it belonged.

"What do it look like?" I asked him.

"Why, that's one there." He pointed me at the punctured skull of a different man at a different time, one who'd come through this street—Main Street, Fatha calls it—in a gas-guzzling racer. He pointed his thick finger and I strained to see, but all that was there was blood and brains. "It ain't right for you. What you need is an honest soul."

That is what we pray for every night.

But now at this time Fatha he cries like he does whenever he's taken a life, and I know why, he told me before. He's afraid, you see, that he'll have to kill every last man on this ugly old earth before he finds me what I need. The tears now they skid down past the rims of his goggles and slide into his big grey beard, covered up for now with his red scarf, the one he always wears when we're outside. I've got one too, but it's black.

"It ain't your fault," he told me once. "You didn't know what you was doing. It ain't no sin when it's from ignorance."

I didn't know nothing about that. I just know Mama ain't here no more, and if I ever want to see her again, Fatha's got to do what he knows best.

"Come, Boy." He turns away from this dead man and heads across the street to the brick building he says was a bank at a different time, a place that used to hold paper for folks who didn't want to share it. "Time to eat now."

I follow, and I hope it ain't cat. I'm getting awful sick of cat.

⋇ ⋇ ⋇

Next day I'm sitting outside all covered up, smearing the ash on the sidewalk with my rear end, taking chunks of broken concrete and breaking them into smaller pieces to throw at the cars and listen to the hollow sounds they make. Ever since the nukes and the EMPs, long before I was born, these rusty old things been sitting here, blocking the road this way. Most all electrics are no good no more, Fatha says.

"What was they thinking?" He mutters a lot when he thinks back on the old days, when the world was green and the sky was blue. I can't even imagine.

It's middleday now and the sun's burning bright and Fatha he's taking his nap inside the bank where it's cool and dark. Ain't nobody ever tries to come through our town this time of day. Only a true fool would. You wait until dawntime or dusktime, that's how you do. Never when the sun's high, because it's too hot and you can't go around sweating out all your water when there ain't much good water to be had.

That's why I sit here in the shade while I sling the concrete and hear it go thunk like a bomb—like I imagine a good bomb to sound.

But there's something buzzing this way now, and I know I should go roust Fatha because that is what I do whenever I hear somebody coming, yet I don't because I know there can't be anybody out this time of day. Would be suicide, Fatha says, and suicide won't get you into Heaven, so who would go and do a stupid thing like that?

I hunker down and keep to the shade while sliding myself under the rusty old car with the dents in the side from my concrete. The ash is real thick down here, but my scarf keeps me from breathing it in, and besides I'm holding my breath anyway and waiting while the buzz gets louder in my ears. It don't sound like that dead man's motorbike from yesterday. That one chugged and Fatha called it a Harly. This one, I don't know, but I can hear it come straight this way, and I can feel my heart thump with it.

The buzz grinds into town from the south and the sound changes like it's speeding up and slowing down, and I know it's weaving around the dead cars and the bodies inside them, and I want to see who it is this time, who would be so foolish to ride under the sun. I should go get Fatha, but no, it's too late for that because I'd be seen—and besides, would he really want to take the soul of one so stupid?

I'm about ready to peek out from under the car when I hear the buzz falter a bit, then a big clatter-noise. A body goes sliding across the ashy street, a body my size, not like all them men Fatha's had to kill up to now—I can't even count how many. This one's covered in rough brown leather and denim and a helmet and gloves and boots. And no crossbow to see.

So I crawl out from under the car and I go straight for the bank to wake Fatha—

But this stranger he's heard me though I moved quiet and quick like a cat, and the black glass on his helmet faces me with my reflection in it. I freeze up.

"Hey," I say before I know it.

He watches me with no words, like he's as frozen as me.

"You hurt?" I notice his motorbike then, but I ain't never seen anything like it. The tires they've got chunks to them, and they're narrow with bigger rims than any I've seen, and there ain't much at all to the chassis.

"My leg." He gestures, and his voice is quiet but I hear fine.

"You want I could—" But I don't want to get Fatha, and

I wouldn't know what to do with the red cross box anyhow. He always takes care of things when we hurt ourselves. "You bleeding out?" If so, it might bring the cats out from the shadows, and they've been mighty hungry lately.

The helmet shakes just a bit, and his hand waves toward his leg again under his other one, but I can't tell if it's broke. Only if I went up to him and checked for myself I'd know, but he might have some kind of weapon I can't see, like a blade or some such, and if I come up too close to him he'll like as not gut me open and leave me out there in the sun to fester with sores till I die.

"You can't be out there too long, you know," I say.

"Wasn't planning on it. Mind sharing some of that shade?"

His motorbike's still running, eating up his fuel, and I know he can't be happy about it no more than he's happy about his leg. I could shut off the engine while he drags himself out of the sun, unless he's just "playing possum" like Fatha says. That's why he's always got his crossbow and shoots dead center in the back so they're no trouble.

I beckon to this small man to join me, and I should go get Fatha and wake him and tell him we've got company— but I don't want him to open up this one's skull for me. This one, he's my size. We could be friends.

He drags himself backward, legs trailing through the dust and ash, and I step quicklike out into the sun and hoof it over to his bike. I pick the thing up and kill the motor and I watch it grind down into quiet.

"Hell, you're a strong one," he tells me, scooting back onto the cool concrete in front of the bank.

I'm holding the motorbike up off the asphalt and it ain't no trouble. Fatha he always says I don't know my own strength.

I set the bike down and prop it up against the car with the dents in the side, and I look for my concrete chunks but now he's sitting with them, this stranger, and he's reaching for his helmet to remove it. I keep my distance, but I know I shouldn't be out here in the sun, even with all the coverings I've got: hat, scarf, goggles, jacket, gloves—

He's got his helmet off, and I see now I was wrong about him, dead wrong. Sure, he's my size, but he ain't nothing like me at all. He's the most beautiful man I've ever seen, and he's looking right at me with eyes like the bluest paint in all the world.

"I don't bite," he says and sets the helmet in his lap, leaning back against the glass double doors. When Fatha wakes up, he'll come straight through there. "You got a name?"

Of course I do. Fatha calls me Boy because that is what I am. "What are you doing here?"

He shrugs slim shoulders. Mine are bigger. "Passing through. You alone here?"

"No." I point past the doors at his back. "Fatha he's here, and you'd best be gone before he comes." Then I really give him a good long look, keeping my distance. There ain't no beard on his face, and it's a narrow face, one that wouldn't look good with a beard anyways. He must be my age or so. And his hair, it's so wavy and long and red like a copper penny, clean like he must wash it every other day. "What's your name?"

"Gwyneth," he says, and it don't sound like no man's name I've ever heard, but I've only heard the names Fatha reads to me from his big book, ones like David and Joseph and Moses. "Call me Gwyn. So, it's just you and your dad here, that it?"

It's always been Fatha and me and nobody else since

Mama, and the ones who pass through don't go no further. But I don't tell Gwyn this; he wouldn't understand; at least I don't think he would.

"You got a soul?" The sun it's burning through to my scalp now and I can't stand out here much longer, but I don't want to be gutted like no dumb cat neither. "In here?" I tap the side of my head.

Gwyn he chuckles, and it sounds like the music Fatha plays on his eyepad on Sundays when he fires up the generator for our weekly devotion time, high and clear and so pretty, and I want him to laugh some more soon as he's done.

"So that's where it is? I've always wondered." He shakes his head, and the copper locks sway back and forth and I want to run my fingers through them. They must feel smooth like Mama's old silk dress Fatha sleeps with. I felt it once when he wasn't looking. "I don't know, kid. Maybe none of us have souls anymore. What do you think of that?"

If that was true, I wouldn't be the only one kept out of Heaven, that's what I think. But I don't tell him.

"You got any food around here?" Another chuckle, just as pretty as before. "What am I saying, of course you do! You've got this whole town to yourselves, right?"

Just us and the cats, that's all. "I'll go and get you some grub." I make to approach him and the doors but remember the back of the bank, the emergency door, and the key I wear around my neck under my jacket. "Don't you go anywhere."

"No chance of that." Gwyn motions toward that leg of his again.

I take off full-tilt around the building and close my eyes with a deep sigh once I'm in the shade of all that dusty brick. I come round to the back where the solid steel door faces a whole lot of nothing out beyond the vacant lot, dry hills grey with ash and what looks like little dots lined up on the ridge way out west. Squinting, I can't quite make out what they are, too far away.

The key comes out easy once I've got my jacket unzipped and I slip it into the lock, knowing there are plenty of protein bars down in the basement where it's cool, locked up so the cats don't get to them. I've got the door open wide when I hear the blast, a sound more like a gawd-awful bomb than any of my concrete chunks against that dead car. I never heard nothing like it, but I know it ain't good, so I run inside, past the offices and vaults and the cot where Fatha should have been sleeping. I run out to the big room in front where folks used to trade their paper, and I stop with my heart pounding like thunder in my ears.

Fatha he stands out front of the glass doors and they're open now, and he's got his crossbow trained on Gwyn who's got what looks like a weapon pointed at Fatha, and there's blood splattered on the glass behind Fatha, and Fatha's jacket is all wet with fresh blood like that man he done shot just yesterday morning, but Fatha he stands tall and strong like always.

"You get back on that bike and you clear out of here," Fatha's saying, and I don't know why he hasn't shot Gwyn yet, but I'm glad of it. We're going to be friends, Gwyn and me. "You tell your bunch they ain't welcome here. This is our town. Y'all had better just move on."

Gwyn chuckles, but it ain't so pretty now. "We've got you outnumbered ten to one, old man. What makes you think you can stand up to those odds?"

I come up slow behind Fatha and squint out through the

dim into the bright sunlight beyond. He's been hurt bad, I can see that, but he don't seem in much pain. He holds the crossbow steady, and if he was to pull the trigger right now, the arrow would go straight through Gwyn's throat.

"Fatha it's okay, he's my friend," I say, and Fatha he almost jumps at me, but he recovers quicklike. "His name is Gwyn and—"

Gwyn he's laughing again, real hard now, and I don't like it. Sounds like he's laughing at me. "Twenty of us against you and that half-wit of yours. You sure you want to make things difficult for yourselves?"

"We mind our own business here. We got no issue with you passing this way." Fatha he tightens his grip. "But you lead your bunch one foot into this town, and you'll be wishing you hadn't."

Gwyn's weapon makes a click-clink sound. "How about I just blow your brains all over that retard of yours?"

Fatha growls deep in his chest and his skin burns red and I know what will happen next, so I let out a "No!" and shove him aside, just to throw off his aim, because he was going to end Gwyn then and there. Fatha's ribs they make a crunching sound where my arm hits him, and he falls off to the side, crashing through the glass of one of them open doors. Limp like a dead cat, he lays there in the bloody glass bits, the crossbow without its arrow.

But it didn't shoot Gwyn. He's fine, staring at me with those big blue eyes of his. The arrow it went straight into one of the flat tires on that car I always hit with my concrete.

"What did you do, kid?" Gwyn he seems mighty surprised.

"He was gonna kill you," I say and kneel down beside Fatha who isn't moving.

Gwyn chuckles again, the ugly sound not the pretty one. "I think you killed him, you dumb bastard." He's got his weapon tucked into his jacket now and is slipping on his helmet. Turns out he was just playing possum after all; his leg is fine and he can walk more than all right. He leaves his black helmet glass open and steps out into the sun. He takes hold of his motorbike and climbs on. "Get ready for some company, kid." He kickstarts the bike, and it buzzes so loud my teeth they vibrate.

Fatha's eyes are closed, his beardy chin on his chest, but he ain't sleeping. He's breathing and bleeding out, but he ain't at peace, that I can tell. I hurt him bad, I'm afraid, and I can feel the tears spill hot down out of my eyes.

"You came with friends, Gwyn?" I remember them dots out on the ridge. Gwyn he must've come on in ahead to look around and see if everything was all right here.

Gwyn twists the handle on his bike and the engine revs up. "You behave, kid, and you won't have any trouble with us."

"Okay." I turn to Fatha and stroke his beard. "Wake up now, you wake up, time to wake up now, Fatha." Gwyn's motorbike tears off out of town to go and fetch his friends. Might be nice to have more folks around. I have long forgot what that's like.

Fatha burps, that's what it sounds like, and now there's blood coming out into his beard. His wrinkly eyelids twitch and peel open to focus his watery black eyes. One side of his face lifts up, and his bloody teeth grin at me.

"About time," he says, and I can barely hear him. He reaches up to touch my face with his hand; this is how he shows his love for me. "You wouldn't let me kill her." He coughs hard, and more blood spills out like tomato soup from the big cans we've got down in the basement. "You'll see your Mama. Now you got yourself a soul." He taps me on the side of my head. "It's been planted, just you gotta let it grow."

"Fatha—"

But his eyes close and his hand drops into his lap, and he don't breathe no more. And in the distance I hear more buzzing motorbikes like Gwyn's, and they're all headed this way. So I pick up Fatha's spent crossbow and I pray he's right, that somehow I've got me a soul now.

I step out into the sunlight to greet my new friends with my insides all tangled up and heavy in my gut. It won't ever be the same here without Fatha, and yet I'm so glad of this one thing: that there will finally be an end to all the killing.

Amen.

OUTER RIMS

TOIYA KRISTEN FINLEY

out•er rims, *n*. *1*. areas of continents flooded in 2014 by rising sea levels due to climate change; the resulting regions.

Why she brought the kids one last time would be the question always troubling her, never finding its reasonable answer. She told herself she wanted them to see the shore before the world changed again. After all, no one regretted last chances unless they weren't taken. Six years earlier she'd thought of visiting NYC, the bistro where she met her husband, to honor his memory. But she fussed over the budget. Her last chance passed her by, after half of New York City had eventually been submerged by the encroaching Atlantic.

She wouldn't rob her children of one last stay at the place they spent summers with their father. Branden and Shannon were more excited about the world changing than losing the shoreline. *Where will the land be next year? One day the whole world'll be underwater!* they said, but they could imagine such things because they would be far from here when the storm's eye came roaring up from the gulf.

Shannon's head lolled against the door crushing her afro puffs, and her neck bent down on her shoulder. Yet she could sleep anywhere at any time, even during the biggest move of her life, and dozed in the back. Branden popped gum in the front passenger seat. He leaned his chin on his sharp knee and looked out the window at the highway. Normally, she would tell him to keep his shoes off the seat, but he was relaxed when he talked about things she thought should unnerve an eleven-year-old boy.

"Where's everybody gonna live?"

"Good question. Maybe they'll stay with family or friends like us before they find their own place."

"Everything's gonna get crowded real fast," he said. "The country keeps getting smaller and smaller. One day there won't be room left."

"Well, when that time comes, maybe we'll live on the moon," she said.

He twirled the bubblegum around his tongue and smiled and went back to the view outside. "All those trees'll be gone." No sadness. No longing. Just a fact.

They were minutes away from the shore when she saw a figure laboring with a sedan on the shoulder of the road. The car slowed and she pulled over. Branden spun away from the window. Under those long, straight lashes, his eyes bulged with disbelief. "But he's a stranger!"

She violated every rule she'd given her children about people they didn't know. "He's having car trouble. I'm sure he's trying to get out of here, too."

She lowered the front passenger's window. Branden

slinked down in the seat. "You need help?"

A young man emerged from under the hood. In the humidity and car's heat, sweat sealed his hair to his forehead. Trees shadowed him, but the redness around his pupils made the blue look like marbles protruding from his eyes. He glanced away from her and down the road, as if he couldn't believe she'd pulled over, either. "There's a parts place off Exit 6. If you could take me, I'd be much obliged."

Branden pouted and rolled up the window.

"Act right," she said.

"Ma'am, I really, really appreciate this," the young man said from the backseat. "Especially with the flooding coming."

"Where you headed?" she said.

"I don't know. Midwest somewhere, I guess. I'm tired of hangin' around the outer rims. Who knows when the next bad storm's comin'."

"I heard that." Her son wouldn't stop staring at the young man. "Turn around, Branden," she said under her breath.

In the rearview window, the young man closed his eyes. He leaned back and angled his face towards the roof, maybe to pray. With eyes wide, his lips parted.

"Mom," Branden said, "he's shivering."

The young man complained of a headache. He scratched his chest until his arms weakened and fell at his sides. But the guilt hadn't come to her yet. She'd take him to a hospital. If she hadn't picked him up, he'd be lying on the side of the highway. The worst that could happen, he'd be admitted; they'd make sure he was evacuated as a patient. But he could be discharged before then. It could be simple heat exhaustion. He'd walk out of the ER in a few hours and be on his way.

Guilt didn't catch up with her until she saw the white

tent in the hospital parking lot and the officers directing traffic. A policeman wearing a surgical mask stopped her. He grabbed his walkie-talkie when he saw the young man in the back.

"Can I get you to park over here, ma'am?" Park away from the ER, where doctors in blue suits and large square hoods waited with pens and clipboards.

She nodded at the policeman. Her son sat up. He put his feet on the floor.

"I'm sorry," she said.

2. an area at the edges of a greater part or whole: *He banished the thought to the outer rims of his mind.*

This woman beyond Cantor's hood respirator did her best to force a polite smile. She rubbed her left thumb with the cracked nail of her right index finger. A bit of dirt clung to the cuticle. Dr. Cantor would rather have a child sitting in front of her, or at least a teenager. She could tell them she was a disease detective who got to wear moon gear, watch them grin or giggle in respect, and downplay the impending rage of water and sickness. But this was her first time wearing the level-4 suit. This woman, with her teeth set firmly against her lips, felt the threat of the hood and the mask.

Cantor felt pushed to find any hint or clue before these people were forced to evacuate, mixing with another population. And already the disease was spreading. This illness that looked like malaria and blossomed in the warm climate. This illness with seemingly airborne transmission and no mosquito bites. The woman in front of her tried to keep her stare on the table, but she'd glance at Cantor's rubber gloves. Crease her eyebrows at the hood and respirator protecting Cantor from the air she breathed.

She thought of all the ways she could make this woman less uneasy, help her drop her guard in this atmosphere. Make her more relaxed so they'd have some flow to the conversation, a greater chance to suss out an answer in an insignificant detail she wouldn't share otherwise. The only way she could consider them connecting was as black women, with so few of them living here now. But they weren't sisters talking over coffee. From the stiffness in her shoulders and the frantic tapping of her heel to the floor, the woman made it clear that Cantor was not on her side.

"I'm... sorry we've made you wait," Dr. Cantor said. "Lots going on." The left corner of her mouth crinkled up, but she didn't know if the woman could see it.

"It hasn't been a fun few hours, I'll admit." She leaned in and raised her eyebrows with her voice. Cocked her chin.

"It's all right. I can hear you fine." It was Cantor who sounded hollow.

The woman leaned back, but her shoulders were still stiff.

Cantor glanced over the pages on the clipboard. "Ms. Burrell, you're from Portland, Tennessee, correct?"

"Yes. We're planning to go up to Ohio."

Cantor grinned like a fool. Burrell's eyelashes fluttered and her eyebrows frowned.

"My aunt lived in Clarksville," Cantor said. "I don't run into many people from the area. I used to spend summers there. My mom put me and my brothers on the 9-Rail."

"9-Rail?" Burrell shook her head. She managed her first real smile. Of fondness. "Haven't thought about the 9-Rail since it went underwater."

"Yeah. Guess you can tell I haven't been home in years."

"Where was home?"

"Alabama. Mobile," Cantor said. "Yeah... Went to school in Milwaukee and decided to stay. But Clarksville, I don't think I've been there in fifteen years."

"You wouldn't recognize it. It turned into a real city almost overnight."

Cantor laughed. "Man, I loved my aunt, but being trapped in that Podunk town?" Burrell laughed with her.

"I'll miss it," Burrell said.

And Cantor composed herself. "Where'd you meet Don Jackson?"

"Is he...?"

"He has a very high fever."

Burrell unclasped her hands and pushed herself forward. "We were on our way back from the shore. His car broke down. I just wanted to help him out, especially with everything going down. I didn't want him to get stuck, or worse."

"When did you notice he was sick?"

She shrugged. She looked down, grinded her lips together like she was having a conversation with herself. "He was working under the hood, you know? And it was hot. He was sweating, and his face was red, but... I don't know. He was in the car maybe ten minutes? He seemed really tired."

"Did he tell you how he was feeling?"

"He said he felt really hot and he was getting a headache. He really couldn't say much."

"And how are you feeling?"

"Fine, considering. Can you tell me anything? When can I get my kids out of here?"

The clipboard fell against the desk. Cantor couldn't look at her head on. Her eyes darted back and forth, back and forth seeking the response that would give Burrell some comfort knowing she and her children would be okay. Burrell stared, demanded an answer from her. "I understand how difficult the circumstances are, but you'll have to stay for observation." And that was the most Cantor would force herself to say. She wouldn't let this woman know that her good deed could leave her whole family dead in a day.

Only Dr. Alagiah was in the makeshift lab. When the disease first manifested malaria symptoms, he'd kept his team optimistic. But as it proved itself to be contagious, the lab became haunted. A place they wished they could avoid. A place for work in silence as the weather reports hung over their heads.

Dr. Alagiah's expressions, even behind the protective hood, were clear. "We've received... We need to..." He dropped his head.

"Dr. Alagiah?" Cantor said.

He closed his eyes. "We got word we're to pack."

When his eyes opened, Cantor found the filtering around her face insufficient. She choked on the fresh air. "We have no idea—"

"We don't get more time. This didn't come from the CDC."

"We're going to *abandon* them?"

Dr. Alagiah cupped her left elbow in his palm. His arm stayed steady, but the rest of him shook. "They're hoping... it'll be the end of the disease. It's spreading too quickly in this heat—"

"With everybody evacuating, they're assuming everyone who's infected is here... or dead already."

He was still shaking. "But we'll have more time after the storms."

She threw the clipboard to the asphalt.

Already, the exposed had been pushed deeper into the hospital. Precautionary measures, they'd been told, to protect non-infected patients. No windows here. A vast, cavernous waiting area with the TVs turned off. To conserve power, they were told, in case there were difficulties during the evacuation.

Cantor and her colleagues collected some samples to take with them. Maybe the blood would reveal answers after the flood, once the disease had been drowned in this outer rim. And the CDC would have a point of attack should it rise again and make its way north. These people were helpful, all things considered. They'd laugh at themselves for being afraid of the needle or picking the worst time to be stuck in a hospital. But when they looked at Cantor, she could feel them screaming, *Please, please let me go now. I'm not sick.*

And at what point would they realize no one would come for them? The doctors and nurses would no longer check on them. The disease detectives would be gone, too. What then? As they realized they'd be left to go under?

Her colleagues didn't make eye contact as they worked as quickly and methodically as they could. They sweated behind their hoods. They said as little as possible. Cantor began to entertain a thought pricking her conscience— *what will happen will happen*. She could ignore it at first.

Kept it at bay with rationalizations about her job and the nature of the disease. But these people... She saw the moment when they realized they were alone. When they freed themselves from this room, but all transportation was gone. When the tidal waves rose up to devour them. Worst-case scenario, she told herself, she at least tried to do something. She wondered if she was being selfish, but she didn't let that bother her for long.

Her daughter draped across her knee asleep and her son sitting next to her vacant-eyed and kicking the wall beneath his chair, she watched Cantor approach her with detached weariness.

"Ms. Burrell, may I speak with you alone?"

3. OUTCASTS; forgotten or unseen persons.

Did he ask about them? He'd meant to. But he couldn't remember. Now he was sure he was awake because he wasn't shaking like this a minute ago. He came in and out, in and out, until being asleep was like consciousness. Then he'd open his eyes and find he'd been to another world and just returned to this bed. When the pain from the headache let him turn his head, he saw all the people in the room like him, stuck in hospital beds, infected with the same damn thing. But they'd multiplied. There was more sobbing. More vomiting. Did he ask about them? Did he find out if they were okay? She had been so kind to give him a lift. Were they still here? Did they get away from the storm, or had the storm passed? The CDC people, he didn't see any now. They were never not around, giving him their "Don, how're you doings?" even in his sleep.

Perhaps he'd asked one of them about that family in his dreams. He would ask now if he could find anyone. At one point, when he could recall being awake, the CDC angels swarmed the room. Their bulbous heads peered into him. Their vacuum-hose wings swooshed even when they stood still. They poked him with their plastic blue skin, asked him lots of questions. He didn't remember a mosquito bite. He didn't feel any, anyway. He was thankful for that. Mosquito-bite itches drove him crazy, and his arms were jelly now. He wondered if some other insect had done this. Mites seemed to be running up and down his arms, his legs, his chest, under his skin when he was in the backseat. And the little boy was angry with him for getting in the car. They were on their way out of this place, and then he came along with his bugs. Did the insects jump off him and onto that little girl? To their mother? To the boy? A woman whimpered and moaned across the room. He listened to his own bed twitch as his limbs rumbled and threatened to snap at the elbows and knees. He wished they would. Then he couldn't feel them anymore. He wanted to apologize. He really should apologize. He killed them. The blues said the family was still here. They were being checked on and poked up, too. If he didn't make them sick, he'd forced the storm on them. Perhaps this was the storm raging in his bones. Like old people used to say they could tell a storm was coming by the creakiness in their joints. He wished it would hurry. He waited for the waters. In this bed he was alone. But if he was going to die, he wanted the sea to pick him up and carry him out where he could drown with everyone else.

* * *

4. ANATHEMA; the accursed. [2014-15]

He pushed his sister's head off his shoulder. She slapped his arm. Her eyes were still closed. "Quit it."

"You're hot," he said.

"I'm not, Branden," she said.

"You're heavy."

Mom talked with adults in the chairs near the corner. Three men and a woman. They were strangers. He didn't understand why she trusted them all of a sudden.

"When we leaving?" his sister asked. She put her elbow on the armrest and used her hand for a pillow.

"Be right back, Shannon."

Mom and the adults shook and nodded their heads at each other. All talked at the same time. Their arms swirled and chopped at the air. Their fingers pointed to interrupt.

"…if we're sick? We get outta here, we'll just make everybody sick and spread it—"

"But there's no reason to know that we are. We won't make it if we don't leave—"

"Go to the media. There's got to be a reporter following a storm here."

"You're crazy," Mom said. "I'm sure they're outside somewhere, on high ground."

"Why'd you tell us if you don't expect us to do anything?"

"I'm confused about the options," Mom said.

"Only one option we—"

"Mom?"

A shock spread through all five of them. Like the worst secret in the world got told and everybody was gonna get in trouble for it. They were scared. Adults. In a panic.

Mom jumped from her seat and grabbed his hand. "I

need you to go wait with Shannon." Her eyes were shiny. The little lines around her mouth got deeper.

"Is that man dead?"

"I don't know."

"Are we sick?"

She didn't say anything for a moment. "I don't know."

Branden tried to free his hand from hers. She shuddered and let him go. "Please, just wait with your sister. Don't tell her. Don't tell anybody."

His chest itched. The itch crawled all over his stomach and his arms. He scratched, but he knew it wouldn't go away. Whatever that man had, whatever those weird doctors asked him about, he had it, too. He wanted to get away from here. But did he want to give the rest of the world *this*? It jumped onto him from that man. And it would jump from him to person to person to person until everybody on the planet died.

"You know you're not supposed to be in grown-up's business," Shannon said.

"Stay away from me!" he said.

Shannon rolled her eyes. She crossed her arms and looked at Mom.

"I'm sorry," Branden said. He sat next to Shannon, but he pulled his arms and legs close to his body.

All the adults came together. Branden watched them get angry and sad. Some of them cried. They hugged. Then they tore pieces of paper and handed them around. They all wrote on the bits of paper and handed them to an old Latino man. They talked some more, and the next thing Branden knew, Mom got him and Shannon and told them to stay with the other kids no matter what.

The quiet boredom in the room was gone. Branden

immediately wanted it back. The men picked up couches. They ran towards the exits with them and rammed them into the doors. Shannon wrapped her arms around Branden's neck. Kids cried for their parents. They huddled into each other and screamed with each *bang*. Adults shouted directions at each other. They told their children to stop yelling because everything was going to be okay.

Hot breath and tears slid under his collar. Hair got in his mouth as kids held onto him and rubbed their faces on his shirt. The sickness hopped from person to person, and it wouldn't matter if they got out of the building or not, if they got away from the storm. Mom watched them bust the doors open. She rubbed her chin when the chains fell, staring out with that same look she had when the man in the backseat started to shiver.

The adults grabbed tables and chairs and pounded through the doors. They pulled their kids from the pack crying in the corner and threw them over their shoulders or ran so hard they dragged them across the floor.

"Mom!" Shannon said.

She turned to them and frowned. "Hurry! Stay with me."

Outside the waiting room, furniture crashed through windows. The hallways burst in shards. Mom pressed Branden and Shannon to her sides, hunched over them and kept them near the back of the group. "Shouldn't have told them. Shouldn't have told them," she said to herself.

Parents pushed their kids through the windows. But their clothes and skin snagged on the glass. Some pounded on the walls until the walls turned red. "Don't look don't look don't look don't look!" Mom said, and they fell to their knees at the sound of heavy boots.

"Don't make me go through the window!" Shannon screamed, and she cried.

Men with thudding voices yelled in the halls. They said they'd shoot. They said to get down. They said to move back in the room, and Branden heard their fists hit cheeks and chins.

"Were they gonna shoot us anyway?" he said.

"Just get down," Mom said. "Just stay here."

"*Were they*?" Branden said.

"I don't know."

"We're not sick. They have to let us go," Shannon said. "Make them, Mom."

"We *are* sick. We're gonna kill people. But I don't wanna stay. Should we stay?"

"Mom—" Shannon said, but Mom was staring down the hall at the men with guns. She mouthed something to herself. Her lips moved faster than the words could make sense.

She pressed them to the floor. Then she bowed her head, too. With his eyes tight to the floor, not seeing anything, he heard Mom say, "I thought it was important, that's all. You didn't need to see it. *We* wouldn't have changed… We make it out of here, you take care of you. Can't be any other way."

He thought the adults had figured it out. He thought Mom told them what they should do. He wanted her to say *we're sick, but we can still live*. But he lied to himself. He wondered why *you take care of you* couldn't keep her from giving that man a ride.

Branden shivered again. He wasn't sure if the sickness made him do it, or Mom's fear rubbing up against him. But the cold and wet tickled his scalp, and he knew it was the wind bringing the rain through the broken windows.

ADVERTISING AT THE END OF THE WORLD

KEFFY R. M. KEHRLI

Five years after her husband died, two years after she moved to a cabin in Montana, and six months after the world ended, Marie opened her curtains to discover her front garden overrun with roving, stumbling advertisements. Marie hadn't seen one since she'd sold her condo and moved out to her isolated cabin. She shuddered.

There were at least twenty of the ads, and for all it seemed they were doing their damnedest to step lightly, her red and yellow tulips were completely trampled. Marie had stubbornly continued to cultivate those flowers despite the certainty that she ought to be using the gardening space, and the captured rainwater, to grow food. Not that it mattered what she'd been growing there. It was all mud now.

The ad nearest her window looked quite a bit like a tall, lanky teenager. It moved like one as well, and might have fooled her except that its forehead was stuck in price scrolling mode. Faintly glowing red letters crawled across its forehead from right to left.

TOILET PAPER... 2 FOR 1 SALE... RECYCLED...

Marie could only recognize the daffodil bed by memory. She snapped the curtains shut. She wrapped a floral print terrycloth robe around herself and hustled from her sparsely furnished bedroom into the kitchen. She was relieved to see the fences she'd put up to keep the deer out of her vegetable garden, while never quite successful, had at least managed to keep her vegetables safe from the ads.

That, of course, would not bring back her flowers.

She glowered at the ads through her kitchen window and filled a glass from the pitcher of well water she kept by the sink. She fumbled open the Tuesday box on her medication canister. Like most mornings, she was thankful that she had filled her prescriptions prior to the end; otherwise she would have none by now.

She would have to go to the garden, and although the advertisements were designed to be perfectly harmless, Marie found she was frightened by the way they lurched over the ground. She suspected this was due to the uncomfortable way their silent progress reminded her of zombie films.

Robert would have been fascinated. A year or so before his death, an advertisement had come up to their door. In those days, the ads had acted more like people than those that now plagued her gardens, and it had stood obediently on the front step until they'd opened the door.

Marie had argued that it was better to leave the door

shut, because if an advertisement left without delivering its pitch, it would learn not to come back to the house. The way she figured it, and the way several of her favorite independent video bloggers figured it, listening to the ads was like feeding a stray cat.

Robert did not seem to be overly concerned that they would never get rid of the ads. "Don't be ridiculous," he said. "They'll last maybe another few years at the most, and then the companies will all move onto something that costs less. Right now, they're cheaper than sending employees door-to-door." He opened the door, despite Marie's protestations.

"Hello," the advertisement said, hands clasped before it. "I was wondering if you had a few moments to talk about your retirement?"

Marie just shook her head and turned back into the house. She busied herself with embroidery, although she still kept an eye on Robert to be sure he wasn't buying anything. No matter how clever her Robert thought the ads were, she did not want to encourage the companies to make more of them.

After a few minutes of animated conversation, the ad left and Robert came into the dining room. He asked, "Have you ever wondered how sentient they are?"

Marie shook her head. She didn't like the ads, and the best emotion she could muster toward them was similar to the way she felt about mosquitoes. Other people thought they served a purpose; she didn't, and it was not worth the argument.

It became apparent that Robert was actually waiting for her answer, and he sat down heavily in one of the other dining room chairs. Marie finished a particularly difficult stitch. "They aren't. They just recognize patterns."

"Yes, but so do we," Robert said. He put both hands on the table and sat up straighter. "How close are they to sentience? They're so much more sophisticated than a recorded ad. They're art."

A few more stitches. Marie laughed. "Art? They're advertisements, not art. It can't be art if it's just meant to sell things."

Robert looked thoughtful. He leaned over the table slowly, put his chin in his hands and looked at her. "And yet you like Mucha prints, and those were all selling something," he said.

If Robert were still alive, and the world had not ended, Marie supposed he would have gone out the front door and immersed himself in a sea of advertising conversation. As it was, she faced the corporate-orphaned menace alone with an old broom and her largest hammer.

She *had* hoped they would simply wander off on their own, but after watching through the window for a few hours, she determined they knew where she was. Marie suspected her RF chip was still broadcasting her ID number. She and Robert had bought them before they truly understood how much advertising money had subsidized the price.

She stood on the threshold of the home she'd purchased with her retirement and the last of Robert's life insurance pay-off, ready to defend it against even the most pernicious of sales pitches.

Marie hefted the hammer over her head and held the broom out like a lance. At least thirty ads were in the front garden now, and more stumbled up the gravel road to her home.

"Get *off* my property!" Her voice only shook a little.

The ads turned to face her. They were designed to understand when they were told to leave. This was meant to limit the annoyance factor. Even in the best of times, the command had rarely worked.

Forehead screens changed from flesh colors to scrolling text. The subtlety had gone out of advertising entirely. She wondered if that was a function of being away from human contact for months on end, or if she was just surrounded by a crowd of defectives.

"Go away!"

The ads crowded in closer, becoming an ocean of words and prices and markdowns, factory blow-outs and email addresses for the next get-rich-quick scheme, male enhancement drug names, tag lines for movie sequels that shouldn't exist, and cash advance loan shark promises.

"Marie… it's been so long."

At the corner of her cabin, just behind her favorite rhododendron, she saw a figure she recognized immediately and might have known by voice alone.

Robert.

Robert as he'd looked when they'd first met, back in the twentieth century, when they had both been younger and he had been alive. He—it, the ad, wore a very simple black two-piece suit, and held a hat under its arm. It looked like the suit Robert had worn to their wedding, but the shoes were different, as though the advertisement had not fully accessed the public files on their marriage.

Through the first three years after his death, Marie had never grown used to the way the ads shifted to Robert's form. Now the image spread out like ripples on a pool, the skin of the ads universally deepening almost to a shade of olive, hair lengthening and straightening and taking on that blue-black sheen she'd fallen in love with.

The forward press of ads stopped just outside of her reach, processing the shift from advertising bot to facsimile of her husband. The ads stopped broadcasting on their foreheads, all except for the broken one, which was now fidgeting from one foot to the other in a way that would have tricked Marie into thinking it was actually human if the sale on toilet paper hadn't been scrolling from one temple to the other.

They were all malfunctioning.

"Have you been waiting?" one of the Ad-Roberts in front of Marie said. She poked it in the chest with her broom handle, and it didn't seem to mind.

Another ad said, "Have you missed me?"

"Lonely out here," said a third.

Marie picked up her hammer and slowly, careful to avoid tripping on the door frame, backed into her house.

She shut the door.

The first time Marie had ever seen an ad take on the appearance of Robert had been only a few weeks after the funeral. She had opened the door one morning to find Robert standing just outside. There was a split second when she found herself wondering if she'd imagined the past few weeks. Then she realized she was looking at an ad. Marie thought about Robert rotting in the ground, dead and alone.

The ads were not meant to use the likenesses of the

deceased. What they could do was almost as bad, but far less illegal—taking those likenesses and shifting them ever so slightly until the ad looked familiar, but not sufficiently to be recognized.

Whether it was an act or not, the ad looked just as surprised as she was. Its eyes opened wide as it accessed her file and, for an instant, it looked like Robert had when he realized he'd said something he shouldn't have. The ad opened its mouth as if to speak, but Marie hadn't wanted to know what it was about to say. She'd slammed the door shut.

It turned out later that the malfunction had been semi-common. Marie could have gotten in on a class action lawsuit but, instead, she'd packed up and sold the condo. She'd moved to the cabin shortly afterward, wanting a place that wouldn't remind her of Robert, who had always loved cities.

All the ads except for one shifted back to their default appearances after Marie returned indoors, but they didn't go away. She kept her shades down and tried to ignore the tromp-tromp-tromping noises of footsteps outside her house.

The gardens had seen better days.

The *most* curious thing was that no matter how content she had been with her hermit's life before, now the ads were outside her door she missed the sound of Robert's voice. She wished she could hear it again, as long as it wasn't a haphazard lead-in to a sales pitch.

Marie sat alone on these mornings, extremely alone, now she had the rustling sounds of the ads to remind her.

That was why, on one fine Wednesday afternoon in mid-April, Marie invited an advertisement in the guise of her dead husband inside for lunch.

They sat together at a white table with a blue-checkered tablecloth and a plate of tiny sandwiches inside Marie's small kitchen. Ad-Robert had attempted to pull her chair out for her, but she would not allow it. She had placed her hammer under her seat before letting the ad in. Even though she didn't think it was dangerous, Marie thought it best to be prepared. Once they were seated, she poured mint tea for them both.

Marie had cultivated the mint herself, of course.

The ad that looked like Robert smiled dumbly at Marie, and the sunlight that filtered into the room lanced brightly across faintly silvered hair. When it smiled, crow's feet spread from the crinkled skin around its eyes. Try as the ad might, however, the months without upkeep had so eroded its ability to keep up with its reference recordings of Robert's inimitable gestures that the resulting attempt looked like a badly choreographed farce.

Marie sipped her tea, watching the ad in silence. It had asked her a leading question, as they'd walked through the front room: something about stock options, which would never draw Marie's interest, even if stocks or money had meaning anymore. Ads were designed not to speak again until the thread of conversation was taken up by a human. She looked out the kitchen window. Ads still filled the back yard. She wondered if they were sharing her location, like bees dancing to show each other the path to fresh flowers. The ads wandered back and forth through what was left of the pansies.

Marie sighed, and Ad-Robert cocked its head.

Either the conversation lag had been too much for its memory banks, or it parsed the sigh as an answer.

The ad asked, "I mean, I don't mean to pry, dear… but you have thought about retirement, haven't you?"

The ad sounded like Robert and, at the same time, sounded like the ad that had spoken to Robert six years before. Marie thought of the hammer under her chair and had to wait to respond because of the sudden thickness in her throat. "Of course I have." It wasn't exactly a lie, but at the same time, the question was moot.

Ad-Robert looked down at its tea but did not drink. It held the cup a few inches above the table and let it steam out into the air. "You ought to be buying biotech. I can help you find the right companies."

Marie said, "I'm sure they're not in business anymore."

The ad tried to do one of Robert's dismissive hand waves, but its wrist motors jerked and the effect was lost. The ad didn't seem to notice. "Of course they're still in business!" Its eyes focused on the space above Marie's left shoulder, as it tried to connect to the Net. Marie was fairly certain that, with the exception of any identification chips she may have, there had never been a wireless connection in a twenty-mile radius.

Marie finished her cup of tea and maneuvered the conversation into a realm she cared for a bit more than imaginary finances. She poured more tea and dumped a spoonful of honey into it. "I've been thinking about planting corn soon, but it's hard to get to a flat patch of ground that isn't constantly underfoot these days." She'd heard rumors that some of the ads were able to carry on regular conversations if prompted properly. A few companies had discovered their ads had been held hostage by lonely people for weeks or months on end.

Ad-Robert didn't move, frozen with what would have

been confusion if it had been human.

Marie waited, but the hope she had for a decent conversationalist faded when Ad-Robert only asked, "So, about your retirement?"

Marie had tried to look for survivors a week after the satellite television signals had gone out. She'd loaded up her old pickup truck with water, emergency bandages, and even a few fall vegetables to share with her neighbors.

One eye on the road and the other on the gas gauge, she made her way down the mountain, looking for turnoffs to the isolated cabins of her neighbors. She hadn't known them well before everything went to shit, but she figured now was a good time to make an exception. It was a beautiful, quiet day. She pulled onto the highway, and no cars passed her in either direction. All the cabins were empty. This confused Marie, since she hadn't taken the people who lived in them to be the sort who would run for civilization at the first sign of trouble. She supposed she had been wrong about them, for whatever that mattered. Marie filled the back of her pickup truck with canned and dried food from their pantries and tried to ignore the smells that emanated from their closed refrigerators.

She only made it halfway down into the valley before the wind shifted to come up out of the south. She gagged, slammed on the brakes of her truck and pulled over onto the shoulder. Even a few miles away, the collective stench of several hundred thousand bodies, rotting sour in the early September heat, was too much for her.

She couldn't imagine anyone living closer. Reluctantly, she had turned the truck around and headed back to her house.

* * *

Marie couldn't destroy the ads. She had trouble even thinking of it because, no matter how wrong their gestures, every ad looked too human.

The ad she kept indoors at least pretended to listen to her from time to time. She could almost ignore the outdoor ads, except for when she had to pass from her house to the well, from the well to the garden, or from the garden back to her house. She had given up on her makeshift pump system the second or third time the ads had trampled holes into the hose. She'd forgotten how hard it was to carry water from the well to the garden by hand, and it didn't help that the ads were always underfoot.

"Get out of the way," she said, exasperated, when the ads stumbled into her few well-worn paths. Even if the ads were not in her garden, it was hard to get enough water to the plants. Every trip with the bucket took twice as long as it should have.

In the evenings, she did not embroider as much as she used to. She was too tired, now, and too worried about whether or not she'd be able to keep her food crops alive and healthy enough to give her a harvest that would last the winter.

Marie grew used to the indoor ad's, "Good morning, sweetheart." It said the same thing every morning, as she passed from her bedroom into the kitchen. The ad always sat in the same chair at the table, in the same position, waiting for her to wake.

When it became apparent that Marie wasn't interested in the ad's sales pitch, it was confused for a long time. It sat and listened, nodding absently to her words in the way

Robert had done just before he'd died, when she hadn't been able to tell if he'd understood or not.

She remembered how her own grandparents had spoken exclusively about the past in their old age. She'd still been studying for her math degree, and she hadn't had any time for those stories.Marie told the ad about other things, about how to know when it was time to pick a pear, about the earth-poison smell of tomato vines and the acid-sharp taste of the fruit.

She was trying to explain the particular crumbling feel of good soil and the moist smell of fresh potato when Ad-Robert interrupted.

It was the only time the ad interrupted her. At all other times, it had been perfectly behaved.

"Have you ever considered your death?" it asked.

Robert had once asked her that. They'd been young, and it had been more a joke than anything else. Marie couldn't look at Ad-Robert when she answered, so she stared out the window at orange-tinged clouds that hung over the forested mountains around her home.

"Yes," she said.

She had been planning to go grocery shopping the day the world ended, after she'd weeded the gardens and picked some zucchini. But she'd turned on the news that morning to pick up the one local channel available from her satellite dish.

Biological agents. Super bug. Nobody on the channel or in any of the borrowed clips they showed could determine if they thought it was terrorism, or just freak random chance. It was a virus, then it was a bacterial infection that antibiotics couldn't touch. Masked and suited reporters questioned the sobbing, quarantined mothers of sick children. Scientists or doctors postulated that if the illness killed its victims so soon after infection, then it couldn't spread much farther.

The rebuttal was simple: there was no way to know how long it gestated, and how long it was contagious. The rebuttal sparked more panic, because the man giving it finished by pointing out that the entire human race could already be infected and not know it.

Marie had turned off the television and sat on her porch in the late summer sunlight for a few hours, and when she'd turned it back on, she hadn't gotten any reception.

A day later, the electricity had been cut off.

One morning when she walked into the kitchen for her medication, the ad did not greet her as it had for the past month. Instead it sat, silent and dark, a life-sized doll made out of LCD and carbon. It no longer appeared to be anything like Robert. It was just a lifeless machine that had grown tired of masquerading as her husband.

She stared at it for a long time, expecting it to come to life with another skewed economics lecture. In case it had a sleep function, she prodded it with a wooden spoon, poking it resolutely in the stomach, the arm, the face. Nothing.

Marie sat down on the other side of the table, leaned far over it and stared at the ad. The face was not really human, but she traced the features with her fingertips, over the smooth hills and valleys that gave the ad a physical presence when it was on. The screen itself was cold to the touch, and she left little skin-oil smudges behind.

Down the neck and across the chest, she could see scratches and scrapes from tree branches and possibly animals. Places where she might have noticed pixels out if she'd looked at it more closely.

Marie sat back in her chair. When she had finished crying, she was left with the problem of disposing of the body. She felt foolish, too… Hadn't she meant originally to kill the stupid things?

The ad was lighter than she'd thought it would be. For all it was nearly the size and build of Robert, it was made of far lighter materials than flesh and bone. Marie was able to drag it with one hand under its left shoulder. She carried her lightweight shovel with her other hand, prodding or swatting any of the outdoor ads that got in her way.

They were still as obnoxious as ever, hovering, surrounding, circling Marie and the dead advertisement like sharks around a sinking boat. The air filled with pitches, slogans, prices.

"We don't have to pay until 2045!"

"I really think you'd like these perfumes, honey."

"Come and visit, the alcohol's free!"

Marie trudged along the thin dirt path that led from her little house, until dry pine needles crackled under her clogs and under the feet of the ads that followed her in a herd. When the ground went flat for a bit, she dragged the ad through a few feet of sparse sword fern.

She dug a shallow grave under a tamarack, and covered the ad with just enough dirt to hide it from view. She didn't think anything would dig it up, but she felt a little bad for not making the grave deeper when the other ads walked over the mound of dirt mixed with pine needles.

Marie wiped her face on the sleeve of her rosebud blouse,

and then she took her sweet time walking back down the mountain, still ignoring the advertisements that seemed entirely unaware of the loss of one of their number.

Marie found the second dead advertisement a few days later, toppled over on the front walkway to her house, scuffed from the feet of the other ads, as motionless and empty as the one that had died in her kitchen.

She thought very seriously about burying it with the other ad, but then she looked at the crowds of them that filled her yard and thought better of it. So Marie dragged the second advertisement out to her shed, and she propped it up between a rake and a hoe, leaving it for the dust to collect on. She realized she could have left it out among the other ads, but she didn't like the idea of her home being surrounded by forgotten bodies.

Every few days she found another, sometimes only toppled over as though its batteries had simply quit, and sometimes sitting tucked against the side of her house as though it had powered down.

She filled her shed with them, and started setting the others up as scarecrows, guarding her vegetables from the birds, though they did nothing to keep away the smaller animals and deer when they didn't move.

The month lengthens and becomes two months, then three, four, five. The ads still come, but there are fewer, and as time goes on, Marie finds that sometimes weeks pass between appearances. Now, when the ads arrive, they are very little danger to her gardens, and she is able to harvest what she needs without them getting in her way.

They come to her to die and sometimes, when it has been a long time between visits, she lets the ads inside, and she listens to them while she serves sandwiches and tea she has made from what she can grow on the plot of land behind her house. The ads that make it to her mountain are moving slower and slower, and Marie is not surprised. She is moving slower these days, too, though she is not sure if that is the weather, leaning in toward winter, working cold into the ragged edges of her joints, or what is left to her now the pills have run out.

Every so often, the ads look like Robert. Sometimes they look like her friends; sometimes they look like her mother. Sometimes they look like nobody she has ever known, and sometimes they look like she imagines her children would have if she and Robert had ever cared to try.

Maybe when the winter is done, she thinks, she will climb down from her mountain to see what is left. The smell of the dead in the city will have gone by then, and there may be other survivors on other hills, looking for her. She holds the slightest of hopes that there are fewer ads because they have found others, and not just because they were never meant to last for so long, lost and alone in a dead world.

HOW THE WORLD BECAME QUIET:
A POST-HUMAN CREATION MYTH
RACHEL SWIRSKY

Part One—The Apocalypse of Trees

During the first million years of its existence, mankind survived five apocalypses without succumbing to extinction. It endured the Apocalypse of Steel, the Apocalypse of Hydrogen, the Apocalypse of Serotonin, and both Apocalypses of Water, the second of which occurred despite certain contracts to the contrary. Mankind also survived the Apocalypse of Grease, which wasn't a true apocalypse, although it wiped out nearly half of humanity by clogging the gears that ran the densely packed underwater cities of Lor, but that's a tale for another time.

Humans laid the foundation for the sixth apocalypse in much the same way they'd triggered the previous ones. Having recovered their ambition after the Apocalypse of Serotonin and rebuilt their populations after the Apocalypse of Grease, they once again embarked on their species' long-term goal to wreak as much havoc as possible on the environment through carelessness and boredom. This time, the trees protested. They devoured buildings, whipped wind into hurricanes between their branches, tangled men into their roots and devoured them as mulch. In retaliation, men chopped down trees, firebombed jungles, and released genetically engineered insects to devour tender shoots.

The pitched battle decimated civilians on both sides, but eventually—though infested and rootless—the trees overwhelmed their opposition. Mankind was forced to send its battered representatives to a sacred grove in the middle of the world's oldest forest and beg for a treaty.

Negotiations went slowly since the trees insisted on communicating through the pitches of the wind in their leaves, which astute linguists played back at 1,000 times normal speed in order to render them comprehensible to human ears. It took a day for a sentence, a week for a paragraph, a month for an entire stipulation.

After ten years, a truce was completed. To demonstrate its significance, it was inked in blood drawn from human victims and printed on the pulped and flattened corpses of trees. The trees agreed to cease their increasing assaults and return forevermore to their previous quiescent vegetable state, in exchange for a single concession: mankind would henceforth sacrifice its genetic heritage and merge with animals to create a new, benevolent sentience with which to populate the globe.

After the final signatures and root imprints were applied to the treaty, the last thing the trees were heard to say before their leaves returned to being mere producers of chlorophyll was this: *At least it should keep them busy for a millennium or two, fighting among themselves.*

* * *

Part Two—The Animals Who Lived as Men

Mankind, as history had known it, was no more. The new hybrids wore bodies constructed like those of mythological beasts, a blend of human and animal features. They scattered into the world's forests, deserts, jungles, and oceans, where they competed with unmixed animals for food and territory.

If some ancient legends were to be believed, men were only returning to their ancient roots as dolphin and lizard, raven and grizzly bear. Other traditions would have been appalled that man had cast himself down from his place at the apex of the chain of being and been consigned to the lesser links below.

Intellectuals became the whale men, who kept their faces, but lost their bodies for the streamlined shape of cetaceans. Their sentience blended with the intelligence already inhabiting those massive, blubbery forms. They indulged in abstract philosophy as they swam through the ocean depths in a silence created by the first absence of shipping lines in five hundred thousand years.

Pilots and acrobats became glider men, acquiring huge eyes, wing flaps, and nocturnal habits which served them well as they arrowed from tree to tree in forests that echoed with their eerie sonar calls. Eight-armed crab men spent their days skittering up and down beaches dancing for the gulls; spotted jaguar men skulked through forests; cold-blooded turtle men inched through years; flattened stingray men lurked on river bottoms, awaiting unwary travelers.

For the first twenty thousand years, mankind peacefully

coexisted in all its forms. After that, the buried genetic contribution of the human mind bubbled to the surface.

"The treaty is an outgrown shell to be discarded," young crab men gestured defiantly with their third and sixth arms. Crab matrons clacked their claws in outrage, but who could control the youth?

The most extreme of the crab men formed a rebel sect called the Weeders. They wove strands of kelp around their eyestalks and ritually cut their seventh arms, searing the wounds with a mixture of brine and gull guano. At first, they expended their rage on symbolic targets: dumb unblended seabirds, or rocks shaped like dolphin men. And then a juvenile Weeder called Long Stalks found an injured seal man bleeding on the beach and dragged him home in time for the evening convocation. The Weeders tore him to pieces, rubbing themselves with his blubber and parading in his fur. The meat they left to rot.

When they discovered the decaying corpse, the crab matrons went to the seal men with offerings and apologies, but the seal men refused to hear diplomacy. They clipped off the delegation's claws and sent the mutilated ambassadors home with a terse condemnation: "You didn't even have the courtesy to eat him."

Seal and crab men hunted each other to extinction in less than a decade. The last crab man sidled four hundred miles inland to a camp of parrot men before expiring with a curse on his lips.

Soon it was hyena man versus eagle man and frog man versus capybara man, then tiger and spider and cockatiel men against snake and giraffe and ostrich men. Amidst the hectic formation and betrayals of alliances that seethed on the battlefield, only one order created a stable federation.

These were the insect men, greatest of all the species of men in their variety and achievements.

Their infantry were the mosquito men, fearsome female warriors with the muscular bodies of amazons topped by tiny, blood-sucking heads. They marched wherever battle raged, drinking the blood of fallen soldiers. They were sliced and swatted, crushed and grasped in giant crocodilian jaws, but still the indomitable parasites survived to carry samples of their victim's blood back to their superiors, the butterfly men.

Oh, the tragedy of the butterfly men, wisest of the insect men, whose useless jewel-colored wings draped from their slender shoulders like robes. These were the descendents of the geneticists who engineered the destruction of mankind, innocent victims of their ancestors' self-flagellation. Forced to subsist on honey and chained to a lifespan of less than a week, these shrewd but ephemeral leaders did not even enjoy the consolation of flight. Instead they lingered in forest glades looking pale and melancholy. Liable to terrible moods, they made love in the underbrush one moment and shredded each other's wings the next.

Yet the geneticists' legacy was not entirely bad, for they had left their descendents the gift of instinct: inscribed into the rapid pathways of their ephemeral brains lay an intricate understanding of DNA and genetic manipulation. Using this knowledge, the butterflies divined their enemy's secret anatomical weaknesses from the blood samples which the mosquito men brought to them. Generations of butterfly men scrutinized each vial in order to create fatal viruses which would massacre their enemy's ranks.

Only when the last disease had been designed did the butterfly men let loose the fruits of their labor.

Simultaneously, a hundred deadly plagues seized their victims, sweeping across the earth in a single night. By morning, only the insect men remained.

High on an isolated cliff in a desert that had once been the Amazon, a cluster of hardy Joshua trees broke their ancient silence to speak once more. Wind rushed through the prickly tufts of their leaves, rustling out a single sentence: *That didn't take long, did it?*

Part Three—The Reign of Insects

Though the butterfly men's cunning won the war, their flighty emotions and brief life spans made them unsuitable for leading a world, and so it was that the cockroach men became the rulers of the earth. Tough enough to survive dismemberment because their brain processes were spread throughout their becarapaced bodies, and possessed of the keen and supernatural senses of scavengers who had once lived among creatures many hundreds of times their own size, the cockroaches had the desire and capacity to enact a reign of fascism on the other insect men the like of which had never been seen before.

Ant men and bee men filled the roles of farmers and drudges. Atlas and rhinoceros beetle men provided brute force. Flea and mite men accomplished those tasks requiring agility.

Mosquito men served as the secret police. The cockroach men sent them to swarm on enemies of the state and drain them dry—and there was never a lack of traitors to keep them fed.

Alas, the plight of the butterfly men was only to

become worse, for the cockroach men were loathe to risk the same end which had befallen their enemies. To ensure their safety from the butterfly's dangerous knowledge, they imprisoned the butterfly men in a dark chain of underground caves where they lived their brief, miserable lives out of the sun's reach. Within a season and twelve generations, all conscious knowledge of how to create viruses from blood was gone, but the butterfly men's unhappy descendents remain incarcerated in their underground cells today.

Above ground, bees and ants marched to the cockroach's well-timed rhythm, carrying crops from outlying farms into the hills of the city. Caravans of traveling gypsy moth men departed each hour on the hour, and the cockroach men began great civil works projects to erect bridges and statues and roads and memorials and temples. Larvae were taken away from their hatchers and forced to work at backbreaking labor past adulthood; dragonfly men journalists reported only that news which drifted on the prevailing winds of fascism; hives were routinely broken up to redistribute the working population. While the other insect men lived poor and wintry lives subsisting on meager grain, the cockroach men gorged on honey, orange peels and moldy bread. Those who dissented disappeared, only to be found as blood-drained corpses swinging from sturdy branches.

Yet all this might have endured, were it not for the deadliest sin of the cockroach men. Ancestrally predisposed to look favorably upon debris, the cockroach men allowed their wastes to build up in giant landfills. Junkyards choked out the fields; garbage seeped into the ground water; rotting trash provided breeding grounds for the nastiest, most virulent epidemics and hemorrhagic fevers. When the first wave of ant men died of a plague that turned their exoskeletons scarlet, at first the cockroach men suspected their old accomplices the butterfly men, but when they went to interrogate them, no one could remember where that unhappy species had been stashed.

The trees cried out against what was happening to them. New bacteria chewed through leaves and blocked out photosynthesis; roots withered in poisoned soil. Things would only get worse, they knew—oh, how they would suffer. Across the globe it would be the same for all things natural: seas would rumble, ecosystems would shatter; even the iron-breathing Archeans in the deepest volcanic vents would perish if the cockroach men were allowed to continue on their path. *This will hurt you too, earth,* the trees wailed, not in the language of wind-in-leaves which they had used to communicate with the humans, but in the language of roots-in-ground and life-in-soil.

And the earth heard their plight. It shivered, cracking the super-continent down the middle like a slice of lightning splitting the sky. *I have seen enough of mankind's ability to make trouble,* it rumbled to itself in the language of magma-under-crust, and it initiated the seventh apocalypse, the Apocalypse of Darkness.

The Apocalypse of Darkness was the most terrible yet suffered by mankind. Untold agony wiped out almost the entire population of the globe.

Three cricket men survived. They woke quaking into the dawn, antennae shivering down their backs. They were two females and a male, and they might have carried their line into future generations, but the three of them regarded each other with dark, compound eyes that reflected the same understanding.

"We must never bear children," said the oldest and wisest. "Or someday we might tell them what we have experienced, and we must never damn another soul to see what we have seen, even by picturing it in their minds."

The others agreed, and the three of them leapt off the tallest cliff they could find, dying in silence. Though the details of the Apocalypse of Darkness are known, it would be disrespectful to the cricket men's sacrifice to record them.

Interlude—Whisperings from Branch to Branch

So, little rootlings, little seedlings, little starting-to-grows, that is why the earth is quiet now. Feel the snails trail across your bark. Listen to the birds trilling in your branches and the insects nibbling your leaves. Hear the snap of monkeys brachiating from branch to branch. With mankind gone, we are free to enjoy these things. Are they not good?

Ah, but by now you've guessed, the time of man is not entirely behind us. Why else would we whisper this tale on a fine spring morning, with winter's frosts sweetly melted?

Before the Apocalypse of Darkness, we did not tell each other stories. Through necessity, we have learned the skill. Next year, you will help us tell the starting-to-grows about The Great Cathedral Mother who stood in the center of the world until her children sprouted up in a ring around her and sucked up all the sunlight. Her trunk remains where she once grew, swollen with dead leaves and congealing sap and blind grubs. Someday, lightning will strike all the way through the earth, piercing her in two, and each half will grow into a tall, straight pine with a tip like a spear: one going up, one going down. And when this happens, everything we think we know about the world will change.

The year after that, we will tell the great love story of The Garlanded Tree and the hive of bees who fertilized her.

But this is our most important tale. Like winter, man will return in his season. By the time he does, little rootling, you may have a great solid trunk like your mother. Or perhaps you will have grown and perished, and it will be your children standing. Or your children's children. Whoever grows when mankind returns must remember how to drop their leaves and huddle naked in the snow.

And also, when man comes back, we wish to return to him his history so that he may hold and regard it like a spring bloom budding on a new-leafed branch, new and yet also old, a gift not unlike the one given last spring. Who knows? Maybe this will be the time mankind can learn from stories.

Part Four—Hands Yearning Upward Through the Surface of the Earth

Stretch your roots into the ground, little seedlings. Listen. Can you hear life rustling under the soil?

Who else, but the butterfly men? The Apocalypse of Darkness did not faze them. Having become accustomed to their miserable state, they could no longer be depressed by the black. They crept anxiously through their underground dwellings, their bright wings beautiful and unseen, and whispered to each other, "Do you feel that? What's happening?"

When the Apocalypse was over, without knowing the reason for it, the butterfly men wept together for twenty-four full hours in cosmic mourning for the human race of which they were now the sole representatives. But since their quixotic moods were often given to fits of communal sorrow, they failed to understand the uniqueness of the occasion.

After that, it was as though a pall had lifted from the butterfly men. They no longer had surface cousins to envy, so they went about making their lives in the dark. Their society flourished. Their stymied flight sense muddled their sense of direction, so they built joyously everywhere, not knowing up from down or left from right. They laughed and fought and made love in the mud and created an entire caste system based on the texture of the useless flight powder that dusted their wings.

Sometimes an unusual prophet among them dreamed of the surface and spoke of things called light and sun, and usually she was buried alive—but occasionally she wasn't, and then a new religion started and some of the butterflies marched off through the dark to pursue their cult in a different set of caves.

In the past millennia, these cults have gained power. Everyone has lost a sister or a cousin or a parent to their undeniable allure. Whispers among the fine-powdered aristocracy indicate that the cults have even gained sympathy among the inbred monarchy in their velvet-draped cocoons. Soon perhaps, every butterfly will believe.

The cults employ a diverse array of dogmas, rituals, taboos, gods and mythologies, but they all share two common traits. All tell of an eighth apocalypse when the earth will open up into a chasm so terrifying that it will unlock a new sensation—a sixth sense—to accompany hearing, smell, touch, taste and desire. And all require their devotees to spend one day of their week-long lives meditating to discern which direction is up, and then to raise their arms toward it, and start digging.

TIGHT LITTLE STITCHES IN A
DEAD MAN'S BACK

JOE R. LANSDALE

From the Journal of Paul Marder

(Boom!)

That's a little scientist joke, and the proper way to begin this. As for the purpose of my notebook, I'm uncertain. Perhaps to organize my thoughts and not to go insane.

No. Probably so I can read it and feel as if I'm being spoken to. Maybe neither of those reasons. It doesn't matter. I just want to do it, and that is enough.

What's new?

Well, Mr. Journal, after all these years I've taken up martial arts again—or at least the forms and calisthenics of Tae Kwon Do. There is no one to spar with here in the lighthouse, so the forms have to do.

There is Mary, of course, but she keeps all her sparring verbal. And as of late, there is not even that. I long for her to call me a sonofabitch. Anything. Her hatred of me has cured to 100% perfection and she no longer finds it necessary to speak. The tight lines around her eyes and mouth, the emotional heat that radiates from her body like a dreadful cold sore looking for a place to lie down is voice enough for her. She lives only for the moment when she (the cold sore) can attach herself to me with her needles, ink and thread. She lives only for the design on my back.

That's all I live for as well. Mary adds to it nightly and I enjoy the pain. The tattoo is of a great blue mushroom cloud, and in the cloud, etched ghost-like, is the face of our daughter, Rae. Her lips are drawn tight, eyes are closed and there are stitches deeply pulled to simulate the lashes. When I move fast and hard they rip slightly and Rae cries bloody tears.

That's one reason for the martial arts. The hard practice of them helps me to tear the stitches so my daughter can cry. Tears are the only thing I can give her.

Each night I bare my back eagerly to Mary and her needles. She pokes deep and I moan in pain as she moans in ecstasy and hatred. She adds more color to the design, works with brutal precision to bring Rae's face out in sharper relief. After ten minutes she tires and will work no more. She puts the tools away and I go to the full-length mirror on the wall. The lantern on the shelf flickers like a jack-o'-lantern in a high wind, but there is enough light for me to look over my shoulder and examine the tattoo. And it is beautiful. Better each night as Rae's face becomes more and more defined.

Rae.

Rae. God, can you forgive me, sweetheart?

But the pain of the needles, wonderful and cleansing as they are, is not enough. So I go sliding, kicking and punching along the walkway around the lighthouse, feeling Rae's red tears running down my spine, gathering in the waistband of my much-stained canvas pants.

Winded, unable to punch and kick anymore, I walk over to the railing and call down into the dark, "Hungry?"

In response to my voice a chorus of moans rises up to greet me.

Later, I lie on my pallet, hands behind my head, examine the ceiling and try to think of something worthy to write in you, Mr. Journal. So seldom is there anything. Nothing seems truly worthwhile.

Bored of this, I roll on my side and look at the great light that once shone out to the ships, but is now forever snuffed. Then I turn the other direction and look at my wife sleeping on her bunk, her naked ass turned toward me. I try to remember what it was like to make love to her, but it is difficult. I only remember that I miss it. For a long moment I stare at my wife's ass as if it is a mean mouth about to open and reveal teeth. Then I roll on my back again, stare at the ceiling, and continue this routine until daybreak.

Mornings I greet the flowers, their bright red and yellow blooms bursting from the heads of long-dead bodies that will not rot. The flowers open wide to reveal their little black brains and their feathery feelers, and they lift their blooms upward and moan. I get a wild pleasure out of this. For one crazed moment I feel like a rock singer appearing before his starry-eyed audience.

When I tire of the game I get the binoculars, Mr. Journal, and examine the eastern plains with them, as if I expect a city to materialize there. The most interesting thing I have seen on those plains is a herd of large lizards thundering north. For a moment, I considered calling Mary to see them, but I didn't. The sound of my voice, the sight of my face, upsets her. She loves only the tattoo and is interested in nothing more.

When I finish looking at the plains, I walk to the other side. To the west, where the ocean was, there is now nothing but miles and miles of cracked, black sea bottom. Its only resemblance to a great body of water are the occasional dust storms that blow out of the west like dark tidal waves and wash the windows black at midday. And the creatures. Mostly mutated whales. Monstrously large, sluggish things. Abundant now where once they were near extinction. (Perhaps the whales should form some sort of Greenpeace organization for humans now. What do you think, Mr. Journal? No need to answer. Just another one of those little scientist jokes.)

These whales crawl across the sea bottom near the lighthouse from time to time, and if the mood strikes them, they rise on their tails and push their heads near the tower and examine it. I keep expecting one to flop down on us, crushing us like bugs. But no such luck. For some unknown reason the whales never leave the cracked sea bed to venture onto what we formerly called the shore. It's as if they live in invisible water and are bound by it. A racial memory perhaps. Or maybe there's something in that cracked black soil they need. I don't know.

Besides the whales I suppose I should mention I saw a shark once. It was slithering along at a great distance and the tip of its fin was winking in the sunlight. I've also seen some strange, legged fish and some things I could not put a name to. I'll just call them whale food since I saw one of the whales dragging his bottom jaw along the ground one day, scooping up the creatures as they tried to beat a hasty retreat.

Exciting, huh? Well, that's how I spend my day, Mr.

Journal. Roaming about the tower with my glasses, coming in to write in you, waiting anxiously for Mary to take hold of that kit and give me the signal. The mere thought of it excites me to erection. I suppose you could call that our sex act together.

And what was I doing the day they dropped The Big One?

Glad you asked that, Mr. Journal, really I am.

I was doing the usual. Up at six, did the shit, shower and shave routine. Had breakfast. Got dressed. Tied my tie. I remember doing the latter, and not very well, in front of the bedroom mirror, and noticing that I had shaved poorly. A hunk of dark beard decorated my chin like a bruise.

Rushing to the bathroom to remedy that, I opened the door as Rae, naked as the day of her birth, was stepping from the tub.

Surprised, she turned to look at me. An arm went over her breasts, and a hand, like a dove settling into a fiery bush, covered her pubic area.

Embarrassed, I closed the door with an "excuse me" and went about my business—unshaved. It was an innocent thing. An accident. Nothing sexual. But when I think of her now, more often than not, that is the first image that comes to mind. I guess it was the moment I realized my baby had grown into a beautiful woman.

That was also the day she went off to her first day of college and got to see, ever so briefly, the end of the world.

And it was the day the triangle—Mary, Rae and myself—shattered.

If my first memory of Rae alone is that day, naked in the bathroom, my foremost memory of us as a family is when

Rae was six. We used to go to the park and she would ride the merry-go-round, swing, teeter-totter, and finally my back. ("I want to piggy, Daddy.") We would gallop about until my legs were rubber, then we would stop at the bench where Mary sat waiting. I would turn my back to the bench so Mary could take Rae down, but always before she did, she would reach around from behind, caressing Rae, pushing her tight against my back, and Mary's hands would touch my chest.

God, but if I could describe those hands. She still has hands like that, after all these years. I feel them fluttering against my back when she works. They are long and sleek and artistic. Naturally soft, like the belly of a baby rabbit. And when she held Rae and me that way, I felt that no matter what happened in the world, we three could stand against it and conquer.

But now the triangle is broken and the geometry gone away.

So the day Rae went off to college and was fucked into oblivion by the dark, pelvic thrust of the bomb, Mary drove me to work. Me, Paul Marder, big shot with The Crew. One of the finest, brightest young minds in the industry. Always teaching, inventing and improving on our nuclear threat, because, as we'd often joke, "We cared enough to send only the very best."

When we arrived at the guard booth, I had out my pass, but there was no one to take it. Beyond the chain-link gate there was a wild melee of people running, screaming, falling down.

I got out of the car and ran to the gate. I called out to a man I knew as he ran by. When he turned his eyes were wild and his lips were flecked with foam. "The missiles are flying," he said, then he was gone, running madly.

I jumped in the car, pushed Mary aside and stomped the gas. The Buick leaped into the fence, knocking it asunder. The car spun, slammed into the edge of a building and went dead. I grabbed Mary's hand, pulled her from the car and we ran toward the great elevators.

We made one just in time. There were others running for it as the door closed, and the elevator went down. I still remember the echo of their fists on the metal just as it began to drop. It was like the rapid heartbeat of something dying.

And so the elevator took us to the world of Down Under and we locked it off. There we were in a five-mile layered city designed not only as a massive office and laboratory, but as an impenetrable shelter. It was our special reward for creating the poisons of war. There was food, water, medical supplies, films, books, you name it. Enough to last two thousand people for a hundred years. Of the two thousand it was designed for, perhaps eleven hundred made it. The others didn't run fast enough from the parking lot or the other buildings, or they were late for work, or maybe they had called in sick.

Perhaps they were the lucky ones. They might have died in their sleep. Or while they were having a morning quickie with the spouse. Or perhaps as they lingered over that last cup of coffee.

Because you see, Mr. Journal, Down Under was no paradise. Before long suicides were epidemic. I considered it myself from time to time. People slashed their throats, drank acid, took pills. It was not unusual to come out of your cubicle in the morning and find people dangling from pipes and rafters like ripe fruit.

There were also the murders. Most of them performed by a crazed group who lived in the deeper recesses of the unit and called themselves the Shit Faces. From time to time they smeared dung on themselves and ran amok, clubbing men, women, and children born Down Under, to death. It was rumored they ate human flesh.

We had a police force of sorts, but it didn't do much. It didn't have much sense of authority. Worse, we all viewed ourselves as deserving victims. Except for Mary, we had all helped to blow up the world.

Mary came to hate me. She came to the conclusion I had killed Rae. It was a realization that grew in her like a drip growing and growing until it became a gushing flood of hate. She seldom talked to me. She tacked up a picture of Rae and looked at it most of the time.

Topside she had been an artist, and she took that up again. She rigged a kit of tools and inks and became a tattooist. Everyone came to her for a mark. And though each was different, they all seemed to indicate one thing: I fucked up. I blew up the world. Brand me.

Day in and day out she did her tattoos, having less and less to do with me, pushing herself more and more into this work until she was as skilled with skin and needles as she had been Topside with brush and canvas. And one night, as we lay on our separate pallets, feigning sleep, she said to me, "I just want you to know how much I hate you."

"I know," I said.

"You killed Rae."

"I know."

"You say you killed her, you bastard. Say it."

"I killed her," I said, and meant it.

Next day I asked for my tattoo. I told her of this dream that came to me nightly. There would be darkness, and out of this darkness would come a swirl of glowing clouds, and the clouds would melt into a mushroom shape, and out of that—torpedo-shaped, nose pointing skyward, striding on ridiculous cartoon legs—would step The Bomb.

There was a face painted on The Bomb, and it was my face. And suddenly the dream's point of view would change, and I would be looking out of the eyes of that painted face. Before me was my daughter. Naked. Lying on the ground. Her legs wide apart. Her sex glazed like a wet canyon.

And I/The Bomb would dive into her, pulling those silly feet after me, and she would scream. I could hear it echo as I plunged through her belly, finally driving myself out of the top of her head, then blowing to terminal orgasm. And the dream would end where it began. A mushroom cloud. Darkness.

When I told Mary the dream and asked her to interpret it in her art, she said, "Bare your back," and that's how the design began. An inch of work at a time—a painful inch. She made sure of that.

Never once did I complain. She'd send the needles home as hard and deep as she could, and though I might moan or cry out, I never asked her to stop. I could feel those fine hands touching my back and I loved it. The needles. The hands. The needles. The hands.

And if that was so much fun, you ask, why did I come Topside? You ask such probing questions, Mr. Journal. Really you do, and I'm glad you asked that. My telling will be like a laxative, I hope. Maybe if I just let the shit flow I'll wake up tomorrow and feel a lot better about myself.

Sure. And it will be the dawning of a new Pepsi

generation as well. It will have all been a bad dream. The alarm clock will ring. I'll get up, have my bowl of Rice Krispies and tie my tie.

Okay, Mr. Journal. The answer. Twenty years or so after we went Down Under, a fistful of us decided it couldn't be any worse Topside than it was below. We made plans to go see. Simple as that. Mary and I even talked a little. We both entertained the crazed belief Rae might have survived. She would be thirty-eight. We might have been hiding below like vermin for no reason. It could be a brave new world up there.

I remember thinking these things, Mr. Journal, and half-believing them.

We outfitted two sixty-foot crafts that were used as part of our transportation system Down Under, plugged in the half-remembered codes that opened the elevators, and drove the vehicles inside. The elevator lasers cut through the debris above them and before long we were Topside. The doors opened to sunlight muted by gray-green clouds and a desert-like landscape. Immediately I knew there was no brave new world over the horizon. It had all gone to hell in a fiery handbasket, and all that was left of man's millions of years of development were a few pathetic humans living Down Under like worms, and a few others crawling Topside like the same.

We cruised about a week and finally came to what had once been the Pacific Ocean. Only there wasn't any water now, just that cracked blackness.

We drove along the shore for another week and finally saw life. A whale. Jacobs immediately got the idea to shoot one and taste its meat.

Using a high-powered rifle he killed it, and he and

seven others cut slabs off it, brought the meat back to cook. They invited all of us to eat, but the meat looked greenish and there wasn't much blood and we warned him against it. But Jacobs and the others ate it anyway. As Jacobs said, "It's something to do."

A little later on Jacobs threw up blood and his intestines boiled out of his mouth, and not long after those who had shared the meat had the same thing happen to them. They died crawling on their bellies like gutted dogs. There wasn't a thing we could do for them. We couldn't even bury them. The ground was too hard. We stacked them like cordwood along the shoreline and moved camp down a way, tried to remember how remorse felt.

And that night, while we slept as best we could, the roses came.

Now, let me admit, Mr. Journal, I do not actually know how the roses survived, but I have an idea. And since you've agreed to hear my story—and even if you haven't, you're going to anyway—I'm going to put logic and fantasy together and hope to arrive at the truth.

These roses lived in the ocean bed, underground, and at night they came out. Up until then they had survived as parasites of reptiles and animals, but a new food had arrived from Down Under. Humans. Their creators, actually. Looking at it that way, you might say we were the gods who conceived them, and their partaking of our flesh and blood was but a new version of wine and wafer.

I can imagine the pulsating brains pushing up through the sea bottom on thick stalks, extending feathery feelers and tasting the air out there beneath the light of the moon—

which through those odd clouds gave the impression of a pus-filled boil—and I can imagine them uprooting and dragging their vines across the ground toward the shore where the corpses lay.

Thick vines sprouted little thorny vines, and these moved up the bank and touched the corpses. Then, with a lashing motion, the thorns tore into the flesh, and the vines, like snakes, slithered through the wounds and inside. Secreting a dissolving fluid that turned the innards to the consistency of watery oatmeal, they slurped up the mess, and the vines grew and grew at amazing speed, moved and coiled throughout the bodies, replacing nerves and shaping into the symmetry of the muscles they had devoured, and lastly they pushed up through the necks, into the skulls, ate tongues and eyeballs and sucked up the mouse-gray brains like soggy gruel. With an explosion of skull shrapnel, the roses bloomed, their tooth-hard petals expanding into beautiful red and yellow flowers, hunks of human heads dangling from them like shattered watermelon rinds.

In the center of these blooms a fresh, black brain pulsed and feathery feelers once again tasted air for food and breeding grounds. Energy waves from the floral brains shot through the miles and miles of vines that were knotted inside the bodies, and as they had replaced nerves, muscles and vital organs, they made the bodies stand. Then those corpses turned their flowered heads toward the tents where we slept, and the blooming corpses (another little scientist joke there if you're into English idiom, Mr. Journal) walked, eager to add the rest of us to their animated bouquet.

I saw my first rose-head while I was taking a leak.

I had left the tent and gone down by the shoreline to relieve myself when I caught sight of it out of the corner of my eye. Because of the bloom I first thought it was Susan Dyers. She wore a thick, woolly Afro that surrounded her head like a lion's mane, and the shape of the thing struck me as her silhouette. But when I zipped and turned, it wasn't an Afro. It was a flower blooming out of Jacobs. I recognized him by his clothes and the hunk of his face that hung off one of the petals like a worn-out hat on a peg.

In the center of the blood-red flower was a pulsating sack, and all around it little wormy things squirmed. Directly below the brain was a thin proboscis. It extended toward me like an erect penis. At its tip, just inside the opening, were a number of large thorns.

A sound like a moan came out of that proboscis, and I stumbled back. Jacobs' body quivered briefly, as if he had been besieged by a sudden chill, and ripping through his flesh and clothes, from neck to foot, was a mass of thorny, wagging vines that shot out to five feet in length.

With an almost invisible motion, they waved from west to east, slashed my clothes, tore my hide, knocked my feet out from beneath me. It was like being hit by a cat-o'-nine-tails.

Dazed, I rolled onto my hands and knees, bear-walked away from it. The vines whipped against my back and butt, cut deep.

Every time I got to my feet, they tripped me. The thorns not only cut, they burned like hot ice picks. I finally twisted away from a net of vines, slammed through one last shoot, and made a break for it.

Without realizing it, I was running back to the tent. My body felt as if I had been lying on a bed of nails and razor blades. My forearm hurt something terrible where I had used it to lash the thorns away from me. I glanced down at it as I ran. It was covered in blood. A strand of vine about two feet in length was coiled around it like a garter snake. A thorn had torn a deep wound in my arm, and the vine was sliding an end into the wound.

Screaming, I held my forearm in front of me like I had just discovered it. The flesh, where the vine had entered, rippled and made a bulge that looked like a junkie's favorite vein. The pain was nauseating. I snatched at the vine, ripped it free. The thorns turned against me like fishhooks.

The pain was so much I fell to my knees, but I had the vine out of me. It squirmed in my hand, and I felt a thorn gouge my palm. I threw the vine into the dark. Then I was up and running for the tent again.

The roses must have been at work for quite some time before I saw Jacobs, because when I broke back into camp yelling, I saw Susan, Ralph, Casey and some others, and already their heads were blooming, skulls cracking away like broken model kits.

Jane Calloway was facing a rose-possessed corpse, and the dead body had its hands on her shoulders, and the vines were jetting out of the corpse, weaving around her like a web, tearing, sliding inside her, breaking off. The proboscis poked into her mouth and extended down her throat, forced her head back. The scream she started came out a gurgle.

I tried to help her, but when I got close, the vines whipped at me and I had to jump back. I looked for something to grab, to hit the damn thing with, but there was nothing. When next I looked at Jane, vines were stabbing out of her eyes, and her tongue, now nothing more than lava-thick blood, was dripping out of her mouth onto her breasts, which, like the rest of her body, were riddled with stabbing vines.

I ran away then. There was nothing I could do for Jane. I saw others embraced by corpse hands and tangles of vines, but now my only thought was Mary. Our tent was to the rear of the campsite, and I ran there as fast as I could.

She was lumbering out of our tent when I arrived. The sound of screams had awakened her. When she saw me running she froze. By the time I got to her, two vine-riddled corpses were coming up on the tent from the left side. Grabbing her hand I half-pulled, half-dragged her away from there. I got to one of the vehicles and pushed her inside.

I locked the doors just as Jacobs, Susan, Jane, and others appeared at the windshield, leaning over the rocket-nose hood, the feelers around the brain sacks vibrating like streamers in a high wind. Hands slid greasily down the windshield. Vines flopped and scratched and cracked against it like thin bicycle chains.

I got the vehicle started, stomped the accelerator, and the rose-heads went flying. One of them, Jacobs, bounced over the hood and splattered into a spray of flesh, ichor and petals.

I had never driven the vehicle, so my maneuvering was rusty. But it didn't matter. There wasn't exactly a traffic rush to worry about.

After an hour or so, I turned to look at Mary. She was staring at me, her eyes like the twin barrels of a double-barreled shotgun. They seemed to say, "More of your doing," and in a way she was right. I drove on.

Daybreak we came to the lighthouse. I don't know how it survived. One of those quirks. Even the glass was unbroken. It looked like a great stone finger shooting us the bird.

The vehicle's tank was near empty, so I assumed here was as good a place to stop as any. At least there was shelter, something we could fortify. Going on until the vehicle was empty of fuel didn't make much sense. There wouldn't be any more fill-ups, and there might not be any more shelter like this.

Mary and I (in our usual silence) unloaded the supplies from the vehicle and put them in the lighthouse. There was enough food, water, chemicals for the chemical toilet, odds and ends, extra clothes, to last us a year. There were also some guns. A Colt .45 revolver, two twelve-gauge shotguns and a .38, and enough shells to fight a small war.

When everything was unloaded, I found some old furniture downstairs and, using tools from the vehicle, tried to barricade the bottom door and the one at the top of the stairs. When I finished, I thought of a line from a story I had once read, a line that always disturbed me. It went something like, "Now we're shut in for the night."

Days. Nights. All the same. Shut in with one another, our memories and the fine tattoo.

A few days later I spotted the roses. It was as if they had smelled us out. And maybe they had. From a distance, through the binoculars, they reminded me of old women in bright sun hats.

It took them the rest of the day to reach the lighthouse, and they immediately surrounded it, and whenever I appeared at the railing they would lift their heads and moan.

And that, Mr. Journal, brings us up to now.

I thought I had written myself out, Mr. Journal. Told the only part of my life story I would ever tell, but now I'm back. You can't keep a good world-destroyer down.

I saw my daughter last night and she's been dead for years. But I saw her, I did, naked, smiling at me, calling to ride piggyback.

Here's what happened.

It was cold last night. Must be getting along winter. I had rolled off my pallet onto the cold floor. Maybe that's what brought me awake. The cold. Or maybe it was just gut instinct.

It had been a particularly wonderful night with the tattoo. The face had been made so clear it seemed to stand out from my back. It had finally become more defined than the mushroom cloud. The needles went in hard and deep, but I've had them in me so much now I barely feel the pain. After looking in the mirror at the beauty of the design, I went to bed happy, or as happy as I can get.

During the night the eyes ripped open. The stitches came out and I didn't know it until I tried to rise from the cold stone floor and my back puckered against it where the blood had dried.

I pulled myself free and got up. It was dark, but we had a good moonspill that night and I went to the mirror to look. It was bright enough that I could see Rae's reflection clearly, the color of her face, the color of the cloud. The stitches had fallen away and now the wounds were spread wide, and inside the wounds were eyes. Oh God, Rae's blue eyes. Her mouth smiled at me and her teeth were very white.

Oh, I hear you, Mr. Journal. I hear what you're saying. And I thought of that. My first impression was that I was about six bricks shy a load, gone around the old bend. But I know better now. You see, I lit a candle and held it over my shoulder, and with the candle and the moonlight, I could see even more clearly. It was Rae all right, not just a tattoo.

I looked over at my wife on the bunk, her back to me, as always. She had not moved.

I turned back to the reflection. I could hardly see the outline of myself, just Rae's face smiling out of that cloud.

"Rae," I whispered, "is that you?"

"Come on, Daddy," said the mouth in the mirror, "that's a stupid question. Of course it's me."

"But... You're... you're..."

"Dead?"

"Yes... Did... did it hurt much?"

She cackled so loudly the mirror shook. I could feel the hairs on my neck rising. I thought for sure Mary would wake up, but she slept on.

"It was instantaneous, Daddy, and even then, it was the greatest pain imaginable. Let me show you how it hurt."

The candle blew out and I dropped it. I didn't need it anyway. The mirror grew bright and Rae's smile went from ear to ear—literally— and the flesh on her bones seemed like crepe paper before a powerful fan, and that fan blew the hair off her head, the skin off her skull and melted those beautiful blue eyes and those shiny white teeth of hers to a putrescent goo the color and consistency of fresh bird shit. Then there was only the skull, and it heaved in half and flew backwards into the dark world of the mirror and there was no reflection now, only the hurtling fragments of a life that once was and was now nothing more than swirling cosmic dust.

I closed my eyes and looked away.

"Daddy?"

I opened them, looked over my shoulder into the mirror. There was Rae again, smiling out of my back.

"Darling," I said, "I'm so sorry."

"So are we," she said, and there were faces floating past her in the mirror. Teenagers, children, men and women, babies, little embryos swirling around her head like planets around the sun. I closed my eyes again, but I could not keep them closed. When I opened them the multitudes of swirling dead, and those who had never had a chance to live, were gone. Only Rae was there.

"Come close to the mirror, Daddy."

I backed up to it. I backed until the hot wounds that were Rae's eyes touched the cold glass and the wounds became hotter and hotter and Rae called out, "Ride me piggy, Daddy," and then I felt her weight on my back, not the weight of a six-year-old child or a teenage girl, but a great weight, like the world was on my shoulders and bearing down.

Leaping away from the mirror I went hopping and whooping about the room, same as I used to in the park. Around and around I went, and as I did, I glanced in the mirror. Astride me was Rae, lithe and naked, her red hair fanning around her as I spun. And when I whirled by the mirror again, I saw that she was six years old. Another spin and there was a skeleton with red hair, one hand held high, the jaws open and yelling, "Ride 'em, cowboy."

"How?" I managed, still bucking and leaping, giving Rae the ride of her life. She bent to my ear and I could feel her warm breath.

"You want to know how I'm here, Daddy-dear? I'm here because you created me. Once you laid between Mother's legs and thrust me into existence, the two of you, with all the love there was in you. This time you thrust me into existence with your guilt and Mother's hate. Her thrusting needles, your arching back. And now I've come back for one last ride, Daddy-o. Ride, you bastard, ride."

All the while I had been spinning, and now as I glimpsed the mirror I saw wall to wall faces, weaving in, weaving out, like smiling stars, and all those smiles opened wide and words came out in chorus, "Where were you when they dropped The Big One?"

Each time I spun and saw the mirror again, it was a new scene. Great flaming winds scorching across the world, babies turning to fleshy Jell-O, heaps of charred bones, brains boiling out of the heads of men and women like backed-up toilets overflowing; The Almighty, Glory Hallelujah, Ours Is Bigger Than Yours Bomb hurtling forward; the mirror going mushroom white, then clear, and me, spinning, Rae pressed tight against my back, melting like butter on a griddle, evaporating into the eye wounds on my back, and finally me alone, collapsing to the floor beneath the weight of the world.

Mary never awoke.

The vines outsmarted me.

A single strand found a crack downstairs somewhere and wound up the steps and slipped beneath the door that led into the tower. Mary's bunk was not far from the door, and in the night, while I slept, and later while I spun in front of the mirror and lay on the floor before it, it made its way to Mary's bunk, up between her legs, and entered her sex effortlessly.

I suppose I should give the vine credit for doing what I had not been able to do in years, Mr. Journal, and that's enter Mary. Oh God, that's a funny one, Mr. Journal. Real funny. Another little scientist joke. Let's make that a mad scientist joke, what say? Who but a madman would play with the lives of human beings by constantly trying to build the bigger and better boom machine?

So what of Rae, you ask?

I'll tell you. She is inside me. My back feels the weight. She twists in my guts like a corkscrew. I went to the mirror a moment ago, and the tattoo no longer looks like it did. The eyes have turned to crusty sores and the entire face looks like a scab. It's as if the bile that made up my soul, the unthinking nearsightedness, the guilt that I am, has festered from inside and spoiled the picture with pustule bumps, knots and scabs.

To put it in layman's terms, Mr. Journal, my back is infected. Infected with what I am. A blind, senseless fool.

The wife?

Ah, the wife. God, how I loved that woman. I have not really touched her in years, merely felt those wonderful hands on my back as she jabbed the needles home, but I never stopped loving her. It was not a love that glowed anymore, but it was there, though hers for me was long gone and wasted.

This morning when I got up from the floor, the weight of Rae and the world on my back, I saw the vine coming up from beneath the door and stretching over to her. I yelled her name. She did not move. I ran to her and saw it was too late. Before I could put a hand on her, I saw her flesh ripple and bump up, like a den of mice were nesting under a quilt. The vines were at work. (Out go the old guts, in go the new vines.)

There was nothing I could do for her.

I made a torch out of a chair leg and old quilt, set fire to it, burned the vine from between her legs, watched it retreat, smoking, under the door. Then I got a board, nailed it along the bottom, hoping it would keep others out for at least a little while. I got one of the twelve-gauges and loaded it. It's on the desk beside me, Mr. Journal, but even I know I'll never use it. It was just something to do, as Jacobs said when he killed and ate the whale. Something to do.

I can hardly write anymore. My back and shoulders hurt so bad. It's the weight of Rae and the world.

I've just come back from the mirror and there is very little left of the tattoo. Some blue and black ink, a touch of red that was Rae's hair. It looks like an abstract painting now. Collapsed design, running colors. It's real swollen. I look like the hunchback of Notre Dame.

What am I going to do, Mr. Journal?

Well, as always, I'm glad you asked that. You see, I've thought this out.

I could throw Mary's body over the railing before it blooms. I could do that. Then I could doctor my back. It might even heal, though I doubt it. Rae wouldn't let that happen, I can tell you now. And I don't blame her. I'm on her side. I'm just a walking dead man and have been for years.

I could put the shotgun under my chin and work the trigger with my toes, or maybe push it with the very pen I'm using to create you, Mr. Journal. Wouldn't that be neat? Blow my brains to the ceiling and sprinkle you with my blood.

But as I said, I loaded the gun because it was something to do. I'd never use it on myself or Mary.

You see, I want Mary. I want her to hold Rae and me one last time like she used to in the park. And she can. There's a way.

I've drawn all the curtains and made curtains out of blankets for those spots where there aren't any. It'll be sunup soon and I don't want that kind of light in here. I'm writing this by candlelight and it gives the entire room a warm glow. I wish I had wine. I want the atmosphere to be just right.

Over on Mary's bunk she's starting to twitch. Her neck is swollen where the vines have congested and are writhing toward their favorite morsel, the brain. Pretty soon the rose will bloom (I hope she's one of the bright yellow ones; yellow was her favorite color and she wore it well) and Mary will come for me.

When she does, I'll stand with my naked back to her. The vines will whip out and cut me before she reaches me, but I can stand it. I'm used to pain. I'll pretend the thorns are Mary's needles. I'll stand that way until she folds her dead arms around me and her body pushes up against the wound she made in my back, the wound that is our daughter Rae. She'll hold me so the vines and the proboscis can do their work. And while she holds me, I'll grab her fine hands and push them against my chest, and it will be we three again, standing against the world, and I'll close my eyes and delight in her soft, soft hands one last time.

For Ardath Mayhar

AFTER THE APOCALYPSE

MAUREEN F. McHUGH

Jane puts out the sleeping bags in the backyard of the empty house by the toolshed. She has a lock and hasp and an old hand drill that they can use to lock the toolshed from the inside, but it's too hot to sleep in there, and there haven't been many people on the road. Better to sleep outside. Franny has been talking a mile a minute. Usually by the end of the day she is tired from walking—they both are—and quiet. But this afternoon she's gotten on the subject of her friend Samantha. She's musing on if Samantha has left town like they did. "They're probably still there, because they had a really nice house in, like, a low-crime area, and Samantha's father has a really good job. When you have money like that, maybe you can totally afford a security system or something. Their house has five bedrooms and the basement isn't a basement, it's a living room, because the house is kind of on a little hill, and although the front of the basement is underground, you can walk right out the back."

Jane says, "That sounds nice."

"You could see a horse farm behind them. People around them were rich, but not like, on-TV rich, exactly."

Jane puts her hands on her hips and looks down the line of backyards.

"Do you think there's anything in there?" Franny asks, meaning the house, a '60s suburban ranch. Franny is thirteen, and empty houses frighten her. But she doesn't like to be left alone, either. What she wants is for Jane to say that they can eat one of the tuna pouches.

"Come on, Franny. We're gonna run out of tuna long before we get to Canada."

"I know," Franny says sullenly.

"You can stay here."

"No, I'll go with you."

God, sometimes Jane would do anything to get five minutes away from Franny. She loves her daughter, really, but Jesus. "Come on, then," Jane says.

There is an old square concrete patio and a sliding glass door. The door is dirty. Jane cups her hand to shade her eyes and looks inside. It's dark and hard to see. No power, of course. Hasn't been power in any of the places they've passed through in more than two months. Air conditioning. And a bed with a mattress and box springs. What Jane wouldn't give for air conditioning and a bed. Clean sheets.

The neighborhood seems like a good one. Unless they find a big group to camp with, Jane gets them off the freeway at the end of the day. There was fighting in the neighborhood, and at the end of the street, several houses are burned out. Then there are lots of houses with windows smashed out. But the fighting petered out. Some of the houses are still lived in. This house had all its windows intact, but the garage door was standing open and the garage was empty except for dead leaves. Electronic garage door. The owners pulled out and left and didn't bother to close the door behind them. Seemed to Jane that the overgrown backyard with its toolshed would be a good place to sleep.

Jane can see her silhouette in the dirty glass, and her hair is a snarled, curly, tangled rat's nest. She runs her fingers through it, and they snag. She'll look for a scarf or something inside. She grabs the handle and yanks up, hard, trying to get the old slider off track. It takes a couple of tries, but she's had a lot of practice in the last few months.

Inside, the house is trashed. The kitchen has been turned upside down, and silverware, utensils, drawers, broken plates, flour, and stuff are everywhere. She picks her way across, a can opener skittering under her foot with a clatter.

Franny gives a little startled shriek.

"Fuck!" Jane says. "Don't do that!" The canned food is long gone.

"I'm sorry," Franny says. "It scared me!"

"We're gonna starve to death if we don't keep scavenging," Jane says.

"I know!" Franny says.

"Do you know how fucking far it is to Canada?"

"I can't help it if it startled me!"

Maybe if she were a better cook, she'd be able to scrape up the flour and make something, but it's all mixed in with dirt and stuff, and every time she's tried to cook something over an open fire it's either been raw or black or, most often, both—blackened on the outside and raw on the inside.

Jane checks all the cupboards anyway. Sometimes

MAUREEN F. MCHUGH

people keep food in different places. Once they found one
of those decorating icing tubes and wrote words on each
other's hands and licked them off.

Franny screams, not a startled shriek but a real scream.

Jane whirls around, and there's a guy in the family room
with a tire iron.

"What are you doing here?" he yells.

Jane grabs a can opener from the floor, one of those
heavy jobbers, and wings it straight at his head. He's too
slow to get out of the way, and it nails him in the forehead.
Jane has winged a lot of things at boyfriends over the years.
It's a skill. She throws a couple more things from the floor,
anything she can find, while the guy is yelling, "Fuck!
Fuck!" and trying to ward off the barrage.

Then she and Franny are out the back door and running.

Fucking squatter! She hates squatters! If it's the
homeowner they tend to make the place more like a
fortress, and you can tell not to try to go in. Squatters try
to keep a low profile.

Franny is in front of her, running like a rabbit, and they
are out the gate and headed up the suburban street. Franny
knows the drill, and at the next corner she turns, but by
then it's clear that no one's following them.

"Okay," Jane pants. "Okay, stop, stop."

Franny stops. She's a skinny adolescent now—she used
to be chubby, but she's lean and tan with all their walking.
She's wearing a pair of falling-apart pink sneakers and a
tank top with oil smudges from when they had to climb
over a truck tipped sideways on an overpass. She's still flat-
chested. Her eyes are big in her face. Jane puts her hands
on her knees and draws a shuddering breath.

"We're okay," she says. It is gathering dusk in this

Missouri town. In a while, streetlights will come on, unless someone has systematically shot them out. Solar power still works. "We'll wait a bit and then go back and get our stuff when it's dark."

"No!" Franny bursts into sobs. "We can't!"

Jane is at her wits' end. Rattled from the squatter. Tired of being the strong one. "We've got to! You want to lose everything we've got? You want to die? Goddamn it, Franny! I can't take this anymore!"

"That guy's there!" Franny sobs out. "We can't go back! We can't!"

"Your cell phone is there," Jane says. A mean dig. The cell phone doesn't work, of course. Even if they still somehow had service, if service actually exists, they haven't been anywhere with electricity to charge it in weeks. But Franny still carries it in the hope that she can get a charge and call her friends. Seventh graders are apparently surgically attached to their phones. Not that she acts even like a seventh grader anymore. The longer they are on the road, the younger Franny acts.

This isn't the first time that they've run into a squatter. Squatters are cowards. The guy doesn't have a gun, and he's not going to go out after dark. Franny has no spine, takes after her asshole of a father. Jane ran away from home and got all the way to Pasadena, California, when she was a year older than Franny. When she was fourteen, she was a decade older than Franny. Lived on the street for six weeks, begging spare change on the same route that the Rose Parade took. It had been scary, but it had been a blast, as well. Taught her to stand on her own two feet, which Franny wasn't going to be able to do when she was twenty. Thirty, at this rate.

"You're hungry, aren't you?" Jane said, merciless. "You want to go looking in these houses for something to eat?" Jane points around them. The houses all have their front doors broken into, open like little mouths.

Franny shakes her head.

"Stop crying. I'm going to go check some of them out. You wait here."

"Mom! Don't leave me!" Franny wails.

Jane is still shaken from the squatter. But they need food. And they need their stuff. There is seven hundred dollars sewn inside the lining of Jane's sleeping bag. And someone has to keep them alive. It's obviously going to be her.

Things didn't exactly all go at once. First there were rolling brownouts and lots of people unemployed. Jane had been making a living working at a place that sold furniture. She started as a salesperson, but she was good at helping people on what colors to buy, what things went together, what fabrics to pick for custom pieces. Eventually they made her a service associate, a person who was kind of like an interior decorator, sort of. She had an eye. She'd grown up in a nice suburb and had seen nice things. She knew what people wanted. Her boss kept telling her a little less eye makeup would be a good idea, but people liked what she suggested and recommended her to their friends even if her boss didn't like her eye makeup.

She was thinking of starting a decorating business, although she was worried that she didn't know about some of the stuff decorators did. On TV they were always tearing down walls and redoing fireplaces. So she put it off. Then there was the big Disney World attack where a kazillion people died because of a dirty bomb, and then the economy really tanked. She knew that business was dead and she was going to get laid off, but before that happened, someone torched the furniture place where she was working. Her boyfriend at the time was a cop, so he still had a job, even though half the city was unemployed. She and Franny were all right compared to a lot of people. She didn't like not having her own money, but she wasn't exactly having to call her mother in Pennsylvania and eat crow and offer to come home.

So she sat on the balcony of their condo and smoked and looked through her old decorating magazines, and Franny watched television in the room behind her. People started showing up on the sidewalks. They had trash bags full of stuff. Sometimes they were alone; sometimes there would be whole families. Sometimes they'd have cars and they'd sleep in them, but gas was getting to almost ten dollars a gallon, when the gas stations could get it. Pete, the boyfriend, told her that the cops didn't even patrol much anymore because of the gas problem. More and more of the people on the sidewalk looked to be walking.

"Where are they coming from?" Franny asked.

"Down south. Houston, El Paso, anywhere within a hundred miles of the border," Pete said. "Border's gone to shit. Mexico doesn't have food, but the drug cartels have lots of guns, and they're coming across to take what they can get. They say it's like a war zone down there."

"Why don't the police take care of them?" Franny asked.

"Well, Francisca," Pete said—he was good with Franny, Jane had to give him that—"sometimes there are just too many of them for the police down there. And they've got kinds of guns that the police aren't allowed to have."

"What about you?" Franny asked.

"It's different up here," Pete said. "That's why we've got refugees here. Because it's safe here."

"They're not *refugees*," Jane said. Refugees were, like, people in Africa. These were just regular people. Guys in T-shirts with the names of rock bands on them. Women sitting in the front seats of Taurus station wagons, doing their hair in the rearview mirrors. Kids asleep in the back seat or running up and down the street shrieking and playing. Just people.

"Well, what do you want to call them?" Pete asked.

Then the power started going out, more and more often. Pete's shifts got longer although he didn't always get paid.

There were gunshots in the street, and Pete told Jane not to sit out on the balcony. He boarded up the French doors and it was as if they were living in a cave. The refugees started thinning out. Jane rarely saw them leaving, but each day there were fewer and fewer of them on the sidewalk. Pete said they were headed north.

Then the fires started on the east side of town. The power went out and stayed out. Pete didn't come home until the next day, and he slept a couple of hours and then went back out to work. The air tasted of smoke— not the pleasant, clean smell of wood smoke, but a garbagey smoke. Franny complained that it made her sick to her stomach.

After Pete didn't come home for four days, it was pretty clear to Jane that he wasn't coming back. Jane put Franny in the car, packed everything she could think of that might be useful. They got about 120 miles away, far enough that the burning city was no longer visible, although the sunset was a vivid and blistering red. Then they ran out of gas, and there was no more to be had.

There were rumors that there was a refugee camp for the homeless outside of Toronto. So they were walking to Detroit.

Franny says, "You can't leave me! You can't leave me!"

"Do you want to go scavenge with me?" Jane says.

Franny sobs so hard she seems to be hyperventilating. She grabs her mother's arms, unable to do anything but hold onto her. Jane peels her off, but Franny keeps grabbing, clutching, sobbing. It's making Jane crazy. Franny's fear is contagious, and if she lets it get in her, she'll be too afraid to do anything. She can feel it deep inside her, that thing that has always threatened her, to give in, to stop doing and pushing and scheming, to become like her useless, useless father puttering around the house vacantly, bottles hidden in the garage, the basement, everywhere.

"GET OFF ME!" she screams at Franny, but Franny is sobbing and clutching.

She slaps Franny. Franny throws up, precious little, water and crackers from breakfast. Then she sits down in the grass, just useless.

Jane marches off into the first house.

She's lucky. The garage is closed up and there are three cans of soup on a shelf. One of them is cream of mushroom, but luckily, Franny liked cream of mushroom when she found it before. There are also cans of tomato paste, which she ignores, and some dried pasta, but mice have gotten into it.

When she gets outside, some strange guy is standing on the sidewalk, talking to Franny, who's still sitting on the grass. For a moment she doesn't know what to do, clutching the cans of soup against her chest. Some part of her wants to back into the house, go through the dark living room with its mauve carpeting, its shabby blue sofa, photos of school kids and a cross-stitch flower bouquet framed on the wall, back through the little dining room with its border of country geese, unchanged since the eighties. Out the back door and over the fence, an easy moment to abandon the biggest mistake of her life. She'd aborted the first pregnancy, brought home from Pasadena in shame. She'd dug her heels in on the second, it's-my-body-fuck-you.

Franny laughs. A little nervous and hiccupy from crying, but not really afraid.

"Hey," Jane yells. "Get away from my daughter!"

She strides across the yard, all motherhood and righteous fury. A skinny, dark-haired guy holds up his hands, palms out, no harm, ma'am.

"It's okay, Mom," Franny says.

The guy is smiling. "We're just talking," he says. He's wearing a red plaid flannel shirt and T-shirt and shorts. He's scraggly, but who isn't.

"Who the hell are you," she says.

"My name's Nate. I'm just heading north. Was looking for a place to camp."

"He was just hanging with me until you got back," Franny says.

Nate takes them to his camp—also behind a house. He gets a little fire going, enough to heat the soup. He talks about Alabama, which is where he's coming from, although he doesn't have a Southern accent. He makes some excuse about being an army brat. Jane tries to size him up. He tells some story about when two guys stumbled on his camp north of Huntsville, when he was first on the road. About how it scared the shit out of him but about how he'd bluffed them about a buddy of his who was hunting for their dinner but would have heard the racket they made and could be drawing a bead on them right now from the trees, and about how something moved in the trees, some animal, rustling in the leaf litter, and they got spooked. He's looking at her, trying to impress her, but being polite, which is good with Franny listening. Franny is taken with him, hanging on his every word, flirting a little the way she does. In a year or two, Franny was going to be guy crazy, Jane knew.

"They didn't know anything about the woods, just two guys up from Biloxi or something, kind of guys who, you know, manage a copy store or a fast-food joint or something, thinking that now that civilization is falling apart they can be like the hero in one of their video games." He laughs. "I didn't know what was in the woods, neither. I admit I was kind of scared it was someone who was going to shoot all of us, although it was probably just a sparrow or a squirrel or something. I'm saying stuff over my shoulder to my 'buddy', like, 'Don't shoot them or nothing. Just let them go back the way they came.'"

She's sure he's bullshitting. But she likes that he makes it funny instead of pretending he's some sort of Rambo. He doesn't offer any of his own food, she notices. But he does offer to go with them to get their stuff. Fair trade, she thinks.

He's not bad looking in a kind of skinny way. She likes them skinny. She's tired of doing it all herself.

The streetlights come on, at least some of them. Nate goes with them when they go back to get their sleeping bags and stuff. He's got a board with a bunch of nails sticking out of one end. He calls it his mace.

They are quiet, but they don't try to hide. It's hard to find the stuff in the dark, but luckily, Jane hadn't really unpacked. She and Franny, who is breathing hard, get their sleeping bags and packs. It's hard to see. The backyard is a dark tangle of shadows. She assumes it's as hard to see them from inside the house—maybe harder.

Nothing happens. She hears nothing from the house, sees nothing, although it seems as if they are all unreasonably loud gathering things up. They leave through the side gate, coming nervously to the front of the house, Nate carrying his mace and ready to strike, she and Franny with their arms full of sleeping bags. They go down the cracked driveway and out into the middle of the street, a few gutted cars still parked on either side. Then they are around the corner and it feels safe. They are all grinning and happy and soon putting the sleeping bags in Nate's little backyard camp made domestic—no, civilized—by the charred ash of the little fire.

In the morning, she leaves Nate's bedroll and gets back to sleep next to Franny before Franny wakes up.

They are walking on the freeway the next day, the three of them. They are together now, although they haven't discussed it, and Jane is relieved. People are just that much less likely to mess with a man. Overhead, three jets pass going south, visible only by their contrails. At least there are jets. American jets, she hopes.

They stop for a moment while Nate goes around a bridge abutment to pee.

"Mom," Franny says. "Do you think that someone has wrecked Pete's place?"

"I don't know," Jane says.

"What do you think happened to Pete?"

Jane is caught off guard. They left without ever explicitly discussing Pete, and Jane just thought that Franny, like her, assumed Pete was dead.

"I mean," Franny continues, "if they didn't have gas, maybe he got stuck somewhere. Or he might have gotten hurt and ended up in the hospital. Even if the hospital wasn't taking regular people, like, they'd take cops. Because they think of cops as one of their own." Franny is in her adult-to-adult mode, explaining the world to her mother. "They stick together. Cops and firemen and nurses."

Jane isn't sure she knows what Franny is talking about. Normally she'd tell Franny as much. But this isn't a conversation she knows how to have. Nate comes around the abutment, adjusting himself a bit, and it is understood that the subject is closed.

"Okay," he says. "How far to Wallyworld?" Franny giggles.

Water is their biggest problem. It's hard to find, and when they do find it, either from a pond or, very rarely, from a place where it hasn't all been looted, it's heavy. Thank God Nate is pretty good at making a fire. He has six disposable lighters that he got from a gas station, and when they find a pond, they boil it. Somewhere Jane thinks she heard that they should boil it for eighteen minutes. Basically they just boil the heck out of it. Pond water tastes terrible, but they are always thirsty. Franny whines. Jane is afraid that Nate will get tired of it and leave, but apparently as long as she crawls over to his bedroll every night, he's not going to.

Jane waits until she can tell Franny is asleep. It's a difficult wait. They are usually so tired it is all she can do to keep from nodding off. But she is afraid to lose Nate.

At first she liked that at night he never made a move on her. She always initiates. It made things easier all around. But now he does this thing where she crawls over and he's pretending to be asleep. Or is asleep, the bastard, because he doesn't have to stay awake. She puts her hand on his chest, and then down his pants, getting him hard and ready. She unzips his shorts, and still he doesn't do anything. She grinds on him for a while, and only then does he pull his shorts and underwear down and let her ride him until he comes. Then she climbs off him. Sometimes he might say, "Thanks, babe." Mostly he says nothing and she crawls back next to Franny feeling as if she just paid the rent. She has never given anyone sex for money. She keeps telling herself that this night she won't do it. See what he does. Hell, if he leaves them, he leaves them. But then she lies there, waiting for Franny to go to sleep.

Sometimes she knows Franny is awake when she crawls back. Franny never says anything, and unless the moon is up, it is usually too dark to see if her eyes are open. It is just one more weird thing, no weirder than walking up the highway, or getting off the highway in some small town and bartering with some old guy to take what is probably useless U.S. currency for well water. No weirder than no school. No weirder than no baths, no clothes, no nothing.

Jane decides she's not going to do it the next night. But she knows she will lie there, anxious, and probably crawl over to Nate.

They are walking, one morning, while the sky is still blue and darkening near the horizon. By midday the sky will be white and the heat will be flattening. Franny asks Nate, "Have you ever been in love?"

"God, Franny," Jane says.

Nate laughs. "Maybe. Have you?"

Franny looks irritable. "I'm in seventh grade," she says. "And I'm not one of those girls with boobs, so I'm thinking, no."

Jane wants her to shut up, but Nate says, "What kind of guy would you fall in love with?"

Franny looks a little sideways at him and then looks straight ahead. She has the most perfect skin, even after all this time in the sun. Skin like that is wasted on kids. Her look says, "Someone like you, stupid." "I don't know," Franny says. "Someone who knows how to do things. You know, when you need them."

"What kind of things?" Nate asks. He's really interested. Well, fuck, there's not a lot interesting on a freeway except other people walking and abandoned cars. They are passing a Sienna with a flat tire and all its doors open.

Franny gestures toward it. "Like fix a car. And I'd like him to be cute, too." Matter of fact. Serious as a church.

Nate laughs. "Competent and cute."

"Yeah," Franny says. "Competent and cute."

"Maybe you should be the one who knows how to fix a car," Jane says.

"But I don't," Franny points out reasonably. "I mean maybe, someday, I could learn. But right now, I don't."

"Maybe you'll meet someone in Canada," Nate says. "Canadian guys are supposed to be able to do things like fix a car or fish or hunt moose."

"Canadian guys are different than American guys?" Franny asks.

"Yeah," Nate says. "You know, all flannel shirts and Canadian beer and stuff."

"You wear a flannel shirt."

"I'd really like a Canadian beer about now," Nate says. "But I'm not Canadian."

Off the road to the right is a gas station/convenience store. They almost always check them. There's not much likelihood of finding anything in the place, because the wire fence that borders the highway has been trampled here so people can get over it, which suggests that the place has long since been looted. But you never know what someone might have left behind. Nate lopes off across the high grass.

"Mom," Franny says, "carry my backpack, okay?" She shrugs it off and runs. Amazing that she has the energy to run. Jane picks up Franny's backpack, irritated, and follows. Nate and Franny disappear into the darkness inside.

She follows them in. "Franny, I'm not hauling your pack anymore."

There are some guys already in the place, and there is something about them, hard and well fed, that signals they are different. Or maybe it is just the instincts of a prey animal in the presence of predators.

"So what's in that pack?" one of them asks. He's sitting on the counter at the cash register window, smoking a cigarette. She hasn't had a cigarette in weeks. Her whole body simultaneously leans toward the cigarette and yet magnifies everything in the room. A room full of men, all of them staring.

She just keeps acting like nothing is wrong, because she doesn't know what else to do. "Dirty blankets, mostly," she says. "I have to carry most of the crap."

One of the men is wearing a grimy hoodie. Hispanic yard workers do that sometimes. It must help in the sun.

These men are all Anglos, and there are fewer of them than she first thought. Five. Two of them are sitting on the floor, their backs against an empty dead ice cream cooler, their legs stretched out in front of them. Everyone on the road is dirty, but they are dirty and hard. Physical. A couple of them grin, feral flickers passing between them like glances. There is understanding in the room, shared purpose. She has the sense that she cannot let on that she senses anything, because the only thing holding them off is the pretense that everything is normal. "Not that we really need blankets in this weather," she says. "I would kill for a functioning Holiday Inn."

"Hah," the one by the cash register says. A bark. Amused.

Nate is carefully still. He is searching, eyes going from man to man. Franny looks as if she is about to cry.

It is only a matter of time. They will be on her. Should she play up to the man at the cash register? If she tries to flirt, will it release the rising tension in the room, allow them to spring on all of them? Will they kill Nate? What will they do to Franny? Or can she use her sex as currency? Go willingly. She does not feel as if they care if she goes willingly or not. They know there is nothing to stop them.

"There's no beer here, is there," she says. She can hear her voice failing.

"Nope," says the man sitting at the cash register.

"What's your name?" she asks.

It's the wrong thing to say. He slides off the counter. Most of the men are smiling on.

Nate says, "Stav?"

One of the guys on the floor looks up. His eyes narrow. Nate says, "Hey, Stav."

"Hi," the guy says cautiously.

"You remember me," Nate says. "Nick. From the Blue Moon Inn."

Nothing. Stav's face is blank. But another guy, the one in the hoodie, says, "Speedy Nick!"

Stav grins. "Speedy Nick! Fuck! Your hair's not blond anymore!"

Nate says, "Yeah, well, you know, upkeep is tough on the road." He jerks a thumb at Jane. "This is my sister, Janey. My niece, Franny. I'm taking 'em up to Toronto. There's supposed to be a place up there."

"I heard about that," the guy in the hoodie says. "Some kind of camp."

"Ben, right?" Nate says.

"Yeah," the guy says.

The guy who was sitting on the counter is standing now, cigarette still smoldering. He wants it, doesn't want everybody to get all friendly. But the moment is shifting away from him.

"We found some distilled water," Stav says. "Tastes like shit but you can have it if you want."

Jane doesn't ask him why he told her his name was Nate. For all she knows, "Nate" is his name and "Nick" is the lie.

They walk each day. Each night she goes to his bedroll. She owes him. Part of her wonders if maybe he's gay? Maybe he has to lie there and fantasize she's a guy or something. She doesn't know.

They are passing by water. They have some, so there is no reason to stop. There's an egret standing in the water, white as anything she has seen since this started, immaculately clean. Oblivious to their passing. Oblivious to the passing of everything. This is all good for the egrets. Jane hasn't had a drink since they started for Canada. She can't think of a time since she was sixteen or so that she went so long without one. She wants to get dressed up and go out someplace and have a good time and not think about anything, because the bad thing about not having a drink is that she thinks all the time and, fuck, there's nothing in her life right now she really wants to think about. Especially not Canada, which she is deeply but silently certain is only a rumor. Not the country, she doesn't think it doesn't exist, but the camp. It is a mirage. A shimmer on the horizon. Something to go toward but which isn't really there.

Or maybe they're the rumors. The three of them. Rumors of things gone wrong.

At a rest stop in the middle of nowhere they come across an encampment. A huge number of people, camped under tarps, pieces of plastic, and tatters, and astonishingly, a convoy of military trucks and jeeps including a couple of fuel trucks and a couple of water trucks. Kids stop and watch as they walk in and then go back to chasing each other around picnic tables. The two groups are clearly separate. The military men have control of all the asphalt and one end of the picnic area. They stand around or lounge at picnic tables. They look so equipped, from hats to combat boots. They look so clean. So much like the world Jane has put mostly out of her mind. They awake in her the longing that she has put down. The longing to be clean. To have walls. Electric lights. Plumbing. To have order.

The rest look like refugees, the word she denied on the sidewalks outside the condo. Dirty people in T-shirts with bundles and plastic grocery bags and even a couple of suitcases. She has seen people like this as they walked. Walked past them sitting by the side of the road. Sat by the side of the road as others walked past them. But to see them all together like this… this is what it will be like in Canada? A camp full of people with bags of wretched clothes waiting for someone to give them something to eat? A toddler with no pants and curly hair watches solemnly like one of those children in those "save a child" commercials. He's just as dirty. His hair is blond.

She rejects it. Rejects it all so viscerally that she stops and for a moment can't walk to the people in the rest stop. She doesn't know if she would have walked past, or if she would have turned around, or if she would have struck off across the country. It doesn't matter what she would have done, because Nate and Franny walk right on up the exit ramp. Franny's tank top is bright, insistent pink under its filth and her shorts have a tear in them, and her legs are brown and skinny and she could be a child on a news channel after a hurricane or an earthquake, clad in the loud synthetic colors so at odds with the dirt or ash that coats her. Plastic and synthetics are the indestructibles left to the survivors.

Jane is ashamed. She wants to explain that she's not like this. She wants to say, she's an American. By which she means she belongs to the military side, although she has never been interested in the military, never particularly liked soldiers.

If she could call her parents in Pennsylvania. Get a phone from one of the soldiers. Surrender. You were right,

Mom. I should have straightened up and flown right. I should have worried more about school. I should have done it your way. I'm sorry. Can we come home?

Would her parents still be there? Do the phones work just north of Philadelphia? It has not until this moment occurred to her that it is all gone.

She sticks her fist in her mouth to keep from crying out, sick with understanding. It is all gone. She has thought herself all brave and realistic, getting Franny to Canada, but somehow she didn't until this moment realize that it all might be gone. That there might be nowhere for her where the electricity is still on and there are still carpets on the hardwood floors and someone still cares about damask.

Nate has finally noticed that she isn't with them and he looks back, frowning at her. *What's wrong?* his expression says. She limps after them, defeated.

Nate walks up to a group of people camped around and under a stone picnic table. "Are they giving out water?" he asks, meaning the military.

"Yeah," says a guy in a Cowboys football jersey. "If you go ask, they'll give you water."

"Food?"

"They say tonight."

All the shade is taken. Nate takes their water bottles—a couple of two-liters and a plastic gallon milk jug. "You guys wait, and I'll get us some water," he says.

Jane doesn't like being near these people, so she walks back to a wire fence at the back of the rest area and sits down. She puts her arms on her knees and puts her head down. She is looking at the grass.

"Mom?" Franny says.

Jane doesn't answer.

"Mom? Are you okay?" After a moment more. "Are you crying?"

"I'm just tired," Jane says to the grass.

Franny doesn't say anything after that.

Nate comes back with all the bottles filled. Jane hears him coming and hears Franny say, "Oh, wow. I'm so thirsty."

Nate nudges Jane's arm with a bottle. "Hey, babe. Have some."

She takes a two-liter from him and drinks some. It's got a flat, faintly metal/chemical taste. She gets a big drink and feels a little better. "I'll be back," she says. She walks to the shelter where the bathrooms are.

"You don't want to go in there," a black man says to her. The whites of his eyes are yellow.

She ignores him and pushes in the door. Inside, the smell is excruciating, and the sinks are all stopped and full of trash. There is some light from windows up near the ceiling. She looks at herself in the dim mirror. She pours a little water into her hand and scrubs at her face. There is a little bit of paper towel left on a roll, and she peels it off and cleans her face and her hands, using every bit of the scrap of paper towel. She wets her hair and combs her fingers through it, working the tangles for a long time until it is still curly but not the rat's nest it was. She is so careful with the water. Even so, she uses every bit of it on her face and arms and hair. She would kill for a little lipstick. For a comb. Anything. At least she has water.

She is cute. The sun hasn't been too hard on her. She practices smiling.

When she comes out of the bathroom, the air is so sweet. The sunlight is blinding.

She walks over to the soldiers and smiles. "Can I get some more water, please?"

There are three of them at the water truck. One of them is a blond-haired boy with a brick-red complexion. "You sure can," he says, smiling back at her.

She stands, one foot thrust out in front of her like a ballerina, back a little arched. "You're sweet," she says. "Where are you from?"

"We're all stationed at Fort Hood," he says. "Down in Texas. But we've been up north for a couple of months."

"How are things up north?" she asks.

"Crazy," he says. "But not as crazy as they are in Texas, I guess."

She has no plan. She is just moving with the moment. Drawn like a moth.

He gets her water. All three of them are smiling at her.

"How long are you here?" she asks. "Are you like a way station or something?"

One of the others, a skinny Chicano, laughs. "Oh, no. We're here tonight and then headed west."

"I used to live in California," she says. "In Pasadena. Where the Rose Parade is. I used to walk down that street where the cameras are every day."

The blond glances around. "Look, we aren't supposed to be talking too much right now. But later on, when it gets dark, you should come back over here and talk to us some more."

"Mom!" Franny says when she gets back to the fence. "You're all cleaned up!"

"Nice, babe," Nate says. He's frowning a little.

"Can I get cleaned up?" Franny asks.

"The bathroom smells really bad," Jane says. "I don't think you want to go in there." But she digs her other T-shirt out of her backpack and wets it and washes Franny's face. The girl is never going to be pretty, but now that she's not chubby, she's got a cute thing going on. She's got the sense to work it, or will learn it. "You're a girl that the boys are going to look at," Jane says to her.

Franny smiles, delighted.

"Don't you think?" Jane says to Nate. "She's got that thing, that sparkle, doesn't she?"

"She sure does," Nate says.

They nap in the grass until the sun starts to go down, and then the soldiers line everyone up and hand out MREs. Nate gets Beef Ravioli, and Jane gets Sloppy Joe. Franny gets Lemon Pepper Tuna and looks ready to cry, but Jane offers to trade with her. The meals are positive cornucopias—a side dish, a little packet of candy, peanut butter and crackers, fruit punch powder. Everybody has different things, and Jane makes everybody give everyone else a taste.

Nate keeps looking at her oddly. "You're in a great mood."

"It's like a party," she says

Jane and Franny are really pleased by the moist towelette. Franny carefully saves her plastic fork, knife, and spoon. "Was your tuna okay?" she asks. She is feeling guilty now that the food is gone.

"It was good," Jane says. "And all the other stuff made it really special. And I got the best dessert."

The night comes down. Before they got on the road, Jane didn't know how dark night was. Without electric lights it is cripplingly dark. But the soldiers have lights.

Jane says, "I'm going to go see if I can find out about the camp."

"I'll go with you," Nate says.

"No," Jane says. "They'll talk to a girl more than they'll talk to a guy. You keep Franny company."

She scouts around the edge of the light until she sees the blond soldier. He says, "There you are!"

"Here I am!" she says.

They are standing around a truck where they'll sleep this night, shooting the shit. The blond soldier boosts her into the truck, into the darkness. "So you aren't so conspicuous," he says, grinning.

Two of the men standing and talking aren't wearing uniforms. It takes her a while to figure out that they're civilian contractors. They aren't soldiers. They are technicians, nothing like the soldiers. They are softer, easier in their polo shirts and khaki pants. The soldiers are too sure in their uniforms, but the contractors, they're used to getting the leftovers. They're *grateful*. They have a truck of their own, a white pickup truck that travels with the convoy. They do something with satellite tracking, but Jane doesn't really care what they do.

It takes a lot of careful maneuvering, but one of them finally whispers to her, "We've got some beer in our truck."

The blond soldier looks hurt by her defection.

She stays out of sight in the morning, crouched among the equipment in the back of the pickup truck. The soldiers hand out MREs. Ted, one of the contractors, smuggles her one.

She thinks of Franny. Nate will keep an eye on her. Jane was only a year older than Franny when she lit out for California the first time. For a second she pictures Franny's face as the convoy pulls out.

Then she doesn't think of Franny.

She doesn't know where she is going. She is in motion.

THE TRADITIONAL
MARIA DAHVANA HEADLEY

I

By your first anniversary, the world's stopped making paper, and so you can't give your boyfriend the traditional gift. You never would have anyway, regardless of circumstances. You're not that kind of girl. You pride yourself on your original sin. It's the hot you trade in.

So you give him the piece of your skin just beneath your ribcage on the right side, where the floating ribs bend in. It's a good part. Not the best. You're like a food hoarder who pretends her larder's empty, all the while running her finger along the dusty ledge that leads to the trick shelves that hold the jars of Caspian caviar. You've always been the kind of liar who leans back and lets boys fall into you while you see if you can make them fall all the way out the other side. You want them to feel like they've hit Narnia. You traffic in interdimensional fucking, during which they transcend space and time, and you go nowhere. When they fall in love, you Shun & Break™ them. Their poor plastic hearts are Pez dispensers topped with copyright violation Mickey mice.

Your boy's not falling for this shit. He simply refuses. He sees through your methods. You met him in a bar on the night of the first apocalypse, just prior, and both of you somehow lived through the night.

He clocked you from moment one, when you bought him a drink and brought it to him, fresh lipstick on your mouth, altering your walk to cause him pain. He drank it. He then took the cherry out of yours and drank your drink too, looking at you the whole time like he was a prime transgressor who was going to rock your world until it broke.

"You gonna try to make me love you now?" he asked. "That your thing?"

"Brother," you said, taken aback by the way he'd just needlessly whacked the rules of flirtation, "I don't even know you exist."

This would have been the end of it, except that five minutes later there was a rending, and everyone was screaming and trying to get away, and buildings were falling down, and the streets were full of the unimaginable.

You were out of your element. You loved the Woolworthing of the world before the apocalypse, the shopping mall fluorescence of flirtation, the IKEA particleboard pushing together of things that would shortly fall apart. You loved paper parasols and plastic monkeys. Everything was your toy. You killed men, but they never got anywhere near killing you.

But he grabbed your hand, and you grabbed his, and you took off running together, dodging crazy, jumping holes in the streets, not stopping to look at the people who were down on the ground already, vomiting up important parts of anatomy.

You didn't actually see the worms that night, though other people did. That was the first anyone heard of them.

When you finally got indoors and safe as you were likely to get given the stakes, given the world situation—sex, you informed him, was necessary, because minus sex? This shit was just monsters and the end of the world.

He wasn't so sure. He'd sobered up, considered lighting out on his own, but you insisted you were better off together. Then you tore off his clothes and climbed him like a firefighter reversing up a pole.

Maybe you love him now, maybe you don't. You don't trust him, but there's nothing new about that.

The apartment you share has big windows, and no curtains. You don't look out. The floor beneath the window has an old bloodstain, but whatever happened there happened a long time ago. In bed, you're rubber and he's glue, and it's hot enough to keep you going.

"This is so you can write on me instead of paper," you say, thrilling at your own *fin du monde* generosity. The rest of the world's in mourning, but you're celebrating your survival.

You roll over to face him. You've outlined the page with a razor blade. The rest of you is unmarked. There's the promise of a quarto. Back before all this, you were both, weirdly, the kind of people who footnoted fucks. You prided yourselves on your grasp of gory details of the philosophical arguments of the 1300s. Now you don't know what you are. Your dissertation is stalled. You used to be the cool girl. Now you're just a live girl.

Your boy presses his cheek to your hipbone.

"You feel like a fossil," he says. "Like a pterodactyl wrapped in fabric."

"As long as I don't feel like a worm," you say.

You know very well that you don't. The people out there who've died, the ones eaten by the worms? First everything liquefies. Then the worm emerges. While it's happening, you feel it like an earthquake inside your soul. There's a reason you're in here. A year of that, and the worms are getting bigger all the time. They start out the size of pencils.

He cuts a word into your skin, and then another, and you gasp when the knife touches you, because here's something you've never done before, and you're a girl who does everything. You have a flash of worry about yourself. There is a distinct possibility that you're flipping backward, your head upturned, everything sweet you've kept hidden sliding out into his hands.

Outside you can hear one of the worms moving through the streets, a big one, about the size of a motorcycle. You blow out the candle. It's not like you're scared.

"Do you remember mimeograph machines?" you ask him. You do. Your grade school had one. Once, because you couldn't stop talking, you were exorcised in the mimeograph room by a substitute teacher using Diet Sprite as holy water. Back then, you couldn't stop anything once you started. You revolved like a bent top, twitched, and bit boys. You cast spells. None of them worked. Now, if you were out there, it would be worse than mimeograph ink. People believe in things they didn't.

"Yeah, I remember mimeographs," he says, and smiles. "The purple ink. It smelled like a hot skillet."

You flip over so you don't have to look at him, and then you roll across the sheet to print the words he's written, grabbing the fuck out of random religion, but isn't everyone?

Hallelujah, Holy, Glory, Be, God, Gone, Gotten, Begat, Bore, Bear, Beginning: in the. End of days.

Out in the street there is a scream, high and wavering, which you both totally ignore.

II

For your second anniversary, he gives you two teeth, wisdom. The traditional gift is cotton, but you've sold most of your clothes. He gives you ivory instead. The teeth aren't quite white, because of the drinking of tea, back before it all. They've been out of his mouth for a while. The world's shifted away from dentistry, or rather, the world's shifted from cosmetic dentistry into tooth-retention, but his were removed before all that. He's lost other things, too. He has no appendix. He has no tonsils. He still owns both his kidneys, though. You only have one.

The thought that he purposefully had organs removed, and didn't even sell them, makes you pissed off with the waste (*wastrel*, you compulsively think, over and over, *wastrel wastrel*) and so you carefully don't imagine his tonsils twitching on a tonsil heap. His appendix like a tiny harp, strumming inside a bath of alcohol.

There is, by now, a black market trade in vestigials, and the wisdom teeth are worth their weight in something. Some people have their mouths studded with other people's teeth. It's become a status symbol. The worms, however, don't care. People are entirely in hiding by now, and still, sometimes, a worm gets in. No one sleeps with an open mouth anymore. There are masks and door seals. If you see a worm, even a tiny one, you're supposed to shine a light on it and stomp on its head. This is not always possible. It takes time, but eventually, the worms get their way.

"Do you love me?" you ask him. It's bullshit to hear yourself. Your voice sounds wobbly. You sound like what you never were.

"I gave you my teeth," he says, but he doesn't say he loves you. You are now plastic in a world where no one needs anything but metal.

You don't say you love him, either. You met during an apocalypse. What kind of fool are you?

"What are your teeth for?" you ask.

"To pay tolls," he says and then he closes your fingers around them. You hide the teeth beneath your pillow. One morning there are coins in their place. Some old traditions, apparently, linger in the world. Or maybe you did that, to try to make him love you. You place the coins on his eyes as he sleeps, and he wakes up laughing.

"Not that kind of toll," he says.

You aren't laughing. You hide his teeth, in case they're ever all that is left of him, and you have to find something to bury. You curse yourself. Even at the end of the world, you're still trying to rig the system. You don't want to talk about love, and so you talk about worms. You casually relate anecdotes of people who died, listing their agonies like ingredients in a complicated recipe, waiting for him to tell you he loves you, waiting for him to tell you he hopes the worms don't get you.

* * *

III

Your skin, by the third year, for which the traditional gift is leather, is covered with words no one uses any longer. He's careful. You're careful. The blood isn't much.

Sometimes he quotes you. "Brother, I don't even know you exist." Then sometimes he laughs. Sometimes he doesn't.

Sometimes you tell him everything you know about him, which is everything except one thing.

Other things have gone wrong outside. You're living in a drifting cloud of ash from some far-off worm-battling explosion, and the lights are out, and the sun's dimmed. You eat from cans opened with stabbing, and you aren't sure what you're eating, but no one says anything nasty. You're still together, in a new little room, this one with only three walls. Your old apartment sank into a hole in the Earth and was gone for good. He traces words on your skin, and then erases them, and then traces new ones over the scars. You comfort each other with childhood.

"Blackboard," he says, grinning in the dim. "Do you remember?"

"Eraser monitor," you reply. "More times than I should have been."

"Chalk dust," he says. "Inhaled."

"Snow," you say. "Back when there was snow."

"There's still snow somewhere," he says.

"I don't think so," you say. "No ice. Remember ice?"

"Of course I remember ice," he says, annoyed, because he's started to forget it. "Your drink had ice the night we met."

"There isn't any ice left," you say, your voice taut against his cheek, and what you mean is, *I'm a new world, fall into me.* You're scared of being by yourself at the end of the world, even though you pretend you're chill. *Chill*, you repeat to yourself, *chill chill chill*. It starts to sound like a word you don't know.

"How would you know?" he asks.

In the dark, you hand him the scar from your inner thigh. In the space where it was, there's now another scar. You've stitched the leather into a purse, on which you've scarred an unsayable word.

"Tetragrammaton," he says, and you feel him tasting the sound of it, not unimpressed with your syllables.

The end of the world has not made you a believer. The end of the word has.

IV

By the fourth anniversary, you've forgotten the traditional gifts. Sex has begun to involve your skeletons. Your boy gives you his scalp. There's a girl one apartment over who was a surgeon, and she comes in with a flat cloth-wrapped packet of knives and little saws like chefs used to carry. She cuts a circle out of his scalp, then out of his skull. You touch his brain, just once, with your fingertip, watching his eyes roll beneath closed lids. Then the doctor replaces the circles and closes his head back up with black stitches so no worms get in.

You give him your heart. Once your chest cavity is open, he looks at it beating for thirteen seconds, and then the doctor closes you back up again. It takes months to heal from that anniversary, but when you finally do, though you no longer have a bed, you lie on the floor and hold hands, and he tells you what your heart looks like at close range. You tell him about the gray whorls of his brain.

"I pretty much love you," you say at last.

"I pretty much loved you the whole time," he says. "Since I saw you standing on top of the bar as the roof fell in. Since I saw you kill that worm with a bottle of bourbon."

This is a new kind of love for both of you, but not a new kind of love for the world. In the pre-catastrophe world, things that loved one another sometimes ate their mates. You both consider this. The thought of lapping at blood and chewing flesh becomes tempting. You're both getting mad scared of the dark.

V

For your fifth anniversary, after the sun is apparently gone for good, you're fully baroque. You cut off your hair and sell it to buy a ring for him. There's still a trade in hair. It's used to weave blankets. It's also used in spells. Magic has started to exist again, in the desperate early mornings.

He's had the bones of his fingers made into a comb for your hair, which is, of course, gone. There's a man who does that, filing the bones down into something spined and wired. The story that inspired these gifts is a cheesy classic, one you both partially remember from childhood, and it's become hot, too, though in its original version it was only about love and pocket watches. Sex at the end of the world is a pornographic, ecstatic recitation of everything that has ever and has never existed, a naming of genus and species, taxonomies of winged creatures and those that slither.

"Lunchmeat," he says.

"Tempeh," you say.

"Hummingbirds," he says.

"Doves," you say.

"Suspender buttons."

"Oak galls."

"Condoms."

"Leotards."

"Illuminations."

"Daguerreotypes."

"Sugarcane."

"Bees."

"The story where the baby gets cut in half."

"It doesn't. It's a threat."

"The story where there are a thousand babies who keep having more babies."

"That story isn't a real story."

You pause in your movements, considering extinctions.

"Carol," you say. "The secretary from the English lit department."

"My grandfather," he replies.

"Blake."

"Rima."

"Geraldine."

"Henry."

"I didn't know Henry died," you say.

"Of course he did," he tells you, but you still don't remember.

"The woman who used to stand at the end of the street, selling meat on skewers."

"That wasn't meat."

"It was, sort of."

"It was shoe soles."

"It was the color of meat."

You lie together in the dark, listening to the world ending. Five years is more than you would ever have expected, given the beginning of this. In the dark, something shines briefly.

"Glowworms."

"Lite-Brite."

"Dungeons and Dragons."

"Breast implants."

"Flaming arrows."

"Greek fire."

"Radioactive waste."

"Fish at the bottom of the world."

He puts his remaining hand up to touch your shaven head.

"There was a gorilla," he says. "Do you remember it?"

"There was a gorilla who climbed the Empire State Building," you finish. You aren't who you were. You've given him all the things you were saving for yourself.

In the world outside your room, the question now is whether to go out and fight the newest version of the worm. This one rears up and bares its teeth. It's got seven rows of sharp: old school multiplex shit. Now it emerges, in the shadowy days at the end of everything. No one has yet seen its tail. It seems to go on forever.

Outside your windows, buildings begin to crumble, and the sidewalks ripple. You are still that loser thinking about love.

"I have to go out," you say.

"I have to go out, too," he replies, and you touch him with your tongue. He tastes like you. Both of you are hungry. You feel like you might explode from out of his chest, or him from yours, writhing and opening jaws, eyeless.

Outside, the worm is rising where the sunrise was. Its flesh is smooth and gray. Your building shakes as the worm moves around it, wrapping it in coils.

"Nylon support stockings," he says.

"Slinkies," you counter.

"William Blake."

"Loch Ness."

A window breaks. He stands up. You stand up, too, and walk out without looking at him again. There's nowhere to look, in any case. It's dark. You start climbing.

The worm makes its way through the streets, turning left and turning right, making a low sound, a slurring rasp. It's a successful worm. The more people a worm gets, the bigger it grows. You walk out under the sky, hunting the worm as the worm hunts you. You're just a normal person who lived through things she shouldn't have. Your fires have gone out. You're not especially special.

Heaven is a cloud of ash, a starless place full of low nests.

You hold your present in your hand, the pronged, sharpened fingers of your man, and below you, you see the worm, shining in the no light.

Fall into me, you think, using your old self, willing the worm to woo. It shouldn't come to you, but it does. Hunger and love work the same way. The spells you knew as a little girl are still part of you. Once you start spelling you're never stopping. It's like you have an audience and a word with a million letters, and you're going to spell it to death. It's like you're a champion.

The worm stretches itself and you stand on top of a building, watching it approach. It's curious. No one comes out in the street anymore. It smells you, or tastes you in the air.

Then, movement. Now you know why the worm is coming.

Your man is in the street, the purse made of your skin held out before him, and on your skin, the unsayable word.

The worm writhes toward him, following your scent, and you're shaking, feeling a this-is-it-shithead situation, but you're here anyway and so is he. You can see your ring, flashing on your man's finger, his remaining hand outstretched. He throws the purse into the worm's mouth, and it laps at it, tasting it, rasping. Its teeth are shining and white, whiter than anything you've seen before. They close on the purse like it's a washrag being wrung. Now the worm's eaten the name of god. In some places, that would be poison.

Its head turns toward you.

You teeter, teeter, and leap, an old movie move showing up in your game plan unexpectedly. You dive for its face, its open mouth, its seven rows of teeth, and they cut you as you go in. No mouth, only throat. The thing is *all* throat. You hold out the comb and claw your way down.

You're going into the center of the Earth. You fall, and you fall, and all around you the stars are falling, too. The inside of the worm is the inside of the world. You claw words into its throat, and you're covered in blood and wet, in cold dark. You're being digested and pulsed, inside a long channel of charnel. You think about all the people this worm has eaten from the inside, and now you're inside it, too. You'll do the same. You're Woolworthing the monster, cataloging it into a bin of like unnecessaries.

You're fucking terrified.

You think about your mother, whom you haven't seen in years. You think about your umbilical cord and the way it wormtangled around your throat. You think about how you lived through that. You hold your man's hand, the sharpened points of the fingers, and around you, the worm convulses and quivers. You stab yourself in, using the bonecomb, finger by finger, and you tear at the worm's simplicity, bisecting it like a bad deed on a summer afternoon.

Eventually there is a larger shudder, a scream, a rasp, and you feel the worm give way.

VI

For your sixth anniversary, you are the woman who emerged unscathed from the worm that ate the city. He's the man who did it with you. You hold his hand in yours, and his other hand, the one made of bone, holds your hair, grown back now, into a twist on top of your head. The sky changes. The ash drifts down. You've given way, just as the worm did, and now, your skin, covered in words, and his body, covered in scars, are what the remaining people know to be the way that leaders look.

Beneath the streets, the worms are asunder, rotting corpses, bewildered by bones.

You met him drinking. He met you drinking your drink. Now you're both in charge of things.

You give him a look for your sixth anniversary. He gives you the same look back.

MONSTRO
JUNOT DÍAZ

At first, Negroes thought it *funny*. A disease that could make a Haitian blacker? It was the joke of the year. Everybody in our sector accusing everybody else of having it. You couldn't display a blemish or catch some sun on the street without the jokes starting. Someone would point to a spot on your arm and say, *Diablo, haitiano, que te pasó?*

La Negrura they called it.

The Darkness.

These days everybody wants to know what you were doing when the world came to an end. Fools make up all sorts of vainglorious self-serving plep— but me, I tell the truth.

I was chasing a girl.

I was one of the idiots who didn't heed any of the initial reports, who got caught way out there. What can I tell you? My head just wasn't into any mysterious disease—not with my mom sick and all. Not with Mysty.

Motherfuckers used to say *culo* would be the end of us. Well, for me it really was.

In the beginning the doctor types couldn't wrap their brains around it, either.

The infection showed up on a small boy in the relocation camps outside Port-au-Prince, in the hottest March in recorded history. The index case was only four years old, and by the time his uncle brought him in his arm looked like an enormous black pustule, so huge it had turned the boy into an appendage of the arm. In the glypts he looked terrified.

Within a month, a couple of thousand more infections were reported. Didn't rip through the *pobla* like the dengues or the poxes. More of a slow leprous spread. A black mold-fungus-blast that came on like a splotch and then gradually started taking you over, tunneling right through you—though as it turned out it wasn't a mold-fungus-blast at all. It was something else. Something new.

Everybody blamed the heat. Blamed the Calientazo. Shit, a hundred straight days over 105 degrees F. in our region alone, the planet cooking like a chimi and down to its last five trees—something berserk was bound to happen. All sorts of bizarre outbreaks already in play: diseases no one had names for, zoonotics by the pound. This one didn't cause too much panic because it seemed to hit only the sickest of the sick, viktims who had nine kinds of ill already in them. You literally had to be falling to pieces for it to grab you.

It almost always started epidermically and then worked its way up and in. Most of the infected were immobile within a few months, the worst comatose by six. Strangest thing, though: once infected, few viktims died outright; they just seemed to linger on and on. Coral reefs might have been adios on the ocean floor, but they were alive and well on the arms and backs and heads of the infected. Black rotting rugose masses fruiting out of bodies. The medicos formed a ninety-nation consortium, flooded one another with papers and hypotheses, ran every test they could afford, but not even the military enhancers could crack it.

In the early months, there was a big make-do, because it was so strange and because no one could identify the route of transmission—that got the bigheads more worked up than the disease itself. There seemed to be no logic to it—spouses in constant contact didn't catch the Negrura, but some unconnected fool on the other side of the camp did. A huge rah-rah, but when the experts determined that it wasn't communicable in the standard ways, and that normal immune systems appeared to be at no kind of risk, the renminbi and the attention and the savvy went elsewhere. And since it was just poor Haitian types getting fucked up—no real margin in that. Once the initial hulla died down, only a couple of underfunded teams stayed on. As for the infected, all the medicos could do was try to keep them nourished and hydrated—and, more important, prevent them from growing together.

That was a serious issue. The blast seemed to have a boner for fusion, respected no kind of boundaries. I remember the first time I saw it on the Whorl. Alex was, like, *Mira esta vaina*. Almost delighted. A shaky glypt of a pair of naked trembling Haitian brothers sharing a single stained cot, knotted together by horrible mold, their heads slurred into one. About the nastiest thing you ever saw.

Mysty saw it and looked away and eventually I did, too.

My tíos were, like, Someone needs to drop a bomb on those people, and even though I was one of the pro-Haitian domos, at the time I was thinking it might have been a mercy.

I was actually on the Island when it happened. Front-row fucking seat. How lucky was that?

They call those of us who made it through "time witnesses." I can think of a couple of better terms.

I'd come down to the D.R. because my mother had got super sick. The year before, she'd been bitten by a rupture virus that tore through half her organs before the doctors got savvy to it. No chance she was going to be taken care of back North. Not with what the cheapest nurses charged. So she rented out the Brooklyn house to a bunch of Mexos, took that loot, and came home.

Better that way. Say what you want, but family on the Island was still more reliable for heavy shit, like, say, dying, than family in the North. Medicine was cheaper, too, with the flying territory in Haina, its Chinese factories pumping out pharma like it was *romo*, growing organ sheets by the mile, and, for somebody as sick as my mother, with only rental income to live off, being there was what made sense.

I was supposed to be helping out, but really I didn't do na for her. My *tía* Livia had it all under control and if you want the truth I didn't feel comfortable hanging around the house with Mom all sick. The *vieja* could barely get up to piss, looked like a stick version of herself. Hard to see that. If I stayed an hour with her it was a lot.

What an asshole, right? What a shallow motherfucker.

But I was nineteen—and what is nineteen, if not for shallow? In any case my mother didn't want me around, either. It made her sad to see me so uncomfortable. And what could I do for her besides wring my hands? She had Livia, she had her nurse, she had the muchacha who cooked and cleaned. I was only in the way.

Maybe I'm just saying this to cover my failings as a son.

Maybe I'm saying this because of what happened.

Maybe.

Go, have fun with your friends, she said behind her breathing mask.

Didn't have to tell me twice.

Fact is, I wouldn't have come to the Island that summer if I'd been able to nab a job or an internship, but the droughts that year and the General Economic Collapse meant that nobody was nabbing shit. Even the Sovereign kids were ending up home with their parents. So with the house being rented out from under me and nowhere else to go, not even a girlfriend to mooch off, I figured, fuck it: might as well spend the hots on the Island. Take in some of that ole-time climate change. Get to know the patria again.

For six, seven months it was just a horrible Haitian disease—who fucking cared, right? A couple of hundred new infections each month in the camps and around Port-au-Prince, pocket change, really, nowhere near what KRIMEA was doing to the Russian hinterlands. For a while it was nothing, nothing at all… and then some real eerie plep started happening.

Doctors began reporting a curious change in the behavior of infected patients: they wanted to be together, in close proximity, all the time. They no longer tolerated being separated from other infected, started coming together in the main quarantine zone, just outside Champ de Mars, the largest of the relocation camps. All the viktims seemed to succumb to this ingathering compulsion. Some went because they claimed they felt "safer" in the quarantine zone; others just picked up and left without a word to anyone, trekked halfway across the country as though following a homing beacon. Once viktims got it in their heads to go, no dissuading them. Left family, friends, children behind. Walked out on wedding days, on swell business. Once they were in the zone, nothing could get them to leave. When authorities tried to distribute the infected viktims across a number of centers, they either wouldn't go or made their way quickly back to the main zone.

One doctor from Martinique, his curiosity piqued, isolated an elderly viktim from the other infected and took her to a holding bay some distance outside the main quarantine zone. Within twenty-four hours, this frail septuagenarian had torn off her heavy restraints, broken through a mesh security window, and crawled halfway back to the quarantine zone before she was recovered.

Same doctor performed a second experiment: helicoptered two infected men to a hospital ship offshore. As soon as they were removed from the quarantine zone they went *batshit*, trying everything they could to break free, to return. No sedative or entreaty proved effective, and after four days of battering themselves relentlessly against the doors of their holding cells the men loosed a last high-pitched shriek and died *within minutes of each other*.

Stranger shit was in the offing: eight months into the epidemic, all infected viktims, even the healthiest, abruptly stopped communicating. Just went silent. Nothing abnormal in their bloodwork or in their scans. They just stopped talking—friends, family, doctors, it didn't matter. No stimuli of any form could get them to speak. Watched everything and everyone, clearly understood commands and information—but refused to say anything.

Anything *human*, that is.

Shortly after the Silence, the phenomenon that became known as the Chorus began. The entire infected population simultaneously let out a bizarre shriek—two, three times a day. Starting together, ending together.

Talk about unnerving. Even patients who'd had their faces chewed off by the blast joined in—the vibrations rising out of the excrescence itself. Even the patients who were comatose. Never lasted more than twenty, thirty seconds—eerie siren shit. No uninfected could stand to hear it, but uninfected kids seemed to be the most unsettled. After a week of that wailing, the majority of kids had fled the areas around the quarantine zone, moved to other camps. That should have alerted someone, but who paid attention to camp kids?

Brain scans performed during the outbursts actually detected minute fluctuations in the infected patients' biomagnetic signals, but unfortunately for just about everybody on the planet these anomalies were not pursued. There seemed to be more immediate problems. There were widespread rumors that the infected were devils, even reports of relatives attempting to set their infected family members on fire.

In my sector, my mom and my *tía* were about the only people paying attention to any of it; everybody else was obsessing over what was happening with KRIMEA. Mom and Tía Livia felt bad for our poor West-Coast neighbors. They were churchy like that. When I came back from my outings I'd say, fooling, How are *los explotao*? And my mother would say, It's not funny, *hijo*. She's right, Aunt Livia said. That could be us next and then you won't be joking.

So what was I doing, if not helping my mom or watching the apocalypse creep in? Like I told you: I was chasing a girl. And I was running around the Island with this *hijo de mami y papi* I knew from Brown. Living prince because of him, basically.

Classy, right? My *mater* stuck in Darkness, with the mosquitoes fifty to a finger and the heat like the inside of a tailpipe, and there I was *privando en rico* inside the Dome, where the bafflers held the scorch to a breezy 82 degrees F. and one mosquito a night was considered an invasion.

I hadn't actually planned on rolling with Alex that summer—it wasn't like we were close friends or anything. We ran in totally different circles back at Brown, him prince, me prole, but we were both from the same little island that no one else in the world cared about, and that counted for something, even in those days. On top of that we were both art types, which in our world of hyper-capitalism was like having a serious mental disorder. He was already making dough on his photography and I was attracting no one to my writing. But he had always told me, Hit me up the next time you come down. So before I flew in I glypted him, figuring he wasn't going to respond, and he glypted right back.

What's going on, charlatan, *cuando vamos a janguiar*?

And that's basically all we did until the End: *janguiar*.

I knew nobody in the D.R. outside of my crazy cousins, and they didn't like to do anything but watch the fights, play dominos, and fuck. Which is fine for maybe a week— but for three months? No, hombre. I wasn't *that* Island. For Alex did me a solid by putting me on. More than a solid: saved my ass full. Dude scooped me up from the airport in his father's burner, looking so fit it made me want to drop and do twenty on the spot. Welcome to the country of *las maravillas*, he said with a snort, waving his hand at all the thousands of non-treaty motos on the road, the banners for the next election punching you in the face everywhere. Took me over to the rooftop apartment his dad had given him in the rebuilt Zona Colonial. The joint was a metaglass palace that overlooked the Drowned Sectors, full of his photographs and all the bric-a-brac he had collected for props, with an outdoor deck as large as an aircraft carrier.

You live here? I said, and he shrugged lazily: until Papi decides to sell the building.

One of those moments when you realize exactly how rich some of the kids you go to school with are. Without even thinking about it, he glypted me a six-month V.I.P. pass for the Dome, which cost about a year's tuition. Just in case, he said. He'd been on-Island since before the semester ended. A month here and I'm already *aplatanao*, he complained. I think I'm losing the ability to read.

We drank some more spike, and some of his too-cool-for-school Dome friends came over; slim, tall, and wealthy, every one doing double takes when they saw the size of me and heard my Dark accent, but Alex introduced me as his Brown classmate. A genius, he said, and that made it a little better. What do you do? they asked and I told them I was trying to be a journalist. Which for that set was like saying I wanted to molest animals. I quickly became part of the furniture, one of Alex's least interesting fotos. Don't you love my friends, Alex said. *Son tan amable.*

That first night I kinda had been hoping for a go-club or something bananas like that, but it was a talk-and-spike and let's-look-at-Alex's-latest-fotos-type party. What redeemed everything for me was that around midnight one last girl came up the corkscrew staircase. Alex said loudly, Look who's finally here. And the girl shouted, I was at church, *coño*, which got everybody laughing. Because of the weak light I didn't get a good look at first. Just the hair, and the vampire-stake heels. Then she finally made it over and I saw the cut on her and the immensity of those eyes and I was, like, fuck me.

That girl. With one fucking glance she upended my everything.

So you're the friend? I'm Mysty. Her crafted eyes giving me the once-over. And you're in this country *voluntarily*?

A ridiculously beautiful *mina* wafting up a metal corkscrew staircase in high heels and offering up her perfect cheek as the light from the Dome was dying out across the city—that I could have withstood. But then she spent the rest of the night ribbing me because I was so Americanized, because my Spanish sucked, because I didn't know any of the Island things they were talking about—and that was it for me. I was lost.

Everybody at school knew Alex. Shit, I think everybody in Providence knew him. Negro was star like that. This flash priv kid who looked more like a Uruguayan *fútbal* player than a *plátano*, with short curly Praetorian hair and machine-made cheekbones and about the greenest eyes you ever saw. Six feet eight and super full of himself. Threw the sickest parties, always stepping out with the most rompin girls, drove an Eastwood for fuck's sake. But what I realized on the Island was that Alex was more than just a rico, turned out he was a fucking V---, son of the wealthiest, most priv'ed-up family on the Island. His *abuelo* like the ninety-ninth-richest man in the Americas, while his *abuela* had more than nine thousand properties. At Brown, Negro had actually been playing it modest—for good reason, too. Turned out that when homeboy was in middle school he was kidnapped for eight long months, barely got out alive. Never talked about it, not even cryptically, but dude never left the house in D.R. unless he was packing fuego. Always offered me a cannon, too, like it was a piece of fruit or something. Said, Just, you know, in case something happens.

V--- or not, I had respect for Alex, because he worked hard as a fuck, not one of those upper-class vividors who sat around and blew lakhs. Was doing philosophy at Brown and business at M.I.T., smashed like a 4.0, and still had time to do his photography thing. And unlike a lot of our lakhsters in the States he really loved his Santo Domingo. Never pretended he was Spanish or Italian or gringo. Always claimed dominicano and that ain't nothing, not the way plátanos can be.

For all his pluses Alex could also be extra dickish. Always had to be the center of attention. I couldn't say anything slightly smart without him wanting to argue with me. And when you got him on a point he huffed: Well, I don't know about that. Treated Dominican workers in restaurants and clubs and bars like they were lower than shit. Never left any kind of tip. You have to yell at these people or they'll just walk all over you was his whole thing. Yeah, right, Alex, I told him. And he grimaced: You're just a Naxalite. And you're a come solo, I said, which he hated.

Pretty much on his own. No siblings, and his family was about as checked out as you could get. Had a dad who spent so much time abroad that Alex would have been lucky to pick him out in a lineup—and a mom who'd had more plastic surgery than all of Caracas combined, who flew out to Miami every week just to shop and fuck this Senegalese lawyer that everybody except the dad seemed to know about. Alex had a girlfriend from his social set he'd been dating since they were twelve, Valentina, had cheated on her at least two thousand times, with girls and boys, but because of his lakhs she wasn't going anywhere. Dude told me all about it, too, as soon as he introduced me to her. What do you think of that? he asked me with a serious cheese on his face.

Sounds pretty shitty, I said.

Oh, come on, he said, putting an avuncular arm around me. It ain't that bad.

Alex's big dream? (Of course we all knew it, because he wouldn't shut up about all the plep he was going to do.) He wanted to be either the Dominican Sebastião Salgado or the Dominican João Silva (minus the double amputation, natch). But he also wanted to write novels, make films, drop an album, be the star of a channel on the Whorl—dude wanted to do everything. As long as it was arty and it made him a name he was into it.

He was also the one who wanted to go to Haiti, to take

pictures of all the infected people. Mysty was, like, You can go catch a plague all by your fool self, but he waved her off and recited his motto (which was also on his cards): To represent, to surprise, to cause, to provoke.

To die, she added.

He shrugged, smiled his hundred-crore ˉsmile. A photographer has to be willing to risk it all. A photograph can change *todo*.

You had to hand it to him; he had confidence. And recklessness. I remember this time a farmer in Baní uncovered an unexploded bomb from the civil war in his field—Alex raced us all out there and wanted to take a photo of Mysty sitting on the device in a cheerleading outfit. She was, like, Are you *insane*? So he sat down on it himself while we crouched behind the burner and he snapped his own picture, grinning like a loon, first with a Leica, then with a Polaroid. Got on the front page of *Listin* with that antic. Parents flying in from their respective cities to have a chat with him.

He really did think he could change *todo*. Me, I didn't want to change *nada*; I didn't want to be famous. I just wanted to write one book that was worth a damn and I would have happily called it a day.

Mi hermano, that's pathetic to an extreme, Alex said. You have to dream a lot bigger than that.

Well, I certainly dreamed big with Mysty.

In those days she was my Wonder Woman, my Queen of Jaragua, but the truth is I don't remember her as well as I used to. Don't have any pictures of her—they were all lost in the Fall when the memory stacks blew, when la Capital was scoured. One thing a Negro wasn't going to forget, though, one thing that you didn't need fotos for, was how beautiful she was. Tall and copper-colored, with a Stradivarius curve to her back. An ex-volleyball player, studying international law at UNIBE, with a cascade of black hair you could have woven thirty days of nights from. Some modeling when she was thirteen, fourteen, definitely on the receiving end of some skin-crafting and bone-crafting, maybe breasts, definitely ass, and who knows what else—but would rather have died than cop to it.

You better believe I'm *pura lemba*, she always said and even I had to roll my eyes at that. Don't roll your eyes at me. I *am*.

Spent five years in Quebec before her mother finally dumped her asshole Canadian stepfather and dragged her back screaming to la Capital. Something she still held against the *vieja*, against the whole D.R. Spoke impeccable French and used it every chance she got, always made a show of reading thick-ass French novels like *La Cousine Bette*, and that was what she wanted once her studies were over: to move to Paris, work for the U.N., read French books in a café.

Men love me in Paris, she announced, like this might be a revelation.

Men love you here, Alex said.

Shook her head. It's not the same.

Of course it's not the same, I said. Men shower in Santo Domingo. And dance, too. You ever see *franceses* dance? It's like watching an epileptics convention.

Mysty spat an ice cube at me. French men are the *best*.

Yes, she liked me well enough. Could even say we were friends. I had my charming in those days, I had a mouth on me like all the swords of the Montagues and Capulets combined, like someone had overdosed me with truth serum. You're Alex's only friend who doesn't take his crap, she once confided. You don't even take my crap.

Yes, she liked me but didn't *like* me, *entiendes*. But God did I love her. Not that I had any idea how to start with a girl like her. The only "us" time we ever had was when Alex sent her to pick me up and she'd show up either at my house in Villa Con or at the gym. My crazy cousins got so excited. They weren't used to seeing a *fresa* like her. She knew what she was doing. She'd leave her driver out front and come into the gym to fetch me. Put on a real show. I always knew she'd arrived because the whole gravity of the gym would shift to the entrance and I'd look over from my workout and there she'd be.

Never had any kind of game with her. Best I could do on our rides to where Alex was waiting was ask her about her day and she always said the same thing: terrible.

They had a mighty strange relationship, Alex and Mysty did. She seemed pissed off at him at least eighty per cent of the time, but she was also always with him; and it seemed to me that Alex spent more time with Mysty than he did with Valentina. Mysty helped him with all his little projects, and yet she never seemed happy about it, always acted like it was this massive imposition. Jesus, Alex, she said, will you just make it already. Acted like everything he did bored her. That, I've come to realize, was her protective screen. To always appear bored.

Even when she wasn't bored Mysty wasn't easy; *jeva* had a temper, always blowing up on Alex because he said something or was late or because she didn't like the way he laughed at her. Blew up on me if I ever sided with him. Called him a *mama huevo* at least once a day, which in the old D.R. was a pretty serious thing to throw at a guy. Alex didn't care, played it for a goof. You talk so sweet, *ma chère*. You should say it in French. Which of course she always did.

I asked Alex at least five times that summer if he and Mysty were a thing. He denied it full. Never laid a hand on her, she's like my sister, my girlfriend would kill me, etc.

Never fucked her? That seemed highly unfuckinglikely. Something had happened between them—sex, sure, but something else—though what that was isn't obvious even now that I'm older and *dique* wiser. Girls like Mysty, of her class, were always orbiting around crore-mongers like Alex, hoping that they would bite. Not that in the D.R. they ever did but still. Once when I was going on about her, wondering why the fuck he hadn't jumped her, he looked around and then pulled me close and said, You know the thing with her, right? Her dad used to fuck her until she was twelve. Can you believe that?

Her dad? I said.

He nodded solemnly. Her dad. Did I believe it? The incest? In the D.R. incest was like the other national pastime. I guess I believed it as much as I believed Alex's whole she's-my-sister *coro*, which is to say, maybe I did and maybe I didn't, but in the end I also didn't care. It made me feel terrible for her, sure, but it didn't make me want her any less. As for her and Alex, I never saw them touch, never saw anything that you could call calor pass between them; she seemed genuinely uninterested in him romantically and that's why I figured I had a chance.

I don't want a boyfriend, she kept saying. I want a *visa*.

Dear dear Mysty. Beautiful and bitchy and couldn't wait to be away from the D.R. A girl who didn't let anyone push her around, who once grabbed a euro-chick by the hair because the bitch tried to cut her in line. Wasn't really a deep person. I don't think I ever heard her voice an opinion about art or politics or say anything remotely philosophical. I don't think she had any female friends— shit, I don't think she had any friends, just a lot of people she said hi to in the clubs. Chick was as much a loner as I was. She never bought anything for anyone, didn't do community work, and when she saw children she always stayed far away. *Ánimales*, she called them—and you could tell she wasn't joking.

No, she wasn't anything close to humane, but at nineteen who needed humane? She was *buenmosa* and impossible and when she laughed it was like this little wilderness. I would watch her dance with Alex, with other guys—never with me, I wasn't good enough—and my heart would break, and that was all that mattered.

Around our third week of hanging out, when the riots were beginning in the camps and the Haitians in the D.R. were getting deported over a freckle, I started talking about maybe staying for a few months extra. Taking a semester off Brown to keep my mom company, maybe volunteering in Haiti. Crazy talk, sure, but I knew for certain that I wasn't going to land Mysty by sending her glypts from a thousand miles away. To bag a girl like that you have to make a serious move, and staying in the D.R. was for me a serious move indeed.

I think I might stick around, I announced when we were all driving back from what was left of Las Terrenas.

No baffler on the burner and the heat was literally pulling our skin off.

Why would you do that? Mysty demanded. It's *awful* here.

It's not awful here, Alex corrected mildly. This is the most beautiful country in the world. But I don't think you'd last long. You're way gringo.

And you're what, Enriquillo?

I know *I'm* gringo, Alex said, but you're *way* gringo. You'd be running to the airport in a month.

Even my mother was against it. Actually sat up in her medicine tent. You're going to drop school—for what? *Esa chica plastica*? Don't be ridiculous, *hijo*. There's plenty of *culo falso* back home.

That July a man named Henri Casimir was brought in to a field clinic attached to Champ de Mars. A former manager in the utility company, now reduced to carting sewage for the camp administration. Brought in by his wife, Rosa, who was worried about his behavior. Last couple of months dude had been roaming about the camp at odd hours, repeating himself ad nauseam, never sleeping. The wife was convinced that her husband was not her husband.

In the hospital that day: one Noni DeGraff, a Haitian epidemiologist and one of the few researchers who had been working on the disease since its first appearance; brilliant and pretty much fearless, she was called the Jet Engine by her colleagues, because of her headstrong ferocity. Intrigued by Casimir's case, she sat in on the examination. Casimir, apart from a low body temperature, seemed healthy. Bloodwork clean. No sign of virals or of the dreaded infection. When questioned, the patient spoke excitedly about a san he was claiming the following week. Distressed, Rosa informed the doctors that said san he was going on about had disbanded two months earlier. He had put his fifty renminbi faithfully into the pot every month, but just before his turn came around they found out the whole thing was a setup. He never saw a penny, Rosa said.

When Dr. DeGraff asked the wife what she thought might be bothering her husband, Rosa said simply, Someone has witched him.

Something about the wife's upset and Casimir's demeanor got Dr. DeGraff's antennas twitching. She asked Rosa for permission to observe Casimir on one of his rambles. Wife Rosa agreed. As per her complaint, Casimir spent almost his entire day tramping about the camp with no apparent aim or destination. Twice Dr. DeGraff approached him, and twice Casimir talked about the heat and about the san he was soon to receive. He seemed distracted, disoriented, even, but not mad.

The next week, Dr. DeGraff tailed Casimir again. This time the good doctor discerned a pattern. No matter how many twists he took, invariably Casimir wound his way back to the vicinity of the quarantine zone at the very moment that the infected let out their infernal chorus. As the outburst rang out, Casimir paused and then, without any change in expression, ambled away.

DeGraff decided to perform an experiment. She placed Casimir in her car and drove him away from the quarantine zone. At first, Casimir appeared "normal," talking again about his san, wiping his glasses compulsively, etc. Then, at half a mile from the zone, he began to show increasing signs of distress, twitching and twisting in his seat. His language became garbled. At the mile mark Casimir exploded. Snapped the seat belt holding him in and in his scramble from the car struck DeGraff with unbelievable force, fracturing two ribs. Bounding out before the doctor could manage to bring the car under control, Casimir disappeared into the sprawl of Champ de Mars. The next day, when Dr. DeGraff asked the wife to bring Casimir in, he appeared to have no recollection of the incident. He was still talking about his san.

After she had her ribs taped up, DeGraff put out a message to all medical personnel in the Haitian mission, inquiring about patients expressing similar symptoms. She assumed she would receive four, five responses. She received *two hundred and fourteen*. She asked for workups. She got them. Sat down with her partner in crime, a Haitian-American physician by the name of Anton Léger, and started plowing through the material. Nearly all the sufferers had, like Casimir, shown signs of low body temperature. And so they performed temperature tests on Casimir. Sometimes he was normal. Sometimes he was below, but never for long. A technician on the staff, hearing about the case, suggested that they requisition a thermal imager sensitive enough to detect minute temperature fluctuations. An imager was secured and then turned on Casimir. Bingo. Casimir's body temperature was indeed fluctuating, little tiny blue spikes every couple of seconds. Normal folks like DeGraff and Léger—they tested themselves, naturally—scanned red, but patients with the Casimir complaint appeared onscreen a deep, flickering blue. On a lark, DeGraff and Léger aimed the scanner toward the street outside the clinic.

They almost shat themselves. Like for reals. Nearly one

out of every eight pedestrians was flickering blue.

DeGraff remembers the cold dread that swept over her, remembers telling Léger, We need to go to the infected hospital. We need to go there now.

At the hospital, they trained their camera on the guarded entrance. Copies of those scans somehow made it to the Outside. Still chilling to watch. Every single person, doctor, assistant, aid worker, janitor who walked in and out of that hospital radiated blue.

We did what all kids with a lot of priv do in the D.R. We kicked it. And since none of us had parents to hold us back we kicked it super hard. Smoked ganja by the heap and tore up the Zona Colonial and when we got bored we left the Dome for long looping drives from one end of the Island to the other. The countryside half-abandoned because of the Long Drought but still beautiful even in its decline.

Alex had all these projects. Fotos of all the prostitutes in the Feria. Fotos of every chimi truck in the Malecón. Fotos of the tributes on the Conde. He also got obsessed with photographing all the beaches of the D.R. before they disappeared. These beaches are what used to bring the world to us! he exclaimed. They were the one resource we had! I suspected it was just an excuse to put Mysty in a bathing suit and photograph her for three hours straight. Not that I was complaining. My role was to hand him cameras and afterward to write a caption for each of the selected shots he put on the Whorl.

And I did: just a little entry. The whole thing was called "Notes from the Last Shore." Nice, right? I came up with that. Anyway, Mysty spent the whole time on those shoots bitching: about her bathing suits, about the scorch, about the mosquitoes that the bafflers were letting in, and endlessly warning Alex not to focus on her *pipa*. She was convinced that she had a huge one, which neither Alex nor I ever saw but we didn't argue. I got you, *chérie*, was what he said. I got you.

After each setup I always told her: *Tú eres guapísima*. And she never said anything, just wrinkled her nose at me. Once, right before the Fall, I must have said it with enough conviction, because she looked me in the eyes for a long while. I still remember what *that* felt like.

Now it gets sketchy as hell. A lockdown was initiated and a team of W.H.O. docs attempted to enter the infected hospital in the quarantine zone. Nine went in but nobody came out. Minutes later, the infected let out one of their shrieks, but this one lasted twenty-eight minutes. And that more or less was when shit went Rwanda.

In the D.R. we heard about the riot. Saw horrific videos of people getting chased down and butchered. Two camera crews died, and that got Alex completely pumped up.

We have to go, he cried. I'm missing it!

You're not going anywhere, Mysty said.

But are you guys seeing this? Alex asked. Are you *seeing* this?

That shit was no riot. Even we could tell that. All the relocation camps near the quarantine zone were consumed in what can only be described as a straight massacre. An outbreak of homicidal violence, according to the initial reports. People who had never lifted a finger in anger their whole lives—children, *viejos*, aid workers, mothers of nine—

grabbed knives, machetes, sticks, pots, pans, pipes, hammers and started attacking their neighbors, their friends, their pastors, their children, their husbands, their infirm relatives, complete strangers. Berserk murderous blood rage. No pleading with the killers or backing them down; they just kept coming and coming, even when you pointed a gauss gun at them, stopped only when they were killed.

Let me tell you: in those days I really didn't know nothing. For real. I didn't know shit about women, that's for sure. Didn't know shit about the world—obviously. Certainly didn't know *jack* about the Island.

I actually thought me and Mysty could end up together. Nice, right? The truth is I had more of a chance of busting a golden egg out my ass than I did of bagging a girl like Mysty. She was from a *familia de nombre*, wasn't going to have anything to do with a *nadie* like me, *un morenito* from Villa Con whose mother had made it big selling hair-straightening products to the africanos. Wasn't going to happen. Not unless I turned myself white or got a major-league contract or hit the fucking lottery. Not unless I turned into an Alex.

And yet you know what? I still had hope. Had hope that despite the world I had a chance with Mysty. Ridiculous hope, sure, but what do you expect?

Nearly two hundred thousand Haitians fled the violence, leaving the Possessed, as they became known, fully in control of the twenty-two camps in the vicinity of the quarantine zone.

Misreading the situation, the head of the U.N. Peacekeeping Mission waited a full two days for tensions to "cool down" before attempting to reestablish control. Finally, two convoys entered the blood zone, got as far as Champ de Mars before they were set upon by wave after wave of the Possessed and torn to pieces.

Let me not forget this—this is the best part. Three days before it happened, my mother flew to New Hialeah with my aunt for a specialty treatment. Just for a few days, she explained. And the really best part? *I could have gone with her!* She invited me, said, Plenty of *culo plastico* in Florida. Can you imagine it? I could have ducked the entire fucking thing. I could have been safe.

No one knows how it happened or who was responsible, but it took two weeks, two fucking weeks, for the enormity of the situation to dawn on the Great Powers. In the meantime, the infected, as refugees reported, sang on and on and on.

On the fifteenth day of the crisis, advanced elements of the U.S. Rapid Expeditionary Force landed at Port-au-Prince. Drone surveillance proved difficult, as some previously unrecorded form of interference was disrupting the airspace around the camps.

Nevertheless a battle force was ordered into the infected areas. This force, too, was set upon by the Possessed, and would surely have been destroyed to the man if helicopters hadn't been sent in. The Possessed were so relentless that they clung to the runners, actually had to be shot off. The only upside? The glypts the battle force beamed out *finally* got High Command to pull their head out of their ass. The entire country of Haiti was placed under quarantine. All flights in and out cancelled. The border with the D.R. sealed.

An emergency meeting of the Joint Chiefs of Staff was convened, the Commander-in-Chief pulled off his vacation. And within hours a bomber wing scrambled out of Southern Command in Puerto Rico.

Leaked documents show that the bombers were loaded with enough liquid asskick to keep all of Port-au-Prince burning red-hot for a week. The bombers were last spotted against the full moon as they crossed the northern coast of the D.R. Survivors fleeing the area heard their approach—and Dr. DeGraff, who had managed to survive the massacres and had joined the exodus moving east, chanced one final glance at her birth city just as the ordnance was sailing down.

Because she was a God-fearing woman and because she had no idea what kind of bomb they were dropping, Dr. DeGraff took the precaution of keeping one eye shut, just, you know, in case things got Sodom and Gomorrah. Which promptly they did. The Detonation Event—no one knows what else to call it—turned the entire world white. Three full seconds. Triggered a quake that was felt all across the Island and also burned out the optic nerve on Dr. DeGraff's right eye.

But not before she saw It.

Not before she saw Them.

Even though I knew I shouldn't, one night I went ahead anyway. We were out dancing in la Zona. and Alex disappeared after a pair of German chicks. A Nazi *cada año no te hace daño*, he said. We were all out of our minds and Mysty started dancing with me and you know how girls are when they can dance and they know it. She just put it on me and that was it. I started making out with her right there.

I have to tell you, at that moment I was so fucking happy, so incredibly happy, and then the world put its foot right in my ass. Mysty stopped suddenly, said, Do you know what? I don't think this is cool.

Are you serious?

Yeah, she said. We should stop. She stepped back from the longest darkest song ever and started looking around. Maybe we should get out of here. It's late.

I said, I guess I forgot to bring my lakhs with me.

I almost said, I forgot to bring your dad with me.

Hijo de la gran puta, Mysty said, shoving me.

And that was when the lights went out.

Monitoring stations in the U.S. and Mexico detected a massive detonation in the Port-au-Prince area in the range of 8.3. Tremors were felt as far away as Havana, San Juan, and Key West.

The detonation produced a second, more extraordinary effect: an electromagnetic pulse that deaded all electronics within a six-hundred-square-mile radius.

Every circuit of every kind shot to shit. In military circles the pulse was called the Reaper. You cannot imagine the damage it caused. The bomber wing that had attacked the quarantine zone—dead, forced to ditch into the Caribbean Sea, no crew recovered. Thirty-two commercial flights packed to summer peak capacity plummeted straight out of the sky. Four crashed in urban areas. One pinwheeled into its receiving airport. Hundreds of privately owned seacraft lost. Servers down and power stations kaputted. Hospitals plunged into chaos. Even fatline communicators thought to be impervious to any kind of terrestrial disruption began fritzing. The three satellites parked in geosynch orbit over that stretch of the Caribbean went ass up, too. Tens of thousands died as a direct result of the power failure. Fires broke out. Seawalls began to fail. Domes started heating up.

But it wasn't just a simple, one-time pulse. Vehicles attempting to approach within six hundred miles of the detonation's epicenter failed. Communicators towed over the line could neither receive nor transmit. Batteries gave off nothing.

This is what *really* flipped every motherfucker in the know inside out and back again. The Reaper hadn't just swung and run; it had swung and *stayed*. A dead zone had opened over a six-hundred-mile chunk of the Caribbean.

Midnight.

No one knowing what the fuck was going on in the darkness. No one but us.

Initially, no one believed the hysterical evacuees. Forty-foot-tall cannibal motherfuckers running loose on the Island? Negro, please.

Until a set of soon-to-be-iconic Polaroids made it out on one clipper showing what later came to be called a Class 2 in the process of putting a slender broken girl in its mouth.

Beneath the photo someone had scrawled: Numbers 11:18. *Who shall give us flesh to eat?*

* * *

We came together at Alex's apartment first thing. All of us wearing the same clothes from the night before. Watched the fires spreading across the sectors. Heard the craziness on the street. And with the bafflers down felt for the first time on that roof the incredible heat rolling in from the dying seas. Mysty pretending nothing had happened between us. Me pretending the same.

Your mom O.K.? I asked her and she shrugged. She's up in the Cibao visiting family.

The power's supposedly out there, too, Alex said. Mysty shivered and so did I.

Nothing was working except for old diesel burners and the archaic motos with no points or capacitors. People were trying out different explanations. An earthquake. A nuke. A Carrington event. The Coming of the Lord. Reports arriving over the failing fatlines claimed that Port-au-Prince had been destroyed, that Haiti had been destroyed, that thirteen million screaming Haitian refugees were threatening the borders, that Dominican military units had been authorized to meet the *invaders*—the term the gov was now using—with ultimate force.

And so of course what does Alex decide to do? Like an idiot he decides to commandeer one of his father's vintage burners and take a ride out to the border.

Just in case, you know, Alex said, packing up his Polaroid, something happens.

And what do we do, like even bigger idiots? Go with him.

BIOGRAPHICAL FRAGMENTS OF THE LIFE OF JULIAN PRINCE

JAKE KERR

Julian Prince

From Wikipedia, the free encyclopedia

Julian Samuel Prince (March 18, 1989—August 20, 2057) was an American novelist, essayist, journalist, and political activist. His best works are widely considered to be the post-Impact novels *The Grey Sunset* (2027) and *Rhythms of Decline* (2029), both of which won the Pulitzer Prize. He was awarded the Nobel Prize for Literature in 2031.

Prince was a pioneer of Impact Nihilism, a genre that embraced themes of helplessness and inevitable death in the aftermath of the Meyer Impact. His travelogue, *Journey Into Hopelessness* (2026) outlined Prince's return to North America, ostensibly to survey the damage to his home state of Texas. The book's bleak and powerful language of loss and devastation influenced musicians, artists, and writers worldwide, giving voice to the genre as a counter to the rising wave of <u>New Optimism</u>, which sprang out of the European Union as a response to the Meyer Impact and the enormous loss of life. [1] [2]

Early Life

Not much is known of Prince's early life. He spoke rarely of his childhood, and with the loss of life and destruction of records during the Meyer Impact, little source material remains. What is known is that Prince was an only child, the son of Margaret Prince (maiden name unknown) and Samuel Prince. He was born in Lawton, Oklahoma, but moved to Dallas, Texas, when he was eight years old. [3] In an interview before his death, Prince noted:

> I was a good kid, a boring kid. I didn't cause trouble, and trouble didn't find me. I studied hard and planned on being a journalist, figuring that I was better at observing the world than shaping it. I graduated high school, and continued with my journalism classes via the net. Up until the Impact, I was thoroughly and utterly average. [4]

Upon earning a bachelor's degree from <u>Khan University</u> in journalism, Prince embarked on a career as a web reporter. [5]

Excerpt from Julian Prince's Nobel Prize Acceptance Speech, 2031

So it is that life, to which we all cling with desperation and joy, prevails. Yet I cannot let go of the memories, the experiences, and the physical reality of those that have passed away. The ghosts are all around us, even as we squint to see through them. It has been said that I deny optimism and ignore our future, but that is not true. It is just that I refuse to let the difficult questions remain unasked. I refuse to conveniently ignore the graveyard that is now half our planet. And I refuse to feel joy that so many have lived when so many—so many—have died.

It is with humility that I accept this award, not for myself, but for the hundreds of millions who are not here with us today. I did my best to tell their story, but they deserve so much more than I can possibly give. If I achieved even a small part in doing so, I am glad.

Pre-Impact Career

Prince spent the decade before the Meyer Impact crossing the globe courtesy of a series of freelance journalism jobs. His first writing job was with AOL Local/Patch in 2010, where he aggregated citizen journalism stories from North Texas and rewrote them for syndicated release to the net. He continued to work for AOL Local for seven years, until he quit in 2017. [6] He wrote about this transition in an essay on the carefree lives of the pre-Impact world in 2031:

I quit because I wasn't excited. Can you imagine

such a thing today? To leave security and stability because your life just isn't dangerous or crazy or exciting enough? Such was the innocence before the Impact. So I left the boring to move to Africa, where the excitement was, and where I could write about things that shed light on life and death, not ennui or entertainment. [7]

Prince took a job with European news agency <u>Star News</u> in 2017. His writing up until the Impact in 2023 was spare and fact-driven, although flashes of Prince's eye for emotion could occasionally be seen. Prince would say of those years, "Everything I wrote back then was worthless, but it was also worth everything—because it was the mind-numbing limitation of facts and cold description that allowed me to view the Impact in its true light." [8] [9]

Excerpt from "Maldives' Last Grain of Sand," reported by Julian Prince (*Star News*, 2018)

Ahmed Manik sits in a rickety wooden boat, watching as a wave crests over a strip of sand. Manik is the grandson of Maldives' last President, Mohammed Manik, and the strip of sand is all that's left of the island country of Maldives, a country wiped away by global warming, rising water levels, and decades of mismanagement. Scientists don't even bother estimating how long this last remnant of the former island nation will remain before it is washed away. It may be weeks, perhaps even days.

Manik shrugs when asked about the lost legacy of his family and former country. "We are all grains of sand, just waiting to be washed away," he says and smiles, which accentuates the heavy creases around his eyes and mouth. He may have accepted the inevitable force of the rising waters, but it has taken a toll.

Impact Year

Prince was already in Africa during the six-month preparation for the Impact and thus didn't have to take part in the Expatriation Lottery. He wrote many news articles during this time, but no fiction or essays. There is no record of Prince's life for the 18 months following the Impact and the immediate global environmental catastrophe it caused. Prince would write about this time often, but never about his own life—only what he had seen. [citation needed]

Excerpt from "Immigration Concerns Dominate South African Presidential Debate," reported by Julian Prince (*Star News*, 2023)

Cheers followed South African presidential candidate Maxwell Mahlangu on each stop of his tour of the country, despite deep concerns that his endorsement of the United Nations Emergency Emigration Plan for North America would upset the entire framework of the country. "Our country's motto is 'Unity in Diversity,'" Mahlangu said at a rally in Port Elizabeth. "How can we let these people die simply because we refuse to accept more diversity?"

Later in his speech, Mahlangu touched upon a common theme expressed by leaders across the globe as countries prepared to take in refugees from North America—no one really knows what the Meyer Asteroid will do to the world. With a massive death toll a certainty, the real economic unit of the future may be people, so taking in immigrants is a good idea: "No one knows what God has in store for us and what life will be like. In the future, with more people, South Africa will be stronger!"

Sitting president Jacob Sisulu rejected Mahlangu's moral and economic argument. He continued to object to the UN's current plan for South Africa to accept up to a million expatriates from the United States. "Such a wave of people would severely stress every part of our country," Sisulu explained during a press conference in Pretoria. "They will starve! China or Russia or Europe should take them!"

"Coming Home"

In 2025, Prince's essay "Coming Home" was published in *Der Spiegel*..[10] It became a worldwide sensation and ironically helped create the New Optimism movement that Prince's later work would reject. In the essay, Prince described the unloading of thousands of North American refugees in various cities along the African Coast, using the metaphor of humanity leaving its doomed colonial past to come home to Africa.

Literary critic Gerald King described the essay as the perfect origin point for both Impact Nihilism and New Optimism, and its publication immediately marked Prince as the leading light of post-Impact literature:

The central concept of "Coming Home" is warm and welcoming. Africa, the cradle of civilization, is welcoming home its wayward sons and daughters, even after their many sins. The deep themes of forgiveness and generosity fed directly into the New Optimism being loudly voiced in Europe. But many overlook that Prince did not flinch in describing the gaunt, guilty looks of those that exited the boats—a few million survivors while hundreds of millions of their friends and family members were doomed to die back home. The language that Prince uses in describing those left behind is very stark and makes it clear to the close reader that one should mourn, as well as celebrate. [11]

The reception of "Coming Home" led directly to Prince tackling the difficult subjects of the Impact and "the Lost," a term for those who died in the Impact that Prince coined himself in *Journey Into Hopelessness*. [citation needed]

Excerpt from "Coming Home" by Julian Prince (*Der Spiegel*, 2025)

Not one person who landed in Africa looked over his or her shoulder. It was as if the direction labeled "west" no longer existed. Sunsets were no longer a thing of beauty but a painful reminder of those doomed across the ocean, a literal dying light. Thoughts stopped at the ocean. It was overwhelming to consider friends and family alive yet suffering with the knowledge of their impending deaths.

Denial was the coping mechanism of choice. No one

that landed in Africa could remember having any family or friends remaining in North America. I asked dozens of refugees, and none would admit to having left anyone behind. Friends, neighbors, colleagues, family—they all somehow made it into the expatriation program.

In Mogadishu I met a man I used to work with. I asked him about several of our former colleagues and whether he knew if they had been chosen to expatriate. He denied ever having known them. I was shocked for a moment, but recovered and asked about his family. He smiled and said that they all made it and were settling across various cities in Europe. He didn't know anyone that had been left behind.

No one knew of anyone left behind.

To know was to be a participant in their death sentence, and that was too painful, too sad, too horrific. But the guilt existed, nonetheless. So they did what they could to avoid it. They didn't look west. They didn't watch sunsets. They never called or messaged North America, even as it still lived. They cut off their former lives and looked ahead to their new ones.

And thankfully, mercifully, Africa was there with open arms. A return to home and hearth, as it had for time immemorial, made everything better.

"The Conscience of a Generation"

Prince traveled back to North America to survey the damage from the impact in early 2026. He spent six months traveling across the continent with a United Nations Blue Team, observing and sometimes helping as they assessed the damage. This experience was the basis for his worldwide best-selling travelogue, *Journey Into Hopelessness*. His stark and often graphic descriptions of a barren landscape, littered with dead flora and fauna, were described by critics as "poetic," "beautiful," "poignant," and "chilling." Prince himself described the trip as the "hardest six months of my life. It was like performing an autopsy on your own parent." [12][13][14]

After returning from North America, Prince spent the next six months working on his first piece of fiction, the novel *The Grey Sunset*. The novel follows the life of Phil Gumm, who is a working-class truck driver from Kansas and a winner of the Expatriation Lottery. The novel is highly introspective, and the narrative follows Gumm's descent from exhilaration at being one of the lucky few to the depths of guilt over those he left behind. The bulk of the novel takes place on the journey from Galveston, Texas to Capetown, South Africa, and the physical journey is an extended metaphor for the emotional and spiritual journey that Gumm also takes. As Gumm physically gets closer to safety and a new life in Africa, he emotionally and spiritually gets closer to guilt, despair, and, eventually, suicide. [15]

The book was released at the height of the New Optimism movement and was immediately heralded as a compelling counter. The phrase Impact Nihilism had already been in use since the publication of *Journey Into Hopelessness* and similar works, but it was *The Grey Sunset* that defined the genre and helped propel its popularity. [citation needed] *The Grey Sunset* won the Pulitzer Prize in 2027, which had been re-established by the Expatriation Heritage Foundation the year before. [16]

Prince shied from publicity, and spent the bulk of the next two years working on what many consider his masterpiece, *Rhythms of Decline*. The novel is a complicated narrative of five families, each of whom lives on a different continent. The centerpiece is the impending impact of the Meyer Asteroid, and how each family deals with an uncertain future. Only one family survives the Impact, although their future is full of doubt as the novel ends.

Literary critic <u>Malcolm Spencer</u> described the book as "the work of unparalleled genius." He described the American Smith family as "the definitive representation of our times. They face impending death with a kind of sad and yet warm acceptance. They live one day at a time, knowing that days are all they have left." Spencer described Prince as "the conscience of a generation" for his unflinching look at the tragedy of the Impact and the guilt and pain it left behind. [17]

Some critics saw the book as a complete repudiation of New Optimism, and this led to significant criticism of Prince. London web daily *The Beacon* called Prince "The Prince of Doom and Gloom." [18] *The Paris Review* printed a scathing review of *Rhythms of Decline*, describing it as "one man's self-absorbed journal of guilt over surviving the Impact." [19]

Prince did a series of interviews in the wake of the criticism. His most famous appearance was on the popular holo *The New Day*, broadcast out of Berlin. When asked about his critics, his reply became one of the most quoted lines of the post-Impact era: "I'll listen to them when they've walked among the three hundred million ghosts that I have." [20]

Despite the controversy, *Rhythms of Decline* won the Pulitzer Prize and led directly to Prince being awarded the Nobel Prize for Literature two years later. [21]

Excerpt from *Journey Into Hopelessness* by Julian Prince (Vintage/Anchor, 2026)

Finally we landed in Texas.

When I was young my parents took me to Palo Duro Canyon in northwest Texas. It was a massive rift in the Earth that my mother told me God himself had carved out of the Texas plains. I didn't see it that way. I saw it as a broken land born of violence, something left behind when the plains and hills had collided. But broken as it was, I saw it as natural and beautiful. The sharp angles and the bare rock acted as a balance to the plains that spread into the distance. And despite the wound in the land, life continued to thrive around it.

There is nothing natural or beautiful in the tortured land that now covers North Texas. The force of the impact stripped away everything. There are no trees, no plants, no grass. There is nothing but scarred land, windburnt ridges, and fetid water. Everywhere there is decay, death, and the certainty that this is a barren land with no future.

Excerpt from an interview on *The New Tonight Show* (Canal+, January 18, 2030)

Phil Preston: Speaking of your trip, there are rumors that you didn't get along with the UN team during your visit to North America.

Julian Prince: Well, we spent six months together, so there were the normal conflicts, but I wouldn't say that I didn't get along with the team. I actually have a funny story about it.

Preston: *You* have a funny story? This I've got to hear.

Prince: Since this was officially a military mission for some idiotic reason, the scientists and I—all the civilians—had to take part in an orientation. The orientation was basically our team leader, Colonel Cooper, telling us over and over again that he was in charge and we had to listen to him. He was this husky bald guy with a kind of soft voice, but he had an intensity that made it clear he was used to people doing what he told them to do. His look and demeanor reminded me of Marlon Brando's character of Kurtz from the movie *Apocalypse Now*, so when he finished I said something like, "Sure thing, Kurtz."

[Audience laughter]

Prince: I thought it was funny, too, but he didn't seem to get it, and he marched over to me, put his nose right up to mine, and said, "The name is Cooper, and you can call me Colonel or Colonel Cooper." Of course I called him Kurtz for the entire six months.

[Audience cheers and laughter]

Preston: I'm surprised he didn't do anything.

Prince: I just assumed that he had no idea who Kurtz was, but during the last few days of the mission I said to him,

"I'm going to miss you, Kurtz." No one else was around, so I hoped he realized that I meant it. He then shook his head and said—and I remember every word to this day—"You have been calling me Kurtz this entire trip, and I had hoped by now that you would have realized how foolish that has been." He then leaned in and whispered in my ear, "You can't go native when there *are* no natives."

Preston: Wow. That's intense.

Prince: I know. And people call *me* the Prince of Doom and Gloom!

[Scattered audience laughter]

Preston: Actually, do you mind that—when people call you the Prince of Doom and Gloom?

Prince: [Pause] Yes.

Preston: Well, you've dated Janet Skillings, so I'm guessing that being the Prince of Doom and Gloom hasn't interfered much with your love life.

[Audience laughter]

Prince: Well, being rich and famous helps.

[Audience laughter]

Preston: So is there anyone in your life right now?

Prince: I'm afraid not. I live life one day at a time.

Preston: So what you're saying is you're only up for one-night stands.

[Audience laughter]

Prince: Life is a one-night stand.

[Uncomfortable silence]

Political Activism

The next ten years of Prince's life were marked by political activism. Violence in Africa and Asia led to the rise of the Repatriation Movement, which fought for the return of former North Americans to their home continent. While most countered the movement on practical grounds— North America simply wasn't habitable yet—Prince saw the movement as something deeper and darker. He felt the movement was about rejecting Africa and Asia and the expatriates' hosts more than a desire to return to their devastated homeland. [21][22]

In a widely quoted speech in 2034, Prince said:

> This is not a movement about returning home. This is a movement about rejecting friends. This is not a movement about finding comfort in familiar lands. This is a movement about fearing those who wish to help. This is not about

repatriation. This is about rejection. [23]

Prince was a prolific essay writer during this period, but nothing ever approached the popularity and power of his earlier work. His essay "Rejecting Home" (*Der Spiegel*, 2035), an acerbic and politically pointed update of his essay "Coming Home," was described by critic Gerald King as "a sad attempt by Prince to leverage his earlier brilliance to make a point about what many are starting to see in him as a naïve perception of unity in people who want no such thing." [24]

Prince ceased his anti-repatriation activism when parts of North America were re-opened for settlements in 2038. [*citation needed*]

Excerpt from *Rhythms of Decline* by Julian Prince (Knopf, 2029)

Simon had hoped that all would be normal in the end. He would tuck Annie into bed, pat Arthur on the head, and then kiss them both goodnight. Jason would wander off, falling asleep to the dull glow of some video game or another. Later, Simon would poke his head in, mutter a goodnight, and then turn the electronics off. Finally, he and Annie would hold each other and let the night take them. That was his dream—that they would fall asleep as a family and never wake up.

Yet, somehow, this seemed better. Their tears, their grief, and their fear tapped into a well deeper than family ritual. They were together in a moment when being alone seemed profane and wrong.

Jason joined Simon and began to cry as they all held each other. No one said anything. They breathed the air that gave them life. They shared the love that made them family. They cried the tears that made them human.

And then they died.

Later Life and Novels

Prince lived the rest of his life in Capetown, South Africa. He only published three more novels; all were well-received but garnered far less praise than *The Grey Sunset* and *Rhythms of Decline*. [citation needed]

Countdown (Knopf, 2040) told the story of a young man named Franklin Proudman who had decided to repatriate to North America. Proudman lands and finds life a lot different than he expected. Much of the book is a rambling series of anecdotes around the hopeless efforts of Proudman to build a life. He eventually dies from starvation, the ground still too damaged to produce crops.

Lost in North America (Knopf, 2045) is Prince's only foray into the science fiction genre.[25] The novel tells the story of the Winkler family, who hide in a fallout shelter in Rapid City, South Dakota. Despite Rapid City being ground zero for the Meyer Impact, the family survives and exit the shelter a year later to rebuild their lives. When it becomes clear that there is no food or wildlife, the family begins a journey, foraging for food across North America. The book has clear allusions to Cormac McCarthy's *The Road*, but the emptiness of the landscape provides for a uniquely Princean view. The book generated significant positive critical press. [26][27]

Prince's final novel, _Crater_ (Knopf, 2056), was released the year before his death. The book continued his exploration of the dark aspects of repatriation.[28] The novel follows a scientist, William Ho, and his assistant Wendy Singh, as they attempt to descend to the bottom of the Meyer Crater. Like Prince's other novels, _Crater_ is rife with introspection. As Ho and his assistant get closer to the bottom, they realize they are in love. It is when they have reached ground zero of the Meyer Impact when the two realize they have found their future together. The novel's ending is ambiguous, as the two are attempting to climb out of the crater but are uncertain if they will ever escape. While thematically similar to his earlier novels, _Crater_ employs a denser prose style, with long paragraphs that often include a stream-of-consciousness technique. Despite its ambiguity and often dark scenes, the novel was marked by some as a return to the optimism of "Coming Home." _Crater_ was a bestseller and re-established Prince as a popular figure in post-Impact literature. [29][30]

Personal Life

Prince was romantically connected to several celebrities during his life, including actresses Renee Diaz [citation needed] and Janet Skillings. [31] None of these relationships lasted more than a few weeks, however. In 2050, unofficial Prince biographer Susan Nillson announced that she had uncovered proof that Prince had left a girlfriend and child behind in North America. The document, a digitized copy of a Texas State birth certificate backed up on a European server, showed that Prince fathered a child named Samuel to a mother named Wendy Reynolds. Prince never acknowledged Nillson's allegations, although most contemporary historians consider the claim accurate. [32]

Excerpt from Julian Prince's final interview (*Paris Live!*, 2056)

Aliette Rameau: You've achieved so much, Monsieur Prince. Do you have any regrets?

[Pause]

Rameau: Monsieur Prince?

Julian Prince: I'm sorry. Your question is a bit overwhelming. My life is full of regrets.

Rameau: Is there anything specific you could share with us?

Prince: No. [Takes drink of water] I'm sorry. Could we change the subject, please?

Death and Legacy

Prince died on August 20, 2057 in Capetown, South Africa, from a self-inflicted gunshot wound. He left no suicide note.

Having died without any heirs, Prince bequeathed his literary estate and assets to <u>The 300 Million Ghosts Foundation</u>, which was founded to record, research, and archive the stories of those who died during the Meyer Impact. [33][34]

Prince's legacy continues to define and influence artists to this day. While Impact Nihilism has fallen out of fashion, Prince's stark images and deep themes can be seen in everything from the paintings of <u>Ellen Winslow</u> to the music of the <u>Bluefins</u>. His use of introspection and stream-of-consciousness has influenced writers as diverse as <u>Joe Lguyen</u> and <u>Isabel Shoeford</u>. [citation needed]

The play "<u>Coming Home</u>" debuted on the anniversary of Prince's death in 2058 at the <u>Globe Theater</u> in London. Adapted by Nobel-winning playwright <u>Andrew Hillsborough</u>, the play was an unabashedly optimistic look at a world that survived an extinction event and came away smiling. Hillsborough noted on <u>BBC</u>, "Oh, I'm sure old Prince would have hated it. But the words are all his. Somewhere along the way he changed. Just because he decided that facing the abyss meant that we were all doomed to fall in, doesn't mean we have to agree with him." [35]

Epitaph on Julian Prince's gravestone

"Finally home."

ACKNOWLEDGEMENTS

Many thanks to the following:

My Publisher/Editor: Steve Saffel, for acquiring and editing the book, and to the rest of the team that worked on the book at Titan Books.

My Agents (past and present): Joe Monti (former) and Seth Fishman (present) for being awesome and supportive.

My Mentor: Gordon Van Gelder, for being a mentor and a friend.

My Colleague: Ellen Datlow for revealing the mysteries of anthologizing.

My Family: my amazing wife, Christie; my mom, Marianne, and my sister, Becky, for all their love and support.

Author/Contract Wranglers: Marie Florio, Ty Franck, Patricia Rogers, Laura Bradford, Kathleen Bellamy, Gavin Grant, and Duvall Osteen.

Second Opinion Corps: Robyn Lupo, Caleb Jordan Schulz, Andrew Liptak, Benjamin Blattberg, Kristin Centorcelli, Lashawn Wanak, Lisa Rogers, Louise Kane,

Paul DesCombaz, Robert Barton Bland, Stephanie M. Loree, Theresa Glover, and Patrick Stephens for providing feedback on the stories during the editorial process.

Intern: Extra special thanks to my former intern, Amber Barkley, who not only provided feedback on stories, but also helped out a lot with other behind-the-scenes stuff on this anthology.

My Writers: Everyone who appears in this anthology.

My Readers (last but not least): Everyone who bought this book, or any of my other anthologies, and who make doing books like this possible.

ABOUT THE CONTRIBUTORS

Ann Aguirre is a *New York Times, USA Today*, and *Publishers Weekly* bestselling author with a degree in English Literature; before she began writing full time, she was a clown, a clerk, a voice actress, and a savior of stray kittens, not necessarily in that order. She grew up in a yellow house across from a cornfield, but now she lives in sunny Mexico with her husband, children, and various pets. She likes books, emo music, and action movies. She writes all kinds of genre fiction for adults and teens.

Megan Arkenberg lives and writes in California. Her work has appeared in *Lightspeed, Asimov's, Strange Horizons,* Ellen Datlow's *The Best Horror of the Year,* and the inaugural issue of the horror magazine *Aghast,* among other places. She procrastinates by editing the fantasy e-zine *Mirror Dance.*

Paolo Bacigalupi is the bestselling author of the novels *The Windup Girl, Ship Breaker, The Drowned Cities, Zombie Baseball Beatdown,* and the collection *Pump Six and Other Stories.* He is a winner of the Michael L. Printz, Hugo, Nebula, Locus, Compton Crook, and John W. Campbell Memorial awards, and was a National Book Award finalist. A new novel for young adults, *The Doubt Factory*, came out in 2014, and a new science fiction novel, *The Water Knife,* in May 2015.

Christopher Barzak is the author of the Crawford Fantasy Award winning novel, *One for Sorrow,* which has been made into the recently released Sundance feature film *Jamie Marks is Dead.* His second novel, *The Love We Share Without Knowing,* was a finalist for the Nebula and Tiptree Awards. He is also the author of two collections: *Birds and Birthdays*, a collection of surrealist fantasy stories, and *Before and Afterlives,* a collection of supernatural fantasies, which won the 2013 Shirley Jackson Award for Best Collection. He grew up in rural Ohio, has lived in a southern California beach town, the capital of Michigan, and has taught English outside of Tokyo, Japan, where he lived for two years. His most recent novel, *Wonders of the Invisible World,* was published by Knopf in Fall 2015. Currently he teaches fiction writing in the Northeast Ohio MFA program at Youngstown State University.

Lauren Beukes (laurenbeukes.com) is a South African novelist, TV scriptwriter, documentary maker, comics writer, and occasional journalist. She is the author of the novels *Moxyland*, *Zoo City* (winner of the Arthur C. Clarke Award), *The Shining Girls*, and *Broken Monsters*. She's also written rollicking nonfiction about maverick South African women, TV scripts, and comics for *Vertigo*. Her short stories have appeared in anthologies such as *Armored*, *Pandemonium: Stories of the Apocalypse*, and *The Apex Book of World SF*.

David Brin is an astrophysicist whose international bestselling novels include *The Postman*, *Earth*, and recently *Existence*. His nonfiction book about the information age—*The Transparent Society*—won the Freedom of Speech Award of the American Library Association.

Orson Scott Card is the bestselling author of more than forty novels, including *Ender's Game*, which was a winner of both the Hugo and Nebula awards. The sequel, *Speaker for the Dead*, also won both awards, making Card the only author to have captured science fiction's two most coveted prizes in consecutive years. His most recent books include book three of his Pathfinders trilogy, *Visitors*; three books in the Formic War series co-authored with Aaron Johnston, *Earth Unaware*, *Earth Afire*, and *Earth Awakens*; an Ender's Shadow novel, *Shadows in Flight*; and book two of the Mither Mages series, *The Gate Thief*.

Junot Díaz is the author of the bestselling novel *The Brief Wondrous Life of Oscar Wao* and the books *Drown* and *This is How You Lose Her*. His fiction has appeared in *The*

New Yorker many times, and also in *Glimmer Train* and *African Voices*. He is the winner of the Pulitzer Prize, the National Books Critic Circle Award and most recently the MacArthur Fellowship. The fiction editor at *The Boston Review* and the co-founder of the Voices of Our Nation Workshop, Díaz teaches writing at MIT.

Cory Doctorow (craphound.com) is a science fiction author, activist, journalist and blogger—the co-editor of Boing Boing (boingboing.net) and the author of young adult novels like *Homeland, Pirate Cinema* and *Little Brother* and novels for adults like *The Rapture of the Nerds* and *Makers*. He is the former European director of the Electronic Frontier Foundation and co-founded the UK Open Rights Group. Born in Toronto, Canada, he now lives in London.

Tananarive Due is the Cosby Chair in the Humanities at Spelman College. She also teaches in the creative writing MFA program at Antioch University, Los Angeles. The American Book Award winner and NAACP Image Award recipient has authored and/or co-authored twelve novels and a civil rights memoir. In 2013, she received a Lifetime Achievement Award in the Fine Arts from the Congressional Black Caucus Foundation. In 2010, she was inducted into the Medill School of Journalism's Hall of Achievement at Northwestern University. She has also taught at the Geneva Writers' Conference, the Clarion Science Fiction & Fantasy Writers' Workshop, and Voices of Our Nations Art Foundation (VONA). Due's supernatural thriller *The Living Blood* won a 2002

American Book Award. Her novella "Ghost Summer," published in the 2008 anthology *The Ancestors,* received the 2008 Kindred Award from the Carl Brandon Society, and her short fiction has appeared in best-of-the-year anthologies of science fiction and fantasy. Due is a leading voice in black speculative fiction.

Nashville native **Toiya Kristen Finley** is a writer, editor, game designer, and narrative designer/game writer. Her fiction has been published in *Nature, Fantasy Magazine, Daily Science Fiction, The Best of Electric Velocipede,* and *The Year's Best Science Fiction and Fantasy, 2010.* She is the founding and former managing/fiction editor of *Harpur Palate* and a co-founder and instructor at GDC Online's Game Writing Tutorial. Her work in games includes *Academagia: The Making of Mages* and its DLC, *Fat Chicken,* and a list of unannounced/suspended-production social-network RPGs and mobile games whose existence shall remain forever a secret (hey, that's the game industry for ya). *The Game Narrative Toolbox* (Focal Press), a book on narrative design she's co-authored with Jennifer Brandes Hepler, Ann Lemay, and Tobias Heussner, came out in early 2015.

Milo James Fowler (milojamesfowler.com) is a teacher by day and a speculative fictioneer by night. When he's not grading papers, he's imagining what the world might be like in a dozen alternate realities. He is an active SFWA member, and his work has appeared in more than 90 publications, including *AE SciFi, Cosmos, Daily Science Fiction, Nature,* and *Shimmer.* His novel *Captain Bartholomew Quasar and* *the Space-Time Displacement Conundrum* is now available from Every Day Publishing, and his other stories can be found wherever e-books are sold.

Maria Dahvana Headley is the author of the upcoming young adult skyship novel *Magonia* from HarperCollins, the novel *Queen of Kings*, the memoir *The Year of Yes,* and co-author with Kat Howard of the short horror novella *The End of the Sentence*. With Neil Gaiman, she is the *New York Times*-bestselling co-editor of the monster anthology *Unnatural Creatures*, benefitting 826DC. Her Nebula and Shirley Jackson award-nominated short fiction has recently appeared in *Lightspeed* ("Give Her Honey When You Hear Her Scream," "The Traditional"), on Tor.com, *The Toast, Clarkesworld, Nightmare, Apex, The Journal of Unlikely Entomology, Subterranean Online, Uncanny Magazine, Glitter & Mayhem* and Jurassic London's *The Lowest Heaven* and *The Book of the Dead*, as well as in a number of Year's Bests, most recently *Year's Best Weird*. She lives in Brooklyn with a collection of beasts, an anvil, and a speakeasy bar through the cellar doors. Find her on Twitter @MARIADAHVANA or on the web at mariadahvanaheadley.com.

Hugh Howey is the author of the acclaimed post-apocalyptic novel *Wool*, which became a sudden success in 2011. Originally self-published as a series of novelettes, the *Wool* omnibus is frequently the #1 bestselling book on Amazon.com and is a *New York Times* and *USA TODAY* bestseller. The book was also optioned for film by Ridley Scott, and is now available in print from major publishers all over the world. The story of *Wool*'s meteoric success has been reported in major media outlets such as *Entertainment Weekly*, *Variety*, the *Washington Post*, the *Wall Street Journal*, *Deadline Hollywood*, and elsewhere. Howey lives in Jupiter, Florida with his wife Amber and his dog Bella.

Keffy R. M. Kehrli is a science fiction and fantasy writer currently living in Seattle. Although his degrees are in physics and linguistics, he spends most of his time in a basement performing molecular biology experiments for fun and profit. In 2008, he attended Clarion UCSD where he learned that, unfortunately, rattlesnakes don't always rattle. His short fiction has appeared in publications such as *Apex Magazine*, *Lightspeed*, and *Three-Lobed Burning Eye*.

Jake Kerr: After fifteen years as a music industry journalist Jake Kerr's first published story, "The Old Equations," was nominated for the Nebula Award from the Science Fiction Writers of America and was shortlisted for the Theodore Sturgeon and StorySouth Million Writers awards. His stories have subsequently been published in magazines across the world, broadcast in multiple podcasts, and been published in multiple anthologies and year's best collections. His young adult novel, *Tommy Black and the Coat of Invincibility*, was released in January 2015 The third and final volume in the series will be released later in the year. A graduate of Kenyon College, Kerr studied fiction under Ursula K. Le Guin and Peruvian playwright Alonso Alegría. He lives in Dallas, Texas, with his wife and three daughters.

Nancy Kress is the author of thirty-four books, including twenty-seven novels, four collections of short stories, and three books on writing. Her work has won five Nebulas, two Hugos, a Sturgeon, and the John W. Campbell Memorial Award. She has also lost over a dozen of these awards. Nancy's most recent work is *Yesterday's Kin*, about a surprising genetic inheritance (Tachyon, 2014). In addition to writing, Kress often teaches at various venues around the country and abroad; in 2008 she was the Picador visiting lecturer at the University of Leipzig. Kress lives in Seattle with her husband, writer Jack Skillingstead, and Cosette, the world's most spoiled toy poodle.

Joe R. Lansdale is the author of more than three hundred short stories and forty novels. His work has been awarded with the Edgar, nine Bram Stokers, The British Fantasy Award, The Herodotus, and many others. He is a member of the Texas Institute of Letters, The Texas Literary Hall of Fame, and is Writer in Residence at Stephen F. Austin State University. He has received the Grandmaster Award and the Lifetime Achievement Award from The Horror Writers Association, and is a Grandmaster and Founder of Shen Chuan, Martial Science. His work has been filmed several times. Among these films are *Bubba Hotep, Cold in July, Christmas with the Dead,* and *Incident On and Off a Mountain Road*. Forthcoming are films of *The Bottoms*, directed by Bill Paxton, and *The Thicket*, starring Peter Dinklage. The Sundance Channel has plans to create a series from his Hap and Leonard novels.

George R. R. Martin is the wildly popular author of the *A Song of Ice and Fire* epic fantasy series, and many other novels, such as *Dying of the Light* and *The Armageddon Rag*. His short fiction—which has appeared in numerous anthologies and in most if not all of the genre's major magazines—has garnered him four Hugos, two Nebulas, the Stoker, and the World Fantasy Award. Martin is also known for editing the *Wild Cards* series of shared world superhero anthologies, and for his work as a screenwriter on such television projects as the 1980s version of *The Twilight Zone* and *Beauty and the Beast*. A TV series based on *A Song of Ice and Fire* debuted on HBO in 2011.

Jack McDevitt has been described by Stephen King as "The logical heir to Isaac Asimov and Arthur C. Clarke." He is the author of twenty one novels, eleven of which have been Nebula finalists. His novel *Seeker* won the award in 2007. In 2003, *Omega* received the John W. Campbell Memorial Award for best science fiction novel. McDevitt's most recent books are *Starhawk*, which follows the young Priscilla Hutchins as she seeks to qualify as an interstellar pilot; and *Coming Home*, in which far-future antiquarian Alex Benedict visits Earth to learn why an archeologist who'd devoted his life to searching for the lost artifacts of the early space age apparently found them but never told anyone. Both are from Ace. A Philadelphia native,

McDevitt had a varied career before becoming a writer. He's been a naval officer, an English teacher, a customs officer, and a taxi driver. He has also conducted leadership seminars. He is married to the former Maureen McAdams, and resides in Brunswick, Georgia, where he keeps a weather eye on hurricanes.

Seanan McGuire was born and raised in Northern California, resulting in a love of rattlesnakes and an absolute terror of weather. She shares a crumbling old farmhouse with a variety of cats, far too many books, and enough horror movies to be considered a problem. Seanan publishes about three books a year, and is widely rumored not to actually sleep. When bored, Seanan tends to wander into swamps and cornfields, which has not yet managed to get her killed (although not for lack of trying). She also writes as Mira Grant, filling the role of her own evil twin, and tends to talk about horrible diseases at the dinner table.

Maureen F. McHugh was born in what was then a sleepy, blue collar town in Ohio called Loveland. She went to college in Ohio, and then graduate school at New York University. She lived a year in Shijiazhuang, China. Her first book, Tiptree Award winner *China Mountain Zhang*, was published in 1991. Since then she has written three novels and a well-received collection of short stories, Story Prize finalist *Mothers & Other Monsters*. McHugh has also worked on alternate reality games for *Halo 2, The Watchmen,* and Nine Inch Nails. She lives in Los Angeles, where she has attempted to sell her soul to Hollywood.

D. Thomas Minton recently traded a warm tropical island for the Pacific Northwest of the continental USA, where he now lives a short walk from vineyards and an alpaca farm. When not writing, he gets paid to "play" in the ocean, travel to remote places, and help communities conserve coral reefs. His fiction has been published in *Asimov's*, *Lightspeed*, and *Daily Science Fiction* and his idle ramblings hold court at dthomasminton.com.

Rudy Rucker is a writer and a mathematician. His thirty-plus published books include both novels and non-fiction books on the fourth dimension, infinity, and the meaning of computation. His novels include *Mathematicians in Love*, *The Ware Tetralogy*, *Postsingular*, *Hylozoic*, *Jim and the Flims*, *Turing & Burroughs: A Beatnik SF Novel*, and *The Big Aha*.

Ramsey Shehadeh splits his time between writing software and writing stories. His fiction has appeared in *Weird Tales*, *Strange Horizons*, *The Magazine of Fantasy & Science Fiction*, *Shimmer*, *Podcastle*, and *The Drabblecast*, as well as in Ann and Jeff VanderMeer's *Steampunk Reloaded* anthology.

Robert Silverberg—four-time Hugo Award winner, five-time winner of the Nebula Award, SFWA Grand Master, SF Hall of Fame honoree—is the author of nearly five hundred short stories, nearly one hundred and fifty novels, and is the editor of in the neighborhood of one hundred anthologies. Among his most famous works are *Lord Valentine's Castle, Dying Inside, Nightwings,* and *The World Inside.* Learn more at www.majipoor.com.

Bruce Sterling is the author of many novels, including *Islands in the Net, Heavy Weather, Distraction, Holy Fire, The Zenith Angle, The Caryatids,* and, with William Gibson, *The Difference Engine.* Much of his short fiction, which has appeared in magazines such as *F&SF* and *Omni,* was recently collected in *Ascendancies: The Best of Bruce Sterling.*

Rachel Swirsky holds an MFA in fiction from the Iowa Writers Workshop. Her short fiction has appeared in venues including *Tor.com* and *Clarkesworld Magazine,* and been nominated for the Hugo, the Locus Award, and the World Fantasy Award, and won the Nebula Award twice. Her second collection, *How the World Became Quiet: Myths of the Past, Present, and Future,* came out from Subterranean Press in 2013. The titular story, reprinted in this anthology, was inspired by a dream—not a good one, or a bad one, but a surreal one. Narrative and many details were added, but female mosquito warriors were there from the start.

Genevieve Valentine's first novel, *Mechanique: A Tale of the Circus Tresaulti,* won the 2012 Crawford Award and was nominated for the Nebula Award. Her short fiction has appeared in magazines such as *Clarkesworld, Lightspeed, Nightmare, Strange Horizons, Journal of Mythic Arts,*

Fantasy, and *Apex,* as well as in the anthologies *Federations, The Living Dead 2, The Way of the Wizard, Teeth, After,* and others. Her short work has been nominated for the World Fantasy Award and the Shirley Jackson Award, and several stories have been reprinted in best-of-the-year anthologies. She has written nonfiction and reviews for such venues as *NPR, Strange Horizons, Weird Tales,* and *Tor.com,* and she is a co-author of the book *Geek Wisdom.* Her latest book is a young adult novel, *The Girls at the Kingfisher Club,* and a new SF novel for adults, *Persona,* came out in March 2015. Her appetite for bad movies is insatiable, a tragedy she tracks on her blog at genevievevalentine.com.

James Van Pelt teaches high school and college English in western Colorado. His fiction has made numerous appearances in most of the major science fiction and fantasy magazines. He has been a finalist for a Nebula Award, the Colorado Blue Spruce Young Adult Book Award, and been reprinted in many year's best collections. His first novel, *Summer of the Apocalypse,* was released in 2006. His third collection of stories, *The Radio Magician and Other Stories,* received the Colorado Book Award in 2010. His latest collection, *Flying in the Heart of the Lafayette Escadrille,* was released in October of 2012.

Christie Yant is a science fiction and fantasy writer, and editor of the *Women Destroy Science Fiction!* special issue of *Lightspeed Magazine.* Her fiction has appeared in anthologies and magazines including *Year's Best Science Fiction & Fantasy 2011* (Horton), *Armored, Analog Science*

Fiction & Fact, Beneath Ceaseless Skies, io9, Wired.com, and China's *Science Fiction World.* She lives on the central coast of California with two writers, one editor, two dogs, three cats, and a very small manticore. Follow her on Twitter @christieyant.

For bonus features including exclusive interviews with the contributors, visit the official *Wastelands 2* website: **www. johnjosephadams.com/wastelands-2**

ABOUT THE EDITOR

JOHN JOSEPH ADAMS is the editor of John Joseph Adams Books, a science fiction/fantasy imprint of Houghton Mifflin Harcourt. He is also the series editor of *Best American Science Fiction & Fantasy*, as well as the bestselling editor of many other anthologies, including *The Mad Scientist's Guide to World Domination*, *Armored*, *Robot Uprisings*, *Dead Man's Hand*, *Brave New Worlds*, *Wastelands*, and *The Living Dead*. Recent books include *Operation Arcana*, *Press Start to Play*, *Loosed Upon the World*, and The Apocalypse Triptych (consisting of *The End is Nigh*, *The End is Now*, and *The End Has Come*). Called "the reigning king of the anthology world" by Barnes & Noble, John is a two-time winner of the Hugo Award (for which he has been nominated nine times) and a seven-time World Fantasy Award finalist. John is also the editor and publisher of the digital magazines *Lightspeed* and *Nightmare*, and is a producer for WIRED's *The Geek's Guide to the Galaxy* podcast. Find him at johnjosephadams. com and on Twitter @johnjosephadams.

WASTELANDS

STORIES OF THE APOCALYPSE
EDITED BY JOHN JOSEPH ADAMS

An anthology of the best post-apocalyptic literature
of the last two decades from many of today's most
renowned authors of speculative fiction.

Featuring prescient tales of Armageddon and its
aftermath, by twenty-two of today's finest writers,
including: Stephen King, George R.R. Martin,
Jonathan Lethem, Nancy Kress, Gene Wolfe, Octavia
E. Butler and many others.

Together they reveal what it will mean to survive and
remain human after the end of the world…

DEAD MAN'S HAND

AN ANTHOLOGY OF THE WEIRD WEST
EDITED BY JOHN JOSEPH ADAMS

From a kill-or-be-killed gunfight with a vampire to an encounter in a steampunk bordello, the weird western is a dark, gritty tale where the protagonist might be playing poker with a sorcerous deck of cards, or facing an alien on the streets of a dusty frontier town.

Here are twenty-three original tales—stories of the Old West infused with elements of the fantastic—produced specifically for this volume by many of today's finest writers. Included are Orson Scott Card's first "Alvin Maker" story in a decade, and an original adventure by Fred Van Lente, creator of *Cowboys & Aliens*.

Other contributors include Tobias Buckell, David Farland, Alan Dean Foster, Jeffrey Ford, Laura Anne Gilman, Rajan Khanna, Mike Resnick, Beth Revis, Ben H. Winters, Christie Yant, and Charles Yu.

For more fantastic fiction, author events,
exclusive excerpts, competitions, limited
editions and more

VISIT OUR WEBSITE
titanbooks.com

LIKE US ON FACEBOOK
facebook.com/titanbooks

FOLLOW US ON TWITTER
@TitanBooks

EMAIL US
readerfeedback@titanemail.com